MY FATHER HAS GATHERED

the BLACK WIDOW
the ARSONIST

the Mild-Mannered
POET
with a penchant for blood

the CROOKED COP
AND, OF COURSE,

the Seattle Slayer.

BOOKS BY
C.M. STUNICH

ROMANCE NOVELS
HARD ROCK ROOTS SERIES*
Real Ugly
Get Bent
Tough Luck
Bad Day
Born Wrong
Hard Rock Roots Box Set (1-5)
Dead Serious
Doll Face
Heart Broke
Get Hitched

TASTING NEVER SERIES
Tasting Never
Finding Never
Keeping Never
Tasting, Finding, Keeping
Never Can Tell
Never Let Go
Never Did Say
Never Could Stop

ROCK-HARD BEAUTIFUL*
Groupie
Roadie
Moxie

TRIPLE M SERIES*
Losing Me, Finding You
Loving Me, Trusting You
Needing Me, Wanting You
Craving Me, Desiring You

DEATH BY DAYBREAK MC*
I Was Born Ruined
I Am Dressed in Sin
I Will Revel in Glory

THE HAVOC BOYS*
Havoc at Prescott High
Chaos at Prescott High
Mayhem at Prescott High
Anarchy at Prescott High
Victory at Prescott High

STAND-ALONES & BOX SETS
Devils' Day Party
Baby Girl
All for 1
Blizzards and Bastards
Fuck Valentine's Day
Broken Pasts
Crushing Summer
Becoming Us Again
Taboo Unchained
Taming Her Boss
Kicked
Football Dick
Stepbrother Inked
Alpha Wolves Motorcycle Club
Glacier

HERS TO KEEP TRILOGY
Biker Rockstar Billionaire CEO Alpha

RICH BOYS OF BURBERRY PREP*
Filthy Rich Boys
Bad, Bad BlueBloods
The Envy of Idols
In the Arms of the Elite

LOST DAUGHTER OF A SERIAL KILLER*
Stolen Crush
Payback Princess
Endgame Romance
Game Over Boys

SCARLET FORCE
Fuckboy Psychos
Unholy Terrors
Vile Bastards
Stalking Nightmares

ADAMSON ALL-BOYS ACADEMY*
The Secret Girl
The Ruthless Boys
The Forever Crew

FIVE FORGOTTEN SOULS
Beautiful Survivors

BOOKS BY

C. M. STUNICH

A DUET
Paint Me Beautiful
Color Me Pretty

THE BAD NANNY TRILOGY
Bad Nanny
Good Boyfriend

FANTASY NOVELS
THE SEVEN MATES OF ZARA WOLF
Pack Ebon Red
Pack Violet Shadow
Pack Obsidian Gold

HAREM OF HEARTS*
Allison's Adventures in Underland
Allison and the Torrid Tea Party
Allison Shatters the Looking Glass

KINGS OF UNDERLAND
a Bride for Beasts
a Marriage of Monsters

ACADEMY OF SPIRITS AND SHADOWS
Spirited
Haunted
Shadowed

THE FAMILY SPELLS
The Family Spells
What The Hex?
The Heart Cantrip
Witch Mates are Fated?

TEN CATS PARANORMAL SOCIETY
Possessed

THE SEVEN WICKED SERIES
Seven Wicked Creatures
Six Wicked Beasts
Five Wicked Monsters
Four Wicked Fiends

THE WICKED WIZARDS OF OZ
Very Bad Wizards

OTHER FANTASY NOVELS
Werewolf Kisses
Gray and Graves
Indigo & Iris
Stiltz
She Lies Twisted
See No Devils
Hell Inc.
DeadBorn
Chryer's Crest
Under the Wild Waves

CO-WRITTEN
HIJINKS HAREM*
Elements of Mischief
Elements of Ruin
Elements of Desire

THE WILD HUNT MOTORCYCLE CLUB
Dark Glitter
Cruel Glamour

FOXFIRE BURNING
The Nine
Tail Game

OTHER
And Today I Die

UNDERCOVER SINNERS
Altered By Fire
Altered By Lead
Altered by Pain

* - Complete Series

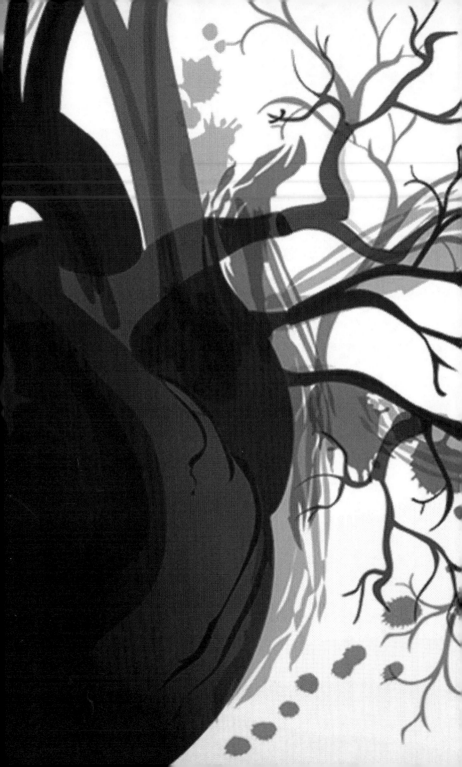

Endgame ♥ ROMANCE

LOST DAUGHTER OF A
SERIAL KILLER

3

this book is dedicated to:

*all of the readers who have sent me messages of encouragement.
I read them all, even if I don't always respond.*

your words of kindness fill my creative well and spill into my work.

*art can be a solo exercise,
but community adds spirit and pizzaz.
thank you for lending me yours.*

PROLOGUE

My hands are covered in blood—and not a drop of it belongs to me.

I realize then that evil doesn't just happen overnight. Sure, some people are born wrong, but others are forged in hate and pain and circumstance. Against my better judgement, against my own will, I am becoming one of those people.

I've just killed a person.

This time, the iron reek that I'm smelling, it's all my fault. This isn't some comatose maid in a wooden box. This is so much more. This is me, Dakota Banks, losing every last part of herself. Every cell. Every molecule. My very essence.

Because I've done all sorts of things I regret in the last few weeks: burned down the theater, slept with my boyfriend's best friend, slept with my sister's ex.

But this is the worst.

Truly, the worst thing that I have ever done.

I look up, meeting Maxx Wright's brilliant green gaze. He

looks as shocked as I am, standing over the body of the person that just died because of me. Really, I was given no choice. It's an ethics problem in real time, and I made the best decision that I could.

I move over to the bushes and throw up, but I can't purge myself of this experience, these awful memories that are going to stick to me like cobwebs. Whenever I brush them away, the venomous arachnid that carries this nightmare in my psyche will simply weave a new web.

"Kota." X puts his big, warm hands on my shoulders, and I turn toward him, lifting those bloodied palms in his direction. The color is oddly beautiful in the early morning light, and the woods around us are picturesque, a true fairy tale at the edge of an aristocratic kingdom.

That's the thing about fairy tales though: they're often dark. They have lessons to impart. I've just learned mine.

No matter how I play this game, no matter how clever or cunning, how intuitive, how tricksy I think that I am, Justin Prior is always three steps ahead. He got me to do what I swore I never would, the ultimate act that has, undoubtedly, made me his child in every sense of the word.

I'm not just his daughter in DNA now, but also the reflection of his image.

He's replicating himself, using me as an extension of his revenge.

My phone buzzes and I slide it out of my pocket.

I don't need to say who sent the text; Maxx knows.

Excellent work, princess. I'd expect nothing less. Congratulations. Take a trophy to celebrate your first win, and then deal with the evidence. Use your pawns if you please.

Pick a friend to live; pick a friend to die.

I chose a piece of myself to die instead, offered up a sacrifice on my chessboard just like Daddy Dearest has been teaching me.

Justin has just checked my king.

We're in the endgame, Dakota. You're *in the endgame, and there are few pieces left on the board. Make your move.*

Only, I should've known Justin better than that, shouldn't I?

I just killed a guy. I just fucking killed a guy.

Maxx takes me into his arms, and I cling to him, but even that can't fix the problem. Even his love and his touch, his kind eyes and confident smile, none of that can save me now.

There are footsteps approaching in the underbrush.

Someone—multiple someones by the sound of it—are coming this way.

What, I imagine, they'll think when they stumble on us is anybody's guess.

Me, with bloody hands and a knife lying beside my boyfriend's foot. A dead man sprawled on his back. Two high school girls, one tied up, the other bleeding from the head.

"Shh, Kota. It's gonna be okay," X whispers as we exchange a look.

No matter what happens here, at least I've got him.

He knows what I've done, and he's standing beside me anyway.

Maxx turns, and I follow the direction of his shifting gaze, expecting more cops. Or maybe a cadre of well-armed serial killers?

The faces that emerge through the trees, I definitely do not expect.

Also, an idea has just struck me, and I can't shake it: no matter what happens here, I'm turning myself in.

Because you can't trap someone in a secret if they refuse to keep it, now can you?

CHAPTER 1

Prom night is an undeniable catastrophe.

A boy I love is missing (again), and the Vanguard house (which I grudgingly admit is also my house) is on fire.

My apologies for the excessive use of parenthetical thoughts, but really? Dual calamities to round out what was supposed to be a night of memory making magic, a respite, a chance to be sixteen even if under the watchful eyes of the Seattle Slayer.

Instead, Justin's gifted gown is a gilded cage that succeeds at keeping me in, but does nothing to keep the horrible, repulsive, and rotten *out*.

Tess is alternately sobbing and making phone calls while she drives. Meanwhile, the three of us sit crushed together in the back seat of her Mercedes, the skirts of my golden gown frothing over the boys' laps. I can't breathe, a swarm of *what-ifs* poisoning my blood as I try and fail not to think of my youngest siblings, trapped inside an inferno.

Maxx, where are you? I wonder, aching for him even as I'm

panicking at the idea of losing a family I never wanted in the first place. But now, here, I'm starting to rethink some of my behaviors. Too little, too late?

I sure as fuck hope not.

My eyes meet Parrish's, the beautiful gold flecks dimmed with emotion. His irises are as black as the ebony night spread across the sky. His hand finds mine, ink-dressed fingers curling through my naked ones. Even though I'm not looking at him, Chasm does the same on my right side.

"Are the two of you dating behind my back?"

Bio Mom's question hangs in the air like smoke, but it pales in importance when compared to either of our other two problems. I glance back at Chasm. He's tugging on his hair and staring down at the phone in his lap, nestled amongst my tulle skirts like a jewel.

"Maxx had dinner with his parents, went into the spare bedroom saying he was tired, and then … disappeared." Chas looks up at me and Parrish, his lips in a thin line. He isn't wearing his lip rings since he's in Seamus-approved mode tonight, but he's just as pretty like this as he is with his lightning bolt colored hair and piercings. "You don't think …"

I do. I am. That's exactly what I'm worried about: did dear old daddy take another boy that I like to hold as a hostage? Then again, he already has Maxine; it doesn't make sense. None of this makes sense.

"Please tell me they're alive!" Tess is screaming, and the three of us cringe in unison. The person on the other end of the phone— a neighbor, I think—says that she doesn't know, her voice weak over the Bluetooth speakers. There's an ambulance, she says. More than one ambulance.

I close my eyes, leaning my head back against the seat. The drive from the hotel is, in reality, only a stone's throw away from the ice palace. Tonight, it may as well be a cross-country drive for how long it feels. I'm in suspended animation here, unable to do or critically analyze anything until I get some answers about my siblings.

Please don't let the kids die because I was too weak to protect them.

It isn't fair to put this on my shoulders. Hell, we don't *know* for certain that Daddy Dearest is behind the fire, but I'd bet my life on it. It reeks of his personal style, after all.

I lift my head up just in time to see Tess push the car into the sea of reporters, rolling down her window and telling the police officers on duty who she is. They usher us through the crowd and past the front gate. Tess hits the emergency brake, but forgets to put the car in park, so Parrish leans between the seats to do it for her as she takes off out the door, car still running.

We chase after her, stepping onto the gravel drive and looking up at the roaring orange and yellow flames that are eating away at the left side of the house. They look like hungry demons, consuming everything that gets in their path. Firefighters are on-site, spraying the blaze with massive hoses as smoke billows up to kiss the stars.

"Holy fuck." Chasm says it for us as Parrish—his face stricken and hands clenched into fists—looks around for our shared siblings. They were all in that house tonight. Ben, Amelia, Henry, Kimber, Paul. Even GG. I highly doubt our new pet is alive.

In typical Tess fashion, she marches right up to the nearest unoccupied firefighter and snatches at the woman's sleeve, commanding attention. For once, it's an appropriate use of her awe-inspiring power. They speak in low tones, impossible to hear over the gathered crowd and the distant popping and spitting, cracking and shattering that comes from the blaze.

There's a strange, still interim there where Tess turns, silhouetted against the light for the briefest of seconds. This is it, a make-or-break moment for everyone in this family. If the kids are gone, then the possibility of us all working out our differences and building something new together is as intangible as the gray plume of smoke trailing up from the ruined corner of the house.

Tess collapses to the grass, sobbing, and Parrish runs up to her, Chasm and me in tow.

"They're alive," she's whispering, over and over again. My heart skips a beat as Parrish falls to his knees beside our mother, clasping her hands in his. "They've been taken to the hospital, but they're all okay." Tess' head snaps up, and I follow her gaze over to something huddled in the grass.

It takes me a minute to realize that it's …

"Maxx!" His name bursts from my lips like a spell, and I find myself gathering up my skirts to run over to him. His head snaps my way, and he rises from the grass, shirtless and with something small bundled in his arms. When my heels get caught in the lawn, I kick them off and sprint the rest of the way to X in bare feet sparkling with dew. He's coughing, but his triumphant grin is almost blindingly white through the soot covering the majority of his face.

My arms go around his neck as I throw myself against him, heedless of the bundle held tight to his chest. Our mouths connect with a sizzle as I dig my fingers into the back of his thick, wavy hair, the chalky feel of ash flaking onto my skin. The fire's heat is nothing compared to the flavor of that kiss, even if Maxx's lips are sooty and gritty, even if he can only kiss me for a moment before his chest seizes with the urge to cough.

That kiss, it only lasts a split-second, but it becomes a memento of my youth, a reminder that the harsh slog of reality can be broken up by brief, breathless respites. It's also a turning point for me, this sudden realization that I can't simply pick a boy. It isn't like that. *I can't choose; I have to let them each decide what they're willing to endure.*

Our lips part with terrible reluctance, but I won't let him get too far away from me; I keep my arms wrapped around his neck. Maxx chuckles but the sound is cut off by a fit of violent coughing that he struggles to get under control.

"Careful, Kota," he whispers finally, nuzzling his face against mine before looking down. I follow his gaze to see what it is that he's cuddling against his chest so carefully. It's GG, our resident white rabbit, wrapped in his shirt. Guess that explains why he isn't wearing one at the moment (which is totally fine with me BTW).

"GG!" I breathe in stark relief, stroking my hand over the bunny's ears as myriad emotions swirl through me. Relief. Fear. *Rage.* Because, while there's the very slim possibility that this was an accidental fire, it's much more likely that this was Justin's doing. The way he smiled at us on our way out of the ballroom is proof enough. "You saved GG?" I ask as I hear footsteps behind me.

Even though it hurts, even though it *aches,* I remove my arms from around X's neck and take a small step back, allowing him room to breathe. The way his gaze catches on mine, and the slow blink he offers me, says that he isn't all about that (the space I mean). He wants to be close to me, and he knows that I know it. Maxx hooks a bit of a smirk, allowing the expression to simmer before the others join us.

Does he know how cocky he is? Turning what could've well been the worst moment of my life into a heart-racing, pulse-thundering, palm-sweating flirtation? What a dickhead. Also, he's a goddamn hero, so if he wants to be arrogant and sexy and kissable, who am I to stop him?

Both Chasm and Parrish move around on either side of me to hug Maxx. That's one of the things I love most about these boys: they're not afraid to show affection for one another.

"I saved the rabbit," Maxx confirms finally, adjusting his grip on the bunny bundle that's pressed to his wide, solid chest. His arms and hands are sooty, but his midsection is mostly clear giving him the appearance of a farmer's tan. Sexiest farmer's tan I've ever seen, can't lie.

"He saved *everyone*," Tess corrects, her voice soft and thick with tears. "Oh, Maxim." I step aside so that Tess can give her son's friend a huge hug. If she noticed that I kissed him, or that our behavior is indicative of intimacy beyond simple friendship, she doesn't let on. "But he needs to give someone that damn bunny and go to the hospital."

X offers up a knowing smile, glancing down at the rabbit. I sort of thought GG was going to be my pet; I'm realizing now that he's actually Maxx's baby.

"Wait. *You* saved everyone?" Parrish asks, tilting his head to the side as he tucks his shaking hands into the pockets of his slacks to hide the slight trembling. God forbid he show any emotion. Parrish is the master of keeping his feelings hidden beneath willful indolence. "What does that even mean?"

"I ..." Maxx starts, licking his glossy lower lip. *I kissed it clean. Me. I did that.* Reaching up, I surreptitiously swipe the borrowed soot from my own lips. X notices, and he exhales strangely, and I *swear* that I can feel him yearning and wanting for me the same way that I am for him. I look up and our gazes clash. It's quite clear that there's something he wants to say but not when Tess is around. "I wanted to be here when you guys got back from prom; the house was already smoky when I walked in the front door."

"He carried everyone outside," Tess declares proudly, glancing down at her phone. It's quite clear she's desperate to get to the hospital, but also that she won't move from this spot until Maxim gets in an ambulance. "Even Paul."

"How many times did you have to go back in there?" Chasm chokes out and then he mumbles something in Korean as he rakes his fingers through his hair. "Holy shit, dude."

"Uh, three?" Maxx's voice is hoarse, almost unrecognizable. Yep, his perky ass is going to the hospital whether he likes it or not. He offers up a small, disbelieving laugh, like he can hardly imagine how he ever gathered the courage in the first place. But it's easy for me—for all of us, probably—to understand. That's just who Maxim Wright is in his heart. He'd give his life to save somebody else's.

It's a comforting and yet simultaneously terrifying thought.

"And you even remembered the rabbit," Parrish repeats as we all turn our attention down to the bunny's trembling body. "You braved a house fire … for a rabbit." There's awe and wonder in my stepbrother's voice, a glimmer that's echoed in Tess' gaze, in Chasm's, in my own, I'm sure.

"Mm." Maxx absently plays with GG's ears, and my heart explodes with love. He might be a dominant dickhead sometimes, and he really can be righteously annoying, but … he risked his life for a bunny that he never even asked for or wanted. That's true compassion. "They won't let me in the ambulance with GG."

"Jesus, X," Parrish murmurs, reaching out to scoop the bunny from his arms. "You need to get checked out; you've inhaled a lot of smoke." I've never quite heard the Prince of Sloths sound so … soft or grateful before. At least, not to anyone but me. As if on cue, Maxx begins a hacking cough that has Tess rubbing his back in small circles.

"Let's go. I'll follow you." She glances up at us. "Why don't … you call your father to come and get the rabbit? Then he can drop you off at the hospital."

My throat tightens up as Chasm scowls, but, if you were Tess and you had no idea of what was really going on, it's a logical conclusion to come to. Who else is going to come and get us? Our friends (that is, if we still had any we could trust) are all at prom. There are other cars in the garage, but although the fire is primarily contained to the second level of the house, it's damn close to the garage. I'm not sure if any of the vehicles will be usable after tonight—including my birthday BMW with the smashed windshield.

Tess doesn't mention the kiss between me and Maxx, but there's no doubt in my mind that she saw it. Add to that the fact that she knows I'm dating Chasm, and now suspects me of dating her son. I'm going to have a lot to answer for once this is all sorted.

So looking forward to that, thanks universe. Tonight is a smooth bar of dark chocolate speckled with clusterfucks. Overall, it turned out okay, but there's a hint of unpleasantness in each bite.

Maxx meets my eyes, reaching up to touch the side of my face as Tess stares at the two of us with a burning curiosity that she works out with a shake of her head. As soon as X drops his hand, she's leading him away toward the ambulance.

"Come visit me, Kota; I'll be waiting," is what he whispers as he passes by, hooking his pinky with mine for a brief instance before we're parted, and I'm pining after him like … a love-obsessed teen? Eww, gross. Is there anything worse?

"She knows," Parrish says, looking after them as he strokes the terrified bunny with a shaking hand of his own. He glances back at me, meeting my eyes with that familiar spark that's been between us since moment one. As soon as I walked in and saw him half-naked, chugging milk straight from the carton, I knew: Parrish Vanguard and I were meant to be. "About us. About Maxx now, probably. Do we have a story?"

"How about the truth?" I query as Chasm groans, running both hands down his face. He looks half-ready to collapse. The relief in the air is palpable, but also, our house is still on fire. We might've just lost everything. I force those thoughts to the side. Life is infinitely more precious than *stuff*, and everyone lived—thanks to X. *Only* because of X.

I have a terrible feeling that five people (six, if you count GG) were supposed to die in the ice palace tonight. *Justin.* I cannot shake the idea that this is part of his plotting. Not the rescuing part, just the murdering.

Panic sets in, but I focus on the current conversation instead.

"While I admire that aspect in all three of you," Chasm begins, punctuating the words by pointing at me, Parrish, and Maxx's back as he steps up into the ambulance, "this is going to come back to bite us in the ass. Tess will *never* accept the two of you together."

"She's going to have to get used to it," Parrish snaps back and then sighs heavily. "Do we really have to call Justin? Isn't there someone else that could deal with the bunny and give us a ride?"

"You mean like Gavin or Antonio? How about Danyella and Lumen? We're running short on friends here, Parrish," Chasm reminds him, putting his own hands in his pockets.

"That's actually not a bad idea," I say, deciding that if we're going to trust Lumen ever again, it should start now. We'll repair our relationship with baby steps. We can't call her directly—Justin would know about that—but there are other ways. "Let's call Danyella."

"You're joking right, *Naekkeo*?" Chas asks, and I guess that Parrish is just too distracted to either notice or comment on the use of a nickname that means 'mine' or 'my sweetheart'. "Sounds to me like Maxx wasn't supposed to be here tonight. Do you understand what that means?"

My blood chills as I look down at GG instead of at his or Parrish's grim facial expressions.

"Justin was trying to kill my siblings," I whisper, and the

horror of that just sinks into my bones, poisoning me against him even further. Because I just *know* this was his doing. He both hates and loves Tess; I think he simultaneously wants to punish her and have her to himself.

How better to do that than to kill her family?

"Tess keeps saying *you kids are my heart* over and over again." I look up to meet Parrish's eyes as he drags in a deep inhale. "I'm not saying it's impossible that this was an accident, but more than likely, it's Justin."

"It was Justin," Chasm confirms, unconsciously fiddling with the spot where one of his lip rings would normally sit. He nearly disrupts the filler and curses, forcing himself to stop fidgeting. "I knew the guy was nuts, but ... he was going to suffocate and/or burn a bunch of little kids to death? That's ... dark."

There are no words to describe how I feel right now, so I don't bother.

"Shit, did Tess just take off with our phones?" I ask, but Chasm smirks at me and reaches out, smudging a bit of soot from the edge of my mouth. He stares down at his thumb for a moment before lifting his gaze back to mine.

"Don't worry: your *oppa* has your back." I kick him in the shin as he snorts and moves away, pausing next to a decorative pot full of flowers. He digs out our phones and then passes them out. Hopefully, Justin wasn't able to hack into our previous conversation.

"I thought it was supposed to be sleazy when a guy refers to himself as *oppa*?" I ask wryly, clustered in the shadows of the yard with the boys while the flames roar and firefighters shout to one another. There's so much going on that I think we're all having trouble processing. Right now, I'd rather focus on teasing and flirtation.

Oppa is a complicated Korean word that can mean anything

from *brother* to *older male friend* to *lover.* The meaning is based on tone and context and relationship status. I *could* very well call Chasm by the term *oppa.* My cheeks flush at the idea, and Parrish rolls his eyes, still stroking the bunny.

"It is sleazy," he agrees, giving Chas a warning look that his friend ignores. "I swear, if you start calling him *oppa,* I'll poison his food."

"That's how you treat me after I suffered so much to bring you home?" Chasm retorts, hitting call on Danyella's number. He's obviously teasing, but there's a pang in those words that can't be faked. Having Parrish back with us still feels so new and tenuous, fragile somehow. To be fair, it's only been a week.

It's like a dream.

Parrish turns away, looking past me in the direction of the house. He affects his usual blasé demeanor, but there's a tightness in his throat when he swallows that tells me he's more upset by this than he's letting on.

I offer him some privacy by redirecting my attention to the screen of my Maxine-phone.

There aren't any messages from the Slayer's number, but there's a text from Justin's regular one.

Princess, I just heard about the fire; I'm on my way to the house. I'd be happy to give you a ride to the hospital.

My stomach goes sour as I tap out a quick, angry message in response.

Already found a ride, but thanks.

I turn the phone off and slip it into Parrish's pocket while he cuddles GG and watches the fire blaze. When his eyes drop to mine, I see a shiny new determination there, one that's edged with violence.

If he could, he'd kill Justin Prior for me.

Only, I can't let him take that burden on, now can I?

"Hey, can you give us a ride?" Chasm asks, and then he pauses, releasing an annoyed huff. "Did I ask to speak with you, Lumen? This is Danyella's phone, asshole." He lets her talk and then scowls. "Yeah, I'm aware it's the same car we smashed up. Do you even care that the Vanguard's house is on fire?"

He hangs up and sighs, and for a second there, I almost believe that they're not coming, that I imagined the talk we shared in the hedge maze.

"They'll be here in a minute." Chasm hesitates, as if there's something else he wants to say, but then he looks down at his phone and shakes his head. He turns, and so do I, so that the three of us are shoulder to shoulder, watching the hoses douse the flames.

But even when the fire goes out, there's collateral damage to worry about.

And yeah, that is most definitely a metaphor for my life.

———

Lumen's pretty pink convertible—essentially a real-life version of a Barbie dream car—pulls into the driveway like it's racing NASCAR. Chasm curses and hops out of the way, running his fingers through his hair.

"Have you lost your damn mind?!" he snaps at her as she flings the door open and stumbles out in bare feet, her heels kicked off onto the driver's side floor mat.

She lifts her phone up and points at it before chucking it overhanded into the grass a good twenty feet away. Very dramatic, but hey, it works. Chasm just raises an eyebrow, gathers up our phones yet again, and *carries* them over to a spot that's hopefully out of earshot of our conversation.

C.M. STUNICH

"OMG, this is actually happening ..." Lumen murmurs, pressing her hand over her perfectly painted mouth. She looks like a goddess with her white-blonde hair in a half-do, twisted into a glorious chignon at the back of her head, the rest of it cascading over her shoulders in gentle waves.

Her pale brown eyes take in the flames and the firefighters and the mess of humanity currently occupying our front lawn before she turns that worried gaze over to me. Before Lumen can get a word out, Danyella's climbing from the passenger side of the freshly-repaired BMW and clearing her throat.

"Dakota." Just that one word. In it, I can hear a thousand different emotions, none of which I have the emotional energy to parse through. My body feels heavy, and it takes all that I've got not to sag to the lawn on my knees and scream.

Justin Prior, the Seattle Slayer, (worst of all) my biological father was willing to *slaughter* my entire ... well, not *family* per se, but like *family.* If that makes sense. Of course it doesn't. Nothing makes sense right now.

I rub at my face with both palms, drawing Parrish's angry visage away from Lumen and Danyella and down to me. He softens his expression and puts one, hot inked hand on the small of my back, lighting me up on the inside like a sunrise. With his other, he keeps GG tucked close.

"Are you sure you want to do this?" he murmurs, his voice strong and comforting, despite the horrific blaze consuming the ice palace. The Vanguard's house. *My* house. Because I've been living here, and I was even starting to feel okay with it. All of my things are in that room, the furniture that my grandmother made me, the antiques, the photograph of Saffron with her arms around me and Maxine. The old, well-loved copies of Harry Potter that Saffron gifted to me. Parrish's art, his sketchbooks, his (hopefully uploaded to the cloud) iPad.

Everything.

I swallow past a lump in my throat, squeezing my hands into fists and forcing myself to look on the bright side: Parrish is alive and he's back, the kids are okay, GG is okay, Maxx is okay. Erm, and Paul … Okay, okay, the guy might be a total bore and an ignorant, pretentious, classist a-wad, but he's not all bad. He has a good heart.

Better than Justin, certainly.

Whereas Paul might be superficial and rude (like, who offers a nose job to a teenager as a gift? especially when said teenager never asked for one), but also, he doesn't kill people. Gotta give credit where credit is due, am I right?

"Hitch a ride?" I query back, glancing over to see those honey-flecked eyes focused on me. Parrish is a vision, even limned against the dying light of the flames. The firefighters in Medina are top-notch, and they've managed to bring the rampaging inferno down to a whisper, a mere suggestion of fire.

"You know that's not what I mean." He frowns at me, his face a pretty, insouciant moue. Parrish gestures at Lumen with one of his elegantly inked hands. "I mean this. Them. The girls who enjoyed stabbing you right in the back when you needed them most."

"Hey!" Lumen retorts, huffing and reaching up to adjust the pins in her hair. "Not fair. I already explained to you that I was being blackmailed. Do you think I enjoyed having my girls kick my crush's ass?"

"Your crush?" Chasm snorts and murmurs something in Korean. "*Dang-geun.*" I think that means … carrot? Or else, I'm totally missing something here (which is the most likely explanation). Then again, maybe it's slang? He gestures at the pair of girls and scowls in turn. "This is your one chance, Hearst. You fuck this up, and I don't care if you've got XX chromosomes—I will knock your ass to kingdom come."

"Real cute, Kwang-seon. Threaten to hit a girl. I'm sure Dakota finds that beyond charming." Lumen flutters her thick falsies as she moves over to stand in front of me, Danyella hovering in the background. She puts her hands on my shoulders, causing both Parrish and Chasm to bristle in annoyance. "Are you okay, sweetie?" When she reaches up to brush hair back from my forehead, I stop her with a gentle hand on the wrist.

"I'm fine." I glance over at Parrish as he cradles GG against the front of his charcoal-colored suit, dress shirt, and tie. That monochromatic outfit with the colorful art on the backs of his hands, his blond-kissed brown hair, and those eyes … It's a feast. If only I had the time or leisure to appreciate it more. "This is Parrish's house, too. His siblings. His dad. His art."

He closes his eyes and turns his head away from me for a moment before opening them again. He stares up at the white cube box that, while a hideous display of modern architecture, maybe wasn't quite as cold on the inside as I'd first thought. Parrish offers GG over to me, and I take the rabbit in my arms.

"I can make new art," he says, his voice as monochromatic as his outfit. "We can't resurrect the dead." The edge of his lip tweaks in a slight smirk as he turns back to me. "Life isn't a video game, right? I'll be okay." He lifts out an arm and pushes his jacket up to reveal more of his tattooed skin. With his eyes on mine, I only see it in my peripheral vision.

I'm consumed by his stare, drawn in and twisted around his heart. It's hard to believe that I walked into this only four short months ago and found him scowling at me, shirtless and holding a milk carton with the words *MISSING CHILD* printed on the side of it.

Like an omen. Like a prophecy. Like clever foreshadowing in one of Tess Vanguard's books.

ENDGAME ROMANCE

"My best art is right here anyway." He taps at his forearm with two fingers as Danyella edges just a bit closer to us, fidgeting with the skirts of her red dress. It pairs well with the slender gold belt at her waist and the cascade of tight braids over her shoulder. Each one ends in a wave of glossy dark brown hair that's kissed with the faintest hint of glitter.

It's the way she yanks on those braids in a nervous gesture that I've never seen before that causes me to draw my gaze away from Parrish and over to her.

"You don't have to forgive us or anything. Just ... let us give you a ride to the hospital."

"Fantastic," Chas declares, clapping his hands together and offering up a cocky smirk that makes my heart flutter. "Because we sure as shit weren't prepared to offer up any such thing." He moves past Lumen, knocking into her with his shoulder and making her scowl.

"You are on thin ice, McKenna," she snaps out, her cheeks reddening slightly with shame as she turns back to me and then, almost reluctantly, over to the house. "Do they know how the fire started?" Lumen's question warbles slightly, and I know what she's thinking: *the blackmailer did it.*

If only she knew the full truth behind that.

"I'm so sorry this happened." Danyella reaches up to adjust her glasses—a brand-new pair in gold to match the gold chain of her belt. "Truly, I am. If you need a place to crash for a while, I'm sure my parents would be more than willing to put you all up."

I smile at her, trying and failing to fully fight back the tears. They prick the edges of my gaze, the salt burning my smoke-irritated eyes. I dash them away and end up with makeup smeared on the back of my hand. Not that it matters.

Who cares about makeup when there's ... this.

"I'm sure Tess will find us a place, but ..." I trail off and look down at the bunny before returning my attention to Danyella's face. "Can you watch our rabbit for us?"

"Rabbit? Since when did you have a rabbit?" Lumen asks, but I'm not about to get into that story just now. I hand the quivering bundle over to her, and she stares down at it like she's never seen a bunny in all her life. "It's, um, cute? But what do I do with it?"

Danyella sighs and moves over to take the poor creature from her friend.

"Lumen can't keep a cactus alive; I'll take care of the bunny for you."

I nod, and my attention swings back to the house.

It's a lot to process. I'm upset about so many things, but I'm the most upset about seeing Justin's full colors bloom.

Or ... should I say color?

Because he's as monochromatic as Parrish's voice, as his suit, as Chasm's black-on-black attire.

Only Justin Prior? Well, his color is *blood-fucking-red.*

The color of death.

If he'd had his way tonight, if Maxx hadn't stopped by ... then the entire Vanguard family save for myself, Parrish, and Tess would be dead.

It hits me yet again, that awful realization, that recurring nightmare of reality.

To stop Justin Prior, I'm going to have to kill him.

Me.

Because there's only one person who he would ever let his guard down around long enough to do the deed. Looking down at my hands, I splay my fingers in the gold tulle of my skirts and try my very best not to imagine that they're already covered in that same vibrant red.

In *blood.*

CHAPTER

2

"Pretend to hate me, okay?" Lumen asked that of us just before we collected our phones and climbed in the car together. Apparently, she's allowed to give us a ride for Danyella's sake (she went with Lumen to prom as a plus-one instead of a date), but nothing more. *Well-played, Justin. Very cute.* I wonder if he expects her to go double-agent?

Chasm's response was a very cheery, *"like that'd be hard."* Clearly, *he* expects her to go double-double-agent. Or whatever it's called when you double-cross and then double-cross again. Wait. Does that just make you a regular agent? *Mindless thought diarrhea, Kota. Chill out.*

Never have I seen an awkward silence that's quite so heavy, quite so sticky, quite so full of unspoken things as this. And trust me: I have seen my fair share. Until you've met your birth mom who also happens to be your favorite author and also who you didn't know existed until like three seconds ago, sitting right there beside your incredibly loving but shell-shocked grandparents, well, you don't quite understand the meaning of awkward.

That is equivalent to this.

There are friendships in this car that stretch for nearly a decade. Some longer. There are broken promises, veiled threats, uncertainty, lies, and just a little sprinkle of hope from yours truly.

Lumen clears her throat and fiddles around with her car stereo.

Even if we were inclined to talk amongst ourselves, we wouldn't, not with all of us carting our phones around. Justin could be listening in on us even now. Speaking of, I received an unsurprising but supremely annoying text from him about five minutes ago.

I'm glad you found a ride; I'll meet you at the hospital.

Because of course. Because serial killers like trophies. Because I'm *sure* that serial killers don't like to have their plans foiled by nineteen-year-old motocross racers. Now, I'm sitting here and fiddling with my phone, waiting for a response from Maxx's parents who are supposed to be at the hospital now. I just want to make sure he's okay, that he's never left alone with Justin …

A familiar song starts to play, one that I inadvertently end up mouthing the words to. I'm stressed, and the music is helping.

At least, it is until I happen to glance over and find Chasm staring at me with a single dark brow cocked in question.

"Mm-hmm." He purses his lips but is clearly trying not to look overly pleased at the same time. He sings an entire line of the song to me—it's all in Korean, mind you—and because I'm still a tad shell-shocked, it takes me a second to realize three things.

One, the song that's playing— *"Some"* a collaboration between SOYOU, Junggigo, and LILBOI—is coming from my phone. Apparently, I left Lumen's car attached to my Bluetooth and she's accidentally started my playlist. A playlist that's titled *Sexy Songs in Korean that I want Chasm to Sing for Me.*

Also, that playlist's name is displayed prominently on the

display in the front of the car.

Also, also, the song features the word *naekkeo* about sixty-billion times.

Yeah, that *naekkeo,* the nickname that Chasm gave me that means 'mine' or 'my sweetheart'.

Erm, also he's just sang it to me, and I'm flushed all over, and he's smirking at me, and I can not only feel Parrish glaring at him from across the back seat, but also both Lumen's and Danyella's confusion from the front.

Right. They're, um, not fully aware of the whole situation. I mean, Kimber ran her mouth around the Whitehall campus about me and Chas sleeping together, and I admitted to Lumen in the hedge maze that I had feelings for Parrish, Chasm, and Maxx. But I'm certain they don't know much more than that. They both might even be under the impression that the 'me and Chas thing' is just a baseless rumor.

I clear my throat as Parrish hisses something out in Korean, and Chasm grins back at him. I'm almost afraid to look over my shoulder to see Parrish's expression.

"What does that line mean?" Danyella asks, her tone conversational but awkward. We've barely spoken a handful of words to one another in the last several weeks, but I'd like it if … Well, despite everything, I still want to be friends.

Does that make me crazy? Pretty sure that it does.

"It means," Parrish begins, his tone low and colored with annoyance, "Something like, *nowadays, it feels like you're mine, it's as if you're mine but you're not.*" He scoffs and I feel my cheeks turning a very bright and very unfortunate shade of red.

The song fades out, and I exhale a small sigh of relief, one that doesn't last very long because …

The lyrics to the next song go a little something like this: *naekkeo naekkeo naekkeo neon neon naekkeo naekkeo neon.*

Basically, it's the nickname that Chasm gave me playing over and over again. The song is *"Mine"* by Team Green.

With a deep groan, I faceplant into both palms, the horror of the fire temporarily pushed back by the powerful hose of shame. Deep, deep shame.

"Dakota Banks," Chasm begins, sitting up and folding his hands behind his head for a moment. "If one didn't know any better, one might think you had a crush on me." I lift my head up just in time to see him wet his lips and then lunge between the seats, switching over to the next song.

It's … yeah, I'm a crazy person: it's titled *"Naekkeo"* by F.CUZ.

"Lumen, turn it off!" I shout, unlocking my phone and trying to stop Chas before he can discover any more of my little secrets.

He switches the song again, over to *"Butter"* by BTS.

"Oh, come on, this isn't even in Korean!" He turns around to look at me as I frantically tap at an Ashnikko song. Now, I'm not only a simp for Ashnikko; I'm a K-pop simp. *Wait, never mind. I was always both of those things.* "My accent is way less extreme, don't you think?"

"Please," Parrish snorts, giving his friend a sneering once-over. "You don't have any accent at all." He reaches up and rakes his fingers through his pretty hair, offering up an urbane expression of unfiltered arrogance. "Not with a vocal coach like yours truly."

Chasm sits back in his seat, but he's not looking at Parrish. Instead, he's *staring* right at me.

"And if you keep practicing, maybe in a couple of years, you could actually visit Seoul and someone might understand you— that is, they might understand you as a foreigner with a heavy speech impediment."

Parrish leans past me to punch his friend in the shoulder, and I can't help but smile. I try to stifle it, but the bromance is too much

24

to deal with. It's so damn cute. Also, also, also … I missed Parrish so much that it still hurts. Seeing him and Chas together again like this, it's priceless.

Chasm leans in toward me, cupping a warm hand around my ear and making me shudder all over.

"*Saranghae,*" he whispers, and then he draws back to slump against the door in his wrinkled ebony suit, rubbing at his chin with pale fingers. My cheeks heat even more as Parrish reaches down, snatching my hand up in his. Chasm's amber eyes shine as he offers me up a dangerous half-smile. "We'll discuss this later, *Naekkeo.*"

"There's nothing to discuss," I choke out, but Chas just offers up a dark chuckle and a shake of his head.

"Sure there is." He looks away, toward the window and the darkness beyond it, the expression on his face losing its warmth. "Before we get to the hospital, the two of you better get your story straight."

"What story?" Lumen demands, her usual audaciousness intact. I'm not exactly ready to spill my darkest secrets around her—far from it—but my relationship with Parrish is a well-known fact around Whitehall, especially since he defended me against Veronica and her girl goons. "Is there more sordid gossip for me to spread?"

I know she's 'acting', but God, it's annoying. Chasm makes a sound of pure frustration.

"The story of … us." I glance back at Parrish, his hand still wrapped around mine. "What do you want to do?"

"You two are officially dating?" Danyella asks, peering at us from around the edge of her seat with GG clutched in her arms. Parrish tosses her a curled lip in response.

"Do you need to know that to report back to your boss?" he retorts, and Danyella inhales sharply, looking over at Lumen. The other girl doesn't acknowledge her, leaving her hands curled so tightly around the wheel that her knuckles are ghost-white. Parrish redirects his attention to me, offering up a grim half-smile. "Should we do it then? Rip the bandage off?"

"Make up an excuse," Chasm demands, leaning in toward us, face earnest. "Doesn't matter how paper-thin it is. Anything is better than the truth."

"I already explained to you: I'm done hiding my love for Dakota," Parrish throws back at him, and Chas scoffs, snorting in Korean under his breath. Only, that trick doesn't work because in their brilliant bromance, they taught each other their native languages. Parrish fires off on him, and Chasm retorts. As they throw foreign curses over my lap, I sit there and stare down at my knees.

The less lies I have to sort through, the better.

At this point, I'm not even sure that I can keep track of them all anymore.

Better to let something like this go than slip up on one of Justin's many requests.

"I'm not saying you're wrong," I tell Chasm, and he groans heavily, slumping back against the door again and putting his fingers to his forehead, eyes closed. "Tess is probably going to kill me."

"You?" Parrish asks, reaching out to turn my chin back toward him. "I'll make it my fault."

"How so?" I ask, narrowing my eyes to slits. "You're her baby, Parrish. I'm … the interloper. Besides, you just came home after missing for nineteen days. Do you really think Tess would blame you for this?"

"*You* are her baby," he retorts, face falling as he, too, turns to look out the window. "Anyway, I'm the guy. It makes more sense to blame the dude in these sorts of situations." His smile shifts into one of smarmy self-confidence. "Trust me: I'll *make* it my fault."

"Bad idea," Chasm breathes, shaking his head again. "Terrible idea. Horrendous. When the two of you come crying to me and Maxx looking to make things better, well." Chas snorts as I glance his way again. "What are you going to tell Tess about me, huh? And, also, not sure if you noticed, but you just Frenched the fuck out of Maxx in front of her, too."

"I'll … figure it out," I mumble, trying my best to ignore Danyella's inquisitive gaze in the rearview mirror. Luckily, the drive doesn't take more than a few more minutes.

Lumen drops us off in front of the hospital in Bellevue, but when she tries to get out, Chasm moves over to her door and pushes it closed, waiting for her to roll down the window.

"What is your problem?" she snaps, but he doesn't budge from where he is, hands braced on the edge of the open window.

"Thanks for the ride, but you're not coming in. We might be willing to accept a ride from you, but we're not all suddenly friends." He shoves away from the car and comes around the front, joining me and Parrish under the overhang. It's just started to rain outside because, you know, of course it would. That can only help with the fire though, right?

"What?" he asks, but I just shake my head.

"I didn't say anything." I look past him to where Danyella and Lumen are clearly arguing inside the pink BMW. Chasm isn't wrong. I *want* to be friends again; I *want* to believe their motivations were similar to mine. That is, that they had little choice in the matter. But I can't forget that even *if* the two of them truly feel sorry for what they've done, it doesn't mean they won't keep doing it.

Knowing Justin, I doubt there's an easy way out for any of us.

I turn around and head inside. We run right into Tess, pacing the lobby and making phone calls. She pauses when she sees us, exhaling in relief.

"Come with me," she commands, tucking her phone away and leading the three of us up in an elevator. With our prom outfits, Tess' notoriety, and Parrish's kidnapping, it's as if the whole world is staring at us. I do my best to ignore them, palms sweating, throat tightening up with myriad emotions.

I'm nervous.

About seeing my siblings, about seeing Maxx, about Tess' question, about Justin showing up ...

We start in Amelia's room, and I'm glad to see she's awake, bright-eyed and bushy-tailed. Henry, too. Ben is already thumbing through another mid-grade fantasy novel, and Kimber ...

Well, Kimber is Kimber.

Even after almost dying, she's got a bit of an attitude.

"How long do I have to stay here? I'm fine," she protests, pushing her hair back and trying to put on a look of beautiful disdain for Chasm. She even manages to give me a disparaging once-over before Tess finally gives up and lets us leave. Paul is next, accepting a hug from Parrish and Chasm both. But my stepdad and me? Yeah, we're not exactly there yet.

Maxx is last.

I'm practically shaking as we make our way down the hall to his room.

"He got the worst of it," Tess explains, pausing outside the door to knock. "He went back in so many times, I ..." She trails off, her eyes—so similar to my own deep brown that it's disturbing —brimming with tears. She places a hand over her mouth for a brief moment to get her emotions under control before returning to the cool, collected star of the bestseller lists that I'm more used to. "Without Maxx, our entire family would've died tonight."

A voice calls out from inside, and Tess finally opens the door.

Maxx's parents—Laurent and Hamilton—are inside with him.

28

ENDGAME ROMANCE

There's a girl, too. A very pretty girl with dark brown hair, a slim, athletic build, and eyes like emeralds. She can only be Maxx's older sister, Tiffany Wright, the motocross star.

She has a high ponytail, and an angry frown on her face as she glances over to look at us.

"I'm still angry with you. Why not leave the stupid bunny?"

"Don't start on me, Tiff," Maxx warns her, his gaze for me and me alone. Does anyone else see that, the way he focuses on me and makes me feel like the only person in the room? Based on the way everyone turns to stare at me, I think they do.

They see it.

Tess gets a little more tense, nostrils flaring, arms crossed over her chest, but she doesn't say anything. Not now. But later. Oh boy, I'm going to pay for so many things later on.

"How are you feeling?" I murmur, choking on the words and clearing my throat as I sidle up to Maxx's bedside. He's dressed in a hospital gown, but it's slid down one of his muscular shoulders, revealing far too much of his chest for my liking.

I've touched this bare chest with my hands; I've licked *that chest.*

I almost groan at my own internal embarrassment, but I tamp the feelings down. *No, bad feelz. Go away. Not right now. Gamer Girl is busy.*

Figures that poor Parrish and Chasm would have their junior prom ruined by Justin.

"Much better, actually," Maxx begins as his sister looks me over from head to toe, coming to a conclusion all on her own. Even Laurent and Hamilton are studying me strangely.

"This is Maxine, right?" Tiffany asks, and I cringe. Wow. Um. How do I respond to that? How do I *explain* that?

With nervous laughter apparently, reaching up to brush strands of lime-green hair back from my forehead. *Tess doesn't know that my sister and X were dating. I'm* sure *this won't come back to bite me in the ass later.*

"I'm Maxine's little sister, Dakota Banks." That entire sentence makes Tess twitch, but she doesn't comment. She will later though, I'm sure. No doubts on that one.

"Oh ..." Tiffany whistles, drawing a thunderous look from Maxx.

"Let it go, Tiff," he grinds out under his breath. Parrish and Chasm take up on either side of me, like honor guards, and I feel a bit better at the show of support. "Anyway, I wish they'd just let me leave. I don't think I even need to be here. How's GG, by the way?"

"He's with Lumen and Danyella," I admit, and Maxx's face tightens up.

"We're taking Maxim home in the morning," Laurent begins, turning to Tess in that odd way anyone over the age of twenty-five does, where they look right over the heads of anyone under twenty-one like they're invisible, as if we're still children in a grown-up's world.

If they only knew all the things we did.

"Back to Portland?" Tess is inquiring politely, and my heart drops.

"I'm not going back to Portland," Maxx interrupts, and all three parents—his and mine—snap their heads over to him like he's sprouted more from his very pretty, very bare shoulder ... I reach out and, with a single finger, hook the edge of the gown, dragging it up to cover his nipple and pec.

Everyone stares at me.

Was that a weird thing to do? It was, wasn't it? It was totally weird.

X hooks a gorgeous, cocksure smile at me before turning back to his parents.

"I don't want to go back to Portland or Eugene, not yet." He clears his throat, and the sound is raspier than it should be. He might not think he needs to be in the hospital tonight, but I do. I'm glad he's here. "It's summer anyway, and the Vanguards are going to need help with cleaning up or moving or … whatever else."

Tess hooks a soft and tender smile, stepping forward and putting her hand over the railing at the end of the bed.

"Don't worry about us, Maxim. You've …" She pauses here to inhale and gather herself together again. Parrish steps up beside her and puts a hand on her back, giving it a small rub. Just a light and casual touch that speaks of love and familiarity, something that I'm not entirely certain that Tess and I will ever have. "You've done enough, honey. You saved my children, my husband." Tess gets a bit sniffly there, but she closes her eyes, and the moment passes.

"You're coming home," Laurent repeats gently, exchanging a look with his dark-haired husband before looking back at Maxx. "If the Vanguards need anything, you know we're always there to help. If your family needs a place to stay—"

"Oh no," Tess chokes out, almost bitterly. I raise my brows and catch Parrish's odd expression. He's surprised by that, too, by his mother's seeming annoyance with Laurent's offer. An explanation comes out soon enough, one that fills me with dread. "We've already been offered the use of Laverne's estate—"

"Grandma's place?" Parrish reiterates, shivering slightly. He hasn't seen his grandmother in person since he was rescued, something that all of us found odd. He had plans to spend time with her tomorrow, after I left to be with Justin.

Looks like we'll *all* be spending plenty of time with Laverne Vanguard.

*Um, like, yay? *insert sad-face emoji here**

If Tess isn't going to like the idea of me dating Parrish, I can only *imagine* what his blue-blooded billionaire grandmother is going to think. We've only met in person once, and she essentially accused me of scheming to insert myself into this family—a family that I *never* asked to be a part of. But now, I mean, after the fire tonight …

I shove those thoughts back.

Dealing with my emotions surrounding the kidnapping, Saffron, Tess, all that good stuff—side quest. Yeah, the most major event in my life is now just a freaking side quest, with an NPC who walks just a little faster than I do, but also way slower than I run (if you get it, you get it). Anyway, I've got the main storyline to deal with here.

That is: Justin and the fact that he damn near killed all of Parrish's and my siblings.

Is it weird that we share blood with four other people? Me and Parrish, mixed up in our brothers and sisters. It definitely makes this entire thing all that much more intense. If I'd liked Parrish even a fraction less than I do, it would've been an insurmountable ordeal. As such, I care about him too much to care.

"Yes," Tess continues, sniffling and also simultaneously gritting her teeth. "We'll be staying with your grandmother, and she's already offered to handle the cleanup and rebuild on the house." By *handle,* I assume she means *pay for.* But who knows? Tess and Paul are wealthy in their own right. Just not Laverne wealthy. Millionaires versus billionaires. Rich versus gluttonous? Ahem.

Chasm shifts slightly beside me.

"If you'd rather stay with me—" That's as much as he's able to get out before Tess is waving her hand dismissively. Pretty sure it's supposed to be a casual gesture, but it comes across as desperate.

"No need. The family will stay together." She lets out a grating laugh that causes Laurent and Hamilton to exchange a knowing look. It must be well-known Whitehall alumni drama that Tess and Laverne don't get along. That, or Medina gossip.

Because, as my bio dad so eloquently phrased it, *this town is cursed in blood and diamonds.*

"I'd still prefer to stay here," X repeats, his tone taking on that resolute edge, the one that says *yo, I know I seem nice but I'm totally an alpha-hole prick, and I'm not going anywhere.* I sweep my hands down the front of my gold tulle skirts, trying and failing to keep my body from having a reaction to that. It's the sort of reaction that makes a person feel all warm and squirmy, like they'd do anything to throw their arms around the other party in question.

Yeah. I want to hug the *fuck* out of Maxim Wright.

"You can bunk with me," Chasm repeats, nodding his chin in X's direction. "Like old times. We'll stay up till three playing games, and Dakota can kick our asses remotely." He crafts this sinful, mischievous little smile that doesn't do anything to help my overactive hormones, but which also falls just a tad short.

He's worried about Seamus, no doubt. Will his father even allow X to stay there? Guess that's a problem for another day. Just so long as we get Maxx's family to back off a bit.

"You're not staying here all summer playing video games with Kwang-seon," Tiffany says, looking over at me yet again, like she'd do anything to solve the puzzle of my relationship with her baby brother. She turns back to him as he frowns. "We should be hitting the track everyday—"

"I can hit the track plenty here," Maxx argues back, and then he does something which surprises the shit out of me. Oh yeah. *This* is why there's a big difference between nineteen and sixteen; he's a legal adult and I'm wrapped up in Tess' umbilical cord and strapped to her back. "I appreciate everyone's concern, but I am *not* going to be leaving Medina for a little while. Please stop talking about it. I've made my decision."

"Maxim Wright," Laurent chastises, but Hamilton reaches down and takes his husband's hand, offering up the slightest shake of his head.

"We agreed that it might be nice to spend some time up here while you get acclimated to your new job. It'd be nice to see the seeds of Justin's company sprout." Hamilton pauses and looks up, a surprised smile lighting his face. "Speak of the devil ..." he starts, and my blood chills.

All of those hot and itchy feelings the boys keep stirring up die inside of me, and I turn just in time to see the Seattle Slayer let himself into Maxx's hospital room—with friggin' *Caroline* in tow.

Caroline Bassett—Parrish's bio mom—is here in the flesh, and this is the first time Parrish has seen her in many, many years.

The three of us—me, Chas, X—turn immediately to Parrish.

The color in his face is completely gone. Sure, he's a white guy, but he's not like corpse-white or anything. I mean, not usually. He looks a bit like a vampire's freshly drained victim at the moment.

"Oh, goodness," Justin says, offering up a hug for Tess. He smiles so passionately and with such empathy that I'm immediately moved by his performance. If the guy didn't enjoy slaughtering teens so much, he could be the proud winner of an Oscar. "Tess, I'm so sorry; I heard about what happened."

She leaves him to stand there with his arms extended, her entire body taut with tension.

"Caroline," she breathes out, choking on the name. Tess' gaze goes right to Parrish, and she steps in front of him, as if to block him from a physical blow.

Yet another talented thespian in the room, Caroline puts a hand to her chest, leaning toward Tess with a look of sheer compassion tainting her Parrish-like features. I can see her DNA written all over his face—just like with me and Tess.

"What a horrific tragedy," she schmoozes in that way that rich people do, when they're pretending to care but actually don't give a shit. All tinged, of course, with frigid gentility and cool politeness dressed in propriety. "I'm so glad everyone made it out okay."

Justin finally drops his arms to his sides, offering up this 'good ol' boy' type look in the Wrights' direction. *Women, am I right, my dudes?* That's what his expression says, and it just ... it fucking *infuriates* me. How dare this deranged Disney-loving maniac Millennial look at Tess like she's the crazy one when he very clearly arranged to have the house set on fire in the first place!

My hands squeeze into fists in my skirts, and I'm gritting my teeth so hard that my jaw aches.

"Relax, Little Sister," Chas breathes, gently placing his left hand on my hip. He's pressed up close behind me, too. Probably a bit too close. I lean back into him anyway, soaking up his warmth and allowing it to chase away the near blind rage building inside of me. "He's grooming you, *Naekkeo.* Always remember that. He wants you to be mad. He wants you to react."

I know Chas is right. I know it. Yet the very act of holding back right now is killing me softly on the inside.

The room goes virtually silent there for a minute, but whereas it was awkward inside of Lumen's Barbie-mobile, this is just plain weird. Weird but also menacing. I feel like a butterfly caught in a spider's web. Thing is, none of the spiders can eat me just yet because they're too busy fighting with each other.

This is definitely deep Medina bullshit, just the next step up from the Whitehall drama I've been dealing with.

"Are you here to see Maxx? If so, we'll step out of the room and give you your privacy." Tess glances back at Parrish, me, and Chasm. "Kids. Let's get something to eat downstairs, shall we?" She turns and moves to head for the door, but Justin reaches out to put a hand on her arm. He stops just short of doing it at a whiplash look from Tess, and then offers a patronizing smile.

"If you need a place to stay …" he begins, and Tess returns the gesture with a caustic snort of her own.

"Thank you, Justin, but we'll be just fine." She continues on, but the Slayer isn't finished. He focuses his gaze on me instead.

"Dakota, at the very least, may as well start staying with me for the time being. Would you like that, princess, to come see your new room?" His blue eyes sparkle, but there's no command here. At least, he hasn't given any. Much as I want to see Maxine, I can't bear the thought of going with the man now. Not only because it would feel like *Slayer, 1: Tess, 0* or something, but because the knowledge of what he did—of what he tried to do—is stirring up equal parts disgust and fury in me.

I can't be alone with Justin, not tonight.

Tess turns all the way around, watching and waiting to see what I'll say. She's testing me. I know that. She's tested me more times than I care to count. Most of those tests, I've failed spectacularly at thanks to Justin's command.

"Tell this fucker to piss off," Chas murmurs from behind me. Parrish says nothing, but he's watching me. Every now and again, his gaze flickers to Caroline, but it comes right back. Either he can't bear to be separated from me or else he can't bear to look at his biological mother. Maybe a bit of both? He hasn't seen the woman since he was three years old; Caroline is as much a stranger to Parrish as Tess was to me. Worse since she *chose* not to have contact with him.

"You don't have to go with him tonight if you don't want to," Maxx adds, sitting up and looking like he must just tear those tubes out of his arm and launch himself at Justin. I'd rather he didn't punch the guy again. As satisfying as that was (as guiltily satisfying as the punishment might've been), I do not want to see what Justin Prior would offer as punishment for a second violation.

"Of course she doesn't have to go with me." Justin frowns and glances over at Caroline who's standing there playing with the neckline of her sweater with the black fur cuffs. It's very, um, Cruella de Vil of her? Somehow, I imagine that fur isn't faux. Based on the woman's overall level of warmth, I could easily see her, like, clubbing baby seals to death for the right outfit.

She's just that sort of person.

"Then I'll see you tomorrow?" It's almost a question. No, it is a question. Much as I'd like to go at ol' Daddy Dearest with a full arsenal of snark, wordplay, and sarcasm, I can't do anything to risk Maxine. If he's letting me skip an extra night with him, I'll take it. But I'm not pushing.

"Tomorrow is just fine, sweetheart."

I turn back to X, reaching out to give his hand a quick squeeze which again draws the attention of everyone in the room—Maxx's sister and parents especially. Tess and Caroline continue to stare at one another, and the tension ratchets up yet another notch.

They tear apart with a clash like lightning and the roar of thunder, and then Tess is clacking her heels down the hallway and Parrish is snatching my hand. He drags me toward the door, Chasm in tow. We manage to make it just past the threshold before Justin lands a hand on my shoulder.

"A moment?" he asks, sweet as pie. The door to Maxx's hospital room closes and Caroline goes about lowering the blinds. Bit of an overreach, maybe? But nobody stops her. Parrish and Chasm linger, but I wave them off. Even the Seattle Slayer can't hurt me in a large hospital full of people. Not that he would. That's not his endgame. What is, I'm not sure, but I aim to figure it out.

Only when I see where he's going can I figure out how to cut him off, how to beat him.

The boys stay where they are, even as I try to push them away, one hand on either of their shoulders.

"Wait at the end of the hallway for me?" I ask, and they look at one another before turning back to me.

"No." They manage the word in near perfect unison, too. Damn it.

Parrish lifts his brown and gold gaze to Justin, and I can see it, that cruel streak in him that's surely the basis of all the Whitehall rumors. What was it that Lumen said to me in the hedge maze?

"They might act like they're your friends, but don't think they haven't done terrible things in the past. They've been just as bad—if not worse—than most."

I trust the guys implicitly; they've proven themselves with actions as well as words. But the way Parrish stares at Justin? I can see right through his decorum and down to the cold, cruel monster underneath.

"How did you think this was going to play out?" Parrish hisses, digging his nails into his palms. "You were going to kill my entire family and we'd still keep doing your bidding?"

If I'm not mistaken, Justin's practiced perfection slips just a tad, like a streaming video skipping to buffer. It's gone as quick as it came, but I know I wasn't imagining it.

The Seattle Slayer is *pissed.*

I'm reminded of his strange behavior in the restaurant when I protested his ordering for me or the way he squeezed the cracker until it crumbled in his hands. Justin is an expert at reining in his temper, but I get the very distinct and nagging sensation that I don't want to see the full fury of his cold rage unleashed.

I might not survive it.

"You'll do whatever I say unless you want Maxine's body dumped on the porch of your ruined house." Justin sighs and brushes at the front of his pale blue suit with his fingers. "Leave us. I'd like to speak to my daughter in private for a moment."

ENDGAME ROMANCE

"Son of a bitch," Chasm growls out, and both he and Parrish exchange another look. Chas' gaze slips to Justin, and dear old dad hooks a perfectly manicured brow. In the end, we don't have many good choices.

Justin has Maxine.

As he did when Parrish was in his custody, he's more than willing to wield my love as a weapon of leverage against me.

"I'll be okay. Go."

The boys hesitate yet again, but they move away as I asked, pausing at the hallway intersection.

Justin steps close, reaching up to brush back a loose strand of my hair.

"I'd like to see your hair dyed a more natural color," he muses, running his knuckles down the side of my face. There's a tenseness to his arm and hand that concerns me, like he might slap me or backhand me if we weren't in public.

Rather than either of those things, Justin smiles prettily.

"You looked beautiful tonight, like a real princess." He taps a single finger on the tip of my nose, like a truly doting and adoring father might. Only, in the case of my bio dad, there's a clear threat in the act. "Do you see how well you fit in here if you only try?" His smile stretches even wider as he sighs and relaxes his shoulders, slipping one hand in the pocket of his slacks. "You've got blue blood, my darling. You and I, we're Medina royalty; we *belong* here."

"You tried to murder my little siblings," I manage to whisper, keeping my own wild temper in check. I look up and into Justin's gorgeous blue eyes, wishing he were a normal person, wishing fervently that his worst sins were as bad as Tess'. She's been awful to me, no doubt, but I haven't been easy on her either. We could … we could work out our differences.

Me and Justin? After the things he's done, we could never have a relationship and that makes me sad. The man is handsome, charming, gregarious, and extremely talented. The Milk Carton app is a brilliant invention, and the schemes he comes up with are legendary. If only he'd put all that energy into bringing positivity into the world instead of, you know, removing people from it.

"Mm. Well, they're still around now, aren't they? And whoever said I set that fire? I was at prom the whole time; you saw me." He continues to smile as I stare up at him with disbelief. I've done everything he's asked. Everything. And yet, he *still* tried to harm the Vanguards. *Kill him, Dakota. Just stab him. End it all. You might go to jail, but at least the world would be rid of a man like Justin Prior.*

I swallow hard.

I'm not ready for that; I don't *want* to do that.

Kill my own father? How would I ever live that memory down? How would I ever live a normal life after finding my hands covered in this man's blood?

"Maxx wasn't a part of your plan, was he?" I ask, affecting a small laugh. It's not a happy sound. Instead, it's crafted of disbelief and frustration. If chance and circumstance hadn't combined into a lucky miracle, we'd be having a very different sort of prom night. "Where does this stop? What can I do to get you to leave my family alone? I've done everything that you've asked."

Justin's hand snaps out, clutching onto my upper arm, fingers digging in so hard that a small gasp escapes me, and I know I'm going to have even more bruises come morning. Not that it matters. I stand here now only because of the miracle of topical filler and makeup. Otherwise, all of the cuts, scrapes, and bruises from Veronica and her girls would have had Tess in a total conniption.

But Justin? He's never handled me quite like this before, with physical violence rather than threats. His 'hug' that he offered up in Tess' foyer was like the coils of a snake, but that could be explained away or forgotten. This is clear and blatant violence, a stepping-stone into much, much worse.

I see my future laid out in front of me, and I don't like what it looks like.

"Your *family*?" Justin breathes on the end of a low, dark laugh. "I *am* your family." He yanks me closer to him, and I hear the boys' footsteps in the hall behind me. I lift my left hand up, stilling them where they are, my gaze locked on Justin's. "Best you remember that or else I may take some of my anger out on sweet, gentle Maxine." He releases me suddenly, and I stumble back, staring at him in disbelief. "I'll see you tomorrow at noon. Wear your hair in a chignon; it looks best that way." He gently pats my cheek with a palm, even as my arm aches from his overly tight grip. "We'll dress you in a tasteful gown, some heels. We're having a special daddy-daughter luncheon."

He moves away from me, back into Maxx's room, and shuts the door behind him.

I don't like that, the idea of him with Maxx.

"Don't worry about him," Chasm promises, coming to stand beside me while Parrish pauses at my back. "Maxx is a tough bastard. That, and he's not as dumb as he looks." Chas does his best to smile at me, reaching out to pull me close, so he can examine the spot where Justin just grabbed me.

There's a very clear set of finger-shaped bruises forming.

Fantastic.

"He won't allow Justin to be alone with him," Parrish adds, releasing a heavy sigh.

He might try to pretend like seeing Caroline isn't hard for him, but I know better; I understand at least some of what he's going through.

"Kids." Tess is waiting at the hallway intersection, arms

crossed, face drawn.

Kids. Right.

I haven't forgotten the question she posed at prom, just before the phone call came in. Who could?

So yeah. We follow her down to the cafeteria, and I ready myself to explain to my biological mother that I'm dating her adopted son.

Fan-freaking-tastic.

CHAPTER 3

I've heard horror stories about hospital cafeterias, but this one isn't bad, more like a restaurant than, well, a hospital cafeteria.

"Thank you," Tess says, smiling as the waiter deposits ice waters on our table, leaving us some space to study the small menu. It's basic stuff, diner food like club sandwiches or burgers, but I'm starving. Pretty sure we all are. She turns her brown eyes over to us next, sweeping them across the three of us before picking up her glass and taking a drink.

For the millionth time that night, awkward silence reigns supreme.

It's Parrish that breaks it. He's the only one who truly could. Not only have he and Tess always been close, but he just returned after a long and extended kidnapping, decorated with nineteen bloody slashes. It'd be hard for him to really test the limits of her patience.

"How bad is the damage to the house?" he asks, not like he thinks Tess actually knows, more like he's probing at the tumultuous waters of her mood. I pick up my own water glass and take a drink, trying and failing to ignore the flutter in my belly or the sweat on my palms.

"I have no idea." Tess sighs and folds her hands together, placing her elbows on the table as she leans in, her eyes flicking to Chasm before returning to Parrish. "We can't go inside until the arson investigation is complete. Then, I'll meet with our insurance agent and get an assessment." She tilts her head down for a moment. "I don't know if there's anything salvageable inside or not, but at this point ..." Tess trails off again and looks up. "Our family is safe, and that's what matters. Thank God for Maxx. Without him ..." Tess chokes on the words, and then washes them down with her water. "After we eat, I'll drop Chasm off at home, and the three of us can stop by a store for essentials and pajamas. I know it's your prom night, but we need to be together as a family right now."

"Which means Chas should stay," Parrish suggests, glancing over and catching his friend's look. Parrish turns back to Tess. "Don't make him hang at home alone on prom night. He's as much a part of our family as anyone else."

Tess inhales again, sips her water like it's wine, and then looks over at me.

Uh-oh.

Here it comes. Brace for impact, Gamer Girl.

Parrish intercepts whatever it was that Tess was about to say.

"About what you asked at prom—" That's as much as he gets out before Tess sits up fully and turns that sharp stare of hers on her son. Parrish hesitates briefly before folding his own hands on the tabletop. He looks so much older in that suit (in a good way). Like, he could play a twenty-something on TV for sure. Ooo, I like the idea of that. Parrish and Chasm in a K-drama. Just so long as I was the leading lady ...

Yeah, my anxiety is clearly getting ahold of me. My mind is slipping over to whatever random and unimportant thoughts pop up. Anything but thinking about this. I've been dreading this moment since my encounter with Parrish in the basement of the Bend house.

"After what we just went through," Tess starts, clearly uncomfortable but unwilling to let this go, "it doesn't seem like quite the big deal it was when I first asked. However ..."

"It's true." That's Parrish. Only Parrish could ever be that bold in the face of Tess' cool, judgmental stare. She just ... well, she just sits there and looks at him. Her face is a beautiful if unreadable mask. I shift in my seat which is a mistake, and her attention flicks my way. "We're dating. We started dating before I went missing—"

"Excuse me just a moment," Tess chokes out, putting up a hand, palm out, and closing her eyes. "Let me process this. I need to ... I need to process this." She stands up suddenly and paces away as the three of us exchange looks on our side of the table, one boy on either side of me.

"Fuck." Chasm sums up the moment in a single syllable.

"This really was a mistake, wasn't it?" I whisper, but neither boy gets a chance to respond because Tess is sliding back into her seat and looking at us with this stricken expression that I can't quite figure out.

"Dakota," she starts, her voice a wounded jab that hits me like a punch to the gut. "What is going on? You kissed Maxx on the lawn; you and Chasm had that ... condom." She trails off and inhales, nostrils flaring. I can't tell if she wants to slap me or hug me. The way she's staring, it could easily be either of those two things.

"We really like each other," I offer up, which sounds lame as hell. Goddamn it. Why am I able to practice such refined loquacity in my head, but when it comes to making words with my mouth parts, I struggle so terribly? "I didn't mean for it to happen, it just … it just did."

"I pushed her," Parrish states firmly, and Tess looks from me to him, over to Chasm, back to Parrish. She doesn't know where to look or what to do. "As soon as I saw her, I knew that I wanted her. I made it happen. You know how I am." He gestures loosely with his right hand, affecting a certain confident nonchalance that I know he doesn't feel all the way to his bones.

His right knee is bouncing slightly under the table. Tess is his mother even more so than she is mine, and I'm her biological daughter. When he told me in the basement that day that he wasn't sure if he could do this, I was upset but I understood. In the end, it could very well mean choosing between a relationship with Tess and one with me.

But Parrish … my Pear-Pear … he chose me, didn't he?

He's choosing me right now.

I reach up and capture his hand in mine, my gaze on Tess. She stares at our combined hands the way someone else might look at a cluster of spider eggs, freshly hatched and swarming. She's skeeved out. She's upset. She has no fucking clue how to handle this.

"That's not entirely true," I offer up, wanting to keep things as truthful as I can. Lies choke, don't they? They clog the throat; they gum up the heart; they stick in the veins like clots. I'm swimming in them, and I have a feeling that the waters are rising, that the tide is coming in as opposed to going out. The end is not yet in sight for any of us. Or, if it is, I'm struggling to accept it. "We liked each other even though we both tried not to."

Tears build in Tess' eyes, and she puts a hand to her mouth.

"What does it matter?" Parrish asks. I'd say he was pleading, but I don't think Parrish Vanguard knows how to do any such thing, not a tattooed, insouciant sloth prince like him. "We care about each other; we treat each other well. It doesn't have to be weird."

"You're my children." Tess drops her hand to her lap, blinking rapidly through the revelation. "You are both my goddamn children." She looks over at Chasm next. "What about you, Kwang-seon? Please tell me because I'm struggling to understand. The condom ..."

Ah. Ah. Yes. That. The fucking stupid condom.

I grit my teeth, freezing like a deer in the headlights.

Right ... Dating Parrish is one thing, but Tess knowing that we slept together? That's a whole other animal, isn't it?

There's a blip of silence there, and I can feel both Chasm and Parrish gearing up to answer the question. But this is my chance to spill the truth, to put it all out there, to claim Chasm and Maxx alongside Parrish. The other boys don't deserve to be treated like dirty secrets.

"We're together, too." I reach down and take Chasm's hand, lifting that up so that my fingers are entwined with both boys at the same time. An arc of energy slices through me, cutting me in half but putting me back together again as a whole new person, someone with sunlight trapped under their skin.

Tess' mouth is hanging open, and she looks a bit ... I guess horrified would be the word?

"The best way to put it, I think," I continue, before anyone else gets a chance to jump in and complicate this, "is to say that they're courting me, the three of them. Maxx, Chasm ... Parrish."

"We're courting her," Parrish agrees with a deep sigh, squeezing my hand in his and meeting Tess' gaze dead-on when she turns to stare at him. "I intend to win, but even if I don't, it doesn't matter. I love Dakota and nothing will change that."

"Are you two having ..." She can't get the word out, but it

seems blatantly obvious to me what she's trying to ask. "Have you ever ... Oh God, maybe I don't want to know." Tess puts her head in her hand, but then lifts her gaze up again. "No, no, I do want to know. Have the two of you been intimate?" Her voice turns to stone, cold and unyielding.

Maxx and Chasm were right, weren't they? This was a huge mistake.

"We have." Parrish fields that question, and Tess' face blanches.

"Since when?" she chokes out. "Under my roof? In your ... in your rooms?!" Tess practically shouts this last part, drawing the stares of the other families sharing the dining hall with us. She seems to realize that this isn't the appropriate place to shout, and settles herself down, but the anger and betrayal in her voice?

I can taste it on my tongue. It's salty, but it's bitter, too, and I don't like it. Not at all. This could very well sever the last thread of goodwill that Tess has toward me. It's possible that, after this confession, we'll never have a relationship, that after I turn eighteen, we'll drift away from one another and become strangers or worse: enemies.

Or shit, maybe Tess won't even wait that long? Maybe she'll give me over to Justin entirely, relinquish her parental rights?

"Before I went missing," Parrish offers up, his mouth this lush, full pout that makes me feel a little bit crazy. "Dakota's the only reason I'm still alive now. When I wanted to give up, when the despair set in ... she's who I thought about."

"Lord help me." Tess puts her face in her hands again, her elbows resting on the table. When the waiter returns to take our order, she asks for a sandwich and then remains quiet until our food is dropped off. I stay where I am, holding the hands of both boys. Neither lets go, as if they don't dare relinquish me for the fear that they may never get to touch me again. "I don't know how to handle this." She lets out a harsh laugh, yanking her plate toward her and biting a cube of honeydew melon in half. "After tonight, I just … I need time."

"I love her." Parrish delivers the words without flinching. My cheeks flush, and I finally manage to extract my hand from his, attacking the French fries on my plate with vengeance. "We love each other." I shove another fry between my lips, glancing over to find him watching me rather than Tess.

He appears resolute.

My heart skips a beat, and I realize suddenly that this was inevitable. Because Parrish and I, we're never going to be able to quit each other. We're never going to be able to hide our feelings. We both fought our mutual pull for as long as we could, fought the tide of our attraction. We ended up in a love-hate dance, picking and poking at one another until … this.

Parrish looks back at his mother.

"What are you thinking?" he asks, a slight eagerness in his voice. He wants so badly for Tess to handle this differently than we feared, than Maxx or Chasm predicted, than I fully and completely expect.

"I don't know, Parrish," Tess enunciates, the words clipped and short. "I have no idea what to think."

"I care about Dakota, too," Chasm offers, swallowing hard. He's as nervous as I am, maybe more so. Tess might not be able or willing to get rid of me and Parrish, but Chas? What if she bans him from the house? What if she bans me from seeing him? Maxx, too.

"I'm taking you home tonight." Tess stands up from the table, leaving her plate untouched but for the three pieces of fruit she's eaten. "The two of you will stay here at the hospital with me until I'm ready to leave. Apparently, I can't let you out of my sight for a second."

"It's our prom night." Parrish rises to his feet just as quickly, his jaw set, honeyed eyes hard. "I got kidnapped by a fucking serial killer." He hisses the words out to keep from yelling them. "I know you're not happy, and I know we're not done talking about this, but let us hang out at the house together at the very least. Everyone else is partying tonight and we're … here. We could've … we could've lost everyone. Don't we deserve to be teenagers for a few fucking hours?"

"Don't you dare curse at me, Parrish Vanguard." Tess stares her son down, and I see that he's at least absorbed—rather than inherited—that cold, unyielding stare of hers. They truly look related in that moment. "I'm so incredibly disappointed in you." The words come out like a whisper, but as she says them, Tess' gaze slides over to me before turning back to her son again. "How can I trust the three of you to be alone at the house? Laverne left town yesterday for a business meeting, and she won't be home until tomorrow morning; I'm spending the night here."

Parrish holds his ground, palms flat on the table, his eyes on our … mother. *Our* mother. Good Gamer God, please help me.

"We can talk more after everyone gets out of the hospital," Parrish pleads. "Look, we're not lying to you; we're telling the truth."

Tess scoffs and rears back, arms crossed, face aghast.

"You told me the truth because I caught you."

"No." Parrish slams his palm down and then stands up straight. "I was going to tell you the truth from the get-go, from the night we lost our virginities to one another."

Oooooh, crap.

Tess' face reddens and she slaps her hand over her mouth.

Yikes.

I stand up, too, and then so does Chasm. Everyone in the dining hall is staring at us for sure now. How could they not? It's drama-central over here. My side quest is rapidly spinning out of control. Looking at Tess now, I wouldn't be surprised if she handed me over to the Slayer herself, just to get rid of me.

"Virginities …" Tess repeats the word, and then frantically digs her wallet out and tosses a wad of cash onto the table. She turns and takes off for the exit, and the three of us exchange looks.

"Dude, this is so bad." Chasm rubs at his face with his palms.

Parrish purses his lips and takes off after her, leaving Chas and me with little choice but to follow.

"Mom, wait." Parrish jogs to catch up, keeping pace with Tess' quick stride. "Listen to me."

She turns on him, quivering and shaking and panting. Completely undone. Tess Vanguard, famous true crime novelist, is unraveling right before my eyes.

If only I had her gift for prose, I might be able to explain the strange mix of relief, fear, and rage swirling more accurately inside her eyes. *Just like the forbidden page plucked from her typewriter, there's a message written into every line of her face that says I'm a mistake. That she doesn't like me. That maybe, just maybe, she'd have been better off with dreams and whimsy than the return of her blood-daughter.*

"I will take the three of you back to the house, but only because I'm having trouble looking at you." She makes another scoffing sound and then shakes her head. "Maxim is involved in all of this?" She stares at me when she asks this question, and I give a very brief, very small nod. "He's nineteen, Mia."

And there it is again, that name. Tess purses her lips, and I know she knows what she's just said and doesn't care. She's that angry with me.

"We're not … he and I haven't …" It's a lie—which I was trying to avoid—but I can't put Maxx in Tess' crosshairs like that. Yes, the age of consent in Washington state is sixteen. Yes, there's that Romeo and Juliet law, but still. Tess has money. She has influence. Mostly, I just don't trust her enough with this one.

"Fuck." She rarely curses, especially in the middle of a conversation with us. Her gaze sweeps the three of us and she shakes her head. "I can't deal with this tonight. Come with me, get in the car, and don't talk to me for the rest of the night."

She makes good on that threat, dragging us to a store for basic supplies—like toothbrushes and toothpaste—but although she lets us pick out some snacks and new pajamas, she doesn't say a single word.

Not one single, goddamn word.

CHAPTER 4

The drive to Laverne's is short, but hardly sweet.

Actually, it's agony. Parrish sits in the front while Chas and I occupy opposite ends of the back seat. Small miracles, Medina might be a cesspit filled with diamond-encrusted leeches, but it's also a relatively contained area. It doesn't take long to get to Laverne's, even from the hospital in Bellevue (these tiny towns are right on top of each other).

When we pull up to the iron gate outside, I'm instantly reminded of the one that led to the Vasquez house, the one that led to Parrish. Wetting my lips, I take off my seat belt and lean forward, between the two seats, eyes wide, mouth ajar.

The gate creaks open—legit, it *creeeaaaaks*—and then we're pulling down a tree-lined drive in the direction of a gothic revival style mansion. Not even kidding: it's also pouring rain and there's *lightning*.

"An Agatha Christie novel come to life," I murmur, and Tess jolts like I've slapped her. She glances over at me, pulling up alongside an old fountain with a mossy blanket stretched over the crowning statue; I can't even tell if it's supposed to be a woman, a man, a horse, a whale. Seriously, it *could* be a whale.

"Agatha Christie ..." Tess trails off, looking out at the looming character of the mansion like it's either an old friend or a great enemy. *"There is nothing more thrilling in this world, I think, than having a child that is yours, and yet is mysteriously a stranger."* With a sigh, Tess turns off the engine.

I turn to look at her, and she does the same. Our faces are uncomfortably close. Because of that, I can see the redness in her eyes, the dark circles underneath. Tess is really being put through the wringer, and I accept that at least some of that is my fault.

I swallow hard.

"Which one of her books is that from?" I ask, and Tess purses her lips together. For a second there, I'm certain that she isn't going to answer. She *did* forbid us from talking to her, after all.

"Her autobiography." Tess turns away from me and opens her door, stepping into a shallow puddle in her nude Louboutins with the red soles. She moves up the wide front steps to the ornately carved double doors, punching in the keycode to unlock them.

"Um ..." I trail off, chewing on my lower lip. "Why did neither of you think to mention that Laverne lives in the house of my dreams? Like, I could eat this house for breakfast, lunch, and dinner."

"Stay with me long enough and maybe you'll inherit it when you marry me." Parrish hooks a saucy smile and shoves his door open, following ... our? ... mom up the steps and into the house. Chasm lets out a tired sigh.

"You might like the architecture, but you won't enjoy staying here: trust me." I glance back at him, but he's staring at the house and not at me. "You've only met Laverne in person once; she's worse with each passing minute." Chasm exits the car, and I chase after him, collecting my skirts in my hands as I clop up the steps and stumble into the soaring foyer, turning in a small circle and feeling a bit like a princess in a fairy tale.

The glittering gold gown, the dark and sprawling mansion, the murders, the boys in their shiny tuxes.

It's all here, with a rags-to-riches storyline to boot.

"How big is this place?" I whisper, my voice swallowed up by the dark and the quiet. The rain continues to pour, the sound creeping in the open front doors, framed by flashes of lightning. A warm summer storm to usher in the start of the season.

And oh, what a summer it will surely be ...

"It's over eleven-thousand square feet," Tess offers up, exhaustion coloring her voice. She reaches up to rub at her forehead. "Eleven-thousand square feet, and none of it is ours." She turns around to look at us, tapping the fingers of one hand against the palm of the other. "We are guests here." There's a pause as Tess glances to one side and murmurs under her breath. "Hopefully not for very long."

She reaches over and flicks a switch, killing the strange umbra of the foyer.

The room—and all of the hallways leading off of it—are flooded with brilliant light. My eyes take in the exquisite millwork, the blackwood staircase, the mosaic tile beneath my feet. Antique furniture fills the space, tastefully occupying the room without overstaying its welcome.

This, I hadn't expected. Having met Laverne in person, I'd have imagined that she'd live in a modern-day igloo (read: cold) with concrete, steel, and glass. Maybe warmed up here and there with some Pottery Barn accents ... This is definitely not that. It's the complete opposite of all that.

"The house was built in 1945," Parrish offers up when he sees my excitement. A smile tints his mouth, but he clamps down on it when Tess turns his way, and frowns instead. "But it's based on a mansion in Tasmania, Australia called the Stoke House which was built in the late eighteen-hundreds."

"Yeah, yeah, you're old money; we get it." Chasm waves his hand at his friend but pauses at a stern look from Tess.

"Come here, all three of you." She heaves a deep sigh, waiting for us to line up in front of her. With her hair wet from the rain and coming loose from its perfect chignon, she appears for the briefest of moments to be somewhat human. But when she narrows those eyes and gets that tone—you know the one—it's hard to remember that she *is* human. She can be a messy, silly author, pacing around and murmuring plot points. Sometimes when she writes, she even makes the faces of the characters or mouths the words they speak.

I like that version of Tess, but a person is, as always, a sum of all their parts.

"Because it's prom night, because of Parrish's ... disappearance." She chokes and swallows a bit, nostrils flaring. "Because Dakota and I have only recently been reunited. Mostly because our house burned down tonight and things could've ... well, they might've been much different than this, I will allow you three to stay here even if I don't like what's going on." Here, she laughs. It's not a nice sound. "I really don't. And I can't ... I can't wrap my head around ..." She stares at me and Parrish, standing shoulder to shoulder in front of her. "My own children. You are *both* my children."

"We're a guy and a girl who aren't related, who never met until *you* brought Dakota here four months ago." Parrish crosses his arms obstinately, determined to ride this thing out. "The stepsibling thing is just semantics."

"Semantics?" Tess asks with a disturbed laugh. "Parrish, you are my *son*. It isn't like I married Paul yesterday, and the two of you just so happened to meet in your teenage years. I raised you; I

gave birth to her. You're supposed to be brother and sister, not …
whatever this is." She lifts up a hand before he can protest any
further. "No, don't. Just stop. I'm going to leave you here with
some money. Order food. Watch a movie in the theater. Figure out
where the game room is and play Scrabble or something." Tess
lifts up a single finger. "But help me God, if you leave this house,
if you bring anyone else over here, or … anything else you think I
might not like, I will come down on you all like a hammer."

Tess removes a wad of cash and a credit card (bourgeois) from
her clutch and hands it all over to Parrish, offering up one, last
look at Chasm, at me. She lingers there, and I wonder what she's
thinking. That I'm a mistake? A disappointment? If she thought all
that before, how could things get any better from here on out?

Tess takes off for the doors, closing them—and the storm—out
with a yank on the metal rings that serve as handles. The
atmosphere shifts as soon as she's gone, and I sag to the bottom
step of the grand staircase in abject relief. Like, I'm glad Tess is
gone, but …

"Holy crap." I rub at my own face with both hands, likely
smearing the work Justin's makeup artists bestowed upon me, and
not giving a single fuck about any of it. "It's like we're on a
rollercoaster that just doesn't stop. It's one loop after another, and I
could really use a barf bag."

Chasm squats in front of me, the position calling to mind that
day he shoved me in the pool, when I popped up and caught him
watching me like a vampire boy from a teen novel that I'd
probably binge read and obsess over for days. The book and the
boy both. There's nothing wrong with falling in love fictionally.

"If Tess kicks you out—or you find yourself suffocating to
death in here—come stay with me. My dad has quite clearly
crawled all the way up your dad's ass, so I'm sure he wouldn't
mind."

"Um, thanks for the rank visual," I quip back as Parrish sits beside me with a groan, leaning his elbows back on another step and using the one above it as a pillow. With his eyes closed, back arched, tattooed hands like a peek-a-boo art show beneath his sleeves, he's a dream. One that I never want to wake up from. And after living with the reality of losing him, I know that there's no price too steep for me to pay.

If Tess doesn't want me anymore, that's ... that's okay.

I can't lose Parrish.

"That went so much better than I thought," he mumbles, and I just stare at him until he opens his eyes and sits back up. He rests his elbows on his knees and clasps his hands together, face wrinkled in consternation. "You don't agree? I thought she was going to kill one or both of us. I was hoping she'd only kill Chasm."

"Yeah, didn't think about that part of the equation, did ya? Either of you." He stands up, effortlessly, and even though I shouldn't notice things like how muscular his thighs are or the way his ebony trousers pull against them, I do. "So now I'm also twisted up in this mess. What if Tess bans me from ..." I'm certain that Chas was going to say *the house,* but alas, that house is no longer.

Sadness sweeps over me, and I grit my teeth.

All that irreplaceable furniture, Parrish's artwork ... those are the two things I'm most upset about. Then again, how could I cry about that when Maxx quite literally saved the lives of the entire family? Even GG. He even saved the damn bunny. Hopefully Lumen and Danyella are down for a quick Rabbit 101 tutorial; he's theirs for a few nights.

"What if Tess bans me from seeing either of you? What am I supposed to do, have some quality one-on-one time with Seamus?" Chasm snorts and stands up, digging around in his pocket and withdrawing a pair of lip rings, picking at the latex on his mouth until he can get them both in. The rain's even managed to clear some of the temporary dye from the lightning bolt design at the front of his hair.

"You'll survive." Parrish isn't looking at either of us now. Instead, he's staring at the inside of the front doors, as if he can see right through them and to the world beyond. *I'm so fucking glad he's back.* The thought slips in as it has so often recently. Not only did I miss the hell out of him, but he's the type of cold, cruel vicious we need to push back against Justin. "For Tess, that was a good reaction. Admit it. She's been worse over smaller things in the past."

"The only reason she didn't flip out was because of the fire. After everyone's home from the hospital, what do you think is going to happen?" Chasm lets out a growl of frustration, letting his head hang back. "Now what?"

"Now what?" Parrish repeats, standing up suddenly. He collects our phones, carries them into the other room, and then returns to pose triumphantly with his hands on his slender hips. "I'm going to fucking kill Justin Prior." He whirls around to look at me, but I just blink up at him. He is not going to kill Justin. I couldn't let him take that burden on. The only person who could possibly take on that burden is *moi.* Man, I am so thoroughly screwed. "Killing a rapist, whatever. Murdering an influencer and her fuckboy? Good riddance. Kidnapping me, I can deal with that. But nobody touches my family." His face goes cold and empty, and I can see that he means what he's saying.

I don't blame him.

I even agree with him. That is, I agree that Justin needs to be … stopped.

If we send him to prison, would that do the trick? Or would he continue to operate from jail like any good crime lord? Is it even *possible* to get him behind bars? It's hard enough to get a conviction when someone really deserves it (only six percent of rapists spend a single day in jail, pretty fucked, huh?) let alone someone with money and influence.

I chew on my thumbnail in thought.

"Are you okay?" Parrish asks finally, turning toward me. "You've barely talked. Here or at the hospital."

"If you knew how long my internal monologues were, you wouldn't think that." I stand up and exhale. "Can we please order some food? I'm starving." I move away in search of the kitchen, but it's … there's a lot of house, let's just put it that way.

Parrish moves ahead of me, gliding through the manor like he was born to rule it. He perfects that slouchy, easy rich boy saunter, spilling his luxe persona into a chair at the overly large kitchen island. My mouth gapes open as I stumble in through a swinging door with Chasm on my heels, looking up at the gold chandelier above the cream-colored stone countertops. The cabinets are custom and soar nearly all the way up to the fourteen-foot-tall ceilings, the pulls carved of some gold-veined mineral into elegant curves that remind me of a swan's neck.

"You like?" Parrish asks, one elbow on the chair arm, his head in his hand. He *appears* to be relaxed, but he's not. Not at all. "I thought you hated rich people?"

"I do hate rich people," I agree, running my fingers over the off-white cabinet doors before I turn to look at him with a smile. "And by rich people, I mean billionaires mostly." A smile teases my face. "But if it's you then I guess it's okay." I pause for a moment and turn my head to the side, a slight frown taking over. "Then again, you're actually horribly insufferable when you're not in love with someone …"

I look up just in time to catch his smirk, watching as he runs his tongue across his lower lip in a move that's disturbingly lascivious. My throat tightens up, and it only gets worse as Chasm strides past me, tickling his fingers along my bare upper back. *Jesus.*

He yanks the fridge door open, but it's just filled with drinks—like Danyella's was. It's that rich people thing again where the damn fridge is stuffed to bursting with expensive bottled beverages, such as fancy waters blessed by immortal nymphs and pH-level this and alkaline that. Organic, fair-trade, carved from the pristine mountaintops of Switzerland. Whatever.

Chasm pushes items around, drawing out an iced green tea for me and sodas for him and Parrish. He tosses a can to his friend, and Parrish catches it in two hands.

"Order the food and then let's keep our phones far, far away from us." Chas looks around the room and then curls his lip. "Too bad we don't have the bug detector … or a car to use to go grab a new one. And now that we're mentioning cars, don't forget that mine is also in your garage." He sighs and leans his ass up against one of the counters. "Hopefully it's not trashed."

"Daddy will buy you a new one." Parrish says it, not me, his eyes glazed over as he stares at the stone countertop in thought. "Liquor's in the cellar." He nods with his chin in the direction of a locked door before reciting a four-digit pin from memory to use on the cellar's keypad. "Go down and grab something nice. I'm not going in there."

My heart contracts as I study Parrish's face, the way he so desperately tries to keep the seriousness of that statement from showing. Of course he can't go down in the cellar right now, after having lived in one for nineteen days.

"I'll do it." I push away from the counter and head for the door. Chasm slides in front of me, holding his arms out to either side.

"*Ani.* I'll do it." He turns away from me, unlocks the door, and grabs for the knob, tossing a smirk over his shoulder. "By the way, *ani* doesn't mean goodnight."

"I know what that one means!" I kick him in the back of the calf, but he just laughs at me, even as he stumbles toward the cellar steps. Then I pause. "Wait, what does that mean again?"

Chasm ignores me, snickering as he sprints down the stairs and out of sight. I kick off my heels, and then I follow after him. Can't leave him down there by himself, now can I? If I were Justin, and I wanted to send a monster to surprise a bunch of teenagers, I'd put him with the alcohol.

Chas is waiting for me as I come around the corner, and he steps forward, causing my back to hit the wall just before he rests a palm beside my face. He leans in and puts his nose tip to tip with my own. He's not smiling either.

My next inhale gets stuck, clinging to my chest and making it feel tight. Making me dizzy. Making me swoon. *Right, it's the breaths not the guy, eh, Kota?* As awful as it sounds, there were parts of Parrish's disappearance that were bliss.

Spending time alone with Chasm. Getting to know him. Developing a relationship.

Getting it on in the hedge maze. Especially that.

Don't get me wrong: I love Parrish. I love him so completely and wholly that it frightens me. I'd have given my life to rescue him, even if it meant he'd live a happily ever after without me. But I miss these private moments with Chas, too.

"*Saranghae,*" he whispers, and then he's kissing me. It's a long, slow kiss, dipped in molasses and dragging in the best possible ways. Though it seems impossible, he tastes just like he smells, like an after-dinner lounge with tuxedos and tulle skirts, trays of peppermint truffles and the faintest whisper of cigars from the smoking room. "I wanted so badly to take you to prom and show you off. In a different life, I guess." He kisses me again, inviting me in with tongue, and then pulling back far too soon for my liking.

"You can't scorch me and leave me on fire," I protest, the words warbly and weak. My fingers dig into the glimmering gold fabric of my skirts.

"Are you asking me to put you out?" he queries, glancing back over his shoulder and cocking a sharp brow. He's really too handsome. It isn't fair. His face is far too pretty for me to keep to myself—especially if I'm carrying one or two other boys' visages in my pocket. Is it wrong, for me to care about three men with the same fervent, violent heat? My emotions are like a filter over my soul, changing the colors, making it impossible for me to see what's really going on underneath.

"Not as such," I respond, which is a total non-answer. I'm still reeling about the fire, to be honest. I'm still reeling about Tess' revelation. I'm … convinced that I'm going to have to murder my own father. Utterly convinced of it. Chasm pulls a glass bottle out of a cabinet by the neck, studying the label. Looking around, I realize how lucky we really were to actually find Parrish. He was in a cellar just like this; there must be dozens and dozens of them scattered throughout the city, hiding all of that liquor in shadows and cool earth. "But you can't just push a girl against a wall, confess your love in a beautiful foreign language, and then beat a hasty retreat. That's against some sort of unspoken romance rule, I'm sure of it."

He chuckles and lets the bottle hang by his side, rifling through others with his right hand.

"After tonight," he starts, pulling out another bottle and studying that label next. But his eyes with their glorious amber irises, they're not staring at the label but through it, to the floor and the molten core of the earth underneath it all. He sighs. "It's not going to be the same."

Chasm turns around, hefting up both bottles.

"Twenty-grand in booze. What say you? Should we drink this and battle it out on the arcade machine downstairs? Honest to God, there's a vintage Ms. Pac-Man down there. You want to kick my ass? It'd really make my prom night extra special."

"You're talking to me like we're about to lose each other." I take a step toward him, and he leans back against the cabinet with a sigh, setting the bottles on either side of him. When he crosses his arms and looks down at the floor with his eyes closed all contemplative like that, he looks like a movie star. "Why is that? Because of the fire? Because of Tess?"

"Because if Justin is ready to light a bunch of kids on fire, then he's escalating the game." Chasm lifts his head up finally to smile at me. "And yeah, add in Tess' fresh carnal knowledge of the situation …" Here he sighs again in clear irritation. "Parrish being back, summer coming, all of it. Anyway, because of all that, I just think we're going to be very busy." He pushes up off the cabinet and steps toward me, reaching his arms around me and tugging me close. As he studies my face, I see it, all of the same tenderness and care he showed during our search for Parrish. "I thought I could give you up for him, to him, because I love him, but I …" He pauses here and reaches up a hand, drawing his knuckles down the side of my face.

I'm trembling now, but that's to be expected, right? It isn't every day that a beautiful boy in a black suit kisses you senseless in an old cellar. It isn't every day that someone you love loves you right back and isn't afraid to tell you so. It surely isn't every day that a handsome man looks at a wanting woman and sees exactly what it is that's inside her heart.

Because he sees it; I know he does.

"But you aren't going to give up, are you?" Parrish asks, sauntering down the last of the steps and walking along the wall of wine, trailing his fingers over the bottles. He turns around at the corner to stare at us and Chasm slowly retreats. But he doesn't let go of me, not completely. "I asked for a week to myself." He raises a single finger. "One week." Parrish drops his wrist, glancing down at the decorative watch he wore for the occasion. "Right on the mark." He lifts his cool gaze up, and my heart thunders. I end up taking a single step back from Chasm. "Well, a few hours early, but close enough." Another pause. "I suppose."

Chasm exhales sharply, reaching up to ruffle his hair with his fingers.

"It's not like that. I'm not trying to undermine you, I just ..." He trails off again as I struggle to find the right words to say. I knew we were going to get here eventually; I just didn't know when or how. But here it is. The first of many talks, I'm sure. "Sex is a bonding exercise more than anything else. We should keep having more of it." Chas shrugs his shoulders loosely and Parrish narrows his eyes.

"Why don't we go upstairs, and we can talk about our food situation?" I suggest, knees weak, palms sweaty. If I have to make a choice, could I? What would I do? Panic sets in then as the corner of Parrish's lip curves up.

"You're right." Parrish steps forward and grabs my right arm from behind with his left hand, causing me to spin, skirts swirling around as I turn and end up falling against him. Talk about a Drama-land moment in real life; I'm smitten. "We should."

He stares down into my face like he has no doubt that this is enough, that I'm fully and completely caught on him.

Chasm's footsteps are soft but sure behind me, and I shiver as I feel his warm breath on the side of my neck, as if he's leaning in to look at me. He murmurs something low and sultry in Korean.

"And that means what exactly?" I whisper back as Chas trails his fingers along the back of my neck, causing my lids to flutter. This is a lot. I mean, they've both fully switched on the charm.

"Who do you want?" Chasm whispers, licking my ear. My ear. My freaking *ear*. And oh my God, it feels fucking amazing. And his question, I mean, it's an easy enough one to answer, isn't it?

Isn't it?

"Both." The word comes out before I can convince myself not to say it. Embarrassment creeps through my veins like poison, and I tug back on Parrish slightly. Not only does he not release me, but I actually end up in a worse position when he steps forward to compensate. I'm now firmly wedged between the two boys, their body heat warming me from either side.

"Both?" they repeat, almost in unison. I can see Parrish lift his gaze from me to stare at Chasm over my shoulder.

"At the same time?" Chasm asks, like the idea never occurred to him before. "Whoa, that's hardcore."

"Um, yeah, not exactly what I meant," I choke out with a laugh, squeezing sideways and unwedging myself from between them. I turn to face the two boys, kinda wishing I hadn't left in the first place.

"You know, why not?" Chasm snaps his fingers, looking at Parrish instead of me. They hold each other's gazes for a hot second before Chas looks over at me. "If that's what you want … but you'll have to say it first."

He turns around and snatches the liquor bottles up, heading for the stairs before pausing halfway up.

"Have to say what?" I demand, but I'm red all over because I know exactly what I just implied and exactly what he's suggesting. "That I want to have a threesome with the two of you?" I snort and shake my head. It's meant to be asked as a question, but Chasm takes it as an affirmative and grins at me.

"Yeah?" He pauses in thought, and his eyes widen slightly. "What should we do about condoms?"

Condoms? Um. Right. Because this is really an option on the

table?

"We can Grubhub some," Parrish offers up, gesturing with his chin toward the stairs. "Grab one of the phones and put in an order; 7-Eleven has food, drinks, candy … condoms. We'll get them delivered." He moves toward me again as I raise a brow in his direction.

"And you know that how?" I ask, and he shakes his head with a small laugh.

"Everyone at Whitehall knows that." He moves past me and pauses, holding out a hand at the stairs.

I'm still convinced they're joking. Once upon a time, Parrish did say something along the lines of, *"If my girl wants to have a threesome, it's my job to make that happen for her."* Mostly, I think he was teasing me then. But right now?

"What do we do until the condoms get here?" Chasm wonders aloud, and because I'm still imagining that they're screwing around with me, I answer like my typical dorky self.

"As Tess suggested, let's play Scrabble."

"Scrabble?!" Chasm chokes as Parrish glances over to stare at me like he's never met me before. "You want to play … Scrabble, on prom night?"

"Drunken strip Scrabble?" Parrish amends, and they meet each other's eyes and smirk before sliding their gazes to me.

"How would you even do the stripping stuff with Scrabble?" I ask dryly, but it was certainly a premature question.

Thirty minutes later, I'm down to my panties, and my arms are crossed over my bare chest.

Both boys are still mostly dressed.

Apparently, any word worth more than a certain number of points or consisting of a specified number of letters allows the person who played it to choose who removes a piece of clothing. I'm running out of choices here. Also, I'm getting my ass kicked.

I'd somehow made the mistake of agreeing to this on the assumption that I was a slightly better wordsmith than the other two. I'm the daughter of a millionaire novelist, right? Tess is like, a big deal in the writing world.

Only … I'm not Tess, and the boys sitting across from me are two of the highest scoring students in the entirety of Whitehall Prep. Parrish might not be in the running for their grade's future valedictorian like Chasm is, but he just came back and destroyed the final exams after having missed weeks of school.

"Are you guys nervous about grades being posted tomorrow?" I choke out, acting somewhat dignified as I sit in my underwear on a stool in the game room. It's a nice room, too, done up in dark greens and richly polished woods. There's an entire cabinet full of board games, a shuffleboard table, pool table, air hockey table, and as Chasm promised, a vintage Ms. Pac-Man arcade machine.

According to Parrish, there's even a hidden vault in the house that's filled with heirlooms, gold bars, and cash. He insinuated that, if necessary, we could rob it and take off together. Once Tess finally gets a chance to process the implications of our relationship, and lays into us, we might have to.

Hey, that'd get Justin off my back, too, wouldn't it? *Except that he'd murder everyone you care about in his search for you.*

I digress. I mean, I purposely digress. I'm mortified, sitting there like that. It's one thing when I'm with one of the guys, and we're both in the moment together. This is insane. I feel exposed, vulnerable … excited.

"I'm only nervous for you," Parrish remarks, reaching out and collecting several Scrabble tiles in his long fingers. He lays them out carefully, one by one, his gaze on me. Unyielding. Unforgiving. Impossible. *I want him so badly.* I shift in my seat. "Also: never do this again."

"Do what?" I query back, my voice a breathy whisper.

68

"Agree to be alone and play this sort of game with two boys you've only known for a handful of months." Chasm records Parrish's score, and sits back in his seat, glancing over at his friend. "You just won."

"He can't have won. We have plenty of tiles left." I indicate the velvet bag that holds the letter tiles with a lift of my chin, but Chasm is already shaking his head as Parrish smirks. They've really fallen into this idea, and I'm not sure what to make of that.

"He won because he just scored enough points to ask someone here to remove a piece of clothing." Chas sits up straight, crossing his arms. He took his jacket off before the game—to make it fairer is what he said, the asshole—and then elected to remove his *own* shirt after scoring enough points. So, there he sits, shirtless but wearing a loose tie and slacks, the ink on his arms and chest visible. "And unless ol' Pear-Pear here wants *me* to remove my pants ..." He trails off and grins. "Dakota, say hello to your birthday suit."

Parrish sighs and relaxes further in his own chair, still wearing his dress shirt but sans shoes and socks. I'm not entirely useless, you know? Not useless, but beet red? Yes, yes, I am.

"Why don't you take those off, Gamer Girl, and I'll get you a robe?" He pushes up from his seat and then points at my panties. "But not until I get back." Parrish takes off, leaving me alone with Chasm again.

"Shouldn't there be a staff here or something?" I ask, swallowing hard and trying my best not to think of how I just lost a word game to two cocky boys, a game that I agreed to play thinking *I* would be the one with the upper hand.

"They'll be back tomorrow when Laverne returns. Just us tonight, but don't get used to this." Chasm studies me and then sighs, getting up and bringing his discarded suit jacket over. He drapes it across my shoulders and then slips his tie off, dropping that over my head. The gesture makes me smile as he crouches beside me. "Don't stress about the grades. Parrish was only kidding; you'll be alright."

"How do you know that?" I ask, terrified that he's wrong, that I'll have failed in at least one class. Not only would I not be able to see Maxine, but the very act of failure might upset Justin enough to drive him into Slayer mode. What if he cuts Maxie the way he did Parrish? What if he starves her? What if he ... just says to hell with it and slits her throat?

"Because I'm an amazing fucking teacher." He stands up straight as Parrish returns, holding a plastic bag in one hand and a white robe in the other, some plush looking thing you'd expect to find hanging on the bathroom door at a five-star hotel.

I take it and slip it on over Chasm's suit jacket, turning away from the boys and stepping out of my panties. I tuck them into a pocket on the robe and then tie the sash. When I turn around, I see that they've moved the Scrabble board off the table and replaced it with junk food galore.

Think: gas station chic.

Hot dogs from the warmer, already cold from the drive over. Hamburgers in paper wrappers. A small cheese pizza.

Condoms.

Like, eight boxes.

"What the freaking freak is this?" I ask, picking one up and gesturing with it. My cheeks must be neon at this point. "We're sort of new to this still, you know. All three of us."

"Buy four, get four free." Parrish unwraps a hot dog and takes a bite off the end of it, sighing heavily and lifting up the bottle of liquor for a drink. Personally, I'm not about to drink anything at all. Not now that this, um, threesome thing is on the table.

No fucking way.

"What a way to spend prom, huh?" Chasm asks, pausing as

another roll of thunder cracks outside. "Not what I expected, but at least we were able to get your ass back."

"Took you long enough." Parrish offers me the bottle, but I wave it away, sitting on the stool in my robe, stuck in a big-ass gothic mansion in the rain with two super-hot guys.

"Yeah, sorry about that," I agree, cringing. "But honestly, I'm not sure there's a better way to spend prom night." I smile. "Maxx foiled Justin's plan, we're together, we're alone, this house is kick-ass, and the storm is welcome." I open one of the chip bags we bought at the store with Tess and dive in, eyeing the Ms. Pac-Man machine. "Any takers?"

"When I said you could beat my ass on that thing, and that it'd be a pleasant addition to my night, I wasn't kidding." Chas stands up and offers out a hand. When I take it, and he pulls me to my feet, our gazes clash, and I feel a shifting in the air.

He guides me over to the machine and Parrish follows.

"What's the highest score you've ever gotten on this game?" he asks as he boots it up and I tap the button for two players.

"Hundred-and-fifty K," I reply easily, wetting my lips. Chas groans as Parrish crowds in on my other side, and I hunker down, steering the yellow ball with the bow that is Ms. Pac-Man around the screen to collect all the dots. The four colored ghosts chase me down, but this is nothing.

The reason Chasm groaned? He knows he's not getting a chance to play for a while.

"You really are a Gamer Girl, aren't you?" Chas snorts again and reaches up to ruffle his hair, looking across the machine at Parrish. "Should we do it?" he asks, and I'm so damn boss at the game that I'm able to flick my eyes over to Parrish just in time to see him stifle a smile.

"We should." He snatches me up and throws me over his shoulder, drawing a surprised gasp from me as he strides off for the door. I watch as Ms. Pac-Man meets an untimely end, and then we're out the door and up a small back staircase to the second floor.

Parrish opens one of many doors down a long hallway, marches in, and then tosses me onto the bed before crossing his arms.

"You better be serious about this," he tells me, exhaling and glancing over as Chasm comes in behind us, closing and locking the door. There's a plastic grocery bag hung over his right arm. "Gamer Girl." He kneels down as I sit up on the bed, staring down at him. His face is neutral, but his eyes are dark with intent. "I've already ratted us out to Tess; she knows everything. We might as well enjoy this. But only if you want to."

I look down at him, shifting slightly on the bed.

"How do we … how does this even work?"

Parrish smiles at me and then rises to his feet, reaching up to take his tie off. He tucks it into the pocket of his suit jacket, and then slips that, too, off.

"I don't know … but we can figure it out." He moves away from me, already barefoot from the game earlier, and then goes about trying to make a fire in the fireplace. He's not very good at it. Chasm either. The two of them rich boy fumble around with the task until I sigh, hop off the bed and shove between them.

In less than a minute, I manage to catch the small fire starter log beneath the wood stack and nurture a young blaze that should stay going for a while.

I sit back on my haunches.

"Where did you learn to do that?" Parrish mutters, rising to his feet. He's unbuttoning his dress shirt, too, nice and slow. He lets the shirt gape open, revealing not only his ink, but the bandages he's still wearing. It's going to take some time to heal completely from what Justin did to him.

"We used fireplaces to heat the house back home." I swipe my hands together, but I'm going to have to wash them. Bit of dirt, bit of sap, some soot on my fingers. Smirking at the boys, I move past them both and into the bathroom.

I've no sooner washed my hands than the boys appear on either side of me. Parrish offers up one of the toothbrushes that Tess bought for us. I end up sandwiched between them and staring in the mirror, a suit-wearing Adonis on either side of me. They're situated at the sinks, and I'm borrowing a bit from each of them.

We're all quiet as we stand there and brush, and I very demurely cover my mouth when I bend over to spit. That makes Parrish snort.

"You were never this careful about brushing your teeth around me before," he remarks, but with the slightest hint of a bemused smile on his pretty mouth. He spits and rinses with a cupped hand, glancing over at me and making my heart jump.

"Are you referring to the time I left my door open, and you saw me brushing my teeth and dancing to BLACKPINK?" I set my toothbrush on the stone countertop and throw what I consider to be a coy look in Parrish's direction. I've never been all that good at those sorts of things. Being coy or flirtatious, I mean. Usually, I just look like I'm having an allergic reaction or something.

"Exactly that." He leans his left shoulder against the wall, crossing his arms. Could he look any more arrogant than he does right now? Or any more attractive? Yeah, negative on both of those things. "Or the many times I've seen you haphazardly brushing your teeth as you wandered downstairs for a snack."

"I always brush them again after I eat," I mumble, rubbing at my face and wondering if this is really going to happen or if the boys were truly just playing around with me. It's been a long, trying night. Justin has escalated the game once again, and I've got a summer of FBI interviews, custody battles, and parental drama to look forward to.

It'll be a summer I will never forget, surely—threesome or no threesome.

"I'm jealous that the two of you get to live together." Chasm opens the shower door and turns it on, glancing over his shoulder at us as he tests the water with his fingers, waiting to see if it's warm. After a moment, he moves back over to the counter, grabs a washcloth along with my wrist, and yanks me over to stand near the shower. "Or live*d* together, past tense. I'm telling you that this thing with Tess is nowhere near over." Chasm wets the cloth with the warm shower water, pushes the sleeves of my robe up, and goes about wiping down my arms.

Shivers take over me, despite the steam, despite the vibrant heat in Chas' fingertips as he gently and carefully scrubs the topical filler and foundation off my skin. He clears the work of Justin's makeup artists and reveals the countless cuts and bruises that Veronica and her friends bestowed on me.

"Don't worry about Tess." Parrish lets those words hang, a definitive statement, pure bravado and unchallenged courage. I just hope none of it is misplaced. What if he can't get a handle on Tess the way he usually does? He practically bullies his way into getting what he wants from his parents, but this time, it may be too big of a deal to breeze past with incuriousness, torpor, and swagger. "I'll handle her."

He moves closer to the pair of us, looking up and past me toward his best friend.

The tension in the room tightens, ratchets around my neck like a noose. I suddenly can't breathe, and I'm hyperaware of all the places that Chasm is touching, the gentle brush of his thumb across the violent throb of my pulse, the way Parrish reaches up and grabs the ties of the robe sash, the pressure, the pull, the tug.

I gasp as the knot comes undone and the robe slides down my

shoulders, catching on my arms and leaving me with Chasm's suit jacket as my only protection against the boys' dual expressions of vigor and heat. *Yikes.*

"I'm going to shower," Chasm hazards, turning his gaze back to mine. "Don't forget about me; I'll be quick."

"How could I ever forget about you?" I ask. It's meant to be a lighthearted, off-handed remark. Instead, it falls heavy and prurient between us, and I start to panic. *A threesome, really?* A slight flick of my eyes over to Parrish shows him frowning, nostrils flared, gaze on the floor and not on my face.

He doesn't release the ties of the robe, and Chasm doesn't release my wrist. Instead, he lifts it up to his mouth and, with his eyes half-closed but focused on my face, graces a molten kiss to my skin. When he drops my hand and turns toward the shower, hands moving down his tattooed midsection to his slacks, I turn away and end up facing off against Parrish.

He moves backward, toward the door to the bedroom, hands still on the ties of the robe. He tugs me along with him, and I comply, gasping as he slams the bathroom door shut behind me. His palms end up on either side of me, and he's leaning in, his mouth precariously close to my own.

"Why did I have to be kidnapped?" he asks, his voice hoarse with emotion. His attention slips from my eyes to my lips, and then he wets his own with his pretty tongue, and I find that I can't look anywhere else. Why would I? Nothing else in the world seems to matter when Parrish Vanguard is pressed this close to me. "If I hadn't, it'd just be me and you."

He leans in and puts his lips on the side of my throat, in the hollow between my neck and shoulder, and I squirm slightly. *If he doesn't kiss me there, I'll die. I'm certain of it.*

"What are we doing here?" I whisper back, attempting to reach up and put my arms around his neck. He stops me by grabbing my wrists, caressing them even as he pushes them back against the door. "Me and you and Chasm." A pause. "Maxx."

Parrish sighs and nips my skin with his teeth, giving me goose bumps from head to toe.

"If you want to be with them—either of them—and not me ..." Here he trails off, using my wrists as leverage to push back and put some space between us. We stare at each other. Him, down at me, brimming with love and affection and fear. Me, up at him, in awe that he survived the things he did, that he fought to live with thoughts of me in his head, that we were brought together by the strangest twist of fate. "If you want one of them instead of me, I can understand that." His voice cracks in a strange way, a glimpse into the real Parrish, the one he keeps so carefully locked away. I've seen it a few times now, but it never ceases to amaze me.

"Once I let myself have you, really have you, I'll never be able to stop."

"You're saying you'd back off?" I ask him, hardly able to get the words out. I mean, if I told him to leave me alone, I would expect that he'd respect my wishes. There's nothing creepier than a guy who won't take no for an answer. *But, but, also ... put up at least a bit of a fight, Pear-Pear.*

He smiles at me then.

This time, it's pure and utter deviance.

"No. I'm saying that's not enough to chase me away." He leans in toward me again, brushing his mouth against mine. Just that, a brush. Not a full kiss. It leaves me aching and wanting and wishing I wasn't wearing the suit jacket on my shoulders. It covers my breasts, and I want Parrish to touch them so badly that they ache. "If you want me to leave, nothing less than a very strong *fuck you, I hate you* will do." He releases me suddenly and steps back, slipping out of his dress shirt and tossing it on the back of a chair. "But I want you to be honest with me." He undoes his tie and lets it hang loose around his neck. "Did you like it better with just Chasm around?" He hesitates here and looks to the side for a moment. "Or Maxx?"

"Every day you were gone, I felt myself dying a little inside," I admit, and then I reach up and slide Chas' jacket off my shoulders, letting it fall to the floor. The robe follows right after, and then I'm completely nude and standing beside the fire.

Parrish's eyes light up, catching on my body before he lifts them back to my face.

"What does that mean, Dakota Banks? You're very good with word games." Parrish picks up a remote and turns on a stereo system. The song *"Pretty Savage"* by BLACKPINK (coincidence much?) starts to play, making me wonder if Parrish didn't connect my phone to the house's Bluetooth speaker system while Chas and I were down in the cellar.

This song is from that very same playlist from the car.

"It means that I love you, Parrish Vanguard. If none of this Justin shit had ever happened, you and I would be … it'd just be us. Forever, I think." Here I pause, crossing one arm over my chest and putting my other hand over my um, bits. I look away for a moment. "No, for sure. Forever." The words come out as a bit of a whisper, but that doesn't mean they're any less true. I look back over at Parrish as he sets the remote down and grabs the neck of the liquor bottle Chas brought up with us. He lifts it to his lips, and then holds out a hand.

"But because it *did* happen …?" He trails off again, but I'm already moving toward him and he's sliding an arm around my waist. I'm sure my cheeks are bright red again, but what can I do about that? It's not like he hasn't seen me naked before. *Oh my God, I might die.*

"I love them, too. I wouldn't have allowed myself to fall for either of them if there hadn't been extenuating circumstances. At this point, all I can do is wait and see what each of you decides; I'm not brave enough to give any one of you up." I reach up and touch the sides of Parrish's face as he scrunches his brow in thought.

"If that's what you're waiting for, you're going to be waiting a hell of a long time." He smirks, but before I can challenge what he's just said, he's kissing me with a wicked-hot tongue, sweeping past my lips and taking over the entire moment.

I almost briefly forget that Chasm is there—almost.

"More Korean music, huh?" he asks, suddenly standing far too close behind me. As Parrish pulls back slightly, Chas leans down and puts his mouth near my ear to sing one of the lines from the song. "*Urin yeppeujanghan savage.*" He chuckles and then his hands are on my upper arms, his grip gentle but possessive.

Parrish lets his lip curl, half-irritation, half-challenge.

"We are pretty savage," he translates which I knew since, yeah, that's the name of the song. I won't talk about the *saranghae* thing. How a K-drama freak like me could've mistranslated that, I'm not sure. Let's just pretend Parrish's kidnapping scrambled my brain. "And we can be, Gamer Girl, if you want us to be."

The bottle of liquor changes hands just as the song switches to *"How You Like That"*, also by BLACKPINK. Chasm snorts again, taking a swig as Parrish slides his hands down my sides, cupping my waist as he dives in for another kiss.

He's much more ... well, *savage* this time, kissing me with these languorous sweeps of tongue, like Chas isn't even there, like he has all the time in the world. Chasm meets him halfway, reaching up to pull pins from my hair and letting the long waves sweep down my back. The feel of my own hair brushing the bare curve of my ass makes me shiver, and the sensation only intensifies as Chas brushes some of it aside and kisses down the side of my neck, over the naked sweep of my shoulder.

ENDGAME ROMANCE

"I love that you love my language, *Naekkeo,*" he murmurs, licking along my skin as Parrish plunders my mouth, lifting up an inked hand to cup my chin. He keeps me where I am, kissing me as my knees go weak and Chasm bands an arm around my waist, just above Parrish's hands. Together, they hold me up as I splay my fingers on Parrish's inked chest, scraping lightly against his skin with my nails. "I love that you're too honest to lie about wanting all three of us. I love that you're bold enough to believe you can have us."

"Can't I though?" I whisper as Parrish pulls back just a fraction of an inch. He licks across my lower lip, his eyes blazing with assumptive defiance.

"Last man standing? Let's see how long you can put up with watching me win." Parrish yanks me away from Chasm and over toward the bed. My back hits the mattress, and then there he is, looming right over me in his slacks, his undone tie hanging around his neck. I touch my fingers to the bandaged wounds left by Mr. Volli (but via Justin's command).

Righteous rage fills me all over again, reminding me that the asshole tried to burn my new family to ashes tonight. On the night of my high school prom, he was going to kill the four little siblings that Parrish and I share, the four siblings I haven't allowed myself to get to know.

The family that I want to fit into it, but still can't figure out how.

Fuck you, Seattle Slayer. You're nothing but a coward.

I'm anything but cowardly tonight: this is what I want.

The Slayer, Tess, whoever … nobody can take this moment from me.

Chasm climbs up on the bed beside us with a towel wrapped tight around his waist, stretching out and showing off his perfect upper body as Parrish kisses me again, pulling back just enough that I have to strain to reach his mouth. He nips my lower lip and then moves down, kissing across my bare skin to my breasts.

I shudder and clutch at his head as he closes his hot mouth over one of my nipples. Turning my head to the side, I can see Chasm staring down at me, his expression twisted up with jealousy, but just as determined as Parrish's.

"I was going to give her up for you," he admits, and Parrish pauses, lifting his face from my breasts. He doesn't look at his friend though, just me. Only me. He keeps his gaze on mine. "I really was."

"I appreciate the sentiment," Parrish purrs, the sound edging into a growl. "It isn't a service I would've ever offered." He licks my nipple again, and I moan, the sound cutting off sharply as Chasm leans in and takes my lips for himself.

Both boys taste like mint and liquor, like promises and pretty, shiny futures.

"Are you guys sure you're okay with this?" I manage to whisper, but I really don't want to ask the question. I just want this. *I could live with doing this every night for the rest of my life. Days wouldn't be off-limits either.*

"I'm sure." They say it in unison, and then turn to look at one another. Lightning crashes between their gazes, and then they're both kissing me in different places. Chasm has my mouth; Parrish presses scalding kisses down my bare belly.

He stops just short of more sensitive areas, sliding his tongue back up toward my breasts.

Chasm pulls back slightly, and the two of them switch. I'd say it was coordinated, but really, it feels more like they're dueling than dancing. Dueling over me. And I love it. The music is loud and well-suited for the moment; it drowns out the strange noises slipping past my lips, disguises the slide of Chas's finger into the wetness between my thighs.

Parrish pauses and looks down, heaving a sharp breath. But then he's kissing me again, and his right hand is massaging my breast, playing with the weight of it as Chasm moves that single finger in and out of me, dropping his own mouth to my belly button. He swirls his tongue in a circle around my dual navel piercings and then very quickly continues the journey that Parrish abandoned.

"I want to be the first person to go down on you."

Just as he promised, Chasm makes sure he's the first one to taste me. He doesn't ask. It happens naturally. My knees bend and I allow him to push my thighs gently apart, dropping his mouth where I so desperately want it to go.

He keeps that single finger inside of me, moving it nice and slow, working his tongue over every square inch of me until there's not a part of me that he hasn't touched, hasn't kissed, hasn't licked.

Parrish makes up for it by kissing my mouth with fervor and passion, alternately pausing to kiss and suck on my neck, my breasts. His fingers trace my nipples, sweep down my belly, tilt my chin toward him so he can get deeper, his tongue down my throat.

I'm not sure that I'm fully coherent in that moment. I mean, I am, but my mind is drifting and wheeling, flying high on the pleasure rippling up from between my legs, the sensation of Parrish's talented fingers playing over my breasts, his skillful tongue.

They keep at it, the pair of them dragging me to the edge of climax, and then right over to the other side. I tumble down, a free-flowing waterfall, crashing into the rocks at the bottom as my body tightens around Chasm's finger, and I shudder against the hot press of his lips.

"Relax, Gamer Girl. We'll take good care of you." Parrish cups my face in his hand, waiting for Chasm to move back up beside me, so that I've got one half-naked, tattooed Whitehall brat on either side of me. "Condom." Parrish holds out his right hand toward Chasm, propped up on his left elbow with his head resting in his hand. "Hurry."

Chas licks his lips and looks down at me, meeting my eyes.

"Thank you. For letting me be the first to taste you." He smiles, and I know he means it—even if it's embarrassing as hell to hear him say it aloud like that. *As embarrassing as you promising to return the favor the last time this was brought up?*

"It had to be you," I promise him, getting lost in the truly epic proportions of his face. Now that he's washed his hair, I can see that yellow lightning bolt so clearly, his lip rings enhancing the fullness of his bottom lip, the sweet shine of it.

"Condom." Parrish repeats his request, and Chas lifts his lip at him, turning over to grab the box. He frees one of the condom packages from it and passes it to me, rather than his friend. I take it and hold it against my chest for a moment, breathing hard, sweating more than I probably should. And all the while, the music keeps going.

I have an extensive playlist; we've got another thirty minutes of BLACKPINK at least before we move onto EXO or Punch or aespa.

Rolling onto my side, I turn to face Parrish, but he's already reaching down with his right hand and flicking the button on his slacks open. My left hand trails gently over his bandages, finding the warmth of him inside his pants. At first, I just stroke him, leaning close so that our mouths are hovering but we're not quite kissing.

Not one to be outdone, Chasm scoots close, pressing his body all along the naked length of my back. He pets me with gentle, questing fingers, drawing the breath out of me with each touch. At the same time, my gaze is all for Parrish, my fingertips brushing and tickling over his most sensitive parts.

"Shit," he breathes finally, losing the slightest edge of his arrogance as I lift the condom up to my lips and tear the edge with my teeth. I pause briefly there to examine it.

"That's sort of a *rule of cool* move," I admit, looking up from the package to his face. "It's honestly not a smart move to use your teeth to open a condom package, just in case a hole gets—" Parrish cuts me off by grabbing my face and kissing my mouth. He yanks the condom from my hand and tosses it aside, only to have Chasm put another in his hand.

This time, it's already open.

I remove the slick ring from the package and put it on while Parrish lays there with half-lidded eyes, breathing heavy, his charcoal slacks pushed down below his ass.

When he pushes my shoulder back and climbs on top of me, I'm completely past the point of rational thought. My fingers dig into his hair as he slides into me. I'm beyond ready thanks to Chasm, and it's easy for Parrish to bury himself fully inside of me.

"I can't believe I'm watching this," Chasm chokes out, putting a hand up to cover his face. But he doesn't leave. He eventually drops his hand down as Parrish curls our fingers together the way he likes, looking down at me as he moves his body. He doesn't look at anything else. Just me. There's wonder, too, in his expression, devotion, promise. "Shit."

More cursing from Chasm, some strongly worded sentences in Korean that I feel like I can almost understand through the sheer emotion in them. And yet ... right now, it's as if Parrish is the only person that matters.

He's back. We brought him back.

And I can never forgive Justin for taking him.

Never, ever.

Sex with Parrish Vanguard is a whole-body experience. He

knows how to touch and pet, how to smile, when to press his face to the side of my throat and chuckle.

"God, I missed you so bad. Doesn't matter how many times I say it, it's true."

"We missed you more. That much I know for sure." I lick the side of his face, and he pulls back slightly, seemingly surprised. That smirk on his face amps up even more, and then he's rocking against me hard and fast and furious.

"You surprise me every day, Dakota Banks," he whispers, and then we're writhing together in a way that I can't spend too much time worrying about how it looks to Chasm. Instead, I let Parrish wrap me up in his arms and his essence, his dewy clover smell thrilling me as much as his touch. I love the way he smells. I'm a creeper, I already know that, thanks.

When he's getting close to his own climax, I encourage him by squeezing him between my legs and murmuring sweet things in his ear. I really don't expect him to take me with him, burying his body deep and driving me right back to that tender edge.

"Kill This Love" is playing now as Parrish rolls off of me, both of us panting heavily, sweating, heartbeats thundering. Chasm stays right where he was, stretched out alongside of me. When I turn my face toward him, he reaches out with a single finger and runs it along the edge of my jaw.

"Was that good for you, Little Sister?" he asks, and then pauses, offering up an apologetic cringe. "Yeah, you're right: I need to scrap that nickname, don't I?"

"Was it good?" I repeat, still breathing hard, and then swallowing the pre-embarrassment I'm feeling from all the things I haven't yet said. "We're not done yet, are we?"

Chas' eyes go wide, and then he's rolling over and scrambling for another condom. I help him out of his towel, shoving it off his hips and onto the floor, and then the condom is on like magic.

"I don't know if I can stay here for this," Parrish breathes, pushing the heels of his hands into his eyes. Both Chas and I pause to look over at him.

"I don't want you to leave," I say, and I wonder if I'm being selfish here. Or if I care. Do I? I mean, I *do,* but I'm also really happy. The happiest I've been in a long, long time. The only thing that might make this moment better would be if Maxim were here …

Whoa there, Gamer Girl. Put the brakes on. You're already dreaming of a foursome?! That's sort of a lot to think about. I push the idea to the side—I'm not sure where X fits into all of this anyway—and roll over toward Parrish to offer him at least some sort of encouragement or comfort. When Chasm follows me and pulls my hips back, an excited and shocked gasp escapes my lips.

Erm. On my hand and knees, him behind me. It's a good deal.

My mouth crashes against Parrish's just as Chasm is pushing into me. Strange emotions flicker through me, the taste of Parrish on my lips, the feel of Chas' hands on my hips …

"Kwang-seon …" The name slips out of me, but Parrish doesn't seem to mind. "Pear-Pear …"

We're kissing hard, Parrish's hands in my hair, my body on fire from Chasm's movements. Parrish is the one who sneaks a hand between us, finding my clit and working the tender flesh with his fingers. I can barely stay upright as I am; it's only Chasm's hands on my body, Parrish's bracing palm on my rib cage, that keep me from tumbling forward.

Even with my shaking limbs, even with my uncertainty, I'm catapulted into bliss. Having them both here with me isn't just twice as good as having one of them, it's … "exponential." I actually breathe the word aloud against Parrish's lips, and he pauses the intricate dance of his fingers. Chasm slows his thrusts, and I swear that Parrish is looking past me at his friend.

"Oh, *Naekkeo*," Chas whispers, part humor, part infatuation. Parrish smiles against my mouth, and then his tongue is taking control of the situation, diving deep, tasting me. Savoring me. Tears prick my eyes because I'm just so happy he's back, that he's here, that he isn't forcing me to choose between him and his friends.

It almost ... sort of ... feels like we're a little family.

Or something.

Chasm tightens his fingers on my pelvis, firing up that wild heat in my blood the way only he can. My reaction to him is so different from my reaction to Parrish, but complementary at the same time. One is red-hot and fervent; one is the cool kiss of a soothing breeze.

My brain is certain that I won't be able to come again, that three times in one night is laughably excessive ... but then it's happening, and Chasm is grunting and groaning from behind me. He moves deeper, harder, rolling his hips against me over and over, and then we're both collapsing onto the bed.

I hear Chas rustling around as he removes the condom and grabs the loose throw from the end of the bed to cover us up with. Then he's curling up beside me while Parrish remains comatose on my left, one arm thrown over his face. I turn my head—not an easy thing to do since I'm lying on my stomach—to find Chasm watching me. He manages a smile on that beautiful mouth of his.

He reaches out a hand as Parrish rolls over, throwing an arm around my waist.

"We should clean up ..." he murmurs, and Chas makes a sound of agreement.

Next thing I know, the three of us are asleep on one of Laverne's guest beds.

Happy prom night, Dakota Banks.

And what a prom night it was.

CHAPTER 5

Our happy bliss is broken by a shrill, warbling scream.

In an instant, we're all awake and moving. Me, I glom on to the throw blanket, wrapping myself up in it. Chasm is on his feet, snatching the lamp from the nightstand and tearing the cord from the wall in the process. He wields it like a weapon before he sees who it is that's just screamed us all back to the world of the living.

"M-mom," Parrish chokes out, sitting on the edge of the bed and frantically buttoning up his pants. He's shaking, his face chalk-white, his eyes as wide as I've ever seen them. Chasm very quickly grabs the towel off the floor and covers his junk with it.

Wait, what? It takes my sleep and sex addled brain a moment to recognize what—and who—it is that I'm staring at.

Tess.

I'm staring at Tess. It was Tess that screamed. *Tess* who is standing in the doorway to the guest room, both of her hands clamped over her mouth, back to the wall, quivering like a wild thing as her eyes flick from Chasm's nearly naked form, over to me (also naked beneath my blanket), and then to her adopted son, his hands shaking so badly that he's missed the button on his slacks about three times already.

Tess' gaze takes in the two booze bottles, the open box of condoms spilling across the nightstand and onto the floor, us. Yeaaaah, mostly she stares at us …

"Oh my God." She turns away suddenly, a bag clutched tightly in her left hand. "Put your clothes on and get out here *now*." She's panting as she storms off, and I'm panicking because I don't have any clothes but for the robe, and oh, I know it already looks bad (it doesn't just look bad, it is bad) but won't it look worse if I come down in a robe?

"My dress." Those are the only words I can squeeze out. Chasm puts the lamp down, raking his fingers through his hair over and over.

"I'll get it," he offers, glancing over at Parrish with a wide-eyed gaze of his own. "What are we going to do? How do we get out of this one?"

"There's no getting out of this." I know immediately that we've just made a mountain out of a molehill. Okay, well, it was already a mountain, but we've just like, Everested the fuck out of this situation. "She's going to send me back to New York; she's going to make me live with *Justin* full-time."

I'm panicking now, truly and utterly panicking.

Parrish scrubs his hand down his face before looking over at me.

"No. I won't let that happen." He pushes up to his feet, collecting his shirt and slipping into it. He's doing up the buttons as Chasm snaps up his slacks and suit jacket, yanking them on before he leaves to fetch my dress. Meanwhile, I sit there wondering if I might actually die because of this. Either due to extreme embarrassment or at the hands of my biological mother.

ENDGAME ROMANCE

With a groan, I do a double facepalm and wish fervently for some sort of natural disaster that might get me out of this. A tornado? Not on the West Coast … What do they have over here? Earthquakes? Too passe. A wildfire? Too depressing.

"Zombies." I lift my face up, eyes glittering. "Yeah, that'd do it. If a zombie outbreak were to occur right now, we'd be saved."

Parrish pauses to snort, but the sound dies off as quickly as it came.

"No such luck this time," he says with a sigh, checking the old-fashioned clock on the wall for the time.

It's just past three in the morning.

"We really blew it, didn't we?" I mumble, tucking the blanket more tightly around myself. Only, it's hard to think of what just happened as a mistake. I enjoyed every single second of it.

"If you have to," Parrish begins, looking over at me with his shirt rumpled, the buttons completely mismatched, several of them not even buttoned at all. "Use the kidnapping card. Use it right off the bat. Use it liberally." He slips out the door as Chasm is on his way back in, tossing the gold dress over to me.

I very quickly hop off the bed, discarding the blanket and trying not to focus on the intensity of Chasm's stare on my bare ass. He's looking, make no doubt about that.

"*Aish,*" he growls out. "I *should* be scared, but …" I turn around just in time to see his face soften up. "I'm not. I'm too happy right now."

"Happy?" I ask, and he moves over to me, reaching around me to help zip up the back of my dress. My heart thunders like crazy, and I swear, I can feel every single spot on my body that he touched. Each one is a sense memory that I'll hold onto for the rest of my life.

"Because we have a chance, you and me." Chas smiles and pats my cheek, pausing at the sound of the door creaking open. I look over to see Tess, arms crossed over her chest, face in a severe frown. If I'd thought I'd seen her angry before, it was nothing like this.

"Get downstairs. Now." She turns and sweeps past Parrish, leaving me and Chasm to follow behind.

That's how the three of us end up sitting at the kitchen island, all of us barefoot and in some post-coital state of deshabille.

Tess has a bottle of red wine open beside her but also a cup of steaming coffee in her hands. It's very, uh, Millennial of her. Wine and coffee. As I said, I just hope that the killing people thing isn't generational.

"What did I just walk in on?" she whispers, and I try my best to conjure up an image of what she must've seen.

Chasm, naked, but with a scrap of blanket over his bare butt cheeks. Parrish, shirtless, his pants in a highly inappropriate state (basically tucked up under his ass). Me ... in my birthday suit. On my stomach. A boy on either side.

I put a hand over my mouth, staring at the counter instead of Tess' face. Her phone lies nearby, so Justin could be listening in. Not that it matters. It's not like he isn't aware of the situation with the boys; he's the one that pushed me into this.

"A consensual act between three people—"

"Three *children*." Tess interrupts Parrish and then sets her coffee aside, snagging the bottle of wine by the neck and chugging it while we stare at her.

"Hardly." Parrish crosses his arms and goes for that princely air with gusto. "There's a lot of pent-up tension between us. Seeing as I went missing for nearly three weeks and almost died ..."

"Oh no," Tess begins with a harsh laugh. "You. And you." I look up to see her point from Parrish to me. "Are not going to use your kidnapping cards against me. Not on this one." She laughs again and takes another swig of the wine. "Is this because of porn?" she asks, as if she's truly trying to understand before she explodes. I don't know what to make of that. She's angrier than she's ever been and yet … not? "Have you all been watching too much porn?"

I rear back like I've been slapped.

"My grandmother used to say that porn is as similar to real sex as *High School Musical* is to a real high school experience. As in, not at all. Less than ten percent of the most popular clips on the internet at any given time actually show people smiling and laughing. People should smile and laugh when they have sex."

"Is that so?" Tess demands, and my face blanches. Oops. She didn't ask for a dissertation on the evils of modern-day pornography. Sometimes when I get nervous, I blurt facts. It's just a thing. It happens. "And you'd know that how? You are … you're my *daughter.* You don't know anything about sex."

"Um." I scratch at the back of my head and try to figure out a clever way to escape whatever punishments she might be dreaming up over there. "Then I'm not sure what just happened upstairs …"

Tess groans and puts her head in her hand.

"I should never have let the three of you come back here. I knew it was a mistake before I even did it." She looks at the wine, curses, and then sets the bottle aside, grabbing her abandoned coffee mug. "As soon as I finish this cup, I'll be taking you home, Kwang-seon. I'll let you know as soon as I get news about your car." Ah, right. Because it was parked in the garage back at the house.

"Understandable," he agrees, hanging his head slightly. But when I catch his gaze out of the corner of my eye, he smiles, and I can't help but smile back.

"Do you think this is funny?" Tess demands, and it's Parrish who answers, certain that he's the most capable of absorbing her wrath. He's probably right, but I don't want him getting into any extra trouble.

"It sort of is, if you think about it," he offers up, trying to lighten the mood. "Mom, it's not like we were doing anything crazy. Just safe, consensual sex."

"I'm going to be sick." Tess chugs the coffee and then sets the mug aside, pacing a tight circle on the kitchen floor. She's barefoot, too, her feet shushing on the ground. She pauses to turn and stare at us. "I can't even believe this. Dakota, was this consensual?"

Well, at least she uses the right name this time. And that's a fair question, considering the liquor and all.

"I didn't drink. Only they did. But I don't think either of them was drunk ..." I trail off and wet my lips. Tess just stares at me, like she has no idea who I am. To be fair, she really doesn't.

Her face was a mess of emotion, rainbow splatter on a ruined canvas; it was hard to tell where the red of anger began, and the purple of disappointment ended. There were more colors there than I'd ever seen in that woman's face, and it changed so many things between us all at once.

The pink parts—the love and affection—those began to show through in the strangest and most obscure of ways.

I never expected a threesome after prom to bring me closer to the woman who had given birth to me.

Those are the things I'd write, if I were to put pen to paper later on and describe this moment.

Let's be frank: Tess was never going to laugh and shrug this off. She's definitely not Regina George's mom from *Mean Girls*, not a 'cool mom' whatsoever. But also, compared to her actions in the past (like taking Parrish's and my doors), this isn't so bad. Proportionally speaking.

"From now on, you and me." She points between the two of us. "We're attached at the hip. If you're on my time, you're by my side." Tess turns to her son next. "When Dakota is with us, you will be with Paul. In fact, I'm going to encourage him to hire you on part-time for the summer."

"I don't want to work at a plastic surgeon's office," Parrish scoffs out, but Tess clearly couldn't care less. "What exactly are you upset about? The three of us being up there? Sex in general? Or is it just because you called me and Dakota your lost babies?" He's breathing hard, but I can see that this is a test for him, too. Because he never liked the way Tess treated me; it bothered him. Her actions toward me, in his eyes, did not match up to the mother she was to him.

The two of them stare one another down before Parrish pulls out another trick.

Or, at least I think it's a trick?

"Caroline is in town. Our house almost burned down. I came back. Dakota came back. Does this really matter? Chasm and I both want Dakota, and she likes us both. Neither of us ... we're not going to make her choose. That's all this is. Me and Dakota. Chasm and Dakota." He exhales and sits back in the chair, watching her.

"Parrish," Tess replies, her voice softening slightly as she exhales. "There's more than one issue here that I need to address." She turns to Chasm next. "You and I, we've already had this conversation, haven't we?"

"We have," Chasm agrees, his cheeks reddening. I've never seen him get embarrassed like this before, but as usual, he accepts criticism with grace in order to salvage the situation. "We really just both wanted to be with her."

"*I* wanted them both with me; I asked them to do that." I speak up because I can't let the guys take all the credit for this.

"Get your things, Kwang-seon. I asked you and Dakota to abstain for the time being, and you chose not to respect that. I'm taking you home. Once we've had time to sort things out here, we'll have another talk."

"Please don't kick me out of the family." Chasm puts his palms together and rubs them in pleading. "I wouldn't survive that."

Tess softens even further, but that hard glint in her eyes is still there.

"I would never do that. But you can certainly spend the rest of the weekend at home without consequence. Put your shoes on. Your father isn't home yet, so if we hurry, you can get yourself together before you talk with him." She moves out of the kitchen, offering us up the briefest sliver of privacy.

"I'm more worried about the pair of you than myself," Chas admits, sliding off his stool. "Tess already knew about us; she found the evidence, remember?" He raises his brows and then steps toward me, looking down into my eyes. Chasm lifts his hands up, pressing his fingertips into either side of my face.

An unconscious breath escapes me, soft and fluttering.

"I'll be with Justin all weekend," I remind him, and he nods, lips pursed tight before he leans down to whisper in my ear.

"Let's use our fathers' relationship with one another to our advantage." He puts his hand on my shoulder. "Hopefully, I'll see you soon. Keep in touch or I'll come looking for you, Little Sister."

Chasm moves past me, but Tess pops her head back in the door.

"All of us are going. You really think I'd leave the two of you here alone?" She scoffs and turns away.

Parrish and I exchange a look, but what other choice do we have?

With a sigh, we stand up and head for the front door—and the still-raging storm—together.

ENDGAME ROMANCE

Chasm is lucky enough to get home before his father. Good thing, too, since he didn't exactly have his filler stuff or spray-on hair dye with him. At least he's got time to do a Sailor Scout transformation into Seamus-approved mode before it's too late.

The last look we share before he disappears through the front door is tinged with melancholy.

I find myself fidgeting in the front seat.

"Let's get milkshakes," Tess suggests, and even though I can't see Parrish in the back seat, I can feel him stiffen up. I turn over to see Tess sighing and pushing mussed hair back from her forehead. I wonder if she got any sleep at the hospital or if she's been up this whole time. She looks utterly exhausted.

We end up driving all the way into Seattle proper to find a place that's both open at this hour and that also serves milkshakes.

"What flavor do you guys want?" Tess asks as we pull up to the old-fashioned board with the handwritten flavors. Someone took the time to draw cute, little smiling fruits, too.

"Strawberry." Parrish and I say it at the same time, and Tess stiffens up again.

I exhale and meet Parrish's eyes in the rearview mirror. I love that we both love strawberry shakes. I'm even coming around to the idea of having been kidnapped and stolen across the country. Because of that, Tess was able to meet Paul and raise Parrish. Who knows who he'd be if she'd never met him? Would I still love him the way I do? Worse: what if I'd grown up alongside him and still fallen in love? That'd have been even harder to deal with.

So, despite everything, I'm happy.

I'm happy ... and I just got caught post-threesome with my bio mom's adopted son and other adopted son. Right. And our house almost burned down. And eventually I'm going to kill Justin.

Yet, I can't think of any of that just now.

Instead, Tess drives us to Admiral Viewpoint which, according to her, actually has better views in the winter since the trees block some of it. Doesn't matter to me. As soon as we park, and I see the glittering lights of the city on Harbor Island, the dark waters of Elliot Bay, I'm feeling okay.

Tess stands between me and Parrish—not something I see changing anytime soon—and sips her drink.

She also prefers strawberry.

So there we are, the three of us sipping strawberry shakes and staring out at the glitter of nighttime Seattle, our thoughts preoccupied. I turn to look over at the two of them. Parrish is staring at the city, but Tess actually looks back at me.

"High school relationships don't last forever," she reminds us, and Parrish scoffs.

"You and Dad ..."

"Met in high school. Did not get together in high school," she reminds him, sighing yet again. "My inclination right now is to slap the both of you, lock you away from each other, and go tell your father." She sucks on her straw again, and then shakes her head. "But I can't do that. I feel too lucky that, after all that we've been through, everyone is still together." A pause here, and I know what she really means. *Alive. Everyone is still alive.* "I'm also not going to let this go either."

"You're worried we'll get tired of each other and break up the family when we split." It's a guess on my part, but it's a good one. It's honestly not a far-fetched prospect. She's right: most high school relationships don't last. *Ours is different.* I feel it in my gut, but then, doesn't everyone? Yeah, everyone thinks that ...

"I wish you hadn't kept this from me." That's how Tess answers. She doesn't confirm or deny my suggestion, but I'm betting on the former. I shiver, my gold skirts swirling in the breeze. It might be mid-June, but this is the Pacific Northwest; warm weather is relative. "When the two of you started having feelings for one another, I wish you'd come to me to talk about it."

"You haven't exactly had an open door," I admit, because at this point, there's no reason to lie. "I thought if you knew, that you'd ..." The words get caught, and I feel myself short on breath. How can I say this? Why am I choosing to say this now? "I thought if you knew that, you'd send me back to New York."

There's a long pause there, the only sounds that of a ship's horn in the distance and the straw-slurp of strawberry shakes in paper cups.

"You wouldn't like that?" Tess questions, rightfully so. She doesn't know the full story, and I know damn well that I can't risk giving it to her. As (pleasantly) surprised as I am by Tess' behavior right now, I know exactly what she'd do if she learned a single detail of Justin's secret coup. She would put Maxine at risk to drive that man into the ground.

But for me, my sister is worth the world. Even if the Slayer kills a dozen more teens before we get this under control. Even if he kills two dozen. The whole situation is seriously like some fucked-up psychology experiment. *There's a train speeding along; it has an option of switching between two tracks. On one track, there's your loved one tied to the rails, but otherwise it's safe. The other ends in a brick wall, which would kill all the people on the train. Which side do you pick?*

I know myself without a shadow of a doubt.

I'd save the person I loved.

I'm not sure if that makes me a good person, a bad one, or just ... a person, really.

"Not anymore." Those words come from me, just the barest whisper, almost invisible when the breeze rustles the branches on the trees.

More silence.

"I don't know how to solve this, not yet. For now, let's get through your weekend with Justin, then we'll figure it out." Tess moves over to a trash can, dumping her empty cup inside. Parrish and I do the same, and we head back toward the car.

Tess stops short, turning around just in front of the hood and looking between the both of us. When she reaches up her hands and places her palms on either of our cheeks, a warmness permeates me that I didn't expect. *What is even happening right now?!*

"As disappointed as I am in the two of you, as frustrated as I am, as confused ... I love you both very much." She smiles slightly, and then drops her hands. "But when we get back to the house, Dakota is sleeping with me. Parrish, you'll take the room next door. The two of you are not to be alone in a room together, is that understood?"

"Understood," Parrish breathes, but his eyes catch mine and something shifts there.

Forbidding us from being together ... is only going to make things worse.

We want each other. Even more than we did yesterday. This morning. Two hours ago.

More, more, more.

"Understood." I climb in the front seat, and we head back to the house. By the time we get there, I'm so exhausted that I slip into the pajamas I picked out, and I'm comatose before my head even hits the pillow.

CHAPTER 6

Tess is awake when I come to, propped up in the pillows and sipping a cup of coffee while I struggle into a sitting position. The whole situation—the room, the expression on Tess' face, my inner awe—is reminiscent of that scene in the 1998 movie *The Parent Trap* when the American twin first visits London and is in bed with her mother, excited and surprised to see what a big deal professionally she is, how pretty she is, how much she missed someone she'd never even met.

I end up sitting with my knees splayed, the blanket draped over my head, an expression of sheer confusion on my face. There's a cup of coffee sitting on the nightstand on my side, hot and steaming. Hesitantly, I reach out and grab it.

The sun is shining this morning, and the gothic grandeur of the mansion seems somehow diminished. Like, we are just in Medina, Washington; this is not an Agatha Christie novel, and my bio mom just caught me in bed with her adopted son—and his best friend.

Such is my life.

"Good morning." She says it first, turning slightly to look at me, her espresso hair falling in a smooth wave over her shoulder. It occurs to me then how young she really is. It's strange, having been raised by my grandparents and then looking at this young woman as my mother. We look so alike, too. It's jarring at times. *Like right now. She's staring at me, and I have no idea where this conversation is going.* "Did you sleep well?"

"What time is it?" I ask, searching around for my phone. But I left it downstairs after our game of strip Scrabble and forgot all about it. Knowing that my bio dad and his goonies can hack into my life whenever they want makes having a phone a hell of a lot less of a priority. I'm not entirely sure that I miss it.

"Ten." She sips her coffee, and I do the same. It's got cream and sugar, and there's a faint vanilla flavor to it. Not bad. "I've already gotten Parrish up and had a talk with him. It's our turn."

I sit there with my coffee, the blanket on my head, and I don't move.

"Okay." Noncommittal, safe. I'm sitting here talking to Tess, but my mind is already on the Slayer and our get-together today. He promised me a lot of things if I could make my grades. Access to Maxine, who I haven't spoken to in weeks. My grandparents who I haven't spoken to in even longer. This is a side quest.

A side quest.

I'm not at all freaked out.

Right.

"What did you want to talk about?" I ask, anxiety rioting inside of me. This is likely the most nervous I've ever been in my life. And it's not because of me and Parrish, not really. It's because this is the last chance I'm giving to Tess before I start to withdraw, before I start to give up on the relationship we might have between us. *Prove me wrong,* I wish, and then I wait.

"I got the details from Parrish—not too many of them." She

shakes her head and sighs, closing her eyes for a moment. "But I can't accept it. I can't have the two of you dating." Tess turns to look at me, offering up an apologetic smile. "I'm not going to hold this over your heads; I'm not going to make a big deal out of this. I just need a promise from you that the relationship isn't going to continue."

I blink at her.

I'm mildly impressed ... and also supremely annoyed.

"We're in love." The words come out strong, surprising me. Tess doesn't seem swayed.

"Parrish already agreed; I suggest you do as well. Then we can just"—she slides her hand away from her, gesturing big—"forget all about this and move on. I have a house to rebuild and refurnish, a family to clothe, and a new series to write. There's a lot going on." Tess looks pleadingly at me, and I'm not sure if she even remotely believes that Parrish and I would actually abide by such an agreement, but ... I don't like it. If he did agree to such a proposal, as Tess has indicated, then it was a lie.

I'm not going to lie.

"I can't forget about this," I admit, taking another sip of the coffee. I appreciate her making it for me, for handling this in a much calmer manner than I expected. "I can't forget about *him* more like." My cheeks—and because nothing is ever easy, my boobs—flush red. "I could just agree with you and lie about it, but I don't want to do that."

Tess sets her mug in her lap, hands curved around it. She's looking at the half-full (or half-empty, depending on your persuasion) cup and not at me.

"Is that what Parrish is doing? Lying to me then?" Tess sounds sad but not surprised. She taps her nails on the side of the mug.

"Not to hurt you," I explain, finally pushing the blanket off of my head. This could very well be the most intimate moment that

Tess Vanguard and I have ever shared. "To protect you. He …
initially rejected me because he didn't want to hurt you."

I turn around and settle into the pillows properly, taking extra
special care not to spill the coffee on the pale-yellow linens. The
room we're staying in has a white coffered ceiling, an ancient
looking chandelier, and oversized pieces of antique furniture.

My mind strays back to the Vanguard house and all of the
wonderful pieces that may have been lost forever.

My throat constricts, but I take another drink to wash the
emotions down.

Far more important things are afoot.

Tess doesn't respond for a while, but I know we're not finished
here yet.

"To protect me." She sighs again and sets her coffee mug aside,
glancing my way. "There's a part of me that's relieved that the two
of you don't hate each other anymore. The rest of me is …" Here
she lets out a scoffing laugh. "The rest of me is horrified. You are
my daughter; he is my son."

"But we don't feel like siblings. The moment I saw Parrish, I
was attracted to him." I chew on my lip, a habit that I picked up
from Maxx. I need to find my phone so that I can check up on X,
make sure everything between Chas and Seamus went okay last
night, and … look at my grades. They should be posted by now.

"Laverne arrived early this morning and the staff is trickling in.
Please keep this to yourself for now," Tess tells me, and then she's
standing up from the bed and gathering her hair together in an
effort to tie it up. "I left some clothes for you in the bathroom."

I don't like leaving things unresolved; I can tell we're nowhere
near to finding a solution to this. But also, I'm supposed to go with
Justin today. I'm supposed to spend two nights with him.

With a sigh, I head into the bathroom, take a quick shower, and
dress in the clothes that Tess left for me. It's all Whitehall stuff—

sweatpants, pullover hoodie, sneakers. I have no idea where it came from, but when I head downstairs to find Parrish waiting for me on the bottom step, I see that he's dressed similarly.

He stands up, turning to face me with an expression of sheer apathy.

I'm not fooled by it.

I pause with my hand on the beautiful banister, lifting my gaze from his as a woman sweeps past with an armful of towels. Staff. Not just one, like the Vanguards and Delphine, but a whole team of them. Turning my head in the direction of the formal sitting room, I see that there are numerous people running around, dusting, fluffing pillows, vacuuming floors that didn't need to be vacuumed.

"How did it go?" Parrish asks, but I'm not even given the chance to answer. Tess pops her head out of the kitchen and gestures for us to join her. "Fuck, I was looking forward to this summer, too." He moves ahead of me, and I follow along, pausing only when he does.

More like, he comes to a full stop, and I slam into his muscular back. My hands come up automatically to brace myself, and I end up with my fingers tangled in the fabric of his hoodie. It's a charcoal colored one with the words *Whitehall Academy—Where the Best Shine Bright* emblazoned across the front. Coincidentally, it's the same type of hoodie he was wearing the day after I met him for the very first time.

"Did you agree to call it off?" he whispers, glancing over his shoulder at me. "The us thing, I mean." I shake my head, and I know he can feel the movement against his back.

"I didn't agree to anything."

Parrish turns around suddenly, withdrawing my phone from his pocket. He lets it dangle from between two fingers and then offers it out to me.

"I charged it for you." He turns away before I can figure out what else to say—if anything—and then he's striding into the kitchen and I'm jogging to catch up with him.

Tess is waiting. Unfortunately, so is Laverne. She's sipping what appears to be Scotch from a small tumbler, her eyes—so much like Parrish's—laser focused on me. I hesitate in the doorway, powering my phone on and cursing Justin out inside my head.

I never *liked* the ice cavern—let's be honest, it's an architectural nightmare—but at least I had my own space there. My stuff from back home. Parrish, across the hall. I feel like I'm free-floating, and the only thing I have to hold onto is the stepbrother-turned-lover who I'm not allowed to touch.

"Sit. I'm making breakfast." Tess gestures at the stools as Parrish moves up to the island and pauses beside his grandmother. Her eyes soften at the edges, and she rises to her feet, putting her arms around him in a snug embrace.

"I knew you'd come home," she whispers, rubbing his back as he returns the hug, and they part so that Laverne can look him over. "Let me see what he did to you." Her voice hardens to iron as she nods her chin in her grandson's direction.

With pursed lips, Parrish reaches down and lifts up his hoodie. My eyes follow the movement of his hand until Tess reaches out and taps me on the shoulder, drawing my attention away from Parrish's midsection. Not that I was looking, not in that way anyway.

I just stare at Tess, but she forces a smile.

"Care to hand me the eggs and bacon from the fridge?" She keeps her tone light, but it's clear that her mind is on last night. So is mine, even though it shouldn't be. *Side quest, Dakota. Side quest. This is just a side quest.*

I do as she asks, setting the items on the counter beside her.

ENDGAME ROMANCE

When she gestures at the empty pan on the burner and offers up a spatula, I join her in cooking. I can't stop myself from repeatedly looking over at Tess, the low murmur of Laverne and Parrish's conversation impossible to hear over the sizzle of bacon fat.

This may very well be the first time that Tess has invited me to participate in an activity with her other than shopping at stores I don't like or going to the country club. *Did it really take the bungled afterglow of a glorious threesome to get to this point?* Still, remember how much I enjoy idioms? Especially this one? *If it seems too good to be true, it's probably a fresh fucking hell.*

I may or may not have modified that one from the original version. Not sure.

"I looked up your grades this morning," Tess continues, a faux nonchalance proving she's a better writer than she is an actor. I pause, my hand frozen on the spatula, the bacon popping and sizzling in front of me. Tess seems pleased; that's a good sign, isn't it?

Turning back to the stove, I fake a terribly inauthentic nonchalance of my own. If Tess and I were strangers before, this is almost worse. Now she knows the secrets of my heart and, because of that, it's entirely up to her to decide what to do with it. Pair that with the anxiety of my grades—and what they ultimately mean for me—and I'm staggered.

I just *barely* manage to hold back a stilted fake laugh. Also, I'm sweating profusely. I take a half-step back from the stove and run my arm across my forehead.

"Oh?" The inquiry manages to reek of desperation, hard as I might try for some of Parrish's disdainful swagger. It's just not my thing, apparently. I pretend to cough into my hand, clearing my throat as I wait for Tess to put me out of my misery.

Whitehall Prep doesn't allow students to log in and check their grades, only a parent can. Well, unless said parent offers their student their password which—obviously—Tess would never do. I'm at her mercy. Hers or … Justin's. I'm certain he has access, code or otherwise.

"If you need to cough, you should excuse yourself from the kitchen." Laverne slips past me and out the door; I almost immediately hear her shouting at the house's staff. Chasm was right: the house is nice, the company not so much. Living with Laverne—however brief—is not going to be pleasant.

"I'll still eat your food, Gamer Girl." Parrish pauses just behind me and Tess, and she tosses a look his way.

"I'd like the two of you at least six feet apart at all times." She points in the direction of the island. "Other side, Parrish."

He tosses her a much saucier look than I would've bet on, especially considering the situation.

"So I'll look at her from afar then." The words are a challenge, one that Tess counteracts as best she can.

"I can't stop you from looking, but I can start taking things away when you do."

"Just so long as you don't take her." Parrish's final challenge echoes through me, and I can barely hold back a sound of surprise. I turn over to Tess, pretending to be disinterested. In reality, all I can think about right now is Parrish and this situation we've gotten ourselves into.

"Please tell me I aced it," I beg, flipping the food with the spatula and hoping nothing sticks.

Tess grudgingly pulls her eyes from Parrish to look at me, and offers up a half-smile in response. It might've been a full smile, really and truly, if she hadn't caught us in the worst possible way last night.

"You did well, Dakota. I'm proud …" A pause here and she sighs as she digs her phone out of her pocket, unlocks it, and hands it over to me. "Of your grades. I'm proud of your grades."

ENDGAME ROMANCE

I ignore the slight, staring down at my scores for the semester.

I'm hit simultaneously by two opposing emotions: well-deserved pride ... and wild terror.

Introduction to Probability and Statistics: 91%
Academic Composition: 98.6%
Technical Writing: 92%
Computer Science 1: 86%
Beginning Japanese: 90.26%
Software Tools: App Development: 99.1%

The school grades on percentiles, but grade estimates are listed below. Anything over ninety percent is considered an A. Anything between eighty and ninety is a B. *So I have five A's and one B.* It's a miracle, to be quite honest.

Or, rather, a testament to the skills of Kwang-seon McKenna.

But also ... *oh God.*

"I want to see all A's on that report card. If you please me, I'll allow you to not only speak to Maxine, but to see her in person."

Justin never specified what he might do if I failed.

"I'm impressed. Waking up to these grades helped my mood substantially." Tess collects the phone from me as I do my best to control my emotions. Panicking won't help. And Justin never mentioned a punishment exactly; he just said I wouldn't be able to talk to Maxine. He'll give me another chance, surely? *I am so fucked. We are so fucked.* "Kwang-seon is an incredible teacher." Her smile intensifies as she passes the phone to Parrish. "In the top ten percent of your class."

Parrish barely glances at the phone screen before switching his gaze to me.

He must be able to tell from my face that it's not good.

"Excuse me, Mrs. Vanguard?" A woman appears in the doorway, dressed in a maid's uniform. It's as ridiculous and clichéd as the one Delphine wore, the one we found that dead girl wearing … Nope. Will not think about that. Remember, I try very hard not to think about the box. "He's here."

"Buzz him in," Tess agrees with an exasperated sigh. Her gaze moves to mine. "Justin's here to pick you up." She pauses and purses her lips. "He's early."

Tess moves out of the kitchen as I pick up a piece of bacon and Parrish raises a brow in question.

"I got a B."

I move past him and into the foyer in time to see the maid open the door, revealing Justin in his beautiful navy-blue suit, shades pushed up into his hair, grinning like a movie star. Such a charming monster. The Seattle Slayer, the perfect techie unicorn start-up serial killer sent to plague the families of other techie unicorn start-ups.

"Condolences again on the fire," Justin offers up sympathetically, slipping the shades off of his head. He smiles at Tess, their eyes fixated on one another. In Justin's, there's obsession and want. In Tess', disgust and hatred. "Are you sure there isn't anything Caroline or I could do to help?"

"Don't you dare come at me with that bullshit, Justin. You brought Caroline Bassett to the hospital when you knew that we'd be there. Nothing you ever do is accidental." She stands her ground, even as he walks past her like she doesn't exist. "And let's get beyond that to the real question underneath: how did you just happen to run into Ms. Bassett? Doesn't it seem odd that you just so happen to be dating my son's birth mother?"

"Love is beyond explanation, Tess." He pauses beside me and then glances back at Tess. "Not that you'd understand any of it. Love and loyalty were never your things, were they?"

Oh shit. Parrish and I exchange a look, and I can see that it's taking every ounce of control he possesses not to kill my bio dad in that moment.

"And now we see it: the real man hiding underneath the glitter." Tess gestures at him as she turns around, looking at me like … and oh God, I hate this … like an equal. For the briefest of seconds there, Tess offers up an olive branch. *If you're adult enough to have sex, then surely you can see how toxic this man is? It's so obvious; it's happening right now. Do you see what I see?* "The gloves come off, and here's the real you, the man who doesn't give a shit that his daughter's siblings almost died in a house fire."

"They lived, didn't they?" Justin meets my eyes and my arm throbs in all the places he grabbed me last night. I have to agree with him. Already, I don't have the grades he asked for. There's no chance for me to get out of this without offering something up in return.

My dignity. Tess' slow and rational approach to a cray situation. My entire fucking life.

"Have you seen my grades yet?" I offer up, shaking and holding that slice of bacon in my hand that I can't eat. I'm squeezing it far too hard; it's weird. I shove the piece into my mouth to keep myself from blurting anything else out.

"I saw them." His smile doesn't change. I have no idea what he's thinking or what this means. Justin glances over at Parrish, offering up an infuriating wink before he turns away again. Parrish actually takes a step forward, squeezing his hands into fists at his sides. Like Maxx, I would not put it past him to actually hit Justin.

And see how well that went last time?

"Just don't," I whisper in fierce warning. "Keep your phone on you. If Tess tries to stop us from communicating … figure it out." I touch his arm and move past, heading for the door as quickly as I can. Anything to get out of that house before Justin starts yet more shit with Tess and Parrish. "I didn't get all A's. What happens now?"

Justin continues to smile as he opens the driver's side door of what I'm guessing is a new car. Sleek, black, expensive. It just screeches *I am a loaded asswad, possible midlife crisis.* And yet, somehow he carries it in just such a way that it's still almost cool.

That's how dangerous this man's charisma is.

I climb in and turn my head to stare at him. He seems to at least pretend to appreciate bravado—most of the time. My hand comes up, unconsciously rubbing at the bruises from last night. Justin notices and chuckles. *That* is what gives him pleasure on this fine morning: the idea of me in pain.

It really hits me then. I mean, I knew it, but there's an emotional punch to the gut when I realize that Justin Prior doesn't love me. Again, I think I knew that in the darkest recesses of my heart, but I didn't expect it to come at me this way. Nobody should ever want the person they love to be in pain. Yet, Justin is happy about my suffering.

All he has in regard to me is obsession and nothing more.

"What happens because of my grades?" I repeat, and he ignores me yet again. This time, he reaches out to turn on a satellite radio station based on hits from the early 00s. *"Milkshake"* by Kelis is playing, and Justin immediately gets into it, tapping his hand on the steering wheel in time to the music.

Fucking. Millennials.

I just stare at him.

Scratch what I said before: seeing as rocking out to old music and singing it loudly and off-key is a proud Millennial trait, I wouldn't be surprised if they truly did enjoy killing people as a whole generation. *Cringe as fuck.* I lick my lips.

There's no point in rushing this. The man murders teenagers. He sets houses on fire with little kids inside of them.

The song ends, and I dare to turn the volume down. He lets me, and I sit back in my seat wondering where we're off to now. I'm supposed to be living with him part-time as of today. What the hell is that going to be like?

"We're going to have a fun summer, Dakota." Justin glances over at me, but I keep my gaze on the trees passing by outside the window. It's just better not to look his way at all. "You did well with that report card." I can hear the squeak of his hands on the steering wheel, and my gaze drops to his knuckles, white with strain. "I know the professor from your Computer Science class." His hands tighten further, and I finally glance up at his expression, almost against my own will. "He's prejudiced against you for being my child, no doubt. Don't worry; I'll deal with him."

"You're going to let me see Maxine? Talk to my … the Banks?" I almost said grandparents. I definitely cannot say grandparents. He *really* didn't like me referring to the Vanguards as my family last night.

Justin pretends to think on that for a minute before reaching out and patting my knee.

"I'm a man of my word, aren't I? In every class that was fairly graded, you got an A." He nods absently, and I find myself exhaling in relief. I'm not going to think about what might happen to Mr. Parker from my computer science class.

I relax back in my seat, but only for a minute.

There's not going to be much relaxation or sleep for the next two nights.

How could there be? I'm bunking with the Seattle fucking Slayer.

And serial killers? They don't do lullabies.

Actually, Justin probably does: I'm just really, *really* tired of hearing him sing. He's a better murderer than he is a vocalist, that's for damn sure.

CHAPTER 7

Justin takes me … to the Vasquez house.

I sit up and stare as the gate slides open before us, and we roll down the driveway I walked down last week to find Parrish.

We're going to be staying in the very house where Parrish was held prisoner.

I almost slip on the damp gravel, still wet from last night's rains. It's going to be much warmer today, but the air's only just started to heat and everything's still dripping. The distant plopping sound of water draining from the trees is the only thing I allow myself to focus on.

"I've got a surprise for you, princess. Come with me." Justin heads up the steps, waiting near the front door for me to follow him in. Because I have nowhere else to go, I do. I'm certain that whatever surprise he has in store for me, I'm not going to appreciate very much.

I step into the shadows of the house, blinking rapidly to help my eyes adjust from the bright light outside. It takes me a second, but I spot a woman standing halfway across the foyer, her hair a brilliant white-blond, designer jeans, bright pink heels. As soon as she hears my footsteps, she turns to face me, and I pause.

She seems somehow familiar ... and yet ... not at all.

"Dakota," Justin begins, inhaling and holding out a hand to indicate the girl. She smiles at me, and I stare at her brown eyes, her wide smile, her flawless makeup. It's so flawless, in fact, that I still don't get it. I'm staring the girl right in the face, and I can't see it. "This is your older sister, Delphine."

I blink a few more times as she moves over to stand in front of me, offering up a hug.

"Delphine?" I say the name, but it takes another few seconds before it registers.

This is Delphine, *that* Delphine, the one who's been working for the Vanguards since before I even arrived in Washington state. The Delphine that Maxx followed home, spied on, and found nothing amiss. The very same Delphine, in fact, that survived scrutiny from the FBI and passed a federal background check.

She's dyed her hair, and she's clearly wearing contacts (or else never wore glasses at all). But this is her; this is most definitely her.

"Dakota." She's still standing there, offering up a hug. In the end, I allow her to embrace me because Justin is standing right beside us and there's nowhere else for me to go. We hold that position for several, awkward seconds before Delphine pulls back and continues smiling down at me.

I'm straight shocked. I mean, I knew there was a possibility that Delphine was involved, but not even in my nightmares did I imagine this.

"Sister?" I say the word again, because I'm having trouble believing this. I'm ... aren't I the Seattle Slayer's only child? *Justin's* only child? He was twenty when I was born, and Delphine is three years older than me. If she were his biological child, that'd mean he had a baby with someone when he was only seventeen.

"A brief high school fling," he replies with a loose shrug, reaching out to brush some of Delphine's hair back. She smiles at him and reaches up to touch his hand. Justin looks at her for a moment before glancing back at me. "I didn't even know I had another daughter until two years ago. I ran my DNA through several databases and voilà, there she was." Justin drops his hand and slides it into the pocket of his fancy slacks. "Me and my girls, a real family." He pauses and looks up at the sound of heels clacking across the floor.

I turn to see Parrish's bio mom, Caroline, striding across the foyer in a tight, black jumpsuit and heels.

"You're here," she says with a bright smile of her own. "Wonderful. What are our plans?"

How is this ... is this even happening?

There's that sense of free-falling again, like I'm tumbling down an endless hole. I'd thought somehow that I was playing on this man's level. Or at least I was close to it. Right now? Getting back at or away from Justin Prior in any shape or form seems to be a distant possibility.

Maxine is—and always will be—my sister.

Amelia is young enough that we can work up to that.

Kimber, I'm struggling to accept as a sibling or even an ornery acquaintance.

Delphine? How can I possibly fit another person into the sister category? I don't even know how to react, so I just stand there as Caroline offers a sly suggestion for a lunch venue, and Justin waves her off.

"No. There's a place in the city that I've been eying. But first, we'll give you girls a moment alone."

Justin moves away with Parrish's egg donor in tow.

ENDGAME ROMANCE

I end up just gaping at Delphine as she forces another shy smile, one that reminds me at least a little of the person she pretended to be as a maid to the Vanguard family.

"It's been hard for me to hold it in all this time," she explains, reaching out to take my hands. The strangest part of all this is that … I'd actually compared Delphine to Maxie in my head. Like when she did my hair for example. This girl *felt* like a sister.

And now here we are.

I get along better with the Serial Killer's little helper than Kimber Celeste.

My life is completely insane.

"You … the bloody sheets … the letter and the skeleton key … That was all you, wasn't it?"

It makes sense; it does. Again, there's a reason we had Maxx tail Delphine. But this? I did not expect this. *Guess that explains why Justin chose that Mexican restaurant, Un Padre, Dos Hijas.* Literal meaning: one father, two daughters.

It seems obvious now, but in the moment?

"Daddy needs our help to get his revenge." Delphine shrugs her shoulders and reaches up, combing that platinum blond hair over her shoulder. I hardly recognize her. From the meek, mousy-haired, glasses-wearing maid to this bombshell heiress with the cocky smirk. *Did I say Justin would be a shoo-in for an Academy Award? Delphine is just as talented, if not more so.*

"Daddy?" I can barely breathe. My chest feels tight, and my fingers are itching to snatch my phone so that I can call the boys. This is breaking news shit. This is … it's monumental. Life changing. My head swims, and I actually stumble. There's nothing to grab onto in the open foyer area, so I end up latching onto Delphine instead.

She smiles down at me in an affectionate sort of way, and my blood runs cold.

Fuck.

The apple does not fall far from the tree. Also, if I'm one of those apples, does that mean I'm just as crazy? Is there a psycho gene just waiting to activate inside of me? *Nature and nurture, it takes both things. The Banks raised you. The Banks. Your grandparents, Maxine.*

And yet ... even Saffron has her issues.

I withdraw from Delphine slightly, but I don't know what to say. I'd really love a moment to myself. I find myself fervently wishing for my bedroom in the ice cavern. Filled with my things from back home, Parrish across the hall, my own, private bathroom.

It might not have been what I asked for, and it might not have been perfect, but I was getting used to it. Where do I go from here? I don't even have a bedroom anymore. I haven't had a clear identity for a while now. Finding out that there are even *more* family secrets to uncover?

It's devastating.

Especially paired with last night, with a fire that I *know* Justin is responsible for, whether directly or indirectly. Kidnapping Parrish was bad enough, but attempted murder? On little kids, no less. His blood daughter's blood siblings.

"Is there a bathroom I could use?" I manage to get the words to come out without a warble or a tremor or a stutter. *Go Gamer Girl, you've got this.* Delphine nods and turns, pointing at a door that I can see just around the corner.

Behind her, there's the hallway where the hidden cellar door was. Only, it isn't hidden anymore. The portrait of Alfred Armando Vasquez is gone, and the secret door is highlighted with white trim that delineates the space. Some of the furniture is the same from the night Chasm, Maxx, and I broke into this place and discovered Parrish. But in all the spots where it appeared that something might be missing—empty side tables, the discolored rectangles on the wall from long-hung paintings, the display stands that clearly used to hold vases or something—are all filled in.

The house has done a one-eighty from when I was last here, and it's only been a week.

One week.

I head for the bathroom as nonchalantly as I'm able, aware even as I do that the room might be bugged, that even if it isn't, I have my phone. This isn't a private conversation in any sense of the word, but I need a minute.

I put my hands on the granite countertop and lean over, staring into the mirror and seeing the small but well-appointed half-bath reflected behind me. Turning the faucet on, I run the water cold and splash it over my face, snatching a hand towel from a nearby ring to scrub at my skin.

With the fabric pressed to my mouth, I let out a small scream of frustration.

On the inside, that maggot of an idea squirms and writhes. *Kill Justin. The only way to end this is to kill Justin.*

No.

There *has* to be some other way. Surely, if he gets outed as the Seattle Slayer, that would be the end of it? Only I know it's not. I know it, but I still can't accept it. I'm not entirely rotten to the core, am I? *Don't let Justin win. This is what he's grooming you to do, to accept that violence like this is normal.*

I bite the hand towel to release some of that frustration, and then chuck it into the sink. Turning around, I hop up on the counter and start a conference call with the boys.

All three of them answer before the second ring, and I smile.

Not only did I meet one amazing human here, I met three. And all three of them are into me. If it weren't for the fire and the humiliation and the killing and the blackmail, I'd be in heaven.

Despite the fact that Justin pushed me into sexual relationships with Chasm and Maxx before I was ready, I don't regret that part of it. I certainly don't regret being with Parrish.

"Please tell me you're safe." That's Maxx, but he hasn't joined in the video call. None of them have which is interesting. It's sound only. Except for, you know, me.

"I'm safe," I respond, and then, because it feels disingenuous, I add, "at least I think I am. For now."

I wish I could see their faces, but if they're not tuning in, there must be reasons.

"I'm in the downstairs bathroom at home, hiding." I can hear Chasm's footsteps as he paces briefly on the other end of the line. "There's been a stream of people in and out of the house all day today. Business stuff, I guess. It's Milk Carton this, Milk Carton that."

"Better than being stuck with Laverne; she won't let me leave her side." Parrish pauses briefly, and I hear a distant murmur of voices. "I've still got my phone for now, but after last night, I'm not sure how long I'll be able to keep it."

"What happened last night?" X asks before I get the chance to bite my own tongue off and swallow it. Because I'm that embarrassed. I'd do it, too, if it weren't so bloody and, like, painful and shit.

"Long story," I blurt before either of the other boys can answer. I'm not prepared to discuss said situation at the moment. My level of mortification from the incident is still sky-high and I'm not ready to come crashing down to reality just yet. *My bio mom found me in bed with my stepbrother and his best friend.* Shivers take over me, but I push them down. Not gonna think about it. I *refuse.* "More importantly: I'm at the Vasquez place."

There's a slight pause there, but nobody's surprised. We were only able to find this place because Justin announced his plans to purchase a house right there in front of us at the launch party. I wasn't aware that he'd be moved in so quickly, but it is what it is.

"That's where you're staying?" Chasm asks, and I sense a small amount of relief in his voice. We're close to each other right now, close enough to walk. That makes me feel a million times more secure, to be honest. One, quick call, and Chas would come running.

"Pretty sure. I can't *wait* to see what my bedroom looks like." Somehow, I imagine that Justin's sense of adventure and love of pageantry will transfer over into the décor. Unlike Tess, I can't see him even offering to take me out and buy me things for my new room; he'd pick them all out himself. Just like he ordered for me in the restaurant. Just like he selected my prom dress. Just like he told me to wear my hair.

I reach up, touching the slightly tangled waves with my fingers. He didn't call me out on disobeying him, but I bet I haven't heard the end of this. The bruises on my arm throb, a reminder that as nice as he appears on the surface, Justin Prior is nothing but a monster underneath. He's a creature; he's a fucking creep.

"I'm guessing you didn't call just to tell us that?" X presses, his voice still a bit hoarse. When I think about what he did for the Vanguard family, I'm overwhelmed with what I can only describe as affection, appreciation … and love. I'm flooded with love for him, and my cheeks heat with the realization. Yes, yes, my boobs also, but at least those are covered.

"How are you feeling?" I blurt out, hoping none of them can tell over the stupid video call that I'm flushed and aching. Lovesick, that's what I am. And it's horrible. And wonderful. And I wish with all of my heart that I could appreciate it more, that I could delve into these feelings and pull them over my head like the blanket this morning.

As it is, I'll do my best to enjoy the small moments. That's what life is anyway, a mosaic of tiny, insignificant things that make up a glorious whole. Kisses stolen in the dark, a sweetly whispered word, a smile on a sunny summer afternoon.

The thought bolsters me somehow, pushes back some of the fear and despair and anxiety. *And yeah, the ignominy of being caught in bed with two guys by one's mom.*

"Much better. I'm actually just waiting for the doctor to sign off, and then I'm leaving. I'll be heading over to Chas' place." Relief fills me at the idea of Maxx being so close as well, just down the block from here. Calling the guys was the right move; I feel better already.

"We're heading to the hospital to pick everyone up this afternoon," Parrish adds, and I lean my shoulder against the wall. "What happened with your grades?"

"Shit, that's right." Chasm exhales, and I smile as I feel his nerves through the phone. He takes his role as a tutor seriously. That or … he's just into me. Either way, it's cute. "What did you get, Little Sister? Break the tension. I'm panicking here."

"One B, the rest A's." There's a bit of silence that follows there. Everything I know, they know. "Good news: it seems like Justin blames Mr. Parker, the computer science teacher, for giving me a bad grade. He's agreed to let me see Maxine."

Collective relief all around, especially from X.

"If you need me there to have the talk, I'll come." There's a pause here and his voice colors with bitterness. "Provided the asshole will let me come over at all."

"I appreciate that," I tell him honestly, but his words do not help reduce the redness in my cheeks. Oh no, not at all. "Chas, I have to know: did you beat Lumen?"

There's a slight pause there, and my heart leaps into my throat. If he failed to snatch that number one spot (he undoubtedly deserves to have it), it's probably my fault. All the tutoring, all the stress about Parrish. Seamus might not hit his son, but he's definitely abusive. What sort of punishment might he exact for this perceived failure?

"I got number one in our class—but just barely." Chasm exhales in relief, but there's some pride to his words that makes me happy. "Not that it matters. Please tell me you're only calling to reassure us?"

Yeah. I wish. If only life were so simple.

"I've got something else for you to chew on." I pause, not exactly for dramatic effect, but Parrish huffs out an annoyed breath.

"Spill it, Gamer Girl, before you kill me with stress. What is it?"

"Delphine is my biological sister." The words don't seem real. Even as they're slipping past my lips, I'm questioning them. Justin had a 'fling' when he was seventeen, and had a daughter he never knew about? Emotions twist inside of me, just like that metaphorical painting of Tess I saw in my mind's eye. So many colors, a rainbow of very human hues. Jealousy (what's that about?), fear, anger, frustration, an odd flicker of bright-yellow excitement, just a stray beam of sunshine in that vibrant chromatic mess.

"Delphine ... our maid?" Parrish queries, the tone of his voice telling me everything I need to know about his facial expression. I can see those almond-shaped eyes of his widening and then narrowing, his ripe, lush mouth getting that pouty tilt to it. "*Delphine?*"

"The very same." I put a hand up to my face, rubbing at my forehead with two fingers. "He claims he had a brief thing in high school and found out through some DNA registry that he had another daughter he'd never met."

"We were right." Maxx scoffs in disbelief. "Who's the old woman she was living with then?"

"I have no idea, but I'll see what information I can get out of them; they're pretty free with it." I pause there, reminding myself that 'they' can hear everything I say or do when I'm in this house, when technology of any sort is in close proximity.

"Keep us updated regularly." Chasm sounds annoyed, but I know that's just a front for what he's really feeling. He's worried about me. They all are. On the flip side, *I* am more worried about them. "And Tess …"

"If you three don't tell me what happened last night …" Maxx begins, his voice a strong warning.

"Tess caught us in the afterglow of a threesome," Parrish explains, and then curses. "I've got to go. Keep in frequent touch with me. All of you." He hangs up suddenly, and I'm left with Chas and X, just like old times.

"You … you had a threesome?" Maxx breathes, and Chasm lets out a choked sound.

"Yeah, uh … I can hear my dad coming. This one's on you, Little Sister." He hangs up next, and then it's just me and Maxim Wright, and this strangely intimate moment that I didn't expect. How can I possibly discuss this, sitting here on a countertop in a strange house (the house that served as Parrish's prison) with just X's voice and my face, and a looming lunch date that sounds like hell?

Yet, I do.

Because Maxx and I, we have magic. Magic that I didn't want, that feels suddenly double-edged and sharp with the prospect of seeing Maxine. But oh, how badly I want to see Maxine … I don't even care if she slaps me. Hell, she could spit in my face, and I'd just wipe it off and keep smiling. I love her too much to lose her; she's my anchor in a cruel and strange world.

Never has anyone in this life been—or ever will be—as trusting or as kind as Maxine Banks. If I'd told her honestly how I'd felt about Maxx, she'd have given him to me. Even if it killed her. Even if she was hurting. She'd smile through the tears and draw a rainbow into the sky. That's just what she's like.

"We … it just sort of happened." I pause again, my voice breathless and small. No, no, not small, just anticipatory. Concerned. I don't want X to be upset. "Are you angry?"

He gives a small, tense laugh, one that causes the fine hairs on the back of my neck to stand on end.

"Angry?" he asks, and then he pauses again, but the silence between us is thick with thought, rife with contemplation. He's exploring his feelings, and I'm content to sit here and wait as long as he needs. Is my heart pounding? Sure. Am I sweating? Always. What can I say? I'm just a sweaty chick. "Parrish was okay with that?"

There's a question buried inside of that question.

Parrish had asked for a week; that week is over. Now what? Am I able to … explore things with Maxx? Should I, considering that he used to belong to my sister? Not in the way he belongs to me, but still. I resolve to ask her when I see her, to state my intentions. That is, if circumstances are favorable. If she's trussed up and bleeding like Parrish, I … *I'll fucking kill Justin.*

I grit my teeth and then force myself to relax.

"Parrish knows there's more to all of this than Justin's demands. He knows. I'm not sure what that means for me and you, Maxx, but I care about you."

"Care about me?" he asks, voice edgy. "I'm falling in love with you, Kota."

I choke on those words, pausing at the sound of a slight knock on the door.

"Just checking in with you. This is a lot to process, I know."

It's Delphine. Either as a caring sister or Daddy's spy, I can't say. Either way, the message is clear: it's time to go.

"Ditto, Maxx." I blurt the word out, and then panic, adjusting my grip on the phone and accidentally hanging up on him. *No! What the hell is wrong with me?!* Delphine knocks again, just a gentle tap, but I'm not about pushing boundaries today, not when I'm so close to seeing Maxine.

I tap out a quick text to X and hit send before I realize what I've just done.

Ditto wasn't the right word. Haha. Just a Pokémon, amIright? I meant to say that I dick you, too.

Dick. I wrote *dick* instead of *like* or else autocorrect is out to screw me.

I hastily punch in another text and send that out.

Didn't mean to hang up on you. Accident. Also, not dick. I meant lick.

That goes out next, and I groan as I see the mistake a second too late.

Dick. Lick. Pokémon?!

I'm on fire right now.

Shoving the phone into the pocket of my hoodie, I slide off the counter and open the door with a smile.

It's not just Delphine who's waiting for me now. Justin stands beside her, looking bemused.

"Come. We don't want to be late for our lunch appointment." Delphine nods at Justin's words, flashing a bright smile and then grabbing onto his arm and clinging to him. The attention makes him laugh as he offers her up a patronizing pat on the head. But his eyes? They're all for me. I'm his stolen property. More importantly, I think, I'm Tess' daughter. And Tess is simultaneously the epitome of both his love and his hate. "Delphi, could you give me a moment with Dakota?"

ENDGAME ROMANCE

"Sure thing." She gives ... our? ... father's arm another squeeze before taking off, her heels loud on the wood floors. I stay where I am, dressed head to toe in athleisure Whitehall gear with a sports bra and department store underwear that don't quite fit. I'm out of my element here. Everyone else is dressed like they're on the way to a fundraiser full of the rich and famous.

"Should I change before we go?" I ask, glancing down at the outfit. Maybe I should've brought the gold gown with me? It's not like I have any other clothes. Not that Tess or Justin couldn't afford to buy them for me. "Is this a fancy place or is this like that Mexican restaurant you took me to?"

Justin chuckles and reaches up, patting my cheek lovingly.

"You appear droopy and sad," he explains, and I just blink back at him. Um, kay? What's his point here other than to be insulting AF? "Which is good." Justin swipes at some invisible lint on the shoulder of my hoodie. "We can't appear too heartless; you suffered a terrible tragedy last night." Here, he hesitates, glancing to the side and offering up a mysterious but disturbing little smile. "Well, almost." He looks back at me and smirks. "Smart move, utilizing your pawns. I'll admit, I assumed Maxim was a liability, but he's proving disturbingly useful, now isn't he?"

"Why did you do it?" I ask, and the hurt shows in my voice even when I try my best to suppress it. "I've done everything you've asked of me."

Justin leans down, putting his hand on the side of my hair. His fingers tighten slightly, and I swallow past a new lump in my throat.

"I'll forgive the hair thing today seeing as last night was tumultuous, but the next time I tell you to do your hair a certain way, you'll listen." He releases me abruptly, turning and striding toward the front door.

It's quite clear that I'm expected to follow.

What even is my life right now? I wonder, but I'm still learning the rules of this game. Until I do, I need to be cautious.

A burst of defiance is only fun if somebody I love doesn't die because of it.

Lunch is a formal affair at a highfalutin Seattle restaurant on the water. Somehow, it feels like everyone there knows Justin and is watching us. Or maybe it's me, in my Whitehall sweats and hoodie. People smile patronizingly at me, and I'm reminded of that initial breakfast with the Vanguards at the country club. Parrish wore his Whitehall hoodie, and all the adults looked at him with a strange fondness and the slightest edge of cruel expectation.

Same deal here.

Caroline is polite, but distant. I can barely stand to look at her let alone speak to her. How dare she waltz back into town on the hunt for romance when Parrish is here and hurting? He might not admit it aloud, but I could see it in his face when he saw her in Maxx's hospital room.

I know all about estranged bio parents and the emotions they can stir up. It's something he's going to have to deal with eventually. For now, I tell myself that Caroline Bassett is simply my bio dad's new girlfriend and do my best not to think about it.

I sip a plain iced tea and try to keep a neutral but pleasant expression on my face. Delphine, I can't get over. I can't stop staring at her, wondering if I missed some crucial family resemblance. *Her nose seems similar, doesn't it? Our nostrils look remarkably alike. How could I have missed that?*

But of course I'm being ridiculous. A vague nostril resemblance does not a long-lost sister make.

Justin is, as always, outgoing and gregarious, full of laughs, constantly smiling.

A royal piece of shit on the inside.

When we get back to the house, he politely (read: menacingly) warns Caroline and Delphine to leave us alone, and then leads me upstairs and down a long hallway to a room with powder blue walls and white moldings, a half-moon shaped addition with a silver velvet chaise, and a large four-poster bed with gauzy curtains. The old windows are all propped open, the light catching on the wavy glass and casting beautiful prisms over the picturesque scene.

There's an antique dresser decorated with various bottles of perfume, an open wardrobe (also probably antique) filled with dresses that shimmer in the cool, June sunshine. I can smell the breeze off Lake Washington, and the distant tang of salt. The house is old (in a good way), architecturally magnificent with details like curved crown molding on the half-moon ceiling, wood floors with walnut inlays, and a view of the charmingly overgrown grounds outside.

Once again, it's the exact opposite of the room that Tess presented me, sterile and strange and cold, with light fixtures from an alien spaceship and hyper-modern décor. This room, it's an antonym. Justin has dressed the bed up in white crocheted throws and fluffy pillows while framed paintings of beautiful girls in bejeweled dresses line the walls like an art gallery.

Upon closer inspection, I see that the paintings share a theme: *they're princesses.* There are crowns and castles and even a unicorn in one. I'm pleased to see that some of the princesses have swords, bloodied swords on occasion. Well, I'm pleased to see that for about half a second until I realize the implications aren't *women defending their own honor* and more like *murdering people is fun-time central.*

The room smells fresh and clean, but there's that slight kiss of mustiness that every antiquer or old house enthusiast understands. It means there's at least a hint of the genuine spirit in the piece or the place, that it hasn't been sanitized and flipped, that there's something real to be gained here.

And of course, I can't appreciate any of it because Justin is standing right behind me, and I know what he's waiting for. He's content, it seems, to actually wait because he wants to see my full emotional reaction to this, how I present myself to him, if I bend or break.

Essentially, we're on a human-sized chessboard, and he's asking me to make the first move in our next game. I run my fingers over the metaphorical pieces, calculating my strategy.

Even as I'm telling myself this room is the opposite of what Tess presented me in so many ways, it's also remarkably similar, too, mirroring my first day in Medina in a strange and discomforting way. It's as if something started that day, and now I'm sliding headfirst down a slope toward the finish line.

I'm just not sure that I'm ready to see whatever might lie at the end of this race.

There's a view of the water, the smell of it, size and grandeur, prominent wealth, an attached bathroom, a whole mansion to explore, a brand-new life.

Tess' initially clumsy attempts at bringing me into the family don't seem so horrible now. Whereas Justin does everything right —takes me to a Mexican restaurant instead of the country club, is open and frank about most everything, fixes up my room just so— he's also broken and empty on the inside. Tess is the opposite.

I spin to face Justin, clasping my hands together behind my back.

"It's absolutely beautiful." I glance back at the bed and the white faux fur rug underneath it, the delicate side tables with the vintage lamps and their frosted glass. To contrast all of the oldies-but-goodies vibes going on in there, a desk sits against one wall with a brand-new gaming computer, the tower lit up and flickering through a series of rainbow colors.

There's a killer monitor to go with it as well as a hot pink gaming keyboard and mouse, a new mousepad with a crown on it, a Secretlab gaming chair, an unopened box with a new headset and mic, and a high-tech webcam.

All the better to spy on me with, I'm sure.

In another world, another version of Dakota Banks, I'd be excited about all of this. Thrilled. I'd be over the freaking moon. It's every gamer girl's dream paradise, and I can't appreciate any of it because I'm too worried about the people I care for meeting an untimely demise. Nothing in this room feels like mine. It's all an extension of Justin's tentacular reach, suction cups popping as he adjusts his monstrous squirm.

"Isn't it? It's exactly what you deserve, my sweet princess." Justin places a kiss on my forehead, reaching out to stroke a strand of dark hair behind one of my ears. "Rest up, shower, and enjoy. I'm sure you'd like a moment to yourself, so I'll leave you for now." He offers me up a condescending pat and then heads for the door, pausing briefly to touch his fingers to a gold shelf with mirrored platforms; it's covered in cosmetics in every flavor, brand, and purpose. "I took the liberty of gathering up whatever is hottest on the internet right now; ten shelves full of trending TikTok goodies. Enjoy." Justin winks and then slips out, closing the door behind him.

So, here I am, about to spend my first night in the home of a serial killer. In the home of the *Seattle Slayer*. Sitting down on the edge of the bed, I take a moment to process. It's been nonstop since I left prom at a run, found Maxx coughing and clutching a bunny, got caught in a threesome, and found out I had yet another sister to add to the mix.

With a groan, I let myself fall back on the bed. I have no doubt that Justin will be watching me in here. If I tried to turn off or get rid of all my tech, he'd know. He'd mention it. On top of that, I'm sure there are cameras and mics in here, and I definitely don't have the bug detector with me.

I'm at his mercy for the time being.

Rolling onto my side, I slip my phone out and text the boys to let them know that I'm alright, and then I fall asleep to a warm breeze and the distant shush of water against the shore.

The nightmares come anyway, swirling around the confines of my pretty, gilded cage.

CHAPTER 8

Delphine is the one who wakes me up in the morning, and for the briefest of instances, I almost believe that I'm back in the Vanguard house, that Parrish is sleeping in the room across the hall, that all I need to worry about today is getting up and heading to school. Lunch with Danyella and Lumen, quips and verbal sparring with Chasm and Parrish, an after-school coffee date with Maxine and X.

Then I blink away the cobwebs to see that Delphine's hair is a brilliant shimmering blond, smooth and luxurious as it curves over her shoulder. She's in her best heiress-chic-influencer outfit, dressed in a white half-shirt, torn baggy jeans, and chunky sneakers, like she's Charli D'Amelio or something. *TikTok, eat your heart out.*

I sit up in bed, realizing as I do that I'm somehow covered up and sleeping in the right place. All the windows are closed, and somebody even shut the curtains. It creeps me out, knowing that either Justin or Delphine came in here and did all of those things for me.

Then again, Delphine has been doing those sorts of things for me for *months* now.

"It was you, wasn't it? That dragged me out of the house that night I woke up in the woods."

It's not quite the morning greeting that she expects, I don't think, and she sits there on the end of the bed blinking back at me with pricey lash extensions. The girl has had a major glow-up, but I'm not sure it's for all the right reasons. Actually, I kind of liked her better before.

"I administered the initial shot, and yes, I put you on a blanket and dragged you to the back door." She shrugs her shoulders loosely, reaching up to pull her pretty hair back. "I even bathed you, laundered your pajamas, and redressed you after. Anything Daddy needs, I'll do."

I sit up suddenly, wanting to plead with her to come over to the dark side with me. Or wait, I'm the good guy in this scenario, aren't I? Good and evil is relative and all that, but like, I don't slay random teenagers, so I've got some moral high ground for sure.

"You haven't known him very long, Delphine," I offer up, wondering how much of Justin's plots she actually knows about. Has she been involved with the killing? Is she simply a gofer? Can I appeal to her better judgment, manipulate her into helping me? "Why are you so gung ho to run his errands for him?"

She smiles then, and I swear that it's genuine. Then again … she was meek and self-conscious and nearly invisible back at the Vanguard house. Gotta give the girl props: she knows how to act.

"I find it strange that you'd even ask me that," she begins, letting out a small, dark laugh. "You've lived in this town long enough to see its shadows." Delphine sighs, staring down at the floor and not at me. "My mother worked her ass off to support me, got paid minimum wage to sweep and scrub and clean, to take verbal abuse and bullshit from the rich assholes she slaved for.

Still, we were basically homeless. We couch-surfed, slept in shelters, rented a one-bedroom studio that sucked up two weeks' worth of her wages." Delphine stands up suddenly and turns to face me. I'm not without sympathy for her story, but I'm also getting nervous. With a backstory like that, and all of this wealth and power laid out before her, how or why would she ever resist? To her, the world is evil. Not Justin. If she believes that, she'll never be on my side. "Then, years after my mother died, I get a call from the sweetest, most loving man I've ever met. He buys me the world, takes care of me, and asks very little in return." Her face hardens up, and she sighs, moving over to the shelf of TikTok trends and rummaging around until she finds some unicorn body butter or whatever the hell it is.

"You knew I was—" Somehow, I can't bring myself to say *your sister.* It feels wrong, like a betrayal to Maxine, a slap in the face. Here I am in the lap of luxury and she's ... well, I'm not even really sure *what* he's done with her. That makes it all that much worse. How could I have fallen asleep when I should've been grilling Justin? "You knew I was related to you all along?" I finish belatedly, and Delphine turns around, rubbing body butter into her arms.

"The first thing Daddy told me was that I had a little sister." She holds up the jar and wiggles it around in her manicured fingers. "Can I have this? It smells amazing."

I nod because—and excuse my French—I don't give a flying *fuck* about anything in this room.

All the material possessions I ever cared about are in the burned-up shell of the Vanguard home. How extensive the damage is, we won't know for a few days yet. Once the arson investigation is done, and the house is deemed safe to walk through, I'll get a chance to scope it out.

"Come downstairs. There's breakfast." Delphine holds out a

hand for me, and I take it, still wearing the Whitehall gear from the day before. With my phone in my pocket, I follow her down the staircase and into a sunny solarium near the back of the house. There's an entire wall of windows looking out at the neglected (but still very pretty) garden, and the back doors are thrown open to let in the morning breeze.

It's not quite ten o'clock, so I imagine the boys are all probably sleeping.

I slip my Maxine-phone out of my pocket and shoot off a quick text, glancing briefly at the million messages they left me over the course of the night.

How can you sleep in Bowser's castle, Princess Peach? This one from X which makes me smile.

The expression only lasts for half a second because Caroline is seated at the table, and there are staff members buzzing around all over the place. Either they're all in on Justin's games or else he's attempting to keep his home and all of the activity surrounding it free from suspicion.

That's what I'd do anyway.

On the other hand, he kept Parrish prisoner in the wine cellar, so maybe not.

Justin's persnickety assistant, Raúl, is there, too, working on a pink MacBook. He gives me a derisive once-over and a sniff of disapproval before returning to his computer. Cool, cool. He's probably a murderer, too, just like Amin Volli.

"Good morning, Dakota." Caroline pats the chair next to her. Styled in a loose, flowing white dress with a delicate daisy pattern, a wide-brimmed hat, and shades, she looks like a model. Her lips are as pouty as Parrish's, and her skin is flawless and free of pores. *A walking filter, my favorite type of human; hide your character flaws under all that pretty.* "Come sit with me."

I can't think of anything that sounds worse.

134

"Awesome." I take the proffered seat, and Delphine relaxes in the chair next to me. When she said there was breakfast, she meant it. The table is, like, catered or something. And not like when Tess ordered food for my birthday. I mean, it really looks like a magazine shoot, the white linen runner piled with silver trays overflowing with pastries, tea sandwiches, and fruit. There are covered trays with breakfast meats, pancakes, and eggs.

I know my spine is absurdly straight, and my fingertips are digging into the front of the chair, but I can't seem to get myself to relax any.

"Did you sleep well?" Caroline asks, lifting her shades up to rest on the crown of her head. She smiles at me, and I'm struck yet again by the number of similarities between her and Parrish. They have the same mouth, same eyes, same nose. It's disconcerting.

"Fantastic, thanks." I'm smiling, but it probably looks more like a grimace. Glower. Pout. Scowl. What have you. I'm not the writer; that's Tess' job. *Only, would it be so bad? I'm not terrible at it.* I can't speak elegantly to save my life, but sometimes my thoughts take on a tint of purple prose. Could I refine that? Do I want to?

It's an irrelevant thought. Pointless, honestly, unless I can figure out a way from under Justin's thumb. Until I do, I belong to him. I won't be allowed to write—unless he says I can. Maybe I won't even want to because my entire family will be dead and buried?

"This is a great house, isn't it?" Caroline continues, slipping her hat off and setting it in the chair beside her. "It needs a gut and a full remodel, but for now …" Here she trails off with a sigh, studying the dark wood molding on the wall like it's a nuisance.

My eye twitches.

Don't say anything; there's no point.

"The wood in here was probably milled from local old-growth

lumber, designed specifically for this house, hand-turned ..." I trail off as Caroline stares at me like I've sprouted horns. It seems that no matter where I go or who I'm with, I freak some people out by speaking up or having the audacity to dye my hair lime-green or sometimes just because I exist.

The righteous annoyance in me summons up some extra bravado.

"I like the house the way it is," I say loudly, just as Justin enters the room. He pauses, dressed in these dark blue jeans, a pale blue button up with the top buttons undone, and expensive loafers. He screams money, power, and privilege as he moves, and also, he too looks like a model.

Again, if he hadn't tried to slaughter my family, I'd like him.

"If my princess likes it, we'll keep it." Justin moves over to pet both my and Delphine's hair, offering us each a kiss on the head. It's surreal as fuck, to be sitting here with him, with Parrish's biological mother, with *Delphine* of all people. My head swims and though I despise the instantaneous familiarity with which this scene is being presented, I endure.

I'll endure as much as I have to for as long as I have to.

"Once you're finished eating, take a walk with me," Justin offers, but I'm already rising to my feet. I'm not particularly hungry. I'd much rather hear about Maxine, maybe schedule a time to speak to my grandparents. Justin seems eager to prove himself as a man of his word, in regard to me anyway.

"I'm ready now."

He raises his brows at that but grabs a muffin from one of the silver trays and turns toward the door.

"As you wish, princess." When Delphine stands to join us, Justin pats her on the shoulder. "Just the two of us this time, sweetheart." He takes off out the door and I hurry to follow. I definitely don't miss the way Delphine's brown eyes track me as I pass, hurt and resentment rising like fog. With a small shake, I can see her mentally dash away the feelings.

I could use this. Maybe not now. Definitely not until I fully understand this game and figure out my strategy, but eventually. Delphine might've been acting before, but I'm not sure that she is now. Her emotions are clear and vibrant, like she believes she's truly come home, as if this is the place she's supposed to be. All her cards are on the table. It might be possible to force Justin's hand, make him choose between me and his other daughter.

What in the actual fuck is wrong with you?

I'm supposed to be playing a game *against* a monster, not becoming one myself. And yet … yet …

I jog to catch up with Justin as he strolls through the yard in the direction of the water. Although the paths back here are overgrown, and the garden beds are quite liberally taking up the space, there's a fairly clear path down to the shore and the private dock on Lake Washington.

"I'd like to get a boat," Justin remarks, and then he stands there, eating his muffin and staring out at the city of Seattle in the distance. I wait beside him, sliding my hands into the pockets of my joggers. The sun feels good on my exposed skin, but the wind coming off the water is chilly, cutting straight to the bone. "Wouldn't that be fun, Dakota? You and I, we could take the boat to the Puget Sound, look for wildlife, stop for lunch in the harbor."

You're nuts. Completely and utterly insane. That's what I'd *like* to say, but then, I'm angling for two very important things in this moment.

"Sounds like somebody else's life," I respond, but with a proper amount of awe in my voice that even though Justin hesitates slightly, in the end he finds my answer acceptable. I'm not lying either. It really does sound like somebody else's life, a fairy tale, a dream that I'm not allowed to have. Because I can never just enjoy a simple day on the water with my dad.

My dad. Even the words are foreign. I know it's true, but I don't want to believe it. DNA tests or no, there's no doubt that we're related. Too many physical similarities. Also, if Tess thought there was *any* possibility that I might not be related to Justin Prior, I'm certain she would have mentioned it.

The thought is depressing, and the feeling hits doubly hard as I stare out at the distant skyscrapers, the lazy boats passing by, the hills in the distance peppered with lush evergreens. It's truly a privilege to be here; the area is stunning. Though ... a quick glance to either side shows yet more giant mansions looming over the water. Not particularly private.

Also, who the fuck wants to live in a neighborhood full of billionaires? *Shudder.*

Leaning a bit farther out, I peer down the coastline to where Chasm's father's estate is. Both he and Maxx are there now while Laverne's estate is on the other side of Groat Point, with waterfront on Meydenbauer Bay. Not that it's *that* far away, I just can't see it from here.

God help me but I miss those boys. So much. Too much.

It's unnatural surely, but what can I do? All those hormones arcing through me and whatnot. I blame them instead of my heart. It's easier that way, to pretend like biology's done this to me.

"What did you want to talk about?" I query, glancing back to see that Justin's still looking out over the water. He turns slowly to face me, smiling yet again. Chills prick my arms, but I don't acknowledge the reaction. That's what the payoff is for him, my reactions. If I don't give him any, it'll be far less fun.

"Tonight, we're having a very important dinner party here at the house." He holds up a hand to indicate the manor looming above us, half-buried behind trees and hedges but impossible to miss regardless. "It's imperative to me that you pay attention to everything you see and hear, every person you meet, every interaction." He takes a step closer to me, folding up his muffin wrapper and tossing it into a trash can full of branches and dead leaves. He then reaches out to take my chin in his fingers, leaning down to peer into my eyes.

I'm supremely uncomfortable right now, but I don't move. Don't fidget. I stand there and stare him right back.

"Trust me: you'll *want* to pay attention tonight. Actually, you'll thank me for it. But first, let's start your lessons off properly, shall we?"

"My lessons?"

Justin releases my chin and takes off, leaving me little recourse but to follow him. He leads me to a small outbuilding, like an artist's studio or something. While the small wooden porch on the outside has clearly seen better days, the interior's been tastefully refreshed with butter yellow wallpaper, cozy furnishings, and a table with a solid wood chess set atop it.

Bio Dad takes a seat in one chair and then holds out a hand to indicate the other.

"Come. I'll teach you how to play."

I begrudge him the seat, and because it's one of the least bad things he could be doing, I decide to begrudge him a game as well.

"I know how to play chess," I explain, reaching down to pick up a pawn. I examine the white-washed wooden piece with its shiny lacquer. It's beautiful, a true work of art. I put it down and then lift the queen, running my fingers across her crown. "And I like that the queen has the most power on the board ..." I shrug, and Justin presents me with a high-handed smile.

"Such a cute little feminist, aren't we?" he asks, and I bristle. "You might know the basic rules of chess, but I assure you: you do not know how to play." With another sigh, Justin slumps back in his seat, reaching out to pick up the black king piece on his side. He toys with it for a minute, stretching out the silence and amping up the anxiety, as per usual.

"Meaning what?"

"Meaning you've got more of your mother in you than you do me." He continues that easy smile without faltering, setting the piece back in place. He crosses one arm over his chest, grips his other elbow, and lazily waves his hand in the direction of the board. "White goes first."

"I'm a gamer," I explain, thinking over what few official strategies I know and then lifting up a knight. I set it back down and Justin immediately moves a pawn forward two squares. "So are you. We're the same—even if I don't want to believe it." We play for a few minutes before he finally deigns to continue the conversation.

"We're similar, certainly, but you don't know how to make the right sacrifices to get what you want." I knock one of his pieces off the board, snatching it in my hand and setting it aside. Justin's smile turns into a smirk, and then he makes his final move. "Checkmate." He rises to his feet. "Study this board and watch your endgame, Dakota."

He leaves the room, and I sit there for a while staring at the board, trying to decide if he really intends for me to learn anything at all. Then I see it: he allowed one of his own pieces to be captured in order to win the game.

Sacrifice.

I don't make the right sacrifices.

Fuck. Tonight isn't going to be good. Not good at all.

I sweep my hand across the pieces covering the board, sending them all flying to the floor. And it feels good. It feels good to be pissed. It feels good to let that anger sweep over me. I'm going to need it in order to get things done.

A normal high school summer just isn't in the cards.

This is fucking *war.*

CHAPTER 9

Rather than call his team of hair and makeup artists for the evening, Justin relies on Delphine to pay me a visit. She helps me select a gown and shoes, twisting my hair into a chignon as requested by Justin. A diamond hair clip complements the oddly familiar tennis bracelet on my wrist, the one that I'm certain my father chose with the one Tess gave me in mind.

I'm swathed in a cute, little strapless cocktail dress. The fabric is soft and satiny, the pattern made up of big white magnolias on an emerald green backdrop. The extra splashes of color come in the form of lime-green leaves, a few shades paler than my hair, but close enough that the hair seems designed to pair with the gown.

"It's an Oscar de la Renta," Delphine explains, handing over a pair of white espadrilles with a lace overlay. "Sit and I'll help you tie these up."

I do as she asks, sitting on the edge of the beautiful old bed in the world's most perfect bedroom. Okay, well, second most perfect in my memory because nobody could ever beat the farmhouse I grew up in. But this is close.

I'm a fly and this is a Venus flytrap. If I move too much, the mouth will shut and swallow me up.

I shiver.

"So who all is supposed to be attending this dinner?" I ask, because nobody's discussed it any further since Justin left me alone with the chess board. I spent the majority of the day talking to the boys over the phone.

The Vanguards are now all safely tucked away at Laverne's. No, there's no news about the house. Tess is apparently brimming with manufactured cheer while also giving Parrish undisguised looks of shocked disbelief. Chasm and Maxx had lunch with their parents while the rest of the day's been spent sitting with their legs in the pool or the hot tub, chatting with me.

I'm not in the mindset to consider what they might be talking about when I'm not on the phone with them. Chasm is tough, one of the strongest people I've ever met. But there's just something about Maxx and Parrish that gets him to back down more than he normally would. The day we first told X that we'd slept together, Chasm was afraid of 'getting in trouble' with his friend. Is this going to be a similar situation? Is Maxx going to grill him about the threesome?

It's hard to say, and we can't exactly get down to the nitty-gritty on these conversations, not with Justin watching and listening. When I wasn't talking to the boys, I chased Justin down in his office and tried to get an answer about when I'd be seeing Maxine, when I could call my grandparents. No luck yet.

"You'll see," Delphine explains, her voice somber, almost grave. She looks up at me, her fingers on my shin. She's dressed in a strapless, white asymmetric minidress with pale pink heels. Her hair is down but twisted to fall over one shoulder, a pair of gold and pink earrings dangling from either lobe. "Tonight is important.

ENDGAME ROMANCE

It's the start of everything." She finishes tying off the shoes and then stands, looking down at me like she truly believes she's my older sister.

Genetically, I suppose she's right. In reality? I only have one sister. Not four. One.

Then again, I can't help the natural big sister type feelings that come over me when I'm around Amelia or even … Kimber. *Fucking Kimber.* I only briefly saw her at the hospital, but even though I'm happy she made it out of the fire unscathed, I still haven't fully forgiven her for what she did.

I suppose we can deal with our issues tomorrow when I see her.

If I have time, I mean.

The custody hearing is on Friday.

I'm sure that'll be exciting, another opportunity to launch a spear straight into Tess' chest. Justin hasn't explicitly told me how he wants this thing to go but based on what he said to me in the foyer that first day—*tell them you want to come with me; beg them; scream; do whatever you have to do*—I can extrapolate and make an educated guess.

"The start of everything?" I ask as Delphine reaches out a hand to help me up. I take it and allow her to lead me over to the mirror. *Whoa.* I definitely don't recognize the young woman staring back at me. She's too polished, too coiffed, to possibly be me. I'm Dakota Banks. I like to hang out in cemeteries sometimes, and I love Ashnikko way too much to be sane; I wear Pokémon pajama pants to elite high school parties, and I really love Tetris and Pac-Man and Final Fantasy.

This person in the mirror looks nothing like me, and I hate it.

I feel like Mia Patterson today.

I *am* Mia Patterson today.

Or worse: Mia *Prior.*

If I hadn't been kidnapped by Saffron, this would have been

my normal. This would have been my *life*. I feel so supremely lucky that I can't breathe. Not lucky that I'm Mia now, but lucky that I was able to be Dakota before. As nice as I look, as much money as I'm wearing, I feel suffocated.

I'm *trapped*.

"Our new beginning." Delphine smiles convincingly, pulling me toward the door and down the long hallway. She laughs as she drags me down the stairs, and I'm reminded of Maxine. The contractions in my chest are becoming sharp, like an emotional heart attack. *When? When do I get to see her?* My mind is full of morbidity, scenes of Parrish slumped in that chair, trussed and bleeding. As I peer into the recent past, Parrish becomes Maxine, and then I'm struggling to breathe all over again.

"How do I look, Daddy?" Delphine asks, pausing in the foyer and giving a little twirl in her white lace dress. Justin pauses to look her over, adjusting his cufflinks before turning his attention over to me. I offer up a smile that isn't real, but I'm definitely not about the skirt-go-spinny thing. I reach up to rub at the side of my face.

"You look perfect," Justin replies, his voice pleased and unbearably smug, as if Delphine and I are dolls that he himself personally crafted by hand. His sapphire eyes sparkle as he studies the pair of us, more of his attention on me than on Delphine.

I'm working on a theory here. That is, Justin cares about me as an extension of Tess. Like, maybe it *isn't* me that he's obsessed with? Maybe it's her. He definitely doesn't look at Delphine the way he does me, and she's at least known him for a couple of years.

"Both of you." Justin shakes out his arms, dressed in another blue suit and white dress shirt. He's not wearing a tie this time, and he's got on gray and white sneakers instead of oxfords or loafers. It's, like, the most stereotypical techie unicorn start-up look I've ever seen. I wouldn't be surprised if he started talking about blockchain technology, NFTs, and Web3, about how Google, Facebook (*ooo Meta, huh, Zucker-pond-sucker?*), and the bird app are old news.

That's his style in a nutshell. It's a vibe, not just a look.

"Our guests should be arriving soon," he remarks, glancing at his watch. It's designer, too, I'm sure, this chunky, wooden watch that screams *Pac Northwest hipster.* I exhale and turn toward the door at the sound of a car's tires on the gravel outside. "Try to have some fun tonight, both of you." He waltzes past and pats Delphine on the head, offering me up a secret, knowing smile as he goes.

Not to answer the door—*the help* can do that, blergh—but to saunter into the lounge and take a seat on a brown leather chair. An employee approaches and offers him up amber alcohol in a crystal tumbler. He holds it like dudes in romance novels always do, fingers on the rim, hand poised above the glass like he's almost too otherworldly to bother with mundane things such as handling his own drink.

I wait in the foyer with Delphine by my side, anxious to see who the first of tonight's dinner guests might be. Music trickles from the house's speaker system, classical music rather than 90s or early 2000s hits.

A butler—no joke, a real be-suited butler—opens the door, and my breath catches in my throat.

Not in a good way either, like when I see the boys after any sort of separation.

Disgust, that's what this is.

On the doorstep stands Veronica Fisher and her parents.

I'd ask why Justin would invite a girl who incited a riot that ended with me covered in knife wounds and a nude livestream floating around the internet, but somehow, the sour feeling in my belly already seems to know. *"It's payback, princess."*

Yikes.

Veronica's parents offer up generic greetings before heading into the lounge to join Justin. Veronica waits in the foyer, looking distinctly uncomfortable but unnecessarily hostile. How dare she look that way, when she's the one that wronged me—on more than one occasion.

I sweep my hands down the front of my puffy skirt, blinking at her and hoping the awkwardness of the situation digs into her skin like needles. *Justin is going to ask me to extract my pound of flesh from this girl.* It's far too obvious for me to think anything else.

"It's the bitch who roughed-up my little sister," Delphine remarks, tilting her head to one side. I glance her way, raising my brows in surprise. She doesn't sound anything like the quiet and diligent girl who cleaned for the Vanguards. Then again, if I really dig into my memories, there were plenty of signs, the way she discussed JJ the missing maid, her curiosity about the boys and my relationship with them.

"Little sister?" Veronica retorts, dressed in a pale pink cocktail dress, her red hair braided and decorated with sparkly pink flower clips. She plays with the length of it over her shoulder as her eyes flick between the two of us. "Aren't you the Vanguard's maid?" She lets out a small, derisive little laugh. "Seriously, Mia? You're related to *the help*?"

When I used that phrase earlier, I was being facetious; Veronica is serious.

Delphine doesn't hesitate, lashing out with a harsh slap that rings in the room like a warning. Veronica puts her hand to her cheek, looking back at Delphine with narrowed brown eyes and a tamped-down scowl. She knows that this isn't her territory, that we have all the cards in the situation.

A small line of red trickles from one of Veronica's nostrils.

"Know your place." Delphine looks the girl over and clucks her tongue. "The Priors settled in this area in the late eighteen-hundreds." She lifts her chin imperiously, flicking her gaze across Veronica as if the girl is little more than pond scum. I can't disagree with that, considering what she did to me, but I'm also trying my damnedest to resist getting violent.

It's what Justin wants from me, after all.

Then again, I'm aware that some situations *must* be solved with violence. Pleasant conversation only gets one so far with a serial killer.

"We were among the richest families in the history of the area until my father was swindled and blackmailed by yours." Delphine forces another smile to her face, one that's dripping with the promise of bloodshed. "If I were you, I'd keep my mouth shut and focus on looking pretty. That's your only job tonight—to behave."

Delphine turns to me and smiles again, and I feel that strange, awful churning inside of me.

Something about all of this strikes me as sad. I can't explain it, but I'm hurting. I hurt when Delphine smiles at me, when Justin laughs, when I look at the shiny new bedroom upstairs. There's this sparkle of *could be, should be, might've been* that makes this whole scene tragic.

I *liked* Delphine from moment one; I wanted to be friends.

We could've been sisters.

"Shall we get something to drink?" Delphine hooks her arm with mine as Veronica stands there, trembling and bleeding. "Bathroom's just around the corner, by the way. Go clean yourself up, sweetheart." She starts to drag me away from the foyer when the front door opens again and Veronica's friend, the nameless brunette (I *know* she has a name, but I can't remember it for the life of me), appears on the front steps.

Ah.

I see.

No wonder Justin was so excited about this dinner: this is his chance to show everyone in Medina that betrayed him who's boss. *Will Tess be here then?* I wonder.

"Scumbag." Delphine growls the word under her breath, pulling me toward one of the sitting rooms. There's a bartender in one corner, and she orders us both cherry cokes. "You know who that is, right?"

"Um, Veronica's brunette bestie?" I reply, because that's all I really know about her.

"She's the daughter of the psychologist who testified against our father," Delphine explains, keeping her voice down so that only I can hear her. The sitting room we're in is vaguely familiar; we definitely came through here when we were snooping around for Parrish.

The memory is truly bittersweet. In hindsight, it was almost fun. In the moment, not knowing whether I'd see Parrish again, it was a living nightmare.

"The psychologist …" I say, accepting my drink and sipping on the straw. The windows in this room are thrown open, letting in a warm, briny breeze that tickles my nose and makes me feel alive in a way that I so desperately need right now.

In January, the rug of my life was wrenched out from under me. Then it happened all over again in February when I discovered I had a different birthday (and, um, I was only fifteen when I arrived in Medina?!), then *again* when Parrish went missing. When he came back. Now.

The pages of my life are flipping by, and I don't even know what chapter I'm on anymore, if the hero can really win against the villain, if by doing so the hero *becomes* the villain. I'm drifting, my feet sliding on ice, and I just want to be able to stand up straight.

ENDGAME ROMANCE

Guests continue to filter in, many of them strangers, some vaguely familiar Whitehall faces. Delphine points them out to me. Well, the adults drift into the study with Justin while the teenagers cluster in the lounge with us. The lawyer's daughter, the psychologist's daughter, the judge's son. Every single person that walks in that door is here because of their role in Justin's downfall, in his framing, the embezzlement charges, the theft of his research.

The room begins to shift and, even though we're *in* Justin's house (also mine, too, if you think about it from a technical standpoint), I can feel that hostility again, the stares, the Whitehall curse. It poisons the room, an apple to my Snow White.

Eww.

Wait, no, screw Snow White. She was a weak caricature of a woman. Make me a Merida from *Brave* or, even better, a Yoon Sae-Bom from *Happiness* (yes, it's a K-drama). I'll take that bad bitch, special police force, zombie killing energy any day.

I pause and turn to see who's here now.

My mouth drops open, and a violent thrill spikes through me. It's so intense that I actually end up dropping my drink, sending ice cubes spinning across the floor.

In the doorway of the sitting room, there are three very familiar silhouettes.

Parrish. Chasm. Maxx.

"I'll get it," Delphine tells me, scurrying away to the bar for a wet rag as I squat down and pick up my glass, rising to my feet as I stare in surprise at my three, um, lovers? That sounds a little … advanced. Boyfriends? I don't know what you want to call them, but there they are, dressed to kill.

Parrish has a white and black varsity jacket draped over his shoulders, a bright pink t-shirt underneath, and black jeans torn at the knees. He's pushed the sleeves of his jacket up to reveal a generous portion of his inked skin, a silver watch on one wrist, and white sneakers on his feet. That thick, chocolate hair of his, kissed with honey, and good enough to eat, is waxed and piece-y, giving him the appearance of some billion-subscriber influencer with bad manners but brilliant bedroom etiquette—if you catch my drift.

Yeah, in short: he's preppy, but sexy as fuck.

Chasm pairs well with his friend's modern-day prince look, outfitted with a shiny black nylon jacket, slick high-top leather boots, and tight black pants. His black and yellow hair falls over his forehead, the lightning bolt freshly dyed, his long bangs razored and sharp. He flicks his tongue against one of the black lip rings that highlight that ripe, lower lip of his. The t-shirt he's wearing beneath the jacket says something in Korean that I can't read but desperately wish I could.

The dark knight has arrived.

Maxx's outfit is designer athleisure chic with an emerald green t-shirt, black cargo pants, and high-top black sneakers with white soles. His coffee-colored hair is tousled and waxed, the frown on his face a very credible threat. He has one hand tucked into his pocket, his confident gaze sweeping the room before landing on me. My throat goes dry, and my palms sweat. The glass starts to slide from my grip again as he makes his way toward me.

I never thought I'd be into a jock-y guy, but all of that hiking and riding motocross has blessed the man with a flat chest, sculpted midsection, and rock-hard biceps.

The preppy rich prince of sloths with the warm heart, the dark knight rockstar valedictorian, and the fiercely protective bunny-saving athlete.

The cup slides from my hand a second time, but X catches it easily and offers up a raised brow.

Every single person in that room is staring at us now, Delphine included. The atmosphere shifts, like wind blowing away the gray and thunderous clouds of an oncoming storm.

"Whoa there, Kota." Maxx sets the drink on the edge of the mantle to my right, and then puts his hands on my shoulders as I struggle to remember my name and what I'm doing here. I've been blinded by boys. Not something I'm used to. Not something I signed up for.

But holy hot damn.

I'm struck dumb as hell by the very sight of them in their business-casual designer clothes.

"You okay, *Naekkeo?*" Chasm asks, cocking a brow.

"She better be." Just that from Parrish as he sweeps that tyrannous gaze of his over the crowd. "Oh, hello Veronica."

"Go fuck yourself, Parrish," she retorts, and he smiles, striding toward her with purpose. I watch in surprise as he flicks his hand out, upending her drink all down the front of her pale pink gown. He leans in toward her, almost like he's going to kiss her, but then turns his head to the side at the last moment, whispering something that makes her eyes go wide. He draws back, turning to study the rest of the students who are staring back at him.

"Did you think I'd come back and everything that happened while I was gone would be forgotten?"

"You're not the only person who has something they want to protect," one of the boys retorts. He's blond and relatively short, dressed in pale jeans and a designer shirt with the brand name stamped across it like an advertisement. Why do people do that anyway? Buy clothes that are walking ads. It's weird as fuck, isn't it?

I think that's Gavin, and he's about to get his ass beat.

Chasm grits his teeth, turning to head in that direction, but I reach out, grabbing onto the sleeve of his jacket, and he stops, glancing back at me. He releases a small, acquiescent breath before looking over at Gavin and the gathered crowd of sparkling, razor-sharp teens.

"You better watch yourself. The last time, you got the jump on me with sheer numbers. When I catch you alone, it's going to hurt."

"Justin Prior's daughter, really? As if you're immune to what's going on in Medina." Another boy speaks up, wearing a hideous oversized sweater that has two shades of green squiggles, and a splash of hot pink over the top. No joke: one of the ugliest pieces of clothing I've ever seen in my life. Also, it's *fuzzy*.

"That sweater." The words choke out of me, and I end up laughing. It's not intentional, really, but it sounds judgmental and disparaging as hell. Not that I care. I know who that boy is, too: Antonio. That is, the very same Antonio whose party I attended, the pool party where I ended up announcing to the entire school that I was 'dating' Parrish and Lumen both.

"This sweater was designed by Loewe," the boy retorts angrily, and I laugh again. It's nervous laughter, but also, like who the hell is Loewe? Is this a designer I should know about? "It's worth more than two-grand, cheap bitch."

Chasm yanks from my grip before I can stop him, and he clocks Antonio right in the stomach, sending him stumbling back to the sofa behind him. The bartender pretends not to notice, passing out Italian sodas and seltzer waters, non-alcoholic beers and sparkling cider. It's a little funny, seeing these kids pretend like they're not passing around a flask behind the scenes.

"Say it again, you little shit," Chas growls out, flicking his gaze to the right as some of the boys step forward like they might get involved.

"What a mess," X murmurs, sticking by my side. I glance over at him, and I know that it's only been two days since we last saw each other, but it feels like millennia. I want to hold him so badly that I can hardly breathe. Okay, correction: I want him to hold me in those strong arms. Our eyes meet and he reaches out for me.

"I'm not going to hide us," he whispers, "not from them."

Then, the author of my world decides she'd like to see what it might be like if one were to throw a pile of dog shit into a fan. Metaphorically, of course. Maxx is reaching for me when he goes completely still, his green eyes on the doorway and no longer on my face.

I start to turn ... and then there she is.

Maxine.

My sister is standing there in a denim skirt with white sandals and a loose, off the shoulder top with yellow flowers. She reaches up to tuck dark hair behind her ear. Her eyes are focused on me. Not her ex-boyfriend. Not Chasm and the boy he just punched. Not Parrish's impossible charisma.

Just me.

I'm shaking now, twisting my hands in the fabric of my skirt.

Maxine.

Every cell in my body screams that I should run to her, throw my arms around her neck, squeeze her close and never let her go. Yet, I can't move. My feet are rooted to the floor and scenarios whiz past in my mind. Justin and his anger at calling her my sister. Tess and her fury at finding our secret coffee meeting. Parrish, tied to a chair.

If I let everyone see how much Maxie means to me ...

I reach up to dash away tears, unsure if I can go through with this, if I can stand here and pretend I don't care that she's here when it's suddenly the only thing (besides the boys) that I care about. The words of her letter filter through my brain like a sweet song.

"I will never give up on you. Never. I know you love me just as much as I love you. Kota, you will be my baby sister even when we're old and gray. I am here for you, no matter what. Whatever happened, whatever she's done, whatever you've done, it doesn't

change the way I feel about you."

I tell myself to stay strong, to stay where I am, to ignore her, tell her off, anything but what I do which is just freaking stand there as Maxine squares her shoulders, lifts her chin, and storms over to me.

"Kota," she says, some of that wild resolve fading as she comes within hugging distance of me. Her lower lip wobbles, her eyes shimmer, and then she's yanking me into one of those classic Banks' family hugs, the big, long, strong ones that warm the heart, body, and soul. "Oh, baby sister, I missed you so much."

It's been two weeks, four days, and twenty-one hours, since I've received a hug from my older sister. I want to scream. And cry. And throw myself into her arms, tell her everything, let her help me puzzle out a solution to all of this that doesn't end with my father's blood on my hands.

She pulls back suddenly, sniffling and looking me over like she's examining me for injuries. If so, she finds some. The wounds I received from Veronica and her buddies are covered with a fine layer of foundation and powder, but my sister is hyper protective and extremely perceptive—especially when it comes to me.

"What happened to you?" she asks, taking one of my arms, her six-foot-one form towering over my own. She turns my arm over, rubbing her thumb across one of the cuts and frowning heavily. Her gaze lifts back to mine, and truth serum sears through me, just as it does when I look Maxx in the face. *They really were a match made in heaven, and I ruined it, and I'm selfish, and I want Maxx for myself.*

"I'm sorry." Those are the only words I can get out, just those two. They're the most important ones that need saying, the only ones, the ones I'd scribe as an epitaph if I died tomorrow. With Justin around, I very well could. "I'm so sorry, Maxie. I'm so sorry, so sorry, so fucking sorry."

"Stop." She puts her hands on my shoulders and leans in, putting her forehead to mine. She smells sweet, like summer flowers and sunshine, like home, familiarity, comfort. I'm such a baby when Maxine is around; she never had a problem filling the empty space where Saffron was supposed to be, that motherly role that I unknowingly craved. I didn't realize it until now, but while Grandma Carmen was, well, *grandma,* Maxie was mom. "Stop apologizing. Just … stop." She sniffs again and reaches out, tucking a strand of lime-green hair behind my ear. "There's no need for it."

Her gaze shifts slightly to the side, to where X is standing, stiff and uncomfortable. He's wearing a frown, but his eyes are apologetic, his hands tucked into the pockets of his cargo pants. They look at each other for a minute before Maxine heaves a long sigh and turns to me again.

"Now that I've got you, I'm never letting you go again." She stands up straight as Parrish and Chasm approach, the tension in the room hanging around us like fog. Thick, soupy fog, the sort that turns a morning sunrise into a watercolor painting, cream and gold and lavender and whipped-honey clouds. It's pretty, but it obscures the whole world beyond it. That's us, trapped in a bubble of tension.

What do I do? How do I handle this?

Justin.

That fucker intentionally avoided my questions about Maxine only to drop her in my lap like an unexpected gift. At the same time, he invited all of the boys, all of his enemies. What do I do now? What move do I make next?

My mind strays to the chess game we played yesterday, to my triumphant snatching of Justin's piece. He made a sacrifice in order to win. The deal for me is this: nobody that I love is worth sacrificing to win this. If it comes down to it, the only person I'm willing to knock off the board is myself.

"Is there somewhere we can go to talk?" she asks me, and I nod, taking her hand. Delphine is standing on the opposite side of X, two fresh drinks in her hands, her mouth slightly ajar in surprise. She didn't know this was coming, that Maxie was going to be here tonight.

And she doesn't like it.

I pull Maxine out of the room without looking at the boys or anyone else.

Up the stairs we go and into my pretty powder blue bedroom, a princess' residence in a stately castle.

"Oh my God," she breathes, peering around the space with wide eyes. And then she smiles at me, and the expression is genuinely, beautifully, stunningly Maxie. "This is gorgeous. Did Justin set this all up for you?"

I spin to face her, dolled up in a dress that costs more than a dress rightfully should. Wearing more makeup than I've ever worn in my life. Sporting shoes that are as likely to make me look cool as they are to end with a broken ankle. I'm shaking from the crown of my head to the tips of my toes.

I thought she was a prisoner; Justin implied it. But what is this? What's going on here?

If he doesn't have Maxine, then does he have any leverage over me? What if I were to steal Justin's keys and take off with my sister, head back to New York without looking back? The temptation is there. At least, it is until I remember all of the extenuating circumstances in my life.

Tess. The fire. My other siblings. Delphine. My grandparents and Saffron and all the legal threats and punishments they might suffer if I were to run. The boys. *My* boys.

There's a soft knock at the door, and I move over to it, peering out to see the three of them waiting.

"Give me a minute, okay?" I close it before I can gauge any of their reactions, turning around and putting my back to the bedroom door. Maxine is peering at me with unabashed curiosity, shameless love, and undisguised pain.

I've hurt her. Because of Justin. Because I couldn't let Parrish die.

"What are you doing here?" I ask her, keeping my voice as neutral as I can. We're being watched in here, no doubt. If Justin isn't looking at us right this minute, peering down at his phone while carrying on a conversation with his mortal enemies/dinner guests, then he'll look later. Tonight, tomorrow. Doesn't matter. Either way, this conversation isn't private. I have to watch what I say.

Maxine wets her lips, shiny with a thin layer of pale gloss. It's the only makeup she's wearing. She'd much rather be hiking or studying than applying face paint and playing princess, no doubt. She takes a seat on the edge of my bed, looking around at the new computer, the shelf full of TikTok goodies, the heavy drapes framing the open windows and the view of the water beyond.

"Last night was your first time sleeping here, right?" she asks, and I swallow hard. I shouldn't feel so awkward around someone I grew up with, someone I've known my entire life. Yet, it feels like we're strangers, and I hate that.

Free-falling, tumbling, spinning.

The sensations inside of me make me feel weightless, but not in a good way. I'm a helium balloon left to drift in the sky, waiting for the inevitable moment when I pop and come crashing down to earth.

"How do you know that?" My voice is small and weak, and Maxine smiles softly and gently, like she's trying to coax a frightened kitten to hop out of the tree it's stuck in and fall into her arms.

"Your ..." She chokes a little on the word, reaching up to sweep brown hair over her shoulder. "Sperm donor told me that. He's been really nice, far more understanding than *that woman.*" Maxine hisses those last two words out, salty and briny with rage. It makes sense that she'd blame Tess for all of this. I would, too, if I were her. "He let me stay here last week, until ..." She trails off again, inhaling and fiddling with her shirt. "Anyway, he let me stay here, and I helped pick out some of the items for your room." Her expression brightens again, and she stands up, taking a step toward me.

I move away from the door, and she frowns at me again. I'm acting like a crazy person, I know, but I'm terrified of what Justin might be planning. If he was willing to cut and bleed Parrish, what will he do to Maxie?

My sister pauses, twitching her mouth in consternation, and then she turns and yanks the door open.

The boys—these arrogant, cocksure assholes in designer clothes—tumble into the room like they're in a cartoon or something, just a mess of men and cursing and slightly flushed faces.

Maxine looks up at the three of them, studying their faces before planting her hands on her hips in that way of hers. She pushes the door closed behind them and hits the lock, as if this situation is normal or average in any way, like a lock can keep out the bad guys.

"Eavesdropping on a private conversation between sisters? That's despicable." She clucks her tongue again. Maxx looks ashamed, rubbing at the back of his head, his entire face flushed. Our eyes meet again, and his feel impossibly deep, like two mossy pools, drawing me down into cool waters.

We not only have the Maxine thing to talk about, but the *dick* and *lick* and *ditto* stuff that he very politely allowed to slide past without commenting on. *Ugh.* This is my first time seeing him since copping to having a freaking threesome with Parrish and Chasm.

It's a lot.

My whole life is a lot.

"Utterly despicable," Parrish agrees, but he doesn't flinch. Chasm shrugs out of his jacket, revealing his inked arms as he tosses it onto my bed and saunters around, whistling and murmuring under his breath.

"Fuck, these are nice digs," he admits grudgingly, but he can't exactly comment on why that's such an extraordinary thing. *Oh my, the Seattle Slayer sure does have an acute attention to detail! He's an interior design wizard. If it weren't for the whole 'being psychotic' thing, he might be cool.*

"Care to explain why?" Maxine asks, unflinching under the boys' combined weight. It's intense when they're all together like this, I won't lie. "What's going on here? Don't try to tell me that it's nothing; I'm not stupid. I saw you punch that kid." She whirls on me, her pretty shirt fluttering in the breeze, tendrils of loose wavy hair falling around her face.

My eyes flick to X, but he isn't looking at my sister: he's looking at me.

"Are you being bullied?" she presses when I don't answer. "Is that where those cuts came from?"

"Did you see the redhead in the pink dress rush past on your way in?" Parrish asks, poking around on the TikTok shelf. He should be sitting on it: he's trending on TikTok, too. Getting kidnapped and then coming back to life has really boosted his popularity. "She attacked Dakota with a group of her friends; they cut her clothes off with utility knives and then posted the video online." He pauses and shakes his head. "Streamed it online more like."

Maxie's eyes widen and sparkle with unshed tears.

"Oh, baby sister …" She moves toward me again but stops herself. She can sense that I'm holding back, I'm sure. If only I could tell her everything, spill all of my secrets. Even so, even with a metric crap-ton of lies between us, even with me taking her boyfriend and *sleeping* with him, she still doesn't look at me with anything less than pure love.

I don't feel like I deserve that.

If only I hadn't come into her life—in the lives of the Banks—then they'd all be safe, and I wouldn't be here ruining everything and causing them pain. *Stop that, Kota. When has pitying yourself ever helped?*

"It's not that big of a deal," I lie, and then I hate myself for doing that. I lean back, resting my hands on the edge of the desk with the fancy new computer I haven't used nor will likely ever use. How can I? It's just a window for Justin to stare into my soul. "Actually … it was awful. Luckily enough, the Milk Carton app has scrubbed every instance of it off the internet—even the dark web. Unless someone downloaded it onto their computer and reuploads it, or if they blurred out my face …" I can't account for everything, but as of now, I can't seem to find the video and—to toot my own horn just a bit—I'm a pretty well-established internet sleuth.

If it was there, I'm certain I would've found it.

Milk Carton. Gah. Yes, it scrubbed the video, but would there even *be* a video without Justin? I still can't decide if Veronica's attack was at his behest or not. When I told the guys that I sensed there were two opposing forces at play, I meant it. It might actually be that Veronica hates me on the basis of being related to Justin, a man that her parents helped ruin for financial gain.

They're all bad guys, all of them, every single one.

And us? We're the vigilantes.

ENDGAME ROMANCE

Maxine looks around at the boys again and then back at me, blinking through her thoughts. I know that look, the one that means she's about to ask something pertinent yet prying. *Fuuuuuuck.*

"Kota, are you dating one of these boys?" she asks me, and I go completely still.

I knew it. I friggin' *knew* she was going to ask that. My gaze shifts over to X. He meets my gaze before looking back at Maxine.

"I'm sure some of the awkwardness here is because of me," he offers up, putting a hand to his chest. "But I don't want to be an obstacle that comes between the two of you." Maxine is staring at him now, her face etched with hurt. I'm sure she really did tell him that he was 'just a boy' and that I was her sister, and I bet she even meant it.

But she liked him. She liked him a lot. Maybe she even loved him?

"Are you two dating?" Maxine asks, her voice calm and cool, free of judgment. Chasm flops onto the bed on his back with a groan, and my sister gives him an odd look. If you think about it, the last she knew we were practically enemies.

"Are they dating or was it a one-time thing?" Parrish clarifies, and now he's looking at us, too, his hands in the pockets of his varsity jacket. The hot pink shirt underneath is striking against his skin tone. It's not just my sister that's asking this question, it's him, too. He wants to know my intentions, X's intentions. He has a right, after all.

"One-time thing?" Maxine asks, and then she lets out a surprised laugh. Just like me. She does the nervous laugh thing sometimes, too. She reaches up to cover her mouth but then just drops her hand at her side. "You know about that?"

Parrish shrugs his shoulder as Chasm snorts.

They all wait for me to explain. This is entirely up to me, after all.

"We're … we're dating," I say, looking over at X to judge his thoughts. His expression softens in a way that makes me feel twitchy; he's gazing at me like he wants to scoop me up and keep me forever. "But we've only … that one time …" I choke on the memory, the feeling of his hips pumping into me, his tight fingers on my wrists, his declarations. I close my eyes and force myself to exhale, reaching up to run my palm over my shellacked and gussied up hair.

When I open them, I find that everyone is just *staring* at me.

"I'm dating all three of them." I say the words with conviction, exhaling and shaking out my hands to release some of the tension. My sister's brown eyes go wide, and she opens her mouth three times to speak before any words get out.

X beats her to it.

"It's a complicated situation," he admits, leaning his broad back up against the dresser, looking confident and sexy as hell. "It's not something any of us would've entered into without … outside influence." It's almost a question, but then, this is Maxim Wright we're talking about. "It doesn't reflect on you at all."

"Of course it doesn't," Maxine replies breezily, but she's as terrible an actor as I am. She's hurt, and even if she tries to squash it down, it's there in the softness of her eyes, the shape of her mouth. "I broke up with you; you didn't want to be with me. Dakota is a beautiful, intelligent girl." She shrugs, and then looks over to Chasm, likely wondering if we've been intimate.

It kills me that I haven't been around to share these milestones with her. Without Justin's influence, I don't know what would've happened. Because I tend to value loyalty, I probably would've stayed with Parrish, been faithful to Parrish, and pushed aside any strange or nagging thoughts in regard to Maxx or Chasm.

Now that I have them all—if only temporarily—I couldn't

imagine choosing one. But if I'd never been allowed a taste? Anyway, without Justin around, if a situation like this *had* developed, I would've told my sister every single detail. The hedge maze. In the school bathroom. With the sun rising outside my bedroom window. Parrish and me on his bathroom floor … All of it.

"I didn't mean to steal your boyfriend," I choke out, because I need to say it. I've needed to say it for weeks now. "Under normal circumstances, I wouldn't have ever …"

Maxine nods, as if she understands. I know she can't possibly, but she thinks she does.

"Dakota, you are dealing with a lot. More than I could handle. And then for Parrish to go missing when you were just finding your groove, the emotions must've been intense. I could never fault you for that." She smiles softly at me, and I ache to go to her.

After a slight hesitation, I do.

Because Justin told me to indulge myself. He told me I deserved nice things. And if he sent Maxine to me tonight, he did it for a reason. I haven't quite figured out what that reason is, but I will. Maybe even before the end of the night.

I go to my sister and allow her to take me in her arms, tucking me under her chin and rocking me as she rubs my back. My head clears immediately, and for the first time in days, I'm able to take a calming breath and relax. Just a little, but it's enough.

When we finally part, her phone—which has been buzzing for a while—goes off again, and she slides it from her pocket. She blinks a few times at whatever it is that she sees and then nods, slipping it back into the sole pocket on her denim skirt.

"We're nowhere near done with this talk, believe me." Her gaze drifts past me to X. "You and I, we should talk, too. But not right now." Maxine smiles sweetly at me and reaches up to cup the side of my face. "I might not like that woman, but the sperm donor, well, he's a pretty great guy."

I snort, and Maxine's brow crinkles, but there's no way I can discuss Justin in this house, not in a disparaging way and certainly not to my sister. He feels threatened by her, and I can't let him have any further excuses to torment the people I love.

"Come with me. He's cooked up a pretty great surprise." She takes my hand and ignores the boys, leaving them behind as she pulls me down the hall. Just like Delphine. Right. I haven't told Maxie about Delphine yet …

Speak of the devil (or at least the devil's daughter) and she will appear.

Delphine waits at the bottom of the stairs, arms crossed, sucking on her lower lip as if she's nervous about something. Her eyes brighten when she sees me, but I really, *really* don't like the way her gaze slips to Maxine.

"This is the Banks girl?" Delphine inquires, forcing a smile. Maxie stops and smiles back at her.

"Dakota's older sister," she explains, pointing at herself, clearly excited by whatever 'surprise' Justin has conjured. Whatever it is, I'm sure I won't like it, but if my sister is okay with it, it's probably not a dead maid in a box.

"Dakota's older sister—biologically speaking." Delphine points at herself just the same, and then the two girls are staring at each other, thunder growling, lightning crashing.

"Um … what?" Maxine asks, and I glance back in time to see all three of the boys on the landing. They appear to be prepping for a photoshoot of some sort, posed all cool and dressed all slick like that. The three of them are watching the events unfold with similar expressions: anger at not being able to help, desperation for some alone time to talk, probably desperation for alone time for other things …

I turn back around and step between the two nineteen-year-olds claiming to be my older sisters.

"This is Delphine, Justin's eldest daughter." I force a polite smile to my face, adjusting my hand over to Maxie next. "Maxine Banks, the big sister I grew up with."

That's a bit of a cop-out, isn't it? To refer to Maxine like that, but it's the best I can do to balance her feelings with my fear of Delphine's or Justin's reactions.

"I … wasn't aware that Justin had other children." Maxine shakes her head slightly, and makes her smile even bigger, even brighter. "It's nice to meet you, Delphine. If you need any big sister tips, I've got them all filed away up here." My sister taps at the side of her head with a pretty white and yellow nail with a daisy painted on it. It's one of the few beauty routines she likes, painting her nails.

"Oh, I'm sure I won't need them. You wouldn't believe how much Mia and I take after our father." Delphine purposefully uses my birthname to throw a barb my way; I ignore it, but I won't forget it. "Your guests are here, by the way." She turns and indicates the foyer, and Maxine's smile twitches.

"Right." She squeezes my hand even harder, pulling me forward just in time for the front doors to open.

For several seconds, I'm certain that I'm the victim of a mirage. I'm lost in a desert of emotions, thirsty for love and familiarity, for a soft place to land. I only *think* I see water, trees, shade, somewhere to rest.

There in the doorway, in the flesh, are the Banks.

My grandparents—Carmen and Walter Banks.

They're standing *right* there, and I don't know whether to laugh or cry.

I realize then that this isn't about Maxine, not in the way it was about Parrish. Justin held Parrish to teach me a lesson. Now, he's just making a promise to enforce it. If I don't follow his rules or play his game—if I don't find some way to checkmate him—I'm committing myself to compliance for life.

Essentially, I'm committing to being his accomplice.

Terror lances through me, but I force a smile to my face anyway. Because, in order to beat someone's game, you have to actually play it.

"I can't believe you're here ..." Tears in my eyes, I move over to embrace my grandparents, the fabric of my green designer gown rustling.

In that moment, I'm pretty sure I just gained a level. In life. I mean, in life I gained a level.

It's a metaphor.

Anyway, I might not be a writer like my bio mother, but I'm definitely a gamer like dear old dad.

He's dead wrong if he thinks otherwise.

CHAPTER 10

The hugs I receive from my grandparents are like buffs in a video game, offering me strength long after they've pulled away, studying me with tears in their eyes. They exchange a quick look with one another that makes me fidget self-consciously before returning their attentions to their long-lost granddaughter. I try not to read too much into it, to wonder if they're looking at one another in disappointment as to what I've become.

Mostly, I'm sure it's all in my imagination.

"You look so grown-up," Grandma Carmen says, her voice choked with emotion. She's wearing her favorite shade of bright-red lipstick, her silver hair twisted into a bun at the back of her head. The dress she's wearing is understated and casual, just a slip of harvest orange fabric with sensible shoes.

She's the most beautiful woman in the room, in my opinion.

"Grown-up in a good way?" I ask, noticing that she's studying my facial expression, primarily my eyes, as she makes her declaration. She's reading all the ways I've matured—either naturally or by force, I suppose. It's not about the dress or the makeup I didn't want to wear, the very pretty but too-high shoes or anything else.

It's the fact that I'm starting to understand Tess and her motivations, that I'm realizing not everything is black and white, that people are complex and strange, and that I myself am one of them.

All of that.

"I'm impressed." My grandmother puts her hands on her hips as my grandfather wipes away tears with shaking hands. He's always been the more emotional, less rational of the two. Also, he takes about twice as long as my grandmother to get ready to go anywhere, and he never knows what restaurant he wants to eat at but always vetoes other's suggestions because his own cooking is superior to whatever we could get when going out and ... Holy Gamer Gods, I missed the man so much that *I* might just start crying again. "You've blossomed, Kota."

"What happened to my baby granddaughter?" My grandfather asks, and I roll my eyes because I know he's about to get sappy, and I want him to, and well, I'm just overflowing with emotions. Maxine stands beside me, beaming proudly, the boys and Delphine just behind, and everyone else *stares.* "Who is this adult person looking back at me?"

"We heard about the fire," Carmen interrupts. "I'm so thankful you weren't in it, and that the family got out." She says 'the family', not 'your family'. I'm not even sure if she realizes it. "All of your things—"

"None of that stuff matters." I make that statement with conviction, but her face crinkles in sympathy regardless. "I'm just so happy you're here."

Justin glides into the room as if summoned, swaggering his way over to stand beside the Banks. His smile is magnanimous and overflowing, his presence saintly and holy. He smiles lovingly at me, acting as if he's not at all bothered by the Banks' references to me as their granddaughter.

We both know that he is; I can *feel* it.

I'm still trembling—pretty sure I haven't stopped since this party began—and yet, I feel simultaneously terrified to have figured out Justin's play and stalwart in stopping it. Seeing my grandparents and Maxine after such a long separation has another simultaneous, dichotomous effect on me. I'm beyond thrilled to see them, but that pain inside of me, the pain that began to bloom when I first saw that awful Netflix show with Sally and Nevaeh, that sprouted when Tess flew to New York, that withered on the vine when I came to live in Washington … it throbs and aches. Limbs regrow from that small, hurtful seed, thorns of emotional torment pricking and poking and making me bleed.

Just as I feared—just as I knew would happen—the Banks feel alien somehow, almost like strangers.

So, I don't belong with Tess and the Vanguards, and I don't belong with the Banks, and I certainly don't belong here with Justin Prior and his shiny new daughter Delphine. I don't belong anywhere or with anyone.

That isn't true. I tell myself that and yet, the pain is there regardless. See, that's the thing with feelings. As Maxine once said, they are neither right nor wrong, they just are. How I process them, how I act on them, that's what matters most.

"You did a beautiful job raising her," Justin praises, still smiling, likely scheming about Saffron and how he can find her. If he does, he'll kill her. I know that as surely as I know that the sun will rise tomorrow; it's just a fact. I breathe out, in, out. It's a struggle, but I maintain a somewhat dignified composure in front of the mixed crowd. "Thank you, but I'll take over from here." Justin laughs and, after the briefest hesitation, my grandparents also laugh.

I do not.

It's not a joke: it's a threat. Mostly, it's a reminder to me that I best keep the peace, or he'll wrench this little bit of happiness from my fingers, wispy white clouds scattering beneath a strong wind.

I keep smiling.

Forced Smile Number Infinity. There is no end to them, and I'm breaking.

"Thank you for inviting us here, for paying for the plane tickets —" Grandpa Walter begins, and Grandma Carmen smoothly takes over.

"First class is nice. Never flown it a day in my life, would never pay such a hefty price for it, but the food was delicious." She smiles at Justin, her perceptive gaze sliding back to me. I wonder if she can sense that something is wrong here or if she's as fooled by Justin as the rest of the world?

The Banks are honest, down-to-earth, hardworking people. They might not consider how nefarious his intentions might be because they themselves don't have such intentions. I'm starting to learn that those who scheme and crawl and creep in the background are always the first to point the finger, to accuse others of backstabbing and plotting because they themselves are doing the same damn thing.

Not that it matters. Actually, it's better. I *hope* my grandparents and my sister remain blissfully unaware. As long as they do, as long as I comply with Justin's wishes, then I won't have to wonder if they're in any danger.

As cunning as he is, Justin knows that once you push someone past their limit, they no longer submit but instead fight back. If he hurts or kills anyone that I love, I won't be his pet. I won't do his deeds. I won't be his dutiful daughter anymore.

"It's divine, isn't it?" Justin agrees, still smiling. Always smiling. Tess is always frowning and griping and complaining, pacing around, switching from crazy hermit writer mode back to polished ice queen in an instant. She's a modern-day Jekyll and Hyde for sure. Yet, she isn't the bad guy here.

Appearances are not always what they seem.

"Dinner will be served shortly; we should retire to the dining room." Justin holds out an arm for me, and because I know my choices here are not good ones, I take it. "Do you see?" he whispers as he guides me away from the Banks, from Maxine, from the three boys with dark but loving glints in their eyes. "Do you see how much I love and cherish you? How greatly and passionately I long for your happiness?"

I say nothing. Better that than a retort he might take the wrong way. Somehow, it feels like I haven't seen the worst of him yet.

Justin pulls out a chair for me at the head of the table and pushes me in, directing Maxine to sit on one side, my grandparents on the other but with a single chair between me and them. He puts X beside my sister which seems odd but isn't entirely unexpected. Nothing Bio Dad loves more than stirring shit up.

The world takes an even stranger turn when I spot Parrish's grandmother, Laverne, in the crowd of glittering wealth. It shouldn't surprise me to see her here, but somehow, I feel like I've been thrown another curveball, one that I better damn well catch before it hits me in the face.

She's seated beside Parrish on the opposite end of the table next to … Lumen.

The blood drains from my face as I sit there and gape, catching the sienna glaze of her stare before she dutifully turns away and takes a seat, dressed in a vibrant pink pantsuit and heels.

As if the sight of her—and her seating arrangement—weren't bad enough, Caroline takes the chair across from her biological son. Parrish pretends not to notice, but the way his hand trembles as he lifts a glass of water to his lips is extremely telling.

Chasm is placed directly next to me while Justin heads up the opposite end of the table, and the other guests naturally find their places.

It feels ... a bit like a chess game. Each piece has been carefully examined and put to its best use, laid out on the board in a pattern that serves Justin and most certainly does not serve yours truly.

I place my napkin in my lap, mostly to hide my shaking hands.

"Are you alright?" Chas whispers, leaning in close to me. Justin notes the interaction, and smiles.

"Is your dad coming tonight? Will Justin tell him about your hair and—" I pause as Seamus enters the room, apologizing for running late as he takes his own seat. Chasm purses his lips and gives a slight shake of his head, clearly not in answer to my question but as a warning to stay quiet.

Something happened to him over the last forty-eight hours. But he's here, and his piercings are in, and his hair is intact, so I'm not sure what to make out of any of it.

"Later," he breathes, and then Justin is tapping a butterknife against his glass and rising to his feet.

"Thank you all for coming," he schmoozes, and I do my utmost to resist rolling my eyes. It takes effort, but I manage to keep it together. For now. "Many of you were present at the launch party for Milk Carton, but I've been eager for a more personal affair, a homecoming and an integration back into the warm embrace of this beautiful town and its generous inhabitants." *Snort.* Oops. That one comes out as an actual sound, and many sets of eyes flick my way. I clear my throat and pick up my water glass, taking a sip and feigning a slight tickle. "I'd like to pay a special welcome to the Banks family, who cared for my daughter for many years as if she were one of their own." Justin lifts his glass, and genteel, murmured praise is spouted by nearly everyone at that table. Delphine gazes up at our shared sperm donor with love in her eyes while I try to get a read on the rest of the guests.

Raúl, Justin's dickhead assistant, is here. Maxx's parents. And, I hadn't noticed him until just now, Amin Volli. He offers me a conspiratorial wink that I ignore to the best of my ability. *This is a pit of snakes, venomous, silver-tongue snakes in bright and pretty colors.*

There are my people here, Justin's people, and Justin's mortal enemies.

I take note of the faces and families present and make the educated assumption that anyone I don't recognize is one of his targets. Keep your friends close, your enemies closer. That sort of thing. Tess is noticeably absent from the event which doesn't surprise me.

Justin seems to enjoy infecting her with as much FOMO as physically possible.

After he takes his seat, and the food begins to come out—served by the staff, of course—I'm able to return my attention to my grandparents. Chasm puts his hand on my thigh beneath the table, searing me with heat, and bolstering my resolve. He's a quiet, respectful presence on my right.

Why did Justin seat everyone the way he did? I make mental notes of each person's position and, as soon as I'm able to, I'll sneak off to the bathroom and draw a map on my phone. Noting where each person is sitting could be vital to figuring out the next step in the game.

"So, Dakota," Grandma Carmen begins, adjusting herself in her seat and attempting not to stare at me like, well, a stolen child. But that's what I am, to both my grandparents and Tess. *To Justin.* I refuse to look down the table at him, focusing on the Banks and this rare and precious opportunity to be together. "Want to tell us about this boy?" She makes the question a joke as she turns to Chasm, but it's not funny. It's almost sad. Because she sounds so normal, so much like home, and I find myself leaning toward her like a flower toward the sun. She clears her throat again, and I can see that this is as difficult for her as it is for me.

We're acting like everything is normal when nothing is.

Seeing them here, it's both rewarding and weird as hell.

I shift in my seat, eyes flicking automatically over to Maxine for help. Growing up, whenever I needed backup or advice in any given situation, I could look to my big sister for help. She doesn't miss a beat, as if we'd never been separated, as if I didn't sleep with her ex-boyfriend like a total creeper.

"Kwang-seon McKenna, right?" Maxine interjects for me, leaning in and putting her elbows on the table. We're the only ones doing it, the Banks, I mean. Everyone else here follows Etiquette and Snobbery 101 and is sitting ramrod straight with napkins folded in their laps, painfully disdainful smiles on their pretty faces. Even Parrish. "You're Dakota's boyfriend." She doesn't mention that I have two other boyfriends, leaving that up to me.

"You can call me Chasm if you want. Everybody else does." He pauses as my grandmother looks him over from head to toe, my grandfather peering around her with a slight frown on his face. "Or … Kwang-seon is cool, too."

"Your first boyfriend," my grandmother says with a long sigh, and my eyes flick down the length of the table to find Parrish, his hazel gaze on Bio Dad and not on me. As if he can sense me staring at him, he adjusts his attention over to me and our gazes crash with a flash of heat.

I swallow hard and reach for my water glass, taking a delicate little sip that's so unlike me that Maxine snorts. She reaches out and gently puts her fingers on my arm.

"Well, not her first. There was Ryan, after all."

"Ryan?" Chasm asks as X narrows his eyes, his mouth a pouty frown as he waits to hear my explanation.

"Ryan who?" I ask, completely blanking on the name. I turn to Maxine and we share a silent sister look, communicating thousands of small minutiae with blinks, raised brows, head tilts, all that good stuff. "Ooooooh." I clap my hands together and every posh asshole in that room turns to stare at me. I ignore them. "Ryan ... Ryan ..."

"Ryan Phillips!" Maxine slaps my arm, and I slap back at her automatically. The warm, snuggly blanket of family and familiarity falls over my shoulders like a cloak, pushing back the strange, dark sea of negativity. "You've been going to school with the guy since preschool, and you can't remember his name?" She chuckles at that. "I don't think she'll ever forget you like that, Kwang-seon McKenna."

"She better not," he says, heaving a sigh and giving me an accusatory look that I ignore. Chasm leans forward and then he, too, puts his elbow on the table. He's good people, that Chasm McKenna. I smile at him as he smirks up at me. "Tell me more about Ryan Phillips. I want to know everything."

"How long have you two been seeing each other?" Carmen continues, her eyes on me and not on Chasm. They ache, those eyes, for all the moments she's missed, for all the firsts and the questions and the emotions she didn't get to see, that she'll continue to miss in the coming years.

"About a month," I admit, realizing how incredibly brief that amount of time really is. Feels like eons—in a good way. I feel like I know Chasm in a way that extends to few others. "But we met as soon as I got here; he's my ... stepbrother's best friend."

Chas sits up and glances down the table in the direction of Parrish. We all do. He turns to see us looking at him and stares right back, ignoring Lumen as she laughs flirtatiously on his left, situated between him and Justin. The hell does that mean? Obviously, Justin's the one who's been blackmailing her, but why sit her next to Parrish?

To mess with me, that's why.

I huff out a breath and reach up, tucking a carefully curled strand of hair behind one ear.

Everything Justin does—from his smiles, to his laughter, to his choice of seating—is nefarious, well-thought, and intentional. I need to do the same, but like, in the opposite way.

"There's a bit more to it than that," I add, and I see Chasm's pretty brows go up. Maxx shifts uncomfortably in his seat, as if he can sense where I'm going with this. My self-preservation instincts encourage me to hide the truth of my situation, but my heart won't allow it.

The world's monsters succeed because of those same-said self-preservation instincts. We need to learn to be brave, to take risks, or else the vast majority of us end up trampled beneath the heels of those more audacious and more vicious than ourselves.

"More to it?" my grandfather asks, picking up his fork and staring down at the … whatever it is that's on our plates. Erm. It looks like a lump of shredded carrots in a spoon. Grandpa sets his fork down and then picks up the spoon, following the lead of the others at the table.

"This is a palette cleanser," Chasm explains, picking up his own spoon and then gagging a bit as he swallows whatever the orange lump is. "Ground carrots and vinegar, I think."

"A palette cleanser?" Maxine echoes, exchanging a look with our grandparents. She leans in, looking so pretty and innocent and *normal.* My heart aches for her. For all the things I've done for her. I want more than anything to spill all my secrets to my sister, but I can't take that risk. I just can't. "Very fancy." Maxie's mouth twitches as she lifts the carrot-spoon to her lips and then chokes a little at the taste.

After eying it for a moment, I do the same. I almost upchuck right there on the fancy table setting. *Oh my God, that's pungent.* It's gross. It's so fucking gross.

"Interesting," my grandmother remarks, pushing her spoon aside. It's whisked away in an instant, and then we're being presented with small bowls of soup.

"I hope you all enjoy," Justin declares from the other end of the table, sweeping his magnanimous hand to indicate the spread. "Wild mushroom soup with a sunken quenelle of risotto."

"What's a quenelle?" I whisper, looking around helplessly. Maxine lifts her brows at me.

"You're the fancy one now: you tell us." She smiles to soften the gentle rebuke, and X leans in, wetting his lower lip in such a way that my attention is irrevocably drawn to his lower lip, to those toothy indents in the plump pink flesh. I blink to clear my thoughts and meet his green eyes.

"A quenelle is an oval-shaped scoop of food, usually with fish or meat—probably mushrooms in this case—and some sort of binding agent, like eggs. Trust me: I've had to ask about this sort of thing before."

Chasm snickers, digging his spoon into his bowl as the rest of us do the same.

The soup, at the very least, is far more palatable than the carrot ... *thing.*

"You were saying?" my grandmother prods, smiling lovingly at me. Her expression feels like the sun, warming my cheeks after a long winter. When the Banks leave here tonight, part of my heart will go with them. If only ...

"Right." I swirl my spoon around in the bowl, and look up, finding X's expression, resolute but prepared. He knows what I'm going to do. Chas, too. "I've somehow ended up with three ... um, suitors?"

"Suitors?" my grandmother asks, exchanging a look with her husband. They turn back to stare at me, waiting for further explanation.

"Chasm ... Parrish ..." I nod my chin down the length of the table in his direction, toward where the Prince of Sloths reclines in his chair, eyes locked on Justin in cold, careful calculation. "Maxim." I flick my attention to the boy in question, wondering how much Maxine told my grandparents about him, what they know. "They're um, courting me? The three of them."

I take a bite of soup. It somehow tastes eighties. I'm not sure how to explain that, but you know how fancy restaurants sometimes just taste old? It's like that. I swear, this soup was the height of fashion in 1983.

"Suitors? Courting?" My grandmother gives a hearty laugh. "How old-fashioned—and lovely." She continues to smile at me as my grandfather eyes the boys in question with a slightly less than excited moue. If Carmen knew I was sleeping with all three of them, she'd probably be wearing an expression more akin to Walter's. "But I thought Maxim was dating Maxine ...?" Here she trails off, and I feel the blood drain from my face.

The soup is spirited away and replaced with a plate of ... oh.

Oh.

These are snails.

There are literally snails on my plate.

"Rich people are so weird," I mumble under my breath, buying myself a split-second to think up an explanation.

Once again, Maxine swoops in to save me.

When she shouldn't. When she should be roasting me alive. When she should, by all rights, hate me.

Instead, she never forgets that she's my big sister.

"We broke up way a long time ago," she says, waving her hand around absently. There's a kernel of hurt in her eyes when I look close, but she blinks it away and hides it with another smile. "We never even kissed." Maxine shrugs and pokes at one of the snails on her plate, swallowing past her initial distaste. Like the badass she is, she picks one up and pops it right into her mouth.

My eyes widen, and I just sit there staring at her as she mulls over the taste.

"Not bad."

"Not ... bad?" I whisper as my grandmother nods in understanding. If she senses there's more to the Maxx situation than we're letting on, she doesn't mention it. She's always been good about knowing when to pry and when to leave things well enough alone.

"Escargot with truffle garlic butter and black trumpet mushrooms," Justin explains, loudly enough that his voice carries to our end of the table.

I don't even know what black trumpet mushrooms *are.*

Oh well. I follow my sister's lead and take a bite before my mental game gets ahold of me. If I think too hard about it—*snail, snail, snail*—I'll puke. It's ... well, it's not as bad as I thought. Kinda chewy though. *I thought Justin was a vegetarian; do vegetarians eat snails then?* I notice then that Justin himself isn't partaking of this particular dish.

Of course not. How barbaric. He couldn't possibly harm a living creature. *Cue expressionless face emoji.*

"Try everything twice," Grandma Carmen murmurs, picking up her own snail. My grandfather does the same, Chasm and Maxx, too.

The relief I feel at having told my grandparents the truth is immense. It carries me through the rest of dinner—a five course affair (not counting the palate cleansers) that continues to baffle us average folk clustered at the end of the dining table.

After dessert is served, we end up milling together in the front room with drinks in hand (nonalcoholic for us youth, unfortunately). With my grandparents briefly locked in conversation with Justin and *Laverne,* blegh, I'm able to get a private moment with the guys after Maxine leaves to use the restroom.

"How are you even here?" I whisper to Parrish, nursing a cherry soda and trying not to fidget under the thrice-gorgeous stare of my boy collection. My *courting suitors,* apparently. Not a bad way to phrase it though, right? "I can't imagine Tess let you out of her sight so easily."

"Laverne put her foot down, Tess put her foot down, and I got trapped in the middle." Parrish releases a heavy sigh, reaching up to brush some of that beautiful hair of his back from his forehead. "As usual, I had to shove Tess under the bus and take Laverne's side to be able to come." He looks disgusted at the admission, and I don't blame him.

Yesterday, when Tess offered me that subtle olive branch in Laverne's foyer, I turned my back on her. Over and over again, we're forced to take the sides of those we disagree with in order to keep the ball rolling.

I don't know how much longer I can keep doing this.

"She yelled ... then she cried. That was the worst part." Parrish sips his own drink, tucking a single hand into the pocket of his jeans as he casts a look in the direction of the clustered Whitehall Prep crowd.

School might be out, but I have a feeling the Whitehall mentality is not limited to the campus grounds. Oh no. It's a pervasive social disease; Medina is a cesspit. *Cursed in blood and diamonds is right.*

"I can't believe Maxine is here, of all places," X inserts, redirecting the conversation. Talking about Tess, and all the emotional pain we're putting her through isn't going to help. Stopping this game, that's the only thing that will. "Why? I thought she was, you know, kidnapped like Parrish."

"Parrish was proof," I whisper as Chasm lifts his lip in a sneer in Antonio's direction. *Dear God, that sweater* ... It looks like an early nineties Nickelodeon cartoon commercial vomited all over it. "Proof that he can and will do what he says. Maxine and my grandparents being here tonight, it's a threat." I suck on my straw, letting my gaze drift back to Justin.

He sees me looking at him, and smiles brightly, offering up a little wave that I ignore.

Delphine is hovering nearby, but she's been cornered in by Lumen. I can't imagine that's accidental. Our eyes meet briefly, and Lumen offers up a smarmy little smile before flipping me off.

Right. We're playing that game tonight. I sigh and turn back to the boys.

"So what are all these smooth-brained bitches doing here?" Chasm asks, studying the gathered crowd of glittering teen models on the other side of the room.

"*Payback, princess,*" I whisper, remembering Justin's words yet again. I know *exactly* what it is that he's aiming for here. I don't even have to guess. "He's going to sic me on these people, that's what."

We all pause the conversation as Maxine returns. She doesn't look at the boys, just me. Only me. It's like I'm the only person in the room.

"Guess what?" she says, offering the only real and true smile in the entire mansion. Even my grandparents aren't fully themselves here. Just my sister. "I'm spending the night."

My mouth drops open, and my drink slides from my hand (yes, again). Maxx catches it like a boss (also, again) and redeposits it in my hand, peeling my fingers open and then curling them around the glass.

"Careful, Kota," he murmurs, and my sister's gaze slides to him. I jerk away dramatically and end up spilling soda all over the toes of my pretty shoes. Maxx is right there, bending down and mopping them up with the napkin he had tucked under his own drink.

I pretend not to notice, but the way Maxine looks at me, I know I'm not fooling anyone. I am hopelessly, stupidly, impossibly in love—with *three* guys. Three. Not one. But freaking three.

"How did you manage to wrangle that?" Chasm asks, and Maxie gives him an odd look.

"Wrangle?" She pauses and considers that for a minute, seemingly coming to the conclusion that he means because of the whole Tess banning me from the Banks thing. "Well, Justin's certainly more reasonable than that woman."

"*That woman*," Parrish grits out. "You mean our *mother*?" he challenges, but all he does is sigh again and shake his head. I can sense he wants to unleash his cold fury on Maxine, drawing back for my sake and mine alone.

"I didn't mean to offend," Maxine offers up, and maybe she didn't, but she isn't going to change her mind about Tess that easily.

Parrish ignores her, reaching over as if he might touch the side of my face. He draws his hand back, but then his features take on a determined cast, and he leans forward, pressing his mouth to mine.

I swear, the entire room goes still.

"Laverne's calling the valet; that means we're on our way out." Parrish puts his hand on the back of my neck, leaning in to put his forehead up against mine. "Stay strong, Gamer Girl. I'll be there when Tess comes to pick you up." He kisses my mouth again, my cheek, my forehead, and then he pulls away and takes off for the front doors, pausing at the last minute to glance back.

He forces a smile that doesn't quite reach his eyes, and then he's turning and heading out the door after his grandmother. Her part in this scheme, I can't quite figure. I have a feeling that she isn't aware of the, um, murdering bits. Probably, she's just supporting Justin because she hates Tess. That's my take. People are complicated, but also ... they're not at the same time. Does that make sense?

I can hardly stand to see Parrish leave; it makes my heart ache. It triggers some sort of anxiety reaction or PTSD or something related to his kidnapping. I almost chase after him, but I manage—with Chasm's help—to stay where I am.

He curls his fingers through mine and holds on tight, so tight that my hand aches, but I don't even care because I like him that much.

"Before I forget: Chas, what the hell?" I murmur, looking over at Seamus, in his usual position beside Justin. Again, not sure if he's in on the homicide part of this deal, but he's clearly in bed with Daddy Dearest.

"You mean this?" Chasm asks, pointing at his lip rings before looking over at Maxine. "My dad doesn't know I have ..." He trails off and gestures at the ink on his lower arms, blatantly displayed in a way I've never seen before. "Rather, he didn't know. He certainly does now."

"Oh?" Maxine raises her brows, likely wondering how a parent could miss their son being covered in tattoos, with piercings in his lower lip, plugs in his ears, and a freaking lightning bolt dyed in his hair. She doesn't know these people like I do. As long as their kids are performing tricks for the good of their prestigious images, then nothing else matters.

"Justin." Chasm purses his lips and looks over at the pair of them, his dad and mine all cozied up with the Banks. "He told my dad to leave me alone and let me do my own thing."

I'm gaping now, slack-jawed and staring.

"It gets better," Maxx explains, looking over at his ex like he isn't sure how much to reveal in front of her. The less, the better. For her own good, obviously.

"Better how?" I ask, heart thundering. Chasm shifts nervously on his feet and plays with his right lip ring with his tongue.

"Uh, Justin implied we might make a nice couple?" He says it like it's a question, and then exhales sharply. "He wants me to propose to you."

"What?!" This is Maxine, not me. I mean, I scream it inside my head, but my sister says it first. "Eww, gross. You're *sixteen*," she hisses, and then her soft brown eyes narrow and she turns a sharp glare on Justin. "Why would he say something like that?"

"It's … different around here," X explains, reaching up to ruffle his hair. He's awkward around my sister, guilt pouring off of him in waves. He cared for her, even if he didn't love her. I know that, and it makes me like him that much more, that he feels this way now. "People here get married young, to whomever their parents tell them to. Think old-school aristocracy in modern-day America."

My sister's face is aghast with disgust as she looks past me toward Justin and then turns to Chasm.

"No offense—"

"None taken," he inserts, and she continues.

"But sixteen is far too young to get engaged."

"Tell me about it," Chasm offers up, shrugging one shoulder. "But uh, I wasn't exactly given a lot of choices." His gaze meets mine again, and I balk. What … what part does this play in everything?

But it makes sense, even on a surface level. Seamus is inextricably tied to Justin; Fort Humboldt Security and Milk Carton are tied. Then it hits me.

Chasm, sitting beside me. Parrish, beside Lumen. X with my sister.

Mm.

I smell a plot.

"Meaning what?" Maxine asks, and Chasm turns to her with a sardonic smile.

"Meaning … no inheritance? Getting shipped off to Crescent Prep?" Chas shakes his head. "For context: Crescent Prep is a school in the middle of backwoods Arkansas where rich families ship the kids they don't want. Something like that."

"So you're going to propose to me soon?" I clarify, cheeks flushing.

"And you're going to say *yes*," Chas whispers in my ear, but not like he's entirely happy about it. I get it. Because I won't have a choice, I'm sure. Justin will be *allll* over this. "But even if we are too young, even if it's a farce … it wouldn't be, inside my heart." This last part, he makes sure to say in such low tones that nobody else can hear us.

"Boys." Seamus appears behind me, and I turn, nearly sloshing my drink everywhere. "It's time to go." He smiles politely, if a little coldly, at me before heading for the doors. Chasm curses under his breath, meeting my gaze.

I can't imagine anything about this is as simple as it seems.

Did his Dad hurt him when he found out about the piercings and the tattoos? He won't say as much right now, but we'll have to find private time to discuss this later. And by private, I mean like, in the middle of a field surrounded by woods or something.

A miraculous, tech-free place without Milk Carton's watchful eyes.

"If you need me, I'm a quick sprint down the road." Chasm leans in and grabs my face. Unlike Parrish, he doesn't peck me on the lips. Oh no. He dives right in, tongue and everything. It's a lot, especially in front of such a crowd. But as soon as he starts kissing me, I almost drop my drink for a third time, and X catches it. Third time's a charm, isn't it?

There's a metaphor there, surely, but I'm too busy having the life kissed out of me by (one of) the world's most handsome boys.

He pulls back, breathless, panting, and his amber eyes meet mine. Chasm turns away suddenly, snatching his jacket as he goes and then ... it's just me and Maxx and Maxine, and why the fuck do they have the same name?!

Ugh.

"I'll give you two a minute." She moves away, heading for my grandparents as I stand there awkwardly, and X stares right back.

"I won't kiss you," he promises, and I nod.

"That's probably for the best," I admit, and his lips tighten. I move forward and put my hands on his big shoulders, rising up on my tiptoes to press a kiss to his cheek first, and then his lips. Light, airy, but full of purpose. "Because I'm going to kiss you."

"Is that so?" he asks, voice cocky and warm, an invitation. I swallow hard as he pauses to set our drinks down on the tray of a passing employee. It's hard to remember that we're actually at someone's house instead of a fancy venue or a country club or something.

Maxx grabs my hand and drags me away, lightning fast. He takes me into the downstairs bathroom and pulls me in before anyone can see that we've just locked ourselves into a small powder room together.

He puts his hands on either side of me, braced against the counter.

"Are you okay?" I ask, choking on the words and acting as if I don't feel the heavy tension between us. Oh, I feel it. Tonight has just been a lot. I mean, a lot, a lot. I'm drowning here and X is a raft. He's a fucking raft. I reach up and put my hand against the side of his face.

He gives a visible shudder and closes his eyes, exhaling slowly.

"Am I okay?" X opens those emerald jewels he calls eyes to stare at me. "You're the one living with a literal serial killer." He pauses then and looks around, narrowing his gaze. Yeah, I wouldn't put it past Justin to stick cameras in the bathrooms. Not because he's a pervert—fortunately, that particular kink doesn't seem to appeal to him (nothing worse than a scum sucking incel scrote, am I right?)—but he had no problem putting cameras in to, uh, watch me and Maxx getting it on.

"I'm sure there are cameras in here," I admit, and Maxx just shakes his head. "I meant: are you okay after saving our entire family, including the damn rabbit?"

"Don't worry about me. The only person you should be worried about is yourself." He reaches up and brushes my hair back gently, leaning in to press his mouth to mine. How is it that each guy kisses so differently? I could identify them in the dark, based on the touch of their lips alone.

"Do we need to talk about the threesome thing?" I whisper, and X sighs against my mouth.

"Actually, this is a good thing."

"It's a good thing that I had a threesome with two other guys?" The words come out, but they feel disconnected from my own mouth. Like, what am I even saying right now? This isn't a kink thing, not some attempt at rebellion or to prove a point. It's just … love. I'm just in love with these boys, and I care about them. That's it.

"Parrish can be stubborn," Maxx explains, nipping at my lower lip and giving me the chills. "I was worried he was going to demand all or bust. If he was willing to be vulnerable and intimate around Chas, then we're heading in the right direction." He kisses my lips again, slow and simple, just his warm mouth against mine.

I raise my own hands to his chest, curling my fingers in his shirt and reveling in the hot, hard feel of him. All of that time on his bike has really honed his upper body, and I want more, more, more of it. As much as I can get.

Our mouths slant together, his hot tongue against my own, tasting one another. It's pure bliss, especially when he reaches down and takes my hips in his hands, lifting me up to sit on the edge of the counter. Maxx's big body ends up between my thighs, his heat making me thrill all over, knocking the sense from me, making me forget where exactly we are and all that's going on.

He pushes against me, and I scoot toward him, heat gathering between my thighs that he encourages by rocking gently forward with his hips.

It would've been a near fairy tale if we'd remembered to lock the bathroom door.

Of all people, it's Maxine that opens it.

X stumbles back, tripping on the toilet and ending up sitting on it as I swallow hard and stare at my sister staring back at me.

I'm an idiot.

Such an idiot.

"I'm so sorry; I didn't realize you were in here." She's completely red-faced and embarrassed, but it should be me who's blushing and apologizing right now. "I was about to come find you anyway. Grandma and Grandpa need to head back to the hotel, I thought …" She trails off, and I nod, swiping my arm across my lips and hopping off the counter. I don't look at Maxx as I pass by, following Maxine into the foyer where Carmen and Walter Banks are waiting for me.

"Your father booked us an incredible room at a nearby B&B," my grandmother says, smiling at me. If she can tell that I was just kissed senseless in the powder room, she doesn't let on. "But we'll be in town for the summer."

"The summer?" I ask, both fearful and excited by the idea.

"The whole summer," she agrees with a smile, offering me up a hug that, when I close my eyes, transports me right back to the Catskills. It's as if I never left, as if my life were normal and easy and simple instead of … well, you know how it is. "And after we leave, Justin's promised you can call or text us as much as you want." She pulls back, and my grandfather gives me a hug next, rubbing my back in soothing circles.

Maxx slips quietly past us and outside, our eyes meeting briefly just before the doors slam shut behind him.

"We'll make chili while I'm here, okay?" Walter says, and I nod, doing my best to hold back tears as he draws back, looking up at Maxine. "Take care of your baby sister, you hear me?" he says, something I've heard many times over the years. When they first started leaving us alone to go to the grocery store, during date night, for weekend trips, and then eventually for a week or two at a time when my grandmother had to travel for work.

It hits me right in the chest when I need it most, like a shot of adrenaline to the heart.

"Always, love you fierce," Maxine agrees, giving them each a hug as well.

"Miss you and love you fierce," I add, a stray tear escaping even when I try to hold it back.

"Don't worry, honey. We'll be at the custody hearing on Friday." My grandmother raises her brows at me like she expects me to be excited about that. In a normal world, I would be. In a world where Tess was just rude and distant and controlling, and Justin was actually kind-hearted and charismatic and loving, this would be ideal.

Use the Banks against Tess in court.

Brilliant.

Except … except, I'm going to have to throw my bio mom in

front of a train. Again. When she really doesn't deserve it.

"Oh, great." I make myself smile, but it feels like a grimace. Carmen can see it; I know she can. Walter is shaking hands with Justin, so he misses the expression, but I turn away as quickly as I can, before either of them can question it.

Mostly, I can't bear to see them walk out of those doors.

If I thought things were going to get better after the dinner party guests left, I was dead wrong. Instead, Delphine is right there waiting, and I end up awkwardly sitting with both her and Maxine in my fancy new bedroom.

Pure. Unadulterated. Hell.

"Tell me a little about yourself," Maxine offers, trying to make polite conversation with my bio sister. Having gone from one to four in such a short period of time is mind-blowing.

Delphine just stares at her like she's the anti-Christ.

"I haven't decided who I am just yet," she offers up, and Maxine forces a smile. She's better at them than I am. That is, her forced smile isn't fake; it's sympathetic. "My dad says I can be or do whatever I want." Delphine shrugs her shoulders, and in that movement alone, I see so much about her all at once.

She hasn't decided who she is? Daddy says she can be anyone or do anything …

I'm definitely not bringing Delphine over to my side unless I break Justin's role of savior in her mind. Thus far, from what I know of my newest blood-related sibling, she isn't irredeemable.

Maybe, after all of this is worked out, we really could be friends?

Chasm would say I'm being too nice, but there's something about Delphine that I like despite myself.

"A refreshingly honest answer. Most people just sticker themselves with arbitrary labels." Maxie chuckles, and I smile. Delphine remains unmoved, lifting a soda to her lips, her gaze on the sinking sun on the horizon and not on either of us.

"What about you?" Delphine returns, cold but polite. She finally redirects her gaze as I shift uncomfortably on the bed, desperate to talk to my sister in private but unsure how exactly to ask Delphine to leave without causing a scene.

"Me?" Maxine grins broadly, lifting up a hand with beautifully painted nails and ticking items off. "I'm a hiking enthusiast who laughs too loudly in restaurants, enjoys focused intellectual debate, and videos about puppies because who doesn't like puppies? Seriously considered being an astronaut for a while, expert in big sistering." She winks at me, just as she always does when she mentions that last bit. Me, and our relationship, have been a part of her personality for years.

"Loyal to a fault," I add, with just the faintest kiss of bitterness. I know I shouldn't be mad at her for forgiving me, but I almost am. I want her to hate me, to yell at me, to tell me off. Because then, maybe, I could tell myself I was being punished properly. That I was getting what I deserved. What am I supposed to do with all of this?

Delphine goes incredibly still, and Maxine exchanges a look with me.

Oops.

The big sistering thing was maybe a bit much for Delphine.

She seems thoroughly invested in proving herself to both Justin and me. She *wants* a relationship like the one I have with Maxine.

"I'm going to shower," she offers, forcing a smile of her own. It's salted, like the rim of a margarita or something. She is *pissed.* "See you both in the morning." She sweeps past me and out the door, pulling it softly closed behind her.

Maxine and I wait for the sound of retreating footsteps before we turn to one another.

It's our first real moment alone all day.

"Oh, Dakota," she says, right off the bat. Maxine scoots over and puts her arms around me, drawing me close. I let her hold me for a minute—because I'm selfish like that—and then I push her gently back. "I've missed you so much, and you have so, so much happening in your life. I feel like a stranger."

I swallow hard and shake my head.

"You're not a stranger, Maxie. You're the only person who truly understands me." I can't talk about, well, any of the Justin stuff with her, so what's left? Anything else. Even boys. *Booooys. I want to do anything but talk about boys right now.* "I'm sorry you had to walk in and see me and X like that."

"He's a cool guy, right?" she says, smiling and leaning back on her palms. She looks up at the ceiling, and I follow her gaze. There are glow-in-the-dark stars being revealed as the evening rolls in, ones that I conked out too quickly to notice last night.

The stars make me think of Parrish.

Justin.

I grit my teeth, but exhale past the anger. He isn't above listening in on any conversation, certainly isn't above reminding others that he heard it in subtle or not so subtle ways.

"He ... is a cool guy," I admit, blinking at her and trying to figure out where we're going with this. Having Maxine here bolsters me; I hadn't realized how much the lack of her presence in my life was affecting me. "But why are you saying that to me? Aren't you angry? You have a *right* to be angry, you know."

She gives me one of her patented looks, and I know I'm in for some trouble here.

"I have a right to *not* be angry, too, don't I? If you fell in love with X, and he fell in love with you, then he didn't like *me* enough. I'm worth more. I deserve more. Besides." She leans forward and cups the side of my face. "I know you, Kota. You were and always will be my kid sister. You're not the type who would set out to steal my boyfriend on purpose; that isn't you."

"But you liked him?" I ask, almost like I'm pleading. I don't know why I'm doing this. Let's chalk it up to extreme stress, okay? Maxine sighs and drops her hand to her lap, shaking her head at me.

"Kota," she warns, looking back up with narrowed eyes. "Don't do that to yourself. Treat yourself with kindness, always. Above all others. If you don't put yourself first, you won't recognize when you're self-sabotaging." She nods knowingly at me. "That's what you're doing right now, trying to get me to punish you."

"I am—" I almost say *not,* but then the word doesn't come out right. She's not lying. Actually, it's the most honest thing I've had anyone say to me for months. Except for maybe *saranghae* and the like.

How did I think it meant goodnight?! What is wrong with me? I watch too many K-dramas to have missed that one. I almost facepalm, but it would be out of context, and I don't want to scare Maxine.

"I am." I reach up and start to pull pins from my hair. My sister scoots forward and digs in, until I'm sighing with relief and shaking out the green and black waves with my fingers.

"Let me get that." Maxine hops off the bed, pops into the

bathroom, and returns with a hairbrush. She sets about combing my hair for me as I flush and sit there helplessly, reverting back to baby sister Kota mode.

It's that easy, with Maxie around.

"You really didn't like him?" I ask, and she sighs, whapping me on the arm with the brush.

"I liked him, of course. If I didn't, I wouldn't allow him to—how did you put it?—*court you* as one of your *suitors*." She affects a faux French accent here that makes me snort. "Nice save, by the way, phrasing it that way for the grandparents. Not that I think they'd care, but they might worry you were being pressured or something."

My mouth opens to spit out the truth—I was pressured but not by the boys, by Justin—but I can't say anything. Instead, I go for as much honesty as I can manage.

"They never pressured me into anything. You know I'd never be with a guy who'd treat me that way. They're all just kind of awesome?" I phrase it like a question and then shake my head. Maxine tsks when the hairbrush pulls because of the motion, and I stop moving. "Parrish was first; I fell hard for him. When he was missing, X and Chasm were there for me."

"I'm sorry that I couldn't be," Maxie whispers, leaning down and putting her chin on my shoulder. "That woman …"

"It's more than that," I explain, feeling this perturbing but insistent need to defend Tess. After all, she lost her house. She almost lost four of her kids, her husband. Because of Justin and all this, she's being sued by her own publishing company for the audacity of wanting to take a break, for taking my feelings into account. It's a lot. I'm not saying the woman and I are suddenly going to be best friends, but she didn't totally panic when she found me with Chasm and Parrish. "It was more than that, but I'm glad you're here."

"Me, too," Maxine agrees, giving me a tight hug and returning the brush to my hair.

We don't bring up boys again for the rest of the night which I'm thankful for.

But that doesn't mean I'm not thinking about them.

Oh no.

Pretty much the exact opposite of that.

Maxine sleeps in my room, sharing the king bed with me. We leave the windows open, listening to the shush and whisper of the lake. It's nice, and it's warm enough that we sleep easily through the night without needing to close them.

Breakfast is an, um, interesting affair, what with Parrish's bio mom Caroline present, Delphine on my right, Maxie on my left … and Justin. He takes the spot opposite me, buttering a croissant as he looks my way with feigned sympathy.

"I'm sorry you have to go back to your mom's today," he tells me, leaning over and plopping the warm pastry on my plate. There's a not-so-subtle look on his face that tells me I better damn well eat it.

I comply. It's the least horrid capitulation I've had to make thus far.

"We'll take care of that at the hearing, I'm sure." Justin lifts his coffee to his lips as Delphine sits up a little straighter in her chair.

"You're going for full custody, right?" she asks eagerly, and I shiver all over, goose bumps springing up on my arms. Maxine goes still, her own croissant halfway to her lips. She pauses there, staring at my arm and then lifting her gaze up to mine. Whatever she sees there causes her to brush off the feeling and take a bite of her food. I almost breathe a sigh of relief.

"As much as I dislike that woman, that seems a bit harsh, if you don't mind my saying so." Knowing Maxine as I do, I know that she actually doesn't care if Justin or anyone else minds, but she has her ways. Feigning politeness in the beginning of any argument is one of them.

If Justin's bothered by her commentary, he doesn't let on. It's so weird, sitting here with the biological father I've always been curious about. Now, Saffron made on that he was some one-night stand, but I'd always wondered about my sperm donor. Now that I'm here with him I can't help but wish I still had those dreams left instead of the harsh, cold glare of reality.

"Tess has been through a lot lately, what with the fire and all." Justin sips his drink, blue eyes focused on his phone screen as he draws it from his pocket. "I could never take her child away from her completely—not even if she's the one who lost the baby in the first place."

Maxine pauses again, looking over at Justin before narrowing her eyes slightly. I glance her way and force a smile that feels like it's being torn from my mouth like a bloody tooth in a dentist's pliers. Even more specifically, like the crazy dentist from the 1986 movie, *Little Shop of Horrors*. That's how fucking bad it hurts.

"Fifty-fifty custody seems fair enough," I suggest, turning back to Justin as Caroline studies me like a test subject and Delphine frowns.

"I've been cleaning that woman's house for a while now. Trust me: taking full custody from her would be a blessing." Delphine pushes her own plate away and looks to Justin for confirmation. "What's your plan?"

"My plan? I don't have a plan." He sips his coffee some more, casual and relaxed in a pale pink dress shirt with the sleeves rolled up, half-buttoned and flashing some chest. He's very swanky, this serial killer tech bro. "I'm simply going to present my case and let the beauty of democracy do its work." He sets his coffee on the table as I struggle not to succumb to hysterical laughter.

The beauty of democracy, eh? That is, utilize his personal connections with the judge to get what he wants out of this. Full custody seems too simple, too neat for a monster such as this.

"Sir." A man pauses in the doorway between the solarium and the foyer. "Mrs. Vanguard has arrived."

I feel my heart clench in my chest, my stomach turning over with nausea.

Of all the ways this moment might go, I don't imagine that any of them will be good.

"Ah." Justin rises to his feet, adjusts the collar of his shirt, and heads for the front door. Caroline doesn't move from her spot, lounging in the sun, but Delphine stands up as well.

Right.

Tess doesn't know about Delphine. I'm sure she's about to find out.

Maxine and I exchange a look, and she ends up following me into the massive foyer where Tess and Parrish both are waiting. Frankly, it's a testament to his silver tongue that he was able to talk his way into coming here.

Tess doesn't seem to know where to look. Well, first, she stares at me, raking her eyes over me from head to toe as if to make sure that I'm still okay, that I'm safe. The brief flicker of franticness there reminds me how traumatized this poor woman really is.

And also, how much worse it's all about to get.

Her attention moves to Maxine next, but surprisingly doesn't linger. Instead, she's staring at my shiny new bio sister.

"Delphine?" she asks, blinking past her surprise. "You work for Justin now?" Tess' eyes narrow to slits and she crosses her arms. "Why am I not at all surprised?"

"Actually," Justin begins, putting his arm around Delphine's shoulders in a fatherly sort of way. He pulls her close as Tess does her best not to gape and fails miserably.

"What on earth …?" she starts as my eyes meet Parrish's. He appears resolute, single-minded, but in a way that makes me feel like the only girl on the entire planet. In the entire galaxy. The only girl that's ever existed.

"Everything is bullshit. You're the only real thing that I have."

"Delphine and I were recently reunited as father and daughter," Justin explains, smiling lovingly down at the Vanguard's former maid. He reaches out and strokes her cheek, and she warms like a flower facing the sun.

"Excuse me." This time, it's not even a question. Tess moves across the floor in Valentino open-toe platform pumps. Right on schedule with the trends, this woman. I feel a similar inclination to be awed by her the way I am with Justin. Whereas it's his kidnapping and death threats that put me off, it's Tess' attitude.

"Lena's daughter." Justin winks at Tess, as if that should mean something to her. Apparently, it does.

"You're Lena Shaw's daughter?" Tess breathes, looking at Delphine and then back at Justin. Parrish moves subtly toward me, and I do the same, until we're nearly touching.

"You look like a doll," he whispers, and I can't decide if he means that in a good way or a really bad one. "Pretty, but not like yourself." That's what he adds, and he isn't wrong.

I didn't choose my clothes this morning, this fairy-tale princess strawberry dress that went viral last summer. It's a real one, too, not a knock-off, a five-hundred-dollar summer frock. It's not my style in the least.

Add in the shoes, the makeup, the fancy hairdo (all gifted by Delphine's clever fingers) and I most certainly do not look like the Dakota Banks who waltzes around in overalls with a strap undone, a loose half-tee with a PlayStation logo on it, and mismatched sneakers.

"Not just Lena's daughter—my own. We were lucky enough to find each other when I was on my search for Dakota. DNA doesn't lie, Tess. As you well know." He gestures toward my bio mom, once again throwing her own ideas back in her face like a grenade.

"And you're Maxine," Tess states, turning away from Delphine and Justin like she's unaffected by the entire conversation. That's about as far from the truth as one could possibly get; I can see it written all over her face.

"Nice to see you again, Mrs. Vanguard." Maxine smiles politely, but I can see that she's struggling to maintain such pleasant social niceties. After all, the last time she saw Tess, it was outside the coffeehouse in the pouring rain.

Tess sighs heavily, but at least she doesn't blow my sister off completely.

"It's nice to see you, too." Tess' eyes catch on me and Parrish and our socially unacceptable proximity (like, who stands with their shoulder touching someone else's like this unless they're in love?). "I hear your grandparents are also in town?"

"For the summer," Maxine agrees, and Justin chuckles.

"I'd have told you, but I read over your agreement with the Banks. No contact with our beautiful Dakota for an entire year? Doesn't that seem unnecessarily cruel, Tess?" He clucks his tongue, dropping his arm from Delphine's shoulders. "Besides, with the fire and all, I didn't feel right bringing it up."

"You son of a bitch." Tess narrows her eyes on him, nostrils flared in anger. She feels like she's the only person in the world who can see beneath his charming exterior to the monster underneath. On the inside, I'm screaming; I'm taking her hands and looking her in the eyes the way she did the night she confessed that Justin raped her, and I'm telling her in no uncertain terms that I believe her, too, that she isn't crazy.

But only on the inside.

On the out, I'm frozen. A statue. A fancy piece of art, wrapped in a glass box and up-lit on its pretty stand near the staircase like the vase I see there now.

"Son of a bitch?" Justin asks, crinkling his brow in mock confusion. He pauses at the sound of heels, glancing back to see Caroline striding into the room. Parrish's eyes go straight to her and stick there. He did an admirable job last night of pretending like his mother wasn't present at the dinner party, that he didn't notice that she didn't care if he was there or not, like he was any other guest.

But I've spent enough time in Parrish Vanguard 101 to see the tiny cracks in his handsome face. He's aching, and he's angry, and every time he looks at her, that pain intensifies just a little bit more.

"Yes. Son of a bitch. I'd call you worse things if we weren't in the presence of minors." And here, Tess gives a harsh and wild laugh, reaching up to run her fingers through her hair. "Or if I didn't think you were secretly filming it in order to use it against me in court." She turns to me suddenly, ignoring Caroline entirely.

"Have you had a chance to check on the house yet?" Caroline asks innocently, but Tess pays her zero attention.

"Are you ready to go? Do you need to grab anything?" she asks, but before I can answer, she turns her attention to Maxine. "Would you like to come with us? At least for the day. I can take you back to wherever you're staying this evening."

"Oh, I'd love that," Maxine blurts as quickly as she can, as if to catch the offer before it disappears. I'm shocked as hell, but happy. Also, not entirely sure this isn't a ploy on Tess' part. Anyway, it's better than leaving my sister with Justin.

"I'll see you on Wednesday," he says, smiling brightly at me. "For lunch." He offers up a little wave as Parrish grabs my hand

and hauls me over to the doors.

Tess doesn't say a word—maybe she doesn't even breathe—until we're in her Mercedes and driving through the gate that I once climbed over in a pretty pink princess dress and borrowed sneakers.

Parrish sits in the front, so that I can sit beside Maxine in the back, but I can see that he'd much rather be here with me. He keeps turning around to look, and our gazes catch and hold.

"That … scum-sucking …" Tess grits her teeth, fingers curled around the wheel.

"Let it out, Mom. Don't hold back. Call him what you really want to call him: a cocksucking, motherfucking bitch-bastard with a shark smile and a personality as rank and distasteful as a Discord mod or a Reddit admin. Just say it."

"Parrish," she breathes, as if she's pretending to chastise his language. Instead, I see her shoulders relax a little. "He's a charlatan, that's what he is. He could sell lumber to a tree." She scoffs at that, and I almost smile.

Or, I would, if I didn't think Justin was watching right now. Listening in, at the very least.

Tess pauses, seemingly remembering that she just invited the sister she previously banished me from seeing into her car.

"I'm sorry, Maxine. Old hurts and all that." Tess looks into the rearview and smiles at the pair of us. "Also, I apologize in advance. We don't have a particularly exciting day ahead of us."

"We're going to the house for the first time," Parrish explains, turning around in his seat to look at me. That causes Tess to tense up a bit, but I'm guessing she won't be mentioning the threesome thing around Maxine. I haven't exactly mentioned it to her either, but not because I won't. We've just had so much to catch up on; it's overwhelming.

"How bad is it?" I ask, wishing I could tear this stupid

strawberry dress off, rip the pins from my hair, and don a *Legend of Zelda* sweatshirt or something. Clothes don't make a person, not by a long shot, but we should at least have the free will to pick out what we want to wear.

"We're about to find out," Tess explains, sighing yet again. "How was the party last night?" Her voice goes a bit icy, but I don't think it's on my account, so it doesn't bother me.

"I'm sure Parrish told you: stuffy, awkward. The only highlight was being able to see my family." The words come out before I can rethink them, and Tess' hands tighten even further on the wheel.

She doesn't ask anything else, and I end up sitting there, kicking myself for the short drive back to the house. The reporters are back, but we ignore them, rolling through the crowd and up the drive.

The side of the house closest to the garage appears to be in the worst shape, whereas the hall where both my bedroom and Parrish's are doesn't seem to be affected much.

From the outside, that is.

I'm sure it's not very pretty on the inside.

Even smoke damage from a small fire can be devastating, and this was a goddamn blaze. My heart seizes again, both in fearful relief of what might've happened yet didn't, but also out of love for Maxim Wright.

He saved the entire Vanguard family.

"Thank you, Maxx," Tess whispers, her throat getting clogged. At first, it seems like she's just following the same train of thought that I am. But then I see him, him and Chasm. They're waiting near the front door with Paul and Kimber. I don't see Ben, Amelia, or Henry, but I imagine they're probably with Laverne.

Tess parks the car, and we climb out together. Maxine grabs my hand straight off, squeezing hard. I explained to her last night what happened, how I was at prom with Parrish and Chasm, how we got the call, what Maxx did for the family.

"Have you been inside yet?" Tess asks, but Paul shakes his head, adjusting his glasses. His gaze is on Parrish, and I wonder if he's thinking about Caroline right about now.

"We were waiting for you," he explains as Kimber's gaze drifts over to Maxine and sticks there.

"What are you doing here?" she blurts out, blinking in surprise. She must recognize Maxine from social media or something, maybe even from the family photo in my room. The two have never met.

"You must be Kimber; I'm Maxine." My sister offers up a pretty smile, and Kimber scoffs.

"What? Are we adopting another one?" she snipes and receives the equivalent of a backhand in the form of a sharp and violent glare from Tess.

"Do not even start on this today," Tess warns her, moving up to open the front door. Before we head inside, she passes out booties for our shoes and masks for our faces. She wrinkles her nose just before she slips one on and then steps into the formerly white-on-white-on-white space. Only now it's pretty much black-on-black-on-black.

Also, it smells like a charcoal barbeque was just thrown in our faces.

"I can't believe you ran back in there so many times," Maxine says to X, and he shrugs, sliding his hands into the pockets of these black *Wright Family Racing* pants that I like the look of; they cup his perky butt quite nicely. I cough to clear the thought as Chasm raises a brow at me.

"Overachiever," he murmurs, and X smirks.

"It's not something remarkable, what I did. It's the least of what's expected of anyone who claims to be human." He smiles and moves into the house, the rest of us following with Kimber in the very back.

I can *feel* her glare like it's a physical thing, but I ignore it, moving into the foyer and looking up at a literal hole in the ceiling. Water drip-drip-drips, hitting the only white spot on the marble floor where it's cleared away the soot.

"The fire restoration people will be here in an hour. If it's marked with yellow tape, don't cross it." Tess sighs and moves forward, toward the living room.

Parrish and I go for the stairs, my sisters and the other boys in tow.

"My clothes are probably ruined," Kimber whimpers, sniffling and then coughing against the harshness of the smell. Before I head up the steps, I look over to see the framed birth certificate on the wall, the one with the cracked and ruined glass in the soot-soaked frame. There's nothing left of the actual certificate; it was incinerated by the heat.

I have a feeling it wasn't my real birth certificate anyway. Because on that one, the space for *Father* was left blank. Tess knew who my father was, and at the time, they were a couple; he'd have been listed surely.

This certificate, it was for her and her alone.

With a sigh, I follow Parrish up the stairs, accidentally putting my hands on the banister and coming away with them covered in soot. The strawberry dress will be ruined before we even make it out the door.

Part of me is glad about that.

"Fucking Christ," Chasm murmurs, studying the cracked glass of the pictures on the wall. He looks to the right, down the hall toward Tess' office, the Vanguards' bedroom, and the rooms where Kimber, Ben, and Amelia and Henry sleep.

That seems to be where the fire started; there's a line of yellow tape blocking off that entire hallway.

"I can't even get to my room!" Kimber cries, pausing with her hands on the tape and staring down the hall. Chasm hesitates beside her for a minute, curses, and then hops over it, turning to point at her.

"I'll take a video, but only if you promise not to move from this spot." He turns, heading down the hallway and making me nervous as fuck.

"Please be careful!" I call out, biting my lip and waiting for him to return. He does, passing his phone to Kimber without a word. She ends up leaning against the wall, heedless of the soot smearing onto her clothes and stares at the screen with tears streaming down her face.

She turns away sharply, as if she can't bear to look at any of us.

"The fire was raging all through Tess' office," Maxx explains, gesturing in that general direction. "By the time I got the little kids out and came back for Kimber, it was in the hallway, too." He shudders and shakes his head, turning and walking down the hall to my bedroom.

With a deep inhale, Maxx tries the knob and then pauses before shoving the door in. I move up behind him and peer around his large shoulders to the room beyond.

Everything is black.

Fucking everything.

Walls, floor, ceiling. My bed looks almost shiny with soot, the family photo on the wall warped from the heat and smoke. The windows looking over Lake Washington are etched and foggy, allowing in a hazy sunlight that bathes the destruction in an ethereal glow.

I run my fingers across the footboard of my bed, the one my grandmother made for me, wiping away soot. If it's possible to clean it off, we might be able to save the furniture.

ENDGAME ROMANCE

The rest of the items … I watch as Maxx pulls one of Saffron's Harry Potter books from the shelf, the cover warped, the pages ashy and wrinkled. *I'm sorry, JK!* I think with a bit of a cringe. More than that, I've just lost an important childhood memento, a gift freely given from Saffron to me, whether or not she ever thought of me as a daughter.

Our last conversation drifts through my mind like a whisper.

"Tess Vanguard doesn't care about you, Dakota. Only I do. I'm your real mother."

Not only that, but Saffron mentioned Justin, as if she somehow knew about him. How? It's a mystery I've yet to figure out.

"It could be worse," Chasm offers up, which isn't much placation, but he's also right. We might be arranging funerals today instead of lamenting lost items. Not that I'm not upset, I really am. My heart aches, especially when I think about Kimber crying in the hallway, but it's also a good reminder that the people we love matter most.

Items can be replaced. Even if they can't, they're still not living, breathing entities. Life is always more important than stuff. GG, the rabbit included.

"Did you hear that he came back in for our pet bunny, too?" Chasm is saying, as if he can read my mind. He looks over at Maxine, and I see her jaw drop as she stares at X. There's a flicker of something there before she shakes her head.

"Holy crap, XY. That's impressive."

"XY?" Chasm asks, sounding out the letters, *ex-why*. "Is that a nickname or something?"

Maxine chuckles and X groans, rubbing both hands down his face.

"Like Maxie, except he can't be Maxie because I'm Maxie." She snorts and shakes her head. "So I started calling him X-ie, and then it morphed to XY because boys have XY chromosomes and girls have XX chromosomes ..." My sister trails off, as prone to blurting out stories as I am.

"XY, huh?" I ask, and Maxx turns a look on me that's half-sympathetic, half-warning. *Don't read too much into this,* he's telling me, but I'm not. I won't. I've put Maxine through enough already. "I like it."

"It's all yours," Maxine says with a soft smile, watching as Parrish and Chasm head into the former's bedroom. I follow along after them, the two Max's crowding in behind us.

The bed where Parrish and I had our first time is as sooty and shiny as my own, the blankets covered in a thick layer of ash. He picks up one of his art books, finding pages stuck together, the pastels or colored pencils he used to create his art melted and distorted. It's not entirely unsalvageable, but it's not good either.

All of our electronics are probably fried.

In fact ... this might be the safest possible place to talk. That is, unless Justin or one of his goons—like that snot-nosed Raúl—came in and put hidden cams and mics around the place.

"Allow me." All three of these boys are mind readers apparently. Maxx slides a bug detector from his back pocket. It looks the same as the one we used before, but it could be a new one. He notices me looking and explains. "I got it at Best Buy on our way over here." X uses it to scan the room, peers out to check on Kimber, and then closes the door.

If I'm going to tell Maxine anything, it's going to be right here, right now.

"What is that?" she asks, wrinkling her nose as Parrish sighs and tries his best to open the window on the far wall. It's stuck at first, but eventually he gets it up with a grunt, releasing a cloud of charcoal smoke in the air that makes the rest of us cough. We pull up our masks and wait for it to clear before yanking them back down again.

"It's a bug detector," I explain, heart racing. "It searches for signals from hidden cameras or mics."

"Why would you ..." she starts, cocking her head slightly to one side. I've genuinely stumped my sister on this one.

"You've heard of the Milk Carton app, right?" It's a leading question, but I have to tell Maxine something. I certainly can't tell her that Justin is slaughtering teens, but plenty of parents spy on their kids and they don't murder people. This is a plausible, feasible reason for me to dislike and distrust Justin that Maxine can understand and process.

After all, Tess put spyware on my phone, too.

Revealing *just* enough of the truth can only help; if Maxine is wary around Justin, all the better.

"Justin's face recognition thing?" Maxie queries, rubbing at the back of her neck. "What about it?"

I give her a look.

"*Track anyone, anytime, anywhere. All in the palm of your hand.*" I quote the press conference because I know that Maxine will have seen it. Even when I was ignoring her, pushing her away, treating her like shit, she'd have searched out any chance at a connection with me.

Her eyes widen in horrified understanding.

"He'd really put cameras or mics in here?" she wonders, and I nod. "I knew something was going on with Justin! He's been spying on you?" Maxine's voice is thick with righteous anger, and she only knows a very small portion of what's happening. "Is there something you want to tell me about him?"

"He's been spying," I agree, looking over at Chasm and Parrish, back toward ... XY. It's a pretty funny nickname, actually, but it also makes me feel like shit. They really had a cute thing going, didn't they? "More than that. He's ... I don't like him."

Maxine blinks at me in surprise before looking over at the

boys. She's perceptive, too perceptive honestly.

"You all know something I don't."

"Many somethings, actually," Parrish agrees lackadaisically, waving an inked hand around. "But there's only one that's truly important: don't trust Justin Prior for shit." He moves past us and opens the door just in time for us to hear Tess and Paul coming up the stairs.

The latter pauses to comfort his daughter, promising to buy her a whole new wardrobe while Tess looks toward her ruined office and then glances back to see the rest of us crowding into the hallway.

"It's going to take some time to make the place livable again." She sighs heavily. "Let's clean up, get something to eat, and we can start looking at places to stay in the interim."

"Grandma said we could stay with her if we wanted," Kimber offers up, but the sour look on Tess' face tells me that is most certainly *not* an option.

In the end, we leave the house just as the crew Tess hired shows up. As she goes about discussing arrangements with them, the mail is also delivered. The post-lady doesn't seem to know what to do with it, so I accept a package and a stack of letters so she can be on her way.

The package is for Tess; one of the letters is for me.

I hand the other items over to Parrish, so that I can open the letter. At about the same time, Tess grabs her package and frowns at it. Using a small letter opener on her key ring, she cuts through the tape at the same moment I unfold the letter.

I'm here now, don't worry. Tell your sister I love you both. Miss you and love you fierce.

Um. Right. In all the chaos, I'd forgotten the unmarked, unsigned letter I received just before prom. Once again, I can only assume it's from Saffron.

ENDGAME ROMANCE

She's here? Like here-here, as in Medina. I look up, as if I might be able to see her standing at the edge of the property or something. Clearly, Justin is looking for her, too, or he wouldn't have asked.

I fold the paper up quickly and tuck it under the neckline of my dress, hoping that Tess won't have noticed. More importantly, *Justin.* Our phones are in the car, and while the electricity to the house has been shut off temporarily, that doesn't mean Justin didn't leave any cameras out here.

The boys saw though, as did Maxine. Kimber, too, unfortunately.

My gamer ass is saved by the contents of the package as Tess lifts the padding and reveals the typewriter she ordered, the one that's supposed to be a replacement for the one that I destroyed. That is, it's the third incarnation of Tess' dream to write on the same sort of typewriter that her grandmother—my great-grandmother—once used.

A silence settles over the group as we all stare down at it. There's no office to put it in anymore, and I do hope that Tess was smart and scanned her working manuscripts into the cloud.

She heaves a deep sigh and closes her eyes for a moment, allowing Paul to put his arm around her as we all wait to see her reaction.

"You know what?" she begins, opening her eyes up and smiling at me. It takes great effort, I can see that, but at least she's trying. "I'm not going to let this upset me. I'm going to take it as a sign." Tess closes the box back up and stands straight. "This is a fresh start. I'm going to work on my fiction novels and focus on my family, and we can all start anew together."

She hefts the box up and carries it to the car herself, platform heels and all.

"Maybe I don't hate her as much as I thought," Maxine muses, and Parrish gives her a look.

"Tess has her faults, but she's good on the inside. Most people in this town are the literal opposite."

He isn't wrong about that one, now is he?

This town is straight cursed.

CHAPTER 12

Tess drops Maxine off at the bed and breakfast where my grandparents are staying. She doesn't wait around to actually see or talk to them though, but I can't expect change overnight. She's doing better than ever before, and far better than I expected after finding out about Parrish and me.

"I have a feeling she's going to have a private talk with us tonight," he whispers as we climb out of the car and he passes by me, *grabbing my ass* in the process. He literally cups it and squeezes, right there in front of Tess. Fortunately, her attention is occupied as she hauls the typewriter out of the trunk.

I'm sure that was the point, but I still sprint after him and punch him in the arm. He smirks at me as he glances over, reaching up to rub at the sore spot.

"Ouch, Gamer Girl. Ouch, ouch, ouch." He chuckles as Paul and Kimber pull up behind us. At the very least, it appears they don't know about me and Parrish being a couple, the threesome, or anything else. We'll have to tell them eventually, but I'd like a space in which to breathe, please and thank you.

"Please stay downstairs," Tess calls out cheerfully, much more so than I'd expect after the day we've had. After we left the house, we toured several others. There are quite literally only six houses for sale in Medina, ranging from five million dollars to *forty* million dollars.

Are the houses nice? Sure. But the inflated prices because of the zip code, that's ridiculous. What a load of crap. As for rent? There are six places nearby, the cheapest four bedroom was eight thousand dollars a month. Like, is that even real? Who can afford that?!

Tess, apparently. Paul Vanguard.

But she didn't like any of them. I mean, we *all* liked the forty million dollar one, but Tess shook her head at the price and walked away muttering about not relying on Laverne for anything. I'm guessing that one isn't affordable without the help of the family matriarch.

Chasm and Maxx headed back after the last showing, driving an entirely different car than I've ever seen. Apparently, Seamus bought his son a new one after finding out the one in the garage at the Vanguard's house won't be drivable for some time until the repairs are completed; the interior is completely smoke damaged.

Anyway, Chas was zipping around in a yellow Porsche (it matches his hair), but he left with Maxx, and now I'm feeling like I already miss them both.

"Crazy girl," I mutter under my breath and Parrish pauses to glance over at me, hooking a sharp and impossible smile. It draws me in like the silver glitter of a fishing lure in the moonlight. *Fuck, that's pretty but also* … I'll probably die. And I don't care. "I am not a fish."

"A what?" Parrish asks, and then a laugh escapes him. It's bright and bubbly, and he slaps a hand over his mouth as Kimber stops to gape at him.

"What the hell?" she whispers, curling her lip up and staring at her brother in sheer horror. "Who *are* you? Did you just giggle?"

"I've never giggled in all of my life," he hisses back at her, dropping his hand just in time to affect an imperious swagger. Parrish smirks again, but it's entirely lacking in flirtation this time, so it just looks like a plain fishhook, rusted and covered in worm guts and all that. So not impressive. *Liar.*

Really though, he looks mean AF.

"Now, get out of my face. You're getting a pass on the bullshit you pulled while I was gone because of the fire, but don't think that extends to further sympathy."

"You're a stupid fallen prince prick," Kimber shoots right back at him, throwing a smirk of her own on her pretty face. The longer I'm here, the more things start to make sense to me. Maxine and I might not have a relationship like this, but this quipping back and forth is Parrish's and Kimber's way of playing with each other. It's actually, almost, a little bit cute. "You're Whitehall's biggest disgrace now, you know that? Everyone thinks it; it's all over social media."

"I could literally give a *fuck* about social media," Parrish breathes, taking a step toward his sister and staring down at her. "You're right: I'm not the prince of Whitehall Prep. I am the fucking *king.* You'd best start remembering that and fall in line, or you're going to seriously regret the entirety of my senior year."

He sweeps past her as she gapes at him. Did I say cute? I meant disturbing.

With a huff, I slip past Kimber and follow Parrish into the living room. Our three youngest siblings are there, entertained with various brand-new electronics. Well, Amelia and Henry are anyway, fussing with their iPads. Ben is reading a book, but he at least looks up and smiles at me.

"Hi, Dakota." He turns back to his page, but I'm smiling anyway. At least I'm being acknowledged.

"No greeting for me?" Parrish asks, and Ben ignores him, turning the page with rapt attention. Parrish sighs and moves past me, toward the stairs that lead down to the game room.

"I said downstairs," Tess calls out, leaning around the corner to peer at us with barely disguised suspicion.

"This *is* downstairs," Parrish posits indignantly, pointing toward the game room.

"This floor." Tess turns away as if that's the final word on it, and Parrish sighs. What? Does she think we're going to run downstairs and rut against the vintage Ms. Pac-Man machine like wild beasts? Oh, that would be nice though, wouldn't it? I'm not totally opposed, but Tess needs to relax.

"Damn it, I was going to fuck you down there," Parrish mumbles, and I shove him in the back. Not to actually hurt him or anything, but more like a nervous reflex. He ends up tripping on the stairs, and even though they're carpeted, and there are only six of them, he falls and lands right on his ass.

I clamp both hands over my mouth, staring down at him as he peers up at me in shock.

"Did you just shove me down the stairs?" he breathes, pushing up to his feet and rubbing at his ass. "Savage. You low-key tried to kill me. I knew you were evil." He comes up the steps to stand beside me as I glance back, relieved to see that none of the kids noticed.

This is all brand-new really, being alone with Parrish like this after everything that happened. This is old-school Parrish versus Dakota, like it's February all over again. We might be in Laverne's house now, and the core of our relationship might've changed, but it's still the same.

"Love-hate, remember?" I ask, even though I'm horrified that I actually could've hurt him. I cock a brow anyway and pretend to be cool when the entire world could see with a glance that I'm anything but. Not in a good way. Some people just don't have that … that Parrish-y swagger.

"Love-hate?" He scoffs. "Sure." Parrish leans down and kisses my lips. I expect it to be a short, simple kiss at best, one that nobody will notice or see. Only … only … he cups the back of my head and pushes in closer, slipping his tongue between my lips and claiming me right then and there.

In front of the *entire fucking family.*

"Oh my God." That's Paul, choking, probably that slamming sound is his back hitting the wall as he stumbles in shock. There's a shriek that's distinctly Kimber, but still, Parrish doesn't stop. He kisses me and then sighs happily against my lips, standing up straight.

I am far too terrified to turn around.

"Did you just kiss her?" Kimber asks, and Parrish very casually looks up to stare at her.

"We started kissing before I went missing. Why would I stop now? I almost died. I'm not going to hold back on the things I want to do. Deal with it."

"Parrish Vanguard," Tess hisses, and then I do it. I finally turn to find her seething and rubbing at her forehead with two fingers. "Come here—*now.*" To her credit, she keeps her voice low, but that doesn't stop me from spotting Laverne's look of grief-stricken horror from across the room.

Guess she didn't notice our kiss at the dinner party?

Whelp. This should do wonders for my blossoming relationship with Laverne. Probably make her like Tess a whole hell of a lot more, too.

Obviously not.

Parrish and I both end up sitting in chairs in the backyard, Tess,

Paul, and Laverne standing before us. To his credit, Parrish is leaning back in his chair, arms crossed over his Whitehall prep hoodie. He looks cool and untouchable, unperturbed yet dangerous.

"What?" he asks as Laverne gapes and Paul sputters and Tess looks like she wants to dig a hole in the yard either to bury us or herself, I'm not sure.

"What?" Laverne repeats, stepping forward and trying to take control of the situation. "You just kissed your sister on the mouth."

"Not my sister," Parrish says with a long sigh, glancing over at me with eyes like honeyed almonds. They're delectable, and so is he, but that's going to get me in serious trouble if I keep obsessing over how pretty he is. "A girl that I met four months ago for the very first time that shares no blood with me."

"Except for four siblings," Laverne corrects with scandal and horror dripping from each word. Parrish sighs again, standing up. I do the same, wondering if I should speak up or if I'll only make things worse.

"There's no reason we can't be together," I state, looking to Tess for support. On the positive side, Laverne's interference seems to have annoyed her enough that she looks like she'd disagree with just about anything the woman said in order to spite her. "We're not hurting anybody."

"This is …" Paul starts, but then he just trails off, like he has no idea what to say. I can tell he resents me a little, but that he wants more than anything for Tess to be happy. I can't say that I'm not bothered by it, but he's not an entirely terrible person either. Clearly, he loves his wife. "Did you know about this?" he asks, looking to Tess as Laverne stares right past Parrish and over at me.

There's something resolute in her face that scares me.

Why was she at Justin's dinner party? Is she a target or an accomplice?

Either way, this doesn't bode well for me.

As I'm standing there and staring at Laverne Vanguard, the multibillionaire bitch who insulted me at the vacation house in Bend, I'm wondering whether she's a pawn or a queen.

Then she turns away and takes off and *that* is when I know I'm in deep shit.

She's an accomplice; I'd bet my life on it. Or, at the very last, all of my gaming skills, the ones that got my subscriber count on YouTube up to six digits. I look back over at Tess.

"I found out during prom," she explains, and I wonder if she isn't going to mention the threesome.

She doesn't.

"Are you okay with this?" Paul asks her, turning to stare at his son. Tess watches her husband for a minute before switching her attention to us.

"I don't know what to do here, to be honest with you," she explains. I appreciate her candor actually. Why do Tess and I always have to make progress right before Justin rat-fucks her with me as his pawn? Because, much as I think we're two players facing each other across a single board, he sees me as one of his own pieces.

By playing with me, teaching me strategies and all that, he's amusing himself. It's not for me, not at all. Whenever I forget that, I just need to recall the pleasure on his face at seeing my pain. That was a telltale sign right here.

He tried to kill my siblings. He kidnapped my first love. He's always watching.

Always.

I flick my gaze up to the camera on the side of Laverne's house. By the looks of it, it appears to be a Google Nest Cam. There is no fucking doubt in my mind that Milk Carton can see right through it, that my face has already been recognized.

Because that's what Milk Carton does: the technology seeks out camera signals, and essentially hacks into them—whether the person who owns the camera wants it to or not. How any of this is legal, I'm not sure. Likely, it doesn't matter. Justin will just bribe whoever he has to in order to make things work.

I turn back to Tess.

"I know you wanted us to agree not to see each other anymore," I start, and Tess' face flushes slightly as Paul frowns and adjusts his glasses with a single finger. "But I can't agree to that. I won't lie to you."

"We could agree not to have sex in the house," Parrish offers up, and this time, it's Paul who turns bright red.

"Or outside of it?" Tess shoots back, raising a brow. "Or at all?"

Parrish purses his pillow-y lips into a flat line.

"We'll use birth control; there's no need to worry. Obviously, since we were virgins, there's no diseases to worry about."

"I cannot listen to this," Tess mutters, turning away and then turning back again just as quickly. She looks at the pair of us helplessly, as both my mother and his, two sides of her warring. Her stolen child and her other stolen child, one that she birthed, one that she knows much better. "Let me think for a second."

I wonder, if Justin weren't in the picture, would her reaction be different? Would she really have sent me back to New York with the Banks? But no, now that I'm seeing her reaction in real time, I don't believe that.

Tess sighs again, and I can see that she's really struggling against her baser instincts here. This, this is her trying.

"Please be respectful of the small things that I ask: doors left open when I say, discretion in public and around your siblings, and an understanding that this is not an endorsement or an acceptance. I'm simply at a loss." She lifts both hands, palms up. "There are no parenting books on how to deal with this." Tess drops her arms and looks over at Paul. "What do you think?"

"I … Whatever you think is best," he finally agrees, but he's staring at his son with an odd expression, like he's still processing that he almost lost him. Or maybe also that he might've died on Friday night. All of it.

"See?" Parrish whispers, turning and heading into the house.

After a small moment of hesitation, I follow.

Kimber is waiting for us, her face torn apart by shock.

"All this, after you stole Chasm from me," she accuses, but she isn't looking at me. Instead, she's focused on her brother.

"They're still dating." He pauses beside her and slips his hands into the front pocket of his hoodie. "If you put this on social media, you're dead. Oh, and I wouldn't deny it either; it'll only make us more popular, not less." He continues on, and I follow after him, skirting a wide berth around Kimber and happy to see that the three youngest kids couldn't care less. Maybe they didn't even notice?

"Fuck you both," Kimber snaps out, but Parrish doesn't pay her any attention, taking off up the stairs. I continue after him, but I swear that I can feel Tess watching us as she slips in the back doors with Paul at her heels.

No doubt she'll be hovering all night.

"That went well?" It's a question, one that I pose in a quiet whisper as Parrish leads me to the very same room where he and Chas and I … did stuff. Ahem.

"Stop living fearfully, Dakota," Parrish says, leaving the door open as he moves into the room and flops onto the couch. He does it with grace, too. That's a skill most people just don't possess, the ability to gracefully flop. It's an innate talent, I'm sure. "Live fearlessly." He leans his head back against the sofa cushions as I perch on the edge of the bed. "This is your room, by the way."

"This one?" I ask, peering around at the generously sized suite and its massive bathroom. "Where are you sleeping?"

Parrish smiles without lifting his head.

"My grandmother put you downstairs next to her master suite; I swapped us."

"Why would she put me so close to her?" I ask, and he lifts his head up, slowly cracking his lids to stare at me.

"She's up Justin's ass, Dakota," he says, but I already figured that out. "Laverne ponied up millions to fund Milk Carton; she's Justin's angel investor."

My mouth must be hanging open because Parrish pushes up smoothly from the leather sofa seat and taps me under the chin with a single finger, leaning in so that our faces are disturbingly close together.

"What's an angel investor?" I whisper as his eyes drift to my mouth, and I can't decide whether the half of me that's more concerned with his warmth or the half that's terrified by what he's just said is more important.

"A grotesquely wealthy person who donates to a start-up in exchange for equity or partial ownership," he murmurs, and even though that's probably one of the driest, least sexy sentences in the universe, it transforms into a come-on when breathed past those pearly lips of his.

Parrish stands up and turns away, moving over to the sound system remote that's sitting on a nearby dresser. Right on schedule, Tess appears in the doorway, looking between the two of us before coming in to sit beside me on the bed.

"How was your visit?" she hazards, trying and failing to be neutral about it. "You must be reeling from everything that's happened. Learning you have another sister, that must not have been easy."

"I always liked Delphine, so it's not too big of a deal." Partial lie. It's a huge deal. But I did like her when she was the Vanguard's maid, so I can at least try to extricate her from Justin's claws.

"Right. And she just happened to be working for us?" Tess turns away and shakes her head. "There's no coincidence there; the man is wicked."

Parrish uses his phone to start up some seriously vintage nineties shit, akin to what Justin might listen to. He fucking rocked it to *"Milkshake"* the other day; there's nothing he isn't capable of.

"Wannabe" by the Spice Girls start to play, and Tess hooks a cute smile at her son.

"Are you trying to butter me up?" she asks him, and he shrugs lazily, as if he doesn't give two shits. Only, he does. He gives a lot of shits, and that's why it's so meaningful that he chose me knowing what could happen with Tess.

With his actions, Parrish is proving that everything he's ever said to me is true

"Remember my eighth birthday party? Maxx's family was out of town, and nobody else came. When I cried, you put this on to dance with me." Parrish smiles saucily, and Tess stares at him for an inordinate amount of time before smiling back. I think she's trying not to cry, to be honest.

"You're a charming little shit, do you know that?" she asks him, and I raise my brows at that. Usually, Tess is harping at Parrish not to curse. This is new to me. "Playing Spice Girls to loosen me up?"

"It's working, isn't it?" Parrish queries back, and Tess just shakes her head with a sardonic chuckle.

"I'm too happy that you're safe to argue with that." She looks back over at me, mollified slightly by her son's attention, but clearly here with a purpose in mind. "Dakota," she begins, and I'm just thrilled that she didn't say Mia. "The custody hearing is on Friday."

Fuuuuuuuuuck.

"I know." I look down at my hands in my lap, fervently wishing for a meteor to crash into the earth so I don't have to go through this. Whatever happens, whatever Justin asks of me, it's going to be pure hell—and it certainly won't go Tess' way. "My grandparents are going to testify on Justin's behalf."

Tess goes completely still, and when I look up, I can see the blatant terror etched into her pretty features.

"What do *you* want to happen there?" she asks me, and it is quite literally the first time she has ever asked my opinion about anything, as if I might actually have some agency over my own life.

I swallow hard.

What do I want to happen? I want to live with the Vanguards in that stupid ice palace, and I want to be friends with Danyella and Lumen; I want to date Parrish and Chasm and Maxx. I want to be a normal teenager; I want to game; I want to post stupid shit online. I want to be able to talk to Maxine and my grandparents whenever I miss them so much that my heart hurts.

I don't want to hurt people. I don't want to be Justin's princess. I wish I had a normal father.

Saffron's letter burns hot in its hiding place, and I lay my hand over it, wondering what, exactly, it means.

What could Saffron possibly be planning?

She kidnapped me once and hid me so well that I stayed hidden for fourteen years, three months, and sixteen days. I can't underestimate her tenacity and scrappiness.

"Does it really matter what I want?" I ask, and there's a plea in there.

Tess doesn't respond to that.

"Justin is going to push for full custody," she tells me gently, but there's a quaver of fear in her voice that I don't expect. Tess is larger than life, right? If anyone could stand up to Justin, it'd be her.

"Write him into a book and kill him off," I say, trying to make myself smile through the joke. "That's what writers do, isn't it? Doesn't hurt anybody, very therapeutic."

Tess doesn't smile back.

"If you don't talk to me, I can't help you," she says, and then it's as if she's holding her breath. The song ends, and Parrish lets it move to another Spice Girls throwback. Saffron liked this stuff, too.

"I know." That's what I say, because I'm such an eloquently loquacious parrot. I can't keep my mouth shut most days, but when it really matters, I clam up. I even pat Tess' hand. I pat it. Like I'm a grandparent comforting their grandkid or something.

With an exhale, Tess stands up and then puts her hands on her hips.

"Don't stay up too late: those agents from the FBI will be here in the morning to talk to you."

Um. Right. Because my life is that weird.

She walks away, but I'm sure she'll be back.

"*It is a curious thought,*" Parrish begins, and it's obvious that he's quoting something. "*But it is only when you see people looking ridiculous that you realize just how much you love them.*" He smirks at me. "Agatha Christie."

"Did you practice that all weekend waiting for me?" I shoot back, and he moves back over to the bed, leaning down to kiss me. He's even pushier this time, leaning into me and causing me to fall back on the mattress.

"Actually, I did," he replies with a shrug, and then he's standing up and gesturing at the TV. There's a PlayStation set up there. Surely not by accident. "Tess' guilt caused her to buy us all new shit yesterday—including you." He picks up a remote and tosses it to me; I catch it one-handed. "If Justin's going to spy on us through tech, we may as well enjoy playing with it."

He takes a seat, and I push the Saffron letter aside to deal with later.

What a mistake.

CHAPTER 13

Agent Takahashi, Agent Murphy. Those are the names of the two women sitting across from me. The former is clearly 'good cop' and the latter is playing 'bad cop'. This is … fun?

I would rather eat my own toenail clippings, I think, but also ew. Also true. Also sorry, not sorry.

"Good morning, Dakota," Itsumi Takahashi, the raven-haired woman with the sharp stare says to me. I fidget in my seat, but not because I'm trying to play innocent here. I'm not. There's no point. Instead, I just let my natural anxiety flow and do my best to roll with it.

"Good morning," I reply as pleasantly as I'm able.

And by morning, she means *ass-end of night, so early it's late.* Okay, fine, it's eight in the morning, but it's summer. I shouldn't be legally allowed to rise before noon.

"Agent Murphy and I just want to have a little chat with you, nothing serious." She thumbs through her iPad for a moment before setting it on the table beside her. We're sitting in Laverne's kitchen at the small breakfast table against the windows. By small breakfast table, I mean rich people sized small. As in, it's like a full eight-person table. The one in the dining room can seat forty FYI.

"You're not in trouble here," Agent Murphy adds, and I cock a brow.

"I didn't kidnap Parrish, so I sure hope not." *Too flippant? Am I being too flippant? This is the friggin' FBI, Dakota, FFS. Get your shit together!* I laugh. It's too weird, isn't it? I bet I look sus as hell.

Agent Murphy smiles. I try to focus on what pretty gray eyes she has rather than the fact that she's *an FBI agent and I'm involved with the Seattle Slayer.*

"Why don't you tell us a bit about your dad?" she suggests, and I almost choke.

"Stepdad, actually," Agent Takahashi corrects, glancing over at her partner. She turns back to me. "Paul Vanguard. What can you tell us about him?" She crosses her arms on the table, all casual and shit.

She is anything but casual; I feel like she's staring into my *soul.*

If I were Tess, and I were writing this book, I'd probably describe it as … No, no, I wouldn't describe it because I would never be such a miserable crab of a writer who'd put her character through such stressful experiences. Fictional people have feelings, too, you know. *Sobs uncontrollably.*

"Paul?" I query, and then I figure we're just working our way through family members. I'll be asked to talk about each and every person in detail, just like when Parrish was missing. It felt like they were talking me in circles with their questions, but I never did figure what the endgame was. "He seems nice enough."

"Seems?" Agent Murphy presses, leaning back in her chair.

She's wearing shiny Oxfords that pair well with her suit, but they're nowhere near the obscene brand-name stuff I see around here. "Why just 'seems'?" She makes single quotes with her fingers, and I shrug.

"He resents me, I think. He wishes Tess didn't have a missing kid. Some stranger lives in his house and makes his life hell, and yeah, he doesn't comment on it, but it's not like I can't tell." I swallow hard and figure I just best get this out of the way. "Also, I'm dating his son, and he seemed pretty upset about that."

Agent Murphy's eyes harden just a fraction, but I'm pretty decent at reading people. Somehow, I'm giving her what she wants right now? Meaning, when we talked before, she didn't know what she wanted.

She sure does now.

Paul? I'm not getting it, not just yet.

"During the period when Parrish was missing, did you ever witness Paul displaying any odd behaviors? Coming and going in the middle of the night? Making excuses to work late or on weekends?"

I'm already shaking my head. As far as I could tell, Paul spent a good majority of that time with Tess. Shouldn't they know this already?

"What about Delphine Shaw?" Itsumi asks, studying her notes again before looking at me with a small smile. "I hear she's your father's daughter?"

"Justin Prior's daughter," I admit, heart pounding. I'm trying not to get too excited here, but is this really happening? They're bringing up Justin and Delphine? Does that mean they're on to him! I refuse to let myself get too excited.

It can't be this easy, not with Justin as clever as he is. You don't design an app that auto-hacks into people's private cameras to search for faces and then sell it for dirt cheap online if you don't have clever tricks, games, and agendas.

"I just learned that, by the way. Like, literally, three days ago."

"Did you ever notice Delphine and Paul interacting with one another?" Agent Takahashi continues. "Maybe she mentioned something about him to you?"

"She warned me against wearing a certain t-shirt because she thought he might not like it." I'm almost too eager to give out this information; I know that. But wouldn't it solve all my problems if, through no fault of my own, the FBI were to nail Justin to the wall?

Only, it wouldn't. I know that. He has too much money and too many contacts. Maybe this is a bad thing?

"She called him Paul, and then freaked a little and changed it to *Dr. Vanguard.*" I roll my eyes a bit, redirecting the attention to Paul instead of Delphine. "Also, he drives a Range Rover with his own name on the license plate. Literally says DCTR P. And everyone knows you can't trust people with vanity plates." I laugh again, and Agent Murphy smiles a hideous smile at me.

She … is still getting exactly what she wants and expects from me.

What have I just done?

"How are Parrish and Paul's interactions with one another? Have you witnessed any fighting between the two of them?" This time, I start to see it, what with the way the redheaded agent is gazing at me like she's going in for the kill.

They're not here for Justin: they're here for *Paul.*

Because, somehow, Justin Prior has figured a way to make Paul look guilty for kidnapping his own child. I know it without even knowing it. They're prodding and baiting me to give up negative intel on Paul Vanguard. Why else?

And of *course* they would never be able to capture Justin, not without a fight. I have a feeling the man would end up walking through a trial of fire and still come out squeaky clean. It's definitely possible to get away with murder if you have money, regardless of who and how many people you hurt or kill.

"They only fight like normal fathers and sons," I reply, almost defensively. "Nothing unusual. Why?" I curl my fingers in the fabric of my Whitehall Prep joggers; they're still the only pants I have right now that didn't come from Justin's pre-determined wardrobe. Tess promised to take me shopping this week, but like, when? After the FBI thang? Maybe before the custody hearing with my bonkers father? And only because of the house fire he set, *obviously.*

"Tell us about any moments that come to mind when you think about Paul. You haven't known him for very long, so I imagine there aren't too many, all of them fairly recent." Agent Murphy leans forward to put her elbow on the table and nods encouragingly at me.

Oh crap. Oh shit. This is not good.

"He didn't kidnap Parrish," I protest, almost scoffing. "That's ridiculous; there's no evidence to point his way."

"Did you learn a lot about the case while researching your online videos?" Agent Takahashi continues. "If there's anything you or your followers might've discovered that we haven't already seen online, I would love to take a look at it."

"It's not about my videos; Milk Carton found Parrish." *Was that too blatant? Should I have even said that?* But I can't watch Paul and, through him, Tess and the kids get dragged through the mud on some trumped up charge.

Fucking hell, Justin!

"Right. But someone took Parrish. A person did that. And we're interested in finding that person because, whoever they are, they managed to evade one of the largest and most expensive manhunts in the country. The Seattle Slayer is killing kids, Dakota, you know that."

Oh.

Oh no.

So Paul isn't just being framed for kidnapping Parrish but for everything? All the murders, like Francisca Cortez and her boyfriend?

I could end this all right now. I could stop it. At any moment, I have the power to shine a light on Justin Prior for the entire world to see. Yet, I know him too well to think he'd go down without a fight. He would send Raúl or his crooked cop buddy or Mr. Volli after Maxine or Carmen, Walter or Kimber, Chasm and Maxx and Parrish.

Let Paul burn to save the lives of everyone else?

Do I even have another humane choice here?

"Paul did not kidnap Parrish." I say it again, just in case they didn't get it the first time.

"Let's not worry about that just now." Itsumi picks up a bottled water and unscrews the cap, and I see that we're nowhere near close to done here. "Why don't you just start from the beginning? Tell us about the first time that you met Paul Vanguard."

After the agents leave, Tess invites me to go shopping with her—and her alone, but I'm too freaked out. I don't want to go anymore. When she asks me what I discussed with the agents, I don't know what to say. I mumble something generic and join Parrish in the game room.

He's sucking ass at Ms. Pac-Man, but I'm not in the mood to tease him for it.

"You let the orange ghost kill you? That's the slowest one." He turns to give me a raised brow, and I sigh. I guess I'm never too worn out to poke fun at poor gameplay. "Scoot." He moves aside and lets me start a game, staring at me all the while. He waits for me to complete the first two levels before he gets in my face.

I ignore him, focusing on my score instead of his expression, all of an inch from mine, boring into my cheek.

"What happened?"

"The FBI wants to frame your dad as the Seattle Slayer." Justin should already know about this, so I don't bother to hide my words or chuck my phone or anything of the sort. He *did* get me a new phone, the latest model, attached my Maxine-phone number to it without my knowledge. It's nice. It's also basically a free, portable spy hole. The heart pin cam was a nice touch, a safe gap measure in case we learned about the tech, but at least we figured that out early.

"Um, excuse me … what? How do you know that?" he whispers, checking the stairs to make sure nobody's about to walk in on us.

"Based on the questions they asked," I murmur, snatching up all four ghosts in Ms. Pac-Man's wide yellow mouth. The level ends, and a ridiculous cut scene starts, but I'm not even seeing it.

What I *am* seeing is Justin foisting off his evil deeds onto Paul's back.

Scandal and ruin for not only the Vanguard family, but Tess in particular. *Famous Novelist Not Only Writes Serial Killers—She Marries Them.* That's what all the headlines would say. Tess would go virulent. That is, like going viral except in a really, really bad way.

"What sorts of questions?" Parrish pushes, reaching out to pry my fingers from the joystick. I let my gaze move to his, getting lost in his scrumptious eyes as Ms. Pac-Man is eaten by Pinky, the uh, well, yeah the pink ghost. Duh. "Gamer Girl, tell me right this goddamn second." He's squeezing me by the shoulders and leaning down to look into my eyes.

His gaze is stricken but steady.

Parrish isn't going to give up. Neither am I. But what to do?

"We should go pick GG up," I remark, and Parrish huffs. He stands up straight, pursing his lips into a line. He knows we can't talk freely here.

We need—and I hate to say this—to go hiking.

We need to find a remote trail, and walk it together, so that we can talk somewhere without Justin's eager ears listening in.

"Don't worry: I already have a plan," Parrish murmurs, rubbing at his chin. He takes off, snatching my hand in his and dragging me along with him. I stumble a bit but manage to find my feet.

All the while, my brain cooks up more possible headlines for this disaster.

The Goddess of True Crime Shacked Up with a Real-life Killer: is Paul Vanguard the Seattle Slayer?

Multiple things occur to me in that moment: whether Paul is framed as the Slayer, or Justin is revealed for who he is, does it matter?

The headlines would be nearly the same.

Either way, our family is humiliated and ruined.

Either way, Tess married the Slayer. Either way, the Slayer is my father figure in one way or another.

What a clusterfuckity-fuck-fuck-fuck.

"This whole world is cursed," I grumble, forcing a more pleasant expression to my face. Whatever Parrish has in mind won't be helped if I'm over here looking like an internet troll without anonymity, you know what I mean? Hideous. That's what I'm saying. I can't be holding onto a hideous expression.

"Let me take care of this." Parrish releases my hand and lifts a single finger. "Stay here and don't move." He slips into the *solarium.* Yeah, this house has a solarium, too. That, and an indoor gardener whose full-time job is based around the plants inside of it.

I wait just outside the glass doors, doing my best not to pace around.

But holy shit.

Attack launched, Justin. I see you. Now what?

I'm reminded of that almost ethereal night where I gamed with all three boys, ate red licorice, and kicked their collective asses. I'd thought I was unhappy then? That was bliss, pure bliss compared to all of this.

Anyway, I remember my character sitting in the attic, waiting for Maxx's alien avatar to find me so I could spring my trap. But when that didn't work, I came up with a backup plan.

Is that what this is? Justin's backup plan? Or was he planning on framing Paul regardless of whether he died in the fire that night?

This shit is sinister. I can practically hear *"I'm The Villain In My Own Story"* from the show *Crazy Ex-Girlfriend* playing. I mean, *I* am not the villain, Justin is. But I can still hear the song in my head. I can't control my inner dork, not even in life-threatening situations.

Parrish reappears a short time later, car keys in hand.

"Let's go," he whispers, heading for the garage door at warp-speed. I chase after him, following him into the cavernous space and noting the multitude of expensive cars parked within. He moves over to the one on the far end, some silver Lexus sedan thing, that he unlocks and climbs into. He glances my way when he sees that I'm just standing there. "Get in before it's too late."

"What about Tess?" I ask, but Parrish just wets his lips and glances away.

"Laverne gave me permission to go. Let them fight about it

later. It's not our problem anymore." He starts the car, and I hurry around to the other side to hop in. I've just barely got the door closed when he hits a button, opens the garage door behind us, and backs out like he's a professional race car driver.

"What about me?" I ask as Parrish heads around the circular drive, and we take off for the front gate. "I can't just leave."

"I told Laverne we were heading to the country club to see Chasm; she knows you're with me." He pauses the car briefly, waiting for the front gate to slide open automatically, and off we go. "Shoot Tess a text right now, and then turn your phone off."

It feels … deceitful.

But if we'd asked Tess? Her answer would've been a resounding no. I'm actually trying to help her here, I really am.

"I haven't had a chance to text Danyella about the bunny yet," I explain, but Parrish just shakes his head.

"She knows we're coming; I already talked to her this morning."

He shifts gears, and we rocket down the road at a much faster speed than is certainly legal. Then again, what does he care? The cops in this town are like private security for the rich folks who live here, and we're driving Laverne's car. Nobody will stop us.

"You talked to her?" I ask.

"I did. Lumen, too."

I try and fail not to be at least a little jealous.

Parrish picks up on that, and his lips twitch in bemusement.

"Don't worry about me and Lumen: you're my only and everything."

I just stare at him.

"Only and everything? You can't say things like that," I whisper, flushing from head to toe.

"Why not? We're in this deep, aren't we? Your dad kidnapped me; you saved my life; we had a threesome. Hell, I told Tess. What would happen if we broke up? Things would be awkward."

"Meaning what?" I ask, simultaneously wishing he'd stop talking and also that he'd keep going. I want to hear more, more, more of this.

"We'll just have to stay together—forever." He shrugs his shoulders like it's nothing, but I'm left completely starstruck. I know it's not possible to guess what the future will hold, nor do I think many high school relationships last, but … some do.

What's the harm in believing anyway?

I slump back in the sumptuous leather seat, fingers digging into the legs of my sweatpants.

The fire restoration crew told Tess that they can probably save some of Parrish's and my clothes; everyone else's might be toast, but they'll try. The closer to the fire, the less chance of saving them. Of course, they can't fix what was entirely burned up.

For now, I'll just count my lucky stars that Maxx was at the house when he wasn't supposed to be. He totally fucked up Justin's plans.

We arrive a short time later at Danyella's place. It occurs to me that I've never seen Lumen's house. I'm sure it's in town—which isn't very big—but where? Why did we never go there?

The pair of us climb out, just in time for Maxx to pull his orange Jeep Gladiator onto the drive behind us. I didn't text them, so this is on Parrish, too. It's nice, having him back; he thinks of everything.

"I've got a hutch set up and ready to go," Chas tells me, sliding his hands into dark jeans and looking me over in such a way that his gaze sets fire to my heart, my soul, and my loins.

Wait. Did I just use the word loins? Who does that? What is my life, an eighties bodice ripper novel with Fabio on the cover? Gross.

"Did you know carrots aren't healthy for rabbits?" Maxx asks, shaking his head. He's decked out in expensive athleisure, as he often is. Sweatpants and kicks, and a muscle tank. The sun catches on the curvature of his biceps, making my—yeah, fine, let's just call it as it is—loins quiver.

Heh. Quivering loins. I guess if I wrote books, I might write them a little differently than Tess.

"They aren't supposed to have them more than once a week," he adds, offering me up the cutest smile known to humankind. Once again, yeah, it's the loins. It's always the loins.

"I … did not know that," I admit as Parrish leads the way to the front door. He knocks once and then opens it, sweeping in like he owns the place.

Danyella intercepts us in the kitchen, wearing a hot pink shirt that matches those fabulous glasses of hers. It reads *There Will Be Drama—This is the Theater, Darling!* on the front, and it pairs well with her white Lululemon leggings and pale pink tennies. It almost looks like … but no.

She couldn't possibly be gearing up for a hike, could she?

"GG's a sweetie pie," Danyella tells us, planting her hands on her hips. Her braided hair is gathered into a high ponytail, and she's got her usual half-stern expression on her face. It's almost like I never burned down the theater and ruined the careful production of *Wicked* she'd been working on all year.

It's almost like she never turned her back on me and let Lumen and the other girls bully me. Almost, almost, almost.

But shit, I miss her so bad that I don't care about any of that.

"The vet says he's about a year old, and she prescribed some orchard grass and fresh veggies. We tried bell peppers this morning, and he seemed to like that." She sighs briefly and looks over at me. "Shall we go?"

"Where are we off to?" I ask, but Danyella just smiles. Parrish smiles. Chasm and Maxx smile.

ENDGAME ROMANCE

"You'll see, Naekkeo. We're starting off your summer the Pac Northwestern Way—with a hike." Chas raises his brows at me, and I gape.

"It's all taken care of," Parrish tells me, stepping forward and sliding both my Tess-phone and my Maxine-cum-Justin phone from my back pockets. Also, he kind of, sort of gropes my ass as he does it.

Let's just say it together now: loins, loins, loins.

He tosses the phones on the table, and the others do the same.

Dump the tech, baby.

The only way to outsmart a tech bro is to go full rogue.

At this point, if I have to become a wilderness expert to beat Justin Prior, I'll do it.

Game on.

CHAPTER
14

We meet Lumen at the trailhead, piling out of Maxx's Jeep together and finding her waiting. While Danyella is done up in pinks today, Lumen has a bright yellow top on, gray hiking pants, and brown boots that look like they've never seen a day in the dirt.

"I am so ready for this," she says, forcing a terrified-looking grimace to her face. "How many miles to the falls?"

"Only about four," Maxx tells us, smiling as he turns to me. Everyone looks at me, actually, pausing as if they're waiting for something.

When Maxine steps out from behind the large wooden sign that marks the beginning of the trail, I'm floored.

"Baby sister," she says, and I gape at her. "I hope you don't mind me joining you. I've been wanting to hike with you for years; this is basically a dream come true for me."

I just stare back at her, fighting back stupid tears. I can't cry, not right now. In this moment, everything is good, everything is happy. Even if there's a moat of shit on all sides, I can appreciate this single, perfect instance.

That's what life is about, appreciating the small things. The distant trickle of a creek, the way the air smells of pine and fresh growth, the filtered sunlight through the trees, the press of good company.

"I've gone hiking with you before," I mumble, but Maxine just raises her brows, her brunette hair in two braids, an old t-shirt paired with her favorite hiking pants and ratty old boots. She's had them resoled two times and swears by them.

"For a half mile—at best." She softens her expression slightly and moves toward me, pausing just in front of me. "I know something is going on, Kota. You can do your best to hide and hurt all on your own, but it's written all over your pretty face." She reaches out to touch my cheek, but I push her hand away.

"Maxine—"

"No." She puts her finger to my lips and shakes her head. "*I* am the big sister. I'm the one who's supposed to protect you, and I've done a pretty shit job at that. I'm coming, and I'm going to pry your worries out, even if I have to use a stick." She marches past me, heading for the trail as I struggle between two warring emotions.

Joy, at being able to see her and spend time with her.

And terror. Pure, undiluted terror.

"I packed you a water bottle and some snacks," Maxx tells me, coming up beside me and putting his hand on my lower back. I look up at him, and he smiles. "If I have to, I'll carry you on my back again, and you can tell me all about how you're no longer a virgin."

I kick him in the back of the leg as he passes by, but he just chuckles and continues on into the trees, following after Maxine.

"I can't believe I'm doing this," Lumen grumbles, offering me up an apologetic smile. I can't forget that she let her friends—no, encouraged them more like—to beat me up. I also can't forget that

I set the theater on fire, smashed the window of my BMW birthday present using my mother's prized typewriter, and slept with my sister's ex-boyfriend.

We all do what we have to in order to survive.

"Hiking. Yay." Chasm makes faux jazz hands, and sighs, looking over at me for moral support. "I've never hiked a day in my life."

"You'll survive," Parrish quips as Danyella hesitates briefly and sets off with the others.

I follow along with the other two boys behind me, and we set a brisk but doable pace. By doable, I mean my gamer ass is dripping sweat, and Chasm is snickering at me.

"Pick it up, slacker!" he calls out, walking backward as Parrish strolls behind me like he's on the runway, this loose, easy swagger that belies his true fatigue. He can't hide the sweat on his own forehead, not even when he scowls at his bestie.

"I was kidnapped and cut up, and I'm still recovering you piss-ant little shit," he growls out, and Chas snorts, still walking backward until he nearly trips over a tree root, and Maxx has to catch his arm to keep him from tumbling into the creek.

"Pay attention to the trail, dipshit," he says as I jog to catch up with the others. The incline is too steep for me to talk while I walk —yeah, I *am* breathing that hard—but even though I know why we're here, I just have to admire the scenery.

Lush green ferns dipped in dew, protected from the sun by soaring trees. Most of them are evergreens, but there are deciduous species mixed in, abloom and bright with color. On our left is a creek that still has a bit of water in it, and bird song is our only companion on the trail beside our own footfalls and heavy breathing.

This close to the monstrous metropolitan beast that is Seattle, a lot of the trails are overcrowded now. Today, this one for whatever reason, is blessedly empty. I only saw two cars in the parking lot earlier which is a huge surprise. We did drive over an hour to get here, but still. I'm thankful for the relative solitude.

When I start to flag a bit, Maxx takes my sweaty hand in his own, gripping it tight, and we turn to look at each other. There's a moment there where everything else falls away, and I find myself so impossibly in love with him that I can't breathe.

Then I remember that Maxine is here, too, and try to pull my hand back.

"No." He says that with every ounce of domineering authority that he usually tries to hide.

See, here's how it goes.

Chasm is a true asshole on the inside, one that tries his absolute best to be nice; it takes effort. Parrish is the opposite, a soft-hearted boy who fights to put up shields against the world. Maxx is a morally upright and devoutly loyal alpha-hole who does his best to squash his bossy urges.

I blink back at him as he hauls me up the trail beside him, and I have to half-jog to keep up.

"No?" I query, trying to keep my voice low. I'm sure they can all hear me anyway, what with how quiet it is out here.

"No, you're not going to run or hide from this. You and me," he starts, wetting his lips and looking past me toward Maxine's back. She's trying to give me some space because she doesn't understand what's going on, but I wish I were walking beside her and chatting like nothing ever happened between us. "You and me, we're not a shameful thing, Kota. I …" Here he lets out a ragged laugh, swiping his free hand down his face.

Did I mention that *he* isn't sweating at all?

This motocrossing athlete son of a bitch …

"I love you too much to act like I'm sorry this happened." He stops suddenly which, you know, causes everyone else to stop,

Parrish and Chasm watching us from my left as I turn to face Maxx and he does the same. Danyella, Lumen, and, of course, my sister are staring back at us from just up the trail. X looks me right in the eyes, making it impossible for me to turn away. "And in a way, I'm grateful that it did."

"We're supposed to be taking care of business here, not marinating hormones in the summer sun," Parrish quips, moving past us as if he doesn't care. But he does. He's still jealous, even if he hasn't said as much.

X rolls his eyes, but he turns and off we go.

I can't seem to stop thinking about his words as we walk.

"I love you too much to act like I'm sorry this happened."

Maxine doesn't say anything, doesn't even seem bothered, but she must be, right?

I put the issue aside as we continue along the four-mile stretch, winding through the woods and up, up, up. Eventually, the trail turns into wooden stairs carved into the hill, and we're scrambling over rocks and small streams.

Thankfully, Maxx is there all the way, helping me along just like the last time we went hiking together. I liked everything about him then, the way he packed water and snacks, took care of my ankle, and carried me on his back. This time, I'm almost, sort of allowed to like him, and it feels good.

He keeps my hand in his, assisting me along the cliff's edge. It's a bit scary, pebbles and rocks slipping out from beneath our shoes and tumbling down the hill. When X pauses, I do the same, turning to look at a majestic view of the Mt. Baker-Snoqualmie National Forest. It stretches out before us in sweeps and dramatic rises, covered in trees and kissing the fog.

"Oh, wow," I breathe out, this feeling of being so small, yet a part of something so much bigger, taking over me.

"This is why I hike," Maxx whispers in my ear, and I shiver.

It's not cold out, not really, especially not after walking so far, but we all know that isn't why I was shivering. We continue on, until we're sitting beside the waters of Bridal Veil falls on a fallen log carved out like a bench.

Well, the girls are sitting there. The boys take up various positions on nearby rocks, chugging water and eating some of the food that X packed. He makes sure to set me up with my water and apple slices first.

"What fresh hell is this?" Chasm murmurs, lounging on his stone seat, back to a tree. He's just recovered his panting breaths, his lightning bolt hair stuck to his forehead. "You call this *fun*? Naekkeo, tell me you're on my side."

"I'm on your side," I reply with a bit of a laugh, enjoying the diffused light of the sun through the trees, and the cool spray of the falls on my right. According to X, the water isn't usually so strong in the summer; some generous summer storms, like the one we had on prom night, have done a lot to add to the majesty of the waterfall.

"What does *naekkeo* mean?" Maxine asks, speaking up for the first time since we sat down. If I said this moment wasn't at least a little bit awkward, I'd be lying. I look over at my sister, seated beside me, her thigh pressed to mine, and decide that I have to do it, tell her at least some of what's going on.

Before I do, I'll need to extract a promise from her to keep quiet about everything. She's like X in that regard, held to high moral standards such that if she thinks telling the world about Justin will save us all, she'll do it. I just don't want her to react too strongly before she fully understands what we're up against here.

"It means *mine,*" Chasm says with a slight smirk that causes Lumen to gag.

"Gross. You would've been better off with me," she adds, and my cheeks flush. Maxine raises her brows, but I'm not about to get into all that just now. Later, maybe.

Parrish says something to Chasm in Korean, and then Maxx butts in, and before I know it, the three of them are having a heated discussion in a language that nobody else here understands.

They wrap it up fairly quickly, but I can tell by their expressions—and the frequent use of the word *naekkeo*—that whatever they were just discussing isn't over.

"Thank you for arranging all this," I tell Parrish, and he inclines his head, a prince offering praise to his subject's acquiescence. I almost roll my eyes. But really, it was sweet. Also, practical.

We're both going to die when we get home tonight.

Rightfully so, I might add.

Lumen and Danyella exchange a look of their own, a stare-off that ends with Danyella rising to her feet and taking off. She doesn't go far, but she moves into the shade of the trees like she needs some space.

"I thought you didn't want Danyella involved in all this," Chasm shoots out, and his academic rival—number two in their class, just after him—stares right back. Danyella was first in our grade, by the way. Overall, she got fifth or sixth I want to say.

"Yeah, well, I guess it's a bit late for that." Lumen looks down at her lap, fiddling with the edge of the single pocket on her pants, one of those small ones made just big enough for a key fob and a phone. Only, she has no phone on her. Nobody here does.

X removes the bug detector from his bag as I raise a brow.

"We can't be too careful," he remarks, which is true, and I wait while he scans us all, Danyella included, and then returns to his rock-chair with a nod. "We're all clear."

Lumen breathes a sigh of relief, reaching up to push her blond hair back from her face. There are a few stray tendrils wafting around, but most of it is gathered into an Ariana Grande-esque ponytail.

"I'm going to cut right to the chase," she starts, and Chas snorts.

"As you better, seeing as you let your girls kick the shit out of Little Sister over here." Chasm nods with his chin in my direction, and my broken fingers tingle with remembered pain. I'm supposed to be wearing the splints for another week, but they don't hurt much so I've been avoiding it. None of the breaks were overly severe, and other than a slight soreness, they don't bother me now.

"Wait, what?" Maxine starts, but we're way past that part of the story. I give her hand a small squeeze.

"I'll tell you later," I explain, and she takes my word for it which upsets me. She shouldn't take my word for anything, none of them should. I could always be lying. Because of the Slayer, I *am* always lying.

Lumen is staring at the ground now, not at me or Danyella or anyone else.

"Parrish and I ..." Here she trails off, and then lets out a huff. She lifts her head up and stares right at him. "I've never been into you; I just need you to understand that."

He cocks a brow like he doesn't believe that, but I'm curious to see where this is all going. She was *just* flirting with him at the dinner party the other night. Why would anyone believe otherwise?

"Okay." Parrish stares right back at her in that way of his. "Explain why you've been panting after me for years then. I'll wait."

Lumen lets out this harsh little laugh.

"Do you hear yourself when you talk?" She turns to look at me. "I hope he's marginally nicer to you than he is to everyone else." Only, he is. A lot nicer.

"I love you, too, Gamer Girl. If this is the last time we see each

other, remember that. And remember that nobody has ever fought for me the way you have."

Yep, Parrish Vanguard is a romantic at heart.

"Why don't you continue with your story before I lose my patience?" Parrish retorts, and Lumen shakes herself out, like she really wants to keep up the bickering, but knows there are more important issues afoot here.

"My family is ..." she starts, and then she trails off with a small sound, putting her face in both of her hands. "We're dead broke."

There's silence all around. I can feel Maxine's palpable confusion on my right, Chasm's judgment, Parrish's quiet contemplation, Maxx's simmering rage.

"The Hearsts are old-money, part of Medina's fabric," Parrish says, frowning hard. "How can you be broke?"

She shakes her head again and then looks up, almost pleading with her pale brown gaze.

"I don't know. I don't watch either of my parents' investment portfolios." She stops and then stands up, like she just can't bear to sit still, pacing a small rut on the wet ground beside the waterfall. The rush of the water means we have to speak up to be heard, but it also obscures our words if there were to be anyone nearby.

Like that hiker, the one that attacked X and me on the trail before.

Mr. Fosser, the pervert rapist who died what was perhaps too easy a death. But at least he's gone and there's some small kernel of justice for poor JJ. Once this is all over, I'd like to find some way—even anonymously—to contact her family and let them know that she didn't run away. I'll spare them the gruesome details, but they have a right to know she's passed.

God, this is so messed up.

At least that poor girl wasn't killed by daddy dearest directly or even via his orders. I can hold onto that for the moment to get myself through the rest of this conversation.

The lightbulb goes off for Parrish before it does me.

"So you were after me for money?" he asks dryly, and then offers up a disparaging laugh. "How very Whitehall of you."

"Aren't you all in high school?" Maxine asks, sounding even more confused than she was when we started this conversation. I take a bite of apple slice and try to remember how insane I found these people when I first got here myself.

"Rich people are crazy," I whisper, and my sister raises both brows.

"I am in full agreement with that one," she mutters back as Lumen whirls to face Parrish.

"Yeah, exactly that. My family is after your family's money. I've been told for years that it's up to me to fix the situation." She pauses there, spreading her hands helplessly. "What was I supposed to do? We've sold off as much as we can, but we're drowning. It's only a matter of time before everyone in Medina realizes that we've lost everything."

She shakes her hands out as Chas cocks a brow.

"This better not be the blackmail you mentioned," he warns, his voice taking on that edge he gets when he feels someone he loves is in danger. It's a little bit scary, but also a lot admirable.

Lumen narrows her eyes on Chasm.

"I haven't gotten to that part of the conversation just yet," she snaps out, reaching up to run shaking fingers through her ponytail. "I'm working up to it, okay? There's more to this."

"Such as?" X encourages, putting pressure on her to reveal whatever else it is that she's hiding.

"I finally told my parents that I didn't want to be with Parrish."

"Could never be with Parrish, more like," the boy in question corrects, but Lumen ignores him, forging on.

"They told me too damn bad," she says with a shocked bit of laughter, looking over and up at the falls like she can find some iota of comfort in the roaring, white water. Lumen turns back around and exhales heavily, as if she's about to drop an atom bomb on us. "Dakota," she begins, and I adjust myself slightly on the log seat, waiting for the explosion. "The person blackmailing me is your father."

"Yawn, tell us something we don't know," Chasm adds as Maxine's face furrows up.

"You *knew*?" Lumen inquires, cocking her head slightly to one side. I stand up, too, and cross my arms.

"We knew," I confirm, looking her straight in the face. She stares right back at me, mouth parted slightly in surprise. Even out here, in a bright yellow athletic top and sneakers, she looks like a model. "But we weren't willing to offer that information up to you." I hesitate and add, "for obvious reasons."

"My parents were involved with what happened to Justin Prior all those years ago," Lumen admits, shaking her head. "My mother is a software developer, you know that? She helped drive your dad out of town once upon a time."

Uh-oh.

Things are all starting to come together, now aren't they?

"Still not hearing anything here that makes me want to trust you." Chasm moves to stand up, but I give him a look and two raised brows. "What? You are far too nice, Little Sister," he warns with another laugh, gesturing at Lumen with a single hand. "This is going to come back to bite us in the ass, mark my words."

"I killed somebody," Lumen says, standing up straight and lifting her chin.

We all go dead silent.

"Excuse me?" Maxine looks at me with sheer terror in her gaze. Her expression clearly asks what the hell I've gotten myself into.

"You did what?" Parrish asks, blinking in surprise as X simply stares.

"That's not what happened at all," Danyella says, reappearing behind us and speaking up for the first time. I turn to look at her, but she's staring at Lumen instead of me. "Don't say it like that; it paints you poorly, and I don't see it that way."

"Explain," Parrish demands, his voice hardening.

"I invited Danyella to a party last year," Lumen admits, sighing again and shaking her head like she's already defeated. But, while I might not know her as well as I thought, I certainly know her better than to think she'd ever really give up. "Even though I know she doesn't like parties, even though I *know* that I left her behind when we started at Whitehall to pursue my own popularity."

"Lumen …" Danyella says softly, but she doesn't refute any of that because it's true.

I remember the words she said to me the first day I met her: *"I wouldn't call her a mean girl or anything, but I also wouldn't confess my deepest secrets to her, you know?"*

"I didn't pay attention to Danyella at the party," Lumen continues, shame coloring her voice. "I left her alone to prove something to my friends. What exactly that was, I can't even say. Something … something happened …"

"I wandered off for some space to breathe." Danyella takes up the story with conviction in her voice. "I just wanted a minute to *breathe*." She looks away and swallows hard; I can see this is weighing as heavily on her as it is on Lumen, if not more so.

I imagine the only reason Danyella hasn't been drawn into this mess by Justin is that her parents had nothing at all to do with his downfall in high society, nothing to do with his being locked up in a psych ward, nothing to do with his stolen research.

"This guy found me out there by myself in the dark." Danyella swallows hard and closes her eyes for a minute. I can see where this is going, and I don't like it. "He tried to force himself on me. He would've succeeded too, if Lumen hadn't stepped in."

"I didn't mean to kill him," Lumen admits, wetting her lips. "It was an accident; it was the only thing I could think to do in that moment." She lifts her chin in defiance. "I would do it all over again if I had to. While I didn't intend to kill him, he certainly had it coming."

"It's not all on you, what happened," Danyella pleads, but Lumen simply shakes her head.

"It is. It's on me. All of this, and my family. That's why I'm here." She turns to me. "My parents are pushing me to pursue Parrish. On top of that, I can't go against anything your father tells me to do. Somehow, he knows about what I did. He even knows where we buried the body."

"Fucking Christ." Chasm again.

Maxine says nothing, sitting there and taking it all in. I imagine she's going to have a buttload of questions, but that's okay. I'll answer them as best as I can.

"There. It's all out there." Lumen lifts her hands up helplessly, as if to ask *now what?* "You basically admitted in the hedge maze that you were being blackmailed, too. So, your own father is blackmailing you?"

Maxine sucks in a sharp breath, digging her fingers into the log bench. I flick my gaze her way but turn back to Lumen instead. I can't tell her about Justin being the Seattle Slayer. Rather, I won't. Not yet anyway. Maxine either.

But this, I can talk about this.

"He's angry about what happened to him all those years ago: he wants me to exact his revenge for him."

"Including Parrish's fake kidnapping, I'm guessing?" Lumen quips, putting the pieces together. I hesitate for the briefest of seconds before nodding. "See, I knew it! It wasn't the Seattle Slayer after all, just some stupid promo for his dumb app, I'll bet."

She isn't wrong about that last bit.

"What is he using to blackmail you this time?" Lumen continues when nobody speaks up. My gaze goes to Maxine, and my sister's eyes widen.

"Me?" she asks, rising to her feet suddenly. "How? Dakota, we need to go to the police with this." She pauses briefly, but I'm already shaking my head. "Why not? The FBI are still in town working on Parrish's case, right? Tell somebody."

"He has too many people in his pocket," I admit. "Cops, for sure. The FBI I don't know about, but you can't underestimate Justin Prior. He's ruthless. Even *if* I were to tell the whole world about him, I have a feeling he has contingency plans up the wazoo." I look my sister dead in the face. "The reason I said those horrible things to you at the coffee shop, the reason I stopped talking to you, even the reason that X and I first hooked up ..." I swallow the hard lump in my throat. "It wasn't Tess' fault: it was Justin's. He threatened Parrish's safety if I didn't comply. Maxx and I had sex, and I guess it just ignited whatever things we were feeling that we'd tried to keep hidden."

My sister is staring at me in horror.

Not because of the Maxx thing, I'm sure. Her mind is blown. This is not the world we were raised in. Horrible situations like this seemed so far off, movie plots or video game storylines, not reality.

Yet, here we all are.

"And I know you, Maxie. I know you're going to want to say something, that you want to step up and do the right thing, but I need you to trust me on this." I reach out for her hand and offer a comforting squeeze. "You'd never do anything intentionally to hurt me, I know, but if you don't let me take the lead on this one, it'll end badly for me."

"Kota …" she starts, but there must be something in my gaze that gives her pause.

"Promise me you won't do anything without mentioning it to me first. That's all I'm asking. Don't challenge Justin in person. Don't even challenge Delphine. If you feel there's something that needs to be done, all I'm asking is that you tell me before you do it."

"I—" She pulls in a deep breath, closes her eyes, and then nods. When she opens them again, she holds out a hand and offers me her pinky. To my sister, a pinky promise is like a binding contract. She takes that shit seriously. "I agree to inform you before I make any moves, but that's it. I'm not promising I won't intervene if you don't like what I have to say."

God, she really is like X, isn't she? I nod, too, and reach out, hooking pinkies and sealing the deal before I turn back to Lumen.

"Besides dating Parrish and luring me out somewhere for a meeting, what else has he asked of you recently?" I ask, but Lumen just shakes her head.

"Nothing else, not yet."

"We need something to use against him, a counter move," I mumble under my breath, rubbing at my chin. Sometimes, in a fight, you can't beat the boss right away, at least in the gaming world. Sometimes, you have to repel the boss a few times before you can actually slay him.

That's what we need right now, something we can use to keep the FBI from nailing Paul with these accusations. But how?

"Got any ideas?" Lumen queries, but I don't. At least not yet.

I look up at her.

"Go ahead and arrange that meeting; I'll show." I turn away, moving back over to my abandoned apple slices and water bottle. I pick them both up and give my sister a look.

ENDGAME ROMANCE

"You will not show," Chasm says with another frustrated scoff. "Are you crazy? That's a recipe for disaster, and you know it. Why on earth would you willingly walk into his trap?"

"I've been studying chess moves online," I admit. Any spare second I have, I'm on my phone researching. "I was reading about this game from 1956, between two famous players named Bobby Fischer and David Byrne. Fischer allowed his queen to be captured and, subsequently, won the game."

"What's your point?" Chasm challenges, moving up beside me and doing his utmost to tempt me with that alluring mint and chocolate scent of his. *Why does he have to smell like ice cream? And not just any ice cream, homemade ice cream with real mint and thick slivers of dark chocolate. Real cream and farm-fresh eggs, for sure.*

This asshole.

"Sometimes, you have to make a sacrifice to win the game," I say, absorbing Justin's lesson to use against him. I turn to look at Chasm, staring down at me with that sharp frown of his. "In this case, I am the sacrifice. I'm not willing to put anyone else out there like that."

"Fuck no," he growls out, but we'll talk about this later.

For now, I need some time alone with my sister.

"Walk with me?" I ask her, ignoring the boys as she follows me up the path a bit further, to another sitting spot with a picnic table. It's wet from the spray, but oh well. I sit on it anyway. "I bet you have a lot of questions."

"I do, but mostly, I want to hug you."

I look up to see her standing there with tears in her eyes, as if I'm the one suffering in all of this. She's worried about *me* when I told her I hated her and stole her boyfriend and ignored her frantic calls and texts …

Maxine moves over and hugs me, whether I feel like I deserve it or not.

"Tell me everything," she breathes, and I do.

Just not the Seattle Slayer part. Because that, it's the most dangerous bit of all, and I won't drag Maxine into it. With this, at least, I hope she understands why I have to do and say certain things.

I hope she understands that I don't mean any of it.

━━━━━━━━━━

When we hit the end of the trail, Lumen leaves in her convertible, Maxine takes off in the only remaining car in the parking lot (I'm assuming it's my grandparents' rental car because it certainly isn't hers) and Danyella moves aside to give me some space to talk with the boys. Maxx has opened up the back of the Jeep so we can sit there together and drink water, wipe off our sweat, and pant and choke from the trek down.

Well, I pant and choke. Chasm is tired, Parrish, too, but somehow, I still feel like I performed the worst today. Go figure. Gamer Girl was not built for the outdoors, my friends.

"Why do you think going along with this will help? It sounds dangerous as hell to me," Maxx says, pulling one knee toward his chest and wrapping his arms around it. He's staring off into the woods, but he turns to look at me as I chug the last of my water.

X already scanned the Jeep with the bug detector, so we're okay to talk here. Although I don't trust any car that might pull into the lot or any person that gets out of it.

"We can't let Justin frame Paul," I say, having already explained what happened this morning to Chasm and Maxx. "It's crucial that we stop him before it's too late."

"If the FBI already think they've nailed Paul, what could Justin do to stop them—even if he wanted to?" Chasm asks as Parrish squeezes his water bottle in an inked hand and stares at the packed dirt of the parking area.

This is his dad, after all. I know they don't get along, but the way Paul looks at Parrish, I know he loves him even if he struggles to show it.

"We need to give Justin a reason to throw the case off-course. He has the power, money, and influence to do exactly that. I'm sure of it." I set my water bottle aside, still trying to wrap my head around the idea that Lumen killed someone. According to her, he was a teenage guy from a high school in Seattle.

I mean, eh, he was also a rapist, so his death doesn't matter much to me, but others won't see it that way. If this story gets out, it's possible that Lumen and Danyella both will face charges. They shouldn't, seeing as it was self-defense, but the criminal justice system isn't exactly known for non-biased fairness.

Ugh.

"Sacrificing yourself to save my father isn't going to happen." Parrish speaks up for the first time since we came down the trail. He looks right at me, and I shift in discomfort. He's just that intense. It's one of the reasons I like him, but also, holy hell, how am I supposed to function around this guy?

"We can't just sit around playing defense, Parrish. We have to strike, and if that means offering up our queen to my father's bishop, then we do it." I stand up and move away before they can argue with me any further, walking over to stand beside Danyella. "I'm sorry about the theater fire," I say, and I mean that. Even though I did it to save Parrish, I still set that fire; I caused her pain.

"I figured out fairly quickly that you wouldn't have done something like that without good reason." She turns to look at me, offering up a smile and adjusting her glasses slightly. "Regardless, I've certainly treated you poorly enough that we're at least even if not tilted more toward me for being in the wrong."

I smile at her, aching on the inside for that friendship we shared almost from day one.

This is too easy, Dakota. Keep your guard up. And I know I should, and I will, but I'm also not giving up on my relationship with Danyella or Lumen just yet.

"I don't hold anything that happened against you," I promise. I really don't. If anything, I'd blame Lumen and still. I see where she's at, trapped between her parents and her crime. It's not a great place to be. "Mostly, I just want to be friends."

Danyella smiles back at me, and then, as if afraid I might turn her down, starts to offer up a hug and then drops her arms. I step forward anyway and initiate the hug myself.

"I've missed you," she tells me, sighing heavily. "Lumen can be fun, but she and I have very different interests. Who else will stay up late rating the top twenty best musicals of all time? Who else will listen to me when I talk about molecular biology even if they hate every second of it? And where will I ever find a friend that listens to both Ashnikko and Italian opera?"

I grin at that last one as we pull back from one another.

"Summer doesn't have to suck; we can salvage this. I believe it."

"Well, you're braver than me," Danyella admits, shaking her head. "I know you can't hang out with Lumen because of all this, but you should come over sometime and spend the night. We have a lot of missed events to catch up on." She clears her throat, putting a fist to her mouth to stifle the sound. "For example, you sleeping with Maxim Wright ..."

"Yeah, a sleepover sounds good," I blurt, cheeks flushing. "But it might not be for a while. We kind of, sort of skipped out on Tess today."

The look Danyella throws me is all sorts of horrifying.

Of course, it's not nearly as bad as Tess herself.

CHAPTER 15

If Parrish thought to use Laverne as a shield, he was sorely mistaken. Tess is actually *angrier* with us now than she was when she discovered the, erm, threesome situation after prom.

Regardless of the fact that I'm locked in Laverne's admittedly pretty guest room by myself, that somehow makes me like Tess more.

She was worried because we both left after a single text from Parrish citing Laverne's permission, a single text from me with the same story, and then turned our phones off for hours. Makes sense why that would upset her more than, well, the other thing.

When I open my door the next morning, I find that I oddly miss a whole bunch of things about living with the Vanguards. Even though this house is to die for, architecturally speaking, it's as cold and formal as the ice palace was when I first arrived. Also, much as I accused Paul and Tess of being wealth obsessed, Laverne takes the experience to new heights.

There are far too many staff members here, so many that it doesn't feel much like a home anymore. Strangers bustle to-and-fro, committing themselves to the massive undertaking a house this size requires. There are people painting, making repairs, gardening, cooking, cleaning, and tidying at nearly all hours.

Besides that, even though I didn't like that she was a maid, it was nice to wake up to Delphine most days, with her dry humor and that deceptive glint in her gaze. I miss that. I really, really miss having Parrish just across the hall.

I stare down at the burgundy rug with the cream-colored peonies, jewel-kissed irises, and sweet pink echinacea, and I ache for not only the old farmhouse I grew up in, but the place I was just starting to think I might be able to call home.

"Today's your lunch date with Justin, isn't it?" a dry voice asks from my right, and I turn to see Parrish lounging against the wall with his arms crossed. He's not shirtless; he never is here. That's another thing I really, really, *really* miss about our house.

It's going to take a month, at the very least, to get the house back in livable condition. Maybe longer. This place is already as suffocating as the old English ivy that coats the exterior walls. Also, I'm aware that it's invasive and damages shit, but it's also pretty.

Like Parrish.

"Choking English ivy vine," I murmur, and he lifts a brow at me.

"Somehow that weird shit you say and do just excites me more," he explains, and I grin at him because I know he's telling the truth. "Who would've ever guessed that I'd end up with the alt-girl?"

"Nobody back home would believe I'd date a preppy boy like you unless they'd seen it with their own eyes. Even my grandparents were shocked."

Parrish just watches me, and I can't remember if I ever told him what happened on my end of the table. There's a lot of this and that happening, and my brain is struggling to remember who knows what.

At the very least, I was able to tell the others about Saffron's letter.

"What's going through your mind this time?" he queries aloud. "Chafed nipples? Summer weather?"

"What about chafed nipples?" Tess asks, appearing at the top of the stairs and crossing her arms. "Are you really going to stand here and discuss that in your grandmother's house of all places? After I begged you repeatedly to behave as a gentleman would?"

"Maybe Dakota doesn't like gentlemen?" Parrish muses absently, tilting his head back slightly as if he's studying the intricate plasterwork on the ceiling. "Maybe she likes assholes?" he drops his head back down slightly and throws out a wild smirk that Tess ignores.

That smile doesn't punch her in the gut the way it does me (obviously), so she forges on.

"Justin will be here to pick you up shortly. He'll drop you off after and then we'll be seeing him all over again on Friday." Her smile nearly cracks her face in half. It's as fake as the ones she started giving me just after we met, the ones that I returned, the forced smiles that have been slowly (very slowly) drifting away.

It's getting more real between me and Tess.

"Okay." Once again, the world's easiest word. It's the only thing I can think to say. I'm not offering my opinion on anything, not giving Justin or Tess information either way.

"I thought you should know that I've invited the Banks out to dinner tomorrow," she continues, and Parrish and I actually exchange a look. "What? I'm not an unreasonable or maladjusted person," Tess says, almost like she's begging the pair of us to see that. "I thought it would be easier for you to transition to living here if you didn't talk to the Banks; I just wanted—"

"Me to be Mia Patterson instead of Dakota Banks?" I ask, and Tess pauses.

"It wasn't easier on you, was it?" she asks, but more to herself than to me. And then, she says something that *really* surprises me. "Maybe it was just easier on me? Because you know what? I blame the Banks. I wish I didn't, but I do. Saffron is their daughter; they raised her. Not only that, but they didn't look into your background the way they should have. Because when you were fourteen and they thought that maybe, just maybe, something was off, they should've tried harder to find the truth."

Tess' cheeks pinken with frustration, but even though she's upset with my grandparents, I can't entirely blame her for it. I might not fully agree, but I understand. I understand, and her honesty is such a refreshing fucking thing that I could cry.

"I know you probably think I'm doing this just because of the custody hearing, but that … that's not it," Tess adds, almost as an afterthought. That's a glimpse right there into the insecurities she tries so hard to hide from the world.

"I'm proud of you, Mom," Parrish says, not something either of us expected I don't think.

"You can stop trying to butter me up," she tells him, but she can't hide the pleasure in her face at hearing those words. "Dakota, you better get ready."

I look down at my clothes—all Whitehall prep gear again. Running shorts, a sports bra with a loose tank over it, and sneakers. I slept in all of it but the shoes, and figured why change? Hey, if I'm lucky, Justin will take me back to the Mexican restaurant. Anything but a repeat of that horrendously stuffy dinner party.

"I'm ready," I say, looking back up, and Tess nods. With great reluctance, she goes to move away, and I step forward just once. Just that one step toward her, the biggest gesture I can display right now. "Thank you, by the way. For messaging my grandparents, I mean."

Tess pauses and looks away, out the window toward the enormous sweep of gardens.

"I'm sure it doesn't seem like much, after Justin went out of his way to bring them here, but I'm glad you appreciate it."

I can't exactly tell her that nothing Justin does is without nefarious purpose in mind, that by bringing the Banks here, he was actually threatening their lives. So, no, I don't hold him in high esteem for the act.

Tess leaves us alone which is a pretty miracle, particularly in light of her anger last night. Neither Parrish nor I thought we had the right to deny her accusations, so we retreated to our separate bedrooms on opposite ends of the house.

I spent every second last night missing him.

"I hate that he gets to take you away, and I can't stop him." Parrish sighs and turns, pushing the door to my borrowed bedroom in. I follow him, and he slams it closed behind me. My back is to the wood, his attention on my lips before he lifts it to my face. "We need a solid plan here, you're right. Not just one overdue reaction to each action that he takes."

"Did you have something in mind?" I ask, and his expression takes a devious downturn.

"Just this." He leans in, capturing my mouth with his, burning me with the heat and solid feel of him. I missed him so much while he was gone. It was a longing and a fear that I'd never experienced before, not even when Tess flew me from New York to Washington state. Not even then.

His tongue is sinful, tracing across my own as he holds the side of my face in his hand. When he pulls back, I find myself drawn forward, and then we're kissing all over again. Parrish puts his other hand up against the side of my face, and then my palm is trailing down his chest, and we're ... we're stumbling toward the bed ...

We fall onto it together, him above me, his palms planted on either side of my head as he stares down at me, looking pained.

"I hate that you're going over there, and I can't protect you. I hate it even more that I got myself kidnapped, and you had to sacrifice so much to save me. Dakota, I'm going to figure this out for both of us."

"Don't break yourself trying to be a hero," I whisper back as Parrish pulls away. Just in time, too, because my phone buzzes in my pocket, and I slide it out to see that ... "Justin's here."

"You just sounded like you were going to the gallows," he replies dryly, but at least he escorts me out of the room and down the stairs.

Justin is at the front door again, smiling wide as Tess stares back at him like she may very well stab him. Does he know how hard he's pushing her? She's only going to take so much before she retaliates.

"Caroline would love to see Parrish," Justin continues, smiling prettily. "She is his mother, after all."

"*I* am his mother," Tess growls out, losing her carefully groomed and coiffed temper. "Caroline hadn't even seen Parrish in person since she left Paul. Not once."

"Yes, well," Justin continues, folding his sunglasses up and tucking them into the pocket on his jacket. "We all arrive at emotional maturity in different ways, don't we?" He looks past Tess and nods in approval at me. "Off we go, Princess, I'm starving."

Parrish grabs me from behind when I take a step forward, hugging me tight, wrapping me up in a sweet-scented hoodie snuggle that reminds me of the day after the talk show, when Tess broke my phone, and he held me so I could cry. And then kissed me. And then ended up rounding second base with me.

I put my hands on his as Tess swallows against her emotions, and then I pull myself from his embrace before I break and just beg to stay here.

Justin and I climb into the car. He starts it, playing *"Party in the U.S.A."* from Miley Cyrus.

Um.

Hmm.

I say nothing, as usual, waiting for him to break the silence.

We end up back at the house instead of at a restaurant which is interesting. Today was supposed to be a lunch date, and that's it. Why are we here?

"Come in, so you can change clothes," he tells me, and we climb out. Justin waits until I'm inside before grabbing me by the arm. I'm not expecting it at all, particularly not when he wrenches me back and around to face him.

Before I fully register what's going on, he reaches out and he backhands me.

And oh my God, it hurts.

It hurts so fucking bad. I stumble back, lifting my hands to my face. I'm biting back a whimper, clenching my teeth around my tongue so hard that it bleeds. But I can't give him the satisfaction of the sound. Even as my head is ringing, and I'm tasting copper, I can't fathom that he'd really do something like that.

Thus far, he's never shown me any physical violence.

I just stare at Justin Prior, a sense of betrayal sweeping over me. Again, I knew this wasn't for real. I knew he was evil. I knew, I knew, I knew, but I …

He just hit me.

Justin sighs and puts his hands on his hips. Blood drips from the curve of my lower lip and hits the pristine wood floor.

"Next time I tell you to wear your hair a certain way, do it." He shakes out his hand and looks me over before reaching out to cup the side of my face. I pull back from him, putting space between us. Justin doesn't like that, but he drops his hand to his side as Delphine comes down the stairs to see me bleeding all over the floor.

"Oh baby sister, what happened?" she asks, looking at Justin for confirmation.

"Dakota slipped and knocked her head into the column," he says with a believable level of sincerity. The look he throws my way is a clear warning: *keep your mouth shut.*

"Come upstairs, and we'll get you cleaned up." Delphine guides me to my 'bedroom' and sits me down on the edge of the bed. She gets a first aid kit to wipe the blood from my face, but most of the pain and bleeding is coming from my tongue and gums. There's not much to be done except to pop a few pain killers and drink some water. "I've always been klutzy, too," she tells me, smiling as she goes through my new wardrobe, selecting a very pretty summer frock in white and blue. It has little bell-shaped flowers all over it.

It's not something I would ever choose to wear.

But I put it on, and I don't say anything. Partially, because my tongue. Mostly because I'm still in shock here.

He's escalating. Of course, I knew that. The fire was proof enough, but somehow, this is more surprising. Because he can see that I'm not coming to heel as quickly as he wanted. When the love bombing and the threats don't work, it's violence that's next on the table.

Lunch today, apparently, is being had in the garden.

We have small sandwiches with cream cheese and watercress,

macarons, and tea. Delphine and Caroline join us, but mostly it's Justin that I'm concerned with. He's as charismatic as always, laughing and joking, but *holy crap-balls, my face hurts.*

I guess I'm either a normal or a lucky person because I've never had somebody hit me like that before. Not once. I don't know how to process it, and it's scaring me. Only, I can't let on. I can't let a single flicker of fear show on my face, or I'm giving the asshole exactly what he wants.

After lunch, Justin invites me to play chess.

As I take my seat at the small table, I put my hand to the side of my aching face, and I quiver with undiluted *rage.* Does any part of me believe this is accidental? No. This is the very definition of grooming: Justin is leading me to the emotions and ideas that he wants me to find.

He *wants* me to be angry.

And it's working. I am. I am fucking pissed.

"Here you go, princess," he murmurs, offering up an ice pack wrapped in a fluffy washcloth. He presses it gently to the side of my swollen mouth, and I wince. "Shh, shh, shh." He releases the ice pack into my grip, and then strokes my hair back, pressing a gentle kiss to the crown of my head.

I'm ripped apart by his actions, torn in two completely opposite directions.

I hate him.

Also, he's exactly the father I always wanted. My heart stutters at the idea that we really, truly could've had this, the closeness he feigns, boat trips to the Puget Sound with lunch and binoculars, games of chess.

Tears prick my eyes, and Justin swipes them away with his thumbs.

"I'm sorry that I hit you like that," he says, and he may as well have just thrown a goddamn glitter bomb in my face. All sparkles and confetti cuteness, and yet, the cleanup is a *bitch*. "I shouldn't have lost my temper."

"And yet, I have a feeling that if we could rewind time, you'd do it all over again."

"Ah, like Hermione's time-turner." He chuckles, but there's nothing funny about this, and even a stupid Millennialism isn't cute or funny anymore. Err, I know *millennialism* technically means belief in an ideal society or something, but whatever. Just add *generational tic* to the dictionary.

"Harry Potter references don't make my face hurt less." I stare him down as he plays with the king piece on his side of the board, absently stroking it and staring out the window instead of at my face. "Don't think I didn't miss your lack of an answer either."

Justin returns his beautiful sapphire gaze to mine and smiles prettily. Only, there's a bit of oil that rises to the surface, the Seattle Slayer coming out to play.

"If I tell you to wear your hair in a chignon, then do it. I've been generous, Dakota. See that? I even call you by your preferred name. I make concessions for you. Why is it so hard to do the same for me?" He sighs and adjusts himself in his seat, gesturing at the board.

Today, I play with the black pieces and Justin, the white.

He makes a move, and I stare down at the board, wishing I could be anywhere but here. The setting itself is beautiful. I mean, wow. This house, these grounds, the pretty little art studio we're sitting in.

"I thought this could be your writing studio," Justin suggests, lifting his gaze up to mine.

It feels like he's just punched me all over again.

I simply stare at him. What else can I do? Not only has he just made the first move in our game, but he's also played one against me in real life.

"Writing studio?" I manage to whisper, getting this funny, twitchy feeling in my spine. "I never said I wanted to be a writer."

He laughs at me then, leaning back and offering a magnanimous, sweeping gesture with a hand decked out in a pewter ring, a new watch at his wrist.

"Of course you'll be a writer," he tells me, and it's as if all the walls in here are crashing down around me. "You're going to write my story, your story, *our* story." Justin scowls, and goose bumps break out on both arms, spiders of terror crawling down my spine. "Somebody has to."

See, here's the thing.

Cool beans, I get a writing studio despite the fact that I've never once mentioned being into writing.

But reality and fantasy are two entirely different things.

He's making me into a mini-Tess. I've just now realized how deeply fucked-up Justin's psychology toward Tess is. I mean, think about it: not only did he try to kill her children, but now he's making me into her replacement.

Thank *fucking fuck* that he isn't a sexual predator. It's the only lucky break I've been granted in this living nightmare.

"Since we're on limited time today, you can start this weekend. I'll read over the drafts and make changes. I've also hired you an editor." He continues to smile at me as I hold the ice pack to my face, wishing I had the guts to just stab him. Right here, right now.

I don't want to be that person. My heart is screaming in my chest, but even though I want to cry and rail at the world, I pick up one of my own pieces and move it. There's no point in arguing with Justin Prior, not when my grandparents and sister are in town. Not when I'm in love with three boys. Not when I'm *just* starting to feel like a part of Tess' family.

I already know about Raúl and Mr. Volli, about that cop guy, the deceased Mr. Fosser. How many other serial killers does Justin have in his pocket? He could simultaneously kill several of my family members all at once and without ever leaving the comfort of his leather armchair.

"What story will I be writing?" I ask politely, barely focused on the chess match at hand.

"It'll start with *once upon a time*—obviously." Justin makes another move, and I do the same. Back and forth, back and forth, just like we've been doing in real life. "We're going to write the story of a king and his princess, and how they were reunited, how they consumed the world."

Justin knocks my king off the table, putting his palms flat on the surface on either side of the board. He stands up and then leans in to peer at me, the spicy smell of his aftershave making my stomach roil.

"Think about how that just happened, how I beat you."

"You made the first move," I counter, and he snorts.

"I've had my software analyze over a million chess matches, and white only comes out on top fifty-five percent of the time. It's not always about the first move, Dakota, but the last." He slides his phone from his pocket to check something as I gaze at the board, studying the arrangement of the pieces and trying to puzzle out where I went wrong this time. "Unfortunately, I have to return you to your mother. Not for long though. Soon, it'll be she who's obligated to return you to me."

He takes off, and I rise to my feet, still holding the ice pack in place and staring at the board for a minute before I follow him through the house and onto the porch.

Delphine sees me off with a hug, one that's almost as good as a Banks signature squeeze.

"Soon, we'll be living together full-time," she murmurs, but if that's supposed to make me feel better, it fails. Actually, I feel *worse*. It's enough to douse the warmth of her hug in ice water.

"What are you planning for the hearing?" I ask, but Justin gives a slight shake of his head.

"What did I tell you, Dakota? You'll be living with me, but as I said before, I'm not a monster. Tess will have you on the weekends."

On the weekends.

I glance over at the old mansion, an infinitely superior piece of architecture to the hideous cube thing where I've been living. Yet, if I could only dub one of these places the ice palace, it'd be this one.

I can't live here, I think, feeling the very first kiss of true panic. Hah.

Little did I know, it was about to get so much worse. Justin wants me to be a writer? I'll writer this shit up for you.

His smile wasn't so much an expression of joy as it was proof that he took pleasure in his own derangement, his Machiavellian scheming. His triumph only came in the form of other's agonies, their tragedies his celebrations. He cared little for the suffering of others unless it offered him a perverse sense of judgment and vindication.

It's not that I don't believe Justin, that I don't think Medina is a cesspit full of rich, calculating creeps. It's simply that he's one of them. In this case, the enemy of my enemy is still my goddamn enemy.

That's how it is in videogames, too. Don't trust two warring creatures. As soon as your avatar approaches them, they'll both turn on you in unison. Case in point: *Monster Hunter.* Unless you've been ragged on by a *rathalos* and a *gore magala* at the same time, you won't truly understand the horror.

We climb into the car together but instead of starting his usual lip-syncing routine, Justin turns to me.

"I'm going to be emailing you a summer itinerary. I suggest

you look it over. I'm also going to send you a list of guests from the dinner party, so that you can send out thank you notes to reward them for their attendance."

"Um, kay." This sounds … disturbingly passe, but alright. I'll send thank you notes. Also, it's a bit prosaic for Justin, certainly. *Yikes.* Where is this going? Nowhere good, I'll tell you that.

"The list of guests is also *your* list, princess."

"My list?" I reply, a wormhole of dread opening up in my stomach. I'm going to get sucked into it and implode, that's what. Whatever news Justin is about to deliver, it's going to blow donkey butt. Whatever that means. I think I just made that saying up? I'm not sure. Could be adopted internet slang. I was saying *Gucci* and *rat-fuck* for weeks before I even fully understood the meanings.

"The people you're going to punish for me," he adds with a smile, and I press the ice pack even harder into my face, even though it hurts, *because* it hurts. Like a pinch to wake oneself up from a dream, except that it's a nightmare this time, clearly. "The monsters who drove me out of town." He grits his teeth and curls his fingers around the steering wheel. "The vultures who stole my money, my work, my wife, my daughter." He hisses, and then forcibly, almost disturbingly, makes himself relax. "Aren't you, my little payback princess?"

Justin chuckles, and I stare as he starts the car and we leave through the front gate. I just stare and stare because I don't know what else to do.

"Then what?" I ask, and he cocks his head slightly, as if he's considering my question. Really, we both know he has a plan in mind already. "What happens if I do it? If I complete your list, if I get revenge on everyone that wronged you?"

"If you do this, I won't ask for anything more."

My eyes widen, but, uh, remember? I *love* adages and idioms and whatnot. Say it with me: *if it sounds too good to be true …*

Yeah, it's too good to be true.

"I'll never hurt anyone you love or care about ever again." There's a pause here and Justin lifts a single finger to indicate an amendment to the rule. "Barring self-defense, that is. Physical attacks as well as judicial ones. In such a case, I retain the right to defend myself."

"You're joking?" I ask, but even though my dear sweet daddy allows me to mouth off, he *really* hates it when I question his honesty. He takes that whole *I will never lie to you* thing seriously.

Justin slams on the brakes, tires screeching on the road. I fly forward, and only by the grace of my seat belt do I avoid another bloody lip and nose.

"I'm sorry," I whisper, hoping to placate him as he turns his head slowly to stare at me. "I shouldn't question your honesty; you'd never lie to me."

His rage dissipates, and he smiles at me again, reaching out to pet my cheek with two gentle fingers.

"Exactly. I don't lie to you, Dakota. You are my everything. You know that, right? Daddy's pretty little princess." He chuckles and shakes his head. "It's too obvious if I do it, don't you think?" He pauses again and looks toward the gate. "I'll need an airtight alibi for every move you make."

"What happens to Tess after this?" I whisper, but Justin doesn't answer. He starts driving again, taking a longer, more circuitous route to Laverne's place than necessary.

"A few more things," Justin continues, and I close my eyes against a rush of sudden fatigue. It's not in my body, though, it's in my heart. I just feel *so damn tired* all of a sudden. "I want you to convince Parrish to date Lumen Hearst."

I go completely still then. Actually, I die a little bit on the inside.

"Huh?" I turn to look at him, and he offers me up this

schmoozy, faux-sympathetic smile that churns my gut.

"Laverne Vanguard reached out to me, honey. She doesn't want you to have a relationship with her grandson."

Bam. Mic drop. I mean, mic drop for Laverne. She has just sunk my battleship.

I knew it. I knew her non-reaction was too good to be true.

"You said … you said that I should ask for what I want." I'm gagging here. I'm dying on the inside. "You said you'd never hurt Parrish; this *will* hurt Parrish."

"Laverne is a very important investor, angel. We need to keep her happy. You can still fuck him if you want, but the McKenna boy is a better match for you." He turns a knowing smile on me as I sit there in abject shock. Hearing your dad say *you can still fuck him if you want* is gross and weird enough, but there's so much more to it than all that, isn't there? "I hear he'll be proposing to you soon. Won't that be nice? Uniting the McKennas and the Priors. Of course, you'll keep your last name. That is, you'll keep my last name after we have it legally changed—after the hearing on Friday, obviously. I'll be made the custodial parent, so it won't be an issue."

I open my mouth (which hurts, by the way), close it. Open it. Close it.

"I'm getting ahead of myself." Justin glances over at me. "You'll say yes to his proposal, won't you, cupcake?"

"I …"

"Just say *as you wish, daddy.* Isn't that cute? It's a *Princess Bride* reference. Have you seen that movie? No? We'll watch it together." He doesn't let me say that of course, I've seen *The Princess Bride*. Maxine and I used to watch it with Saffron. But that is an answer that will result in his temper, so I keep it carefully tucked away.

"As you wish, daddy." On the outside, I'm calm, placid, almost submissive in nature. On the inside? I'm on fire.

"One last thing," he says as we pull up to Laverne's beautiful gothic revival, and I see Parrish leaning against a column, waiting for me. Our eyes meet through the windshield, and metaphorical lightning crashes. "Maxim and Maxine, they make a cute couple, don't you think?"

"Does it matter what I think?" I whisper, and Justin chuckles again.

"As I said, keep fucking him if you want. But he *will* date Maxine, do you understand?" Justin leans in toward me to whisper. "I may not have Parrish tied to a chair anymore, but you know when your Daddy means business, don't you?"

"Why?" I choke out. "You said I deserved nice things, you said —"

"And you do. This isn't about that, is it? Parrish and Lumen; Maxx and Maxine. You and Chasm. I'm arranging my pieces on the board, Dakota. I suggest you do the same." He leans over me to open the door, and there Parrish is, pulling it wide and staring at the ice pack on my face.

"You hit her," he breathes, his face coloring red with rage.

"Not at all: she ran into a column, didn't you, princess?" Justin's stare is a challenge, one that Parrish takes up. Before the two of them can kill each other, I'm launching myself up and out of the seat.

I take Parrish's arm in my own before it's too late.

If Justin and Parrish come to blows—verbal or physical—only one of them will make it out alive.

I love Parrish, and he's incredibly calculating, absurdly powerful in personality, but he cannot beat Justin Prior, not as such.

"Just let it go," I whisper, dragging him away.

Justin gives a little honk, offers up a wave, and then I hear

"The Sign" by Ace of Base blasting as he jets off.

"Gamer Girl." Parrish gently takes my chin and turns me toward him. He must see the horror in my eyes, his own searching my face before he swallows past a lump of emotion. "Tell me what happened, tell me everything."

The tears come again, but I'm not ashamed of them, allowing Parrish to bundle me up in his arms and hold me close. He strokes my back, and he waits, and he says nothing, but I can't escape the nightmare of a directive that was just given to me.

Parrish and Lumen, Maxim and Maxine.

The only good part of this whole scenario is the me and Chasm bit.

Clearly though, there are two things the Seattle Slayer doesn't understand: love and loyalty. He thinks he can drive us apart when all he's doing is pushing us closer together.

And together, we are stronger.

CHAPTER 16

Pick my pawns wisely, one of the first lessons my father taught me. Guess I did that, huh? Because my pawns are here, all around me, and we're in this together despite threats to our lives, attacks on our characters, and divisive blades poised at the throats of our intimacy.

If Maxine didn't love me the way she does, and me her, we might not have survived the Maxx thing.

If Parrish didn't love Chasm the way he does, and Chasm him, they might not have survived us cheating on him.

If Lumen didn't have a good heart beneath all her sass, we'd still be at war.

As such, we're all (sans Lumen) sitting together on the sand at Medina Beach Park. It's a fairly chill day, with only a single family seated on a blanket nearby. Otherwise, it's just the six of us —me, my boys, my sister, and Danyella—digging our bare feet into the sand and listening to the patter of Lake Washington on the shore.

In a fortuitous twist of irony, Justin's obsession with technology and his all-seeing eyes have chased us away from our phones and computers, PlayStations and iPads. While everyone else at our school is busy chasing clout and boosting their subscriber counts at the price of their own dignity, here we are, drinking fruit sodas from glass bottles, eating superbly ripe watermelon, and watching the sun set.

"I'm not sure that I've ever just sat and watched the sun go down like this," Chasm admits, seated on my left with his knees up, his arms wrapped around them. "Not since my *halmeoni*—err, my grandmother—died, anyway." His face tightens up a bit, and he exhales. He doesn't have to say in words that he misses his grandma; his entire aura shifts to one of melancholy. But only for a second. Chas is not one to let his own issues get in the way of anything else. He *still* has yet to tell me the full story of what happened between him and Seamus.

I can't imagine that Justin simply said *let the boy be,* and voilà, it was so.

Much as he likes to think it, he isn't a god.

"It's pretty, isn't it?" I ask, admiring the view of Mount Rainier in the distance. "There are so many colors. Have you ever tried to take a picture of a sunset? It never turns out right, not even with the best phone camera in the world." I take another bite of watermelon as Parrish wraps his arms around me from behind and holds me close, resting his chin on my shoulder.

We're all caught up now, this little group of ours.

Just … not on the Slayer stuff. The boys and I are keeping a few select things to ourselves. I can only hope that's not a colossal mistake.

"Why on earth would he want us to date?" Maxine asks, glancing over at me from my right. X is lying on his side, one hand propping up his head as he gazes out at the water, but I can see the way his muscles tense up at the question.

"Nothing Justin does is single-minded. Every move he makes has two hidden motives, at the very least." I pick up a ruby red square of fruit and place it on my tongue, closing my eyes as I savor the watermelon's natural sugars. Is there any other food that screams *Americana summer* the way this fruit does? "Likely, he wants to isolate me further from everyone that I love."

"That's the most horrible thing I've ever heard in my life," Maxie mumbles, playing with her braid. It's surreal, seeing her here, sitting on this small beach in Washington state with the stepbrother I hated (okay, fine, love-hated) from moment one, his best friend that I got mixed up in multiple misunderstandings with, and ... and her ex-boyfriend. Oh, and Danyella, of course.

I feel bad for Lumen and the fact that she can't be with us right now, but it is what it is. Eventually, I'll find a way to free her from Justin's influence. It's as if everyone I know has been sucked into this dark fairy tale, cursed by the evil wizard.

It's up to me to set them free. If I have to be a princess, I'll be the warrior princess who rides into battle atop a steed, sword raised, a bow and arrow strapped to her back.

But right this second ...? I glance over my shoulder to see if I can't spot Tess and my grandparents sitting at the picnic table. True to her word, Tess extended the dinner invitation herself. Originally, she'd offered to take them to some fancy five-star restaurant in Seattle, but then I mentioned Justin's stuffy dinner party and how the Banks (myself included) aren't particularly into that sort of thing.

I suggested we pick up barbeque from a nice takeout place and hit a park.

Surprisingly, Tess accepted.

For once, she listened to what I had to say. And now, the very family she banned me from speaking to is sitting here in the warm evening air with the sparkling water, the distant laughter of people strolling down the docks.

I could never have predicted this back in February.

Anyway, when I glance over my shoulder, I don't see anything but Parrish's face, soft and gentle in the molten light from the setting sun. He offers me up a smile that makes my heart pitter-patter, and I feel my pulse skyrocket. Our faces are so close, and it'd be so natural to just kiss him right now.

My lids get heavy, and his do the same, and then we're leaning in together for—

"Teenagers will be teenagers, now won't they? Hormonal surges during puberty are so unbelievably disturbing." Danyella makes this scoffing sound that sends a vibrant pink blush to my cheeks and chest that I hope I can blame on the sunset. As I go to turn away, Parrish catches the edge of my face with two gentle fingers and presses a soft kiss to my mouth anyway.

It's the sort of stupidly innocuous kiss that tricks onlookers into thinking it's romantic, but chaste. Only, that's not true at all. It's like a hidden strike of lightning, zinging through the body, pebbling my nipples, rushing straight to the spot between my thighs.

Ugh, no!

I turn away sharply, and Parrish lets me go, hyperaware of my injury. Yesterday, after Justin dropped me off, Parrish fetched me a fresh ice pack and pain killers but made sure to keep it from Tess. It's just the sort of wound that monsters like Justin excel in, the kind that hurt the soul more than the body. It's not obvious from a distance.

Maxx and Chasm don't know yet, but I'll tell them as soon as I get a chance.

The former glances back to see what we're doing as Chasm slips out a cigarette and looks back, trying to see if he can get away with smoking it here.

"I'm still struggling to get used to the idea of you two dating," Danyella admits as I swallow hard and blush all over, shifting as if to move away from Parrish. He locks his arms even tighter around me, but it feels too good to resist. I could sit in his arms on this beach, watching the sun set, forever and ever.

Even amongst thorns, there are roses, after all.

"Weird as fuck, isn't it?" Chasm offers up with a harsh laugh and a shake of his head. He cups his hand around the cigarette and lights it, taking a quick drag as he continues to peer over his shoulder in search of Tess. Guess he figured the whole *get out of a threesome free* card used up all of Tess' goodwill toward him. "I'm still struggling myself."

"Why don't you swallow a bag of dicks and be quiet?" Parrish retorts, his breath ruffling my hair and bringing goose bumps up on both of my arms.

Maxine makes a small noise of surprise, unused to the boys and their methods of showing affection. From down the beach, Kimber sits on a towel by herself and pretends not to be interested in us. She lost her phone privileges for one reason or another, so at least we don't have to worry about Justin watching us through her.

Anytime she thinks we're not looking, she openly stares in shock at the sight of her brother cuddling up to me. If she weren't so afraid of him, I imagine she'd find a way to convince Tess to come over and see us like that. I'm not entirely sure what her reaction would be.

"Why don't you stop rubbing all over Kota and let her breathe for a minute?" Maxx turns the rest of the way over, grabbing a piece of watermelon for himself. I can't seem to resist staring at his lips as they turn glossy with juice.

"I should've expected this," Danyella murmurs, unconcerned with the boys quibbling. She's used to it, after having gone to school with them for so long. "Remember when you confessed to being in love with Parrish in the theater? That was back in, what, February? March at the latest."

"Hah!" I blurt, and Chasm offers up a dark look as Parrish sighs heavily and happily behind me.

"I knew it. Right from the start, I fucking knew it." Mostly, Parrish mumbles under his breath, but Maxx can hear it, and he struggles to maintain a neutral expression.

"No, no, no, I never said I was in love with him. You're thinking of the conversation where you asked if I liked him, and I said I wasn't sure if I did or if I hated him." Danyella listens to me as Maxine looks on in rapt attention, absorbing every word of this conversation. Then my former friend turned enemy turned friend again snaps her fingers and adjusts the pair of bright yellow glasses she's wearing today.

"The micropenis," she says, and everyone there goes quiet. Chasm just *stares* at his friend, and X allows a smug smile to tease his pretty mouth. "You accused him of having one that day."

"Not surprising," X murmurs, grinning and catching Parrish's foot before he can kick him in the chest.

"I do not have a micropenis." Parrish offers up with a breezy laugh, sitting up and leaning back on his palms. I scoot forward because I swear, he's getting hard behind me, and I can feel it, and I'm not very good at resisting the people I love.

Last night, Tess corralled us in the theater—yes, Laverne's house has a legitimate theater with rows of seats and everything—and encouraged us to watch a movie as a family. Parrish and I complied without complaint for several reasons: first, we owe Tess for being cool about the threesome; two, he's been home less than two weeks while I've been 'home' for about four months; three, we both sensed that she's in full survival mode now.

Tess isn't sure when or if we'll have a chance to be together like that again. Not just because of the fire, not just because both Parrish and I were kidnapped once upon a time, but because of tomorrow's custody hearing.

I am most definitely not looking forward to it.

Because of the impending hearing and Tess' need for family time, Parrish and I haven't, erm, you get what I mean. Blue ovaries? Is that the female term for blue balls? Close enough. Blue clit sounds weird, and blue vagina is just ... this isn't an alien romance, so no, we won't go there.

"Blue nipples," I murmur, and then I chuckle, and everyone is staring at me like I've lost my mind. Oops. My cheeks flush, and I sputter a quick response. "Um, I was wondering what the lady term for blue balls is ..."

"And so you said blue nipples aloud? You're the weirdest person I've ever met," Chasm declares, and then he leans forward and kisses my lips with the faintest hint of tobacco on his own. My mouth tingles as he pulls back and blinks those jewel-like amber eyes at me. *Mosquitos get lost in amber, right? All amber is really, is fossilized tree sap.*

"Fossilized tree sap eyes." I say that one on purpose and then tap Chas on the nose. "That's what you've got, *oppa*." That last part, I add on breathlessly, almost wistfully.

He blinks back at me in confusion, and then wild laughter slips from him. He points at me with the cigarette.

"*Oppa* ... I am officially in love." Chasm makes a circle with his hands and shouts it out for the entire beach to hear. "You got that, Medina? I'm in love!"

I slap at him as Kimber openmouthed gapes at us, and Maxine chuckles. Danyella recoils a bit, and Maxx makes this sour face that precedes him rising to a squat. He puts his big hands on either side of my face, and then he's kissing me with his tongue tainted with watermelon, forcing my mind right back to the lady blues all over again.

"If you're talking about blue balls, you must have ideas in mind," he whispers in my ear, quiet enough that only I can hear. I'm still reeling from his kiss as he sits back on his haunches, elbows resting on his knees. "You never confirmed or denied the micropenis thing."

"I'd rather not know anything else about Parrish's penis," Danyella admits, and then she's standing up and he's scowling.

"You don't know anything at all: I do *not* have a micropenis. Tell them, Gamer Girl."

"It's appropriately sized. Now can we drop this?" I hiss this part out, glancing over at my sister in complete embarrassment and total shame as she sits there with a hand clamped over her mouth to hold back laughter. I realize then that Maxx and I just kissed in front of her, and I don't know if I should just accept that she'll have to see us together eventually? If we should hold back around her?

I don't know the answer to any of this.

"Baby sister, I don't even know how to take this in." She waves a hand around in my direction and plants an elbow on her knee, resting her head in her hand. Her eyes are warm, so it's hard to say if she's bothered by me and X, but maybe I should ask? "You've grown up a lot. I'm only sad that I missed it."

"If only we could work on that cardio so that we could go on long backpacking, trips," X offers up, raising both brows at me. Maxine chuckles and shakes her head.

"You're barking up the wrong tree, XY. Never gonna happen."

I look between the two of them and wonder yet again if I didn't make some sort of mistake, hoarding three amazing people to myself when I should only rightfully have one. Unless, I mean, I guess equal wealth distribution does not apply to boyfriends.

"Come sit with us," my grandmother's voice calls out, and I

rise to my feet with Maxine. The boys follow, too, and we end up arranged around the wooden picnic table where my grandparents and Tess requested a minute to talk amongst themselves.

It's not difficult to assume they were discussing me.

All eyes turn my way as I grab a paper plate and add some corn and mashed potatoes to it, acting as if I don't notice the attention. Never in my life have I been the center of attention the way I am here, with Tess and Justin, with three love interests, with the Banks reunited. It's a little unnerving, a little nice.

I focus on my food, not on the fact that Tess is staring at me, and I realize I've just subconsciously chosen to sit on her side of the table across from my grandparents. Maxine is on my right, and I suddenly can't tell if I did the right thing, made a mistake, or just … fell into something entirely new altogether.

"What were you guys talking about?" Parrish asks, the slightest edge in his voice, as if he thinks I might truly get sent back to New York or something. He parks his elbow on the table and lets his head sit in his hand, drooping a bit like the whole thing is just too heavy to hold up. It's a lie: the King of Sloths has claws.

"We were discussing the custody hearing tomorrow." Tess' voice is neutral, but strained, and she glances back three tables over to where Paul is entertaining the kids. Kimber slogs our way, realizes there isn't a place to sit, and then begrudgingly heads in that direction.

"Here," Danyella offers, rising to her feet and taking her food with her. "I'll go sit on the bench and sketch; this seems like a personal family conversation."

"You're welcome to stay—" I start, but it's too late. She's heading off to an unoccupied bench, and now Kimber is sitting beside my grandfather and he's smiling at her.

"You and Dakota look so alike, it's incredible," he says, and Kimber's eyes widen like she might protest. I guess she has enough social graces not to go down that road, so she says nothing, turning away from them and pretending to be interested in buttering a roll.

Walter turns back to me, and I know he notices that I sat down next to Tess somehow.

I flush—yes, again—and pick up the ear of corn in my hands.

"We were going to testify on Justin's behalf at the hearing tomorrow," Carmen reiterates, and I find myself wishing I had the guys around me right now. Instead, they're all clustered on the opposite side of Tess and out of reach.

Since I first arrived in Washington, they've been my constants. It was rough at first, but Parrish started taking care of me almost against his own will, standing up for me, explaining things to me, ushering me out of the TV studio, holding me while I cried. And then when he went missing, and I was going through the worst of it trying to get him back, I had Chasm and Maxx. They're not just lovers, they're friends. The best I've ever had, actually.

Well, besides Maxine, of course. But she's a sister, right? They're either the worst or the best from what I hear. Maxine is one of the good ones. Delphine and Kimber are up for questioning. Amelia is too young, but I see promise there.

"What were you going to say?" I ask, taking a bite of the food and finally raising my gaze to meet hers.

Carmen folds her hands on the table, her lipstick refreshed and bright as always, a cherry red color that she's worn my entire life. Her eyes are sharp, and she's a cunning woman, but the Banks have *no* fucking clue what they're up against here.

I just remind myself of my own naivety upon arriving at these shores.

"That after having raised a young woman who we believed to be our own flesh-and-blood granddaughter for fourteen long years, the unnecessary separation between us is causing undue emotional distress."

I nearly drop the ear of corn, a deep, sad frown etching itself into my mouth.

She isn't wrong.

Tell me about this same scenario months ago, and I would've jumped for joy at the thought of going to court and getting another chance at this. But after everything that's happened? My stomach is a void of pure dread.

Tess says absolutely nothing. Her face is a blank mask, one that I can't even begin to read. Parrish, though, he's an expert. He's looking at her with a disturbed expression that makes me wonder what it is exactly that he sees.

"If I agree to some sort of visitation schedule, will you reconsider?" Tess poses the question, but I'm immediately on edge. What happens if she does that? It's not through my own actions, but what if Justin retaliates regardless?

Then again, he never specified that this couldn't happen, and he's all about the honesty thing. But is it worth the risk?

"Dakota, what do you want us to do?" It's my grandfather asking this time. Maxine puts her hand on my leg for support, but it only helps a little. This is basically my worst nightmare come to life. I want to scream at them all about Justin. Most everyone I care about is right here with me in this moment.

If I asked to see those FBI agents today, and we all stayed together like this, would I be safe from Justin's machinations?

Likely not.

A man who reinvents himself after an historic downfall, who's a computer genius that's at least partially responsible for today's technology, a guy who makes an app that can hack into basically any camera and then sells it for only fourteen bucks to the public … that is somebody you don't take chances with.

You create a plan, and you execute it.

That's what I was missing yesterday, when I lost the chess match with Justin. I wasn't paying attention, and I had no plan. I gave a *bit* of thought to each individual move, but not to the situation as a whole.

See, that's the problem.

I set the corn down and wipe the salt and butter from my fingers with a wet wipe that my grandmother hands out to me. Tess watches the interaction with a slightly sour expression on her face, one that I don't quite understand.

Why is every move that Justin makes preset to make me look like a total asshole?

It was bad enough in front of my peers, Paul, Tess, worse in front of Maxine. In front of my grandparents? Fuck. My. Life.

"What sort of deal did Justin make with you?" I ask instead, because asking a question—even one as rude as this—is better than giving a definitive statement of any kind. Tess lets out a small exhale, but then tries to hide the reaction by picking up a can of seltzer and chugging it.

"He was generous and polite," Carmen begins, exchanging a look with my grandfather. He doesn't respond, but they share one of their famous couple stares, and I just know telepathy is a possibility because they're for sure using it. How could they not be? My grandmother turns back to me. "He said it'd be your choice when you called us or Maxine. Actually …" And here Carmen goes about trying to tidy up the table until Maxx stands up and offers his assistance, carrying several paper plates with used corn ears to the trash. "He suggested he'd fly us in for major holidays and even send Dakota to New York for part of the summer next year."

Tess *stares*.

I have a feeling none of those things are an offer she'd be willing to make.

"Done." Just that. One word. It surprises the shit out of me, and I sit there gaping, wishing fervently that she'd go back to ice-cold dragon mode, snipping and sniping at everyone and everything. She can't realize her mistakes and improve her parenting now, can she?! This so messed up. "All of those things. I'll put it in writing even. I'll ... Saffron can visit her as long as I'm present."

Uh-oh.

That's when I know for sure this is getting bad.

By offering even supervised visits with my kidnapper, I know that Tess is desperate. She doesn't think she can win this thing tomorrow and neither do I. In fact, I know that she won't. There's not a chance for her, even if the Banks don't testify.

"We won't testify against him because, unless Dakota knows something we don't, there's no reason to." Carmen turns toward me, but I can't possibly say a word, now can I? The best I can do is absolutely nothing. She studies me for a minute before looking back at Tess. "We can agree to sit on the sidelines—but only if we get something in writing beforehand."

Tess is a shrewd businesswoman as well as an author (lucky), and she nods. She'd expect nothing less. Normally, my grandparents are the type who'd do a deal on a handshake, but not here, not after Tess Vanguard swept in and ripped us apart.

"Can I tell a story?" Tess offers up as I just sit there like an idiot and swallow back the urge to scream. My father truly is incredible at his work: I am just as trapped, just as tongue-tied now as I was when he literally held Parrish captive at knifepoint.

Because now I know, now I understand the true scope of his reach.

There is nowhere he cannot find me, no place he can't get access to me. Even now, knowing that after I gave a very hammy and embarrassing speech about leaving our phones in the car for family time (shockingly, it worked), it's a possibility that I might've missed a camera here or there and that Justin could be watching and listening.

It's staggering, how horrific the idea of that truly is.

"Tell your story, Mom." Parrish takes her side, but it doesn't bother me anymore. It's cute, really, and a good indication of the true character beneath his royal sloth skin.

Tess glances my way, worrying at her lower lip in a way I'm not used to seeing. This is that crazy, kooky author side of her peeking out, the one that wears messy buns and laughs at her own storytelling, sitting in that chair and crafting entire worlds with her fingers.

I raise my brows in a noncommittal but hopefully encouraging way.

It's such a shame that, at the beginning of our relationship, Tess and I both bungled it up when we had every opportunity to make it right. Now, here I am, shackled to Justin's whims, and I can only keep quiet and strategize.

"Did I ever tell you how Saffron and I met initially?" Tess offers up, and that surprises me. Surprises Maxine, too, I think, because I can feel her shift behind me. Nobody expected our conversation to go in this direction.

"I wasn't aware that you knew her at all," I admit, surprised and shocked and fascinated all at once. This is almost like hearing the classic *how I met your mother* story except Saffron was my kidnapper before she was my mother which, you know, is a different take on the whole deal.

"We met at a women's shelter in Vancouver." Tess purses her lips and looks back at the Banks. "She had her baby with her when I first arrived." Tess swallows and closes her eyes, as if she's gathering her resolve together. This story is costing her some pride, I see that, and my heart aches.

Maxx is now sitting beside Maxine. Pretty sure he moved to

this end of the table to be closer to me, but also … the two Max's make a perfect couple. His green eyes meet mine, and the intensity of his stare cuts right through me. I want a moment alone with him; I haven't had one since … like fucking forever ago.

I want him to envelop me in his strong arms and hold me against his broad chest, and more than anything else, I want him to run his fingers through my hair and kiss me. I want him to whisper things like, *feel me, touch me, all over* like he did on the one and only night we spent together as lovers.

With great reluctance, I tear my gaze away from his, stop the metaphorical bleeding with an emotional band-aid, and focus back on Tess.

"She had the real Dakota Banks," I amend, and then Maxine is speaking up for the first time since we sat down at the table.

"*You* are the real Dakota Banks." Her voice is firm, uncompromising. Our eyes meet, and I end up letting her put an arm around me so I can rest my head on her shoulder. Tess stares at me like she was staring at Carmen handing me the wet wipe, and—although I'm no bestselling author—this is what I see.

For the first time, she saw them not as the kidnapper's accomplices, but her daughter's loved ones, the people who'd bandaged scraped knees, and helped with school projects, the people who held her when she cried, the people who made her laugh, who took care of and nurtured her for her entire known life.

They were not aggressors: they were family.

Anyway, that's what I'd write if I ever wrote this down. I might have, if Justin hadn't creepily started pushing me in that direction.

Now I might not just to spite him.

"She had her baby with her, and I had mine." Tess sighs and picks at the red and white checkered tablecloth with a fingernail. "I was there because Justin and I were getting a divorce, and he'd been abusive, and I had nowhere to go." Her breath warbles a bit on the release, but this is Tess Vanguard we're talking about here. She rallies as Maxine keeps me tucked close and listens.

Chasm is staring off into the distance, but I know he's paying attention; it's all in the eyes with him. Parrish, too, is pressed close to Tess for moral support. Kimber isn't looking at anyone or anything, but I can tell that she isn't totally checked out here.

I can tell that neither of my grandparents expected to hear the word *abusive* in the same sentence as Justin's name, but that they believe Tess, too. How could they not? The look on her face, the tone in her voice, it's genuine. Or maybe I just think that because I had that very same man backhand me just twenty-four hours prior?

"We made friends there. I genuinely enjoyed Saffron's company." Tess sighs. "We were both there for, God, six weeks or so? I managed to obtain temporary housing, and Saffron just said she was ready to move on. We lost touch, and yet, I might not have remembered her name, but I thought about her often after that."

This explains how they seemed to know one another when they spoke on the phone, that shard of betrayal in Tess' voice.

"How did you piece together that the woman in the shelter was Saffron?" I ask, and Tess lifts her eyes from the tablecloth to look at me, *really* look at me. She takes me in like it's the first time all over again, and I can't decide if it was Parrish going missing and then coming back (a truly significant miracle considering she'd experienced a once in a lifetime event like that before) or if it was the fire or something else altogether, but I can see her shell cracking.

Maybe, just maybe, it isn't a shell at all? Maybe it's a shield that Tess has been holding up against the world all these years to keep the pain of Justin's abuse at bay, to hide behind to avoid the pain of losing a child? I might be back, but that doesn't mean she can ever recoup those lost years and stolen memories, the chance at raising her baby in her own image.

It's all gone. Saffron took all that. And yet, here I am. I'm sitting right here, and it's like she just finally understood that even if she wants to hold that shield up against the rest of the world, she can't hold it up at me or else we'll never understand one another.

"As soon as I saw her face, I recognized her," Tess admits, looking back over at my grandparents again. She doesn't say it aloud, but there's this sense of betrayal in her words, in her expression, as if she believed she and Saffron shared a connection that was then exploited. Sympathy floods me, for both Tess *and* Saffron. "I'm not sure if you heard this part of the story or not?"

"We hadn't," Carmen agrees with a long sigh, staring down at her folded hands atop the table's surface. "And we have no idea where Saffron is now. It's not unusual for her to go missing for stretches at a time like this, so really, she could be anywhere, but who knows?" My grandma glances my way, but I'm still processing.

Maxine, likely, is still processing.

That baby Saffron had with her at the women's shelter, that was Maxine's biological sister.

I stand up after a minute and move away from the table, circling a large tree and sitting down with my back to it. The lights in the small parking area flick on as the sky darkens, and I close my eyes.

When I hear footsteps coming my way, I just assume that they're Maxie's.

Right name, wrong person in mind.

"Are you okay?" That smooth, cool voice belongs to Maxim Wright, the very cute boy named after a very unfortunate magazine. I smile at him, but without ever opening my eyes.

"What happened to Maxine?"

"You know your sister too well, don't you?" he asks, and then he ruffles up my hair, and I'm cracking a single lid to look at him, strong and handsome and limned in the faint glow of the parking lot lights. Maxx stills his fingers slightly and then drags them down through my hair, fingertips whispering across my scalp. My breath catches, and my throat tightens, his green eyes shimmering with undisguised interest. "I moved too quick, that's all. She's avoiding me just a bit, so that probably explains it."

With a small sigh, he turns and puts his back to the tree beside me, our shoulders touching. Maxx is facing more toward the water than I am, just around the curved side of the trunk.

"Is it awkward, seeing her again after everything that happened?" I ask. I mean, I realize he's seen her since we had sex, but not for any extended period of time.

Maxx hesitates before answering, and then he curls his fingers though mine, pressing our hands into the grass. He rubs a thumb across my knuckles as he thinks.

"I feel bad," he admits, and I turn to look at him only to find he's already turned to look at me. He allows a cocky smile to take over his mouth, and I wonder then how I didn't notice back in the coffee shop what an arrogant little shit he actually is.

"Bad about what?" I ask, and then Maxx leans in closer to me, his mouth brushing across mine.

"That I'm happier with you than with her."

"Don't say that," I tell him, but then he's releasing our hands and turning toward me fully so that we can look at each other more easily.

"Dakota, do you know how I felt when I thought we were a onetime thing? How I felt just the weekend before last when Parrish came back, and I was relegated to fetching clean pj's and watching the door?" I flush a bit at that one, but Maxx doesn't let me roil in the emotion. He reaches up and cups my chin, staring at my mouth and then my eyes.

It occurs to me then that I haven't been in Maxim's crosshairs until now. Before, he assumed at every turn that he was about to lose me, that I was going to go back to Parrish, and that him being my sister's ex (albeit it a platonic one) had precluded us from ever actually being together.

Like Tess, he'd thrown up a shield across his heart.

It's down now, I can see that, and it's making it impossible to breathe.

Right then and there, it seems as if—given the choice—I'd choose Maxx over anyone else in the world. Just me and him, together like this, it's perfect.

I can't breathe; my fingertips are digging into the dirt; the whole world spins.

"I know how you felt," I admit, my voice a whisper. I do, because I was sitting on that countertop in Parrish's bathroom after … well, we made love, and then Maxx knocked on the door to give us pajamas, and for a split-second, just a flicker, our eyes met. That's how I know. "And I'm sorry."

"I love Parrish; I've known him since before I can remember. But I have to admit that I liked having more of you and your attention. Do you really love him? Do you want to be with just him? If so—"

"You can't be serious," I murmur back, and then I'm turning and sitting on my knees, so close to him that it's probably kind of weird to see from a distance. He blinks at me, his lashes long and dark, his hair like coffee with a drip of cream.

"You really want us to do this?" He pauses here and lets his gaze slip to one side before redirecting it back to me. My relationship with each boy started differently and took an entirely different path. But X? I was able to experience that tumbling, skydiving, frothing, fluffy, wild, sparkling sensation of love at first sight. Our gazes met in line at the coffee shop, and I was immediately giddy, wondering if I might be able to get a number from a cute boy and start something exciting.

But my sister? I know her like my own mind. She loved Maxx, and I took him. That's a hard pill to swallow. Without Justin's interference, I never would have experienced this with him. It's difficult for me to say that I regret it, because … it's that good.

I'm that excited by it.

"Why did you go back to the house really?" I ask him, because I feel like I'm missing something here. That, or else he never specified. Hell, maybe he just hasn't had a chance, a moment for me and him? We're like an *us* here all of a sudden which is new. I've felt like an *us* with Parrish at times, with Chasm, too. But not Maxx, not yet. The closest was when we were kissing in the tasting room of the winery, but that's it.

This is better.

I'm looking at Maxim, and he saved my family, and he's the type of selfless, brave individual that people dream about, write about, make movies about, craft poetry for … but they rarely exist. Here one of them is, and I feel guilty for even thinking he could be mine.

Because even with a gun to my head, I'd have trouble choosing one of the three boys and leaving the other two to move on without me. Nope. Nope. Can't do it. Or *won't* rather. They're going to have to leave me, that's what.

If that never happens …? The thought trails off, and I don't chase it. I'm not ready to face the possibility of that just yet, because it's too amazing and, as Maxx assumed all along that he'd never have me, I assume that I'll never quite reach that dream.

And not just because of the guys and how impossible it is for me to fantasize over this but also because there's a sick feeling in my gut that says I may very well die before any of this is over.

It's a pipe dream and not because I don't believe that—out of all the many billions of souls in this world—that if anyone could make a situation like this work, it'd be these three guys. It's a pipe dream because I don't know how to get out of this without losing myself in the process, one way or another.

"Don't look so sad, Kota," Maxx says, smiling softly. Of all the people I've met in Medina, both good and bad, he's the only one who picked up my nickname and used it on the regular. Or like at all. He reaches up and rubs a thumb along the side of my face, giving me the chills. "You're not alone in any of this."

After a moment of hesitation, and a quick glance back at the rest of the group, X curses under his breath and then wraps his arms around me, pulling me to his chest. He takes my spot against the tree and holds me like Parrish did earlier.

It feels different, but just as good.

I'm not even sure how that's possible, but it is.

"I know that I'm not alone, but I'm also scared. However this ends, it won't be good. Even the best possible scenarios have terrible downsides."

Maxx listens to me for a moment, the savior of the Vanguard family, a hero who doesn't even consider himself to be one, and then he speaks so softly that if his lips weren't pressed up against my ear, I probably wouldn't have heard him at all. Also, he's speaking in such low, sultry tones that I know that while his heart might be in the right place, his body has other ideas.

"I'm almost embarrassed to admit it," he begins, but I snort. It's a very unladylike snort, and I don't give a shit. What is ladylike anyway? If I'm a lady, then everything I do *is* ladylike. So okay, fine, I give a very lady-esque snort.

"You're not embarrassed about anything. I'm almost convinced that you're unaware of what that emotion actually entails." I put my hands over his, and I, of course, being an expert at embarrassment am fully aware that this is a new and shiny moment for me and Maxx Wright.

We've never allowed ourselves to really cuddle up like this, and I'm loving it. Also, I'm pretty sure nobody at the picnic table can see us where we're sitting, especially as the darkness sweeps in over the landscape.

Learning that Saffron and Tess knew one another, that Tess met the 'real' Dakota Banks, it alters my perspective on things a little.

"I get embarrassed," Maxx argues, but then it's as if he's searching for an example and can't find one. He quickly changes the subject, and I stifle a smile. "The reason I left my parents' place so quickly was because it hit me all at once, and I couldn't wait long enough to explain things to them. I had to leave, right then and there."

"What hit you, exactly?" I whisper right back, wishing we had fireflies in Washington. Somehow, summer feels like it should have fireflies. We have them back home, in the Catskill Mountains. Although, the longer I'm here, the more I connect with the people in Medina that I care about, the more that line between here and there blurs.

Home is—yes, it's another adage, I'm sorry—where the heart is.

Truly.

"I wanted to wear that boutonniere, Kota. I decided that I was going to prom even if I had to go as a chaperone, even if I was the weird old guy instead of just your date." He lets out a sultry, little laugh that has goose bumps taking over my bare arms and legs. The night is cooling off quickly, but Maxx's warmth is more than enough to make up for it. "I went back to the house to get my suit."

There's a pregnant pause there, one that sits as heavy and obtrusive as the big, white moon in the sky.

If Maxx hadn't made that decision—which is fucking adorable, by the way—the laughter of the children that I can hear in the distance, it would be gone forever. Tess would break; Parrish would bleed; I would lose a chance to get to know the family that I might've had if Saffron hadn't stolen me.

But if she hadn't, then what? Justin never forgot about me, clearly, so what would my life have been like?

My biggest questions remain unanswered. Why did Saffron choose me? Because of my looks? Maybe. But doubtful. And how does she know about Justin? If I were to take Tess' story and Tess' story alone, it would seem that at best, Saffron heard secondhand tales about the man.

Only, when I spoke to her, it didn't feel like that, now did it?

"Not every person would go inside a burning building," I say, and Maxx pulls me just a little closer. I can feel his heart beating against my back.

"To be fair, I wasn't aware it was on fire until I went inside."

"You're saying you wouldn't have gone in if you'd known?" I retort, but he has no response to that because we both know that he would have. "And somehow, you went back in three times, but didn't know the second and third time?"

"Like I said, I did what any human in my position should do."

"Should." That's the only word I have to say. We're both aware that the majority of people would not have done what Maxx did. Even among those who would go in to save the children, they certainly wouldn't have bothered with the bunny. Which reminds me ... "How is GG doing?" I ask, and Maxx laughs.

"Same old, same old. He's young enough that if we get him neutered now, it might help reduce some of his, uh, bad behaviors. Seamus doesn't like having him around though. That might become a problem."

We pause our conversation at the sound of footsteps and there's Tess, looking down at the pair of us all wrapped up together like, well, lovers.

"We're packing up and heading out," she says, studying us like she doesn't know what to think. I carefully extricate myself from Maxx's arms and rise to my feet, swiping grass off my butt. More than anything else, I wish I could go with him and Chasm, take Parrish with me, and have a sleepover with the four of us.

Those few days after Parrish came back, when we were all able to sleep in the same room, that was heaven.

Maybe at some point, but not tonight. Not with the hearing so early in the morning tomorrow.

It's dark out, and we've already checked the area for cameras. There don't seem to be any, so … this is as safe a place as any.

"You two aren't—" she starts, but I don't care what she was going to say (it's probably better that I don't know), and I throw my arms around her neck. The hug surprises the shit out of Tess. She even takes a step back, but it's already too late because it's happening anyway.

With my mouth near her ear, I whisper what I hope is an encouraging but not damning statement, something that even *if* Justin heard about it, it wouldn't matter.

"Don't ever stop fighting." Just that. It's all I say, and then I pull back and head toward the picnic table to bid goodnight to my grandparents and Maxine.

Tomorrow can't be over soon enough.

CHAPTER 17

There's less media attention on this court battle than there was during the last one, but it's not as if the paparazzi have up and decided to leave us alone. The fire roused their interest; Parrish's return roused their interest; Milk Carton has roused their interest.

I can't breathe, finding myself sitting in a wooden chair at the front of the room.

I'm supposed to be talking now, I think, but I can't. My throat has closed up, and my head is swimming. Anxiety rockets through every one of my limbs, and even the presence of both the Banks and the boys in the audience can't calm my nerves any.

Everyone is fucking *staring* at me, and if I could fully be myself and tell the truth here like I did during the last hearing, it would still be bad. As it stands, my tongue is chained, and Justin has me held like a marionette. His expression upon hearing that the Banks would no longer be testifying, that was scary. It was quiet and contemplative on the outside, but there was this dangerous glint in his blue eyes that promised Tess' stunt would not go unpunished.

"Tell them you want to come with me. Beg them. Scream. Do whatever you have to do."

The directive, given to me on the very first day that I met Justin in person, hangs heavy in the back of my mind. Justin did not give me explicit instructions today the way he's done in the past. Why? Because, as I said, the Banks are in town for a reason.

I'm expected to understand and perform to his wishes *without* crystal clear directives.

Yet, here I am, suffocating.

One of the lawyers—this one is Tess'—is asking me questions, but I can't answer them because I can't hear. My ears are ringing, and my vision is fogging at the edges.

"Excuse me. I need to use the restroom." I shove up to my feet, and practically sprint down the aisle and out of the courtroom, bent over and wheezing, hands on my knees. The boys are right there behind me, Maxine alongside them.

"I told Grandma and Grandpa you needed a minute," she whispers, helping me over to a bench as Chasm sits on one side of me, Maxx on the other, and Maxine kneels in front of me with Parrish standing behind her. "Do you need some water? A granola bar? I could grab something from the vending machine."

I'm on the verge of a panic attack, I'm sure.

"I can't do this. It's not like it matters what I say anyhow." I let out a sharp, degrading laugh and run my hand over my face.

"Hey, Little Sister," Chasm murmurs, taking one of my hands in his. "There's no shame in like, passing the fuck out on the stand. They can't make you talk if you're not conscious, you know what I mean?"

I turn to look at him.

I mean, he isn't wrong.

"I can't pass out on command," I hazard, but I don't think

that's what Chasm is saying. He cocks a brow at me.

"No, but you can *pretend* to." He flicks his gaze around the mostly empty lobby. We're at the courthouse in Kent, and I must say, the building's a lot uglier than the one in New York. *Focus, Dakota. This is not a moment to fixate on architecture.* "Look at me." Chas puts his hands on either side of my face, his touch a source of calm as it was while Parrish was missing. "Just ... roll your eyes back and flop onto the floor."

"What can Justin possibly do if you refuse to talk?" Maxine suggests, because she doesn't know he hit me the other day. I couldn't bear to tell her. She also doesn't know about the, err, serial killer stuff. "I know he has that app, and that he has money, but bullies can't be allowed to continue their torments."

I just stare at my sister, and I wonder if I shouldn't tell her everything.

How can she possibly understand my motivations if I'm not totally honest with her? At the same time, I don't know if my sister can *handle* an overload of information like that.

"Have you ever been up against a billionaire?" Maxx asks, and my sister turns an irritated gaze his way. "What? I'm just saying, it's not like any other feud. If he wanted to, Justin could afford to pay someone to kill one of his enemies and have little to no connection to any of it."

My sister just stares at him, even though he's speaking hyperbolically.

"The thing about Tess is," Parrish begins, exhaling and closing his eyes for a moment. I imagine that this is the very reason he allowed himself to pretend to hate me in the first place. By being here, I'm hurting Tess with every breath. "She seems tough, but she forgives too easily. Just push through however you need to. She'll move past it."

I'm not entirely sure if I believe that or not, but even if he's only saying it to make me feel better, I appreciate it.

"It's okay." I close my eyes for a minute to gather myself. "I can do this. There's a way to get through this." I shove up to my feet before anyone else gets a chance to respond and open the courtroom doors, slipping back in.

I'm asked how I feel, if I can continue, all that good stuff, and I end up back at the front of the room to give my own testimony. Smoothing my skirt against my thighs, I take a seat.

This case is over, no matter what I say. I'm certain that Justin has handpicked the judge. Looking at Tess when she walked in here this morning, I imagine that if Justin didn't also have Laverne's backing, she might have been able to pull a trick.

As such, check and mate.

"Who do you want to live with, Dakota?" the lawyer asks me again, offering up a small smile that doesn't quite reach her eyes.

"I don't know enough about either of them to choose" I admit, which is hurtful enough toward Tess. I know them both more than well enough to understand that Tess has the personality of a Brillo pad, but genuine character. Justin? His heart is made of slime, but it sparkles with glitter from afar. "It doesn't matter to me what happens here."

I answer a few more questions, doing my utmost to ignore the dual stares of my biological parents. The other lawyer takes a turn, but my answer remains the same.

Justin told me to *do whatever it took.*

Well, all it will take is for me to do nothing.

The Seattle Slayer has this rigged; it's in the bag.

And there's nothing that I can do about it.

So, because I know moments like these are few and far between, that I may never get them again, I make myself enjoy seeing both of my parents at once, in the same room. Growing up with the Banks, I never wanted for anything.

But also, Saffron was never around, and I didn't have a dad, so ... I just take it in.

Tess, looking at me like she's failed, but also as if she can't help being disappointed. Justin, with a cool half-smile that belies the rage beneath.

He is *furious* with me.

How on earth am I going to pay for this one?

———————————

"I take it there's a reason behind your defiance." Justin's words are as cool as the smile he wore during the court proceedings which, I don't think I even need to say, swung his direction. That is, not quite as I expected, but most definitely in his favor.

Justin is the full custodial parent meaning he has the final say on everything as far as legalities. Changing my name, for example. Or allowing me to leave the country with a passport.

As far as parenting time, Tess is given unsupervised weekend visits.

That's it.

Only two days a week to escape, to see Parrish, to get a break.

Rather than Tess' place being my default, it's Justin's.

I am stuck with Justin.

Fortunately, it's Friday, so I'll be able to return to Tess in the morning. But for now? While he's in an endothermic rage? I'm with Justin. *Trapped* with Justin. It was bad enough that Caroline was in the audience, along with Delphine, but even weirder when Justin basically told his other daughter off so we could drive alone together.

Fucked.

I am so fucked.

"You told me to cry, scream, beg, whatever it took. Well, it took my doing nothing. I did nothing, and it worked out exactly as you wanted it." His hands squeak as they tighten around the wheel, but there's a hot pit inside of me, dredged up by the anxiety I felt in court.

"Word games again, Dakota?" Justin asks blithely, as if he doesn't care. He does. "After the incident with the rabbit, I believe you were warned?"

"I did exactly as you asked," I say, feeling angry tears threaten. "Do what it takes. It's done. I'm yours."

"And the Banks? Is it a coincidence they chose not to speak up today? Is it also a coincidence that Tess' scumbag lawyer tried to dig up the past and use it against me?" I assume he's referring to Tess' claims of past abuse, the cases she filed against him that she managed to dredge out of obscurity. The things Justin had done his best to bury—that he'd scrubbed almost entirely off of the internet —rose to the surface like corpses from the grave.

"That was all Tess, the latter part. I can't say what my—the Banks were thinking. Maybe they struck a deal with her?"

Justin doesn't respond, waiting until we get back to the house before he yanks me from the car by my arm. I tear away from him and stumble back, panting heavily as we face off against one another in the driveway.

"Stop it!" The words explode from me, entirely unbidden. I know I'm risking a lot here, but he's also pushing me. Pushing, pushing, pushing. I can't take it anymore. I stare at him, breathing hard, watching his sapphire eyes shimmer like gems. "You jerk me around, you pick my clothes, order my food, dictate my schedule." I'm panting heavily, running on steam and pure, unfiltered adrenaline. It won't last though. I've just backed myself into a corner, and I need to find a way out of it. And *quick.* "You," I start, and then I force my voice to soften even when I'd rather grit my teeth, "you're charming, and handsome, and intelligent, the sort of father I always dreamed of having."

"Flattery will only get you so far, princess," he says, his words a sibilant hiss, a clear warning. I'd better work this out or I'm in serious trouble.

"You said that it was important to ask for what I want, that I deserved nice things. I deserve a father that doesn't hit his daughter, for starters. Don't hit me again." I do my best to make it sound like a request, but it's not. If he keeps escalating the physical abuse, I don't know what I'll do.

I might snap.

I might make a stupid, split-second decision that costs someone their life.

I can't allow things to escalate like that.

"How can I be a real daughter, and you a real father, if this keeps happening?"

Justin exhales, as if he's releasing some of his tension, and then he smiles at me.

It's not a good smile, I'll give you that.

"I find a bit of pushback amusing. You're not a doormat like your sister." He glances toward the gate of the property as if in annoyance. I'm not sure where Delphine and Caroline are, but they should be here soon. He looks back at me, affecting a slouch that isn't entirely unlike Parrish's. I guess it's just a 'grew up a rich boy' thing. Justin's confident, easy swagger is sharp and dangerous and volatile in a way that Parrish's just isn't.

I'm on edge, wondering if I shouldn't run, if I've just blown all of our careful planning, plotting, and maneuvering.

"Lesson in sacrifice indeed," he murmurs, and then he looks right at me. "Choose somebody to die."

"Excuse me?" I whisper, putting my hand up to my throat and resting my fingers against my pulse. *Thump, thump, thump.* This thing became real the moment I saw Parrish strapped to a chair and bleeding, when Chasm and I opened that dreaded box, the one I try my best not to think about but do anyway.

Somehow though, until today, I didn't want to believe what I already knew.

"Choose one and show me you're mature enough to accept the consequences of your actions. Ah." Justin pauses to lift a finger as I stand there trembling, wearing an unobtrusive white summer dress with my hair twisted into a careful chignon, just as he asked. Even though I left Laverne's house with Tess this morning to attend the hearing, Justin told me exactly what outfit he wanted to see me in. "This is another lesson in chess. I'll give you an example next time we play." He pauses here to scowl at me, giving me a once-over that has me chilled to my very bones. "I'd been planning on playing a game with you after our celebration dinner this evening, but I find that your scheming has soured me on the idea."

"My scheming?" I repeat as he moves closer to me, and I stay rooted to the spot, but aware that I'm essentially allowing a cougar to sneak up on me. Soon enough, his teeth will be in my neck, and I'll be left as so much meat.

Fucking hell.

"Encouraging Tess to come at me like that. You must've said something in order for her to get her claws out like that, seeing as you aren't her favorite person on the planet. Do you see the way she looks at you? More than likely, she's glad to be rid of you." Justin moves past me, and I have no choice but to follow, up the front steps to the porch, into the house, the kitchen where the picture of Alfred Armando Vasquez hung, the clue that ultimately led us to Parrish in the first place.

I hate the things that Justin is saying to me now. I despise them. On the inside, I am beyond terrified that they're true. *Don't listen to him, Kota. If he's saying these things, you should be* less *likely to believe them, not more.*

He wants me to hurt.

Right now, my enemy is throwing lightning bolts my way. Like the heroic Link in any Zelda game, I need to lift up my metal shield and return those bolts on Ganondorf. I know, I know, the video game thing, but still. The metaphor is there.

"I'm going to ponder on the rest of what you said. I'm not an unreasonable man, and I find your resistance to me admirable. Most can't hack it, princess. It's why you, and not your sister, are destined to follow in my footsteps." He continues on toward the garden, and I keep up, my kitten heels loud against the pristine floors.

Classical music drifts from the solarium as we pass through and Justin pauses, sliding his phone from his pocket to change the selection. Within seconds, I'm listening to *"Hot N Cold"* by Katy Perry. It's catchy, but um, the lyrics make my skin crawl. Especially as Justin sings them.

Blech.

We continue outside together and, to the tune of Katy's poppy bubblegum voice, he says it again.

"Pick one to die, Dakota. I don't care which one. A pawn, a friend, a family member." He turns an imperious look over his shoulder that has my brain working on overtime. *How do I get out of this? What's my angle? What's my move?*

Because, as much as I despise Justin, I am learning to play his games.

Just not alongside him.

Against him.

Always against him.

"You have thirty seconds." Justin sets a timer on his watch, turning fully to face me. The overgrown garden is slowly being manicured to perfection, and I find that each day it gets closer and closer to tamed and further from wild, I like it less. Less and less and less.

I am that garden. I *feel* like that garden. Pruned. Pushed back. Shaped. Pulled out. Replanted. Walled in.

I exhale.

"Don't you ever wonder what would happen if you just stopped? Crush them with your success. All those people that screwed you over." I move closer to him, slapping the back of one hand into the other. He eyes me as if he's listening, but who knows? I believe that he has some legitimate mental health issues. Not that I think there's any psychologist in the world that could fix this crazy. No, once you cross that line, to murder, to torture, to rape, it's all over. "We really could just be father and daughter. I could live here, and go to school, and we could ride boats and play chess and—"

My eyes brim with tears.

Justin frowns at me.

Am I softening him up? I can't tell.

"Justin, please—" He reaches out like he might hit me, but I don't flinch. I stay right where I am, and he smiles at me. It's a shark's smile; he's scented blood in the water.

"I *told* you before, Dakota. Call me daddy. I call you by the dead baby's name, don't I?"

I flinch at that. Where the strike couldn't do it, this does. I'm the child of a killer.

I'm a serial killer's daughter.

"You are not responsible for the consequences of other people's actions."

Maxx's words echo in my head. I make myself listen to them, allow them to repeat over and over again, to bolster me, push me, strengthen me. Just because my father is a bad person, it doesn't mean I have to be. I'm not responsible for his choices, his actions.

I am my own person.

"Pick one in thirty seconds or they all die." This time, the words are a growl. He holds out the watch face for me so that I can see the numbers, the hand ticking in a circle around it. My eyes lift to his, and I wish, and I hope, and I hate that it has to be this way.

Despite everything, I wanted to love him.

"Twenty-five seconds." He continues to stare at me, laughter drifting from a family that's passing by on their boat. The water sparkles and shines; the sun is high, air is warm, flowers bloom.

I close my eyes.

My brain runs through frantic calculations, and then my eyes snap open.

"Twenty seconds."

Is there a knife nearby? A weapon of any sort? My eyes drift over to a shovel on the ground, and then I lunge, snatching it up in both hands. I rise to my feet, remembering briefly the feeling of that hoe digging into Justin's flesh the night he kidnapped me out of my bed at Tess' house.

I swing the shovel at his head, even as my heart screams, and he catches it.

A sharp point digs into my side, and I look down to see the glimmer of a knife. My gaze drifts to the side and I find Raúl, looking annoyed in a white suit with a pink dress shirt, and bright yellow leopard print glasses.

"Drop the shovel, Miss Prior," he tells me, ignoring me in favor of turning his attention on Justin. My bio dad yanks the shovel from my hands and tosses it aside.

"Were you imagining I had no idea you wanted to kill me?" Justin asks, and then he laughs. He lifts the watch up. "Ten ... nine ... eight ..."

"Saffron!" The name bursts past my lips, and then I drop to my knees. Not because I'm weak, but because the grass is warm from the sun, and the earth beneath it is soft. *Raúl, I knew it. I knew he was in on it.*

"Saffron?" Justin repeats the name like he's equal parts pleased and pissed off, dropping his arm to his side. "You'd sacrifice your adopted mother, hmm?"

I reach into the pocket of my dress, pulling out the folded paper that I've been keeping with me just in case. While I didn't expect this exact scenario—what sane person could?—I figured that keeping the letter around and presenting it during a crisis might just help me stay alive.

I lift it up to Justin.

"Here. I received it this morning. I thought you might want to know."

Justin stares at the page, his fingers tightening around it. And then he curls his lip and scowls again, turning away to face the water instead of me. Raúl stays by my side, but he's disappeared the knife into his clothes, and there's no sign that he just stabbed it into my waist. Glancing down, I see a small red bloom on the side of my too-white dress.

Oh, Gamer Girl. You are in deep. You are in this so deep.

"Saffron …" Justin trails off, and I stay as still as I can.

Does he know why I picked her?

First off, I know for a fact that he doesn't know where she is, and that he can't find her. Now, there aren't many people on this earth with the capability to track a person the way Justin can. I'm damn near certain he's already plugged Saffron's face into his software.

Which means she either knows about it from watching the press releases, or she just rolls like it's 1988 … or something. Ahem. I'm not really up on my recent history, but pretty sure you could sort of disappear in the eighties. No smartphones, few computers, lack of GPS trackers, that sort of thing.

Anyway, Justin asked me about Saffron's whereabouts on the phone the morning after we found Parrish. He was obviously annoyed and getting frustrated.

The second reason I picked her? The moment that he sees that woman, he's going to try to kill her. And that was true even before I blurted her name out like she was some sort of scapegoat.

"Get out of my sight," Justin commands, just as Delphine appears at the back door. She's smiling brightly, her blond hair bright, her makeup soft and tasteful. She's wearing a white dress, too, but hers has a satiny black belt around the waist, and matching flats.

"We're going out to celebrate, right?" she asks, and then her voice falters and trails off as she sees me sitting there in the wet dirt. The grass is damp from the sprinkler system, and my legs are now covered with mud and bits of grass.

"Maybe later, sweetie." Justin blows her off and continues into the garden with Raúl sighing and absently flicking the wheel on a lighter as he tags along like the pathetic lackey he is. I put my face in my hands and try to breathe.

Delphine offers out her hand, tugging me up to my feet.

"You didn't actually want to live with the Vanguards, did you?" she asks, sounding genuinely concerned. I ignore her, pulling my hand from hers and retreating to 'my room' for some (relative) privacy.

I don't text or call the boys or the Banks or anyone else.

What's the point when Justin can hear my every word?

CHAPTER 18

Later that evening, I change into the most palatable outfit Justin's left for me: a pair of white jeans and a hot pink hoodie with Milk Carton's logo on the front of it. The logo is black and white with a silhouette of an actual milk carton—and a picture of my face on the side of it.

Yep.

I feel like that kid in the zombie high school K-drama *All of Us Are Dead* whose mom put his face on her chicken restaurant logo. *More like, you're in the* Squid Games *trying to carve an umbrella shape from a piece of honeycomb with a needle while at the end of a gun barrel.*

What's the difference between that show and my life? Rich people manipulating poor people for sport? That's my reality. Sort of. Also, the rich people are trying to kill each other. It's an extra layer of fun.

"Daddy," I say politely, pausing in the doorway to his office. It's on the first floor, thankfully, and about as far from my bedroom as can be. He pauses, turning away from his laptop to smile at me.

"Yes, princess?" he asks, acting as if I didn't try to hit him in the head with a shovel earlier. Maybe he liked it. Probably he did. Because his whole goal here is to mold me into his image. What did I do? I sunk to his level, and I'm already regretting it.

Who would I even be if I killed my own father?

Certainly not the Dakota Banks I grew up knowing on the inside.

"I want to go out with my friends." He just stares at me, considering. It's a gamble, but I decide to bring up my bio mom. "Tess never lets me go anywhere or do anything; I was hoping you'd be different."

Justin sighs and rises to his feet, coming over to stand in front of me.

He reaches out to touch my chin, and then he digs his fingers into my skin in a way that hurts but that I refuse to acknowledge.

"Who are you planning on seeing, hmm? Your future fiancé? Because I could support that." He drops his hand down and turns away, pausing once to glance over his shoulder. "Leave the Vanguard boy out of it—at least for tonight. He'll soon be your stepbrother on both sides of the family. It's a bit weird, don't you think?"

"Both sides of the family?" I ask, going cold on the inside. "You're going to marry Caroline?"

"Well, of course." Justin sits down and turns from his laptop to one of the ... I count *nine* screens on his desk and mounted to the wall behind it. There's so much going on, I don't even try to make sense of it. Even though I'm learning all sorts of things about computer science and coding and app development over at Whitehall, I hate it.

Now, I can't tell if it just isn't my thing or if Justin has tainted it for me. Either way, I don't believe I'll be following in his footsteps. Just because you like to do something, doesn't mean you have to get behind the creation of it. That is, I like playing video games but *fuuuuuuuuck* working in tech.

"Did I ever tell you her story? It's fascinating." He clicks and types, clicks and types, pauses, swivels back around in his chair to look at me. "I mean, other than that she birthed your boyfriend and then …" He makes two running fingers and trails them through the air. "Skedaddled. Want to know why?"

I glance over my shoulder, as if I expect Caroline to waltz in at any moment. Nobody there, and I *am* curious … I look over at Justin.

He turns back to his computer and hits a single button.

The Milk Carton app launches on all nine screens, and he taps a name on a list labelled *Chocolate Milk.*

"Cute or too complicated?" he murmurs, and then he's staring at and through me again. "The milk names. Saved contacts is *Chocolate Milk,* the aging software is *Strawberry Milk* …"

"Too complicated," I whisper back, and he nods.

"We have two finished applications, slightly different UIs. I'll make a note." Justin leans back in his chair as Caroline's face appears onscreen. She's in her room, sitting at a vanity and brushing her long hair. It's absurd, how similar she looks to Parrish. It's also absurd how easy it was for Justin to locate her.

He returns to the main screen, taps another button. There's Delphine in her room, practicing some viral hip-hop dance. It's almost cute. I mean, it would be if I weren't watching her on our daddy's facial recognition software.

"Want to see what else it can do?" he asks, and then he clicks another name.

Tess Prior.

Um.

Yeah.

Right.

Not gonna unpack that one just now.

My biological mother appears, two empty bottles of wine on a desk beside her. She's in one of Laverne's guest rooms, the one I woke up in with a cup of coffee waiting. My heart seizes as I watch her angrily smash the keys of her new typewriter. *Clack, clack, clack.* So Justin really does have hidden cameras inside of Laverne's place.

Figures.

He returns to the main screen, selects another name. There's Parrish pacing a rut in the floor of his borrowed bedroom, hands clasped behind his head. He is *pissed*, and it isn't hard to see why. Even though he knows Justin is watching our every move, he's been texting me nonstop since I left the courthouse with Daddy Dearest.

"Even better." Justin switches to Maxine, sitting in the hotel room with our grandparents. They're watching a movie together. Not a one of them looks as if they're paying much attention to it. With a sigh, Justin then switches his focus to Chasm.

He's in his room, but Maxx is nowhere to be seen until ... he comes out of the bathroom with only a towel around his hips. *Oh my.* I force myself not to notice the droplets of water clinging to his skin.

Chas and X must be aware that there's a camera in the room with them, but I'm sure there isn't much they can do without being blatantly obvious. If Justin gets too wise to the fact that we're ditching his tech when necessary, and acting for the camera at other times, he'll evolve to handle the challenge.

The man does not need to get any cleverer.

He turns back around in his chair yet again, contemplating me.

I'm not stupid enough to miss the fact that this demonstration was a warning of his power. And also ... he's going to sell this app to the public?! Can you imagine what humans will do if they can track each other for fourteen bucks and the click of a button?

Doooooooom.

I try not to make an *Invader Zim* reference and fail because I am, and always will be, the 'alt-girl', as Parrish so eloquently put it.

"Can I go see Chasm and Maxx then?" I ask as Justin crosses his legs and bobs his foot.

"You don't want to know about Caroline?" he retorts. I do. But I'd much rather get out of here.

"Some other time? It's summer, and it's Friday night, and I'd rather not hang out with my dad." It's a teasing quip, something I might play on my grandpa. Only, he'd laugh and ruffle my hair, and we'd both know that I do actually enjoy hanging out with him.

As I expected, it pleases Justin, and he waves me away.

"Just tell the driver where you need to go." He focuses back on his program, and I make the great escape. I almost hesitate because of Delphine. As far as I can tell, she's only partially in on Justin's games.

Pretty sure she doesn't kill people.

Unless ... I wonder what happened to her grandmother? If that woman was truly her grandmother.

In the end, it's not worth it.

I'm suffocating, and I need to get out of here.

I ask the limo driver for a ride to Chasm's place, not bothering to call or text him in advance. Instead, I just show up and wait at the front door until X appears to open it.

"Saw you arrive on the gate cam," he admits, dressed in the *Wright Turn Barcade and Adult Fun Center* apron I've seen him wear before. Ah, that's right. His parents own a barcade—that is, a bar with arcade games for adults—and he works there. I'd almost forgotten. "I'm on my way to work."

ENDGAME ROMANCE

He nibbles his lower lip as I stand there awkwardly and try not to fidget. Maxx's gaze drifts down to the logo on the front of my shirt, and he frowns. It's a very stylized milk carton (quart style) silhouette in stark white with my baby picture in a grainy black on the front.

Milk Carton. Track anyone, anytime, anywhere. All in the palm of your hand.

That's what it says, right beneath the logo. It's absurd, and I hate it, and I want to set it on fire.

"Is Chas in his room?" I ask, and Maxx gives a slight shake of his head.

"He's at night classes." This news is delivered deadpan style, but I'm standing there gaping in shock.

"School *just* let out, and he's at a night class? On a *Friday*? He was first in his class—in the whole school, too."

Chasm is … he's fucking smart as shit. He tutored me and Parrish *and* wiped the floor with the competition, academically speaking.

Maxx offers up a sympathetic look, and then shrugs his shoulders.

"You haven't spent much time around Seamus, have you?" he asks as I admire the imposing silhouette he makes in the doorway of the mansion. X steps out, quite close to me I might add, and I'm instantaneously reminded that we've only had sex once, and that *he* has only had sex once *period.*

Eeee.

"Guess not." I reach up and scratch at my forehead with a single finger. Maxx has a smell that's suited to summertime, like a pretty drink with a fresh fruit base, a squiggly straw in a bright color, and a tiny paper umbrella. That's Maxx. Makes about as much sense as *dewy clovers,* eh? Here's the thing: I don't traffic in hyperrealism; I'm all about vibes. "Justin told me not to see

Parrish tonight, but he never specified that *we* couldn't hang out."

The edge of X's overconfident mouth lifts up, and he studies me like he's trying to decide what to do with me.

"If I put an apron on you, do you think you could pass for eighteen?" he asks, and I raise a brow. Maxx laughs, the sound loud and confident, untamed and without restrictions. It rings in the warm, evening air, further distancing me from the nightmare of this morning. "Sounds creepy, right?" He tousles my hair again, but then pauses with his hand on the side of my head. With a determined tightening of his lips, he steps forward and reaches out, pulling the pins from my hair until the black and green waves tumble down to my ass.

I'm surprised by how intimate the moment feels, standing there in the sweet summer breeze, the one that reeks of freshly bloomed jasmine and spicy sweet box flowers. X's fingers are strong and sure as he picks the bobby pins from my hair, and then smooths his palm down the back of my head.

"Sorry, I meant to explain my creepy comment: you have to be eighteen in the state of Oregon to serve alcohol."

"I have to serve alcohol?" I whisper, because I can't seem to get my voice to sound any louder than that. I want to ask X why he likes to tousle my hair, what it means when he does it.

"You can't think I'd actually take you to a bar for any other reason, right?" He offers up this devastating smile. I'm not sure I've ever seen this particular one before. We haven't had many chances to spend alone time together. Usually, we're with at least one of the other two boys. My mind strays back to lying on Parrish's bed beside Maxx, watching Patrick Swayze and Jennifer Grey make love … I mean dance. Watching them dance. *Gah!*

The smile Maxx is giving me now cuts right through my heart, bleeds me dry right there on the sprawling front porch of the McKenna home. It's completely unfettered, that smile, offered freely and without restraint.

"And I thought you were trying to win me over before ..." I mumble, and both of Maxx's dark brows go up.

"You thought I was trying? Kota, I was trying *not* to." He reaches down and scoops me up, just like that, into his arms as if I weigh nothing. Our eyes meet, and I struggle to breathe all over again. "Remember what I said when we ..." He searches for the right term. "Had sex?" Mm. Very vanilla choice. "I thought it was a one-time thing. I'm going to start romancing you."

"Right now?" I manage to stutter out, praying that Justin isn't watching.

"Right now."

Maxx loads me into the passenger seat of his Jeep, and off we go.

Wright Turn Barcade and Adult Fun Center is located in the Georgetown neighborhood of Seattle, about an hour from Medina in traffic. Maxx says it takes half that to get home after the bar closes at three.

Since I don't know anything at all about Seattle proper— Medina is basically a world away despite the views and the geographical proximity—I look up Georgetown online and see that it's advertised on the city's website as an (and I'm quoting here, so don't hate me) "industrial-hip" neighborhood. Pretty sure it was unironic. When a government website starts using terms like *industrial-hip,* what it means is *bourgeois-gentrified.*

The bar is cool though, housed in an old brick building on a main thoroughfare. The sidewalk is bustling as we ease past it and into a parking lot plastered with *No Parking Signs;* it's only six spaces worth behind the building, and it's just enough for employees.

Maxx takes me through the back door, outfitting me with an apron of my own and then pointing at me with a single finger.

"Stay on my ass tonight, okay?" He snatches up a visor with the words *Wright Turn* stitched into it, and situates it over his gloriously thick hair.

"You want me to stay on your ass?" I repeat, and he smirks, shaking his head and turning away. X heads out the door and into a large, tiled space behind a wooden bar. The room is dark, but lit up with laughter and lights, pings and beeps, the flashing of old arcade machines.

Oooooh, fun.

I wet my lips and crack my knuckles, and Maxx's deep chuckle follows me from behind the bar and into the thick of it. People laugh and drink, flirt and squeal, situated at *Primal Rage* or *Mortal Kombat*, *Space Invaders* or ... *Gauntlet Legends*. The sight of that particular machine makes me think of Parrish, and then I think about Tess, and—

I need a mental break.

I need one so badly that I didn't tell Maxx about Justin while we were in the car. I didn't tell him that I almost killed the man with a shovel, and I most certainly didn't tell him that my father demanded that I choose someone to die.

Or that he's almost guaranteed to go through with it.

Pausing in front of the Ms. Pac-Man machine, I decide to make up for my loss (not really mine though) from the game that Parrish distracted me from. As I play, a waiter in a uniform appears by my side and deposits a drink on the waist-high table between my machine and the next.

"A mocktail, just for you," Maxx tells me, and I shiver all over, tongue stuck to the corner of my lip as I try to master a 1981 classic. "Mixed it special. I call it the *Cool Blue Wave.*"

"If you're really calling it the Cool Blue Wave, we can't be together."

He snorts at me, dropping the tray by his side as he watches from over my shoulder.

"Um, holy shit."

"Holy shit is right," somebody else says, and then a small crowd of people forms behind me, pressing close as my score edges up toward the high score displayed in the center of the screen. The yellow circle of Ms. Pac-Man is moving so quickly that I can't actually blink, avoiding ghosts, collecting dots. *Points, points, points.*

I almost go numb when I play like this. I mean, I zone out. There's nothing else in the world but for me and this game. Somehow, that experience frees the rest of my brain. Like, all my anxiety and attention and worry is hyper focused on the screen.

Now what?

Justin will not be easy to kill. I wasn't aware that Raúl was around; he surprised me. Now, I have a small sore spot on my right side, and I don't even know who the fuck I'm supposed to be.

Literally, I just picked up a shovel and tried to kill a guy.

A ghost—it's Pinky because, I mean, it's *always* Pinky— gobbles me up for the final time, and the crowd groans as I fall just short of the high score. I take a small break and let somebody else play, but I'll be back.

Mark my words.

The place is so busy that X isn't able to stay with me for long, returning to slinging drinks as I wander around and get a look at the laser tag area, the various claw machines packed full of stuffies, and an area of advanced VR.

I wait my turn at one of the rooms and head inside, donning the gloves and boots and goggles. It's good stuff, fairly modern in terms of realism, but I've seen better. *Gamer girl's a game snob, no doubt.* I move on and end up back at the bar again.

There are myriad people gathered around, but I notice after a moment that all of them are girls. I mean it. Every single one. Maxx is mixing drinks and passing them out with a smile, but he doesn't react to any of it, the over-the-top flirting, the requests for his number, the touches of fingers on his arms or shoulders.

Eventually, he finds his way over to me, putting his forearms flat on the counter and leaning in.

"What can I get you, Kota?" he asks, and I exhale. This moment that we're having, it's supposed to be the *only* thing I have to worry about at this age, whether or not the cute boy on the other side of the counter is going to kiss me.

Serial killers? Not so much.

For a split-second there, I pretend Maxx is behind the counter at a soda fountain in a black-and-white movie.

I lean up and press my mouth to his, causing a shocked ripple to go through the crowd of girls. They all watch in surprise as X opens up to me, tracing my tongue with his own, giving it back to me twice as hard as he's getting it.

Not only does he smell incredible, he *tastes* incredible.

I'm not ready for Maxx to pull away, but he does, serving me another drink before moving back to the rest of the crowd. Several of the girls drift away after that, looking disappointed.

With my mind wandering the way it is, I soon end up at a late nineties game: the original 1998 *Dance Dance Revolution.* Grinning, I climb up and hit start. The Barcade charges an entry fee, so there's no need for cards or phone payments or … like quarters? None of that.

The machine is huge, pink and blue and silver. On the ground, there are arrows, ones that I'll tap my feet against as I dance in time with the arrows flashing on the screen. It's a fun game, more cardio than *Elden Ring*. Unless, you know, you get up and throw things when you're pissed the way I do.

I hop on, drawing a crowd of drunken *DDR* enthusiasts and ending up sweaty as hell, my apron hanging around my waist, my pink hoodie tossed aside. I'm left in a tight black wife beater that catches Maxx's attention on his next round through the arcade. His eyes lock on mine, and I wonder if he's even going to be able to pull away, or if he's going to stand around and watch me dance.

Since *DDR* can be played between two people, I'm thrilled when a guy steps forward, and we go at it like we're arcade brats from the eighties and nineties. Not gonna lie, I enjoy modern gaming, modern graphics, solitude, but there's something to be said for the wild energy in here, the laughter, the chatter.

I'm enjoying myself.

Despite everything, I'm having a good time.

Also, I'm at least five years younger than every other person in here save Maxx.

He waits for me to finish dancing, but my opponent gets to me first.

"Hey, you're pretty good at that," he says, wicked hot, flashing a sharp smile that makes my brows raise. He looks like … mmm … Suga from the K-pop band BTS. He looks young, so not much past the legal drinking age I'd bet. "You want to exchange numbers, and we can do it again sometime?"

I almost open my mouth to say yes because I'm as dense as a box of rocks, but then X is right there, standing behind me with his arms crossed over the front of his apron.

"She's too young for you," Maxx tells the guy, that overprotective note in his voice again. I give him a look, and my DDR opponent raises a pale brow, pierced through with a single silver hoop.

"She can't be any younger than me," the guy retorts, and then it occurs to him as he sees the apron hanging around my waist. I'm not twenty-one and here to drink; I'm here to work. He must assume eighteen, since legally I shouldn't be in here unless I am. Not that it matters. I wish I could come here every night.

"I'm her boyfriend. Fuck off." Maxx sighs as he adds these last two sentences on, and I flush red all over at his words. "Your boobs are blushing," he tells me, after having finally chased the other guy off. He takes a step forward, and I lift my head to look at him.

"You're not going to unironically start calling yourself a sigma male, are you?" I ask dryly and Maxx snorts at me.

"I'm a lone wolf," he says, cupping his hands around his mouth and pretending to howl. When he drops them, he puts his palms on my shoulders, leaning in and just *barely* brushing his lips against mine. It's a tease, nothing more.

I pout at him in annoyance.

"*Sadge,* my kiss," I murmur, and he chuckles.

"Don't start speaking Twitch at me," he warns, turning and then glancing back at me over his shoulder. "I start kicking people out in fifteen. Wait for me."

As if I have anywhere else to go.

I'd like to go over what happened with him anyway, before he takes me back to Chasm's and, eventually, to another house that I don't want to call home. At least with the ice palace, there was hope. Even in the bleakest moments, there was hope. With Justin's place, there's none.

I'll never be able to relax there.

If I'm talking emotes aloud, my brain must really be scrambled from earlier.

Kota, you tried to kill your sperm donor with a shovel. That's next level messed up.

To keep myself distracted, I wander back into the sea of bright lights and happy chirps from the arcade machines. I'm standing in front of an *Indiana Jones* pinball machine when Maxx finds me again, leaning close and letting his breath tease the fine hairs at the back of my neck. *Holy shit, that feels good,* I think, hating myself and finding it impossible to resist.

Do I … have to? Is there really any good reason to resist Maxim Wright at all?

Maxine. There's Maxine. And yet … he isn't 'just' my sister's ex-boyfriend anymore, is he? He's my friend. Because of Justin, he's my lover.

"Fucking finally. Shooing drunk people away from shiny objects is not an easy feat." He sweeps the hair back from my neck, putting his face up against the side of my throat. My chest tightens, an almost painful sensation stirring in my lower belly.

With my gaze locked on the flashing lights of the pinball machine, I tap my fingers against the buttons on either side, playing the game as best I can with such a distraction. The arcade is dark and nearly empty now. Blessing or curse? Both.

Oh yeah. Both.

I'm not even sure how to respond to Maxx's words, whispered so fiercely against the throbbing pulse in my throat. *I thought you were nice,* I want to say, *but I almost like it better that you're not that nice.*

"I wouldn't know; I've been drinking mocktails all night. Mostly, I've been drinking *Blue Waves*." I shift rapidly to one side, breaking Maxx's hold, but only because he lets me. He's even stronger than I suspected he was, dressed head to toe in lean muscle from the motocross, from handling such a huge bike …

I immediately engage myself in another game. And by another game, I mean Ms. Pac Man. Again. A favorite of mine. I'm clinically obsessed.

"You have no idea how difficult it was to resist touching you."

He moves up behind me again, penning me in against the machine with his arms on either side of me. I clutch the joystick for luck and focus on that instead of the heat behind me. Or the very masculine chuckle in my ear. "Nearly impossible if I'm being honest with myself. It made me question who I even *was*."

"You think it was easy for me?" I quip, and then ... *no, why did I say that?!* I'm terrible at flirting, total shit. I act as if I'm this slick, cool gamer chick but I'm just a dork. Complete and absolute.

I turn around suddenly, finding X very, very close to my face, his eyes on my mouth. If anyone were strong enough to lift me up onto the edge of this machine and ... do whatever with me, it'd be him. It'd be Maxx Wright for sure.

That's, I think, what makes this whole thing a little more fun.

We're starting a game.

Like the one I was just playing.

Opposite to the one I'm still playing against a serial killer.

A game.

"I should probably get you home," he hazards, looking to one side, possibly thinking about the time or about Justin or Chasm or a whole bunch of other things. In all honestly, I'm wondering how easily that resolve might break or shatter if I push on it. Does that make me terrible? If so, if it does, I'm not sure that I care.

Justin keeps pushing at my boundaries, breaking them down, destroying them, yet look at me. I'm still here. I almost killed a person and I'm *still here.*

"It's past three am."

I give him a look.

"As if that's my fault," I retort, and then his mouth is just on me.

He tastes a bit different than earlier, more like adventure, like an experience, a feeling that's entirely intangible. His tongue is sharp, but his lips are kind, the same sort of dichotomy as his personality.

My arms wrap around his neck, my eyes closing against the flickering lights of the arcade, the darkness that lurks in every corner. It's just the two of us in here now, but as always, anyone could be watching.

That terrifies me.

"We should probably stop here," I mumble, but Maxx just frowns before turning me back around to face the machine. This is not what I was expecting. His hands slide up and over my hips, coming to rest there.

I wonder what it'd be like, to try to play the game while he ...

"Play for me." It's a sultry suggestion, offered in a very husky voice. Maxx holds onto me as I exhale and hit the button for single player. I'm only half paying attention, but it's more than enough to keep the levels flowing. Meanwhile, X finds my neck again, kissing and licking, tasting me.

I wonder what I taste like to him? I almost ask, but I'm not *that* weird. Usually. Sometimes, I do say things like 'blue nipples' out loud, so there is that.

"Holy shit." I lose my first life on the game as X's strong fingers slip down and tease me from behind, stroking slow and confidently along the aching heat between my thighs. Unconscious sounds slip past my lips, but I bite them back, trying to maintain my gamer dignity by staying alive—at least until I beat that high score.

Maxx readjusts his grip to my hips, holding tight. One might think it would be slightly less sexual, having him hold my pelvis like that, but it's not. It feels ... anticipatory. I continue to play the game, watching his face reflect back at me from the screen when it goes dark for the 'cut scenes'. Really, it's just these ridiculous, oversimplified cartoons of Mr. and Ms. Pac-Man getting their romance game together.

"It really is late," X begins, considering the situation. "But I don't want to take you back there." I can hear the anger in his voice, directed at Justin and not me. "Not now, not ever."

"Are you sure you don't have ulterior motives?" I push, and Maxx laughs, his breath stirring my hair a bit. I'll have to remember to put it up again before I head back to Justin's which, really, just makes me even angrier. I have to put my hair up? Or what? He'll hit me. He'll escalate things.

He made me pick a family member to die today.

And I haven't told Maxx about any of it.

I open my mouth to start, but then Maxx is stepping back from me. He tears the apron over his head and tosses it aside, onto the surface of one of the other machines. The atmosphere changes very, very quickly.

His hands return to the curves of my waist, reminding me that I left the hot pink Milk Carton sweater on the DDR machine. *Not that I care if I never see it again.*

It's just my black tank between X's hot hands and my suddenly too-tight skin.

"Are, you, um." That's what comes out of my mouth. *Are, you, um.* Wow. Loquacious, aren't I? *Tell him that when he's around, you forget that you're involved with a serial killer, that he makes you feel normal in the best way possible. Tell him that he makes you feel special, too, but not the sort of special that comes with being kidnapped and returned to your birth family after fourteen years, but the sort of special that makes you realize you are unique, that you have something worthwhile to contribute to the world simply by existing.*

"Am I what?" Maxx returns, stepping up close to me again and wrapping his arms around my waist from behind. He rests his chin on the top of my head, taking advantage of our height difference to peer over me at the screen. "Hitting on you? Yes, I am."

"Did I ask that?" I sputter right back, but then he's pressing a kiss to the side of my neck, and I realize that if I wasn't asking that —I was—that I should be. "Could we even feasibly, you know, in here? Will anyone else be coming by or …?"

"Could we feasibly do what?" he returns, smooth and confident. The dickhead knows exactly what I mean. "Nobody else will be coming in. It's at this point in the night that I lock up and head home. I'm always the last one out of the building."

I die again—on the game, not IRL—and curse up a colorful storm as Maxx's palm slides up my stomach to cup my breast. My eyes go half-lidded, and the game becomes a distant, secondary thing to the heat of his touch.

"Sex, Maxim Wright. You know damn well what I was talking about."

"Does being flippant make it less embarrassing?" he teases, and I elbow him in the stomach. Have you ever elbowed a wall of granite? If so, try it. That's what X's abs are like.

"You're inhuman." The words come out like a displeased grumble, but underneath the actual sentence, there's a simmering heat.

"Shall I prove that to you?" He reaches into his pants pocket and withdraws something, tossing it onto the console beside my joystick. My eyes flick down to see the small, square shape of a condom package. *Oh Lord.* This is like, gamer fantasy central.

Me and Maxx, surrounded by vintage gaming machines, protected by shadows, all alone.

I left my phone in his Jeep because, well, obvious reasons. But if Justin wanted me home by a certain time, he'd have said something before I left. I'm fairly certain he doesn't care how long I'm out. Anyway, he just proved to me that, with the click of a button, he can see exactly where I am and what I'm doing at any given time.

X reaches around me, unbuttoning and unzipping the white jeans. His hand slips in, fingers stroking my most sensitive spot. I sag a bit, but I'm determined to keep my hand on the joystick. The game continues, my score ticks up, and Maxx pleasures me with his fingers. He strokes and pets, and my lids become heavy, half-closed things.

"Do you like this?" he asks me, but I can't talk. All I can do is lean against him, arching my back slightly so that I press up closer to his warmth.

Maxx continues until my legs are jelly, until I'm coming apart at the seams. I lose my last two lives on the game, and then he's picking the condom up off the console and leaning down to whisper in my ear.

"You should probably take it all off," he murmurs, and I do, even as I'm flushed all over, my hands shaking. I kick off my sneakers, peel off my socks, pants, underwear. Everything. Maxx pauses to pull something from his apron—it appears to be an antibacterial wipe—and then he wipes the surface of the machine down.

"What are you doing?" I ask, wondering if I should take my shirt and bra off, too. Maxx doesn't reply right away, and I hear the further crinkling of clothing being discarded. Just as I'm deciding that yes, I will take my top off, there are hot hands on my arms and I'm being spun around.

I don't really expect Maxx to *lift me up* onto the surface of the game. I can feel the buttons pressing into my ass (this is a new machine, outfitted with Ms. Pac-Man, not an original like the one in Laverne's game room). Just FYI.

Ahem.

Anyway, my bare ass is situated between two red joysticks, and my face quickly heats with a blush.

"Hey there, Kota," Maxx murmurs, his face fairly close to my own. We've evened out the height difference between us just a bit. Also, his parts are lined right up with my parts, so …

"Hello Maxim the Men's Magazine," I quip back, and he laughs. Then he's kissing me, and my hands are dropping to his broad shoulders. He's taken his shirt off, thankfully, so I use the opportunity to feel him up again, just as awed by his physical form as I was the last time we did this.

Last time.

I thought it was the first and last time.

I'm so glad that's not true.

Looking down, I see the tip of him poised between my legs, teasing my body and already fully encased in the condom. I lift my gaze back to his, and he meets it, using his hand between us to help push himself into me.

We're just *staring* at each other as it happens, and I love every second of it. I feel like I can see the full and honest truth of who Maxx Wright is in his eyes, in the shape of his mouth, in the way his lids droop just before he kisses me again.

We dive into the moment fully, him pushing all the way into me, giving me that delicious feeling of fullness. It'd be too much maybe if he hadn't worked me up beforehand. As it stands, it's just right. It's perfect.

He sighs against my lips, brushing a hand over my hair in that way of his.

"Oh, Kota," he murmurs, and then he kisses me again, and I can't think of a single damn thing except for him, and the way he feels as he works himself in and out with slow, confident strokes. There's no rushing to the finish line, oh no. He knows exactly what he's doing, working me up so that my face feels hot, and my entire body goes limp under his ministrations.

This time, there's no threat to Parrish's life.

This time, the guilt—although still present—is much

diminished.

The arcade machine is firmly bolted to the floor to keep drunk folks from stumbling into it and knocking it over, so it easily supports Maxx's deep, confident thrusts. He adjusts his hands to my ass after a while, cupping me tight and pulling me closer to the edge of the machine.

With each subsequent movement of his hips, he grinds into me, and his warm, hard body works my clit without my hands or his even needing to be involved. I throw my arms around his neck, digging my fingers into his soft, dark hair, keeping his face close to mine.

We only stop kissing when my heart rate skyrockets, and my legs begin to tremble. Maxx pulls away slightly to look at me, resting a palm on my chest. *I really wish I'd taken off my damn shirt!*

"So fast," he murmurs, and then he's looking me in the face again, and his hips are moving. He cups my ass with his hands again, squeezing tight, bringing our bodies together again and again until …

Oh fuck.

The sensations sweep over me, and I let my head fall back, hair pooling on the surface of the machine behind me, thighs clenching tight of their own accord. I can't escape Maxx's grip—wouldn't want to—so I surrender to my own orgasm even before he gets his. It's glorious, and all-consuming. I see stars or maybe I'm just looking at the flashing lights of the other arcade games against the ceiling.

Either way, it's ethereal and transcendent.

X doesn't stop, picking up the speed and intensity of his movements until he's coming, too, and we're both slumping back against the screen, sweating and panting together. He's the first to laugh, but when I do it, too, he hisses and pulls back, taking off the condom and tossing it into a small trash can on the floor beside another machine.

I remember what Parrish said about me laughing during, um, coitus, and smile.

"Too tight to handle?" I ask and then *why the hell did I just say that?!* Clearly, I'm incurably dorky.

"Unbelievably so," Maxx admits unashamedly, as cool as I'm decidedly uncool. He helps me down from the machine before fastening his pants. I snatch my own off the floor, yanking them on and then … we turn to look at one another.

He smiles at me, and my heart breaks and then reforms all over again. Stronger. Reinforced.

"That was fun," I offer up, and he cocks a single brow at me.

"That's good to know." Maxx snatches up his *Wright Turn* visor and parks it on my head. The way he looks at me, it's enough to buckle my knees. I just barely manage to stay standing by placing a hand on the arcade machine beside me. It's *Galaga* this time. "If it wasn't, I'd have to excuse myself to the bathroom and cry."

He grins at me, but I don't expect that X cries very easily. Or at all.

He steps toward me, putting his hands on the curve of my waist. My thundering heart pounds even harder, and I get dizzy on my bare feet, looking up at him like this. *Seems like your fantasy of doing it on a Ms. Pac-Man machine has come true, eh?*

Brilliant.

He takes my face between his hands, leaning down to kiss me in such a way that my lips tingle. He knows exactly what sort of dose to deliver to keep me interested.

"Do I really have to take you back there?" he asks, more to himself than to me, I think.

"I …" I exhale because I don't want to go anywhere. I want to stay with Maxx and have him hold me close, and I don't want to think about the fact that Justin hit me, that he legally owns me now, that he made me pick a family member to die. "There are some things I have to tell you, but this feels too good, and I don't want to."

He pulls me closer, consuming me with his warmth and his scent, and then strokes my back until at least some of my anxiety has retreated. *Did I really just sleep with Maxx Wright again? In an arcade of all places?* I blush all over yet again as we separate, and he smiles knowingly at me.

"I love that you blush across your chest," he tells me, trailing a finger across the air in front of my reddened skin. "It makes you so easy to read."

"What do the pages say exactly?" I challenge, lifting my chin in pure and utter defiance. "If they don't scream *let's do it again* then you're reading me wrong."

Maxx exhales sharply and then reaches down for his pants again, unbuttoning them and proving in no uncertain terms that he's already hard again. My eyes take in the sight of his fingers wrapped around his shaft, and then I'm turning around in such clear and blatant invitation that I doubt I'll be able to look him in the eye after.

He swipes another condom—how many does he have exactly? —from his apron pocket, and then he's bending me over the pinball machine and sliding into me a second time. I grip the sides of the game as Maxx rides me hard and fast, smoothing a palm up my spine, curling a hand in my hair. He grasps the long waves in a firm but gentle grip, encouraging me to lift up just slightly, to arch my back.

Also, he thrusts hard. Hard, hard, *hard.*

"Move *with* me, Kota," he says softly, but it's a clear command. And damn it, I do it. I move back against him, and the pleasure doubles. Triples. I can't breathe for the feel of him inside of me, taking up all the empty space in my heart. "That's it. That's it, Kota."

He comes first this time, shuddering against me, making these dark, masculine sounds that have me so beyond embarrassed that I don't know what to do with myself. Luckily for me, Maxx does. He turns me back around, steps close, and then slips his hand between us. As he kisses me full on the mouth, like some sort of white knight prince, his fingers dance a devil's dirty deed on my aching body until I'm collapsing against him with a near-sob, ripped in half by a second orgasm.

"That's my girl," X whispers, holding me close and stroking a hand down my back until I can finally find my feet again. As expected, I most definitely can't look him in the eye as I yank my pants back up and button them. "You're not embarrassed, are you? You can't be. I was just inside of you."

I almost kick him, but then he gestures with his chin in the direction of the bar. When I finally gather the courage to look at his face, he's grinning.

"Come. I'll make you a drink, and you can get everything off your chest."

CHAPTER 19

Maxx's demeanor shifts from happy and sated to enraged by the end of the discussion. He even reaches out and gently takes my chin in his fingers, searching for signs of trauma from when Justin hit me. Only, there's nothing to see because Justin Prior is a very careful monster.

"I wish you'd told me that sooner," he whispers, struggling to hold back his temper. He releases me and rakes his fingers through his hair. "But thank you for telling me."

"Please don't try to kill him." The words rush out of me, but the way Maxx returns my stare, I can easily see that happening. He attempted to punch the guy before, so I can only imagine what he'd do if he got his hands on Justin again. "Raúl was right there, like a shadow. I didn't even see him coming." I take another sip of the *Cool Blue Wave* and breathe out, refocusing myself. "Don't jump the gun and get yourself killed, Maxx Wright. I can't lose you."

He stiffens up slightly, but then relaxes, moving back around the bar to offer me up another hug.

ENDGAME ROMANCE

Since he doesn't directly respond to that statement, I imagine he's thinking it over.

In the end, I can't stay here forever, so we head back to Justin's in the orange Jeep, and I check my messages. Texts from Parrish, from Chasm, Maxine, and even Tess. She knows about my second phone now because Justin gloated to her about it, and she's been using that number instead of the new one she got for me.

Although, looking at it now, I actually preferred her version of spyware over Justin's. His is infinitely worse.

Are you holding up okay? is what she asks me, but I don't have the energy to answer that. I have two choices: answer with a lie that hurts us both, or tell a truth that hurts us both. I just can't with it.

I set my phone aside and spot a utility knife—the sort people use for camping—in one of Maxx's cupholders. Absently, I remove it and twirl the polished wood of the handle around in my fingers. It's a pretty knife, probably not super useful in a fight, but handy.

"Do you want that?" X asks me, glancing my way. "You can have it; I have another one on my key ring."

I raise a brow and then shrug, slipping the knife into my pocket. Maybe it's about time I consider carrying a weapon with me? Something better than this would be ideal. A hunting knife? A … gun, if I could get ahold of one.

If I did, I could just walk up to Justin and—

No, I'm too tired to focus on that right now.

Maxx takes me back to the house, his green eyes absorbing the monstrous mansion with its climbing ivy, and I can see the barely suppressed need in him to fight back, to step in front of the speeding bullet that is Justin Prior in order to protect me.

We kiss briefly, and he looks me dead in the face.

"If he hits you again, please call me."

I nod, but my tongue is tied, and it feels impossible to speak.

Maxx surprises me yet again by being a consummate gentleman, walking me up to the door and all that to make sure that I'm safe. Thing is, in this particular instance, what's *inside* the house is far more dangerous than what's outside of it.

"Dakota, I—" he starts, pausing as the front door opens and Justin appears. He's smiling, but then, he's always smiling. I bet he smiles when he kills people, too.

"Mr. Wright, thank you for bringing her to the door." He makes this shooing sort of motion with his hand. "But that's quite enough of that. On your way now. Dakota will be engaged to Kwang-seon soon enough, and how would it look if the two of you are seen cavorting around together?" He raises his eyebrows in a not-so-subtle threat, and Maxx bristles.

At the same time, my phone goes off again, and I look down to see a text that makes my stomach drop.

Can you meet me? I know it's early, but it's urgent. Like, really urgent. It's from Lumen. At five o'clock in the morning, it's early to some people, late to others. There's a string of emojis that follows after, ones we worked out in advance to secretly signal that this was 'it', the meeting arranged by Justin.

I look up and Maxx meets my gaze, but I can feel Justin watching me, studying me.

"Are you okay?" X asks, because he isn't afraid of anyone or anything even if he rightfully should be.

Justin lets out a small laugh and steps back, opening the door even wider.

"You're just fine, aren't you, Dakota?" he asks, ushering me inside. My eyes meet Maxx's, and I wonder if I shouldn't say something about Lumen's text now. "I've been more than generous, and it's getting late."

There's a command there, one that I can't risk unleashing on

340

Maxx. Because if he feels like he has to, Maxx will go after Justin to protect me. And Justin? Well, he'd kill Maxx if he had to. No doubts about that. He wouldn't lose a wink of sleep over it either.

"I'm okay." The words are soft, but I step into the house and allow Bio Dad to shut the door behind me. He watches Maxx pace a bit on the porch, entangling his fingers together behind his head, before he eventually heads back to the Jeep and then waits there, staring at the house like he's considering knocking or breaking in.

The consolation prize of returning to Justin's home at sunrise is that he doesn't seem to mind that I was out late. Not that he didn't text me; he did. It's just that he didn't care if I came home early or not, if I stayed out and … did my own thing.

"Maxim Wright rather than Kwang-seon McKenna?" he asks, picking up a cup of coffee from the side table near the door. He takes a sip and then tsks his tongue at me, turning away and disappearing into the solarium.

Raúl is sitting at the breakfast table working on his pink MacBook. He glances up at me in disdain as I enter the room, reaching up to adjust his brightly colored eyewear. Today, it's a pair of rainbow glasses.

"Am I being punished?" I ask, and Justin sighs, continuing past me to sit on the back porch. I can't decide if he's just getting up or if he never went to sleep. Either way, it looks like he's gearing up to watch the sun rise.

"Did you think I wouldn't know what Lumen was up to?" Justin asks casually, crossing his legs as he reclines in the chair and stares out across the water. "So, go. Save your 'girlfriend'"— and here he makes a quote shape with a single finger, holding his coffee in the other hand—"just be aware that someone *is* going to die tonight. You can bring your boyfriends with you if you want, but I wouldn't recommend it."

I just stare at him.

I really messed up, didn't I? By challenging Justin the way I did.

"Is this because of the things I said after the hearing?" I ask him, and he turns his head oh-so-slowly to look at me.

"Actually, yes. But not in the way you might think. I'd been planning on letting you make the decision yourself as to whether you'd meet Lumen alone or take your harem." He says it unironically, too, the harem thing. He really and truly doesn't care about that part of the equation, now does he? "I wanted to see if you were independent or overly reliant on your pawns. But"—he holds up a single finger—"I appreciated your gusto and bravado in terms of challenging me. This is a *favor*, Dakota." He sips his coffee again and then points at his cheek. "Now, give me a kiss and say *yes, Daddy* and go meet your friend."

"The friend you blackmailed into beating me up, into tormenting me, into revealing not just personal information about me and Parrish but also about how I destroyed the students' cars."

"I never made you do that; it was a choice." He taps his cheek again. "And one day, you'll thank me for what I did. Do you think I asked Veronica Fisher and her friends to cut your clothes off and post you naked online? I did not. I cleaned the internet of your images, Dakota. By using Lumen Hearst, I was proving to you what you already know: everyone in Whitehall—in Medina—is a monster."

I bend down and kiss his cheek, chills creeping across my skin. "Yes, Daddy."

The words are wooden as I stand back up, heart pounding as I run through any and all available options.

Someone is going to die tonight? Who? Saffron? Lumen?

One thing I do know: it won't be me.

Justin doesn't want me dead.

I move away and into the house, sliding my phone from my

pocket.

Where are you? I reply, and Lumen responds almost instantly with an address.

There's a text from Maxx, too, asking me if I'm truly alright, if I need anything, if he should stay the night. Cute. Would Justin allow that? It's not like he cares what I do with boys—in fact, he encourages it.

I'm totally fine. Get some sleep. I send that before I can stop myself, hoping that Maxx really will go home and stay out of this for the time being.

My choices are not good. Tackle this alone, which sounds like a really bad idea. Or bring one of the guys along which also seems like a really bad idea.

"Just be aware that someone is going to die tonight."

I make my decision and then wake Delphine up to bum a ride.

———

Delphine doesn't mind being woken up. Actually, she seems excited that I sought her out, showing off the beautiful new convertible that Justin bought for her. I'm not surprised in the least, not about the car or the fact that she says he'll get me one as soon as I'm able to drive.

He'd like that, providing an even nicer and fancier car than Tess did.

I force those thoughts aside, focused on the moment at hand instead. Because whatever is going to happen tonight, I'm not going to like it. We head to the address together—it just so happens to be a diner that either stays open all night or else opens up really early—and Delphine drops me off.

Lumen is waiting at a table inside, and I watch almost forlornly as Delphine leaves again.

"You made it," she says as I approach the table and take a tentative seat across from her. I tossed my phone under a bench outside. If it gets stolen, eh. Honestly, it might be a blessing. The two of us stare at each other for a moment before she leans in toward me. "I accidentally left my phone in the car, so I wasn't sure if you got my last message."

"Mine's outside under a bench," I add, and Lumen smiles. Not to say there aren't cameras in here. There very well could be. "What's up? Justin seems to know that we've been communicating. Unfortunately, that doesn't bode well for either of us."

Lumen just stares at me, blinking a set of falsies that I wonder if she put on just now or has been wearing all night. Her blond hair is loose and hanging in a glossy wave over one shoulder, and she's dressed herself into a white t-shirt with gold letters on the front and a pair of blue jeans. Pretty sure the letters constitute some luxury brand, but I could be wrong. It could just as easily be a political slogan of some sort.

Lumen is hardcore conservative in many ways; Danyella is mostly the opposite; I float between them. Somehow, all three of us got along just fine before Justin's interference. Imagine that.

"What did he say?" she asks, her voice a strangled, tired thing. A waiter brings over a pair of coffees, and I order a plate of eggs and bacon, wishing I could enjoy this moment. It could be fun if there weren't extenuating circumstances involved. I just had sex with one of the hottest guys I've ever seen in my life—in an *arcade* of all places—and now I'm here having breakfast with a friend, and I should just be gushing over my experience …

Instead, I keep wondering who the hell is supposed to kick the bucket and if I made the right decision by *not* informing the guys and … *I could text them now, let them know that I'm out with*

Lumen, but not give them the address. At least then they'd know something was going on. If I did give them the address, the three of them would show up within minutes. Guaranteed.

It's a nice feeling and simultaneously threatening.

On the other hand, I know for a fact that Justin won't allow anything to happen to me. *I* am not the one at risk here; there's no immediate threat against my life. It makes sense for me to handle this on my own.

"One second." I head back outside, slide my phone from under the bench and message the boys anyway. Hey, they might track my phone and show up here, but … I can't lie to them. And I can't just leave them out.

Eating breakfast with Lumen; she really wanted me to meet up and talk. I'll message you when I get home safe. I hit send, head back inside, and slide into the booth across from Lumen.

"Sorry about that." I clear my head and try to remember where we were. Ah. Right. "Justin said *you didn't think I knew what she was up to* or something along those lines." My food arrives almost as quickly as I ordered it, and the waiter leaves the plate in front of me as Lumen sits there staring back at me.

"You're sure that's what he said?" she asks, and I nod, taking a bite of scrambled egg and realizing as it hits my stomach how damn hungry I was. Part of me wants to go outside and see what the boys' responses are. On the other hand … gah.

I make myself eat. Maxx tired me out, I won't lie. *Two times in quick succession, and my stomach is still in knots. I want to be naked in bed with him, licking and kissing every square inch of his body for hours, for days, for a week.*

Someday, maybe.

"I'm sure."

Lumen signals the waiter back over and orders this massive heaping pile of pancakes with chocolate chips, strawberries, and whipped cream.

"I was on a diet but screw it. If I'm going to prison, who cares?" She digs into her food with a sigh, but because I'm, well, me, I can't let that comment slide.

"You don't need to be on a diet, Lumen. First off, you're in great shape. Second, diets aren't helpful for anybody. Eat healthy eighty-percent of the time, and do your own thing the other twenty-percent."

She sighs heavily and stuffs a huge bite into her mouth.

"You're too awesome, you know that?" she murmurs, but she doesn't agree or disagree with my statement.

I lean in to whisper so that the few other patrons in the room won't be able to hear us.

"Besides that, you used justifiable force to protect Danyella. I don't necessarily believe that you *would* go to jail over that sort of incident." I sit up straight and down some of my water before taking another sip of coffee. Too much caffeine without water makes me feel ehh for some reason.

"Not after burying him and keeping it hidden." She sets her utensils aside and puts her face in her hands. "Why didn't I just report it then and there?" I'm not actually sure if she's talking to me or herself. "Maybe I should have? But I was afraid. These cases don't always go the way they should, you know."

She isn't wrong, but it's a moot point now so I don't argue it.

Instead, we sit together and eat breakfast at six in the morning while the sun peaks its head above the horizon.

"What are we supposed to do now?" I ask her, wondering how murder comes into play in this particular scenario. We finish our food and Lumen pays, despite my protests. I've got some cash on hand thanks to Justin. He practically throws it at me.

"I have no idea." She takes me outside, and I grab my phone from under the bench. Unfortunately, it's still there. I almost wished it had been stolen.

If you don't message me back now, I'm tracking you and coming over there. It's Parrish. He could be on his way here at this very moment.

Little Sister, I swear to fuck. CALL US. X is panicking—also, he's pissed.

Nothing more from Maxx himself though, not after our last conversation. I find that to be odd, but I don't reply to them. I know that they *can* track my phone because I let them add software to mine for that very purpose.

"We should go." I encourage Lumen to leave the parking lot, just in case one of the boys shows up.

"Where *are* we going?" she asks absently, and I shrug.

"Back to Justin's place?" I ask, my heart thudding oddly in my chest. Justin didn't send me out just to have breakfast with Lumen and then bail. Something else is going on here, but I can't quite put my finger on it. Am I missing something? Is this yet another lesson that I'm just not getting?

On the way back, a cop car pulls up behind us and turns on its lights.

My mind immediately goes back to the cop we saw that night in the Vasquez house, the one that came around the corner opposite Mr. Volli with a freaking gun in his hand. It would make sense, wouldn't it? Who else could it possibly be?

"Don't pull over," I say, clutching at the edge of my seat with tight fingers. "Just don't."

"I can't not pull over," Lumen insists, but she keeps driving anyway. "Why? What's going on?"

She wouldn't know about the cop because we didn't exactly tell her that part.

"Justin has cops in his back pocket," I explain, as quickly and succinctly as possible. "I don't know if the person following us is one of his pets or not. Are you willing to take the risk?"

We end up back at Justin's place—only to find that the gate is closed.

It's closed, and the street here is a dead-end with another manor across from ours, only their gate isn't on this side of the property.

We're trapped.

Lumen is no Scarlett Force (famous action star/stunt driver extraordinaire) so outrunning and outmaneuvering a cop car isn't an option. We exchange a look as the guy tells us to get out of the car, and to do so with our hands raised.

This is … not good.

Not at all.

I'm not great with faces, but I'm pretty sure the uniformed officer that climbs out of the car is the same guy I met in the wine cellar. I wish I'd looked at his name tag the last time we saw him.

He walks right up to us, Lumen on one side of the car, me on the other.

"Walk," he commands, using the gun to gesture us into the woods at the end of the street. Oh no. No, no, no. This is not good.

"Someone is *going to die tonight."* Justin wasn't kidding around, was he? Not that I assumed he was.

Lumen and I exchange looks, but what can we do?

Justin closed the gate on purpose; this is exactly where he intended for us to end up.

Lumen and I do as we're told, turning and heading into the shadows of the trees. The sun might be rising, but it's still early morning, and the sun's rays are weak. They barely penetrate the copse of trees. Pretty sure this is the Fairweather Nature Preserve. It's not a big space, but at ten acres, it's certainly large enough for us to get lost in.

We walk slowly, crunching across the debris on the forest floor.

ENDGAME ROMANCE

The morning is cool and misty, but I can tell it's going to heat up quick. Not … that I'll be able to enjoy any of that. *Oh hell no, whatever happens here is going to dictate the course of my life.*

Somehow, I can feel it in my bones.

What we see when we reach a small clearing shocks the hell out of me.

It's Danyella. She's unconscious, arms tied behind her back, but there's no mistaking her distinctive pink glasses or the black *SIX* sweatshirt with the white crown that she's wearing.

Lumen makes a small sound of surprise, but I remain silent, even as the cop commands her to get to her knees beside Danyella's quiet form.

He turns to me, his face impossible to read. It's neutral, but almost disturbingly so. There's nothing there. His eyes are empty in a way that Justin's aren't, and I'm reminded of Mr. Fosser all over again. This guy gives me the chills in a similar way.

Please don't let this man be a pervert, I think, but I'm not about to let anything happen to any of us. Not at all.

I'm not an idiot: I didn't come here emptyhanded, after all.

"Pick one." The cop's words are eerily similar to Justin's from earlier, and I get the chills all over again. This moment has been planned for some time; Justin intended for me to end up right here, just like this.

And, by turning Lumen into the bad guy, he almost guaranteed who I would choose.

Lumen Hearst, the daughter of the woman who stole Justin's research.

Shit.

I put my hands up to my face, as if I'm having a panic attack. Sort of am, sorry, not sorry, but I don't let my anxiety control me. Not here, not now. What good would that do me?

If Justin didn't send me out here with specific instructions, then he's waiting for me to make a move.

I put my hands on my hips, and then I bend over, putting my palms on my thighs.

"Why are you doing this?" I ask, my voice shaky with unshed tears. I look up at the brown-haired man with the more than average face. He could be anybody, really. He's fairly young, not any older than Justin certainly, and he's handsome in the traditional sense.

Not a man you could pick out of a crowd.

Monsters hide in pretty skins sometimes, don't they?

"None of your goddamn business, that's why." The man's voice stays neutral, but then he *smiles* at me, and I go cold all over. *Where did Justin find these creeps anyway?!*

But the answer is obvious: Milk Carton. He probably used his stupid app to find perverts and killers, started rounding them up as pawns. I shudder. Did he use unsolved crimes to find wanted murderers?

That wouldn't surprise me at all.

I lift my head up slightly, aiming to go for the knife in my back pocket, the one that Maxx just gifted to me.

What are you going to do, Kota? I ask myself, but I already saw what I was willing to do earlier. If somebody I love is in danger, then I have to be willing to bend my principles. What good is morality when it serves no practical person?

I love these girls more than I care about my morals.

I know exactly what I'm willing to do to get out of this. Justin wanted to teach me about sacrifice? What if the only person I'm willing to sacrifice is *myself*?

"The man you're working for," I begin, standing up slightly, hand moving slowly, so slowly ... "You should know that he's the Seattle Slayer. How do you know that he won't come for you next?"

ENDGAME ROMANCE

The cop guy just stares at me, and then he laughs. The sound is remarkably pleasant, like this guy would be the last person you'd expect of being a killer.

"He's not the Seattle Slayer," the man begins, cocking his head slightly. "*I'm* the Seattle Slayer."

I just stare at him.

Huh? But Justin … No, I know without a doubt that he's the Slayer. What the fuck is this guy talking about then? Lumen makes a small sound from her spot on the ground, and I flick my eyes her way, noticing that hers are focused on the cop in a disturbing way.

Like, she might rush him and get herself killed in the process.

She must think that she's going to die anyway.

"Dakota, let Danyella live," she tells me, her voice resolute, and I know that I'm running out of time. There's no chance to find out what the guy means by his statement.

Instead, I whip the knife from my pocket and charge him. I bury the blade in his stomach, and it's … it's awful. It's so awful. There's a horrible popping sensation, and then my hands are covered with blood and I'm stumbling back in total shock at what I've just done.

A small knife to the abdomen doesn't drop an attacker! My brain is screaming at me, but I'm still standing there staring at my palms and panting. I look up just in time to see the guy throw a punch at my face.

The impact rocks my head back, and I stumble, but I don't go down so easily. Instead, I charge him and so does Lumen. The man is too focused on me to notice her, so she's able to get the upper hand, knocking him off balance enough that he drops the gun. Rather than pick it up, he backhands her and sends her stumbling. She knocks into a downed log and tumbles backward as I rush forward yet again.

The man shoves me back, but I don't stop, scrabbling for the knife in his stomach. I manage to grip the handle, but then we're falling to the ground together, and he's grunting from the pain, his hands reaching for my throat ...

They don't make it there because someone shoves him off of me, and I'm able to suck in a deep breath.

It's Maxx.

He wrestles with the guy and manages to pin him as I sit up, somehow clutching the bloodied handle of the knife. X is grappling with the cop, but then ... the man is shuddering and going still beneath him.

It takes Maxx a few seconds longer to realize, but then he pauses and looks down at the guy, panting heavily. He's still wearing the same jeans from earlier, a green and yellow Oregon Ducks hoodie on the top. It's smeared with blood as I scramble over to him, and Lumen moans, pushing herself up to her feet and swaying.

She rests a palm against the trunk of a tree as Maxx and I look down at the cop on the forest floor, bleeding from *a fucking stab wound.*

"Is he ..." I start, and Maxx checks the man's pulse. It takes longer to die than that, doesn't it? Only I don't know anything about this because ... because ... *it is so ROYALLY FUCKED UP.* "He's not dead, is he?" I whisper, but Maxx is already standing up and staring at the ... it's not a body, is it?

I move away from the guy, staring down at the knife in my hand, and then I drop it on the ground and move away to throw up. Just like Chasm did when he saw JJ in the box.

This isn't real. It can't be real. I don't believe that it's real.

"Kota." X's voice is soft, his hands warm on my shoulders as I spin around and lift up my palms. They're covered in blood. It's jewel-bright in the sunlight, wet rubies spattered across guilty skin.

No.

ENDGAME ROMANCE

No, no, no.

A text comes in on my phone and, because I know exactly who it is that's going to be messaging me, I pull it out. I don't even care that it's now smeared with blood.

The text has come from Justin's burner phone, not his real one.

Excellent work, princess. I'd expect nothing less. Congratulations. Take a trophy to celebrate your first win, and then deal with the evidence. Use your pawns if you please.

I realize then that, as usual, Justin's plan was multifaceted.

If Lumen died, he got his revenge on the Hearst family. If Danyella died, he broke me just a little more. If the cop died … if the cop …

Sometimes, people are grown. Sometimes, like that garden at my father's house, they're cultivated, planted, nurtured, watered, weeded, and then plucked. A perfect flower, just right for the vase.

No matter what I did here, I lost.

Justin has just *checked* my king, and I can feel it in my gut.

We're in the endgame, Dakota. You're in the endgame, and there are few pieces left on the board. Make your move.

Only, I should've known Justin better than that, shouldn't I?

I just killed a guy. I just fucking killed a guy.

I don't realize I'm saying it out loud until Maxx wraps me up in his arms and pulls me close, crushing me against his firm chest hard enough that I can hear his heart beating. His smell, that sporty citrus tease, cuts through some of the horrid iron smell.

There are innumerable things that I regret about the last few weeks, such as smashing my mother's typewriter into the windshield of my birthday present. I regret delivering JJ's body to her killer. I regret saying and doing horrible things.

But this? Wow. I mean, this is by far the worst thing I've ever done, and I've been at that threshold multiple times over the past few weeks.

The bar just gets lower and lower and fucking lower.

"Shh, Kota. It's gonna be okay," X is murmuring, stroking his hand over my hair. I hear more footsteps in the underbrush, and panic. I look up, finding X's emerald gaze on mine. Even in the sweet, soft sunshine of early morning, his eyes are dark.

Dear old Daddy didn't give me much say in this matter, did he?

And yet, my actions are my own.

Thanks for showing how much you love me, eh, Dad?

Maxx turns, and I follow the direction of his shifting gaze, expecting more cops. Or maybe a cadre of well-armed serial killers? I definitely don't expect Parrish and Chasm to appear, both of them red-faced and panting and panicked.

"Naekkeo." Chasm is choked up. Parrish is … he struts right for me, grabbing my arm and yanking me from Maxx so that he can wrap me in his arms.

"How dare you scare me like that," he whispers, pulling back slightly to check me over. Chasm appears on my right side, turning my face to his with a single finger. He's distraught, completely broken with worry, but I can see him carefully cobbling himself back together as he looks from me to the body, back to me.

"How did you guys get here so fast?" I ask, wondering if they tracked my phone.

"You're lucky we got here at all," Maxx snaps out, but then he exhales sharply and goes to ruffle up his hair. He pauses and then stares at the blood on his own hand before swiping it on his sweatshirt. Doesn't help much. There's too much of the red stuff. It's everywhere.

"Justin blocked us from tracking your phone," Chasm tells me, and he curses in Korean, swiping a hand over his face. "Maxx followed you, and he told us where to find you."

I glance his way, but he isn't looking at me: he's staring at the body on the ground.

I follow his gaze, but Parrish steps in front of me, blocking my view.

"Don't." Just that one word from him, and my knees collapse. He catches me and helps me to the forest floor as I hear Lumen moaning as she stumbles over to Danyella.

"Yeah, I'm fine, thanks for asking," she snaps, and Chas curls his lip at her. "Danyella, honey, wake up." She gives our friend a shake as Maxx pulls his keys from his pocket, opening up a utility knife on his key chain to cut the ropes off Danyella's wrists.

The girl stirs but doesn't wake. That might be for the best. I don't want her to see this.

"I'll back the Jeep up as close to the woods as I can," Maxx is telling Chasm. "And then we'll load him up. One of us can drive the cop car—"

"No." My voice is much steadier than I expected. Maybe because Parrish's hands are on my upper arms, smoothing up and down, soothing me with his honeyed gaze, his dewy clover smell as powerful as Maxx's. "No. That's not what we're doing." I go to move, but Parrish won't let me.

"What do you need? Tell us. You shouldn't have to ... well, you shouldn't have to do anything at all." He pauses as I lean in, putting my lips to his ear, so that Justin's camera ... or cameras? ... won't be able to hear us.

"Get the GoPro off the front of the guy's shirt." I distinctly remember seeing one there. If so, it won't be any official police gear. I mean, obviously not considering the guy was going to shoot a teenage girl in cold blood. "Get it and take it away. If you have the bug detector, bring that over."

Parrish pulls away from me and then lifts up a cool, reassuring hand to my forehead.

"Close your eyes," he tells me, but I shake my head and lean away from him. Not because I don't want him to touch me, but C.M. STUNICH

because I don't want this man's blood all over Parrish. He frowns hard at me, but then stands up, extending a hand to yank me back to my feet.

I've come to a conclusion, but I can't voice a single word of it aloud. Not just yet. I hand Parrish my phone, and he doesn't question it. He knows what to do.

"No?" Maxx asks, exchanging a look with Chasm before they both turn back to me. "What do you mean?"

I give a slight shake of my head as Parrish removes the camera pinned to the man's shirt and then carries it off toward where the cars are parked. How long do we have before somebody comes across the abandoned vehicles? There's only one estate at the end of the road near us, but their gate faces the crossroad. Only someone looking for Justin's place would come this way.

I'm surprised there aren't any paparazzi out here, but there could be. There's a chance they just don't know where Justin lives. Yet. It's always a yet with those creeps.

When Parrish returns, he does indeed have the bug detector and he uses it, helping us locate the other two cameras positioned on the space. These ones are so small that I look at them and smile before crushing them in my fist.

"What's the plan?" Lumen asks, her voice laced with pain. I glance her way and see a stream of her own blood draining down her temple.

That's when I turn back to the boys. Chasm is giving me this *Naekkeo, I oughta drag you back to my cave and keep you there* sort of look. He's mad. He's not the only one. Maxx is quietly furious, and Parrish is shaking, overwhelmed by those intense emotions of his.

"You three are going to leave—" I start, and you'd think I'd slapped each and every one of them.

"*Shiro,*" Chasm declares.

356

"Hell no." Maxx.

"Absolutely not." Parrish.

I force myself to inhale, exhale, inhale.

"Listen to me," I start, but they're all up in arms and overprotective, and it's *really* cute, but— "BOYS!" I shout the word and they pause, turning their collective stares on me and making me wish I could just have a normal summer vacay with them.

One day. Eventually. Nothing lasts forever, right?

All things must end—including this.

Justin told me specifically that any information given to the police that led to his arrest was off the table; he never told me that I couldn't frame one of his cronies the way he's trying to frame Paul.

Lesson learned, old man.

This is exactly the move I needed to escape the check he's just driven me into. He thought he had me trapped in a corner? Fat chance. I may not be checkmating him just yet, but I'm moving my pieces around to save my ass. I *will* control the center of this board.

This will keep the FBI off of Paul for a while. At least, it'll prevent them from charging him (I hope). I might go to jail for the rest of my life, but … like I said, if I was going to sacrifice someone, I'll only choose myself.

Just like the game of the century between Bobby Fischer against Donald Byrne, I'm offering up my queen in the hopes of using my bishops for the win. Or whatever. Direct metaphors don't matter.

"I'm turning myself in." I raise my chin as the three of them gape at me, and Lumen chokes.

"Naekkeo, we talked about this self-sacrificial crap. As in, *you're not fucking doing it.* You like when I speak Korean? Here it is again." He repeats himself—presumably—in his native tongue. "And a third time in Japanese." And he does, he says it, crossing his arms obstinately over his chest.

"I won't go to jail; Justin won't let that happen." I'm bluffing now. Maybe he would, just to teach me a lesson? But there's an equal chance that he'll get me out because my serving prison time most definitely does *not* serve his ends.

"Dakota, it's not worth the risk," Parrish begins, but then Maxx is bending down and picking up the knife. He turns as if he, um, might like stab the body or something? Oh God. I rush forward and wrap my arms around his waist, squeezing just like I did in the coffee shop bathroom that day when I begged him not to watch that video.

He did it anyway, but … I put every ounce of love I feel for *him* specifically in this move, and he goes still.

"Please don't," I murmur, rubbing my cheek against his broad back. "Please listen to me. I know what I'm doing." Maxx peels my hands off—yes in a similar way to back then—and turns around to stare down at me. It occurs to me then that he was likely pulling my hands off because he wanted me in that moment, because he liked my touch too much to bear.

The thought warms me, bolsters me, gives me the courage I need to commit.

"Kota, this is nuts." He's practically pleading with me, teeth gritted, hand shaking around the knife. He may have already fucked this whole thing up by touching it, but we'll see. I take it away from him and rub the hilt on my clothes. His DNA and fingerprints will be on the knife, but it was his knife; he gave it to me. It's plausible so long as *he* isn't tested for the cop guy's blood.

And why would he be?

I'm going to confess that I did it.

"If we do this, bury the body together, we're deeper into

Justin's hole. He has yet more evidence to use against us."

"What the ... what are you even talking about?" Lumen asks, sounding confused. I remember then that she ... oh. Right. She doesn't know that Justin's a serial killer. "This cop said he was the Seattle Slayer! Of course we should turn him in. Nobody will blame us for this."

Mm.

Yeah, might be time to bring her up to speed ...

"Also, your fucking *dad* is the one who sent us here. He a killer, too? It's sus as hell, Dakota." Ah, Lumen really is too smart for her own good. Give her a few hours and she'll probably figure out the entire plot.

I give her a look of warning.

"Just follow along with the plan for now, okay? I'll explain later." I turn back to the boys. "Please leave." I look between the three of them, but I can see that they're not convinced. "Burying this man won't set us free; I won't live the rest of my life in hiding or at the edge of a knife."

"Fuck." Chasm gets it first because, well, he always does. He turns away and paces a small rut before spinning back to point at me. "If you end up in jail, I'm springing you free and we're running away to another country together."

"Same." This from Parrish as he side-eyes his friend. "But that won't happen." He turns back to look at me. "Tess would never let that happen. You should see her, Dakota. She's bringing out the big guns to get you back."

I want to ask him what that means, but there's no time right now. The sun is climbing higher in the sky; each second we delay there's a risk of someone stumbling on us. There are hiking trails throughout these trees, after all. Plenty of locals go poking around here for fun, too.

"I'm going to leave, but only if you look me in the eye and tell me the absolute truth." Maxx steps forward, and I find my gaze impossibly drawn to his. How could I bear to look at anyone else? "I asked you via text if you were okay, and you lied to me."

"I—" But I did. I had good reason for it, but he isn't wrong.

If he hadn't sensed that something was amiss and followed me out here, something really, really bad might've happened. Honestly, if I had known the guys were coming and made different choices, I might not be in this situation ATM.

Justin was right though: somebody did die tonight.

"What do you want to know?" I ask, twisting my hands in the lower half of my shirt. The very same shirt where Maxx laid his hands just a few hours ago, made love to me against an arcade machine. *Screwed me against one afterward.* I exhale. "I don't *know* that I won't be charged or that Justin won't save me, but I highly doubt it. Think about his motivations: he's grooming me. He wants me to be his little helper … or his Tess replacement. I'm not exactly sure, but he did tell me to collect a trophy from my kill."

I shrug my shoulders and Maxx turns away for a moment in thought.

"I mean it, Little Sister. You, me … I think South Korea extradites to the US, but we could get new identities in Seoul or something."

I almost smile at that because I'm pretty damn sure that he's serious. Like, actually serious.

"I told you: Tess won't let that happen." Parrish turns to Maxx, and the two of them stare at each other for a long while, and then, as usual, they start to speak to each other in Korean. Chasm rolls his eyes and shakes his head, turning to Lumen and Danyella and ignoring his friends.

"Don't mess this up for her or I will *destroy* you. Understand me? I'm still debating on whether or not to tell the whole of

Whitehall that you're dead broke."

Lumen stares right back at him before flicking her gaze to mine.

"Tell the authorities everything," I say, trying to keep my voice even. "Except about the boys and Justin. Anything else is fair game."

"Why?" Lumen asks, not flippantly, but with a tense curiosity in her voice.

"Because if you don't listen to what I say, we're all dead."

CHAPTER 20

By the time I sit down on the edge of the bed in Laverne's guest room, I'm half-ready to collapse. *Half-ready? Kota, you are trashed.* I fall back and throw an arm over my eyes, fatigue dragging me down into blissful, shadowy darkness.

"Dakota, can I come in?" Tess asks, but she's just rapped on the doorframe and she's moving into the room without my consent. Parrish is with me, but he stays a few feet away and doesn't sit on the edge of the bed, leaving room for … our? … mother.

Mother.

I don't let myself dig too deeply into the fact that I've dropped the 'bio' bit from Tess' mother title in my brain.

"Sure." I'm barely conscious, won't lie. Already, I'm drifting.

What the hell just happened to me?

Here's what: I had Parrish return my phone to me, and then after the boys were safely gone, I called that FBI agent chick, Itsumi Takahashi. I called her, and she called the local police force, and then Lumen, Danyella, and I were whisked away.

362

ENDGAME ROMANCE

After checking us for injuries, our clothes were collected for evidence, and then we were questioned.

I told them what I knew: Lumen and I met for breakfast (boy troubles, teehee, gag), and then on our way back to Justin's, we were pulled over by cop dude. He led us into the woods where Danyella was waiting, told me to choose one of my friends to die, and I attacked him with the utility knife that Maxx gave me cause, like, we've been hiking together a lot.

Oh yeah, and I also told them the guy identified himself as the Seattle Slayer.

That was easy, right? Because he did. He did, and I'm still struggling to figure that one out. Unless ... the Seattle Slayer isn't a single person but a collective?

Justin isn't *just* the Slayer by himself, is he? Add in Mr. Fosser, Mr. Volli, Raúl, the cop ... Holy shit. I bet that's it! It is; it has to be.

Anyway, both Tess and Justin showed up at the police station for me.

And oh fuck. Oh fuuuuuuck. I did not like the look on his face.

My phone was looked through by the agents and then returned back to me. Mysteriously, the text from Justin's burner phone had already disappeared. Even if they check the phone records, or hits on the nearby cell towers, I'm sure Justin can scrub all that stuff, too.

He's that good.

Luckily, it's a weekend, and Tess asserted her parenting time so, here I am.

I killed someone; I'm a murderer.

Whatever happens in the end, Justin won.

He got me to do something that I swore I never would. He made me a killer in his own likeness and, even if that man's death was justified, I'm heartbroken.

"Honey, I'm worried about you." I feel Tess' hand on my elbow, and I lift my arm away from my bleary eyes. I blink at her as Parrish picks up a remote and presses a button, dropping these fancy-pants shades over the windows. In an instant, the room goes from vibrant and summery to pitch-black.

He moves over to the nightstand and flicks on the lamp, adding a warm glow to the room. Coincidentally, it's the same lamp that Chasm picked up to use as a club when Tess walked in on our threesome.

Looks better as a lamp than a weapon.

"I just need to sleep, and I'll be fine." I don't know if that's true or not, but I'm so damn tired. So tired. I just want to rest and pretend like the world doesn't exist for a minute.

"You've been through a lot tonight," Tess says softly, her hands shaking as she reaches out and rests her fingers against my other arm. I'm not used to being touched by her, but I don't dislike it. She should do it more, show physical affection like that. The image of her marching into the police station, ash-faced but dressed to kill, that was comforting in so many ways.

Tess doesn't know what she's up against when it comes to Justin, but she isn't some weak, cowering thing either. There's a strength in her that I respect. Her stance, her posture, her commanding tone, they belied a cool, easy confidence at the station.

In her eyes, I could see the truth.

She was afraid.

So afraid.

She's been through too much, and I'm sure this is just the icing on the cake. Not sure how she feels about having a killer as a daughter either.

The narrative, however, works. The Seattle Slayer kidnapped Parrish, right? The only target out of fourteen to escape his knife.

It makes sense that he'd come back for his 'sister'.

Maybe, to many people, this night was one of relief.

I'm worried that I've just been too clever, that Justin is going to punish me for it.

We shall see.

But I did walk out of that station, so there's that.

It's not over, not entirely, but as of right now, it seems like an obvious case of self-defense. Lumen's story matches mine. Danyella has no story because the last thing she remembers is falling asleep.

Somebody got her out of bed—just like they did me.

Fortunately for her, she didn't wake up until after she was in the ambulance. She won't have to suffer repeat nightmares about dead cops or blood on her hands or the horrible impossibility of having to choose between loved ones.

"The Banks want to see you," Tess continues, as if she can't decide what she meant to say or ask before that. Parrish remains silent, shoulder leaned up against the sloped wall to his left. The bed is partially tucked into a nook with its side tables, and the wall slopes up from there, peaking fourteen feet above our heads. The architecture here really is magnificent.

You're losing your goddamn mind, Kota.

Architecture? Lumen and/or Danyella almost just died. I killed somebody. My future is a series of too many balls in the hands of a juggler. One wrong move, and it all comes tumbling down.

"I want to see them, too, but I'm so tired. Please let me sleep first." I roll onto my side away from her, my lips cracked and dry, my body freezing cold all of a sudden. I know this feeling. I've stayed up for enough midnight game launches—and then played well into the next day—to know what fatigue looks like.

For me to turn down seeing my grandparents and Maxine, that tells you how tired I really am. I can barely think. In fact, I don't *want* to think. It hurts too much, and all I care about right now is closing my eyes. Even if it meant letting Justin win the game of life, I'd probably still do it.

I'm that worn-out.

She was a liar, that girl, that Dakota Banks. She swore she'd rather kill herself than harm another. But that wasn't true at all, was it? Like father, like daughter. The lost spawn of a serial killer indeed.

I feel so empty inside. This is so much bigger than having my door taken away or being scolded over a stupid pastry. What's just happened to me, it's so extensive, so deep and invasive, that while on an intellectual level, I understand how bad this is, I can't process it.

Maybe I don't want to process it?

Maybe I *can't* if I still expect myself to keep functioning? That must be it.

Surprisingly enough, Tess finally sighs and relents, rising from the bed. She looks at Parrish for a moment and, without a word, she exits the room and leaves the door cracked.

"I trust that you'll leave this open?" she asks, and Parrish nods before Tess finally moves away.

"Did that just happen?" he asks as I sit up on my elbows, wearing WHPA gear all over again. It's what Tess brought to the station for me to change into. Justin? He brought me a cute little sundress that made my stomach roil.

Oh his eyes ... his eyes ... I can't think about his eyes right now.

Also why I left my phone in Tess' car on purpose.

Also, also why I asked Parrish to quickly go over this room with the bug detector. He does that now, sliding it from the front pocket of his gray Whitehall hoodie. Once the room is clear, he turns the light off and pushes me into a proper position on the bed, yanking the covers from under my butt and then tossing them over me.

He climbs in beside me, too, and he's not wearing a shirt.

Score.

Sort of.

I'm too tired to appreciate it, but his skin might feel good if … I sit up briefly and chuck my hoodie, leaving the tank on underneath because I just don't think Tess is ready to see us skin to skin in here. I can still feel him though, his arms touching my arms, his belly pressed to that bit of bare back between my shirt and pants.

"Belatedly, yes, that just happened. I must've finally blown Tess' last rational brain cell to smithereens." Parrish offers me up a low snort, but he doesn't allow himself to laugh. Instead, he strokes hair back from my forehead in a soothing gesture.

"You scared me so much tonight," he whispers, pressing a kiss to my temple. "I love you, Gamer Girl."

That's the last thing I hear before I conk out.

But it's a good one. Oh yeah, it's fucking fantastic, as good as a night ending in murder can really get.

I don't wake up until *Sunday* morning. Literally. I sleep all through Saturday, wake briefly in the middle of the night for another shower and some snacks that Parrish brings me, and I'm out again.

We wake up together, bodies intertwined, and I sit up. He blinks sleepy eyes up at me, and I smile down at him, reminded of those first few days that he came home. I've never felt such relief and joy in my whole life; I might never again.

"Thanks for keeping the nightmares at bay," I murmur because, honestly, I didn't have any while he was holding me. He sits up, too, and then pulls me in for a kiss that I won't let get beyond the lips because, well, I really want to brush my teeth, but …

It makes my heart flutter and sparkle.

Eww. Kota, come on. You're gross AF when you're in love.

It's something I wouldn't have known until like just now. Not for sure anyway.

My cheeks flush as Parrish watches me, his gaze dark and hard to read.

"I still can't believe you tried to do that on your own." He shakes his head. "Gamer Girl, you're killing me. I knew from moment one that you were stubborn as hell, but this …"

"I wasn't willing to risk your life or anyone else's," I tell him, our conversation cut short as Tess opens the door without knocking. Parrish considered locking it after we got our snacks last night, but neither of us could go through with it.

Poor Tess.

While she seems a tad disturbed to see her shirtless son sitting in bed with me, she doesn't remark on it. Well, not in the way I might've suspected. *How can she not possibly believe I'm more trouble than I'm worth at this point? How?*

"I was wondering why the two of you went from hating each other to snuggling after Parrish came home." Tess blinks at us like she's finally putting all the pieces together. "Were you … together when we were in Bend?"

"Not yet," Parrish admits. "I was trying to decide if I trusted you enough."

That gives Tess pause. Me, too.

Trust her enough? I thought he was choosing *between* me and her. That's what he originally said anyway. But now, it makes so much more sense.

"Trusted me?" Tess echoes, and she seems completely sniped

at this point. Parrish got her in his crosshairs. Game over. "What do you mean?"

"I didn't know how you'd react, if you'd punish Dakota or punish me, if you'd separate us or panic." He spills his heart out, just like that, and I remember all over again why I like him so much. Parrish Vanguard is packed with heart; he cared about Tess all along, so much so that he practically (or did) hate me for disrupting her life on more than one occasion. "Maxx and Chasm, they begged us not to tell you."

Tess just stands there, listening. She says nothing. Does nothing.

"What changed your mind?" she asks after a time. I don't even know how to weigh in on this conversation. In the end, I was willing to trust Parrish's judgment, but I didn't know what Tess Vanguard would do.

She's surprised me in ways both good and bad. She is painfully, fallibly, honestly human.

"Your love for us." Parrish is unashamed as he says this, swinging his legs over the side of the bed so that he can fetch his shirt. He yanks it over his head, and I can barely stand the way the fabric catches and slides over his face, dragging his pouty lower lip down as he pulls it into place. "You love me, and you love Dakota too much."

Tess' eyes fill with tears, but she blinks the emotion from them and turns her head back toward the hall.

"The Banks are here. Get dressed and come down please. I'd say pajamas were fine, but ... Laverne. Dakota can wear whatever she wants, but Parrish, you should change." And here her voice hardens slightly before she leaves the room, pauses with her hand on the doorknob, and then turns back around. "Actually, I *would* feel better if you changed clothes in different rooms."

A ghost of a smile kisses Parrish's full mouth, and he casts a saucy look in my direction.

"I'd rather get *un*dressed in Dakota's presence."

"Alright, I don't love you *that* much. Get in your room and put your clothes on," Tess snaps, but there's a joy in her voice that she's even able to boss us around. Parrish was kidnapped and returned. After fourteen long years, I was brought back. Her family did not die in a fire. I did not die at the hands of a serial killing cop.

Supposedly.

Now that I really think about it, what the man said made sense.

The Seattle Slayer is a collective not an individual.

That scares me for so many reasons. Does Justin even have blood on his hands? He might not. He might, like the leader of a cartel or mob or something, be completely clean. That's what RICO—Racketeer Influenced and Corrupt Organizations—charges are for. It's a way to nail a crime boss who orders dirty work but never does it.

Could … could that work on Justin?

Parrish puts his palms on the bed, leaning forward to press a kiss to my cheek. I flush neon red as he heads for the door and Tess lingers to stare at me.

"If he ever stops acting like a gentleman, tell me." She closes the door, and I smile to myself. It doesn't last overly long because then I remember that I killed a guy, and even if he was a murderer, it's … it's a lot.

Not to mention, I'm having flashbacks of shooting Mr. Fosser's corpse and that was … it was fucking horrendous. I think I might have some mild form of PTSD or something.

With a shake, I knock off the emotions and force myself into, well, my hoodie. With the sweatpants, it's basically an outfit, and you know what? Fuck Laverne. I don't care if this is her— admittedly gorgeous—house, I'm in a mood.

ENDGAME ROMANCE

I don't let myself dwell on the idea that, despite this move on my part, Justin got exactly what he wanted. The boys clocked it from moment one: he was grooming me to kill. I killed. I took a person's life, which is the very stepping-stone Justin was hoping for from the start.

I head downstairs to find Maxx and Chasm waiting for me, one of each boy toy leaning against the newel post and wall respectively. They both straighten up substantially when they see me.

Chasm sprints up the bottom three stairs and then, when he's a stair below me and we're more or less at the same height, he digs his fingers into my hair and kisses the shit out of me. My knees nearly buckle as he slides his tongue up against mine, but he catches me around the waist and keeps me standing.

"I was so fucking worried," he mutters, pulling back as my cheeks heat and Maxine appears from around the corner. She pauses as Chasm moves aside, and we stare at each other.

"Baby sister." Her eyes well with tears as I hit the bottom step, and then she's dragging me into her arms and crushing me against her. "It's all over. It'll be okay. It's going to be okay."

I wish she was right.

Her words and touch are soothing, but just like the last time she tried to calm me in the coffeehouse, it's not necessarily true. I feel the urge to tell her everything—Lumen will have to be fully brought into the fold—but what about Maxine?

I just don't know right now.

Maxx and I exchange a look, one that communicates volumes, but he's far too respectful of my relationship with Maxine to get between us right now. Instead, he and Chasm follow me into the eat-in portion of the kitchen where my grandparents are waiting.

I'm still hugging them and letting them cry over me when Parrish enters the room, dressed in his usual preppy chic with khaki shorts and a white sweater. He looks like maybe he could join a yacht club, but then, with the tatted hands ... guess he's the rebel preppy boy?

Or else, labels are stupid as fuck and not worth anyone's effort? Truth.

Tess is seated beside Paul and, although I can tell she's uncomfortable with how close I am to Carmen and Walter, she says nothing. Instead, I think she's gripping Paul's hand beneath the tabletop. They really do make a darling couple, don't they?

Anyway, I sit between my grandparents, Maxine beside Carmen, and the boys fanned out between her and Paul. There's plenty of food on the table, but it's hard to feel hungry with so much scrutiny.

Everyone is staring at me.

"I don't mean to press you, honey," Tess begins, and I can see that this is about to go in a very Tess Vanguard sort of way. "But would you like to speak to a psychiatrist?"

Not particularly. But it's a reasonable idea.

Maybe later, after this situation is sorted out. I mean, if Justin doesn't kill me for this beforehand.

"Not at this time," I say as politely as I can, exhaling and slumping a bit in my seat. I slept practically all of my Tess-time away, and as nice as it was to cuddle up with Parish, I'm terrified of going back to Justin's. "Maybe later. I'd really like to push past this and have as normal a summer as possible."

"The Slayer already took enough time from us," Parrish adds, speaking up for the first time. He butters a piece of toast and then tosses it onto Chasm's plate. The two of them glare at each other, and I swear I hear Parrish say something like *meokda* which means eat, or you eat, or I eat or ... I'm not very good at Korean. Hence, the *saranghae* means goodnight stuff.

With a dramatic sigh, Chasm finally picks up his toast and

takes a bite.

"Well, it's certainly something to consider." Tess does her best to soften the rebuke as Paul adjusts his glasses and gives his son a *not your business* sort of a look. Oh, if he only knew. "Are you … okay with going back to Justin's tomorrow?" she asks me, but even if I were able to tell the truth and say no, is there anything she could do to stop it?

"Definitely." The lie makes my teeth hurt, but I choke down a gulp of ice water to force the truth back into the shadows where it, unfortunately and hopefully only temporarily, belongs.

"Tell your dad if he wants more snails for dinner, I can get them out of my garden and ship 'em over."

It's a dad joke, for sure, despite Walter being our grandfather.

Both Maxine and I groan in near unison, and we make polite, if awkward, conversation for the rest of the meal. Everyone here knows what I did, that I murdered a guy. Nobody—least of all me —knows what to do or say to make it better.

I am beyond ready to escape by the time the adults drift away to talk.

The boys and I end up in the backyard together with Maxine. Surprisingly, Kimber saunters out and gives me a strange once-over.

"Thankfully you're not dead. If you had died, Mom would be in Godzilla-bitch mode for months." She stares at me as if daring me to retaliate, and that's when it hits me. Is she? Is she treating me … like she treats Parrish? Am I supposed to insult her back or something?

It's how the two of them exchange affection, bizarre as it seems to me. When Parrish went missing, Kimber was clearly devastated.

"If *you* don't piss off, you're the one who's going to end up dead." Parrish takes care of the insult for me, and Kimber scoffs, fluffing her blond hair and giving Maxine … is that a jealous glare? My older sister blinks in surprise and watches as her rival struts off and slams the French doors behind her.

"Is she always like that?" Maxine queries, and again, Parrish answers for me.

"Worse, usually." He tucks his hands into his pockets, and then we all just sort of stand there.

"I killed somebody on Friday night." A pause. "Err, early Saturday morning. Let's just kick the elephant's ass right out of the room. I'm a murderer, plain and simple."

"You do realize you have over a million subscribers on Twitch, right?" Maxine asks, and there's a teeny, tiny part of me that's excited by that. The rest of me is straight wrecked because I killed a dude, and my crazy serial killer father is breathing down my neck, and I've avoided all of his inevitable texts and calls by leaving my phone purposefully off and on the front seat of Tess' car …

"Over a million you say?" I wish I'd been able to gain that many followers with my actual gaming abilities and not because of the kidnappings or the serial killer stuff. I mean, that's impressive, but I'm not interested in fame based on tragedy. From the way the guys are looking at me, maybe they're not totally thrilled either.

"As long as you don't start doing hot tub streams," Chasm mutters, sliding out a pack of cigarettes and then returning them to his pocket as if he's thought better of it. Maybe he's trying to quit smoking? That'd be nice. I won't pressure him—at least not now —but good for him if he is.

"Hot tub streams are a hard no from me." This is Maxx, crossing his arms over his chest as I roll my eyes.

"As if I'd ever dress down to a bikini and stream games from a hot tub just so nasty ass old perverts online can jack off. That's fucking sick. If I ever catch *you* watching a hot tub stream, it's over." I make an X with my arms over my chest, and he raises a brow at me.

"Deal. I won't watch them; you won't do them." His lips twitch slightly and, even though I can sense that he's still slightly angry at me about the other night, he teases. "But about that OnlyFans account ..."

"Excuse me?" This is Chasm. Parrish has already heard this before, so I'm fairly certain he knows it's a joke. Maybe not though, what with the way he's staring at me.

"OnlyFans?" Maxine's eyes turn into huge saucers, and I rush to explain, waving my arms like a crazy person or one of those, like, weird blow-up things they put outside of used car sales lots. Pretty sure *Family Guy* calls them *'wacky waving inflatable arm-flailing tube men'.* That's me. I am a wacky tube woman.

"Not really. Never. You know how I feel about that kind of stuff. It's a joke." I give Maxx a look, but he just smirks at me. "Mr. Men's Magazine, back me up on this."

"It better be a joke," is what he says, all sultry and shit. "The only fan that gets to see you naked is me." Hah. I see what he did there. I flip him off, and he laughs, but it doesn't last long. I can tell by the gleam in his eye that he wants to speak to me. Alone, possibly. Or at least without Maxine.

We take a walk through the gardens together in the early morning light, and I refuse to allow my brain to fixate on the sight of the cop's body, bloodied and still on the forest floor. Instead, I keep the conversation chipper and upbeat, until Maxine runs inside to use the restroom.

That's when Maxx stands in front of me, hands on his hips and gives me a dark look.

"Yes?" I ask, as innocently as possible. It almost works; I can tell.

"Dakota, do not *ever* lie to me again," he repeats, just as he did in the forest that day. "You have to trust me." He pauses here and swallows, like he's choking on his own pride or something. "You have to trust *us*. If we do this thing"—and here he points between me and himself, me and Chasm, me and Parrish—"what I need from you is pure honesty at all times. Unless Justin has a gun to your head or the head of somebody you love, talk to us." He looks away slightly and then shakes his head. "I was afraid we were going to lose you."

"Justin never intended for me to die—" I start my protest, but I don't finish it. X offers me up such an impossible look that I remember all the things that Chasm told me, about his rigid morals, about how he'd die to uphold them. This is one of them, and I respect him for that.

"There's more than one way to die, Dakota." I know what he means. I can feel it, just a little bit, a tiny fungus growing and multiplying on the shadowy underside of my heart. I won't let it take root, but it's there, and it's insidious.

"How did you know to follow me in the first place?" I ask, and Maxx offers up a wan smile.

"I could tell based on your face when you got that text, when you told me everything was okay after I texted you. It was the same look you had when Parrish was missing, and I asked if you knew where he was."

I sigh.

Having one super cute, super perceptive, super *possessive* boy on my ass would be hard enough. Three of them? What am I supposed to do with three? *Too bad that foursome shower was lost in the fire.* But it won't be forever, and I'm seriously not even remotely thinking about that because I might be thirsty, but I'm not insane.

"No way on the foursome thing." It comes out of my mouth like things often do, blurted and without regard to my own safety, sanity, or dignity.

"No shame, Little Sister," Chasm cackles, as Parrish allows a partial smile to tease across his perfect mouth. He exchanges a look with Maxx, and I can't decide if it means *yeah, sure, bro, I'd do it* or *no fucking way am I sharing with you.* They definitely have more tension between them than either Chasm/Parrish or Chasm/Maxx.

"I was thinking *no* on the foursome thing," I argue, pausing as I see the back door open and Maxine heading our way again. "It was in the negative sense."

"Sure it was," Chasm quips, bumping me with his hip as he saunters past.

The rest of the day is peaceful, if not a little weird and awkward with Tess hovering around so much, but it's nice. I'd have preferred more sex and less peopling, but c'est la vie.

Same deal that night, but at least Parrish is there to cuddle me.

The nightmares, too, are shoved into a corner of shadows, buried, and forgotten.

At least … temporarily.

CHAPTER 20

Monday morning, we get news from the agents that they're still working on the Seattle Slayer aspect of the case, but that it's a pretty cut-and-dried case of self-defense on my part. That doesn't mean we're done with questioning, oh no, but I've got a small reprieve.

Justin, too, is contributing his assistance, having plugged in the cop's face to Milk Carton. Oh, wow, total surprise, the guy is like, guilty of a bunch of violent, horrific crimes that were mysteriously caught on camera. None of which prove that he was the Seattle Slayer, but still.

It appears I'm not going to do time for this—at least it doesn't seem that way now.

On the other hand, Justin is a rolling storm of fury when he picks me up in the morning. He's so angry, in fact, that he doesn't play his usual vintage pop songs or sing one of my favorites—seeing him mouth the words to Ashnikko's *"Maggots"* was a real treat—and instead we sit together in the car in dead fucking silence.

"I only did what you taught me," I admit finally, hoping to get the jump on this situation before he strikes me again. Or kills somebody I love. Or forces me to sleep with Lumen or something.

"How so?" he responds, quiet and dangerous, seething and frothing on the inside. I was right to push this conversation ahead; if he gets me back to the house and we haven't resolved anything, I'm going to be sorry.

"You taught me to make sacrifices in my games. I sacrificed my queen in order to—" I'm not even allowed to finish my argument before Justin is turning the music on as loud as he can, drowning me out to the tune of AFI's *"Miss Murder"*. Um. It's a very telling song choice.

That is me now. I am Miss Murder. I am ... tainted.

If Justin really is going to make me start writing that book, I'll begin it like this.

Once upon a time, there was a girl. She was loud and opinionated and she loved more than anything to get lost in other worlds, in video games or books or television shows. Mostly, this girl wanted to live. She didn't realize that until much later in her young life, that while she adored those other worlds, she wanted to stay in this one with the family she knew, the family she did not know, and the boys she was desperate to know more about.

We return to the house and Justin climbs out of the car, but not before demanding that I follow him. He leads me to the 'writing studio' where the chess board is set up, and then plucks the white king from the board, putting it right up to my face.

"You are *not* the queen, Dakota." And here he laughs before turning and chucking the piece at the wall so hard that the top portion of it breaks off from the base, the pieces rolling across the floor. "You are the king, silly girl. Was this really a lesson I needed to teach you, hmm?" He spins back toward me, raking his eyes over me in disgust. "You're damn lucky I'm here to clean up your mistakes."

I blink at him.

It's the only move right now that seems unlikely to piss him off.

"You best hope that this fiasco doesn't lead the authorities to my doorstep. You understand what will happen if this takes a wrong turn, don't you, Dakota darling?" He turns and points at a laptop in the corner. It's brand-new, as frothy a bubblegum pink as Raúl's.

"Sit down and write. As punishment for your actions, you won't be going out today." He turns and leaves the room, slamming the glass doors hard enough behind him that I'm surprised they don't break.

I cringe a bit and then reach up, sweeping my palms over my artfully slicked-back hair. I had Maxine give me a twisty bun at the base of my skull. Clearly, part of Justin's plan is testing my limits, sniffing out my boundaries, and then slowly edging me closer and closer to crossing them. A person can only be pushed so far before they break.

I'm doing the same with him.

I turn toward the computer, a deep sense of dread taking hold in me, thorny vines wrapping my arms and legs. I close my eyes and shake them off, fighting past the memory of a dead, bloodied man lying in the woods.

With a sudden exhale, I swoop into the chair and sit down hard. Flipping up the lid, I open a word processor, and then I just sit there and stare at the blank page. *How does Tess do this?* I wonder, the blinking cursor like a well-laid curse, a promise of the infinite. There are literal universes trapped inside the black and white type of a well-laid word.

Once upon a time ... I write because, well, Justin told me to. But then I sit there and wonder if this is what writer's block feels like, like there are whole people and vast stories and endless landscapes bursting but stuck, vibrant but clogged, poised, breathless.

I crack my knuckles.

Once upon a time, there was a princess trapped inside a tower. Her dresses were hoodies, her crown a headset, and her tower a mansion on the shores of Lake Washington. Unconventional, surely, but she believed in the premise of the modern-day fairy tale.

That is, there's always a happily ever after waiting at the end of the rainbow.

<hr>

Midway through the day, Delphine interrupts me for lunch, and we end up sitting together on the edge of the boat slip. Our legs dangle in the cool water, but the sunshine is more than enough to make up for it.

The bright crisp crunch of the apple in my hand provides a welcome accompaniment to the rhythmic lapping of the water, the distant bird song from the garden, and the voices of our neighbors on their boats.

"Are you excited for the garden party tomorrow?" she asks me, and it takes several seconds for me to register what she's talking about. Oh. That's right. Justin sent me that itinerary …

I lift up one butt cheek, so I can slide my phone from my rear left pocket, and I smile at the encouraging texts from the boys. I told them I was writing all day today, and they seemed equally surprised.

At first, it sort of freaked me out. I mean, it still *does* freak me out that Justin would try to turn me into a mini-Tess, but it's actually, almost, sort of, kind of … fun? Though I'm not sure that Justin would appreciate my version of the manuscript where he's the villain and not the king as he so perceives himself to be.

I take another bite of apple, navigating past the vast proliferation of texts to my email.

Ooo. Vast proliferation? I look up the word *proliferation* to make certain that I've used it correctly. Score! I write it down on my phone's notepad and Delphine gives me a look.

"Oh, baby sister …" Her words trail off and then she's scooting closer to me, and I'm stiffening up. I mean, we shared some moments back at Tess' place, such as when she French braided my hair, but we're not really *that* close. Also, she stole the nickname 'baby sister' from Maxine, and I'm not sure how I feel about that.

I glance her way as she gives me a sideways hug, and I wonder how deeply she's really into all this?

"Don't feel sorry for me," I assure her, even if, when I close my eyes during the day, I see splotches of bad memory. Parrish kept them at bay during the night, but what's going to happen now that he isn't here? Five fucking days trapped in my tower before, ironically, I can go back to Tess and Laverne's place as a semi-free woman. "You lost your grandmother recently, and you've barely talked about it. You must be hurting, too."

Delphine hesitates, sitting up straight and turning her attention to the water and the view of the city across the sparkling surface of the lake. I knew her mousy act was just that—an act—but I didn't expect all of this, the bright blond hair (it suits her honestly) or the designer clothes, the new car, the overdone bedroom that she claims to have decorated herself …

Sitting like that, our legs pressed close, my phone and my apple still held in my hands, her arm around my waist, I can see the faintest shine of tears in her eyes that she does her best to hide.

"She passed away of natural causes," she says, as if that

somehow makes it easier. "And she was really old—"

"Doesn't mean you loved her any less. Probably, you loved her more." It's meant to be a soothing statement, but Delphine closes her eyes tight and withdraws her arm, putting her hands in her lap.

"That's true," she admits, but then she does her best to give me a comforting smile, and I feel myself sympathizing with her. Maybe I shouldn't, but I can't help myself. *Chasm is right; I am way too nice, aren't I?* "But even though I miss her, I feel …" She rubs at her face as if she's ashamed of whatever it is that she wants to say. "Relieved. I feel relieved. I've been taking care of her for years, and I'm tired."

I put what I hope is a comforting hand on her leg, and then I let her be as she stares at the view, eyes still shimmering with tears.

I look at the email from Justin, the one that I just barely glanced at before.

There it is. *Garden Party at Whitehall Gardens. Noon. Dress code: upscale summer casual.*

Oh.

Fantastic.

Is this really still happening? I'm not sure how far the news of the 'Slayer's' capture has spread, but I bet the whole town knows. I'm surprised there still aren't any reporters. At least they can't get to us on the water. If they could, they would, but there are rules in place seeing as so many famous douchebags live around here. I won't name names, but think of a billionaire dumb enough to shoot himself into space in a penis-shaped vessel that looks like it belongs to Dr. Evil in the movie, *Austin Powers: the Spy Who Shagged Me.*

Anyway, no reporters. Good thing. Great thing, actually.

But a garden party? What even *is* a garden party?

"What's a garden party?" I ask Delphine, and she turns to me, blinking those big doe eyes of hers.

"Uhh." She laughs and reaches up to rub at the back of her head. "I honestly don't know. A bunch of rich people eating tiny sandwiches, drinking tea or wine, and milling around a garden?"

I just stare at her, and she laughs again.

My next question just bursts out of my mouth. I'm starting to like this girl, but I have so many questions that need answering.

"Where did the blood on my sheets come from?" I ask her because, surely, she's the only person capable of having done that.

My shiny new sister seems surprised at the question, offering a nervous laugh as she tucks that pretty gold hair behind one ear. She looks sidelong at me, offering up a sheepish smile.

"Oh, it was only pig's blood," she tells me, but somehow, I'm not convinced.

Later in the day, I find myself in Justin's office, waiting behind Raúl as he taps on the doorframe.

"The unruly one wants to see you," he drawls, as if he's bored out of his mind. Justin turns slightly in his chair and nods, and I push past Raúl. He has the fashion sense of a K-pop star, but his personality is that of a hedgehog. A hedgehog with rabies. A hedgehog with rabies with a stick up its ass.

I flip him off as I walk by, but he ignores me, spinning on his crocodile skin loafers and storming off.

"I don't like him," I tell Justin, hoping my frankness will please him as it sometimes does.

"Nobody likes Raúl," he says, also appearing bored out of his mind. "Would you like to kill him, too? If so, I'll give you a gun, and you can walk right up to him and blow his brains out." Justin turns back to his computer with its nine billion monitors and starts typing. There's a bunch of code on the screen, but it may as well be an alien language to me.

On the inside, I feel nauseous. I sway, like I'm on a boat set wild by a tempestuous sea. On the outside, I remain disturbingly calm.

"Was it really pig's blood?" I ask, exhaling and wondering if Justin will know what incident I'm referring to. "On my sheets that day, after Delphine changed them—"

"It wasn't pig's blood." Justin doesn't look at me, but my entire body breaks out in goose bumps. "Would you like to know whose blood it was or, better yet, remain blissfully ignorant?" He continues working on his computer, and I make my exit.

Outside his office, I put a hand to the wall, bent over and panting.

With my eyes squeezed shut, I can see so many images that I wish I'd never been exposed to. Parrish, on his deathbed. JJ, curled up and cold. Mr. Fosser's corpse quivering as I pressed the trigger. The cop guy—his name was Heath Cousins—in a bloody pool in the morning sunshine.

I shove back up to my feet, spotting Raúl as he passes through the solarium. He's flicking a lighter again, playing with it like it's a tic he indulges more often than not. Once again, I can't help but wonder …

The front door opens, and I turn to see Amin Volli, my sixth period teacher, waltzing into the mansion like he owns the place. I'm surprised he's here, to be honest. Seeing as he's the one who carries out much of Justin's dirty work, isn't it a bit suspicious for him to hang around here?

"Hello, Miss Prior," he greets, and even though the sound of that name makes me cringe twice as hard as being called *Mia Patterson,* I let it slide. "How are you?"

"How *am* I?" I choke out, but he just adjusts his bow tie, glasses sliding down his aquiline nose. "You're kidding me, right?

How do you think I am?"

"*We should meet in another life, we should meet in air, me and you.*" Mr. Volli chuckles, dressed in a tweed suit and very fine shoes, like he always is. "Sylvia Plath. We could be friends in another life, Miss Prior. You're so very clever."

I just keep staring at him.

"Your manuscript?" he begins, raising a single brow. "It's been updating to the cloud as you've been writing, and well, I've been reading it—"

My face drops, and I shudder all over.

Justin is one thing, but my teacher?

I look over as my bio dad waltzes out of his office, adjusting his watch.

"Amin," he greets, and then his sapphire eyes fall on me. "You think she has any talent?"

"Her writing is raw," he begins, and I feel my face heat. Not only did … I … well, I lost something important and vital to who I was, to who Dakota Banks was supposed to be, but now I'm being humiliated? It's almost too much. "It relies a bit much on prose and metaphors, but I can see Tess' influence in her writing." Mr. Volli leans down, putting his palms on his upper thighs and offering up a patronizing smile. "You must've read her novels over and over again, am I right?"

"Well, at least that's something," Justin says with a sigh, eying me like I'm a nuisance. Oh how I wish. I wish I truly were a nuisance to him. But no. He's just temporarily annoyed with me. Underneath that itch of annoyance, the obsessive glint is still there.

After all, in the scheme of things, I did exactly what he wanted, didn't I?

I killed somebody.

Like father, like daughter.

I can't resist the mantra.

ENDGAME ROMANCE

"Enjoy the rest of your afternoon to yourself, but if you set foot outside of this house ..." Justin trails off, and then smirks at me. "Well, you'll be in serious trouble, young lady." He moves over to me and kisses me on the top of the head.

Delphine's footsteps precede her as she moves into the room, Caroline close on her heels. Parrish's bio mom—I am still completely and utterly weirded out that Justin is dating her—has an expensive designer bag on one arm, a black dress that makes her look like a venomous spider (or maybe that's all in my head) and a pair of red-bottoms on her feet.

"I was planning on inviting Dakota to join me to shop for my wedding dress," my new 'stepmom' offers up. Her eyes move from Justin to me, and she offers a red-mouthed smile. Her lipstick is similar to what Ms. Miyamoto wears, or maybe even the shade that my grandmother favors, but somehow it's impossibly more garish and disturbing. "We could do lunch afterward? I know a great place on the water. The seafood is world-class."

"If you stay with your stepmother, then I suppose it's alright." Justin lifts up a finger, like he's a real dad and not some psycho who threatened to kill my boyfriend if I didn't fuck his two best friends. "But no boys. You hear me, cupcake?" He taps me on the nose and then turns to leave.

"Keep up the good work on the manuscript; I'll send over my edits at the end of the week." Mr. Volli follows Justin out the front door, and I turn to find Delphine smiling at me. Caroline is smiling, too, but somehow it feels like she's about to bite me, wrap me up in a web, and save me for later.

I almost shudder.

"If you'd rather stay home and rest, we'd understand," Delphine offers up, but frankly, the idea of sitting around this huge house by myself—and by that, I mean with dozens of staff members who look at the floor and not my face—then the answer is a resounding *hell no*.

Much as it sounds like literal torture to go out with Caroline Bassett, I'll do it.

Just so I don't have to think about the guy I killed.

Just so I don't have any idle time for my brain to remind me that I am, without a doubt, the lost daughter of a serial killer.

Shopping with Caroline and Delphine is not so dissimilar from my second day here in Washington when I went out with Tess and Kimber. Granted, Delphine is far nicer to me than Kimber, and Caroline's tastes run slightly more expensive and heaps less conservative than Tess, but still.

It's awkward as fuck.

I redirect my thoughts away from bad memories and from the curious stares of other shoppers by thinking about Justin's taunt about Caroline. *"Did I ever tell you her story? It's fascinating."* As much as I wish I could claim that I'm not interested, I am. I do want to know. I want to know why Caroline left Parrish and Paul, why she's never even attempted to have anything to do with her son.

He's such an amazing person, that's all I can think about as she laughs and makes nice with me and Delphine. The newest addition to my sister collection, well, she doesn't seem to mind or notice that our father's 'fiancée' is as fake as press-on-nails, but I'm not fooled.

"When did you get engaged anyway?" I ask, wondering why there wasn't some big fanfare, a party or celebration of some sort, a piece on a local news website, gossip and hubbub in the society pages.

Caroline pauses, her glass of wine halfway to her lips. We're seated on a balcony that hangs out over the water, the cries of gulls a sweet accompaniment to our meal. The food is good, I'll admit that, but I can't get over the nervous itch I feel whenever I look at Caroline.

"Justin wanted to keep it quiet, what with everything else going on. How would it look if we announced our engagement while your brother was missing?" She blinks her eyelash extensions at me and takes another sip of wine before holding out the glass for a waiter to refill. "Besides, we've both been married before; I didn't want to make a big deal out of it."

Huh.

Caroline seems the type who enjoys attention; I can't tell if this 'quiet engagement' is bothering her, or maybe if it was her idea all along? Either way, I allow the conversation to drift to less important things.

I'm a bit surprised when all three boys—and Tess—show up at the same restaurant.

Only one of the four people staring at me is surprised.

That is, Tess. Tess is surprised.

"Oh, Dakota …" she starts, and then her gaze drifts to Caroline, and holy *fuck,* her dark brown eyes go hard, and the edge of her lip twitches as if she might scowl. "Caroline."

"Tess."

The two women glare at one another as I look between them, my own attention drifting over to Parrish. He glances at his egg donor, but then his gaze shifts to mine. As soon as our eyes lock, I feel myself getting twitchy.

How on earth did I lay next to this gorgeous boy and not attempt to take things to the next level? I mean, it makes sense in the context of what I went through, but as I stare at him, standing with the sunshine highlighting the blond bits in his brown hair, raking long, inked fingers through the gentle waves, his pouty mouth slightly parted ...

I tap my own chin to close my mouth, and then frantically dab at my lips with my napkin to make sure I'm not drooling. He notices my weird awkwardness and smiles at me. It's devastating.

Chasm, on the other hand, is not quite so subtle. He walks right up to the table and leans down beside me, putting his lips up to my ear.

"Tomorrow is supposed to be our engagement party. Please say yes." He licks the curve of my ear, and I shudder all over just before he disguises the action by pressing a not-so-chaste kiss to my cheek.

Does Tess know about the engagement thing? I highly doubt it. If she does, there's nothing she can do about it unfortunately. If we're just getting engaged and waiting to get married, she can't really stop that. At seventeen, I could marry Chasm with parental consent which, since Justin is the custodial parent, he could give regardless of Tess' wishes.

Also, eww. Eww to all of it. I like Chasm. I'm ... in love with Chasm. But I don't want to get married in high school.

At least Washington state requires both parties to be at least seventeen. There are US states where there's no minimum age to marry, states like Massachusetts that allow *twelve-year-olds* to marry. To amp up the skeeve factor even more, most states have younger minimum ages that girls can marry than boys.

Why do you think that is? Fucking. Gross. And we're talking about the USA here, not some distant, barely imaginable country across the world.

I digress.

Chasm rises to his full height, his lightning bolt bangs falling prettily across his forehead, his lip piercings switched out for black studs, his short-sleeved shirt showing off his ink.

"Kwang-seon," Tess warns, and he smirks at me, offering up a wink as Tess approaches the table to stand beside him. "This looks fun. What are you three up to on this beautiful summer day?" You'd think she was declaring war the way her voice sounds, the way Caroline tenses up and narrows her eyes.

Both of these women dated Paul, had children with Paul. Both of these women dated Justin Prior. Most especially, one of these women raised the other woman's child. Snippets of shouted conversation drift to me from the period when Parrish was missing.

"I honestly don't know what to say to you, Caroline. Yes, well, he is your biological son."

Tess, pleading with Caroline to care that Parrish was missing. And even though I couldn't hear the other end of the conversation, I can only imagine that she didn't care. No, she was too busy dating and getting engaged to Justin, I guess.

"Wedding dress shopping." Caroline's bright mouth twists into a smirk as Delphine leans back in her chair, looking between the two women as if she has no horse in this race. She doesn't like Tess, and I don't blame her. The way Tess ordered her around, ehh, I wouldn't be a huge fan of the woman either.

I *wasn't* a huge fan of the woman, and I'm her daughter. When did that change?

I look up at Tess' face, and I like how fierce she looks, how calculating. She isn't done here; she hasn't given up. I know that, and I appreciate it more than I can put into words.

"Oh?" Tess asks, raising both brows. "You and Justin …?"

"Yes, me and Justin," Caroline snaps, sitting up and clearly losing the silent battle of wills. Tess' composure hasn't crumpled, but I can already see Caroline losing her cool. Maxx studies the two women before looking at me, and I find that I ache for him in a new and different way.

He saw right through me, came for me, was willing to give up his freedom to take the fall for the cop's death. I wish I could stand up and throw myself into his arms, but I can't take Justin's warning—even delivered as mildly as it was—lightly. He winks at me though, and I flush red-hot. Nothing unusual there.

"He didn't want you to sign a prenup the way Paul did, eh?" Tess asks, and then she gives this terrible laugh. It's full of Big Bitch Energy, and I am living for it. She tosses her dark hair—worn loose for once—and turns to me, dismissing Caroline entirely. Tess pauses briefly to look over at Parrish. "And don't worry, honey: your father never asked *me* to sign one." Tess bends down to give me a kiss on the forehead. "I will *never* stop fighting." She whispers this last part in my ear before standing back up and offering a beauty queen esque little wave. "Enjoy your lunch."

She takes off toward a table at the corner of the balcony, but the boys linger.

"How are you feeling today?" Maxx asks me, and just the soft, easy way he asks the question makes me want to break down. Instead, because I can't bear to break down in front of Caroline or even Delphine, and especially not in public, I make myself smile.

"We'll talk tomorrow. You'll be at the garden party, yes?"

"I'll be there," he confirms, exchanging a look with Chasm. Parrish takes a step forward, putting himself between the two other boys. It suits him, that spot. Because as devious and intelligent as Chasm is, as alpha male and confident as Maxx is, Parrish is still the boss.

He puts his palms flat on the table and leans in.

"Caroline," he says, surprising me. Delphine pauses with a bite of seafood pasta on her fork, and Caroline freezes with her wine glass pressed to her red lips. "Justin suggested that, now that you're back in town for good, we should spend some time together. A little mother and son bonding, what do you say?"

392

ENDGAME ROMANCE

The woman stares at him like she's just received a fatal checkmate.

"Well, whatever Justin says," she mumbles, gaze shifting to the side.

Parrish smiles at her, one of his cruelest smiles, the one he wore when he was rating me a three on his fuckability rating scale on TikTok.

Oh how far we've come.

"Laverne is taking me to the garden party, so I'll be there, too. Stay safe, Gamer Girl." He doesn't kiss me, and neither does Maxx because, well, Justin might be able to overlook my 'fiancé' giving me a cheek kiss, but the others are likely to piss him off.

I would rather not draw his ire their way.

The guys drift off, and I feel impossibly, absurdly lonely. Lonelier even than when I first got here, and all I wanted to do was go … home.

What that means right now, I'm not entirely sure.

All I know is that home is not and never will be as a princess trapped in Justin's tower.

CHAPTER 22

As soon I step foot in the garden area of the country club, I'm greeted by a sea of familiar faces. There's a select few who are genuinely happy to see me, a large portion that stare at me in that strange, calculating way that both Whitehall students and Medina residents use to assess competitors and/or prey, and a fairly sizable chunk that are hostile.

Veronica Fisher, for example. Her brunette friend whose name I've surely heard but can't be fucked remembering. The guy with the Nickelodeon gak sweatshirt (he's not wearing it today, but still), and his friend. Their assorted cronies. Etc., etc., etc.

Laverne is there, lips pursed, sipping from a teacup at a table near the hedges. Lumen is present as well, as is Danyella. Even Maxine and my grandparents are there. *Thank God.*

Mostly though, you know where my eyes are.

On the boys, all dressed to kill, like a K-pop band that has yet to debut. Parrish is decked out in a tucked-in white tee with his silver Baphomet necklace hanging low. I'm not sure why he wears it seeing as it's sort of an obscure icon, some long-forgotten deity that was supposedly worshipped by the Knights Templar.

Whatever the reason, it lends him this edginess that would otherwise be impossible seeing as he's wearing a pair of casual gray wool trousers, a black belt with the end hanging down like a fashion statement. Add in the black and white Chucks, and I'd say he was going for a 'soft boy' aesthetic.

Soft boy is sort of like a fuckboy but without having a nasty attitude. Supposedly, the trend and the look is supposed to accompany artistic and sensitive personality traits, both of which Parrish has.

But, eh, screw labels.

Whatever you want to call him, he's a stunner, especially with the new black watch on his right wrist, the casual slouch of his body, and the violent glimmer in his eye as he surveys the crowd.

X is wearing a white hoodie with the hood up, a black wifebeater underneath, and loose white jogging shorts with bright red sneakers. He pushes the hood back as soon as he sees me, and I swear, these guys must practice in the mirror for this. All those sexy flourishes that boy bands use? They do that. It's as if they're taunting me.

Oh, and Chasm?

Holy *shit.*

Chasm is *allll* dressed up. He's wearing dark slacks with these yellow, black, and white sneakers that I only know are Balenciaga because Kimber had to tell me *all* about them the last time he wore them. He's got on a pullover sweater—also in black—with a crisp dress shirt collar peeking out of the neckline. The black and white stripes on the collar add that gothic edge that he likes so much.

He turns toward me, and his smile, it's practically dripping with innuendo.

We haven't had any alone time recently, but I'd love to get his thoughts on this engagement thing. It's not just me who's being forced into this against my will; he's paying the price for falling into Justin's web. At the very least, Chasm's involvement is more because of his dad than it is because of me, but still.

Besides that, I want the full story of what happened when Seamus discovered the tattoos, piercings, and colored hair. The latter, maybe, isn't such a big deal. But the metal? The ink? Seamus must've been furious.

"*Mu-seun ir-i-ya?*" he asks, but it may as well mean goodnight, so … Chasm grins at me. "Oh, come on. You aren't as much a K-drama simp as you pretend to be." He moves up beside me, the other two trailing slightly behind him, as if they can sense the energy here.

That is, Justin watching us all.

And not over tech this time, but from like, right there.

"Daddy!" Delphine skips down the steps to give him a hug, buying me a moment with the boys.

They don't ask me how last night went because they know. I logged onto my shiny new PlayStation, and this time, when we played that game, the one with the aliens and humans where I kicked Maxx's ass, we were all on the same team.

Our conversation, monitored as it was, remained light and airy, as if this were any other summer. It's one that I don't think any of us will ever be able to forget, regardless of what happens next. As far as that, I haven't the faintest clue.

I have another meeting with those FBI agents this week, but that's about it.

After the information that Justin obtained through Milk Carton was forwarded to the police, nobody would ever blame me for that man's death. He's done some, oh God, some admittedly horrible things that I'd rather not talk about just now.

The only consolation in hearing about his evil deeds was that my guilt was assuaged somewhat. The boys know all this, as we discussed it over a private Discord server last night. I'm just thankful at this point that Justin hasn't cut me off from them entirely. He could, if he really wanted to, but I know why he hasn't.

He doesn't want to break me; he wants me to be loyal, subservient, an accomplice to his crazy. It's why he rewards and punishes me in equal measures, a Stockholm sort of thing.

"Do you think we could take a walk?" Chasm asks it first, scratching at his forehead as he gives Maxx and Parrish a look. The former exhales heavily, but nods. Maxx knows he was the last one to step in and lay claim to me, so he doesn't push as much as I believe he would've had he been first.

Had he been first, I don't think we'd be entertaining the idea of suitors and courting and whatnot. It'd just be, *pick me, Dakota, and don't look back.* I almost swoon thinking about that, but then, I couldn't bear to let Parrish or Chasm go either.

In an odd way, it worked out for the best. Parrish and Chasm aren't exactly the sort to share, but Parrish was missing, and things just sort of fell into place this way. It's the only part of this entire scenario that I don't regret.

"Alone? Don't let this engagement thing get to your head." Parrish gives me a once-over, taking in my emerald-green satin skater minidress with the silver heels. I didn't choose any of this—makeup, hairstyle, outfit—but at least it's a somewhat better fit than the princess gowns that Justin's been draping me in. "I let you call her naekkeo. I let you take over the end of my week. I let Maxx and Dakota do it on a Pac-Man machine—"

"Ms. Pac-Man," I correct. Not that it matters. It really doesn't. I'm just embarrassed.

"That's right, Pear-Pear. It was *Ms.* Pac-Man," Maxx purrs out, and Parrish scowls at him. "And also, an *Indiana Jones* pinball machine."

"That reminds me!" I pause and dig around in the bag on my arm, pulling out a few t-shirts that I picked up while we were out shopping yesterday. I didn't see anything I wanted for myself, but Delphine came home with a maxed-out credit card (actually, she spent thousands and it never maxed-out, but you get the idea). Caroline did the same. She picked her wedding dress out, too, this casual but absurdly expensive mini with a plunging neckline.

Me, I picked up things for the boys.

I'd have grabbed a gift for Maxine, but there was absolutely nothing in the stores we went to that she would wear.

"Here." I hand Parrish the white t-shirt, and he takes it. He lifts it up and stares at the design on the front before letting that scrumptious gold and brown gaze of his drift past to me.

"It's a pear." He says that with a sort of mystic bafflement that makes me chuckle.

"It is. It's a pear." I point at him. "Because you're Pear-Pear, get it?"

He isn't unamused, but he scoffs anyway, and crumples it up in his hand. I pass over Chas' t-shirt next, and he gives me such a disparaging look that I can't help but be defiant and flippant as I look back at him.

"What? You love BTS," I say, because that's what I got him. A cute pale pink men's cut tee with the black BTS chevron logo and seven male silhouettes.

"I swear to fuck, Naekkeo," he warns me, but he can't hide his grin.

"Can't wait to see what I got." Maxx tucks his hands into the pockets of his shorts, but I can see that he's eager to see what I picked out for him. His confidence won't allow him to think otherwise, that I didn't get him anything at all.

I did.

I pull out the last shirt and pass it over, watching as his lips twitch into a smile.

It's heather gray, with black block letters that read *I Love Hiking & Maybe Like Three People* on it. Perfect, right?

"You little shit." Chasm chases me down the steps, but I don't get very far in my heels.

Next thing I know, I'm trapped in a corner of the hedge maze, spinning around to see him poised directly behind me. He lifts one brow, and I feel my heart leap into my throat. I can't be the only one remembering that we had sex for the very first time in a hedge maze. At school. While under threat of Parrish's death.

Chas swings the tee over his shoulder and leans in so close that his dark chocolate and mint scent mixes with the fragrant sweetness of freshly bloomed flowers, and the sharp, bright scent of just-cut grass.

"BTS?" he asks, stepping even closer, so close that I have to tilt my head back to avoid staring at his chest. "This is what I wanted to talk to you about, after I saw that playlist in the car."

"Um, right." I'd almost forgotten about that. Almost, because embarrassing moments are so sticky that some random stupid thing a person did in, like, elementary school can pop up ten years later and be like *hah, hijacked your mind!* In the darkness in the middle of the night, have you ever just laid in bed and cringed at some shit you said five years ago?

Yeah, uh, me neither. No way. I do cringe-worthy stuff on a daily basis, so it's hard to parcel through it sometimes. Only, I'll remember that moment for the rest of my life, I'm sure.

"I'm being too weird about your heritage—" I stop talking when he puts a hand over my mouth.

"No. I'm going to start teaching you to speak my language. I never did get to properly tell you how proud I was of you for getting those grades." He smirks at me and leans in even closer.

"Remember what I said? That if you passed Japanese, I'd start teaching you Korean?"

That lights me up.

Chas points to himself and smirks.

"We're going to start with a word that describes me: *jalsaenggyeotta*."

I blink a few times and then try it out, rolling the world around in my mouth and making corrections to my pronunciation based on Chasm's critiques.

Finally satisfied, he stands up straight and nods his chin.

"Exactly that," he says with a grin. "Your pronunciation isn't half bad. Parrish has a terrible accent." That makes me smile, even if I'm pretty sure he's teasing and not exactly complimenting me.

"What's it mean?"

He parks his hands on his hips, and I realize with a pang how much I've missed him. We spent a lot of time alone together searching for Parrish; we were a team. Even before Maxx joined us, it was just me and Chasm and that vase of sunflowers and the handful of condoms he gave to me and Parrish and—

My eyes get teary, and he gapes at me in surprise.

"Don't cry, *Naekkeo*," he murmurs, tilting his head slightly to one side. "It's nothing bad. It just means handsome."

Handsome. Of course he'd describe himself as handsome.

I throw my arms around his waist and squeeze hard, even as he stumbles back a bit, and then puts his arms around me in turn.

"*Oppa*," I whisper, putting all of my strength into the hug.

"Oh my God." Chasm exhales, his breath coming in rapid, staccato pants. "This is … this is too much, Little Sister. I'm supposed to stand up in front of all those people—including my dad—while pitching a tent?"

I don't care if that is the case. I just hold him as tightly as I can. You never know when it's the last time you're going to hug someone, so it may as well be as hard and fierce and full of love as possible.

When I pull back, it's just enough so that I can look up into his pretty amber eyes.

"Thank you for the BTS shirt," he says, hooking a strange half-smile. "I'll kill you if you admit this to anyone else, but ... I really do like their music." That makes me laugh, and I give him another squeeze for good measure. "You're a pretty good dancer, going off that Ashnikko dance you showed me at the lake. Wanna try to do one together? We could start with the dance from *"Butter"?"* That makes me smile, and I stand up straight, reaching up to swipe the small tears at the edges of my eyes.

I'm not sure why I'm crying exactly.

Because my life is strange and weird, and I just really appreciate Chasm being by my side? Whatever the reason, I can't seem to stop.

He beats me to it, swiping a tear from either one of my eyes with his thumbs.

Footsteps on the path draw both of our attention, and I look past Chasm to see Justin strolling toward us, hands in his pockets. Chas' lip curls up, and he scowls so deeply that Justin actually laughs.

"Cute, Kwang-seon. Very cute. Are you having fun trying to hack into my work?" Justin turns to look at me as I raise both brows. I wasn't aware that Chasm had tried to do that. "You hear that, princess? Your fiancé is an extremely talented hacker. Of course, he's no match for me, but you've got years of growth to catch up to—and maybe even surpass—me." Justin shrugs his shoulders loosely and looks us both over. "If you behave for me today, I'll send you both on a little trip. Would you like that? A few days to yourselves?"

It makes me suspicious as hell. As I said before, nothing Justin does is ever single-minded. He has plans within plans within plans, and he's always got fail-safes and backups for everything.

"You'd let us go away together?" Chasm asks, sounding just as baffled as I am. "No offense, but what are you and my father up to? Pairing us together like this?" He pauses there and flicks his eyes to the side before looking back at Justin. "Not that I'm complaining." Chasm stands up straight, one hand tucked into his pocket, chin raised. *My dark knight.* "I love Dakota."

"Sure you do," Justin quips, as if Chasm's declaration is nothing more than mud on the bottom of his boots. That *really* digs into Chas' skin, but I grab his free hand before he can retaliate. Not that I think he would. That's more Maxx's deal, allowing his emotions to carry him in the heat of battle. Chasm is better at holding back and striking later, the way he did when he had his female friends beat Lumen up. "Seamus and I were best friends in high school, you know that? He was one of the only people who stuck by me through the scandals. Before I was run out of town, I gave him the money to fund Fort Humboldt Security. Think about it: you two were destined to be together before you were ever born."

Justin is turning me into the book writing wife, and Chasm into the computer genius husband. Just like him and Tess. It's like, he's recreating the life he was supposed to have. I don't understand it, but am I supposed to?

I don't think Justin cares what anyone else thinks.

"What do you need?" I ask him, because he didn't follow us into the hedges just to chitchat.

The smile that takes over his lips tells me how right I am about that.

"Veronica Fisher is badmouthing you at your own engagement party. Are you going to allow that behavior?" It's a rhetorical question. I'm not supposed to answer it. "Punish her. Show her that the Fishers have *nothing* on the Priors. Assert yourself, princess. I'll be watching." He taps at his temple before turning and leaving me and Chasm alone in the hedges.

"Fuck, that guy gives me the creeps." Chas shivers all over and shakes his head, turning to me. "Punish her? This, at least, is an easy task. I've been thinking up ways to repay Veronica for what she did to you."

"You've been hacking into Justin's shit?" I ask him, and Chas lets a brief smile flit across his lips.

"I'm not good enough to stop him from spying on you," Chasm begins, licking his lower lip. He leans in toward me, cupping his hand around my ear to whisper. "But I am good enough to follow him quietly down the tunnels he makes." He stands up straight and puts a finger to his lips.

"Be careful." I follow him as he continues down the path. After a moment, Chasm looks back at me and smirks.

"Catch me?" he suggests, and then he's running ahead and disappearing around the bend in the maze. I chase after him, passing strolling couples and canoodling couples and well, mostly just couples being couples.

The maze here is much smaller and less complicated than the one at the school, but I find myself lost anyway, stumbling out into an empty area with circular brick patios and bistro tables. It's entirely unoccupied, but I swear, I can *feel* somebody watching me.

Spinning around, I look back toward the exit—or entrance?—of the maze, but there's nobody there. I've got this eerie feeling though, like eyes on the back of my head. Surely, Chasm is around here somewhere. Justin certainly is, and he's likely got his goons in tow.

I'm certain I'm being paranoid.

And then a hand clamps over my mouth, stifling my sudden

scream, and I'm dragged backward into the bushes.

———————————

"Shh." There's a familiar voice near my ear, and then the hand is removed from my mouth as I turn around to see …

"Mom," I breathe. But not my bio mom, my adopted mom. If we're going to get technical about it, my kidnapper.

Saffron Banks is standing right in front of me, her hair swept up into a high pony on the back of her head, her eyes dark, a leather jacket slung over her shoulders. I have no idea what to say or how to react. Is she kidnapping me a second time?

"What are you doing here?" I choke, filled with an ice-cold terror. Justin asked me to pick a family member to die, and I chose Saffron. I chose her, and he was going to kill her anyway, and oh my God. "You can't be here."

"I already know," she whispers, her voice hushed, eyes flicking around in frantic paranoia. I've seen her like this many times in the past. Once, during a family dinner, she just stood up and sprinted out the door, took off in her car, and didn't come back for three months.

But right here, right now? Her life is really, truly in danger.

"You already know what?" I whisper back as I hear my name being called. Chasm is looking for me, and he sounds worried, but I can't move from this spot. I can't do anything that will give Saffron away.

Thank the gods I left my phone in the car again.

It's getting to the point where I'm quite literally repulsed by the damn thing. I don't want to be spied on by Justin or Mr. Volli or anyone else. It's difficult to realize how important privacy and boundaries are until you're entirely stripped of them.

"I know about Justin," she hisses, sighing and reaching up to run a palm over her hair. Wavy tendrils have escaped to bob around her face as I take in the rest of her outfit: dark jeans, combat boots. Not the usual Saffron-esque attire. I always sort of thought of her as like, a hippie I guess? She liked peace sign necklaces, and seventies music (despite the fact that she's only thirty-eight), and long, flowing dresses. "Don't you wish she'd told you about him sooner?" she asks me, sounding exasperated.

"Justin?" I ask, remembering that conversation outside the coffee shop when she asked if Tess had told me about my father yet. "What do you know?"

"I can't stay here for long," she tells me, looking past me to where Chasm's just wandered out of the maze. He's starting to look panicked, and I don't want that. We've all been traumatized enough over the last few months. "Give this to your sister." Saffron takes my hand in hers and presses a folded note to my palm. She cups my face between her hands and looks into my eyes. "I love you girls so much, you know that?"

"Mom—" I start, and then wonder if I should be calling her Saffron now. If I want to start calling Tess, Mom then do I need to change the way I address Saffron?

She kisses my forehead, both cheeks, and then drags me into a tight, fierce hug. I return it because well, I missed her. For as long as I could remember, she was the only mother I ever had. How and why she picked me, exactly, I still don't understand. Is it just because she'd met Tess at the women's shelter, and saw a similarly aged baby with comparable coloring to her own? Or is there something more to it?

"Do you want to see Grandma and Grandpa?" I ask, but she's already shaking her head and looking past me toward the hedge maze. There's a purposefulness to her stare that bothers me. What is she up to?

"Not today." She looks back down at me and smiles. "He's

always watching. That's why I couldn't contact you." Saffron looks around the shady area where we're huddled, as if searching for hidden cameras. To be fair, there could be some. Who knows? "But I'm here. I'm going to protect my girls, no matter what. Just stay strong for me."

"I don't understand—" I pause at the sound of footsteps, glancing back to see that Chasm is coming our way. He can't possibly see us from where he is in the bright sunshine, but as soon as he reaches the shadows ...

I turn back to Saffron to find her watching me.

Just as Tess' perfume was familiar to me, Justin's aftershave, so too, is this woman's scent. You hear things about scent, how inextricably it's tied to memory, but right here, right now, I'm swept away in an old memory. There's a field of flowers, too much sunshine, and me and Maxie laughing as Saffron took turns spinning us in circles. This smell, like daisies and warm grass, it's distinctly hers.

"I'll check in with you whenever I can, but I can't let him know I'm here. If he finds me, he'll kill me." Oh. Well, at least she knows that. But ... how does she know that?!

"You know about Justin?" I whisper, and Saffron gives a curt nod.

"Stay safe and be careful. I won't let him hurt either of you." And then she's slipping away just before Chas parts the thick leafy branches with his hands and peers in at me.

"Jesus, Naekkeo. You scared the fuck out of me. What are you doing hiding in here?"

I can't answer him because I'm too busy staring after Saffron. She ducked under some branches and then scrambled over the short brick wall at the rear of the property. From what I can tell, there's just woods on the other side. It's the Wetherill Nature Preserve, I believe. I only know this because Maxx knows all the local hiking and nature spots.

"Are you okay? You look like you've seen a ghost."

I glance down at the note in my palm and unfold it.

I love you and your sister. I'm always watching over you, even if you can't see me. Love you fierce.

That's all it says.

She wants me to give this to Maxine? I'm not sure how good of an idea that is. Then again, Saffron is more her mom than she is mine …

I turn to Chasm suddenly and lift up on my tiptoes, curling my fingers in the fabric of his sweater. "Saffron was just here," I whisper to him, and his eyes go wide.

We're interrupted by a group of Whitehall students—neutral ones, this time, thank fuck—that stumble into the patio area laughing and playing with their phones.

Chasm purses his lips and then takes me by the hand, leading me back to the main area near the country club's main building. On our way back, we pass Veronica on a small stone bridge that spans a jellybean-shaped koi pond.

She sneers at me and opens her mouth to say … whatever. I honestly don't care. I'm too freaked out by Saffron's sudden appearance. *What is she doing here? What does she mean she's going to keep us safe?*

And when she says that Justin will kill her, is she being metaphorical? Or does she know more than she's letting on? Does she know, somehow, that he's the Slayer?

Parrish is waiting just beyond the bridge, but as soon as he sees us, he strides forward with purpose, taking initiative and knocking into Veronica so hard that she stumbles back. Her thighs hit the railing on the stone bridge, and with a squawk of fear, she catapults over the edge and into the water.

Her friends gasp and rush to help her as does an older woman in a khaki suit with short red hair. I imagine that's Veronica's mother? She glares up at Parrish, but he's strutting past as if nothing at all happened.

"Savage," Chasm murmurs, raising both brows as Parrish gestures with his chin in Maxx's direction. He's situated in a filigreed metal chair, hands steepled, astute gaze surveying the gathered crowd. He snorts as Veronica is helped from the water, a lily pad stuck to her head. I kid you not, like an actual lily pad.

"Got us a table near your grandparents." That's all Parrish says in response.

Justin is smiling at us from across the patio area. He gives a small nod and a wink which I ignore. *Saffron.* This is a new and unexpected development. I find myself chewing my lower lip, a habit that I picked up from Maxx. I also picked up nibbling nervously on my thumbnail the way Parrish does. Wonder what habit I picked up from Chasm? If I haven't grabbed one yet, I'm sure that I will eventually.

As much as I'd like to tell the other boys about Saffron, this is not the right place to do it. I pocket the note for Maxine, stunned at the audacity of these people. I just killed a cop. Like, that literally just happened. Everyone is staring at me, but nobody's acknowledging it.

A town full of WASPs. Medina is a wasp nest. Heh. Get it?

I shake my head to clear the nervous laughter that wants to escape, and then force myself through my rounds, greeting my grandparents with hugs. They ask me how I'm feeling and fuss all over me, and I feel so guilty that I can't tell them that I found their daughter. I know how they worry about her when she disappears like this.

But I can't tell them. Not at all. I'm not even sure how to tell Maxine about this.

Maxx helps to distract Maxine for me so that I can talk to

Lumen and Danyella, but … it's weird to see them together, especially with Justin pushing for them to start dating again.

The man's manipulation knows no bounds.

"Girl, we need a sleepover," Lumen whispers as Danyella tucks her hands into the pockets on her red and white polka dot dress and looks me over. "I need all the tea. You're keeping a lot from us, aren't you?"

Danyella gives her bestie a harsh look and then turns back to me.

"Are you feeling okay? I can't imagine this is easy on you psychologically." I just stare at her.

"I'm not the only one who went through some shit the other night." As soon as the words leave my mouth, I see Danyella cock a brow at me.

"Don't downplay your feelings because you believe ours are more valid. Dakota, you saved our *lives.* I'm only sorry that I slept through it all. I can't say that I would've been as brave as you, but I wish I'd at least been awake to offer moral support."

I give Lumen a look, but she offers up a slight shake of her head. She hasn't told Danyella the full truth, and maybe that's for the best? If we keep Maxine and Danyella ignorant to what's going on, they have less of a chance of getting directly involved with Justin.

"I'll see if I can't convince Justin to let you guys spend the night. He's pretty chill about that stuff?" I add a question mark onto the end of that sentence because, yes, while my bio dad is easygoing in certain ways, he's fucking nuts in so many others.

"At least we can talk to each other again," Lumen whispers, giving Justin a side-eye. Now that she's my, um, 'pawn', I'm responsible for her well-being. That doesn't bode well, I don't think. The Hearsts are on the list that Justin sent me, one of the families that contributed to his being kicked out of Medina, stripped of money and title, and committed.

They won't walk from this unscathed.

"At least there's that," I agree, and then Maxine and the boys rejoin us. We spend the next hour or so eating and chatting, phone-free, sitting in a small group as far away from the rest of the gathered crowd as possible.

Once Seamus arrives, dressed in a blue suit, and a small frown, Chasm shudders and I know for damn sure that he held back on his story. *I bet he hit him. If he did, I'll—* But I don't let myself finish that thought. I'm sure the guys had the same idea about Justin.

Not super stoked on the idea of killing any more people.

I shove the thought aside as violently as I can, squashing it into one of those little boxes and burying it deep in my psyche. Tess is probably right that, at some point, I'll need to talk to a psychiatrist.

For now, I'd just like to survive the summer, thank you very much.

After a while, I notice that Chasm's drifted away from the group. When he returns, he's soaked in sweat and looks nervous in a way that I've never seen him before.

Uh-oh.

It's coming.

He's going to propose.

I never expected this to happen to me during high school; I'm not even sure that I *want* to get married. On the other hand, some part of me is excited, too. It's sort of like we're LARPing—live action role playing—a possible future between us.

If I look at it like that, it's not so bad.

Chasm moves over to where I'm seated and then pauses. He clears his throat loudly enough to catch the attention of everyone around me, and then he picks up a glass and taps a fork against it. The glass breaks which is sort of funny, and then he awkwardly helps Parrish and Maxx mop up the drink and gather the glass shards together while everyone stares.

My grandparents—who don't know this is coming— along with Maxine who does, Justin who's gloating, Veronica who's glaring, Lumen and Danyella who appear sympathetic, and Maxx and Parrish who are both jealous as fuck.

Mr. Volli is there, too, which bothers me, smiling as he delicately lifts a finger sandwich to his mouth and chews thoughtfully. Caroline is seated beside him while Raúl hovers in the background on his iPad. He lifts it up, and I sigh as I realize he's filming this.

Fantastic.

But then Chasm curses under his breath, and I'm pretty sure that I hear him say *fuck it* like he did just before he kissed me against the tree by the lake. Oh, and also like he did just before he devirginized himself with me in the hedge maze.

'Fuck it' seems to be our couple motto.

He drops to one knee, like a knight pledging allegiance to the princess.

See, when I wrote about him in the story I'm penning at Justin's place, I referred to Parrish as a prince, Maxx as Robin Hood, and Chasm as a dark knight. It fits, doesn't it? If I have to be the princess in a tale I never asked to star in, they may as well act as a stellar supporting cast.

As if matters weren't complicated enough, *Tess* steps out the back doors of the country club, dressed casually but nicely in a sleeveless, ruched dress with sexy cutouts on the sides of it. The very instant she appears, Justin's hungry gaze is on her and not on me.

Further proof that I am a means to an end. Tess is the true endgame for Justin. The only question that remains is what he plans on doing with her.

She pauses, turning her head to look at me, and our eyes meet in this moment of sheer, fucking terror.

It goes like this, right?

Tess handled the me and Parrish thing admirably. He really and truly thought about their relationship and came to the correct conclusion by trusting in her. Now, here I am, about to get engaged to another guy. Granted, she knows I'm dating all three of them (or however she frames it in her mind), but this is a whole other level.

I'm sixteen and getting engaged; Tess doesn't know we're being blackmailed.

Crap, crap, and triple crap.

She stares at me before her eyes drift to Chasm, and the box that he's pulling out of his pocket. Mm. It's a very distinct looking box, black velvet, small, square. It's a ring. There's nobody in the world that would mistake the size and shape.

Before I can catch Tess' expression, I concentrate all of my attention on Chasm.

As his amber eyes meet mine, I exhale, and I allow the rest of the world to fade and blur at the edges until it's only me and him. It's not that hard, really. I mean, right now I'm sort of using my love for him as a survival technique so I don't have to see the inevitable look of horror on Tess' face, but still.

Chasm is sunflowers and second chances, loyalty and earnestness, cunning and intelligence. He's dark and devilish on the inside, but he fights so damn hard to be nice. He tutors girls who tease him for not wanting to go home to his abusive dad, and all he asks is that she keep it secret that he helps out drunk girls. Not because of his reputation but because of *theirs*.

"Yes."

Fuck.

Chasm blinks at me in surprise, and then grimaces slightly.

"I haven't asked anything yet, *Naekkeo*," he whispers, snapping open the box. There's a small, delicate band with a yellow diamond. I see money written all over the damn thing. I also don't see a lick of personality, so … Justin picked this ring out?

I wouldn't be surprised.

Ahem.

Not that it matters.

Did I just make an ass out of myself? People are murmuring and whispering all around us, but Chasm just laughs, looking down even as he lifts the ring up.

"There goes my speech," he says, and he can't seem to hold back the laughter as I snatch the ring from the box and Chasm snaps it closed. He lifts his face up to look at me, still smiling. "Dakota, will you marry me?"

"Mm-hmm." The sound barely scrapes out and then Chasm is slipping the ring on my finger and pressing a kiss to my knuckles, still on his knees, ever the knight kneeling before the princess.

"Thank fuck." He lifts up and kisses my cheek and then my lips. Polite, genteel clapping surrounds us, and I can sense the mood of the crowd: *well-played.* That's what they're thinking here in this blood and diamond, ultrarich town. An heir and an heiress, whose fathers just combined their ultrapowerful companies, uniting aristocracy and increasing wealth. Just as Lumen is being pushed to get with Parrish.

If something like this had happened at, say, a barbeque back home, do you know what the reaction would have been? Shock and horror, that's what. Laughter, maybe? Disbelief? A sixteen- and a seventeen-year-old getting engaged? How silly and inappropriate.

But this is a whole other world, isn't it?

"Tess is here," I whisper in Chasm's ear, even as I put my arms around his neck, and he lifts me up from the seat, wrapping his arms around me and squeezing me so tight that I actually bend both knees, lifting my heels up and dangling in his strong embrace.

"I'm going to die," he mutters, his face pressed against the side of my neck. "Write my epitaph, Tess 2.0."

And somehow, even amongst the craziness of the moment, I take that as a compliment.

———————————————————

"You have lost your fucking *mind*." Tess is hissing this at Justin when I head down the small hall toward the country club's bathroom. There's a large room at the end there for corporate parties and whatnot, but it's empty today.

Except for Justin and Tess, obviously.

The door is slightly cracked, so it's not exactly eavesdropping, but …

Parrish, Maxx, and Chasm are at the end of the hall waiting for me. As I said, overprotective but all things considered, we have been through a lot. Anyway, they exchange looks and then join me, crowding around the door to listen.

The time period between Chasm holding me and now, I'd like to … I'd like to permanently erase it from my mind. Instead, it's absolutely destined to stick in my brain and flare up at inopportune moments, such as during a job interview or in the shower or while lying in the dark before bed.

As soon as Chasm and I separated, people were coming up to congratulate us. Mostly, people I didn't know were coming up to congratulate us. Justin was there, Seamus, Caroline, Delphine.

Then my grandparents approached me, looking terribly confused.

"Dakota, could we get a minute to talk to you alone?" Carmen asked. I'd nodded and well, we haven't exactly gotten that moment just yet, but the watery smiles on her and Walter's faces, the exchanged glances, the beaded sweat on their brows … not good.

Then Tess … Oh, Tess. Tess, Tess, Tess.

Somehow, even though the romance takes precedence in my mind more often than not (I've realized that's just sort of part of falling in love), this is all really about me and Tess. My story, I mean, the one I'm writing for Justin. It's about me and Tess.

She said nothing to me. Instead, she went up to Justin and, after a tense bit of whispered conversation, they retreated to this room.

It doesn't take any sort of expert to see that Justin is simping for Tess.

He wants her so badly, but I don't think he knows if he hates her or loves her.

"I've lost my mind?" he queries back at her, like he's a total innocent in all this. "By uniting two great Medina families? Our daughter is set to inherit the world." He lifts his arms out to either side and turns, as if to indicate the universe at large. "I don't understand how you could possibly be upset by this."

"Well," Tess starts with a gruff laugh, running her hand over her face. I hate that she keeps being painted as the crazy one, the unreasonable one. In all reality, she's the only person who continuously calls Justin Prior out. "She's sixteen, for one, and he's not much older. Beyond that, Kwang-seon did not come about my wedding ring all on his own." She crosses her arms over her chest and stares Justin down as he drops his arms to his sides and smiles.

"Are you accusing me of something? He asked my permission for Dakota's hand in marriage. I accepted, and then offered up the ring which—if you recall—you threw at my face and told me to shove up my ass. So therefore, it is *my* ring. It cost me a fortune, and it reminds me of happier times. Why shouldn't I give it to my best friend's valedictorian of a son?"

"I know these kids." Tess points at the door. I think she was intending it to be metaphorical, but then her gaze slips to the side and she spots us. *Shit.* She purses her lips and marches over, opening the door and gesturing us in.

We move in together and then stand there, drowning in awkwardness.

"What is this about?" Tess asks, but even though anger simmers beneath the question, she maintains her calm. She looks from me to Chasm to Parrish. Briefly, she glances at Maxx, but there's some confusion there. Like, doesn't it seem as if he has no horse in this race and yet, here he is? That's my guess as to what she's thinking.

"I love Dakota." Chasm projects his usual chill, lifting up in his shoulders in a shrug. He looks about ten years older on the outside, but in his eyes, I can see it: there's true fear there. And it isn't of Justin or even Seamus, it's about Tess. It's about the possibility that he might lose her, the woman who is essentially his mother.

"I practically raised him." That's what Tess said to me about Chasm before. He's always at the house, even when we happen to be grounded. He gets special privileges, is welcome in family moments, treated like any other Vanguard child.

This is his greatest fear, and Justin is doing his best to facilitate it.

"I wanted him to ask me." I step in and step up, moving forward as if to single myself out. Parrish clenches his jaw, but what can he really say? Chasm stares at me like I've lost my mind, but Maxx wears an approving look.

We exchange a quick glance, and I can tell he understands and appreciates my motivations. I turn back to Tess, preparing myself to launch into some serious bullshit.

Lies, really. I'm about to peddle in lies. I've been spinning them a lot as of late, and I hate every fucking second of it.

"No." Tess lifts up a finger, and my eyes widen in surprise. She turns back to Justin and points at him. "This is one of your schemes."

"And if it were, Mrs. Vanguard?" he asks, sighing as if in annoyance. "If it were, so what? What are you going to do about it?" There's a challenge in his voice, one that makes the muscle in Tess' jaw tick.

She's *furious* right now, but she's holding it all back.

I see then that maybe some of her WASP-y behavior might have to do with this, with learning to navigate the minefield that is Justin Prior. She shed him years ago, but even so, all he had to do was waltz back into town and take control.

He's a master of abuse.

"What have you done?" She turns back to us. "Whatever it is, if you tell me, I'll make it right. Anything. But you have to talk to me." Tess waits there as Chasm and I exchange a look, and he shakes his head at her.

"I'm just in love with Dakota, and I was having trouble watching her date Parrish and Maxx—"

"I wanted a commitment." The words come out in a rush, and I do my best not to fiddle with my dress. Instead, I channel that same energy from the day of the Martina Cortez interview when I told Tess sorry, not sorry and refused to give up my phone. "I told the three of them to prove themselves. Chasm … he did."

Tess does not look convinced, not at all.

I rub at the ring with my thumb, disturbingly aware of the fact that Tess, herself, got married to Justin Prior in this very piece of jewelry. It gives the whole moment an entirely different aura.

"We'll talk about this when I see you on Saturday." Tess turns to leave and pauses beside Parrish. "Come home with me, please."

He stares her down and swallows hard, glancing over at me. I give a slight nod of my chin. *Go.* Tess has been through enough and yet, she's standing up for us today. I'm impressed. I don't want to see Parrish put up a fight and take Laverne's side yet again just to stick around.

The pair of them leave, and then it's just me, Chas, Maxx, and Justin.

"We'll be heading home soon. You can pack your things and get ready to head to the cabin with Kwang-seon." Justin adjusts his dress shirt sleeves, rolling them up to reveal his forearms. "Say your goodbyes to the Banks and meet me out front."

He doesn't mention the ring and its disturbing origin story, Tess' defiance, or anything else.

I sigh as soon as he leaves the room and then put my face in my hands.

"This is like the condom thing all over again." I'm mumbling, but I know the boys can understand what I'm saying.

"Yeah, well …" Chas trails off with a tired laugh. "It is what it is. Let's try to look on the bright side. What did he mean about the cabin? Where are we going?"

I drop my hands but force a smile even as Maxx lifts his white hood up over his hair, his green eyes trailing Justin down the hallway.

"He said he'd give us some time alone as a couple, but I have the feeling we're not going to like the motivation behind the act." I stare down at the ring as Maxx turns back to me.

"Your grandparents are incoming," he murmurs, and I see that they have, indeed, spotted me from the other end of the hallway. Even though I know they're no longer my legal guardians, that we share no DNA, the Banks are and always will be my grandparents.

I'm legit terrified.

Maxx excuses himself which I don't like. I want the four of us to be in on this together. That's how it's been this whole time, the four of us against the world. There's no time to address it before Carmen and Walter are moving into the room and my grandparents are staring at me like they've never seen me before.

I was afraid that when they saw me again for the first time, they wouldn't recognize me. That they wouldn't look at me as their granddaughter any longer. They surprised me—in a good way —and pulled me right back into their embrace, reassuring me without words that we were still family.

But this?

Now they're staring at me as if I'm a whole different person than who they thought I was.

"Dakota, what's going on?" Carmen looks over at Chasm and then back at me, and I feel so damn guilty I could croak. "Chasm seems like a nice boy, but this is ... you're only sixteen. This is a big commitment to make at your age."

She's right. But what do I do? How do I fix this?

The answer is: I don't. I can't fix this right now.

All I can do is kill people and turn myself in. That's my big revolt, my grand move, the way I push my pieces around the board. That's not enough. *Kill him, Dakota.* I shudder all over and shake out my hands.

"It's a rich people thing," I explain with a strangled laugh. My grandparents exchange a look as Chasm tries to interject.

"It's pretty common for people around here to get engaged young and marry later, for family connections and all that." He makes himself smile big. "There's no rush to the finish line or anything. Engagement doesn't mean marriage just yet."

"It's like a promise ring," I blurt, wishing I could kick myself just for that comment alone. "We're sort of just ... committing to each other. Nothing more than that, really."

They look slightly mollified, but Walter shakes his head.

"I still don't know how I feel about this. If it were up to me, I'd ask you to take the ring back and take a step apart from one another to think this over." There's an unspoken *but* hanging in the air.

But it's not up to Walter anymore. It's not even up to Tess. It's only up to Justin.

"We'll think on that," I promise, but we won't.

Fuck, I hate lying.

I hate myself even more for doing it, and isn't this Justin's plan working exactly as he wants?

It is.

He really is winning this goddamn game, now isn't he?

CHAPTER 23

Justin drives me back to the house and then sends me upstairs to pack a bag. Apparently, I'm staying at the guesthouse with Chasm, the very same one where we first discovered GG. It's not an around the world bonanza or anything, but the idea of being alone with him there, without Justin or Tess or anybody else, it sounds a lot like heaven.

By the time I get downstairs, already pondering Justin's motives behind this decision (of which there are many, I'm sure), Raúl directs me to the artist's studio where I find Justin waiting beside the chess board.

I take my seat and we begin to play. I notice that the king piece he broke last time has been glued. Still, it's impossible to miss that crack in it. Its flaws are visible for the entire world to see.

As I'm moving one of my pawns, Caroline pops her head in to show Justin something related to the wedding. He barely glances at her phone screen before agreeing and then shooing her out the door. The way he looks at that woman, it's impossible to believe he gives a single flying rat's ass about her.

"I thought you were in love with Tess?" I ask, wondering if that's a dangerous question to ask right about now.

Justin pauses, but he doesn't seem upset, making his move quickly and then sitting back in the chair. He chuckles, like I've just said something particularly amusing but impossibly childish.

"Oh, Caroline's nothing." He watches me make my move, and then flicks one of my pawns off the table to land on the floor. Dramatic, but the guy did say he liked pageantry. And he *did* let his crony wear a black stag mask during a hostage situation, so … "She's just a user and a loser who will do anything for money, a black widow who thinks she's getting one up on me."

That gives me pause. I'd made a spider analogy about Caroline before, but does he mean black widow literally? As in, a woman who kills her husband in order to inherit his money. Usually, I just think of that sort of thing as a misogynistic trope. Then again, have you *met* Caroline Bassett?

"Wait. You said you had a story to tell me about her. Was this it?" I hover my fingers over the board, calculating my next move the way I'm doing in real life in regard to Justin. I can't live like this forever, so what's my endgame?

What is my freedom worth to me?

"Did you know that the reason Caroline left ol' Paulie and their newborn baby was because Laverne wanted her son to force his future bride to sign a prenup?" Actually, I *did* know that because Tess said as much at the restaurant the other day, but I keep my mouth shut. I'd rather listen than talk right now. Any scrap of information could be helpful here. "Caroline only cares about money. A prenup would have done her no good. So, she abandoned her baby and left Paul at the altar."

Justin wins the game as he usually does, and I sigh, taking out my phone to snap a photo of the board so that I can study it later.

"Is that why you called her a black widow?" I ask, and Justin snorts.

"No, I call her that because she *is* one. She's killed three of her husbands thus far. I'm sure she plans on getting the jump on me next. Only, she isn't half as clever as you, now is she?" He stands up, but then slides his phone from his pocket.

I get a notification that he's just emailed me, and I look at the information sent over. It's a series of links to news articles about wealthy men who passed from various natural causes, each from a different country. The name of the grieving wife is different in all three, but the pictures are clearly Caroline Bassett.

Wow.

"Did you pick her on purpose to upset Tess?" I ask, but Justin just smiles slyly at me.

"Actually, no. That was a mere bonus. Milk Carton found her, of course." He takes off out the doors, and I follow, running into Delphine on the way.

"I didn't get a chance to properly congratulate you earlier," she says, holding out a small package. Just seeing her reminds me that I never had the opportunity to give Maxine the note I got from Saffron. There was no privacy to be had at the club. None at all.

"Stay safe and be careful. I won't let him hurt either of you."

Oh, Saffron. What on earth are you up to?

"Thank you," I tell Delphine, looking up and into her overly eager face. I still have no idea how involved she is, if she actually commits violent acts under the name of the Slayer, but I hope not. I unwrap the package to find a tarnished silver bracelet and look up with a raised brow. "Um, no offense, but what is it?"

"This was my grandmother's," she says, her voice faltering a bit. She reaches out and touches a finger to what's likely an important family heirloom or at the very least, an antique. "For a wedding, you need something old, new, borrowed, and blue, and a sixpence in your shoe." Delphine grins. "My grandma used to say that anyway. So … here it is. Something old."

She offers me a kiss on the cheek before moving away, and I have to admit, whether she's a serial killer or not, I'm touched.

I hold the bracelet to my chest and watch as she disappears in the direction of the dock.

Chasm picks me up in his new car, climbing out and lifting a pair of shades into his hair. He's wearing the same outfit from earlier which is a huge bonus because he looks drop-dead gorgeous in it.

"Keep your phone on you at all times," Justin tells me with a smile, as if he's just a normal dad and not some psychotic creeper. "And Dakota." He leans in, and I take it he's dead serious about this. "Leave the other boys out of this, do you hear me? These next two nights are for you and Chasm."

He pats me on the head and retreats, leaving me with my duffel bag on the porch. Chas jogs over and hefts it up for me, slinging the strap over his shoulder.

"Come on, Naekkeo," he says, letting his gaze drift up the imposing brick front of the building. "Let's get out of here before he changes his mind."

We hop in the car, and Chasm holds out his hand for my phone.

"Let's attach it to the Bluetooth, and you can listen to your crappy K-pop songs."

"You said you liked BTS," I retaliate, clutching my phone to my chest. "But, um, if you wanted to sing something to me—" He snatches the phone from my hand which also sort of brushes his hand across my boob, and then we're staring at each other.

I'm reminded of the day I bailed on the TV studio, how Parrish put me into his best friend's car and sent me on my way. He accidentally touched my ass when he was pulling me back in the window that day; the tension was there.

It's certainly *still* here. The only difference now is that we've already acted on it. We'll act on it again today and tomorrow and the next day, I'm sure.

"What the hell are you thinking about right now?" he challenges, and my face and chest flare with heat. "Your lips parted, and your pupils ..." He makes an explosive gesture with his hands. "They blew out and got huge. Also, you're sweating. Also, you're red, like, all the fuck over."

"So are you." The retort is petty, but it's not untrue. His forehead and cheeks are red, and he's using his tongue to tease the black stud of one of his lip piercings.

"So I am," he replies, and then he does exactly what he said, hooking up my phone and tapping the playlist titled *Sexy Songs in Korean that I want Chasm to Sing for Me.*

It starts with *"Pain"* from Isaac Hong. It's a dramatic ballad with both Korean and English parts.

Chasm just snorts and shakes his head.

"If you think I have the range for this, you're going to be sorely mistaken." He starts the car and I relax back in my seat, allowing my eyes to close. It's as if my life has been on warp speed since prom night.

I just want to breathe.

Chas seems to sense that, driving us first to get milkshakes—he gets a chocolate monstrosity and I do strawberry again—and then the next time I open my eyes, we're at the guesthouse, the one by the lake.

It gives me the chills to see it again, thinking about the day we found GG. Not only that, but these are the same woods where Justin and—based on what I know now—probably Mr. Volli chased me and then stuck a needle in my neck.

What the purpose of that was, I can't say. A show of power? A test? I could probably ask, and I bet Justin would tell me.

"The screaming/silence cabin is *ocupado,*" he tells me, and I give him a look.

"You speak Spanish, too?" If so, I swear, I'm considering myself a failure at life. He gives me this sly, little look and then opens his door.

"All of like six words." He nods in the direction of the house. "But don't worry: you can still scream and nobody will hear you." He climbs out, and I scramble to follow, sucking on the straw of my milkshake as he hefts bags out of the trunk and drapes one over each shoulder.

"What should I grab?" I ask, but he just pokes me in the back of the leg with the toe of his shoe.

"Nothing. I've got it."

I give him a look and he raises an eyebrow at me.

"What? I can't be a gentleman for my fiancée?"

Oooo. I almost die. Fiancée?

I dart around him and snatch some of the bags from the trunk, even as Chasm grumbles at me, carrying them up the porch steps and waiting for him to punch in the code for the front door.

"Set all that on the kitchen counter," he commands, and then he pounds up the steps to deposit our bags upstairs. When Chasm comes back, he's got the bug detector in his hand. I say nothing as I start to unpack the bags, finding glass containers with brightly colored lids.

I pop one open, aware that I've got my phone tucked into the pocket of the pullover sweater I draped over my dress. I've also switched my heels out for flip-flops because, yeah, I'm not about to go traipsing around in stilettos for fun. Irreversible damage to leg tendons, nerve damage, bunions, ingrown toenails. How sexy do high heels sound now, huh?

ENDGAME ROMANCE

Anyway, Justin can hear us, but he can't see us unless he's got other cameras and mics in here. After a quick sweep, Chasm shakes his head and tosses the bug detector on the counter.

We share a look, but all I can guess is that Justin didn't particularly want to watch us get naked together. My cheeks flush again and Chasm leans in toward me, putting his elbows on the counter.

"You're blushing again, Little Sister."

"What's in these?" I ask, lifting the lid on one of the containers as he smirks at me.

"Side dishes." Chasm watches as I reveal the bean sprouts in the dish. They smell like sesame oil, and I can't resist picking one up and popping it in my mouth. *Yum.* I take a small clump and eat them as Chas smiles at me. "You like?"

"I love." I put the lid back on the dish and then open another one, lifting it up to my face for a sniff. My eyes move back to his. "Kimchi?"

"Oh, so you *do* know what kimchi is?" he teases, and I stick my tongue out at him. I set that one aside and continue my exploration. It occurs to me as I'm tasting various items that none of this stuff is packed like it came from a store.

"Did you make all of this?" I ask, and he chuckles, standing up straight.

"I did." He crosses his hands together behind his head, his gaze trailing over the sea of containers. There's a melancholy there that cuts right to the bone, and I wonder if Chasm isn't thinking about his grandmother.

"This must've taken a lot of work," I prompt, and he smiles. Again, the expression is tinged with old memories and heaps of melancholy that he tries hard to hide.

That's the thing about Chasm: he doesn't like to show his emotions. Not like with Parrish where there are so many that it's overwhelming. More like, Chas feels that even the most basic of emotions are a burden to others. His emotions, that is. He has no problem helping others with theirs.

"It is. But don't get too cocky: I make my own side dishes from time to time. It's like, a childhood thing." He drops his arms and then grabs one of the containers, popping it open and then pulling a set of wooden chopsticks from another bag. He uses them to pick up what I think is a rice cake and offers it out to me.

Our eyes meet as Chas places the food in my mouth, and I chew it carefully, appreciating all the hard work he must've put in to make this stuff. For me? If he did, he won't admit it. *Ass.*

"Sweet, spicy, chewy."

Chasm puts one in his own mouth, chewing thoughtfully as he looks around the place. I remember then that there are photos in the hallway, of Chas as a kid with his grandma. It takes on a whole new meaning now that I know Chasm better. Last time I was here, he'd just kissed me, but he was also telling me he had a crush, and I was convinced he was scamming on drunk girls.

Don't judge a book by its cover, eh? Or even the title or blurb really. I had to dig deep into Chasm's story to see the real him.

"I wish I could just live here with you," he remarks, and I blush. I'm going to have to stop blushing around Chasm. But it's a lot, to go from being a never-been-kissed virgin whose sole experience with dating is holding hands at a school festival. Once. That was one time. "I've always wanted to just live here, away from Seamus."

"I feel like there's more to the story of this"—I gesture in a circle with my finger at his appearance—"than you're telling me. I don't believe for a second that Justin just waltzed in and told your dad to leave you alone and all was peaceful."

Chasm stands up straight, setting the chopsticks aside, and then he heads out the front door and I follow. We collect the last of the bags, and he closes the trunk, heading back inside and depositing it all on the counter.

He pulls out a head of napa cabbage and glances over at me.

"We're going to make dinner together tonight." He pats the cabbage, and, although I'm freakishly excited at the idea of cooking with Chasm, I want to know more. As always, I'm aware that Justin is listening, but there's nothing about this conversation that he would care about.

"What happened with Seamus?" I repeat, and Chas sighs, removing a container of soybean paste, a green chili pepper, garlic, a small bag of flour, and a bag of … fish?

"Dried anchovies." Chasm pokes the bag, and then grins at me. "We're going to make *baechu-doenjangguk*." I'm not going to try to pronounce that just yet, but I'm excited by the idea, especially when he takes out an apron and tosses it to me.

It's pink with cakes and loaves of French bread, jars of jam and cupcakes, and two cats—one black, one white.

"This is a *Kiki's Delivery Service* apron," I breathe, referencing one of my favorite Studio Ghibli movies. That's a movie studio by the way; they make iconic Japanese anime films. Remember my soot spirit pen? That's from *Spirited Away*, another movie by the same company (and director).

"I had to brave a *Hot Topic* to get that for you," he says, and then shudders like the store itself is poison. "Besides, isn't the black cat's name GG?"

I give him a look and slip my sweater off, tossing it aside.

"It's *pronounced* like GG, but it's spelled differently." Still, when I go to put the apron on and Chasm rushes around the counter to do it for me, I can't deny that I'm pleased. He takes the ties on the back and uses them to drag me closer to him, my back to his front. "You're charming me, but you can't escape the question, *oppa*."

"You know exactly how to manipulate me, don't you?" he asks, yanking the ties so tight that I gasp and a warmth travels through me. I'm hyper-aware of his body heat, his breath stirring my hair, his hands as they deftly tie the apron and then come to rest on the curves of my waist.

He reaches up and, like Maxx the other night, pulls the pins from my hair. I make sure to glance over my shoulder and put a finger to my lips. I don't want Justin to know about that. I'm not sure if his order to wear my hair in a chignon extends to a moment like this, but I'd rather not find out.

As soon as my hair tumbles down my back, Chasm threads his fingers in it and puts his nose up against the back of my head. He breathes in, and I close my eyes against the electricity in his touch, at the tension between us.

"I've missed you," he admits, and my throat gets tight. I've missed him, too. We spent nearly every day together for three weeks. And I saw him almost every day before that. Lately, we've been spending a lot of time apart.

I miss the ice palace, I admit it. I want to go back to living in the room with all my things from back home, with a view of the lake, Parrish across the hall, Chasm as a daily visitor, Maxx as a frequent guest.

I turn suddenly, and throw my arms around Chasm's neck, and then we're kissing and I'm stumbling back. Without skipping a beat, he lifts me up onto the edge of the counter, stepping between my thighs, his tongue working against my own, his lip studs teasing my skin and making it tingle.

He tastes so good, and he feels even better, pressed up tight against me like that.

When he pulls back slightly, I make a small sound of protest, and Chasm bites my lower lip gently. His teeth graze over my skin, and my lids get heavy, sliding closed as he adjusts his mouth to my neck.

He kisses my pulse and pushes the satin of my green skater dress up my thighs, the touch of his palms on my bare skin stirring up heat in my core.

"Shit." Chasm chuckles against the side of my neck, and I get goose bumps, squeezing him between my thighs. I can feel the hard press of the bulge in his slacks, and suddenly, I don't care so much about making soup. "We haven't been here ten fucking minutes ..."

He picks me up, and I let out a noise.

We stare at each other, and he smirks at me, all cocky and shit.

"I've always wanted a guy to pick me up like this," I admit, and he laughs again.

"Like I said, I'll be the hero in your drama, *Naekkeo.*" He puts me on the couch and climbs over me, his mouth fervent for my own, his fingers playing with my hair. I do the same to him, grabbing a handful and yanking as we dive into each other.

It heats up then, as he grinds against me, and I wish I wasn't wearing this (admittedly adorable) apron. I want to take everything off. Instead, Chasm surprises me by pulling away and sitting up.

He's completely breathless as he looks down at me, some of his dark armor stripped away to reveal a tenderness in those amber eyes that makes me fidgety. He yanks his sweater off and chucks it to the floor, his fingers reaching for the buttons on his black and white dress shirt.

As soon as he undoes it and reveals all of that ink, I'm sitting up, too, and putting a hand on his chest. I can feel his heart thundering wildly beneath my palm, and I close my eyes.

"I have a question for you," he asks, and I open my eyes again to see him watching me. "Remember when I said I wanted to be the first to taste you? And then you let me, and I loved it?"

Oh.

Oooh.

He never told me liked it that much …

"That option is on the table—right now." It's supposed to come out sounding coy, but I'm all breathy and nervous. Also, I really am sweating a lot. Chasm smiles at me and then leans down, taking my lips again in a searing kiss.

He leaves my apron and dress in place, but his fingers curl devilishly around the waistband of my panties. He drags them down my legs and deposits them—with flair—onto the floor, flicking his fingers as if they've personally offended him.

I'm so nervous that words fail me; I don't know what to say.

Maybe I'm not supposed to say anything?

Chasm notices that I'm sitting up, reaching out and putting a finger to my chest. He pushes me back so that I'm lying half-propped on some pillows.

"Relax," he purrs, and then he's adjusting himself on the large sofa. It's deep and long—the sofa, I mean—and surprisingly perfect for this. He scoots down and I suck in a breath as his face gets close to the aching spot between my legs.

This is a whole different experience from last time. It's light outside and, although the curtains are closed, there are no shadows to hide anything. Not my body, not my face, not my reactions.

"Are you okay?" he asks me, and I nod. I can't speak right now, but I do relax, leaning my head back and closing my eyes.

The first touch of his tongue is charged, galvanic. I'm not even prepared for it. The sensation zips right through me, causing my fingers to dig into the white cushions of the couch, scratching across the fabric as I exhale. *Long, slow breaths.*

His hands find purchase on my hips, and he locks his grip down, holding me still while he laves me with the hot heat of his mouth. It's a much slower build than the other things we've done, and I have to actively force myself to chill out.

Mostly, I want to scream. In the end, I drag a pillow over my mouth and bite down on it. When Chasm laughs at me, and his breath touches *everything,* I rock my hips and he dives back in like it was an invitation.

He's slow and patient, and he makes these breathy sounds, these moans of want and excitement that start this ball of energy growing in the base of my spine. My breasts ache, my skin feels too tight, and my thighs quiver as he not only tastes me but *devours* me.

I'm not expecting him to slide two fingers in, but as soon as he does, we're both making rather telling sounds. His are deep and full of longing while mine are light, mere whispers on the wind. How could I do anything else but surrender to the hot heat of his mouth? His blatant enjoyment of the act only makes it more enticing, and I squirm as Chasm explores me in ways I'm not even sure I've fully explored myself. He pets and strokes with his thumb, presses gentle kisses with his lips, teases and flicks with his tongue.

My hands fist tightly in his hair and he grunts, murmuring something that could be in any language and would still be easily understandable. He likes me. A lot. More than I think he was expecting. Certainly, I like him more than I thought I would. He was *such* a dick at first, but once Chasm commits to a person, he's all in.

It's almost obsessive, but there's a healthy respect that keeps our relationship just this side of reasonable.

"Don't stop," I manage to whisper, and he chuckles again. Ah, the feel of Chasm's laugh against my overly needy body makes me writhe, digs my fingers harder into his scalp, pulls him closer. My hips thrust unashamedly against his face, and I wonder if—like with Maxx—I'll even be able to look Chas in the eye after. *Oh, gamer gods help me.*

"Never."

Chasm takes his time, working me to the edge of orgasm until I'm trembling beneath him, and then he pulls back, kissing my belly, my thighs, the insides of my knees. Once he deems that I'm fully recovered, he dives back in. His fingers thrust slowly in and out, a hypnotic rhythm that's equal parts pleasurable and also frustrating.

I want to finish, but he won't let me. Not yet anyway. Instead, he repeats that process multiple times, making me believe that I'm about to come, and then taking the opportunity away again. I'm almost mad about it; there are literal tears in my eyes.

"Please." Another whisper from me, another chuckle from him. "*Oppa.*"

That seems to do the trick.

He slides one, hot palm up my stomach and under my dress, sucking on my clit, adding a third finger, and then he's slamming all three into me hard and fast. This time, the climax comes on too quickly for Chasm to knock it back.

I'm coming hard enough that fireworks blossom behind my closed lids, and I worry for the briefest of instances if I'm ever going to be able to breathe again.

Chasm rests his cheek against my stomach as I pant, the decorative pillow falling from my face to the floor. I throw an arm over my eyes, completely and utterly breathless. Wrecked, ruined, satisfied. I'm shaking all over, too, and it's undeniably embarrassing. Or maybe I just get embarrassed easily?

"That was … amazing." There's awe in my voice that he picks up on because, of course he does, he's a cocky fuck. Chasm sits up, putting a palm on either side of my waist, and I open my eyes to find him staring down at me.

His lips are shiny, but I pretend not to notice. I try to look away, but he tilts my face back toward him with a single finger on the side of my jaw.

"Ah, *Naekkeo,* you're not allowed to do that, not after everything we've been through." His eyes shimmer with emotion before he closes them briefly. I make myself stay where I am and when he opens them, we're looking right at each other. "See? That's better, isn't it?" he murmurs, and then he moves to kiss me and hesitates. "What's the etiquette for this sort of thing? Am I allowed to kiss you? Is that weird?"

"It's my own body, and if you put your mouth on me, why can't I put my mouth on you?" I grab him by the back of the neck and bring him toward me for another kiss. There's an unfamiliar taste there, but it's faint and sweet, and it doesn't bother me.

We kiss for a long time, longer than I think either of us realizes. By the time Chasm breaks away from me for a breath and looks up, there are long shadows being cast across the room. Granted, it was late afternoon anyway, but it looks like we're gearing up for sunset which, since it's summer, is at like nine o'clock.

"Do you want me to …?" I reach for his pants, but he grabs my wrist in strong fingers and offers a small shake of his head.

"That was offered freely." He kisses my lips and then the tip of my nose before standing up. He snatches my panties as he goes and tucks them into his pocket as I frown, yanking my dress back into place.

"You're not keeping those, you perv." I stand up from the couch and then decide that maybe I should pop into the bathroom real quick to clean up. When I come out, Chas is in the kitchen with a black and white striped apron hanging loose around his neck, and he's got the cabbage quartered and laid out on a wooden cutting board in front of him.

There's a pot on the stove filled with water that's on its way to boiling and Chasm is doing … something to the dried anchovies.

Oh. Tearing the heads off. That's not at all serial killer-y or creepy.

I move up behind him and put my arms around his waist, and he groans.

"I've wanted a girlfriend since I was a freshman for this exact purpose."

"So you can rip fish heads off for her?" I query, and he snorts.

"No smart-ass, so that she could come up and hug me from behind and call me *oppa* and look all cute and shit." He glances over his shoulder at me as I lift my head up. I can't imagine I'm the first girl to ever grab him like this.

"How … many girls have you kissed?" I ask, and he rolls his eyes at me.

"I don't know. A handful?" He pauses and then his beautiful face takes on a decidedly smug expression. "Are you jealous?"

I snort, as if that's total nonsense. It's not. I am jealous.

I move to stand beside him, the cabbage sitting in front of me.

"You're not going to answer? I take that as a yes then."

"You mean like you answered all my questions about Seamus?" I look at him, and he sighs, using his own knife to point at the cabbage.

"Throw that in the pot, stir it a bit, and then let it boil for, like, a minute." I follow his instructions, but my gaze is focused on his hands and the way he wields the knife. Chasm finishes with the fish and then goes about peeling and mincing several cloves of garlic. "You really want to know what happened with my dad, huh?"

"I care about what happens to you." My words are quiet as I stare at the ring on my finger. Part of me likes it there, because Chas is my fiancé and even if I didn't want one and we're way too young, well, I like him. The rest of me wishes I could take it off and throw it down the sink.

Justin forced Chasm to propose to me with the very ring he laid out on his diner bill when he asked Tess to marry him. So cringe.

"Justin outed me," he says with a long exhale, chopping the pepper next. "He came over and *accidentally* let the information slip, something like, *'what happened to your hair?'* or whatever. That's how it started."

I feel my lip curl, but I don't dare a say word of dissent aloud. Surely, Justin or Mr. Volli or hell, Raúl, is listening in. *Eww, Raúl.*

Chasm puts the knife down and washes his hands, glancing over at me and gesturing with his chin. It occurs to me that he just went down on me, and then I'm blushing again. He notices and crooks a sultry half-smile. "Rinse the cabbage in cool water, then chop it up."

He bends down and retrieves a rice cooker from under the counter, setting it up and filling it with dry rice and water. He presses a button and voilà, it's just a waiting game.

I do as he asked with the cabbage, but when it comes to chopping it, I suck.

Chas ends up behind me, his arms around me, and he gently shows me how to use the knife. The sound of it slicing through the leaves, the feel of his body, the cadence of his breath, it's easy to forget what a mess my life is.

"My father lost his temper. He came at me, but Maxx wouldn't let him hit me." Chasm sighs heavily, rustling my hair. "Justin called him off, but he won't speak to me now. Not even via text. He's acting as if I don't exist."

That makes me sad. I can hear the pain in Chasm's voice, and I ache for him.

"I only got all of this ink because ... well, I mean it looks dope. But really, I got the first tattoo to see how long it would take Seamus to notice. I mean, I hid it, but not very well. It wouldn't have taken much for him to figure it out, you know? If we spent any time together at all, it would've been inevitable, him finding out." He sighs. "If it weren't for Tess and Parrish, I would've grown up lonely and bitter."

We finish chopping the cabbage, but I don't look directly at Chasm, not yet. I don't want him to see that I'm choking back tears. He adds the ingredients to the pot and then slips a pair of plastic gloves on. He churns the mixture with his hands, and then drops the lid on the pot.

"We've got about thirty minutes until this is done." Chasm turns to me, and his expression softens. He takes the gloves off and puts his bare hands on either side of my face. "Don't look so sad, *Naekkeo*."

"You don't have to hide yourself from me, Kwang-seon."

He just stares at me, but I can see that this is hard for him. He's not used to letting loose, to allowing others in. So far as I can tell, it's only Parrish and Maxx that he's ever fully embraced. *And Tess.* I remember the pleading in his voice that night we came home and she was drunk, when she yelled at him for treating me like a conquest.

"I'm glad you're here," he says, and then he gets choked up. "I miss my *halmeoni*, and I hate my fucking dad, and I …" He trails off, and then he kisses me. "You make it all better, Dakota. You made it better even when Parrish was missing, and I wanted to die." He looks into my face, and I find myself tongue-tied. How do I respond to that?

By being honest.

Because I'm already drowning in lies.

"When you're not around, I think about you all the time. Home is where the heart is, Chas, and I'm starting to wonder if New York isn't it anymore. You and Parrish and Maxx …" I trail off as he sighs and presses his lips to mine again, soft, easy, comfortable.

"You want some soju?" he asks me, and I'm pleased that I actually know what that is, a mild tasting alcohol that usually comes in green glass bottles. I nod, and Chas stands up, unpacking yet another bag. He must've spent hours preparing this stuff. "I stole it from my dad, as per usual. He keeps it around so he can drink and stare at a portrait of my mom that hangs on his wall."

Ouch.

I don't comment on that as Chasm pours two small shot glasses for us. We clink them together, down them, and then he pours us each another. The alcohol content on soju isn't as high as say, vodka or Jäger, so there's not much risk of overdoing it.

"Want to do a love shot?" he asks me, but I don't know what that is.

"Like the song *"Love Shot"* by EXO?" I query, naming another K-pop tune. Chasm snorts as I blink at him in confusion, hooking his elbow around mine. We take our shots with our arms linked, and I can't help but smile.

"Can we start learning that dance?" I ask, because he did promise me.

Chasm groans, but he's not getting out of this. Besides, I want to see what sort of dancer he is. I was impressed during prom, but we shall see.

I find my discarded sweater and pull my phone out so that we can look up how-to videos. *Eat your heart out, Seattle Slayer. Watch this all you want, you asshole.*

We spend the rest of the night dancing, eating cabbage soup and side dishes, and talking until long after dark.

And then, into the bedroom it is.

CHAPTER
24

Sunshine stabs into my eyes like knives, and I blink myself awake to see Chasm standing at the window. He's just opened the drapes, and he's wearing these black sweatpants that hang so low on his hips that I can see just *this* much ass crack.

It's … some stupid ass crack. Really stupid ass crack. As stupid as Parrish's stupid muscles and Maxx's stupid smile. All of them, just plain stupid.

Stupid good, that is.

"Why are you doing that?" I grumble, rubbing at my eyes as I sit up. It takes me a second to remember that I'm *naked,* and I choke out a sound, gathering the sheets to my chest as Chas turns around to look at me.

He raises a brow but says nothing.

It makes zero sense for me to be embarrassed after last night. We had sex several times. It was like my first night with Parrish all over again except that this time—for the first time—there was no rush. No hovering parents (I put my phone in the attached bathroom and shut the door). No life-or-death ultimatums. Just me and Chasm and a proper bed and time.

It was heavenly.

"It's two in the afternoon," Chasm says, and then he props the window open, perches on the edge of it, and lights himself a cigarette. He stops just short of smoking it and stares at the burning tip. "I'm trying to quit," he explains, and then he's grabbing an ashtray off the desk and stabbing the cigarette out. Chasm sighs and rubs at his face with both hands, but when he drops them to his lap, he's smiling. "I had fun last night."

"Me, too." I exhale, and then I drop the sheets. Chasm's eyes drop right down to my chest and he rakes his fingers through his hair, leaning his back against the jamb of the window. The summer sunshine falls across his inked chest and arms, his amber eyes like jewels, heavy and half-lidded. His pretty lips are parted, and his tongue is teasing one of the black studs. "You look like a model."

"*You* look like a model," he retorts, eyes on my face instead of my breasts.

"No, *I* look like a model."

The sound of a voice in the hallway scares the shit out of both of us. I let out a scream and, following Chasm's lead, snatch the lamp from the nightstand to use as a weapon. Chasm grabs a knife off the desk, one that he brought up from the kitchen last night.

The bedroom door swings open and there's Parrish.

Also, there's me. I'm naked with a sheet clutched against me, a lamp raised high like a sword. His eyes take in my silhouette, just *barely* covered with bits of sheet. Mostly it hangs across one boob and my crotch. That's it.

"Well, hello there, Gamer Girl." His voice is a kaleidoscope of emotion. There are bright streaks of happiness, the deep red of lust, the vibrant emerald of jealousy. He lets his almond-eyed gaze shift to Chasm. "Just so you know: we brought a signal jammer." Parrish hefts up a hand inked with a sunburst and shows us a black device.

"I don't see any other cameras or mics," Maxx says, appearing behind his friend. He, too, stares at me with blatant emotion in his green gaze. Only, his isn't a kaleidoscope. There's stark appreciation, a softening of affection, and then he flicks his eyes to Chasm and his possessive alpha-mode kicks in.

I set the lamp aside and clear my throat, adjusting the sheet to cover both boobs.

"Signal jammer? Aren't those illegal?" I ask, but Parrish just stares at me with slitted eyes. He's breathing harder than he should be, but even though I'd love nothing more than to jump into his arms, I'm worried. "Do you think that'll really stop Justin?"

"Illegal is relative when battling a serial killer, I'd say," Maxx declares, stepping around Parrish and then filling the room with his huge form. His confidence oozes into the air, silky and inviting.

This situation makes me think of the shower back at the ice palace, big enough for four. I don't want to accidentally blurt out *foursome* again, so I shift my thoughts back to the matter at hand.

"Justin forbade me from inviting you here." They know this already since I texted them. I was never told that I couldn't, so that was fair game. "If he finds out—"

"We hiked over from the skate park." Maxx speaks up, soothing me a bit as he smiles. "Don't worry, Kota. We were careful. We carried the bug detector"—he lifts it up to show me —"and the signal jammer with us. Anyway, we won't stay long."

"How do we explain to Justin what happened to the phone signal?" Chasm asks, sounding annoyed. I think he was enjoying having me all to himself.

A lightbulb goes off in my head as I sit back down on the bed.

X joins me, and the mattress dents in his direction. I slide toward him a bit and my bare hip bumps his denim-clad one. We both look down and then back up at about the same moment.

His eyes find my lips as Parrish steps up close to me, reaching out and taking my face between his hands. He's set the signal jammer aside, so he's free to hold me and kiss me as X heaves a sigh.

"You are so damn dramatic sometimes."

"So says the man who scammed my girl out from under me while I was *kidnapped.*" Parrish talks with his mouth against mine, and then kisses me again. He tastes so damn good, and I'm naked, and I want to hold him so bad … He draws back and stands up, turning a look on Chasm. "And you. You're no better. Worse, maybe."

"I never lied about being into her. In fact, I let you two go at it, prepared myself to step back and give up. But you know what? That's not how things worked out, is it?"

"Wait." I stand up suddenly, but the sheet gets caught under my foot and rips from my hand. I'm completely and utterly naked beneath a thrice-multiplied boy gape. Rather than panic and cover myself up, I simply lift my chin. Yeah, one of the side effects of being naked is that they can now see the full extent of my boob blush. "Please don't fight. That's Justin's goal here, sending me and Chas off like this. He *wants* to break us apart."

"He can't break us apart," Parrish says, sounding aghast at the very idea. "Don't you know by now that we're always like this? The only difference now …" Here he steps close to me, wearing a black pullover sweatshirt with pushed up sleeves and dark blue jeans. He leans down again, so that we're nose to nose. It riles my blood, to see him like this, and I totally understand now that all of our fighting and bickering was based on tension and want from the very beginning. "Is that we all want *you.*"

"I ... I know that." I lean away from him, but he drops his hands to my waist and I gasp. "We ... Justin. I don't want anything bad to happen to you." Parrish stares at my mouth before lifting his milk chocolate and toffee eyes to mine.

"We'll leave before he gets overly suspicious. Mostly, we came to tell you that we followed Raúl last night." I raise a brow, but Parrish just purses his lips and turns away, swiping his hand over the lower half of his face. I sit back down beside Maxx.

"And?" Chasm asks, snapping his fingers. "What happened?"

"He set Philippa's house on fire." Maxx is the one who speaks up, and several things hit me all at once.

Fire. The lighter. The Vanguard house.

Justin, obviously, was at prom as a chaperone, offering him a squeaky-clean alibi for the night. Seamus, too, was there by his side. But what about Raúl? He could've set the fire.

Parrish must be thinking the same thing which is why he's so upset.

"Who's Philippa?" I ask, and Chasm snorts.

"This is one of the reasons I like you so much." He stands up from the windowsill and moves to stand closer to the foot of the bed. Maxx surreptitiously lets his hand cup mine, fingers entangling. My heart sings a bright song, but I tune it out for a minute to work through this. "These Whitehall brats strut around like the world owes them a favor, and you can't even be fucked to remember the name of one of the bullies who cut your clothes off." As soon as Chasm says it, he softens his face. "It's a good thing. I respect you for not giving a shit."

"I know." I smile at him. "I wasn't offended. So ... who's Philippa?"

"Brunette girl, always kissing Veronica's ass," X explains. Oooooh. So that's her name. I know I've been introduced to her

444

several times, but Chasm is right. A person only has so many fucks to give, and I wasn't about to pass one out to some asshole who tried to help her bestie chuck me off a third-story building. "Psychologist's daughter, the one who helped get Justin committed."

"What happened?" I ask, because as much as I dislike the girl, death in a burning building is not something I'd wish on her. She's just a spoiled, rotten brat following her parents' orders to go after me—not so different from me. Let's be straight: Justin is my biggest problem, but the other families in Medina are not blame-free.

Actually, they do deserve some karma (although dead teenagers is a bit much). They framed Justin, stole his research, stole his money, had him committed. They're bad guys, too. They are *all* bad guys.

"We put it out," X continues, and I turn to look at him. He's wearing a *Wright Family Racing* sweater in black over a green tee. His hair looks wavy and soft, and his expression is eager and bright with interest. Because of me. Or maybe it's because I'm naked?

"Does Justin know you put it out?" I ask, feeling this tightness in my belly that has nothing to do with last night or the stares of my three 'suitors'. We've already screwed up several of his plans. Right now, he's still convinced he can have everything: his revenge, his success, his wealth, his daughters. But if we push him too far, he'll retaliate.

"I hope not." That's Parrish, of course. He tucks a hand in his pants pocket and stares at me. "How many times did you guys do it last night?"

"Seriously?" Chasm groans, letting his head fall back and putting both hands over his face. "Show yourselves the door. Make like trees and get the fuck out of here." He drops his hands and gives Parrish a look.

Maxx surprises me by pulling me into his lap and putting one of his hands on my upper thigh. The touch is impossibly intimate, so close and so far away from the spot I wish he was touching.

That devious hand of his slides up and over the curve of my hip, coming to rest over my pelvic bone. He gives a little squeeze, and I exhale.

"We came here to check on you and tell you about Raúl. Mostly, we came here because we were jealous." Maxx leans in and captures my mouth, claiming me as he kisses me, and he's entirely unapologetic about it.

We pull apart reluctantly and Chasm clears his throat.

"We made *baechu-doenjangguk* last night. Take some home. Take some side dishes, too."

"You made her side dishes?" Parrish asks, and Chasm gives him a look. "Wow. You really are in love." Chasm kicks him in the back of the leg, but Parrish ignores him, tossing an imperious look over his shoulder. "Get dressed and come with us."

He parks himself in the doorway, his sloth-like tendencies causing him to slouch against the jamb.

"Do you want us to leave and give you some privacy?" Maxx asks, but I just shake my head.

"You've all seen me naked anyway." I feel my face heat, but I try really hard to be cool as I move over to my duffel bag and bend down to dig through it.

All three of them groan, and I drop to my knees beside the bag, glancing back at them. The boys all have their hands over their eyes. Oops? I snatch my Ashnikko hoodie and yank it on, dragging a pair of sweatpants on.

"Better?" I stand up with my arms out, and they all drop their hands.

"Definitely not," Parrish remarks, and Maxx gives him a look. "I liked you better naked."

"Don't be an asshole." X stands up as Chas sighs and mumbles something like *so much for my relaxation time,* and we head downstairs together. Chasm quickly packs them some soup in an airtight container, and hands over what's left of the side dishes and soju.

"Don't forget the kimchi," he adds, and X gives him a quirky little smile.

"You sound like an *ajumma,*" he murmurs, and Chas cocks a brow.

"Could an *ajumma* get it up six times in one night, huh?" He smirks at X, curling his lip in challenge.

"What's an *ajumma* again?" I ask, but all three of them just laugh at me.

"You're the worst K-drama simp ever," Parrish mutters, and it's true. I really am. "*Ajumma* are older women that elbow you in public, nag too much, feed you a lot of food, and wear vinyl jackets and year-round visors." He taps at his forehead with a single finger, and I see Chasm offer a secret smile that he tries to hide behind his hand.

He might've been separated from his culture all this time, but his friends have kept it alive. How cute is that? They're the perfect bromance trio, aren't they?

I'm sad to see Parrish and Maxx go, and my heart aches a little when they walk out the back door, but I know what I have to do.

I have to check my fucking phone.

I excuse myself to the upstairs bathroom and sit on the closed lid of the toilet, turning the screen on with a vicious churning in my gut. There are messages from nearly everyone in my life, but nothing urgent.

Even Justin has yet to say anything about the signal jammer, and I'm not about to bring it up. I tuck the device in my pocket and head back downstairs to find Chasm bent over the counter, playing with his own phone.

"You know how it felt when Justin made us … express our feelings?" Chasm asks as he looks up at me. I nod. "This is just like that. I'm *happy* that I'm being forced to stay here and chill with you, even though I know he's probably up to something." He slides his phone across the counter to me. "Pick some food and place an order. We're not going anywhere today except maybe to the lake."

"I thought you couldn't swim?" I ask him, because that's what he told me the first day we met, when he accused me of making Tess cry. Maybe I did, I don't know, but it certainly wasn't intentional.

"I can hang in the water with a floaty or fuck around in the shallows, but no, I can't actually swim." He cringes a bit and bites at his lip stud. It gives him this pouty look that I quite enjoy.

"I could teach you," I suggest brightly. "You teach me Korean, and I teach you to swim."

Chasm appears skeptical, but he shrugs and then stretches his arms over his head. His tattoos—of which one entire arm is full of flowers, thorny vines, bees, and moths—are even prettier in the midday sunshine. If we go down to the lake, he likely won't be wearing a shirt for the majority of the day, and I'm totally okay with that.

"Deal. Let's do it."

I pull my own phone out once more, but still, there's nothing.

That freaks me out a little.

As it should, apparently.

ENDGAME ROMANCE

The lake we're using isn't a public swim spot; it's a part of Seamus' property, so we have the whole thing to ourselves. It's unseasonably warm out today, so even though the water's a bit cold, it's refreshing.

As guilty as I feel for spending my day hanging out and not actively trying to figure out ways to deal with Justin, I realize how much I needed a rest. Since the day Parrish went missing, it's been nearly nonstop. Each small reprieve I was granted usually came with something horrible to hang over my head.

Today is blissfully normal.

Except for the fact that I'm now a murderer.

I shove the thought down where it belongs —buried in shadows like a ticking time bomb—and I concentrate on teaching Chasm to swim. He's smart, and he's well-built. I bet he picks it up quick.

We don't go back to the cabin (except for quick bathroom breaks) until late evening, and then we're both so exhausted and sun-warmed that we end up on the bed together.

"We should nap," Chasm mumbles, eyes closed, his pale skin tanned by the sun. He'll have a funny line where his swim trunks sat. As soon as my thoughts go in that direction, I'm looking down and I'm tempted to peek.

My fingers trail down his chest, and he lets out a small groan.

When I push his waistband down, he goes completely still.

"What are you doing?" There's a tenseness in his voice, layered with excitement. One might think we had enough fun last night, but is there really such a thing? I don't stop what I'm doing. Actually, I just push his swim trunks down the rest of the way, revealing that tan line I was curious about amongst other things.

449

Namely, my attention is on his dick.

I reach out to touch him, and he doesn't stop me. When I adjust myself so that I'm straddling his legs, he stares at me from beneath half-closed lids.

"What are you up to, *Naekkeo*?" he asks, but I don't want to tell him just yet. Instead, I sweep some hair behind my ear and bend down, pressing a kiss to his lower belly and enjoying the way his stomach muscles contract.

My hair slips out from behind my ear and brushes over his skin, making him shiver and bringing up goose bumps on his skin that I run my palms over. Down his legs I go, until I've taken the swim trunks off and tossed them onto the floor.

"Dakota—" It's the only word that he gets out before I straddle his legs again and wrap my fingers around the base of him. I give him a squeeze to test his reaction and, when he closes his eyes and starts to relax, I lean down and give him a quick lick, just a single flick of my tongue.

You'd think I gut-punched the guy.

"Is this actually happening?" he mutters, but he doesn't stop me as I taste him in the most intimate way possible, using my lips and tongue on him the way he did me. Well, the plumbing is different, but the intent is the same.

Chasm grabs the sheets in two handfuls, groaning and arching his back. My hair teases across his skin, tickling and summoning more goose bumps in its wake. When I take him in, his hardness pressed against my tongue, he loses it pretty quick.

Next thing I know, he's grabbing me and hauling me up the bed.

Chas flips us over so that he's on top and then he destroys my mouth with persistent, hungry heat. He's licking and kissing and nuzzling at my mouth, my neck, yanking my bikini top down to access my breasts.

He gives my nipples as much attention as I did his dick, and then he's untying my bikini bottoms with deft fingers.

"Are you sure you don't want me to finish you with—"

"I'm sure." He snatches a condom from the nightstand and puts it on, diving back in to kiss me. At the same time, he pushes between my thighs, and then he's pressed tight against me. My body welcomes his in, and ecstasy rolls through me.

Chasm is even more vigorous than usual, lifting up above me so that he can look down and meet my eyes, rolling his hips into me again and again and again. If someone had told me that the guy that shoved me into the pool that day would be inside of me, making me feel this good, looking this deeply into my eyes, I would not have believed them.

Only, it feels right. Something about Chasm just makes sense to me. We've been through a lot together, so much so that it seems like our relationship has blossomed and grown in maturity beyond the span of a few months.

It feels like it's been years.

I let myself truly relax into the moment, running my hands down Chasm's back, pressing the metal of the ring into his skin. He can feel it, too, I know he can.

He kisses my mouth, and he tells me something in Korean that I feel in my soul but that I don't understand. It's not the time for translation, so I don't ask. I just enjoy. The feel of his body, the taste of his mouth, the cadence of his words.

More things I don't understand, whispered frantically, fervently in my ears. Fast, faster. He matches the movement of his body to his voice, kneading my breast with strong fingers, nuzzling my throat. I throw my head back into the pillows, locking my ankles together behind his back.

"Let's stay like this forever," he mutters, voice sloppy, almost accented. And he never has an accent. I must be that good, right?

Only, I feel like I'm just lying there, so I reach up and put my hand on his chest, encouraging him to roll over so that I'm on top. "Or like this."

For a second there, I'm not sure what to do, but then biology takes over and I'm rocking my own hips against him. Riding him, that's what I'm doing. It feels incredible, especially when he lays his hands over mine, pressing them into his chest and looking up at me.

I follow the cues in his face, his body, his breath, adjusting my movements accordingly. When he climaxes, I slow the rolling of my pelvis and just watch, a gasp of surprise escaping me when Chas pulls me down to him and rolls us onto our sides. He's panting against the hollow of my throat, arms wrapped tight around me. We stay that way until his breathing evens out, and then scoot back a scant few inches from one another.

I prop myself up on a single elbow, reaching out to trace one of his tattoos. I can see Parrish's hand in the design, and that reminds me that Chasm can work a tattoo machine himself.

I lay my head on his chest and he strokes his fingers through my hair, swallowing three times before he's able to speak.

"That was … your mouth … I'm going to have nightmares about it."

"That bad?" I ask, and he laughs, the sound as deviant as the look in his eyes when he turns to me.

"That wicked good." Chasm pushes me onto my back again, kissing his way down my body. I'm beyond shocked when he drops his head between my thighs again, but how could I possibly complain? My fingers dig into his pretty hair as he puts his tongue *in* me this time, something we didn't quite get to on the first round.

My orgasm is slow and stubborn, but Chasm doesn't give up. He doesn't seem to get bored or tired of servicing me, putting three fingers in again and running his tongue over my clit in a way that triggers every nerve ending to fire.

I finish with his fingers still in me, and he sits up, looking smug with himself.

"The way you squeeze …" he starts, and I kick him in the leg. With a haughty laugh, he falls onto his back beside me again, and we lay there looking up at the long shadows on the ceiling turn to full dark.

"Which tattoos of Parrish's did you do?" I ask, and even though I can't see his face, I can feel him shift slightly.

"Basically all the spots he couldn't get. His back, his chest. I only learned so I could tattoo him, to be honest. It's his art; it isn't mine."

I think about Parrish's tattoos and the blue dragon comes to mind.

"Did you do the dragon?" I trace my finger over Chas' chest, and he captures my hand, pressing it against his skin.

"I did."

"What do you want to do, if you don't want to do art?" I ask him, genuinely curious. He's so busy being student body president and valedictorian, tutor and best friend and now boyfriend. Poor Chasm. Does anyone ever ask him what *he* wants out of life? "Also, it's weird that you have night school three times a week in the summer."

He makes a scoffing sound.

"Oh, you have no idea." There's a pause there where it seems like he's thinking about something. "I don't really know what I want to do, to be honest with you."

"Well, you're smart enough to do literally anything; there's no rush." I snuggle closer to him, and he wraps me in his arms, hugging me tight. My heart swells, lying there with him like that.

"You really are the best, Pokémon pants," he murmurs against my hair, but even though he's teasing, I can tell that he means what he's saying.

"*Saranghae,*" I whisper, and this time, it means both 'I love you' and goodnight. But that last part is only inferred.

"*Nado saranghae.*" Chasm returns the affection and that's it, light's out.

CHAPTER 25

The ringing of my phone sends panic surging in my chest. I roll over and snatch it up, fear roiling in me as I see that the number of the screen is from Justin's burner phone.

Chasm is awake just as quick, sitting up behind me and panting heavily. As soon as I grab my abandoned hoodie from the floor and slip it on, I answer.

I'm surprised to see Mr. Volli in the black stag mask, a throwback moment to the day Parrish disappeared.

"Hello, princess," he says, and my heart begins to race. If we're bringing out the pageantry again, then this is something huge. This is Justin shifting his pieces on the board, blocking me in, preparing to win the game yet again. Because, every time we play, no matter how clever I am, he always wins in the end.

"What do you want?" I check the time and see that it's just past eleven in the evening. We've only been asleep for maybe an hour at most.

"You surprised me in so many ways," Mr. Volli à la Justin says.

Figures that he'd give his underling an earbud and then make him get on camera. My bio dad refuses to do a thing that could ever get him charged with a crime.

It seemed like a hopeless fantasy even when I thought I could get him arrested—and then suffer through him tracking me via lackeys whilst in jail. This, this is a reminder that he isn't responsible for anything, that he hasn't *done* anything.

If Raúl went out to set Philippa's house on fire—with her inside of it—then it stands to reason that he might have set the fire at the Vanguards as well.

So. They truly all are the Seattle Slayer, aren't they? Justin's killers. Raúl. Amin Volli. The cop. Mr. Fosser. Caroline? I have no idea on that last one, but it seems feasible that he's planning to add her to his roster in the future. Justin tracked down a murderer with Milk Carton and brought her into his life intentionally.

"How so?" I ask, sitting up and forcibly keeping myself calm. It's my form of rebellion against Justin, after all the things he's made me do. Killing that man in the woods was … it's a heaviness in my stomach, like a ball of lead, but I won't let it break me. In the name of self-defense, especially in defense of those I love, I did it and I would do it again.

Justin knows that; he's *counting* on it.

"I'll admit, I didn't expect you to kill Officer Cousins. I was hoping you would, but I didn't expect it. As for turning yourself in?" Mr. Volli offers up a smooth laugh, and I see now that while he's attempting to imitate Justin's swagger and confidence, it's not the same. "Impressive. And very, very brave. Were you truly prepared to spend the rest of your life behind bars?"

I say nothing; it's a rhetorical question meant to upset me.

I won't let it.

"What do you want now?" I ask, doing my best to sound bored, almost annoyed. Better than what I really am which is exhausted.

Body, heart, soul. I should've figured this mini staycation with Chasm wasn't going to last.

"You and your new fiancé are going to prove yourselves to me. I'm tired of the games, princess. You're quite clever, and I appreciate that, but I need a commitment from you." He reaches down and picks up a gun, some sort of long-range rifle that sends a shard of ice through my chest at the sight of it. "I'm going to give you the rest of the summer—that is, before the first day of school at Whitehall—to get rid of Veronica Fisher."

"Pardon me?" I choke out, and if I wasn't already sitting down, I'd have collapsed. "What do you mean *get rid of her*?" But I know what he means. I know exactly what he means.

He wants us to kill her.

Because that's what the Seattle Slayer has been doing all this time, isn't it? He's been killing teenagers, mostly the ones related to his revenge plot but a few others here and there, just to throw off the pattern. That's how callous he is. Or should I say 'they'. It's like a '*My name is Legion, for we are many*' sort of thing.

The Seattle Slayer wants *me* to continue his work.

He wants *me* to become the Seattle Slayer. Or, one of them anyway.

"Get rid of Veronica, show me the proof, and then get rid of the body. Otherwise." And Mr. Volli picks up the rifle, displaying it prominently on the camera. He's seated in the wine cellar again, the bottles of Secret Cache wine—the very wine from the winery where my parents had their first date—stacked on the racks behind him. "It won't just be Saffron on my hit list. You'll have to pick someone else. Who would it be this time? Kimber? Danyella? Or would you get creative and go for Tess herself?"

My teacher's eyes sparkle at me from behind the mask, but it's not really him that's looking at me, it's Justin. Through him. Because he controls Amin Volli completely, just the way he wants to control me.

And we're getting there.

He's already destroyed my moral fiber in so many ways, torn it to bits, shredded it, reworked it into a design of his own making.

"Veronica Fisher. This is a task for the two of you alone. You'll learn soon enough that marriage is a commitment; this is a great first start."

The camera feed cuts, and then Chas and I are just sitting there in the dark.

Kill Veronica? Show him proof? How the *fuck* am I supposed to get out of this one?

I could play a thousand games of chess, and I'm not sure that I'd ever find the answer.

"Don't panic," Chas tells me, pushing the blankets back and finding his clothes. "We'll figure this out."

I make my final decision then. I've considered it over and over, but I haven't allowed myself to accept the inevitable. Even when I picked up that shovel, I didn't think I was actually going to *kill* Justin with a single hit. What I would've done after that is a mystery: tied him up, turned him in, had this epiphany sooner.

Regardless, I know that it's time to start plotting.

Justin expects that I'm going to try to kill him?

He's giving me no choice. Ironically, he's creating the very monster he's always dreamed of. Whether I follow his directives or not, I'm on the path, fulfilling my role as the Slayer's dutiful daughter.

What could be more dramatic than a daughter stabbing her father in cold blood? Just like the ending to Tess' book, the one with all the clues, *Fleeing Under a Summer Rain*. I've read the book so many times now that I could quote it by heart.

The knife is gripped tightly in my hand, but I'm disconnected from the blade, that sharp-edged sliver of violence that's stained with the red of my shame. My fingers release, and the weapon—the very same weapon he once used on my mother—falls to the floor.

I collapse along with it, knees hitting hard wood, eyes blurred with tears.

My destiny was chosen for me long ago, before my first memories, sealed and signed in blood. I look at my reddened palms, and the tears come unbidden, each salty drop diluting the ruby color to the palest pink.

Once upon a time, my mother fled my father's violence under a summer rain. The night was warm, but the droplets were cold.

My tears are made of ice, and my heart is broken.

Justice has been served, but I didn't expect the bitter taste on my tongue, or the sad requiem playing in my soul. Be careful what you wish for, they say. Sometimes, you might just get what you ask for.

We sit outside on the back patio, side by side, looking out at the very woods that serve as a prologue to this nightmare. I should've told Tess that night what I'd experienced. Would it have changed my fate? It's impossible to know the answer to that question, but I wish I'd said something.

"Don't ever stop fighting."

During my lunch with Caroline and Delphine, she promised she wouldn't. Then, after the engagement, she called Justin out on his shit. Maybe it's beyond Tess' wildest imaginings that he could ever be the Seattle Slayer, but she knows something isn't right.

I sigh and Chasm pours me another shot glass full of soju.

I know for a fact that we're not going to kill Veronica Fisher.

I'd sooner march up to Justin and take my chances on him. Veronica is a cruel, awful brat. Would she have really pushed me off the third-floor courtyard? I have no idea. But I'm not killing her.

"Do you want to talk about it?" Chasm asks, and I sigh, glancing over at him. His eyes are shadowed in the darkness, but that bright yellow lightning bolt almost glows. I point at it, and he raises his brows.

"Did you use glow-in-the-dark dye?" I ask him, and he flashes a saucy smirk.

"You're just now noticing? Damn. I must be a genius in the bedroom." I elbow him, but he just laughs. My phone is lying face-up on the pavement, but at best, Justin can see the stars. He can hear us, too, which is why Chas has a notepad and a pen on his left.

I detach myself from the situation, pretend it's a plot in one of Tess' books. What would a clever main character do? What would a girl in a video game do when faced with this dilemma? There's an answer here; I just have to find it.

Chasm picks up the notebook, passing it over to me. I take it, but I have nothing to say just yet.

"You know, there's parties happening nearly every night in and around Medina," he offers up, speaking aloud. "I bet Veronica will be at most of them; she never misses a good party. One of the favored spots for Whitehall brats is the old summer camp out near Kellogg Lake." He downs his soju and then holds out his glass so that I can pour him another. According to Chasm, it's better if someone else pours your soju for you; it's a communal drink.

Okay, so she'll be easily accessible at a party. I gather if there's an abandoned summer camp, it's a fairly remote location (that is, remote being relative since we're so near to Seattle). That's good. It gives us a chance to play games with Justin. He can't possibly bug the entirety of the woods, now can he?

My biggest opportunity at getting the leg up on him is using his own audacity against him. He believes his tech gives him all-seeing eyes, an omnipotent view of the world. My thoughts stray back to the moment in the bathroom with the heart pin camera (RIP, fire).

A lukewarm kiss hardly satisfies those sick little desires you're harboring.

It was Justin's own words that gave me the clue I needed to figure out the heart pin. Then, in the hedge maze when Chasm and I first consummated our relationship, we had no cameras. Justin had no eyes. And yet, when I acted as if I thought he could see us, he played along with it.

That's the key here, using his own arrogance and overconfidence against him.

I nibble on my thumbnail and find myself reminded of Parrish. I miss him. I miss Maxx. I wish the four of us could live together the way we did during finals week. I want that back. *I want that forever.*

"Do you think we'll be doing this long-term?" I ask, and Chasm snorts.

"Fuck, I hope not. Didn't your dad offer you an out? After we, uh, take care of these brats, you're free to live like normal, right?" Neither of us actually believes that he'd be so generous, but the man is monitoring our conversation so, it is what it is.

"I meant …" I don't tell him what I actually meant. That is, me and him, Parrish and X. It can't possibly last forever, right? It is, as I suggested to my grandparents, a case of them courting me, trying to win my hand like old-school knights in a jousting competition. The thought of letting any of them go makes my heart ache in a way I can hardly put words to.

If Parrish had never been kidnapped, I wouldn't have known how truly amazing all three of them are. They've really proved themselves to me, shown me their true colors, and oh what glorious hues they are.

I blink and then hold out my glass for another splash of soju.

Kidnapping.

I down my drink, set the glass aside, and then lift up the pen.

I jot down the word and add a big fat question mark after it.

Chasm's eyes widen as he lifts his gaze from the page to my face.

We trade the pen and paper, and he writes a question of his own for me.

What happens after? What's the endgame?

Endgame indeed, because even if we somehow pulled this off, convinced Justin that Veronica was dead, what then? We can't hold her captive forever. Which means that if we do this, I have to finish this thing in fairly quick succession.

I look up and our eyes meet. I don't have to write down my thoughts; Chasm can see them all over my face. He's frowning hard, and I know him too well at this point to think he has any idea in mind other than to take over this task for me.

We return to drinking soju and plotting, using the pen and paper to discuss the logistics. We never stop talking aloud, however. Because Justin is far too clever to miss a prolonged silence such as that.

Only, he never mentioned the signal jammer.

Is this task retaliation for that? Or did he somehow not notice? If so, could we use the signal jammer again? Just enough to make a clever move. Here or there, signals must cut out due to unforeseen events. Wi-Fi can go down; there are pockets with no cell reception. Is there a way to manipulate that?

Either way, we'll figure this out.

We always do.

CHAPTER 26

I never thought it would be such a relief to head back to Laverne's mansion, that Tess would actually be a breath of fresh air in my life. She's waiting in the kitchen area when I walk in, sipping a cup of coffee.

Chasm comes in with me, but holy shit, he's nervous as hell. He most definitely is *not* relieved to be here.

Tess' dark brown eyes—clearly since Justin's are blue, I inherited my eye color from her—watch us as we shuffle in together. Parrish is there an instant, skidding around the doorjamb from the direction of the staircase in a pair of socks.

They slip and slide on the floor, and then he's right there in front of me, wrapping me up in his arms and pulling me close. He hugs me like he wasn't sure I'd make it through the week alive.

"I hate being separated from you," he murmurs, and then he notices Chas' spazzy behavior and narrows his eyes to their usual slitted formation. He pulls back slightly from me and turns to face his mother. "You promised you would be nice."

She gives him a look and sighs, setting her cup down on the countertop.

"I did. I just don't understand this ... relationship." Tess pauses again as Maxx moves into the room, his hair wet from a shower. His smile is pretty enough to crack hearts. Certainly, it's pretty enough to crack mine. I wonder if he's been staying here while Chas was gone? I wouldn't want to stay with Seamus by myself, that's for damn sure. "All three of you are still courting my daughter? Despite the fact that she's now ... *engaged.*" Her voice cracks and she lifts her fingers up to massage her temples. "Yet another thing I don't understand."

"I explained it to you." Parrish stands guard over me and Chasm as the latter fiddles with his shirt, hands twisting in the fabric.

"Oh, stop that, Kwang-seon. I know I'm scary, but I'm not *that* scary." Tess sighs. "Can I pour anyone else a cup of coffee?"

"Please." I practically leap at the offer, taking a seat on one of the stools. Maxx and Parrish take up on either side of me while Chasm hesitates, his hands on the backrest of the fourth stool.

Tess sets out three cups of coffee, some of her weird flavored creamers, and ... fresh cream. Our eyes meet, and I remember how she made me green tea with honey the day that Chasm and I delivered JJ's body.

Fuck.

I almost wish she were as awful as I first thought; it would make this easier. I wouldn't care about hurting her feelings or disappointing her or wanting her to like me.

"So." Tess leans her forearms on the counter as we all go about preparing our coffees. Well, not Maxx; he hates coffee. I notice that the kettle's on, and I wonder if Tess doesn't already know that. "Let's talk about this engagement thing."

I lift my mug up and take a sip, trying to wash down the

anxiety. *What a clusterfuck.*

"Our dads think it's a good idea," I offer up, forcing a smile. "What with Fort Humboldt Security becoming part of Milk Carton and all that."

"And yet, you're still dating Parrish and Maxx. Am I understanding this correctly?" Tess remains calm which can't be easy. Not only did her house burn down, and her family just barely make it out alive, she had a second child kidnapped, lost a custody battle, and is being sued by her own publisher for refusing to write *Returned Under the Guise of Night.*

I feel myself warming toward her yet again. Has she said and done things that I don't agree with? Oh yeah. That whole 'it's my body, I made it' comment was creepy as hell. But I don't have to agree with every single thing that she says in order to respect her. And I do, now more than ever. Maybe for the first time, honestly.

"I explained this to you," Parrish repeats, sipping his coffee with pizzazz like the foppish rich boy that he is. "We're still in love; this engagement is about business."

"Uh-huh." Tess is not buying what we're selling, but even though her eyes drop to the ring—her ring, once upon a time—she doesn't add anything more to that.

"I'm here for Dakota, for as long as she needs me to be," X adds, and then the tea kettle whistles and Tess goes about making him a green tea and honey concoction that makes me blush. I love that we love our tea the same way. Maxx and I are opposites in a lot of ways, but that's one of the reasons that I like him. He's refreshing, a breath of new air to push me out of my comfort zone.

Tess purses her lips, but she eventually leaves the kitchen, and it's just the four of us and a buttload of information to catch up on.

"Why is she being so calm?" Chasm asks, anxiety coloring his words. "This isn't possible."

"I told her this was Seamus and Justin's wish more than your own." Parrish sets his mug down and glances my way. "That's not against the rules, is it?" He drawls this last question a little louder, as if it's truly meant for Justin's ears.

With a sigh, I toss my phone onto the counter, but there are no incoming texts. *Thank fuck.* Now that I'm here, I'll see if we can't ditch our phones and find somewhere to talk. One plus side of Justin flexing on me and showing off some of his hidden cameras is that I've got a better idea of where they are and how he likes to position them.

"We should go hiking," Maxx suggests, putting his elbow on the counter, his chin in his hand. He glances askance at the rest of us and hooks the most charming all-American smile I've ever seen. "I've made a list of all the places within three hours of here. I assume we'll be tackling most of them before the end of summer."

"I hate you sometimes, you know that?" Parrish says with a deep sigh.

We finish our coffee and off we go.

⸻

I should've known better than to think Tess was going to leave me entirely alone for the weekend. As soon as we're back from the hike, Chasm and Maxx head back to Seamus' and Tess corners me in my borrowed bedroom, waiting for me on the edge of the bed while I shower.

"Um, hey …" I start, pulling my t-shirt down and hesitating in the threshold between the bathroom and bedroom. Today's hike was longer and harder than the last one, so I'm sore as hell. On the plus side, we're all caught up with one another and the ideas are flowing.

This Veronica thing is going to be tricky, but I think we can manage it.

ENDGAME ROMANCE

Once we execute the plan, we'll have a very short window in which to wrap up the whole Justin thing. I wish I knew what Saffron had meant when she said she was going to keep me and Maxine safe. She's got a lot of issues, so I should know better than to be hopeful, but … what if she has a plan?

"Come, sit." Tess is looking through movies on the TV, and there's a bowl of popcorn on my bed.

Things are getting weirder by the minute.

I do as she asks, taking a seat on the bed beside her, the popcorn bowl between us. On my nightstand, there's a bottle of iced tea and a package of Bon Bons, chocolate coated ice cream balls essentially. Also, there's a package of red licorice, a box of Milk Duds, and a bag of peanut butter M&Ms.

"I thought we could have a movie night together?" she suggests, and I just stare at her.

"Um. No offense, but why are you doing this now?" I'm not trying to be rude; I'm genuinely curious. I'd never wanted to come to Washington, to live with her, to give up my old life for a new one on the basis of something that happened to me before I was even a conscious being.

But … I couldn't stop myself from being interested, from wondering what it might be like to have a parent who didn't take off on a whim and disappear for months, to be my idol's daughter, to see who Tess Vanguard really was. I waited for her to offer me driving lessons, to ask me about school, to invite me to do something that *I* wanted to do.

Eat at a hole-in-the-wall restaurant, shop at a store that wasn't designer, take a walk, have a pleasant conversation, go to a pottery class together … something, anything.

I'm tentatively pleased with the situation, but I don't understand how Tess appeared so cold and impossible when I was trying to please her, and now that I'm under Justin's thumb and doing horrible things against my will (that fucking typewriter-windshield scenario was so cringe), she's being nice?

Tess doesn't look offended. Instead, she ponders the question for a moment, grabbing a handful of popcorn and putting it in her mouth. She chews thoughtfully as I settle into the pillows, folding my hands across my stomach and wondering how long it'll take Parrish to show up here.

He will, no doubts about that.

He suggested we shower together, but Tess quite literally passed by my room as we were heading into the bathroom, so … She gave him a look, repeated the word *gentleman,* and here we are.

"I was trying to give you space," she admits, taking another bite of popcorn. It appears appropriately buttered—as in, soaked, drenched, dripping—so I snatch a handful for myself. "I know I can be controlling. I'm not sure if it was your kidnapping that triggered that in me, or if I would've been this way regardless."

I exhale and sit up, dragging my wet hair over my shoulder and using the brush I brought from the bathroom to start detangling it. Having ass-long hair is sort of awesome, but it also sucks dick at times. Washing, combing, drying—it can take an hour or more.

"You came across as controlling in other ways," I admit, and Tess stiffens, then deflates a bit.

"Yeah, well, I've had a bit of a reality check as of late." Her eyes harden, and I know she's thinking about the custody battle. Parrish told me she sobbed for hours after, and then went ice-cold. I know she's plotting and scheming; I just don't think she can beat Justin's omnipotent menace. "Does Justin … I mean your father, does he treat you well, Dakota?" She looks over at me, and I see it yet again, that vibrant pleading. Somehow, she knows. She senses Justin's true intentions.

The urge to spill it all is there.

This Veronica Fisher thing, it's a big ask. Hearing about Raúl trying to burn Philippa's house down? That's insane. Is Justin truly planning on killing the teenage children of all his former classmates/conspirators? Is he truly planning on having *me* kill them all for him?

Probably.

"He treats me like a princess." The words are true, if only said princess lived in a tower. I blink at Tess, and she frowns at me. In as silent a manner as possible, I get up and grab the hot pink Milk Carton hoodie that I accidentally took from Justin's. I say accidentally because I tossed it on my duffel bag, and it somehow got mixed in with other clothes.

I would never under normal circumstances choose to bring it with me.

I sit back down and smile, and Tess' gaze drops to the logo. As soon as she sees it, her lip twitches a bit and she turns to look at the TV. If this display has revealed anything, she doesn't let on.

"Do you really love my son?" she asks me, which was a question I wasn't expecting.

"P-pardon?" I feel my face flush because while we declared this openly to her, the way she's asking now ... *my son.* She's asking almost as if she's Parrish's mother, and not mine.

"I asked him this same question: do you really love my daughter?" Tess explains this, as if she could read my mind or something. "I won't give you his answer—if he wants to share, that's his choice—but I'd like to hear from you in private. I'm struggling to understand how the two of you went from hating each other, to being ... intimate, to wanting to reveal said intimacy to me." She stares me down, and I feel myself fidgeting, overwhelmed with discomfort.

Thanks a lot, Justin, you dick. I'm here because of him, in this awkward situation because of him, and I don't doubt that it was all intentional. If he wanted to kill Tess, he could. Hell, he could have every single one of his enemies killed.

But that's not his intention: he wants us all to accept him as a genius, a god, to see him rise. It's extremely important to him. On top of that, I'm pretty sure he wants Tess back but knows he can never have her. Short of kidnapping her the way he did Parrish, there's nothing he can do. What he *can* do is strip her of her heart —her children—take her husband away, ruin her career, burn her house down.

Ruin her relationship with her lost daughter.

"After all that," Tess continues, turning to me fully and crossing her legs on the bed. She fucking stares me down again, and I know without a doubt that she's onto something. Onto Justin, specifically. "You accept a marriage proposal from Chasm? Why even tell me that you were dating Parrish then? It would've been much simpler to just lie to me and say you were with Chasm and Chasm only."

She's so close to getting it.

So close and yet … a rational person doesn't hear a creaking on the stairs and automatically assume it's a ghost. A rational person doesn't see a flash of light in the sky and automatically assume it's a UFO. A rational person doesn't see a girl acting irregularly and assume there's a serial killer controlling them like a puppet.

No matter how smart she is, could Tess ever really figure it out?

"The condom that the FBI found, the one that Chasm threw away … it was mine and Parrish's."

That seems to surprise Tess. She sits up a little straighter and then, after closing her eyes and shuddering slightly, she opens them and takes a handful of popcorn from the bowl. It feels like we are *this* close from making a big step forward.

Only, we can't.

I can't give her the answers that she wants.

"You lied to me?" she asks, and her voice is edging on that cool, angry tone I've come to fear. With considerable effort, she seems to get herself under control. "Why would you do that, knowing that my son was missing?"

This one's on me. Justin didn't ask me to lie to Tess about sleeping with Parrish. At least in this, I can correct my mistake.

"I was afraid that you'd blame me," I whisper, tears welling up in my eyes. They're spilling over and down my cheeks, hot and shameful. I don't even care if Justin hears them; I can't hold them in. At least in this moment, I need to let it out.

I killed a guy. His blood was on my hands. I'm afraid of what's going to happen with Veronica.

"Blame you?" Tess asks, her own face taking on a blush. As it does, I notice ... I notice that her chest just above the scooped neckline of her shirt turns red, too. We blush the same. I'm shaking as I turn my head away, but she reaches out and turns my face back to hers. "Why would I blame you?"

"Because you love Parrish more—and that's okay—and I'm a huge fucking disappointment. I smashed your typewriter into the window of my own birthday present." I'm sobbing now; it's just all coming out. "I never wanted to do that. I didn't mean to do that." I put my face in my hands. I've been good about taking all of my emotions and stuffing them into boxes, pushing them into the shadows with my foot. I knew before *any* of this Justin shit started happening that I was already filling them up too quickly, that I was running out of room.

My entire life was flipped on its head because of a Netflix show, because of a woman who's running around Medina without a phone, who seems to know exactly how to avoid Justin's disturbing app. I lost everything; I gained so much more. I ... I wish I could just live my life on my own terms.

Being beholden to someone else, it never works out. My case might be extreme, but it's never a path that leads to true happiness. Never.

"I read your manuscript, remember? I know how you feel about me." I drop my hands to my lap only to see that Tess is also crying. Her face is as wet as my own, and her mouth is turned down in an impossibly beautiful frown.

"What I wrote there, I ..." She starts and then stops, looking away and heaving a deep sigh. "I lied to you, too." I don't understand what she's talking about, so I sit there, and I wait, and I look at the movie theater snacks she made, and the fact that the movies she's scrolling through aren't movies at all but K-dramas because she knows that's what I like. "I don't write because it makes me money." She turns back and then looks down at her lap. "I write because I have to, because I'd go crazy if I didn't, because I see such beautiful things inside my head, and I want to share them. You were right when you told me that I was an artist. I just ... I was angry."

"Why?" I ask, trying to understand, trying to figure her out. Clearly, our main issues stem from simply not understanding each other.

"The most beautiful thing that I've ever seen in my head was ... it was you." She sniffles again, fresh tears rolling down her cheeks. "Finding you. And I did. But you ... you didn't want me. You didn't remember me. You hate me."

"I don't hate you," I protest, but Tess just shakes her head at me.

"You did, and I understand why. It took me some time, but I let my anger get the best of me. I'd imagined things going a certain way so many times, written it down, scrapped it, rewrote it again and again until it became this sacred, perfect thing. I was so busy wondering why my dream wasn't playing out the way I wanted to realize that I was getting exactly what I needed which"—and here she laughs—"is clearly far more than I deserve."

"Don't say that—" I start, and she gives me a sharp warning look.

"I'm the parent; *you* are the one who needs me," she declares, and then she's reaching out and grabbing me. Tess Vanguard, Ice Queen. She's so cold, she's practically fucking Elsa. But ... when she pulls me into her arms and wraps me up like I'm a baby, I let her. Because Saffron robbed her of this experience.

Next time that I see her, I have to ask. I have to know. I want to understand.

Tess strokes my hair back.

"What happened to you with the police officer—"

"I don't want to talk about that." My voice hitches strangely, but Tess persists.

"It's okay to be upset; it's okay to be confused. About me, about Justin, the custody hearing, the Seattle fucking Slayer." And here she lets out a bitter laugh. Right. She thinks the man who took her son almost got me in the end there, too. Once again, so damn close to getting it. "I just want to lock you up in a box and stand guard all day and night."

"If only it worked like that," I whisper back, but having her hold me like this, I feel better somehow. "And I don't hate you. I don't."

I notice the door is cracked slightly, but as soon as my eyes catch on Parrish's in the shadows, he turns away and very carefully pulls the door shut to give us privacy. As much as I miss him, Tess and I need this.

I just hope there aren't going to be any repercussions because of it.

Parrish wakes me up by stroking a finger down the bridge of my nose.

"Rise and shine, sleepyhead," he murmurs, buried under the covers beside me. In fact, they're draped over his head and he's positioned above me on all fours. His body is braced on his knees and left palm, his right finger tracing over my lips. They tingle with his touch, and I reach up, gripping his inked arm in tired fingers.

"Don't do that."

"Why not?" he asks dryly, raising a brow. "Because you'd rather have my mouth there?"

He drops his lips to mine, and I let out a desperate sounding groan. Parrish's kisses are like fireworks lighting up a night sky, bright bursts of color in an otherwise ebony expanse. He lights up the darkness, drives away the shadows. For a while there, I really and truly believed I would never see him again.

My life would have been a shell, empty and echoing. I'm not sure how I would've survived losing him.

"Whatever you did to Tess last night, she's in a much better mood this morning. We're going out to breakfast."

"At the country club?" I groan as he pulls away from me and sits up, just in time for Kimber to open the door. I push up onto my elbows, cheeks heating as she wrinkles her face at the pair of us in bed together.

"Fucking sick. Mom, they're trying to have sex!" she yells out, and Parrish grits his teeth, flying out of the bed and storming over to the doorway.

"I'm going to make your sophomore year a living hell," he grinds out, but she just crosses her arms and smirks at me while peering around him.

"You see this? You think he's actually a nice guy? It's total bullshit."

Tess appears beside Kimber and gives us both a stern look.

"We're going out to breakfast as a family."

"Sans Laverne?" Parrish queries, and Tess does her best to quickly bury a smile.

"Don't talk about your grandmother that way." Her chastisement is complete crap, but at least she's trying. "She seems busy; I didn't want to bother her." Tess' polite way of saying she doesn't want her to go. *Thank God.* I don't think Laverne is in on the serial killer stuff, but she greatly dislikes me, hates Tess, and seems happy to play social games with Justin. "It's a new place; I've never been."

My heart soars at the idea of skipping out on the country club, and I hop out of bed.

Parrish reluctantly leaves the room so that I can change, and we meet downstairs. The white limo is waiting there, and I get the strangest sense of déjà vu. It's like my second day here and yet, it's completely different. In so many ways, it's better. In a lot of ways, it's worse.

This time, instead of writing snotty messages on his phone— Parrish puts an arm around my waist, and Tess' eye twitches. She says nothing, but her gaze does drop to the ring on my finger and sticks there.

"Remember when we sat in this limo and you typed out *'get lost, Dakota. I don't do incest'* on your phone?" I whisper this in Parrish's ear, and he turns one of his fine, princely glares down on me.

"Why do you have such an impeccable memory? I doubt that's what I said."

"It's exactly what you said," I whisper back, and he heaves a sigh, his face as dismissive and devastatingly handsome as it always was. Only, it's mine now. There's a glimmer in his gaze that he can't hide, not even if he wanted to. Because I'll always remember that he told me I was the only real thing he had, that he accepted he might die in order to free me from the Slayer's demands, because when he looks at me I know that he'd take the burden of this from me if he could.

Paul stares at us and adjusts his glasses, shaking his head like he can't quite believe what he's seeing.

"The two of you ... I still don't quite understand."

"Nobody asked you to," Parrish retorts, and Tess gives him a look. He does his best to soften his expression, but his words are firm and uncompromising. "You almost died, so I'll forgive you."

"You're magnanimous, son." Paul sighs and says nothing for the rest of the drive. Kimber pretends to be zoned in on her phone, but I can tell that she doesn't have her earbuds in this time. And the kids? For once, they're not on their iPads (or in Ben's case, buried in a book).

When they actually talk and spend time together, the Vanguards aren't quite so cold and odd as they first appeared. Mostly, they're distracted. By work, by deadlines, by the internet. But right now? This is nice.

I'm totally surprised to see Maxx and Chasm waiting at the restaurant, but I'm happy that Tess invited them. She did say the family was going out to breakfast, didn't she? It wouldn't be right if they weren't there.

Everything seems to be going smoothly until the subject of Caroline comes up.

It's actually Paul that introduces it, bringing up the idea of Justin and Caroline getting married.

"They've sent out invitations already," he says, sounding annoyed. Not because he gives a shit about Caroline—other than that she's in town and acts like her son doesn't exist—but likely because it's another direct shot at Tess.

Her ex, Paul's ex.

It's not a coincidence.

I'm probably one of the only—if not *the* only person—that knows why Justin truly picked her to be his bride. First and foremost, it was her violent nature he was seeking; the fact that her presence in Medina would upset Paul and Tess was just a bonus.

"The wedding is next week?" Tess asks, letting her gaze drift over to me. I was aware that Justin and Caroline were planning on getting married soon, but I didn't know when. This is the first I'm hearing that a date's been set.

"Our family received an invitation, right?" Parrish says casually, and we all stop what we're doing to stare at him. Well, not the kids but everyone else does. "I'd like to go."

"Absolutely not." Paul is adamant about this in a way he is about few other things. His eyes meet his son's, and the two of them enter into a silent staring contest the likes of which I haven't seen since Parrish lied about me being at the school and got his car taken away.

"Uh-oh," Chas murmurs, just before Parrish's eyes flash in defiance. I know why he wants to go—to be with me—but to someone else looking in, it might seem like he's interested in his bio mom.

"Why not?" he demands, gaze slipping briefly to me before returning to his father. "I've also been invited to dinner at their house on Wednesday; I've accepted."

"Who invited you to dinner?" Paul asks before Tess gets a chance. But I can see her bristling from here, and I don't blame her.

"Caroline and Justin." Parrish stabs a, well, it's a slice of pear which is sort of funny. Did I mention that he's wearing his pear t-shirt today? Paired with a black sport coat that's currently hanging on the back of his chair, and gray pants, he makes the tee look elegant. "Apparently, Caroline wants a chance to reconnect with me." Tess and Paul exchange a look, but Parrish is quick to add, "not that she could ever be a mother of any sort to me, no worries on that. I don't expect much out of it, but I'd like to at least see what she has to say."

The conversation is clearly not over, but Tess and Paul turn a shared look on one another, and the subject is dropped for the remainder of the meal.

"I'll admit that I was wrong about Tess and the deal with you two dating," Maxx says after, once we've crossed the street to a park. Amelia and Henry spotted it from the front porch of the restaurant and Tess was so excited to see them interested in something in the real world as opposed to on a screen that she fervently agreed.

She's over there now, *playing* with them.

"But?" Parrish asks, turning to look at his friend.

"But I don't think you should push her on the Caroline thing." X tucks his hands in his pockets as Chasm picks at the edge of his own. I know he's thinking about cigarettes or, rather, his lack thereof. "I know you want to be with Kota, and so do I, but it'd be much easier for Chasm to step in."

"Outsourcing your supposed girlfriend's safety, huh?" Parrish retorts, but X just sighs and shakes his head.

"I'm trying to keep you from making a huge mistake. If Justin invited you over there via Caroline, he has something in mind that you won't like. It's better that you just stay away, period. There's a reason that he chose you to kidnap, you know what I mean?" Maxx sighs and looks right at me, like there's something he wants to say but isn't quite sure how to put. Our phones are in the limo, and it's doubtful that there are any cameras where we're standing. I mean, maybe there are security cameras at the edges of the park or something, but video isn't an issue right now: audio is. We're safe in that regard. "I have an idea, by the way." He sits down on the bench and puts his elbows on his knees. "I'm sure Parrish has told you about the secret passage in Laverne's house?"

Parrish pauses and turns to Maxx suddenly as Chasm stands up a bit straighter.

Parrish did actually mention that, the day of prom, right before our ... our threesome. Ahem.

Wow. Sally and Nevaeh wouldn't even know what to do with me now. I feel a bit bad as I haven't messaged them recently, but on the other hand, they've only messaged me about newsworthy events such as Parrish's kidnapping or Justin's app, never just to check on me or to talk. Never just to say that they miss me.

I've been friends with the pair of them since forever, and it makes me sad when I think about drifting apart from them, but I guess that's just part of growing up, huh? There's always a sea of loneliness that goes along with it. I've learned a great lesson here though, with the boys, with Danyella and Lumen, even Tess.

Sometimes, we lose something and gain something in the same breath.

"We could keep Veronica there." Parrish makes the connection and snaps his fingers. "It's perfect."

"It's only perfect if we can get past all the fucking cameras." Chasm sighs and sits down hard on the bench opposite Maxx. "I think I'm having withdrawals. Remind me why I ever started smoking in the first place?"

"In the hopes that Seamus would notice and reprimand you? A desperate cry for attention? Certainly it was that; I *did* warn you." Parrish turns away and Chas rolls his eyes. I'd be annoyed with Parrish if I didn't know he was teasing. "What if we used the bug detector to go through and map them? More accurately, what if *you* went through and mapped them?" He points at Maxx. "While the rest of us are at dinner?"

"If you're going, I'm going." X's statement rings with finality; he won't be budged. Parrish rolls his eyes in annoyance.

"Fine. We'll do it together then," he snips, curling his lip in Maxx's direction.

"Our goal is what then?" I interrupt, still standing on the sidewalk in front of the bench. "Kidnap Veronica and get her into the vault? What if someone stumbles on her?"

"Nobody will." Parrish seems confident, even if he is wearing the stupid pear t-shirt. It's so fucking cute on him that I can barely stand it. He casts that cool gaze my way, and tremors run through me. It's like a natural disaster in my heart. He can destroy cities with a single look, countries with a touch, my whole world with an embrace. "Only Kimber and I even know it's there; we stumbled on it once when Laverne was coming out and we were playing hide-and-seek. Even Paul doesn't know it's there."

"What if Laverne goes down and finds a Whitehall Prep student locked in her vault?" I ask, but Parrish shakes his head.

"She rarely goes down there and anyway, I'll keep watch." He sounds confident, as he always does. Very few people know there are any cracks in the prince's crown. But I do. Because he cried for me, and he holds too many feelings inside, and fuck, I just love him. A lot.

I move toward him, and he takes me in his arms, dragging me in close.

"Miss me, Gamer Girl?" he asks, and I nod against his chest.

"Can I live across the hall from you forever?"

"No." The word is firm, and it brooks no argument. "We'll be married, and we'll share a room, of course."

"I feel like there are factors in this living situation that you're not considering properly." X leans back on the bench and crosses his arms behind his head, locking eyes with Parrish over my shoulder.

"Yeah, like the fact that we're engaged? Can we circle back to the vault thing?" Chasm pauses, and I swear, I can hear that brilliant mind of his ticking as he works through this. "What if we worked it so that everything—up until the last minute—*is* on camera? That's what Justin wants anyway. He won't be happy if we try to screw around. But ..." Chas stands up as I pull back slightly from Parrish. He's staring at the sidewalk now and not at either of us. "If we had just one split-second between one camera and the next, we could make a switch."

"How so?" Maxx clarifies, and in the way the three of them plot together, I can totally see how they were unholy terrors roaming the halls of Whitehall. "Like, say, we switch Veronica out for a decoy? Bury something else in the woods on Laverne's property?"

"If we were dragging a tarp," I add on, tapping at my lower lip, "and then the two of you"—I point at Maxx and Parrish, since according to Justin's instructions, they're not allowed to be involved—"are waiting in the dark space between two continuous camera feeds? We leave the real Veronica behind and drag an identical tarp with like, dirt in it or something?"

"That might work, if we drug Veronica." Parrish hazards a glance at Chasm, and he lifts his gaze to meet his friend's stare. "I could steal some of Tess' sleeping pills. If we catch Veronica at a party, she'll be drinking. If we get her early enough and dump the pills in her cup, we can get her comatose without killing her."

"God, this is so fucked-up." Maxx exhales and rubs at his forehead. "Tess has sleeping pills?"

"Everyone in Medina gets prescribed sleeping pills. Sometimes it feels like you're from another planet, you know that? I could walk up to any person in this town and find a pharmacy in their medicine cabinet, purse, or glove compartment." Parrish scoffs, and X gives him a look.

"Yeah, well, if I'm from another planet then Dakota is from the *same* planet. Just remember that." He pauses as Kimber makes her way over to us.

"What do you want, shit-for-brains?" Parrish asks, and she glares at him. Her eyes drift to me and the ring that's on my finger. That day she caught me in Parrish's room with Chasm was a literal nightmare. *"How dare you?"* She looked at me then like she wanted to kill me. Now? I have no idea what her expression is supposed to encompass.

"Everyone in town knows the four of you are in some sort of weird, poly relationship." She states it as a fact, but what can I say. I don't really know where this is leading, but none of us seems concerned with that right about now. There are more important matters to sort through. "It's bizarre."

"Did any of us ask for your opinion? No? Then fuck off." Parrish crosses his arms obstinately, but Chasm at least tries.

"I know you had a crush on me, Kim—"

She looks him up and down like he's lost his fucking mind.

"I did not."

"You did," Parrish corrects, and Kimber turns a glare on him before glancing at me.

"I don't understand how or why you'd put up with him as a boyfriend; it made more sense when you hated each other. At least now I know why you were acting so weird when he was missing." I blink at her, but she doesn't know the half of it.

"Are you here to wave the white flag?" I wonder aloud, and Kimber looks at me like I'm speaking an alien language.

"Wow. You really aren't from around here, are you?" she asks, as if that wasn't obvious before. She looks to Parrish next. "Dad wants to see you." She turns and points at Paul, waiting down at the end of the sidewalk with his hands tucked into his pockets. He gives a small wave and Parrish sighs.

"I guess he almost died, so ..." He trails off and then turns to me suddenly, taking my face between his hands for a smoldering kiss before he draws back and looks me dead in the face. "I have a surprise for you later; don't go too far."

He takes off, leaving me breathless and wanting behind him, and I turn a look back on the other boys as Kimber pretends not to be listening, but let's just be frank, she's a terrible actress and she's totally eavesdropping.

"Don't tell me what the surprise is—I don't want to know." Chasm sits back down on the bench, and I smile at him, absently twirling the ring on my finger. "No, wait, actually I *do* want to know. Every detail."

I roll my eyes that time, but Maxx just smiles.

"Are we sure we don't need to go hiking again to get some details sorted out?"

"At this point, I feel like you're just taking advantage of the situation." I sit down between the two of them and watch Tess across the street, playing with Ben, Henry, and Amelia. Part of me wonders if I would've liked growing up with Tess, having her play with me like that.

The rest of me is convinced that Justin would've gotten his claws in me sooner. Then again, he told me that he was waiting to come back into my life as someone powerful and respected, that *"nobody wants a disgraced father living in exile."*

The only person who *might* know the answer to that question is Saffron Banks.

CHAPTER 27

Parrish starts the night off by showing me the vault. There's a hidden door in the floor of Laverne's wine cellar. There are no cameras in here, thankfully. My guess is this: Justin and his cronies would have a difficult time getting into Laverne's house to plant them. So who could've done it?

The staff.

It makes the most sense. There were no cameras here before the staff arrived, and plenty after. None of the members of Laverne's household have access to the cellar, so it all makes sense.

"We'll steal some alcohol while we're down here to make it more plausible," Parrish remarks, checking the labels on the bottles before selecting one. It doesn't seem random, more like he actually knows something about wine.

"Are you picking at random or is there something about that bottle that you like?"

"This bottle is worth about fifteen thousand dollars. I want to drink it just to spite my grandmother." He turns it around to look at the label, and I raise my brows. See what I mean? How does he even know that?

"You're seventeen," I say, and he turns a look on me.

"So? You're sixteen, and you're engaged and also have two other boyfriends—the most important of which is me. We all have our idiosyncrasies, don't we, Gamer Girl?" I glare at him because, as sexy as he is, as much as I love him, he is also a consummate asshole. I refuse to admit that his surly, imperious attitude is at least *part* of the reason I like him so much.

He looks down at the hidden door but doesn't bother to open it.

"I don't know if there's an additional alarm on this door now, but I'll find out."

"How?" I ask as he looks up at me, and I feel that familiar shiver of delight at being under his hungry gaze. I know what Parrish wants tonight, and I want the same thing. I don't care if we have to sneak around like we used to; I just want to be with him.

"I'm my grandmother's favorite; I'm set to inherit her company and her fortune. She hasn't given any of her other grandchildren—let alone her own son—such a privilege. Come on." He takes off up the stairs, checking carefully to make sure there's nobody waiting in the kitchen, and off we go.

He leads me down a long hallway lined with oil paintings of old people (rich folk *love* oil paintings of old people, particularly when they're related to them or, if old themselves, portraits of them). He opens the door to an opulent bedroom done up in heavy dark woods, gold, and cream. It truly looks like the enclave of a prince.

On the desk, there's a notebook with a cluster of loose colored pencils beside it. Also, I see a tattoo machine and dozens of ink bottles, and my throat clenches tight. Parrish called me a canvas once, and I can't help but wonder ...

I spin to look at him and clap my hands together.

"Is my surprise a tattoo?" I ask, and I don't even bother to hide the gleeful excitement in my voice.

Parrish sets the wine bottle down and turns to face me, leaning his (perfect) ass up against the edge of a piece of furniture. His expression unfolds like a flower in bloom, and I wonder if it's mostly just me who gets to see him like this. Not as a little lordling prince. Not as a sloth god. Just … Parrish, raw and real.

"Tess bought me everything brand-new," he explains, and then I remember the beautiful design he made for me just before he went missing. A lot of items in the house—especially in his room and mine—can be salvaged, but likely not that single sheet of paper. I don't have much hope. "She caught me once tattooing myself with a ball point pen and a needle and made me pay a visit to an established tattoo artist to learn what the job truly entailed."

"You gave yourself a scratcher tat?" I ask, and Parrish smirks, reaching up to tap two fingers against his upper arm.

"Covered up, Gamer Girl, but nice try." He stands up to walk toward me, and I feel the urge to run. I don't know why, but I do. Maybe it's because of the intensity in his stare, the way he looks at me like something he wants but can now really and truly have? I'm still shocked by it, both by the look and also by his careful, if reluctant, acceptance of Maxx and Chasm as my … boyfriends.

Three boyfriends.

That's … a lot. *Oh wait, two boyfriends and one fiancé actually.*

"I'm starting to see that you were right about Tess: she isn't as terrible as she first appears."

He pauses directly in front of me, his multi-colored irises simmering with heat. The gold flecks seem to burn bright, like they're molten and the brown parts darken to hungry shadows. He lifts up both of his tattooed hands and hovers them over my upper arms. I want him to touch me so badly that I pull in an exaggerated inhale, just so the breath will cause my body to expand through the microscopic amount of space between us.

His palms graze my skin, and then I exhale, and we're separated by like, literal atoms. I almost feel him, but he's not touching me, and it's infuriating. I reach up and grab his wrists, pushing his hands where I want them to go.

"Pushy, aren't we?" he teases. "Don't think because Chasm and Maxx move at warp-speed that I will, too. I want this to ache, Dakota." He draws his arms away from me and moves past, heading in the direction of the sketchbook. "Although, I have to say: the idea of them touching you at all still bothers me a little."

"Even after the threesome?" I ask, and then like *why the fuck did you just say that?!*

"Especially after that." He sighs and picks up the notebook as I turn around, flipping open to one of the pages and then holding it out to me. "Here. Take a look."

Instead of one rose like there was in the original drawing, this one has a heart. To be more specific, this one has *three* hearts. I look up and meet Parrish's eyes as my fingers tighten on the edges of the notebook.

"The rose is the state flower of New York, but I wasn't sure that you needed that anymore. Hearts seemed more appropriate."

"Three hearts?" I ask, biting my lower lip like Maxx does. Parrish just slits his eyes and then points at me.

"Give it a proper go-over, and don't be too nice. You complained that girls are raised to be people pleasers, right? Prove the world wrong. Don't be too nice, Dakota. Not in this, not in anything else. It's more important to stand up for yourself than to be nice." He moves toward me again, and my heart begins to beat a frantic, staccato rhythm. "Tell me if you want this as your first." He points at it and lifts a brow. "If I need to make changes to the design, I'm more than happy to do it."

"Tell me if you want this as your first." As if the sexual innuendo dripping from that sentence was an accident. What a tease.

I turn my attention back to the drawing, to the three anatomical hearts, pierced through with what I first assume is an arrow, but that I come to realize is actually a *quill pen*. The tip of it shines with blood, but it doesn't come across as ominous this time. Somehow, it feels like an acknowledgment of growing pains, the sort that I've been up against for months.

The hearts are green like my hair but softened at the edges with dark shadows and black branches that sprout directly from them. The whole design is painted as if by a watercolorist's brush, a few splashes of pink and green and black here and there to break up the hard, defined lines of the branches, the quill pen, and the hearts themselves.

It's as dynamic as the rose piece; I can feel the hearts beating on the page in my hand. *More like, your heart is beating so fast and so hard that you can feel it in your fingertips.* Either way, I love it. It's an evolution of the rose drawing—which I would've happily allowed him to ink into my skin—and I can't imagine ever regretting it.

Even if I do, that's what life is all about, isn't it? Make some decisions for yourself, regret them. Learn anew. The only thing we can ever count on is the present, and I want this so much it physically hurts. My chest is tight, and when I exhale, it's shaky and rife with excitement.

"You sure you wouldn't be more comfortable with a butterfly or a flower or some shit?" Parrish asks this question with a heavy dollop of inference, and I look up, blinking a few times as I try to get the joke. *"No, of course not. You should know me better than that, Flor."* This next tease is said in a false feminine voice as

Parrish bats his lashes at me, and I narrow my own eyes at him.

"Have you been reading *Stepbrother Inked* again?" I demand, and he grins at me. "You memorized those lines *just* to spit them back at me in this moment, didn't you?"

"I aim to please," he teases, breezing past me to open a box of gloves. They're black latex, and I can't resist the flutter in my belly as he snaps them over his inked fingers. "Besides, I wanted to see if the dude character Florian had any tricks that I could use in the bedroom—"

"Nope." I hold the notebook out toward him, and he turns fully around to stare at me.

"What do you mean *nope*?" he asks, as if he didn't just give me a speech about standing up for myself. "The composition is perfect. The color is—"

"You are not going to get tips from Florian Harper Riley," I declare, naming the book's hero. "He's a manwhore, and you were mine first. Get your tips somewhere else." I cross my arms, and Parrish stares at me.

"You have three boyfriends now. Don't I get three girlfriends? I could save Lumen's family from financial ruin—" I walk up to him and grab his face, kissing him to shut him up. He sighs as I pull away, and our gazes meet. "Damn it, Dakota. I can't even tease you with that, can I?"

"You said I was the only real thing you had …" I start, my gaze flicking away for a moment. Justin is probably watching, but what does it matter? He clearly knows how I feel about Parrish or else he wouldn't have chosen him to be the one he kidnapped. There's no hiding my feelings now. "I know it's selfish." I look back at Parrish, pleading with my eyes. "It's one-sided, and fucked up, and it never would've happened if Justin … I mean, I don't regret it now, but I wouldn't have done this to you if given the choice."

His face softens, and he pats me on the cheek with a gloved

hand.

"I know, Dakota. Don't stress. You risked your life to save me. Don't think I've forgotten that." He pulls out the desk chair and then takes a seat in a dining chair that he must've dragged in here from somewhere else. "Where do you want me?" he asks, and I don't think he misspoke. The smile on his face tells me that his words were intentional. "What I mean to say is: where should I penetrate your skin and inject my—"

"Here." I lift up the left leg of my shorts and point to my upper thigh. It's the exact spot where Parrish's fingers brushed my skin when he called me a canvas. "Horizontally, so that it'll show if I wear the right shorts."

His face tightens up with some sort of intense emotion, and then he exhales.

"I was hoping you'd say that. Stay standing for me."

I do, and he goes about cleaning the area, using a razor to get off the fine hairs, and then lifts his eyes to mine.

"I'd like to freehand it," he tells me, and I blink back at him.

"Okay. I don't really know what that means, but I trust you."

"Do you?" he retorts, and I nod. I've seen his work, both on himself and on Chasm. I've seen his sketches, too, and all of those creepy silicone body parts that are very Justin-y in nature. That is, they look like something only a deranged serial killer might keep.

"I do."

Parrish picks up a marker from the surface of the desk and then bends down, recreating the sketch itself in the most basic of ways. He follows the natural curve of my thigh and adjusts the size of the piece so that it'll fit easier onto my leg.

"My dad is worried about me spending time with Caroline." Parrish continues marking me up with the pen. I can barely stand the brush of his gloved fingers, the damp kiss of the pen tip like an extension of his hand. He's very close to the, uh, promise land, and

I'm starting to feel fidgety. It doesn't help that he keeps looking up at me from underneath those long lashes of his. "Don't squirm too much, or we might end up doing something other than tattooing."

"This won't stop us from—" I start, and Parrish's pen goes still.

He smiles wickedly at me and then shakes his head.

"We'll put an aftercare bandage on it; I bought a roll of Saniderm." I have no idea what he's talking about, but I nod my head like I understand. "And don't worry." Parrish drags his gloved fingers down my leg and then sits up, leaving gooseflesh in his wake. "I'll handle you with care."

"You were saying about Caroline?" I continue, clearing my throat in a way that does absolutely zero to distract from my body's blatant displays of excitement. My nipples are hard, and they hurt, and there's no shortage of lubrication between my thighs.

"Mm." He studies the ink on my leg, and then makes a few more marks with the pen. "He gave me this long, weird speech about how he was in love with Tess all along, but that he was jealous of her and Justin. That, he claims, is why he ended up with Caroline in the first place." Parrish nods and sits up straight. "Go look in the mirror, tell me what you think, and then I'll have you sit, and we'll see how it moves."

I follow his instructions, but it's hard to see what the piece is really going to look like. The pen marks are obscure, and the basic outline doesn't capture the splash of color or the dynamic shapes and movement of the sketch. Still, I trust Parrish enough that it's all I need to see.

"Perfect."

I sit down in the chair and Parrish makes a few, last lines with the marker before switching it out for the machine. My fingers dig into the sides of the chair—this high-backed baroque throne-like thing that I actually like—and he leans down.

"It doesn't hurt as bad as people say," he assures me, and then he's pressing the needle to my skin. I exhale automatically, shivering at the sharp sting of it, the vibration chasing me to my core. The first few minutes are the worst, but I control my breathing and Parrish goes slow, keeping an even pressure, and occasionally pausing to swipe away beads of blood.

I don't let myself think about Tess or Justin or my grandparents or anyone else. I've been doing what everyone else wants me to do lately, and I'm making this decision for myself.

"According to my dad, Tess really should've been my mother all along anyway." He continues his work, eyes focused on my leg, but voice thoughtful, raw. It reminds me how I feel when I play video games sometimes, that zone you get in when you're really focused on something that's important to you. "I think he's afraid that I actually *want* Caroline's attention."

"Don't you?" I ask, and Parrish snorts. He looks up at me again.

"We both have parents who are killers: you tell me how you feel about it."

Parrish goes quiet again and continues his work as I mull the question over.

"I wish Justin was just a father," I say, and I don't care if he's listening at this very moment. "I wish he cared about me more than he cared about his revenge plot. Even now, somehow, I still can't fully shake my wish."

There's no response from Parrish for a while, and I wonder if he, too, isn't giving some serious thought to his own question.

"Caroline wouldn't marry Paul with the prenup in place because she didn't care about me or him or anyone but herself." The buzz of the machine provides a pleasant backdrop to his careful words. "She gave birth to me and then took off, but not after attacking my dad and breaking his nose." Parrish shakes his head. "No, I don't care about her or wish things were different. I *liked* having Tess as a mom. I think we both have valid points of view."

"I agree." My voice is a bit breathless, a tad strained.

We take a break so that I can use the bathroom, and I realize maybe that I should have taken my shorts off before getting started. Parrish ends up helping me out of them, and then he presses this hot kiss to my lower belly that somehow turns the strange, tingling sensation in my thigh to pleasure.

He retreats so that I can pee in peace, and then I wash my hands and rejoin him in the bedroom. He offers me water and a snack, and we get right back to work. This time, I can't help it: I reach out and stroke my fingers over his blond-kissed brown hair, and he shudders.

"Do you want me to mess this up?"

"I couldn't help myself," I admit, and that at least, makes him smile. "I like knowing that I can rile you up now."

He offers me a disparaging look, one that's pure dramatic thespian, and then lets this slow-cooker smile stretch across his face. By the time it's done roasting, I'm hungry for it. *OMG. Please no. Thank goodness people can't read other people's thoughts. What sort of metaphor was that?!*

"You riled me up from moment one. I was fully prepared to despise you; I'd set myself up for it. Then there you are, gorgeous and perfectly weird, and apologizing for responding to *my* rudeness ..." He trails off and huffs, reaching up an arm to swipe at some of the sweat on his forehead, and I find myself mesmerized by the action.

Parrish and I are into each other, make no mistake about it.

"I try. I think people get too caught up on being right or winning. It's okay to admit to making mistakes or not knowing things." I shrug my shoulders, and he sighs, but it's a wistful sound.

"Are you, like, sixty or sixteen?" he asks, and I snort right back at him.

"Benefit of being raised by grandparents instead of parents?" I wonder, and then my mind drifts to Saffron, and I wonder where she is and what she's doing. By keeping her appearance a secret, am I really helping her? At the same time, Justin's omnipresent eyes would be sure to find her if I told basically anyone but the boys.

My eyes follow the sure, steady movements of Parrish's hand. He was born to be an artist. It's not just in the practice or the talent, it's the vibe. He's having a conversation with me, but I can see that his focus is wholly consumed by his art. He's fully embroiled in the creation; it isn't mere action for him.

As the tattoo comes to life on my leg, I'm even more thrilled by the design. He was right about the free-handing; it's shaped to the contours of my own body, lending the piece even more freedom of movement.

"Are these three hearts supposed to represent you and the boys?" I ask, and Parrish lifts up a surprised face to blink at me.

"No. They represent you and Tess and Saffron." He stares at me, and I stare right back at him, and then I'm blushing so furiously that he offers me up yet another charming smile, one dripping with sheer decadence. That's Parrish Vanguard for ya.

"You wanted a tattoo that represented me and my best friends?" he asks, and I'm too embarrassed to even sputter out a response of any sort. "Mm. Well, now that you've mentioned it …" He trails off and then gestures at the quill pen. "You thought the pen was you? Do you *like* writing? I was under the assumption that you were only doing it because Daddy Dearest was making you."

494

"I ..." I'm not sure how to respond to that, so I just keep my mouth shut and focus on not embarrassing myself for the remainder of the tattoo session. It takes about seven *hours.* Yes, seven full hours. Tess only invites herself into the room once during the entire session, but that's probably because she's seen us intermittently through the day and night. When we stopped for snacks, Parrish wrapped my tattoo, and I wore pants to keep it hidden when we went into the kitchen.

I feel bad about not telling Tess about the tattoo beforehand, but like I said, I came to Washington for Tess. Went to Whitehall for Tess. Changed my entire life for Tess. This is for me.

When she did come into the room (without knocking, some things never change), I just so happened to be in the bathroom and Parrish was sitting at the desk absently sketching something on a blank page. If she had seen what we were doing, would she have stopped us?

She left the door open on her way out, but I think the fact that Laverne's bedroom is right next door repels her like salt to a ghost.

Just when my eyes are starting to get heavy, and I'm slumping slightly forward in the chair, Parrish reaches out and puts his arm on my shoulder.

"I'm adding some highlights and then that's it—we're done."

Any joy I might've felt from that statement is obliterated the moment he starts to apply white highlights over my already sore and swollen skin. Like, girls deal with period cramps (the equivalent of a pumpkin scraper grinding down the sides of one's uterus), and so the tattooing isn't that big of a deal.

But the white ink? Oh, the white ink.

I'm wondering if I'm even going to be able to make it when Parrish sits up and studies my leg with an artist's eye.

"Can you stand up for me?" he asks, and I do. He looks the piece over again as I peer down at it, some of the fatigue and pain numbed by the adrenaline of my excitement, and then nods. "Yep." He sits back and exhales. "That's it. It's done." He closes his eyes for a minute and then opens them to blink up at me. "Go check it in the mirror and tell me what you think."

I do, and I ... I can't quite believe this tattoo is mine, right there on my upper thigh.

I feel almost silly now for automatically assuming the three hearts were for the boys—and also, that at sixteen I'd even *consider* getting a boyfriend tattoo, even one as obscure as this— and now my heart is filled with pride at the meaning Parrish imbued it with.

Me, Tess, Saffron.

"I love it."

Tears prick, and Parrish looks a tad concerned as he hovers behind me with a concerned frown.

"You don't have to—" he starts, but then I'm spinning and my arms fly around his neck. I do this weird 1950s leg pop thing as I kiss him, but only to keep the fresh tattoo from rubbing against his pants. Our mouths collide, and then things are happening like ... his hands are sliding up my bare back beneath my t-shirt, and I can't tell where his tongue begins and mine ends.

My back hits the mirror, Parrish hitches my left leg up, and our kissing is so much more than just kissing. I can't breathe. I'm consumed by him. My thigh aches and burns, but each throb and pulse reminds me of that deep furrow in his brow while he was working, the way he closes his eyes to recenter himself, the thought he put into the sketch ... all of it becomes innuendo and arousal.

He's the one who regains consciousness first, breaking away from me and carefully lowering my leg to the floor. He turns away, paces three quick ruts, and then spins back to me. It takes him several swallows to get any words out.

"As much as I want to fuck you right now, slam your ass into that mirror …" He chokes off and puts a gloved hand to his mouth. It seems to occur to him that there might be some of my blood on that glove, residual ink, whatever. He pulls it away slowly and sighs. "Right. Infection. Nothing is less sexy than infection." Parrish turns and points at the chair. "Sit."

"God, you're bossy," I mumble, and he slaps my ass as I pass him by. I turn and manage to get a nice hard slap on his tight cheeks before he can stop me.

"I swear, if you didn't have a big open wound on your leg right now …" Parrish's voice is a warning, one that I want to defy, to break, just so that he'll come at me with all of that heat and want that's burning like a doused fire inside of him. It just needs a little stroke, a breath of oxygen, a dash of kindling … it's all set to rage wild.

"You have a lovely rump," I declare, and then I sit down in the chair and cross my arms over my chest. "And if you're going to slap mine, I sure as hell am going to slap yours."

"Lovely rump? What planet are you from?" He sits down with a sigh. "The only positive thing about the fire is the loss of those weird horse statues. You truly are an alien creature, Gamer Girl."

"I bet the fire reconstruction crew salvages all of them. Don't be surprised if you wake up one day to find one staring back at you from your pillow." I let my voice swell with smugness, but then Parrish is wiping down the tattoo again, and *ohshitohgodithurts*. My eyes close and I force myself to exhale through the pain as he bandages me up with a roll of what appears to be saran wrap. "Is this, like, kitchen stuff? Like 'wrap up the leftovers' plastic?" I ask, and Parrish shakes his head.

"Not at all. This is breathable, but it's also waterproof. Before you leave for"—Parrish's mouth twitches, and he scowls—"*his* place, I'll take the bandage off, wash it, and after the tattoo dries, apply a new bandage. You can wear that until next weekend provided there's no excessive weeping or fluid." He stands up, snaps his gloves off, and flicks them into the wastebasket. "Voilà. My work here is done."

"Your work here is just getting started."

I … don't know why I say that. It just happens, and then Parrish's mouth is curling up at the edges.

Devious, that's what he is.

"Okay, *now* I can fuck you and slam your ass into that mirror." He moves away, and I gape at his back, rising from the chair and wincing a bit at the soreness in my thigh. There's another, more pressing feeling *between* my thighs anyway, and I wonder where it is that he's going.

He opens his nightstand drawer and withdraws one of the eight condom boxes that he and Chasm ordered via Grubhub. My face flushes red all over again thinking about that night, but mostly, I'm excited. When he was missing, I craved him so desperately that I thought I might break apart from want. Now that he's back, I appreciate him more than I might have otherwise.

A near miss with mortality is a surefire kick in the ass.

Parrish turns back to me and then he reaches over his shoulder, snatches a handful of his t-shirt, and yanks it off. He meets my eyes as he tosses it aside, and I take a few steps closer to him. I remove my own shirt and chuck it on the small sofa that graces the foot of his enormous bed.

"No Super Nintendo controllers this time?" he laments, and I look down to see the black lace bra that I meant to wear during our first time but totally forgot to put on. "I think I liked that better."

"You don't like this?" I ask, pointing at the lacy cups, and then Parrish is shoving his pants down and kicking them aside. He grabs a condom on his way over to me, and then he's taking me into his arms and kissing the life out of me.

ENDGAME ROMANCE

My hands drop to the button on my shorts, tearing it open, and then Parrish is offering an assist; he shoves the white-starred blue denim over my ass and then lets it slide to the floor. I do my best to kick it aside, but not at the expense of *not* kissing him because we're young and needy, and we like each other, and he almost died, and all I care about right now is the feel of him pressed against me.

"What have you done to me?" he mutters against my lips, and I brace myself for more Parrish-isms, that is, life-changing declarations of love and loyalty. He's better at them than anyone else, that's for damn sure. "You soften all my sharp edges, Dakota." Parrish pauses and takes my face in his hands, putting his forehead to mine. "All the emotions that brim over and spill out of me, I want to give them to you. Just you. You're the only one for me."

He pushes his tongue against mine before I have a chance to respond.

I'm not sure how I would anyway because I'm confused, and I don't know what to do.

I'm in love with three boys, and yet, Justin is telling me that I have to force two of them onto other girls? Why? Because he knew. Because he's that smart. He knows that a four-way relationship isn't a likely outcome.

In the end, somebody is going to get hurt.

In the end, I might … have to choose.

My heart wails in brief melancholy, but it's drowned by the ferocity of Parrish's love, the way his hands worship over me, his acute and careful avoidance of my freshly bandaged tattoo. This time, when he hefts my leg up, there's nothing stopping us.

He's somehow managed to get the condom on in the midst of our vigorous groping, and then he's lifting me up, and my ass really does hit the floor-length mirror that's (hopefully) well-attached to the wall behind it.

Our bodies slide together, and it's like that first night all over again.

Emotions run hot and high, and I'm sweating, and I'm staring at him, and he's staring right back at me. We kiss, and it feels fervent. We kiss, and it feels impossible. We kiss, and I know that at least in my endgame, Parrish is one of the pieces that I save.

He moves slowly and purposefully at first, looking at me, kissing me, but then the heat and friction are too much for both of us and we forget to be human. We're two bodies, and two hearts, and nothing else matters. Not Justin. Not Tess. Not the Banks.

It's me and Parrish; we're an unbreakable unit.

Just when I'm starting to see stars, and the feel of his body wrapped tightly up inside of mine becomes the single most important point in the universe, Parrish moves us away from the mirror.

"Oh, the view …" he murmurs, and I realize he's staring at my ass. His bends his knees and lets us fall to the floor together, putting my back on the plush white rug in front of the mirror. We're both entirely naked now, and I can feel him everywhere, touching everything.

It's amazing.

"Faster, harder," I mumble, and he grunts at me in approval.

That's when the moment shifts away from 'lovemaking' and more to … I don't know, mating?

As soon as that thought hits me, I'm embarrassed all over again, but the friction between our bodies quickly erodes the shame. It's just pleasure and fun, and my hands are sliding down Parrish's back and feeling up his beautiful body. I can smell that dewy clover scent, fresh and bright, and I press my nose to the side of his neck just so that I can breathe him.

He does the same, his face next to my hair.

ENDGAME ROMANCE

"Why do you taste and smell like sponge cake?" he mumbles, pausing and panting above me. Our eyes meet again, but I can't speak because I can see the whole world in his irises. Maybe, because in that moment, he *is* my world, and I'm his. "Cake, fresh cream, fruit. That's your smell, your taste."

Parrish adjusts my leg, pushing it up but also making sure he's not hurting me, and then he moves so fast that I can't breathe, that I run my thumbs over his nipples and toss my head back. There's no give on this floor though the softness of the rug keeps it from hurting. It's just his pelvis slamming into mine, heat, movement, and then ... then ...

I finish first, stars exploding in my open eyes, and I'm crying out, and he covers my mouth while apologizing profusely for it. We can't get caught, not right now, not like this. I'd die. And also ... these walls have eyes and ears.

Parrish comes next, digging his feet into the floor, driving even more deeply into me than I thought possible, and then I'm slapping my own hand over his mouth to stifle the sounds. A small squeak escapes me when he very lightly bites my palm, but with his hand still over my lips, it doesn't go anywhere.

With a heavy sigh, he pulls away from me and slumps back against the edge of the sofa.

I stay where I am, but I roll onto my side, pillowing my head on my hands, and then we just look at each other. He smiles first, and I smile back, and then we're both just laughing. We don't stop laughing, not even when our stomachs hurt, and he's bent over, and tears are streaming down my face.

Even in the midst of hell, there are bright spots.

This moment, it'll get me through the inferno of next week.

At least ... I hope it does.

CHAPTER 28

We both forget to move me back to my room afterward, so the first thing I'm greeted with in the morning is Tess, staring down at the pair of us in Parrish's bed. I'm so startled to see her that I scramble up like I've been slapped, wearing panties and a tank top and nothing else, and her eyes drop right to the tattoo on my leg, covered with plastic but obvious, nonetheless.

Oh shit.

Apparently, I must say that aloud because Tess gives me a sharp look in response.

"Oh shit is right. Parrish, get up." She reaches past me to flick him in the nose as he slowly comes to, spots her standing there, and then curses. "I'm at a loss for words right now. Maybe I've been too easygoing on the pair of you? After everything this family's been through, I'm really trying here. But this? Not only did I ask the pair of you to abstain …" She trails off, but she doesn't need to explain what it was that we were supposed to be abstaining from; we all know she means sex. "But how the hell did you think this was going to be okay? The minimum age to get a tattoo in this state is eighteen. How do I explain this?"

It hadn't occurred to me until that moment that she's right, that Justin could use this against her as a case for incompetency.

"Beyond that, because we've all been through such hard times lately, I've been more lax than I should be, but I can't just sit around and let you drink and have sex and tattoo indiscriminately." She picks up the empty wine bottle as proof, and I cringe.

Yeah, we weren't thinking very clearly last night, were we? After we wiped the tears from our eyes, we showered, drank the wine together, and then had sex ... many more times. I don't know what counts as a session, but it was ... it was a lot.

"I didn't think about the custody stuff," I admit, and Tess sighs, closing her eyes so tight that her face wrinkles up a bit.

"He's already here. At this point, your best bet is to hide it and hope he doesn't notice. You." She points at Parrish. "You're off to the office with your father for the day, but we'll be discussing this when you get home." She turns to me next, and her expression mollifies even though I can tell she wants to be angry with me. "We'll talk when you get back. Put some pants on and then go upstairs to change."

Tess waits for me to do that, following me out of the room. She even trails up the stairs after me and stays in the hallway until I come out of my room. She's leaning against the wall with one shoulder, arms crossed, and our eyes meet.

I'm beyond flustered, even though she already knew about me and Parrish being intimate.

Also, maybe I feel like we disrespected her a little bit? She truly has been more understanding than I ever expected or dreamed of. I guess almost losing four of your children in a house fire will put things in perspective. That, and the double kidnappings, and me killing a cop ... Yeah, I think I'm only alive right now because Tess has seen the bottom of life's barrel recently.

"This isn't a stamp of approval for your behavior, but ... do you want me to take you to get birth control pills?" She hesitates there for a minute and then exhales. "I know there are male birth control pills now—and I'll offer the same deal to Parrish—but I don't know that I'd ever trust that someone else was taking proper precautions. It's best if you only have to rely on yourself."

I just stand there, and I don't know what to say.

Yes? Thank you? No? Dear God, please help me?

All of the above.

She's right: there *are* male birth control pills now. For years, the research was stymied because the men participating claimed 'side effects' but then people realized women had been suffering those exact same side effects on a worse level for years, pulled their heads out of their asses, and approved the drug.

"Are you *sure* you're Tess Vanguard?" I ask, trying to be funny as a means of deflection. Instead, she strips some of that softness from her face and gives me one of her bestselling author ice queen glares.

"If you weren't on your way out the door with a man I'm convinced is a literal psychopath, I would be behaving quite differently. I still can't ..." She reaches up and rubs at her forehead, closing her eyes tight. "I can't believe you would get a tattoo without talking to me first. I'm not an entirely unreasonable person, Dakota."

She calls me by the right name again, and my heart swells with both respect and guilt.

"I'm sorry," I whisper back at her, thinking about our movie night, and the way she cried, and all the wonderful things that she said to me. "I just wanted to do something that I wanted to do and not care what anyone else thought."

ENDGAME ROMANCE

Tess opens her eyes to look at me, and then pauses as Justin's bright, easygoing laughter drifts up to us. I hear Laverne's harsh tones followed by Paul storming out of the kitchen in the direction of the backyard.

"We're not done with this conversation," she repeats, and then she's standing up from the wall and heading down the stairs with me following behind her.

Parrish catches my arm at the bottom of the stairs, and Tess turns a look on him.

"I have to clean and redress it." When she doesn't relent immediately, Parrish adds, "I promise we won't fuck in the interim."

"Oh, you only think you got off lightly, son. When you get back from work today with your dad, it's going to be me and you having a private conversation." Tess flicks her hand at us and sighs again. She sounds so damn tired; I don't blame her. I'm tired, too. Pretty sure we're *all* tired. "Go. I'll deal with Justin."

She heads into the kitchen and Parrish pulls me quickly back into his bathroom.

"I used the bug detector," he whispers, squatting down in front of me as I sit on the closed lid of the toilet. I lift up my dress to reveal the tattoo—and also my panties which catch his eye for a hot minute. "Are those aliens on your underwear?"

"It's *Invader Zim*," I hiss back, as if that's proper repartee, as if wearing cartoon alien panties from some obscure early 2000s show is normal behavior. "You used the bug detector for what?"

Parrish wipes the tattoo clean, applies some ointment and then fans at it with his hands as if to dry it off. Meanwhile, he talks quickly.

"I'm coming to dinner on Wednesday; I went in the kitchen just now and accepted Justin's invitation."

"Is that why your dad stormed out of there?" I ask, and Parrish

505

offers up a quick nod. "Did you use the Laverne defense against him?" Another nod. Satisfied that the tattoo is now dry, he applies a fresh bandage … and then slides a finger right up along the crotch of my panties. My breath releases in a rush as Parrish stands up and hauls me to my feet.

"My grandmother despises Caroline, but she also enjoys making Tess sweat." He exhales and then wraps me up in a hug. "We'll get this sorted, okay?"

I nod, and then I kiss him, and it's like an old movie kiss where the characters aren't sure if they'll ever see each other again.

Because you never know what plans the Seattle Slayer has in store, now do you?

———

Justin is unusually quiet as we sit together in his fancy car and make our way back to the house. He waits until we're inside and the door is closed behind us before he reaches out with a single finger and lifts my skirt.

His lips purse as I gasp and slap the fabric back into place.

He isn't perving on me, but still. Nobody should lift somebody else's skirt like that.

"A tattoo?" he asks and then sighs heavily. "How crass. At least it's in a spot where nobody can see it. If I hadn't already gotten my way in court, Tess is right: I certainly could've used this against her." He smiles at me and then reaches out to pinch my cheek. Hard. Way too hard.

I almost wince, but through sheer force of will manage to maintain a stoic expression.

"You're not going to kill someone I love over it?" I quip right back at him, and he goes completely still. The pressure on my cheek intensifies until my skin is screaming, and Justin is tugging me a step closer to him.

"Don't test me, princess." He releases me, but then raises a finger. "I enjoy seeing you indulge in your wants at the expense of Tess' happiness." Ouch. He certainly knows how to phrase things to highlight the worst in them, now doesn't he? "And at least your hair looks nice, although I'm torn on the color." Justin crosses his arms and leans back to study me.

I've worn my hair in a careful bun, as he suggested. Worn one of the dresses he purchased. And I dislike myself for doing so, for capitulating to a terrorist. If I'd brought a knife along with me from Tess', could I end this thing right now?

The temptation is there.

I hate the way my fists clench, and the idea of getting blood on my hands (again) doesn't seem so unappealing. I'm trapped in a cage with invisible but very strong bars. Each one of them is the life of a person I love and care about, and I don't know how else to escape except to bleed the one who put me there.

"You said to ask for what I want? I want to keep my hair this color." I stand firm, hoping that Justin enjoys the slight slant of defiance. "I won't get any more tattoos. Does that seem fair ... Daddy?"

The word comes at the end of a choking cough, but it's there.

He smiles at me.

"Go write your pages for the day, but before you do, take a look at Amin's notes. He's a competent editor, don't you think? With some work, we might be able to get you to Tess' level." Justin turns away and stalks off in the direction of his office, leaving me to sag against the newel post.

Mondays have never been my favorite day of the week, but now? They're pure torture.

Five days a week with Justin Prior is five days too many.

The following morning is spent as they often are here in the Prior house, sitting around the breakfast table in the solarium with Caroline, Delphine, Justin, and Raúl. The latter despises me. He wrinkles his nose whenever I talk, scoffs at my suggestions, and gives off an air of general distaste.

Feeling's mutual, buddy, I think as Justin lists off an array of tasks, and Raúl scurries to accomplish them like the good little go-fer he is. Whenever there's a down moment, he reaches his hand into his pocket and plays with his lighter. I could see the tip of it earlier when he was waiting for Justin to come down the stairs.

He's the one that set the fire.

So, Justin dug up an arsonist to do his dirty work for him? Why the hell not? He already has the poet with a penchant for blood. The black widow as a future wife. Two dutiful daughters. He lost the crooked cop and the useless raping pervert. Who else does he have working for him? Seamus? The Wrights? He had Lumen on strings, too. Shit, maybe he still does, what do I know?

I rest my chin in my hand, my eyes drifting over to Caroline. Does she know that her future husband is the Seattle Slayer? Or rather, does she know that her future husband is *one* of the many moving parts that makes up the Seattle Slayer?

An idea begins to percolate, one that simmers and then boils throughout the day as I retreat to my writing cave (it's being forced on me, sure, but there are worse places to be on this property) and then spend the rest of the afternoon eating ripe pineapple with Delphine.

I like her, even though I probably shouldn't, even though I can't help but remember all of the times Maxx told me that he didn't trust her. He's a damn good judge of character, that boy. At this point, anyone in Medina is capable of anything. As far as I'm concerned, I can only trust the boys and only because they've proven themselves with both actions and words so many times over that I've lost count.

In the evening, I seek Caroline out. She's seated on the deck that overlooks the water, sipping wine and flipping through the pages of a glossy magazine. In the decadent colors of sunset—all that molten fire bleeding into delicate peach and softening to an azure kiss above the clouds—she looks so much like Parrish that I ache for him.

I had an adopted family that loved me. I had a bio mom that fought tooth-and-nail to get me back.

Parrish's bio mom? She barely acknowledges his existence. I suppose she could be worse; she could be Justin.

"Hello Caroline," I say, plopping into the seat across from her.

Her gold-flecked brown eyes lift from the page to my face, and a tiny furrow (microscopic really, because of the Botox) appears between her brows. It's similar to the one Parrish wore as he inked me last night (only similar because, again, the Botoxing), and I find my breath catching in my throat. I *do* talk to the boys while I'm here, but it's all baseless dribble.

We discuss video games or—in Maxx's case only—new hiking routes, Whitehall gossip, social media trends, summer bucket lists, that sort of thing. I'd enjoy all of that if the conversations were private, if I had any true free will, and if I wasn't stressed out about Veronica Fisher, and the Slayer's looming request.

I have until the end of the summer to kill a girl? To slaughter one of my peers? To punish the adults in Justin's life who betrayed them by murdering their child?

Now, if he'd asked me to straight punch Veronica, I could do that. I mean, I did it once, and I'd do it all over again in a heartbeat. If he'd asked me to vandalize her new Tesla, or throw her MacBook in a lake, dump a steaming hot cortado on her, then sure. I would do all of those things because she had her girls cut me up with knives and livestreamed it.

But killing her?

No.

Not gonna happen.

"Hello Dakota." Caroline forces a smile that's as fake as the ones I used to put on for Tess.

I stare at Caroline, and she stares right back at me. I hesitate for so long that she actually turns her attention back to her magazine and keeps reading. *It's now or never, Kota. Make your move.* I've thought about what I'm about to do all day, and no matter how many times I run through plausible scenarios, I come to the same conclusion.

Justin prides himself on staying true to his words—when it comes to me, that is.

He never specifically told me that I couldn't, um, 'communicate' with Caroline Bassett.

I reach into my back pocket and withdraw a packet of papers, tossing them onto the table beside Caroline's wineglass. She glances down at them before looking up at me, and I smile. It's a real smile this time because, this part of the game at least, is going to be fun.

You hurt Parrish. Your presence in Medina continues to hurt Parrish; it hurts Tess, too. I hope this moment sucks serious ass for you.

"What's this?" She closes the magazine, sets it aside, and then takes a long, slow, indulgent drink of her wine before finally deigning to unfold the printed pages. Caroline's slim shoulders stiffen up, and she spends an inordinate amount of time looking at the first page before quickly parsing through the others.

She lifts her gaze to mine. There's a fear there, but also a righteous rage. She wants to retaliate against me, shut me up, threaten me, but then her eyes flick to one of the security cameras attached to the house's exterior wall, and I know she's thinking about Justin.

If she kills his kid, she can't marry him. If they *had* already been married, I might've gone about this in an entirely different manner.

"Three dead husbands, three big fortunes." I reach out and tap the edge of one of the pages with a single finger. "Their deaths were a bit shocking considering all three were in good health prior to their kicking the bucket, but you know how these things are."

Caroline carefully folds the pages and then sets the stack on the surface of the table.

"Clever, bringing up my dead husbands." She smiles at me and then reclines in her chair, crossing her legs and allowing her silk gown to drape luxuriously around her. "But if you think dredging up my past misfortunes will keep me from becoming your wicked stepmother, you'll be sorely disappointed. Justin knows my history, including my failed engagement to Paul Vanguard. It's all out there."

"Did he tell you that he was the Seattle Slayer?" I ask, hoping like hell that he hasn't. If he already has, then this is a pointless exercise, one that I'm sure he'll chastise me for later. If he hasn't, then maybe I can use Caroline against him?

She's the black widow type, right? Clearly, she's here for his money. If she is or isn't planning on murdering husband number four, I have no idea. But if she found out he was a notorious serial killer? How easy would it make things for her? She could claim self-defense. She could win Justin's fortune without having to hide his death or move; she could stay right here in Medina with the elites she so fervently wishes to be a part of.

"Excuse me?" Caroline seems genuinely confused, and I feel the first surge of triumph in me. Maybe this will amount to nothing? Maybe—likely—Justin was already planning on telling Caroline the full truth after the wedding, recruiting her to do his killing instead of her own? That's my guess on this one. If so, there's a possibility that all I've done is speed up the process of her finding out.

But it's worth the gamble, for sure.

"Well, part of the Seattle Slayer anyway," I correct with another smile. "There are multiple people involved; he's simply the head of the beast, so to speak."

There's another long, awkward pause there, and then I stand up, heading into the house and up to my room. I don't run into Justin, and he doesn't seek me out. That's an important clue. It means he doesn't have the manpower to watch me every single second. After all, he only has so many cronies and they have other duties to attend to. As for the man himself, he's quite busy preparing for the public launch of Milk Carton (and arranging murders). Oh, and also, he makes me watch Disney movies with him.

Villainennial. Do you like that one? Villain plus Millennial? Too much, huh?

Regardless, it shows me that it's possible for Justin to miss something here and there.

He isn't a god, much as he thinks he is. No, he is painfully, impossibly human like the rest of us.

CHAPTER 29

Maxx's bike clears a jump and catches air. For a beautiful instant, there he is, silhouetted against the sun in his lime green and black riding gear, and then he's hitting the dirt track and taking off at dizzying speeds that have me leaning forward and curling my hands around the edge of the fence that lines the track.

"You look like a worried wife," Tiffany Wright says, pausing beside me and chuckling. Other than our brief acquaintance at the hospital, this is the first time I've met Maxx's sister. She, too, seems to prefer calling him X, and the pair of them remind me of Maxine and me.

It was a little odd at first, seeing her sling her arm around Maxx's broad shoulders and rubbing her fist against his hair, but after about an hour, I realized that size doesn't matter. Once an older sibling, always an older sibling. She is the clear boss, despite how his alpha male hide might prickle at the idea.

"Do I?" I ask, and then I do my best to curl my ring finger up in my fist so that it doesn't catch the sunlight. There's not a single

513

person in Medina—or connected to anyone in Medina in any way, shape, or form—that doesn't know about Chasm's proposal.

Tiffany looked at me oddly at first when Maxx reintroduced me as his girlfriend, but then she just mumbled something like *crazy rich weirdos,* and I knew we would get along great. He also made her promise not to tell anyone which she took in stride. Her dark brows went up and her face, so similar to her brother's but with a decidedly feminine cast to her features, proved that she wasn't buying what her little brother was selling.

Still, she agreed to keep our secret and moved on.

If only it didn't *have* to be a secret.

Damn you, Justin, and your bullshit directives. Encouraging me to get Maxx and Maxine back together, how cruel is that? As if they ever could or would reunite after he slept with her little sister. I cringe and rub at my face, but I can't keep my gaze from tracking Maxx's progress as he takes the turns nice and tight, and hits the throttle just before every jump.

"He's been at this his whole life," Tiffany explains, crossing her arms on the edge of the fence. She's dressed all in black today, with *Wright Family Racing* stitched or printed on all of her clothing. "Don't worry so much." Tiffany pauses and then frowns, glancing over at me and then cocking a suspicious brow. "Unless you're just checking him out? Either way, that stare of yours could melt plastic."

I flush all over and Tiffany howls with laughter. She's raucous and loud, and I knew I liked her within the first thirty seconds of meeting her again. At the hospital, she was slightly more subdued —for obvious reasons.

"It's fine, it's fine." She waves a hand at me. "Every female friend I've ever had has been into my brother. You are not the first." Tiffany—or, I guess, everyone just calls her Tiff—looks me up and down with emerald eyes that match her brother's. "Could you be the last? He gazes at you like you're the only human being on earth."

I open and close my mouth, but no words will come out.

The hot sun beats down on my back, and I wonder if Oregon is aways hotter than Washington, or if it's just today. It was pleasantly warm, but with a nice, sea-kissed breeze back in Medina. Here? It's sweltering. I can feel sweat dripping down my spine and beading on my forehead, but I tell myself that only has to do with the heat and not the words that have just left Tiffany Wright's mouth.

Maxx finishes his final round on the track, parks his bike, and takes his helmet off. Does he mean to shake his thick, lush hair out with his fingertips as the sunshine turns it a burnished chocolate? Does he know what he's doing when he accepts a metal water bottle from his father and splashes it onto his handsome face? Is he even aware of what it looks like when he drinks deeply, and the strong column of his throat moves with every swallow?

We drove down to Portland—or rather just east of Portland—to meet his father and sister on the track. The drive took about three hours, but we left early enough that we got here right around lunch. Chasm had some tutoring thing today and Parrish, well, he's not allowed to skip work at Paul's office. Seems Tess is dead serious about that.

So, here we are, just me and Maxx. Justin didn't seem to give a shit when I asked if I could go, other than to warn me that Chasm is my primary concern and that, of course, everyone in Medina has affairs, but that they know how to keep them to themselves.

Eye twitch.

Anyway, Maxine took our grandparents down to Eugene for the day to show them where she lives and goes to school, and this was the perfect opportunity for me and Maxx to spend some time together.

On the way down, we listened to Emerald City Murder Podcast and all their theories about Heath Cousins, the cop that I killed and that I try very, very hard not to think about. But it's there, always in the back of my mind, the strange popping sensation of the knife, the reality that, when it came down to it, the Slayer really and truly could get me to murder someone.

Exactly as he wanted.

The small thrill I got from turning myself in has faded around the edges, and now I'm just dreading my next conversation with the two FBI agents.

Maxx's father—Hamilton, the one with the dark hair—is speaking to him in hushed tones, and I can see the tightness in X's shoulders. As soon as he climbs off his bike and stalks back toward the large toy-hauler that's parked nearby, I chase after him.

His face is set in an annoyed frown, but he smiles as soon as he sees me.

"Did you like watching?" he asks, which comes across dirty as hell, but probably wasn't meant to. That is, until that smile hooks a little sharper, and he lets his gaze trail down my body and then back up again. "Did I impress you? I was trying really hard, in case you couldn't tell."

"According to Tiffany, you've been at this since forever, and that's how you always ride." I lift my chin in mock defiance, closing my eyes for the briefest of instances and then opening them to see Maxx Wright in my face.

His smell … I wish I could explain the way it makes me feel. There's that faint sporty-citrusy scent to him that there always is, but fresh sweat? I'm attracted to the smell of *fresh sweat*? I won't lie. I surreptitiously Googled it on my phone (yes, even knowing Justin would see) and discovered that there really are chemicals in dudes' sweat that arouses women (straight and bisexual ones, anyway). Old sweat doesn't have the same effect, just those shiny, brand-new droplets from working out in the warm sun.

"Are you saying you weren't impressed?" he asks me, tilting his head slightly to one side. He could kiss me if he just moved in a fraction of an inch. *Please, please move in that fraction. A half inch would do it, just a half freaking inch.*

"Not in the slightest," I blatantly lie, but I'm only teasing and he knows it.

"Would you be more impressed if I used these muscles to lift you up and fuck you against the side of this truck?" The words are breathy and, as soon as he says them, Maxx's eyes widen and he blinks several times before cursing and turning away.

I jog after him as he heads in the direction of a brown brick building that apparently houses a women's locker room on one side, and a men's on the other. I can't follow him in there, but I do go all the way up to the threshold before skidding to a stop.

X pauses to glance back at me, turning fully around in his green and black gear and peering at me from the shadows. I cannot even deal with the way his long-sleeved riding shirt stretches over his muscles, or the way his boots buckle around his thick calves.

"Why did you run from me?" I ask him, knowing there isn't anyone else in the locker room. We're the only people at the track right now. "You can't say something like that and then run."

"Kota." Maxx walks right up to the doorway and then puts his arms out, bracing his elbows on either side of the doorjamb. "I can and will run away after saying something like that. I told you before that I don't trust myself. You're my first real girlfriend, my first kiss, my first ..." He trails off and closes his eyes, breathing in deep and then exhaling sharply. "My first—and hopefully only —sexual partner."

Oh God.

Oh my God.

Oh my fucking God.

What did this boy just say? Why am I living for it? How do I deal with the fact that, when I'm with each boy by himself, he's the only one I want? When I'm with them all, I'm … confused. I rub at my face.

"You ran away because you're scared?" I ask him, remembering all the things he told me during our first sexual encounter together. He doesn't trust himself. He might not, but I do. "I have full faith in you, Maxim Wright. If you would relax a little, I think you'd see that you're not a sadist or a pervert or a brute, just a bit cocky, a tad dominant, way overconfident—but in a good way."

"Oh, I see," he says, leaning down so close that I'm tempted to bite the plump, pinkness of his lower lip. "Overconfident? You think that's all this is? Dakota, if my father and sister weren't here, I really would peel my pants down, lift you up, and screw you against the side of that truck."

"Prove it sometime." I put my hands on either side of his face, and then I kiss him. He goes completely still, and I decide that I can't push this any further, drawing back—

Maxx yanks me into the locker room, shoves the door closed, and pushes my back up against it. His mouth descends fiercely on mine, taking control of the kiss as I rest my hands on his broad shoulders. I can't get enough of his smell, his taste, the sounds he's making or the way he's pushing up against me like he might really and truly do it, throw caution to the wind, and have sex with me right here and now.

One of his gloved hands finds my breast through the fabric of my shirt, and then he's squeezing and kneading it, dragging moans up that he kisses right off of my lips.

"If I had a condom …" he starts, and then he moves away from me with considerable effort, like ripping a piece of taffy in half, the way it clings, it sticks, it pulls. "I almost don't even care."

I gasp at that and clamp a hand over my mouth, and Maxx gives me a strange, little half-smile in response.

"See what I mean? But no, you're in high school. That's fucked. We can have babies in our late thirties." He points at the door behind me. "Now go away and let me shower; I smell."

"You smell amazing to me." I'm not sure why I say that or why it's any more or less embarrassing than anything else we've said to each over the last fifteen minutes, but I turn and sprint the hell out of that bathroom like I'm on fire.

I can hardly breathe as I bend over, palms on my upper thighs, and struggle to control the raging surge of hormones inside of me. It's not as if I never touched myself before sleeping with Parrish. Most everyone does. But … but …

"Stupid boys. Stupid sweat smell. Stupid full, pouty mouths."

"Wow. You've got it bad, don't you?" Tiffany asks, surprising me enough that I have to choke back a scream as I stand up straight, doing my best to act nonchalant and impossibly cool. I say impossibly because I am one-hundred-percent, undiluted, fair-trade, ethically sourced dork. Her eyes drop to my breasts, and I wonder for a brief minute if she isn't gay or bi and is checking me out. But then she snorts and clamps a gloved hand over her own mouth to stifle the sound.

I glance down to see that Maxx has left dirty handprints all over my white Lululemon exercise top. Justin picked it, as he does everything else, and I don't entirely feel like myself in it, but … *there's a hand-shaped dirt splotch over my right tit. Fantastic.*

"Do you need to borrow a new shirt?" Tiff chokes out and, cheeks and chest red with shame, I nod.

She fetches one for me, and I slip into the women's locker room to change.

I take my sweet time, washing my hands, fluffing my hair (I let it down as soon as I left Justin's) and hoping that Tiffany will be on the track by the time I come out, so we don't have to talk about what just happened.

Instead, both her and Maxx are waiting outside the door, him with his arms crossed over the front of the t-shirt I bought for him, and her with her hands on her hips.

"Hey there," she calls cheerily, and Maxx gives her a sharp look of warning. "Does the shirt fit?"

It does. It's a bit tight in the, um, chest region, but that makes sense since Tiffany has a taut, athletic build, and I've got ... well, boobs. It's lime green with *Wright Family Racing* written on the front in black cursive. It rides up just a tad in the front, showing off the dual piercings in my belly button.

X's eyes catch on them and he swallows hard, tearing his gaze away—the taffy thing again—to look at Tiff.

"Really?" he asks her as I move up to stand beside them, and he adjusts his gaze to look down at me again.

"What? Does it look that terrible?" I ask, tugging at the bottom of the shirt. Maxx reaches out and grabs my shoulders, turning me around as Tiffany snickers. He traces something on my back, and I shiver as his finger glides over the t-shirt's smooth fabric.

"*X Wright's Fangirl,*" he reads, and Tiffany's snicker turns into deep belly laughter. I spin back around, smacking Maxx in the face with my hair, and causing him to do one of those weird, sharp inhale things. "You're hilarious, you know that?" Maxx turns an apologetic look on me. "Do you want me to get a different shirt? We have a whole box of plain *Wright Family Racing* tees in the truck."

"Why is there a shirt that says *X Wright's Fangirl* on it?" I ask, and that just causes Tiffany to laugh harder. Hamilton makes his way over to where we're standing and places his hands on his hips.

"Oh, you gave her the fangirl shirt." He chuckles at that, too, and Maxx rolls his eyes to the sky. It's my first time really seeing him around his family, and I like it. He's less stern and domineering, and his behavior is more akin to a regular nineteen-year-old's. "We had a whole set of those made for Maxx's first professional race way back when. Well, mine and Laurent's said *Fanboy,* but otherwise they were the same."

"We should probably get going," Maxx tells his dad, putting his own hands on his hips, and then the two men are staring at each other, and I can see that Hamilton is bristling with things he wants to say. I wonder if it's about Maxx's career in motocross or about his staying in Medina for the summer or something else entirely.

I can't forget that Maxx's parents encouraged him to date Maxine, to get back together with her after they broke up, or most especially that they talked badly about me to him before we'd even met. With Laurent scoring a brand-new job at Milk Carton, a remote work job with three times the pay as his position in Paul's office? I smell Justin's handiwork.

"Where are you off to?" Hamilton asks, but Maxx just shrugs his shoulders as if he doesn't know. Only, he does because he has a bicycle in the back of his Jeep and also this really cool seat with a backrest that attaches over the rear wheel. Yes, folks: Maxim Wright is going to take me on a scenic bike path, and I don't even have to pedal.

Is he real? I stare at him, and his eyes flick to me. There must be something in the way I'm staring at him because he lifts both brows, and then wets his lower lip before reaching out and snatching my hand in his.

"We're taking a bike ride, but we haven't decided where just yet. Whatever strikes our fancy." Maxx pulls me along with him, and I wave goodbye to both Tiff and Hamilton before we're climbing into the Jeep together. "Thank fuck that's over," he murmurs, and then he starts the vehicle and off we go.

"Is everything okay?" I ask, and now that I know the origin of the shirt I'm wearing, I'm actually sort of thrilled to have it. Tiff said I could keep it, too.

"Why were you looking at me like that just now?" he asks, glancing over at me as he pulls off the dirt road that leads to the track and onto the pavement. The road we're on is close to Portland, but it's buried amongst logging country; it's basically a different world out here.

"Like how?" I wonder, because I'm not even sure I remember what he's talking about.

"Like …" And here Maxx trails off, and a smile crosses his lips again. He has a habit of doing that, you know, smiling all cute and whatever. "You were lucky."

"I *am* lucky. You're taking me on a scenic bike ride, and I don't have to do any work. What more is there to say?"

He continues smiling, but some of the hardness in his gaze softens.

"Do you want to tell me what you and your dad were arguing about?" I ask, but he shakes his head.

"Not really. It'll just piss me off all over again, and I don't want to be pissed off today." He glances my way, and there it is again, that gorgeous fucking smile. "I want to take my new girlfriend out on a bike ride and show her the prettiest places that other people don't know about." He pauses there, and his hands tighten slightly on the wheel before he looks my way again. "We're there, aren't we? At the girlfriend thing? I mean, if I jumped the gun and—"

I feel my cheeks heat, but I'm waving my arms around again like the noodle-man, so clearly I'm not as cool as I think I am. Which, to be fair, isn't very cool at all. I explained that to you.

"You didn't jump the gun, not at all," I assure him, leaning back in the seat and staring down at my lap. I'm wearing Lululemon pants, too, in a teal color that totally clashes with the lime green shirt I'm wearing now. Not that I care, but I bet Justin would. He seems determined to mold me into the perfect, little socialite/serial killer. Those two things might seem at odds at first, but really, they have a lot in common.

Case in point: both require a cold detachment, a sense of selfishness and entitlement, and a lot of acting and posturing in social situations. See? Socialite/serial killer. It's just the murdering people thing that sets them apart.

"So we're dating? Like, officially dating?" he asks, and he doesn't look up directions on his phone or his car. He seems to know exactly where it is that we're going, leading us further away from the track and into the Tillamook State Forest. Some of the areas we drive past have been clear-cut, but there are baby trees sprouting here and there. Hey, I'm all down for logging land; it's infinitely better than tract housing. "I realized last night that we hadn't actually had a conversation about this."

He's gesturing now with his right hand, and I get the idea that maybe, just maybe, Maxim is nervous.

I turn in my seat to stare at him, and he stops gesturing, firmly planting his hand on the wheel as I reach out and run my fingers through his thick, dark hair.

"Kota," he warns, back to using that stern voice of his. "Do you want to crash off the side of this mountain?"

"How many girlfriends have you had in the past?" I ask him, trying and failing not to think of Maxine. God, he really is perfect, especially for her. But maybe he's more perfect for me? I chew on my lower lip and then pinch my own thigh so that I'll stop doing it.

"Three?" he says it like it's a question, and I keep staring at him. "The first two barely counted. We hung out a bit, went to a few dances and school events together, and held hands. Only Maxine ... Still, we didn't kiss. You can ask her again if you don't believe me."

"Why wouldn't I believe you?" I retort, and he opens his mouth, snaps it shut. Sighs.

"Why are you doing this to me?" he wonders aloud, like he's just stumbled on something so strange and unique that he's awestruck. Whether good or bad, I can't tell.

"Doing what?" I ask as we pass through shadowed forest roads with thick, dewy undergrowth. There are ferns everywhere around here, Jurassic looking ones. Everything is wet and moist, and moss clings to the trees. Hell, there are even *ferns* growing out of the trees. It's beautiful and very, very remote. I check my phone to see that the service has cut off, smile, and then chuck it into the back seat. Going hiking regularly has made Justin believe that I like hiking, and so he doesn't say anything about it.

Really, it's just the perfect way to ditch his tech.

That's all I want to do right now anyway, throw technology out the window and do things. I love gaming—it's built into my identity—and I can learn and execute a viral TikTok dance like nobody's business, but the feeling of being watched and monitored all the time, I can't deal with that. Anyway, the more I get out and try new things, the more I'm thinking that I might actually like them.

"Acting too cute for words," he says, and I bite my lip so hard that it hurts. "Telling me it was love at first sight in the coffee shop and expecting me not to think about that comment obsessively for, like, years."

"It's the first and only time I've ever felt that way," I explain, looking down at my lap and forcing myself to breathe normally and not pant like a crazy person. "When I met Parrish, when I met Chasm, there were strong emotions there, but not the butterflies-in-a-spring-garden-inside-your-heart-thing."

"Do you purposefully make shit like that up or does being cute come naturally to you?" he asks me, sounding breathless. Maxx turns left up a bumpy hill, and tree branches scrape the sides of the car as we plunder over potholes. This road isn't well-kept which means it isn't well-used which means privacy and no people, thank the gods. "Anyway, I want you to be my girlfriend—officially. Even if Justin doesn't want us to be public about it, we can hide it until we deal with him. I only care about how you and I feel, and how Parrish and Chasm are responding to it."

"I want you to be my boyfriend, Maxim Wright Men's Magazine," I tell him, and he stops the car right then and there. He puts it in park and then turns to look at me, and I find that I'm leaning away from him because the urge to kiss him and then crawl into his lap is just *there*, and it's strong, and my entire body is having a wild, desperate reaction to touch his.

Yeah, no wonder we were so uncomfortable around one another before; our sexual chemistry is off the charts.

"Okay, it's official. You're mine; I'm yours." He reaches out to take my hand, rubbing his thumb over my knuckles and stealing away my will to live. *You're a boy crazy nut, Kota.* I never thought I would be one. Actually, I don't think that I am. I think I'm a hopeless romantic who just happened to be pushed into a high-stakes situation with three really awesome dudes, and fell hard and fast. "If Parrish or Chasm has a problem with it, we'll talk it out with them, but I don't want that to be what ends us. If we're enjoying being together, I just want to keep doing it."

"You're saying you don't mind sharing?" I ask him, and he snorts. His grip on my hand becomes something more. A tad possessive, a lot sensual, an invitation.

"Oh, I mind," he tells me, and his tone shifts enough that I lift my gaze from our joined hands to his handsome face. "I just don't think it's a deal-breaker is all." He releases me, and I feel that blazing heat of his touch go with him, leaving me in the cold.

We continue on for a ways after that, but neither of us is

talking. I do notice when I glance over at him that he's smiling to himself and, when I flip the visor down on my side of the car, I see that I'm smiling, too.

We're into each other.

That's a straight fact.

When we arrive at the parking area, I'm surprised to see a wide dirt path that disappears into the trees. I'd expected something a bit more rugged, but there's a sign nearby that claims the trail itself is upkept by a local bicycling club.

"This is amazing," I admit as I climb out and look around the lush vegetation, the soaring trees, and the distant trickle of water that turns out to be a small stream under a bridge. The wooden bridge is the start of the path, and then it winds casually and lazily through the woods until it disappears from sight.

I'd be worried about riding on the back of the bike if, you know, Maxx didn't have the body of Adonis. I learned today that it's not really a good idea to go two-up on a dirt bike, but this is a compromise I can live with.

"Helmet," he says, passing one over to me. It's black, and it fits perfectly, even with my mass of black and green hair cascading out from underneath it. He puts one on himself—this one is lime green —and then flips open the seat on the back of the bike. As I watch, X unloads a small cooler with two metal water bottles, and a glass container that I'm pretty sure came from Chasm. The food inside is different though; I see veggies. "Lunch," he explains as he fills the seat up and then snaps the cushion closed, locking it in place.

I remember how our first hike went, how the dude had everything but the kitchen sink in his bag.

A warm thrill takes over me as I watch him, strong and confident and capable. That's what he's sensing in himself: his competence and his capabilities and his natural tendency toward leadership. He perceives those things as somehow making him this hulking cave-bro who drags women around by the hair. He's afraid of that, but fortunately for us both, that isn't the case.

He's just a planner. He's a caregiver. He's a leader. He allows Parrish to take control because Parrish is like a shark fin in the waters of Medina; he knows when to strike and bite and bleed. Maxx would prefer to be up on the boat looking down with a spear in hand. Chasm is the first mate, charting the course, taking over in rough seas, and swabbing the deck.

"Alright, Kota, climb on," X says, and he can't hide the thrill in his voice. The guy just spent over an hour riding around a dirt track in the hot heat, and he's excited all over again at the thought of exercising.

"You're so weird." I chuckle as Maxx swings his leg over the bike and then turns to watch as I climb on behind him. There's only one way to sit, and that's with my arms wrapped around X's hard, warm body. Extra bonus that he's wearing the t-shirt I bought him. Parrish did, too. Now all I need is Chasm to don that BTS merch like an ARMY fanboy to make things right.

"How so?" Maxx asks, and then off we go. I can't help but notice the muscles in his arms and upper back as he steers the bike, or how powerful his legs are; he has absolutely no problem peddling me around, not even when the terrain gets a bit rougher around the corner. We approach a moderate incline and still, he doesn't slow.

"You make me feel cared for. I like that. I'm not somebody who gets up early to make breakfast and lunch for myself, who remembers to pack a towel on a hike, who sets up a bike with a special passenger seat just to make a day out that much more comfortable."

"You like that sort of stuff?" he asks absently, and I push up a bit of his shirt so that I can see a hint of the angel wing tattoos that he has on his broad back. *Delicious.* "Is that attractive to you? It just sort of seems … normal to me."

"It's weird to me, and I love it."

He rides for a few minutes before responding.

"You're weird to me, and I love you."

Oh. Um. Okay. I'm not at all embarrassed and freaking out and obsessing over his words.

We go quiet for a while, and I rest my cheek against his back, wishing I didn't have to wear a helmet so I could rest more comfortably. The sunlight falls through the trees in a dappled dance, stirred by a gentle breeze that's offset by the warmth of the day. There are birds singing in the trees and several small waterfalls that surprisingly still have a trickle, even in an especially hot, dry summer.

We bike for nearly an hour before X pulls over and sets up our picnic. There was no room for a blanket, but there's an old picnic table seated beside the creek. The water weaves back and forth beneath the path, covered with metal grates or sometimes proper bridges. Even with the picnic table as an option, we opt to sit on the moss-covered embankment instead.

"How do you feel now compared to when we sat in front of that waterfall and talked?" he asks me, biting into an apple and staring into the woods with those brilliant green eyes of his. They truly are jewel-like, two emeralds in a classically handsome face. "Last time, you said you were afraid that Tess would never feel like a mother, and that you might go back to New York and not fit in there either."

"You listen," I say, and I'm impressed. A lot of people *hear* but they certainly don't listen, and even if they do, they don't commit what they learned to memory like that. "And you told me that I shouldn't wait for the world to make space for me, that I had to carve some out for myself."

He smiles at that, letting his gaze slide my way as I open the lid on the glass container to find sliced cucumber, baby carrots, cherry tomatoes, and hummus. I dip a carrot and snack on it as X watches me.

"You listen, too," he replies, and then we both go silent, enjoying the relative solitude and the absence of traffic, plane, or people sounds. It's more refreshing than you might think. I see now why the insult *go touch grass* is so popular on the internet. Maybe more angry people need to go outside? Who knows?

"Tess and I are making headway," I admit. It's true. And it's also surprising considering the intensity at which Justin has tried to sabotage our relationship. I had to beg her to tell me about Justin Prior right after Parrish went missing, painting myself as a callous asshole. I had to look her right in the face as she admitted that Justin raped her and do nothing. I had to ignore her pleas the day after the fire when she begged me to see what a crazy fucker he is. "I, um, want to show you something."

I sit back on the grass and then I shimmy out of my pants just enough so that X can see my fresh tattoo. When I glance his way, I see that his eyes are wide and that he's looking not at the tattoo but at me with my pants shoved down like ... well ... um.

"The tattoo." I point at it wildly, and his eyes finally land on the square of plastic stuck to my thigh. He looks at it for a moment before his gaze drifts to my panties, and I yank the pants back up with a huff. "Parrish gave me my first tattoo."

"Parrish is selfish for firsts," X growls out, and I shiver all over. "Tess knows about this?" He does his best to soften his voice, but I'm not sure that it's working. There's a brand-new tension in the air that's clinging to my skin like bits of dandelion fluff. I swipe at my arms, but it clings stubbornly.

"She found out on accident when she walked in on me and Parrish in bed together."

X groans and puts his face in his hand.

"I like the tattoo, but I don't like the idea of that, you and Parrish having sex." He bites into the apple again, finishing off the last of the pale flesh, and then chucks the core into the woods. He offers me up an explanatory look. "It's biodegradable; I wouldn't otherwise litter."

"The fact that you found that information immediately pressing to relay to me tells me all I need to know about your personality."

There's a brief lull there as I set the container aside and put the lid on it.

And then Maxx is rolling over, and his huge body is positioned above mine, and we're kissing like we've been separated for eons. My hands roam over his back and shoulders as he sears my mouth with the promise of heat and pleasure.

"Could we actually … right here?" I ask, and X pauses, reaching into his pocket and withdrawing a condom. The smirk that stretches across his face is an easy *yes* to that question.

"You told me to prove it. This is me, fucking proving it."

Um.

Wow.

"Did you really just say that?" I breathe, and then he's looking at me with an almost painfully serious expression on his handsome face.

"I really just said that," he whispers, lips hovering close to mine. He leans in and captures my mouth with a fierce, hungry kiss, one that speaks volumes more than words ever could. *I want you to be mine; I wish you were mine; you always should've been mine.* X pulls back before I can even fully register the power of that kiss, and then he puts his forehead to mine. "I thought I was going to break that day at the coffee shop, after you ran Maxine off and made her cry."

"Justin …" I start, but Maxx knows. He knows everything, and I know I wouldn't have made it this far without him by my side.

Not only has he been solid and reliable and comforting, but I'd be four siblings short if he hadn't intervened.

If he hadn't wanted me so badly that he went back to get his damn tux.

"When you grabbed me, Kota, I felt it everywhere." He offers me up a look and then uses his right hand to push against my chest until I'm falling back into the soft bed of moss, listening to the gentle trickle of the creek, staring up at his face silhouetted against the lush canopy. "It hurt to untangle your arms from around my waist."

When I move to put them around his neck, he stops me, grabbing my right wrist with his left hand and locking his fingers around it. He presses it down into the moss, and I suck in a sharp breath.

His green eyes are deadly serious right now.

"What are the chances of somebody stumbling on us here?" I ask, and Maxx offers the slightest shake of his head.

"I have no idea. Unlikely?" There's a clear question mark attached to the end of that word. "Does it matter? I want you right now." He exhales, expression set and determined. "If you don't want this, you can tell me, and I'll back off." X lifts his brows, and all the things he said to me after our first night together come drifting back.

"I pulled your hair and flipped you over to do you from behind during my first time, and that was only a fraction of the things I wanted to do."

"I know you're afraid of yourself, Maxim, but I'm not." I relax and exhale, closing my eyes as Maxx releases this growling sound of frustration under his breath, putting his lips to the side of my throat and breathing hard against my skin. I can smell that sporty fragrance of his, but I'm too scared to ask if he's wearing cologne or body spray or something.

It's been well-established at this point that I have a scent fetish, and that I smell dewy clovers, mint chocolate ice cream, and *Cool Blue Wave* mocktails when there no such things around.

"Your personality smells nice."

That's what comes out of my mouth, on this dream-like romantic afternoon with Maxim Wright, a dude who's built like a fitness model, who's overprotective but fiercely gentle, who picked up a knife and considered taking the rap for a murder he didn't commit.

"My personality?" Maxx starts, and then he shakes his head, and the motion causes that dark chocolate hair of his to brush against my skin and make me writhe. I dig my heels into the soft earth, close my eyes tight, and arch my back. "I'm going to fuck you, okay?"

"Are you asking me?" I whisper, but I don't open my eyes. I keep them shut so that I can focus on the sensation of his hand as he lets it drift down to the apex of my thighs. Maxx flicks a finger across my aching heat, and an involuntary gasp escapes me.

"Not exactly." He retreats a bit, tearing off my shoes before he goes about yanking my pants entirely off and tossing them aside. Still, I keep my eyes closed. I hear birdsong. I feel the heat of his palms. I sense the frenetic energy brewing inside of him.

He likes to be in charge. He likes to make snacks and plan hikes, to gripe at Chasm and Parrish for not doing things the way he likes things to be done. And to be fair, he's good at all of that. If we listened to Maxx as much as we ignored his advice, we all might be in a better place.

When his mouth presses up against the skin just north of my bellybutton, my eyes fly open and I fist my hands in his hair. *Shirt, off.* It's the only thing I can think about, shedding my clothes so that I can touch him more, feel his muscular body pressed tight to mine.

But when I try to grab hold of it, he snatches my hand in tight fingers.

"Leave the shirt," he tells me, eyes glittering. "I like the *fangirl* thing."

Maxx lifts up onto his knees and undoes his pants, opening the condom package and unrolling it over his shaft as I sit propped on my elbows to watch. Our first time, we were in a rush, harried and afraid for Parrish, pressured and lacking necessary privacy. Our second (and third) time, we were in the arcade, and it was more hormonal and needy than anything else.

This is … I'm not sure exactly what this is, but next time, I'd love to do it in a bed, alone, in the dark, and without any time constraints.

"Thoughts?" he asks me, exhaling heavily and wrapping his fingers around his dick. I'm mesmerized by the sight of that, and it takes some effort to look up at his face.

"I was thinking about the next time we have sex."

"Already?" Maxx asks, and the smile that he gives me is devastating. He's a heartbreaker, this one. I just hope I caught him early, cutting off that career right in its tracks. There shouldn't be any hearts to break if he only ever holds mine in his hands, right? "I love that."

He drops back down, straddling me on all fours, palms on either side of me, knees on either side of my own. The heat between us seems to burn, that tension we carry twisting and morphing into an impossible monster.

"I don't want you to be engaged to Chasm," he murmurs, annoyance coloring his voice as he gets up close and personal with my lips, talking against them more so than he's kissing me. It's almost frustrating, but I like the anticipation too much to complain. "You deserve better than some rich asshole. You and me, Kota, we're from the same planet. We don't eat risotto quenelles and garden snails for dinner; we don't think it's normal to get a BMW for a sixteenth birthday present; I went to *public* school once upon a time."

"Are you saying us middle-class folks should stick together?" I murmur, wishing that he'd just kiss me and knowing that he's holding back on purpose. "Because if so, I support that idea. Eat the rich."

"I'd rather eat you." Maxx says it. Then it's happening. His mouth is on mine, fierce and protective, claiming me. In that kiss, I see his intent to win, to beat the other boys, to come out on top. He's willing to sit and wait and hold on.

The fingers of his right hand slide across the back of my neck, pulling me close as he nips at my lips and tongue. The way he kisses is punishing; he won't let me get enough. He keeps drawing back just slightly out of reach, forcing me to push up onto my elbows, to lean into him, to chase him.

"I want your full consent," he mutters against my mouth, his own eyes half-lidded, his gaze so dark and intense that he looks a part of these woods, some long-lost forest god struggling to survive in the modern world.

"You have it," I whisper back, wondering why he's pressing this so much. He's still afraid of himself? That's the only explanation I can come up with.

"If you give it to me, I'm going to go nuts. It's one-hundred-percent or zero. And if it's zero, then it's *zero*." He exhales against my mouth, and the feel of his breath against my moist lips drives me completely up the wall.

"I understand and accept." The words come out a bit mumbled, a bit annoyed, and he laughs as he puts his forehead up to mine again.

"I hear you, Kota." Maxx shoves my wrists down into the moss, hovering over me, kissing and tugging on my lower lip.

"You picked up my bad habit." He licks the corner of my mouth, and I squirm, squeezing my eyes shut tight. "Oh no. If we're going to do this, we're going to do it with your eyes open."

When I don't immediately comply, Maxx stops kissing me, and he waits. He waits for so long that I have little choice but to look at him, opening my eyes to see him poised above me, his face set in clearly defined resolution.

I'm reminded all over again about all the things Parrish and Chasm told me about him, how he has his own set of rules, how if he thinks he needs to do bad to achieve right, he'll do it.

"He has these annoyingly rigid morals. Sometimes it takes a while to figure out what they are, but once you know, you can be assured that he'll never break them."

"Look at me." X sits up fully, tugging his shirt off and tossing it aside. He takes my hands and puts them on his chest, encouraging me to touch him the way he did on our first night. I don't mind. I want to feel everything, every groove and hollow of his muscles.

When he adjusts himself, using one knee to nudge my thighs apart, my lips part in surprise.

"Don't look so shocked," he warns me, smirking and angling my hips with his hands. "This is just the beginning; we're going to have a lot of fun together, Kota."

"You think so?" I start, but then X is thrusting hard and deep and fast. I lose whatever silly quip I was going to make as he comes down on me, arched above me, kissing and sucking on my neck. The sensations are almost overwhelming.

I end up clinging to his back, fingertips digging into his warm skin, wearing his fangirl shirt, pants-less and fucking on a forest floor in the middle of nowhere.

His thrusts are so impossibly consuming; it's all I can do to catch my breath between one and the next. His strong arms end up sweeping under and around my waist. He lifts and turns us so that I'm more or less sitting on his lap and looking into his eyes, his back to the nearest tree.

Our discarded veggie box gets knocked over, the lid popping off as it spills to the earth, our water bottles toppled.

X studies me with an intriguing expression on his handsome face, part awe, part satisfaction, part … anger? I'm not sure what that last bit is about, but I don't care because he smiles at me, and it's devastating.

It's devastating to see him smile while he's inside of me and holding me so close like this. I can feel a blush creeping into my skin, but he kisses my cheeks, my neck, drops his lips to my chest.

"Don't be embarrassed, Kota." He lifts his eyes to my face, and I get lost in the emerald hue. I don't know if it's the woods or the pleasure swirling up from the very core of me, but they seem ethereal, impossible, unreal. "Not with me."

"I trust you, Maxim Wright," I tell him, and an almost sad smile stretches across his mouth before he's kissing me again and encouraging me to move with him. It's a completely different position than I'm used to, my hips rolling to meet his upward thrusts, the mossy ground soft and spongy beneath my knees.

"Whatever it takes." That's how he replies, and then he's kissing me so hard that I forget we're in the woods, that I forget about Justin, that X is the only person and the only thing that matters.

I might have a serial killer for a father, but I've got this romance thing in the bag, right?

"Whatever it takes," I promise him back, and then he makes this snarling sound that has me covered in goose bumps. Maxx rolls us over until my back hits the moss, leaves and twigs tangling in my long black and lime green hair.

He thrusts so hard that my ass makes an indent in the soft

ground, and he takes a handful of my hair, pulling my head back so that he can kiss me. It's the movement of his lips and tongue more than anything else that drag my climax out of me, that make me writhe and cry out, throwing my arms around him and shuddering in his strong grip.

"You'll always have a place to call home with me," X whispers, and then he exhales against the side of my throat. "When I want something, I really am willing to do whatever it takes—especially for the right girl."

X lifts up to his knees, pulls my left leg up to his chest, and then works himself into me with deep, slow thrusts, grinding our bodies until together he reaches his own climax. Seeing him above me like that, sweat-dappled and perfect, it makes the world seem just that much less menacing.

He's strong, capable, loyal, a friend for life.

That's Maxx Wright for you.

His body shudders as he finishes, and then he's rolling off to the side and onto his back, panting and staring up at the leafy canopy.

"Was that you at a hundred percent?" I joke, referencing his earlier comment. Also, I'm blushing, and this is sort of a weird scenario, so I think I'm trying to deflect a bit, too.

"That was me at the starting line." He sits up and looks down at me, quirking a brow.

Then, he surprises the shit out of me by dropping down and pushing my thighs apart, his lips and tongue finding my molten core until I'm coming all over again.

"Just the start." Maxx finishes me and wipes his mouth off on his arm, offering me up another apple and a smile. "We should probably get dressed before we get arrested for indecent exposure, huh?"

He crawls over to retrieve my pants and underwear, helping me into them before he yanks on his own pants. His shirt, at least, he leaves off for a minute, gathering up the disturbed veggies and water bottles.

"I love you, Maxx Wright," I tell him, and he goes completely still before glancing over his shoulder and flashing me the most heart-warming smile I've ever seen on a boy's face.

"I love you, too, Kota Banks." He packs up the bike, tugs his shirt back on, and then offers me up a sympathetic look. "We might want to walk back."

"Why?" I ask, blinking innocently at him. Until I stand up that is. "Oh."

"Oh is right." Maxx smiles tightly at me and then lets the expression turn into a smirk. "I'm a little big for you, I know. I wouldn't want to make you uncomfortable by having you sit on such a narrow seat so soon after taking me."

I pick up a handful of leaves to chuck at him, but he just laughs, green bits stuck to his chocolate covered hair as the sun slants through the trees and warms the forested shadows around us.

CHAPTER 30

When we arrive back at the parking area, I see a second vehicle beside Maxx's Jeep, and my cheeks heat. We just had sex out in the open where anyone could've seen. I trusted that X knew this place well enough to know we wouldn't encounter anyone else, but the sight of that car makes me nervous.

Then I notice the familiar figure waiting with her back to a tree, staring up at the canopy as sunlight falls across her closed eyes. I have no idea how Saffron found us out here. I'm assuming she tailed us? If so, she didn't follow us into the woods, did she? If she saw us in that state ... I pretend like I don't have a bit of moss stuck in my panties, and hop off the bike, moving over to stand beside her.

"Which boy are you dating?" she asks me, which is a really odd question if you think about the circumstances. Still, this is Saffron Banks we're talking about, and for all intents and purposes, she is my mother. There's a reason why Parrish inked three hearts into my upper thigh. Saffron drops her dark gaze to mine and looks past me at X.

He's leaned the bike up against the rear of the Jeep and his moving toward us cautiously, as if he trusts Saffron as much as he trusts Lumen. That is to say, not at all. I turn back to her and try to figure out how to explain the situation.

"They're all courting me," I explain, using the same old-fashioned terminology that seemed to work on my grandparents. "Think of them as suitors."

"You don't need three boyfriends," she tells me, but not unkindly, reaching out to stroke the sore spot on my cheek. I thought I'd done a decent job of covering it up with makeup, but Saffron rubs it away and reveals the injury as if she knew it was there all along. Her gaze hardens and she drops her hand by her side. She's wearing that quilted leather jacket again, the same boots, the same jeans. Only her shirt is different. It's green and yellow, a University of Oregon tee that I wonder if she got from Maxine? I haven't had the chance to give my sister the note from the garden party—there hasn't been a safe or silent moment since then—but I still have it. "You don't need any boys at all. It's okay to want them, just don't start to think that you *need* them."

"What are you doing here?" X demands, crossing his arms so that he looks big and scary and protective. Saffron looks at him, but only for a moment before glancing over at me again.

"I didn't track you; I followed you." It's not really an answer to X's question, but that's just how Saffron is. I look back in the direction of her car, this sleek and sexy purple muscle car that's probably from the sixties or something. I have no idea where she got it, but it has a New York state license plate, so I'm assuming she drove all the way over to the West Coast in it.

It's probably stolen, I think, but then, I had my crush stolen and I now know how little a car actually means in the scheme of things. I can't bring myself to care other than for the fact that I don't want Saffron to end up in jail locally because of it. Or anywhere, really. If she goes to jail, Milk Carton will sniff her out, and she'll be dead within twenty-four hours.

"He can't see us out here," she adds, as if I was confused about something. I wasn't, but I am now.

"What do you know about Justin Prior?" I ask her, knowing that if she followed me all the way out here today, it was for a reason.

"Let's take a walk, just me and you, mother and daughter." She says it like that, as if it were so damn simple, as if to the world she isn't a kidnapper, just my adoptive mom. There are so many strange feelings being stirred up in me, but I don't know how to interpret any of them without talking more to Saffron first.

"Hell no. If you want privacy to talk, I'll hang back, but I'm not leaving Kota alone with anyone." Maxx's gaze meets mine, and softens slightly, but I know that he isn't softening at all. He means what he says, and there's no way for me to dissuade him from it. Not that I would; I don't fully trust Saffron either.

"Kota." Saffron sighs and shakes her head. "I always loved that nickname for you."

"Was that also the nickname you gave your own child?" I ask her, surprising myself by bringing up a subject that doesn't actually matter in terms of current events, but that I realize I'm almost desperate to know. I lived somebody else's life with somebody else's family wearing somebody else's name. I need to understand that to make sense of my own life.

"Walk with me." Saffron takes off down the path, and I exchange a look with X.

"Go. I'll keep you safe." He squeezes my hand, and then does just that, taking up a careful but respectable distance behind me and Saffron. Poor guy. First, the motocross, next the cycling, and then the err, extra credit exercises on the moss, and I can't believe he's not passed out.

"Do you like it here?" Saffron asks me, and I know she doesn't mean the Tillamook State Forest. She's talking about Medina and maybe even Tess. For some reason, I don't think she's asking me about Justin. Obviously, based on her behavior at the garden party, she knows something's up with the guy. How much, I can't tell but hopefully I'll find out now.

"I didn't at first," I admit, happy to have the freedom of truth once again. Justin isn't here; he can't see or hear me. Saffron certainly isn't going to tell him anything. "I hated it. I hated Tess, and I hated her house, and I hated everyone in it."

Saffron acts like she's listening, but it's hard to say. She can be absentminded at times; her thoughts tend to wander. It used to hurt my feelings when I was younger, but now I realize that's just how she is. She isn't being rude intentionally, and it's not that she doesn't care.

"You don't feel that way now?" she asks me, and I stop walking, turning to face her. She does the same, and then we're just staring at each other. Me and my mom. Me and my kidnapper.

"What do you know about Justin Prior?" I repeat for the fiftieth freaking time. "Tell me, *please*. You have no idea how much it would help to know that I've got someone else on my side."

"I know that he's the Seattle Slayer," she tells me, her voice darkening at the mention of Daddy Dearest's moniker. "I know that he hurts people, that he kills people, and that he's threatening both you and Maxine."

My mouth is hanging open.

X whistles sharply from my left, but I can't turn and look at him because I'm so busy gawping at Saffron.

"H-how?" I whisper. I can't seem to make my voice any louder than that. Here is one more person who knows Justin's true colors, and I can't particularly rely on her for anything because Saffron isn't a normal, rational adult. She's always been a bit broken, sometimes on drugs, sometimes in facilities, always a wanderer. But still, I'm intrigued.

"I saw him once," she tells me, in that very Saffron-y way of hers. "Kill a person. Just around the corner of the women's shelter that I stayed in with Tess."

My heart begins to beat so furiously that I feel faint, and I end up putting a hand to the tree trunk behind me. Parrish had insinuated—during one of his strangely cruel but also helpful moments—that Saffron had chosen me to steal because I looked like her deceased child. Tess had implied that it was their friendship that had drawn Saffron to me.

But this? I feel like this is the core truth of the entire fiasco, the single pinprick that every other aspect in my life revolves around, the sun of its own solar system if you will. I'm only the person I am today because of whatever Saffron is going to say; I only lived the life I lived because of it.

"Who?" I ask, trying to piece this whole thing together.

"I have no idea," she replies, and I'm even *more* confused, rather than less. "Two days after Tess left the shelter, Justin came looking for her. He showed everyone pictures and videos of his wife and child, asking for information. I was the only person who knew where Tess had gone, but I told him nothing. Tess had confided in me far too many stories about her ex for me to give her up like that."

"How did he end up killing someone?" I ask again in total shock. "And how did you end up seeing it?"

"Happenstance." Saffron sighs and then turns back toward the path, continuing on before adding, "fate."

I jog to catch up with her.

"Several nights later, Justin was back and showing Tess' picture—and your picture—to a homeless man in the alley outside the shelter. I was on my way back for the night and happened to pass by. The man told him that he didn't give a fuck about his missing family, and then Justin shot him in the face."

All I can do at this point is stare at her, but she isn't done.

No, it gets worse. With Justin Prior, it always gets worse.

"He turned around and shot another man who was sleeping on the ground and then, when he saw a third man walking by carrying a bag of groceries, he shot him, too. And then he put the gun away and walked off." She reaches up and frantically smooths her palms over her slicked back hair, over and over again. It definitely makes her look a little neurotic, but I'm used to it. "If he'd seen me, he would've killed me, too, even while I was carrying my baby. I'm sure of it. All the things Tess told me, and then my Dakota died, and I knew I had to protect you."

She stops walking again and looks over at me, her eyes brimming with tears.

"I protected you, Dakota, when nobody else would. Tess went back to Medina, of all places. How did she not know Justin would find you there eventually? She didn't care, Dakota, but I do. I saved you from that. I'm your real mother." Saffron turns away from me yet again and continues walking.

I stay right where I am, lost in the idea of that, of Justin shooting three random people because he was ticked off and in a mood. I knew he was dangerous, but I've been wondering as of late if he ever did his own dirty work. Clearly, he does.

Is there a way to connect him to those murders somehow? What if Saffron leaked the information, and he got arrested for something totally unrelated to me or anyone else in Medina?

It's a nice thought, but unlikely. It wouldn't surprise me if Justin had the ability to hack into databases and remove DNA samples or fingerprints from his past crimes. After all, when I first looked his name up online, it was a ghost town. For someone as big and prominent as Justin, as high up in polite society, to suffer such a downfall from grace and yet have zero evidence floating around the internet? You know the man is skilled, if nothing else.

"How did you know he was the Slayer?" I ask and Saffron turns, walking backward with her hands clasped behind her.

"It's obvious, isn't it? He kills people. He hurt Tess. He tracked you down. Fourteen teenagers in fourteen days? Each one with fourteen tick marks on their skin? You were missing for fourteen years. It's him. I can see the hurt and pain in your eyes, and I won't let it keep happening; I'll protect you, Dakota."

She turns away again and continues down the path while I stand there and stare, unsure if I'm relieved to finally know some of the hidden truths I've been wondering about since I saw that damn Netflix show. Or if I'm even more upset than I was before.

"This is fucking insane," I murmur, but then Maxx is sliding his arms over my shoulders from behind. He's big and comforting and he still smells amazing. I'm also a tad sore from earlier, but in a good way. I lean back into him and close my eyes, easily able to fight off my usual embarrassment in the scope of bigger and badder things.

"What do you think she's planning to do? Why does she keep saying she's going to protect you?" X pauses and then I open my eyes to see him looking down at me. "You don't think she's going to kill Justin, do you?" he wonders, and am I bad person for hoping something like that could actually happen, that I could be free from Justin's control?

"No," I say, and I sigh heavily. "Saffron is … weirdly perceptive about certain things, but she doesn't have it in her to carry out an execution. I don't know exactly why she's in town, but I think it'd be best if we convinced her to leave."

It's worth a try, even if I don't have much hope of her listening to me. She's as stubborn as Maxine.

By the time Saffron returns back to the car, it's getting later and the air is chilly in the shadows. I didn't mind sitting and waiting for her since I had Maxx and snacks and space away from Justin. I told him all about my Caroline subplot, about Parrish officially accepting the dinner invitation, and caught him up on my writing journey.

"Mr. Volli was weirdly good at teaching the app development class, but he's a fucking asshole of an editor. He red-pens every line, and he asks too many questions. *Do you need a metaphor here? Is this word too advanced for a general audience? Do you really believe this pop culture reference is timeless, or do you think it'll date your work?*" I huff out a breath and Maxx raises his brows.

"What was the pop culture reference?" he asks, and I throw a grape at him. He catches it in his mouth, cocky asshole. "It was a K-drama, wasn't it? Ashnikko? No, some sort of musical …"

"Fine. Yes. It was a K-drama reference, are you happy now?"

We both pause at the sound of footsteps and Saffron reappears. She comes straight over to where we're sitting in the Jeep's truck bed with the tailgate open.

"I should probably go now, and so should you." She puts her hand on my knee, and I swallow down a lump of emotion. "Don't do anything you don't want to do, Dakota. Don't compromise yourself. No matter how much he tries, he'll always try to turn you into Mia Prior."

I shudder all over. I'd thought Mia Patterson was a scary fate, but Saffron is right: Mia Prior is so much worse.

"I want you to leave town, Saffron. Justin *is* going to kill you if he gets a chance, and he can track anyone he wants—"

"Not me," she assures me, and I realize her choice of car was likely intentional. A classic like that doesn't come with a hackable computer system or biometrics or dash cams. It's much more difficult to trace. Saffron clearly knows what she's doing as Milk Carton hasn't been able to find her just yet. "And I'm not leaving town, Dakota. I'm sorry, but I have to do this."

"You don't have to protect me anymore, Saffron," I assure her, even though I wish she could. With all my heart, I truly wish it were possible. "Justin made me choose a family member to die as punishment. The only person I loved who wasn't directly in his sights was you. I … I offered your name."

Saffron just stares at me and then pats my leg in a comforting manner.

"That was the right choice, Kota. What else could you do?" I hop down from the truck bed to give her a hug, and she wraps me up in one that feels so heartbreakingly familial, impossibly maternal, and as overprotective as Maxim Wright.

"Please, please, please just leave. I don't want anyone that I care about to get hurt." I squeeze her tighter—Banks family style—and then pull back, but I can see from the stubborn set of her face that she isn't planning on listening to me. "Saffron, you don't understand the power he wields or the lengths he'll go to in order to get his way. It's not *just* about killing people; he wants respect and social standing and clout. He's desperate for it."

"I'll find a way to get to him; he's very well-guarded, unfortunately." That's her answer, and then she's turning and taking off. Just before climbing into the car, she pauses to glance back at me and offers up a smile. "And no, Kota was never my baby's nickname. It was only ever—and will forever be—yours." She closes her car door as tears sting my eyes then pauses briefly on the gravel drive leading away from the parking area to wave, and then just like that, she's gone.

Nothing unusual about that, unfortunately. For as long as I can remember, I've been used to seeing the tail end of Saffron Banks, on her way out the door to some adventure or another.

I didn't get to ask all the questions I wanted, but I know so much more now than when I set out today.

"I hate that I have to take you home," X breathes, and I know what he's thinking.

It's what we're all thinking: when is one of us going to get the chance to end this once and for all?

It would only take one small blip of inattention, a moment of deep sleep, a quiet shadow ... but the punishment for failure? He won't hurt me because he wants me more than anything to be by his side, but he'll start killing people I love. He'll kill *them* if they try to get him and fail.

It just has to be me, but I can't mess this up. I can't take a risk like I did that day with the shovel.

And so, with Saffron's piece moving on its own across my board, I plot.

CHAPTER 31

I arrive home to Ice Palace 2.0 and slog tiredly up the stairs to my room. Justin doesn't bother me, and I don't see Delphine anywhere, allowing me enough time to shower and change into pajamas as I mull over the answers I just got from Saffron.

I wanted to know, didn't I?

The thought makes me sick.

I wasn't kidnapped because I looked like baby Dakota, not just because Saffron had a mental break, but because of Justin's violence. Literally. It was his act of shedding blood that catapulted us into an alternate reality.

As Saffron suggested, did she really save my life?

What would've happened if Justin had found me and Tess when he was in that state? If he'd been able to get to her before she built herself up with power and wealth, married into the mightiest blue-blood family on the block, had her name cast in lights over her true crime novels.

I can't let my mind go there. Already, I have enough shit to worry about.

Instead, I fixate on the highlights of the day. That is, Maxim Wright. Cut out the Saffron/serial killer bits, and it was essentially the perfect summer day.

I towel dry my hair, twist it into a loose knot on the top of my head, and then head downstairs to find something to eat. There's always plenty of food prepared and left covered in the fridge for reheating, but I decide against it.

I'd rather cook something. It's an easy way to clear the mind but keep the hands moving. I find it therapeutic. Because I'm tired of eating quenelle and buttery snails, I settle on something simple and decide to whip up the same cornbread recipe that I used at Tess' house.

I'm still in the process of laying out the ingredients when Delphine moves into the room. She, too, is in her pajamas, her newly dyed blond hair curved over one shoulder. She looks at me like I'm insane for a minute before opening the fridge and revealing all of the carefully prepared meals available to us.

"Don't you just want to heat something up?" she asks, but I shake my head.

"Nope. I want to cook more than I want to eat, to be honest." I start looking through cabinets for a bowl, a whisk, a pan. This kitchen is vast, far larger than Tess' and with a lot more square footage than Laverne's. Hers is compact, but luxuriously outfitted. This one's a bit simpler, and clearly hasn't been renovated since the early 2000s.

I don't mind though: why on earth would granite countertops ever go out of style? That's raw stone, and it's beautiful. I smooth my hand over it as I gather what I need, pleasantly surprised at how well-stocked the place is. All the better for Justin's servants to cater to our every whim, am I right?

No wonder Delphine looks so repulsed.

"I'd understand why you wouldn't want to," I assure her as she creeps into the kitchen step by step, almost as if she's physically repelled by it. "You probably did a lot of cooking for your grandma?" I don't mean to hurt her by bringing the subject up, but I only realize after I say the words how callous they might sound. "I'm sorry. If you don't want to talk about it—"

"No, I …" Delphine pauses and looks down at the sea of items on the island, and then picks up the bag of yellow cornmeal. "I didn't say that; I'm fine talking about my grandma. Why shouldn't I be? She's not here anymore, so the only way I'll get to feel like I'm by her side again is to tell her stories." She sets the bag aside and then looks up at me. "Do you want me to look up a recipe?"

I tap the side of my head as I set a cast-iron skillet on the counter with a smile. Somehow, I swear it tastes better baked in cast iron than in glass.

"No need. Recipe's up here." I preheat the oven and then push the mixing bowl in front of Delphine. She looks nervous, almost as if she's on a first date or something. I get it. She wants me to like her. I want to like her, too. It's just … I can't trust her, now can I? But we can certainly bake together.

There's gotta be some sort of ancient, fucked-up fairy tale rhyme about two daughters of a famous killer baking up a storm … or whatever. If there isn't, there should be.

"Go ahead and add the flour, cornmeal, sugar, salt, and baking powder and then whisk it together." I make a spinning motion with my finger, and Delphine looks at me in a way that reminds me of her expressions back at the Vanguard house. Tentative, reserved, but with that gleam in her gaze that promises a sharp wit underneath it all.

"Okay …" She goes about following my instructions, and I pick up my phone, linking to the room's Bluetooth sound system and starting up a playlist. No, it is not Ashnikko or K-pop. Yes, it's a playlist of my favorite musical hits, so sue me. "Now what?"

I continue directing Delphine through the process of making the corn bread and, since we're at it, I try some small talk, too.

"What do you and Justin like to do together?" I ask her, wondering if she's got a revenge list the same as I do. Also, I'm curious. Do they ever go out to eat, just the two of them? Do they ever take walks? Has Justin ever offered to take her on a boat to the Puget Sound?

"We haven't spent much alone time together," she admits, and there's a thread of melancholy in her voice that I pick up on and cling to. Ah. See. Maybe I really could pry them apart or turn them against each other? Well, I could turn Delphine against Justin. I would never purposefully try to turn him against her.

I would not put it past the man to murder his own daughter.

"Do you want to spend more time with him?" I ask, and she pauses to look up at me, the shell of a cracked egg held in her hand.

"Of course I do. He's our dad. Don't *you* want to spend more time with him?"

I'm not sure there's a way to answer that question appropriately without a blatant lie passing my lips so I just shrug, and we continue on with our cooking project.

Once it's in the oven, Delphine and I sit together on stools beside the counter, her with a seltzer water, me with a glass bottle of iced tea. She's showing me some songs that I've never heard of and that I actually like (maybe I can finally expand my listening horizons) when Justin comes in and sees us sitting together.

"Oh, this just warms my heart," he purrs, putting a hand to his chest as he moves into the kitchen and peers into the oven. "You're even cooking together? I'm impressed." He turns back around and directs his gaze to me. I lift up my eyes to meet his, and I see that he truly is surprised.

ENDGAME ROMANCE

He didn't expect me to warm toward Delphine at all. More than likely, he expected us to spar. Here's the thing though: I just don't have the energy to fight on another front. That's an important lesson, too, in video games or chess or life. Don't fight so many battles that you can't win any at all.

Delphine, regardless of her level of involvement, is a problem that can wait.

Justin turns around and approaches the counter where we're sitting. I can only imagine what he's going to do next. Stir me and Delphine up by dropping another secret? Purposefully set us at each other's throats? Or maybe he's going to pet each of our heads and tell us what good girls we are?

Gross.

Whatever it was that he was planning on doing, it's interrupted by the sound of the front door.

Justin frowns and pauses, glancing over his shoulder as slow, dragging footsteps approach. There's a rasping sound, harsh and wet that freaks me out. Zombie invasion? It literally could be. That's exactly what it sounds like right now, the shuffling, the wheezing.

Amin Volli, the studious poet/devoted teacher/murderer, grabs the edge of the wall and drags himself into the kitchen. His suit jacket is hanging loose, his dress shirt torn and stained with red, and he's actively bleeding all over Justin's floor.

"What on earth happened to you?" my father asks, as if his friend showed up with a bit of dirt on his collar. He turns around and studies the man as he pants and Delphine sucks in a surprise inhale, her eyes widening as she studies Mr. Volli's brutal state.

He looks as if ... somebody tried to kill him?

It wouldn't be undeserved.

Justin turns to glance at me as Mr. Volli struggles to catch his breath. He looks like he's in need of immediate medical attention, but Justin doesn't appear to care. Instead, his eyes narrow as he studies my face.

"Do you know anything about this?" he asks me, and I blink back at him in shock.

"How the hell would I?" I retort back, aware that I should probably toe the line right now. There's a heavy tension in the air that's scaring me. If Justin truly believes I had something to do with this, what'll his next move be?

"It was that woman," Mr. Volli breathes out, quivering and panting as he turns and puts his back to the wall of cabinets. He ends up sliding to the floor as Delphine pushes up from her chair. She disappears into the downstairs bathroom and returns with a first aid kit. After peeling back his shirt, her face blanches and she looks up at Justin.

"He needs real help, Daddy. This looks serious."

I don't move from where I am, frozen in place, an onlooker with a curious mind. *Who did this? Whoever they are, they're my hero. But also ... that woman? Does he mean Saffron? Does he mean Tess? Lumen?*

"Who." Justin pulls his phone out, but he doesn't dial 911 or anyone else. He waits for Mr. Volli to take a drink from the water glass that Delphine presents him, and then raises his brows. His foot taps at the floor in clear impatience.

"I'm fairly certain—but only fairly—that it was the kidnapper." Mr. Volli reaches up and wipes some of the blood from his mouth, staring down at his hand in fascination. It almost looks like he might *lick* it, but then he shakes his head and turns his battered face up to Justin. One of his glasses lenses is shattered, his right eye is swelling and turning purple, and his lower lip is split right down the middle. "It was dark, so I couldn't see properly, but I'm positive it was a woman."

Justin looks back at me again, but I don't have answers for

him.

Could it have been Saffron? I mean, it's possible. It's also really hard for me to imagine my adopted mother trying to murder a dude. Does not compute. Then again, she *did* say she was going to do whatever it took to keep me safe.

Have I found my savior in Saffron yet again? Or is this going to make life worse for me?

"I'll check the cameras," Justin confirms, and then he finally makes a quick call to Raúl. "Bring the car around and get Amin to the hospital." He hangs up and puts the phone away, moving back over to where I'm sitting and putting his palm flat on the countertop. "You went hiking again today, did you?" he asks, and I nod.

There's a lump of cold fear in my throat that I can't seem to swallow past.

I'm aware of the sharp knives stuck in the wooden block to my left. Do I need to grab one to defend myself? Justin notices and grabs the block, shoving it onto the floor and sending blades scattering. He leans in so close that I can smell his aftershave, can see striations of color in his irises.

"You best *hope* that Saffron was responsible for this, and that you and your pets had nothing to do with it. If I find out that you organized this, I'm going to be *fucking pissed*. Do you understand me, princess?"

"You never said that I couldn't hurt Mr. Volli," I retort which was a stupid, fucking thing to say.

Justin raises his hand like he might very well hit me again, but then draws it back and smooths his palm down the front of his dress shirt. Our eyes lock, and I feel a renewed vigor inside of me. I've got a vigilante on my side, don't I?

Someone is out there, fighting on my side, and I'm glad that I don't know who it is for sure.

If I don't, then Justin can't blame me for it.

"You have other enemies," I add, thinking of Veronica's family. It could've been her, right? Or her mother? Clearly, the Fishers are unhinged. "That's another lesson in chess: don't underestimate any of the pieces."

I stand up and pad away, heading up the stairs to my room and leaving Justin to deal with his bloodied pawn. There's a note on my desk that wasn't there before, and my eyes widen, glancing over at the open window with its curtains dancing in the breeze.

Did someone climb in here and leave this for me? If so, how did they get past all of Justin's cameras?

I move quickly over to the note and unfold it, glancing down at the familiar handwriting.

I'm sorry I missed him. I'll get him next time. Miss you and love you fierce.

Holy shit. My adopted mother really is going after Justin. I'm so stunned that—after flushing the crumpled note down the toilet —I sit down hard on the edge of my bed and force myself to breathe. I'm worried about Saffron's safety, but … she really is fighting for me in her own way.

A text hits my phone, and I lift it up absently to see who it's from.

I pulled some strings. We're revisiting the custody issue next week. I'll be personally texting Justin to eat shit. Just thought you should know ahead of time.

I set my phone aside and carefully peel my pajama pants down so that I can see the still-healing tattoo through the plastic.

Three hearts.

One for me, one for Tess, one for Saffron.

Parrish could not have chosen better symbolism, and I could not have a better team at my back.

In chess, the endgame is when there are few pieces on the

board. But that's not the finish line, a checkmate is. In videogames, the endgame is when the storyline is done or max level is achieved, but truly, it's when the fun stuff really starts.

In romance, it's the final pairing of the story's main love interests. That bit? That's the easy stuff. Maxx, Chasm, and Parrish are solid.

Apparently, so are both of my mothers.

As worried as I am, I cannot wait to see this play out.

I cannot wait to be free of Justin.

Because after the endgame, it's the coda, the conclusion.

And me, I want my happily ever after so bad that I can taste it.

I only hope that it doesn't leave the bitter tang of iron on my tongue.

Music can set the tone for any scene.

Foreboding pipe organs bring to mind soaring gothic revival churches and vampires. Pop music conjures sunshine and laughing teenagers, arms thrown around one another's shoulders. And this? The tune that's playing now?

It may as well be a death knell.

As soon as I head down the staircase and realize that Céline Dion's 1997 smash hit *"My Heart Will Go On"* (from the movie *Titanic*) is playing, my stomach twists into an impossible knot of dread.

It's hard to breathe.

I am fucking *terrified.*

Around the three-and-a-half-minute mark, when the song gets super extra, and Céline is just belting out those lyrics, I come around the corner to find Justin lip-syncing the words with true heart, clutching a fist to his chest and everything.

I swallow down a lump of sheer terror. I haven't spoken to the man since last night, but Delphine popped in earlier to let me know that Amin Volli was already on the mend and wouldn't be spending more than a day in the hospital.

But … I mean, go Saffron. She snuck up on one of the Seattle Slayer's many faces and put him in the ER for the night. Could she really be my ticket out of this? Am I selfish for wanting her to do the dirty work for me?

No, Dakota. It has to be you. You have to kill this man.

He's almost cute like this, singing nineties songs the way he is. The thought of taking his life, I … I'm going to do it. I've made my mind up. In the process, I'll be killing Dakota Banks once and for all. In the process, I will truly and utterly become Mia Prior in the way that Justin has always wanted.

Just like the main character in Tess' novel, *Fleeing Under a Summer Rain,* I'm going to kill my father in cold blood.

I force a smile as the song ends and … Shania Twain's *"Man! I Feel Like a Woman!"* starts to play.

Err.

"Don't you love nineties music? So fucking cheerful," Justin bites off, smiling at me, but with far too much teeth. That, and he doesn't often curse unless he's truly angry about something.

"It's nice—" I start, but then he's storming across the solarium and snatching my arm in tight fingers. He yanks me toward him so violently that I almost lose my feet. In an instant, our faces are pressed close and he's looking into my soul with those sapphire eyes of his.

"Where is she, Mia?" Justin grinds out, squeezing my arm so hard that my fingers go numb from the pressure.

"Who?" I ask, playing dumb even when I damn well know who's talking about.

ENDGAME ROMANCE

Saffron.

She's his ultimate enemy. Everyone else in Medina? They're almost too easy. It isn't hard to knock people like that off their thrones, particularly when they're swimming in devious secrets the way everyone in this town is.

But Saffron? Saffron stole his child. Saffron is penniless, jobless, relationship-free. She barely has a relationship with Maxine. She evaded him for over a decade; she's evading him now.

"Goddamn it, Mia." He grabs my other arm and shakes me so violently that my teeth clack together. "I know you know where she is or at the very least, you've seen her recently." He draws back and then ... he hits me again. He backhands me right across the face, and I taste blood on my tongue. "Where is she?"

I'm holding my cheek and panting heavily, eyes on the floor. He never said he wouldn't hit me, so I guess this isn't him breaking his word, but it sure feels like it.

Mia. He keeps calling me Mia. It's like the script has flipped all over again. Tess is calling me Dakota now, and Justin is calling me Mia. It's as if everything prior to this moment was upside down, and I'm finally seeing the whole truth of the situation.

I look back at Justin, seething in front of me, dressed in a handsome charcoal suit with blood-red sneakers on his feet. He's okay with a little pushback when he's winning, but when he's losing?

"You got Tess' text then, I take it?" I query, and I can't help it: I quirk a smile. As soon as he lays eyes on the expression, he lifts his hand again. If it weren't for the ringing of the doorbell, he might've struck me even harder.

Justin squeezes his hand into a tight fist and drops it by his side.

"You think I won't simply walk up to your mother and shoot

her in the head?" he queries, quite dryly I might add. The color drains from my face as he scowls at me. "I'd much rather Tess was where she belonged: by my side or on her knees in front of me. But if I can't have her? And you won't come to heel?" And here, Justin actually laughs. "Maybe I've been too nice, hmm? What do you think, Princess?"

He skirts past me as I stand there trembling, swallowing my own blood down.

Did he ... did he really just say those things?

I turn around to see Raúl opening the door which is strange seeing as the butler usually does it. That freaks me out almost as much as the Céline Dion thing. The staff isn't present today even though we're having a dinner?

With the boys as guests?

Shit.

I turn around to see Parrish strolling in the front door, hands in his pockets. His face is set in its usual apathetic sloth formation, but the moment he looks my way, his gaze widens and he's sprinting over to grab me by the shoulders.

I give an involuntary cringe and pull in a sharp intake of breath.

"Did I hurt you?" he whispers, loosening his grip. His fingers are so gentle that I want to cry, but I can't. No. More like I *won't*. I refuse. Justin thrives on reactions, and I'd be betraying myself if I let him have my tears.

"I'm okay," I whisper, but clearly, there must be a visible mark on my face because Parrish is swiping his thumb over my lip and cursing. Before I can stop him, he pulls away and grabs a knife off the carefully set dining table. "Parrish!" I yell, but he's far quicker than I am, heading straight for Justin's office.

I chase after him, but Raúl (that *snake*) throws out a leg, tripping me and sending me onto my knees right there in the foyer.

The pain knocks the air out of me, but I don't let it slow me down. Instead, I move even faster, scrambling up to my feet and rounding the corner just in time to see Justin shoving a full magazine into a handgun.

Parrish is standing there with the knife in his hand, red-faced and panting. But what can he do with a steak knife when Justin's holding a semi-automatic?

"Go clean up, Princess." Justin gazes at the gun with apparent disinterest before lifting a smarmy smile up to my face. "Now." That last word, it puts the fear of God in me. I snatch Parrish by the shoulder and he drops the knife, unresisting as I drag him out of Justin's office and back into the foyer.

"Don't." The word comes out of me in a similar fashion to Justin. A sharp, harsh command, brooking no argument. "If someone's going to do this, it can only be me." This last part is a whisper; I can't seem to summon any more energy than that.

"Absolutely not," Parrish returns, taking my face between soft and shaking hands. "How could I let you give up a part of yourself like that? I'm already mean, Dakota. I'm already cruel. You … you're the sunshine that breaks through the clouds."

I pull away from him. Not because I want to. But because I don't want to show any further emotion around Justin. Instead, I take off up the stairs just as the front door opens again.

"What the fuck?" It's Chasm. I can hear his footsteps paired with another even heavier set—Maxx—and then I'm in my bathroom splashing cool water on my face while the three of them cluster behind me, triple gazes reflected in the mirror. *It's probably a goddamn camera, too.* "Little Sister, what's going on?"

"We're going back to court," Parrish says as Maxx forces me onto the closed lid of the toilet and examines my face. Ah, that's right, the sports medicine thing. My future doctor. I almost let myself cry again, but I swallow the tears back. "Tess, I mean. I don't speak legalese, but we're getting another go at the custody thing."

"Is that what this is about?" Maxx asks, using his strong fingers to offer a gentle suggestion to my lips. I open wide for him, and he checks my tongue and gums. "That fucking piece of subhuman filth," he growls out, but I just close my eyes and let myself fantasize about X punching Justin in the face. I let it play over and over in my head, a therapeutic memory to help wash away some of the pain.

It's more emotional than physical, as always.

I would've just called you Daddy if you'd been one, I think, but it's a moot point. It's a lost cause. Justin is never going to change. Justin tried to set my siblings on fire. Justin kidnapped Parrish. Justin killed three random people in front of Saffron. Justin hit me —more than once.

"He feels like he's losing; he doesn't like to lose." I hold the side of my now swollen face as Chasm digs through the cabinet for a first aid kit, finding one beneath the sink and passing it to Parrish who hands it to Maxx. "Add in the Mr. Volli incident and I imagine that's why he lost his temper." I pause there and in the name of honesty decide to add, "also, I might have taunted him a little."

"Little Sister ..." Chasm grits his teeth and exchanges a look with Parrish as Maxx goes about tending to my wounds. "What the hell do we do here? You can't control Tess or Saffron. How is any of this your fault?"

"I don't know," I whisper, closing my eyes against X's gentle touch. "I really don't." I look over at Maxx and try to force a smile. Only, it hurts too much, and he gives me a look.

"Don't make yourself smile for my benefit," he chastises, like he's the parental figure of the group or something.

"I was thinking about the woods yesterday," I tease, and he

pauses, his own mouth quirking at the corner before he gets control of himself.

"The woods, really?" Chasm asks, but there's only a fraction of his usual teasing in there. The three of them are far too upset to play around right now. Parrish has his arms crossed tight; he won't even look at me. "What the hell is this dinner really about?"

"Whatever it is, it won't be good." I look back at Maxx. "You shouldn't be here."

"I couldn't not be here," he whispers back, his face stricken. "Is scumbag Volli going to live?" I nod and Maxx exhales, putting his hands on his hips. "Shame."

"Tell me about it," Chas murmurs, and then he notices his bestie's sullen state. "Something else happen besides ..." He trails off and then reaches out to press a soft thumb against my lower lip.

"I tried to stab Justin with a steak knife." Parrish uncrosses his arms and moves into my bedroom, looking around the room with a deep frown etched into his gorgeous mouth. In a fit of rage, he grabs onto the mirrored TikTok shelf and yanks it over, spilling items all over the ground.

Delphine comes running, panting as she opens the door and sees the state of things.

"What the hell happened in here?" she chokes out, staring at Parrish and then looking over at me next.

"You know he's the Seattle Slayer, right?" Parrish asks, looking at Delphine like she's a traitor or something. "Sweet old Daddy Dearest?"

"Parrish!" Maxx grinds out, snatching his friend's arm and jerking him back. "Are you trying to get somebody killed?" he whispers, but only loudly enough that Chasm and I can hear.

Delphine blinks, almost too slowly to be real.

"Huh?" she asks, as if she has no idea what Parrish is talking about. "Are you nuts? He's the sweetest man in the world," she mumbles, moving into the room and helping Chas right the toppled shelf. It's completely ruined by the way; all of the mirrored shelves are shattered. The makeup, lotion, whatever else was on there (I haven't looked) is spilled in a vibrant rainbow across the white rug beneath my bed. "I don't like violent boys." Delphine pauses to look at Parrish, and the two of them stare each other down. "And I don't appreciate people talking shit about our father."

"Your father?" Parrish laughs, and the sound is dark and full of strain. "Your *father* just hit your little sister across the face? If my dad did that to Kimber, I'd do worse in response. You say you love Dakota? That you're her big sister? Prove it." He takes off and leaves the four of us standing in silence in my pretty fairy-tale bedroom.

"He hit you again?" Delphine asks, and it's the word *again* that really gets the cogs in my mind turning. She knows about last time? If so, why didn't she say anything? Why is she still defending Justin? The newest addition to my sister collection just shakes her head and puts her fingers up to her temples. "Do you need any help getting ready?"

"Did you hear what he just said to you?" Chasm retorts, but I shake my head and Delphine nods. She opens her mouth like she might just say something but seemingly decides against it. She pauses several seconds before speaking again.

"Daddy would never do something like that." Delphine lifts her chin defiantly, but it's her eyes that scare me the most. They're almost ... empty. Have I underestimated this girl? Is she more involved than I originally thought?

A cold fear begins to creep into my limbs, taking over my fingers, my toes.

"Parrish must've misheard me," I say, hating the lie even as it slips past my lips. "I said that I tripped again."

Delphine smiles prettily at me, but the expression still doesn't reach her eyes. Not at all.

"Do you need anything, baby sister?" she asks, and there's a genuine thread of concern in her voice as she steps toward me and holds out a hand. In the end, she drops it by her side and purses her lips slightly. "It'll all be okay." She smiles again, and Maxx goes completely stiff beside me with anger. Chasm scoffs, shoving his hands into his pockets and standing guard on my right side. "You'll see: Daddy knows best."

She turns and heads out of the room, leaving me there with the jewel-toned kiss of crushed makeup painted across the floor.

"I'll clean this up," Chas offers, but I just shake my head.

"We don't dare be late to dinner," I whisper, and then I head after Parrish.

Who knows what might happen if he's left unsupervised?

Justin sits at the head of the table in the solarium with Caroline on his left, Parrish on his right. I'm seated beside Chasm and Maxx at the opposite end with Delphine shoved haphazardly into the middle of it all.

As I watch, Justin lifts up his wineglass and takes a careful sip.

"So, Parrish," he begins, as if they didn't just face off against one another with a knife and a gun. As if Justin didn't just hit me for the second time. As if he didn't just disparage and threaten Tess in front of me. "You must be happy to have this opportunity to reunite with your mother."

"I only have one mother and that's Tess Vanguard." Parrish's words are firm, almost aggressive. He's sitting ramrod straight, having chucked his sloth persona for the cold, cruelness that lies beneath. "Just as Dakota has no father—"

Justin throws the wineglass on the floor and leans in toward Parrish in warning.

"You're quite lucky I made Dakota a promise in regard to you." Justin sits back after a moment and snaps his fingers, summoning Raúl with a clean wineglass and a rag. With a scowl (that man is always scowling), Raúl goes about mopping up the mess, using a middle finger to shove his pink and blue glasses up his nose. "Now, Caroline …" Justin continues, turning to face her.

As for her part, Caroline attempts to remain the cool, civilized socialite she so desperately wants to be. But I swear, there's a tremble in her hand that wasn't there before. It's impossible to miss as she lifts her own red wine to her lips.

"Yes?" she asks, turning to look at her fiancé.

"Aren't you excited to see your one and only flesh-and-blood son?" Justin parks his chin in his hand, and Maxx shifts uncomfortably beside me. Delphine seems oblivious to the tension, but only an alien could miss the suffocating pressure in this room. Now I'm even more confused as to her motivations.

What the hell is going on here?

"Oh, of course." Caroline looks Parrish directly in the face for what might very well be the first time ever. She forces a smile to her painted lips, but there's zero reaction from Parrish. He picks up his own water glass and takes a drink.

"This is what he excels at," Chasm whispers, leaning in. "This sort of … blue blood sparring thing. Just watch." He sits back in his seat, and then nods in his friend's direction with his chin. Glad to know that Chasm has faith in Parrish.

Personally, I'm finding it difficult to simply lift the fork to my mouth. What are we even eating? I can't taste any of it. Probably because Maxx put some sort of numbing stuff on my tongue. Apparently, I cut it pretty badly with my teeth.

I poke the fork into what I think is quinoa, listening to the strained and continued silence of the solarium.

"What's your favorite subject in school, Parrish?" Caroline asks, and I wonder then who named him that. Surely not her? Who named me Mia? Both Tess and Justin seem fond of the name.

"My favorite subject is destroying people who deserve it." Parrish delivers this in an entirely deadpan voice, crossing his arms over his chest and leaning back in his seat. "Do you deserve it, Caroline Bassett?"

She just stares at him before turning a perplexed expression Justin's way.

"I'm not going to sit here and take abuse from this boy," she says, her voice hardening, taking on a sharpness that makes me question if I truly saw the trembling in her hand or if I'm oh so slowly losing my mind here. "You're the one who wanted to have dinner with this brat in the first place."

Ah. And there it is. I knew I smelled a plot. Just what that plot is, I can't ascertain.

Justin picks up his steak knife, and my heart seizes in my chest. Telling me that he won't hurt Parrish is one thing. But what if he simply decides he doesn't care if I call him a liar? What would it matter if Parrish were already dead or bleeding?

The boys seem to have the same idea, rising on either side of me until Justin's harsh laugh breaks through the quiet, and he tosses the blade onto the table. It skids and slides over to me.

"Daddy?" Delphine asks, and Justin's face takes on a hard cast.

"Go to your room, Delphine," he tells her, and she blinks wide, confused eyes at him. "Now."

"But Daddy—"

The look he throws her way is pure poison. In the end, Delphine is red in the face with frustration, but she shoves to her feet and takes off, pushing her chair in so hard that it hits her plate and subsequently knocks over her water glass.

Justin waits for her footsteps to disappear up the stairs, for her door to close, and then he nods his chin at me and crosses his arms over his chest.

"Did you think it was cute, telling Caroline over here our little secret?"

I go stone-still, one hand on my fork, the other clutching Chasm's hand as he trembles beside me.

"What secret—" I start, but Justin grits his teeth, and I realize I'm skating on very thin ice here. "You mean the Slayer thing?"

"Pick up the knife, Mia." Ah, and there it is again. Mia. I'm now officially Mia.

I do as Justin asks, figuring that at the very least, I can stab *him* with it in a pinch. My eyes flick to Raúl, standing beside the open back door with his lighter in hand. He flicks the wheel menacingly, and I wonder if I shouldn't stab him, too, while I'm at it? Justin ordered the fire set, sure, but it was clearly Raúl who did the deed.

No wonder I never liked the guy.

"I want you to stab Caroline in the leg with it."

I gape at Justin as Parrish rises to his feet, and Caroline gasps. She puts a hand to her mouth and this time, it's quite obvious that her hand is trembling around the stem of that wineglass.

"Wh-what?" I choke out, and then I'm standing up, too.

"You heard me." Justin stares me down unforgivingly. "Caroline over here was planning on marrying me for my money and then killing me. Isn't that right, sweetie?" He turns to his fiancée who's now pale-faced and gaping. "I was going to invite you to play *with* me, but ..."

Justin reaches into his pocket, withdrawing some papers that he hands over to Caroline. Much like I did, actually, when I showed her the printed articles that Justin had given me. These don't look like articles however, more like credit card statements.

"Did you think I wouldn't notice the sorts of things you were spending your money on?" Justin queries, glancing her way and then hooking a smile. Caroline shifts through the papers, her mouth opening and closing several times before she gives a nervous swallow.

"It's not what you think, darling," she offer up with a little laugh. The sound of it makes my teeth hurt. "These are my own personal cards; I wasn't spending your money on any of it."

Justin raises a brow as he glances her way.

"It's not the source of the money, Caroline, darling. It's the intent." He flicks his fingers at the papers. "You're a very important asset to me." Justin reaches out, snatching Caroline's delicate chin in hard fingers and forcing her to look at him. "And the wedding must go on, of course. But do you think I'd let you plot my murder and not say a thing about it?" He tsks his tongue and then gestures at me. "Mia, this is an order. Stab that knife into Caroline's leg. Maybe you'll kill her, maybe you won't if you're careful with your aim."

"Daddy," I whisper, hoping the name will mollify him a little. It doesn't. "She could bleed to death."

"I will not ask again." He turns back to me. "Do it." There's an unspoken *or else* resting on the tip of his tongue. "What should it matter? You already killed a police officer. It's not as if you're an innocent any longer, now are you?"

I suddenly find it impossible to breathe.

My vision swims, and the knife gets loose in my fingers before finally dropping to the table. Maxx grabs me before I can fall, but even in his arms, I'm tongue-tied. I'm frozen. I'm suffocating.

"You destroyed your mother's life. You cheated on your boyfriend. You betrayed the kidnapper's sweet, little daughter. What more can you *possibly* do, Mia?" Justin continues to taunt me, throwing everything he made me do back in my face. "You set the theater on fire and ruined your friend's dream over what? Some blue-blooded little brat with a nasty temper who has a money-grubbing whore for a mom and a father who stuffs silicone tits into socialite's chests for a living."

Parrish snatches the knife before I can make a move, and then he's moving and Chasm is trying to stop him.

But it's too late.

He shoves the blade into Caroline's thigh, and she lets out the most horrific scream I've ever heard in my life. The dizziness fades and I shoot to my feet, tearing from Maxx's grip. He's two steps ahead of me, grabbing one of Parrish's shoulders while Chasm takes the other. They wrench him back, but he's already released the knife and put his hands up, palms out.

Caroline is groaning, clutching at her leg and hyperventilating.

"He's my pawn!" I shout, throwing myself in front of Parrish and doing my best not to look at the blood draining from Caroline's leg. "It doesn't matter if I did it or he did, it's all the same, right?"

"Now you're finally thinking like a proper king," Justin says, smiling up at me and lifting his brows. "Kings do not make their own moves, now do they? In all reality, they're useless pieces, aren't they? We play with our knights." He gestures at Chasm with a hand. "We fight with our bishops." He flicks his fingers at Maxx. "We run through opponents with our queens." He stands up and winks at Parrish. "Who raised you? What sort of boy stabs his own mother?" Justin snorts and then takes off, leaving us at the table with a bloody Caroline and a whole fuckload of emotional trauma.

In the end, Raúl escorts Caroline to the hospital, and I end up sitting on the dock with the boys in total silence. We're staring out at the water, pressed close together in a line. I'm holding both

Chasm's and Maxx's hands, but Parrish isn't interested in being touched, his face turned away from us.

"Do you want to talk about it?" Chas whispers for what must be the third or fourth time.

"There's nothing to talk about," Parrish mutters back, finally turning his attention to us. His face is blissfully empty. "I did what had to be done."

"You stabbed your mom—" Chas starts, and Parrish bares his teeth at him.

"I only have one mom," he repeats, his voice low and menacing. "I don't give a shit what happens to that woman in there."

"Dude, you don't have to front with us. Just be honest," Chasm pleads as Maxx heaves a tired sigh and runs a hand down his face.

"No way in hell we're leaving Kota here by herself tonight," he declares, doing his best to change the subject.

"The only thing I care about in regard to Caroline is that she upsets Tess," Parrish continues, ignoring Maxx and making me wonder if this isn't a case of *thou doth protest too much*. He exhales through his nose and then looks back at the water. "And no, of course not. We're not leaving Gamer Girl with that freak ever again."

"It's not as if any of you have a choice." I let my feet dangle in the water and allow my mind the space to work on a plan. I've got to stop Justin before this gets any worse; I'm running out of time. With Tess fighting back on the legal front and Saffron creeping around the shadows, I'm as likely to lose either or both of my mothers before the summer is over.

That, and my own sense of self, my morality, my heart, my soul.

If I haven't lost too much already, that is.

"Will he even care if we stay the night?" Maxx asks, looking down at me.

It's a valid question. Would Justin? Probably not. What better place for the boys to be than in his house, under the stifling view of his all-seeing eyes. How could we possibly plot against him here? Here's a clue: we just fucking *can't*.

"Probably not, but remember: he told me that you needed to date Maxine." I look over at Parrish next, playing with Tess' ring on my finger. "And that you needed to date Lumen. Don't think he's going to forget about all of that."

"I haven't forgotten about it either: I invited Lumen to the wedding." Parrish shoves up to his feet, looking down at his hands. He's washed them multiple times already, and I don't actually believe he got any blood on them in the first place. He's upset, even if he doesn't want to admit it. "X, I suggest you do the same with Maxine."

"Where are you going?" Chasm asks, following Parrish up to his feet.

"Tess will fall apart if I stay the night here. Not that I blame her." Parrish pauses there to look down at me, hazel eyes softening. Chas offers him some space so that he can step close, squatting beside me. Parrish reaches out to brush some hair from my forehead and that urge to cry hits me all over again. "Don't be sad, Gamer Girl. Not on my account anyway."

"What you did tonight—" I start, but Parrish reaches out and puts a very gentle hand over my lips.

"What you did for me the entirety of the time I was kidnapped, I could spend my whole life trying to repay you and never make a dent in that debt." He tries to smile at me, but smiles were never Parrish's favorite expression in the first place. It's even more difficult for him now, when there are so many other things to worry about. He drops his hand from my lips and takes my chin in his fingers. "I'd like to spend my whole life trying, at the very least."

"Just remember: you were kidnapped by *my* father." The words are barely more than a whisper, almost fully obscured by the sound of the water lapping against the shore.

"I was kidnapped because Justin wanted to dig a needle into Tess' heart and make her hurt; I was kidnapped because she loves me so damn much. And *you* remember this: Justin is as much your father as Caroline is my mother. As in, not at all." Parrish stands up, giving Maxx a look first then Chasm next. "Keep her safe for me tonight?"

"Are you sure you don't want to stay? Laverne would stand up for you." Chasm tucks his hands into his pockets and drops his chin before looking back up at Parrish.

Parrish simply shakes his head as Maxx stands up and pulls me along with him.

"We'll keep her safe," he promises, locking eyes with Parrish. "Let's get through the wedding and then hit the next available party at the Kellogg Camp."

The name sounds familiar, but it takes me a minute to place it. Ah, that's right. The abandoned summer camp that Chasm mentioned. A high school party. A *Whitehall* high school party.

Sleeping pills.

Veronica.

A kidnapping.

I can't fucking wait.

"There's one planned for next Friday," Parrish offers, sighing heavily. He closes his eyes and lets his head fall back. When he opens them, he's clearly looking at something in particular. We all follow his lead, finding the moon sitting pretty in a sea of sparkling stars. It's still light out, but it's as if the sunset is kissed with just a whisper of night.

"Friday," I repeat, because I know that as soon as I pull the trigger on this plan, I'm on a strict timeline. However we go about this, no matter how clever, no matter how cunning, we cannot keep Veronica Fisher—pathetic snot-nosed brat that she is—captive for very long. It's not right. Even the idea of containing a person and taking away their freedom of movement disgusts me, but this is the only way.

We kidnap Veronica, convince Justin that she's dead, and when his guard is down … when it's down, I …

"Friday." I say it again, dropping my chin and staring out across the water in the direction of the Puget Sound and the boat trip with my father that I'll never get to take. "Friday."

I turn and head up the path toward the house and the boys follow.

Chasm and Maxx curl up in bed with me, but nothing sexual happens. How could it, after the day we've had?

There is one thing that I notice. It's small—probably it's nothing—but I do take note of it. At two separate times during the night, one or the other of the boys is missing. I tell myself they're using the bathroom but, even though I don't keep track of the exact time, they're gone far too long for that to be plausible.

That, and the attached bathroom in my bedroom remains unoccupied.

"Where were you?" I whisper as Maxx climbs back into bed with me. He goes completely still before turning a smile my way that's almost ominous in the strange shadows of night.

"Grabbing a snack," he tells me, leaning down to press a kiss to my forehead.

In the morning, I get the same story from Chasm. And why, oh why, would I think anything else but to believe them?

CHAPTER 32

I'm not entirely certain how I make it to Saturday morning, but when it comes, I'm downstairs waiting on the porch when Tess shows up. I must've truly and utterly disgusted Justin with my behavior because he hasn't spoken to me since our glorious dinner party.

Thank God.

He could never speak to me again, and I'd be beyond thrilled.

"Never thought I'd see the day ..." Tess starts as I yank the rear passenger side door of her BMW open, sliding in and slamming it shut with an audible sigh of relief. At this point, I'm not entirely certain that I care if Tess notices that something is going on.

Actually, as both she and Parrish turn around to look at me, I know she's onto us.

"Are you okay, Dakota?" she asks me, narrowing her eyes slightly before flicking her gaze over to the imposing brick manor on our right. "Do you need me to go in there and speak with him?

575

Did something happen?"

"I'm fine." I stare at my lap, but I know I'm breathing heavily, that I'm acting beyond abnormal. I'm just so beyond relieved to get out of Justin's house that I'm having trouble remembering that I'm supposed to lie, lie, and lie some more.

I am so fucking sick and tired of lying.

"Our new hearing is set for the Monday after next," Tess tells me, reaching out a hand and then pausing with it hovering in midair between us. I look up as Parrish undoes his seat belt and goes to climb out. *Please, just touch me,* I think at Tess and then I just end up reaching out and taking her hand with my own. Her eyes widen in surprise, but I guess I've just realized that she's not a mind reader. If I need more from her, I have to speak up.

"Could we go hiking?" I ask, four words that I never, ever, ever expected to come out of my mouth. Parrish scoots into the seat beside me and closes the door. Tess wets her lips and gives him an odd look but doesn't comment.

"Hiking?" she asks, and I nod briskly. "Me, you, and Parrish?"

"Me, you, Parrish, X, Chasm, Maxine, my grandparents ... I don't even care if Kimber comes." I shrug my shoulders again. "Let's just go for a nice, long hike somewhere remote."

"Remote?" Tess repeats, and then I'm releasing her hand and she's turning back around and shifting the vehicle into drive. I've thoroughly and utterly stumped her. As we drive, she attempts to make conversation, but I can't talk in here with Justin listening.

"I'd much rather Tess was where she belonged: by my side or on her knees in front of me."

Fuck you, Justin Prior. Just, seriously, fuck you to hell and back.

I scrub my hands over my face and do my best to rally.

One way or another, I'm going to end this soon.

One way or another, I'm either going to kill Justin or I'm going to force him to kill me, and that'll be it. He can't weasel his way out of that one. Tess will never let it go. Saffron will never let it go. The boys will … oh, they'd be heartbroken but furious. They'd get revenge for me and then, eventually, they'd move on and find new girlfriends and I'd fade away into a distant memory …

I blink away tears for a scenario that hasn't even happened.

That is most definitely not *going to happen. Are you seriously going to let Justin of all people drag you down like this, Kota? That's not like you at all.*

With a sniffle and a serious rallying of my spirit, I reach down and curl my fingers through Parrish's, looking up with a bright smile on my face.

"Let's go as far away as we can, to a place where the trees are so thick that the forest floor is dark, somewhere that has a bumpy road and coordinates instead of an address."

Tess thinks on that for a minute and then nods, checking my face in the rearview mirror. What it is that she sees, I'm not sure, but her expression becomes more resolute.

"I will never *stop fighting,"* she'd said.

And I believe her. I do.

I look over at Parrish and our eyes meet. He offers up another smile before lifting my knuckles to his lips. Tess allows it—for a minute. But when he sucks one of my fingers into his mouth?

"Parrish Vanguard," she gasps in complete and utter disgust, and he reluctantly drops my hand to his lap, offering up a wink in response. That makes me laugh, and even if it's a bit forced, a little bit sad, at least there's real mirth in it.

We'll get through this together, I promise myself.

Because I can't let Justin win. I can't even let him tie with me. And if I died, that's what it'd be, a stalemate. Oh no. I'm going to checkmate his king, flip the board, and then I'm never, ever going to play a game of chess for as long as I live.

Tess surprises me by inviting everyone on my list to join us not just on a hike but at a cabin she's rented for the night. It sits on over two hundred acres of land with private trails threaded throughout.

Also, there's like zero cell service out here.

A smile lights my lips as I wait on the porch with Pear-Pear and X, watching as my grandparents climb out of their rental car with Maxine.

"This is a first," my grandfather says, looking around at the trees, the impossible sunshine slanting into the clearing where the 'cabin' sits. Um. I guess it's only a cabin in the sense that its walls are made out of logs. In reality, it's a mansion. I mean, it can sleep up to sixteen people. "Dakota Banks, eager to go hiking. What are the odds?"

I'm smiling, and it's not entirely unreal.

"If only we didn't have to head back into town so soon for the … wedding." Tess can barely get the words out as she joins me on the front porch. Her eyes follow Maxine as my sister bounces up the steps and throws herself into my arms, offering me up the biggest, best Banks signature hug known to mankind. It's like, something registers in Tess' gaze right then and she glances away, moving back into the cabin to give us some space.

"Not that I think it's okay for *that man* to spy on you," Maxine begins, and my lips quirk up at the new nickname, "but I'm beyond giddy at the idea of you taking up hiking as a new hobby."

"She's dating me; she doesn't have much choice." Maxx offers this up with a slight nod of his chin and a cocksure smirk that has me simultaneously annoyed and excited all at once. He parks his hands on his hips and then notices my grandmother lifting her bag from the trunk, sprinting down the steps to grab it for her.

He ends up coming back with all three of the Banks' duffel bags slung over his broad shoulders.

"Show-off," Chasm murmurs, coming out of the house and crossing his arms over his chest. He offers Parrish up a dark look. "You didn't think to run down there and help with their bags?"

"They're *your* future in-laws after all," Parrish whispers back, but I know he doesn't entirely mean that. Or, if he does, he doesn't mean that the Banks would be Chasm's in-laws alone. Sure, multiple marriages aren't exactly legal in the US (probably for the best, to be honest), but there's no rule that says we can't live together, love together, and be happy forever after, right?

"Boys," my grandfather greets and, even though my grandparents are a long ways off from following sex-class stereotypes, he doesn't seem to mind taking on the overprotective father role. "Kwang-seon." Grandpa's eyes drop to the ring on my finger, even as I'm still half-hugging Maxine, and his mouth twitches.

"*Abeoji*," Chasm greets, offering up a polite bow. He flashes a pretty smile when he rises to his full height and, as per usual, gets the brunt of a situation he has little to no control over.

"Please tell me that means *I'm sorry*," Walter grumbles, but he offers up a smile anyway, and moves past us into the house. There's something in his gaze however that gives it away.

He's upset, but he's not upset at me *or* Chasm.

Does he know something more is going on behind-the-scenes? Did Tess tell him? I can't decide if I'd like that or if the idea terrifies me. I don't want my family to be in danger, but if they can believe in me even throughout all of this nonsense ... Wow. Just ... wow.

My grandmother pauses in much the same way, reaching out to take my hand. She rubs her thumb over the ring but says nothing in regard to the marriage.

"*Eomeoni*," Chasm says, offering up another bow as one of Parrish's perfectly manicured brows twitches in annoyance.

"I'm glad we finally get to spend some time together," Carmen offers up, and she says this to Chasm and not to me. I mean, I know she's happy to spend time with me, but she's curious about these boys, too. Her gaze slides over to Parrish and then, as he comes back out of the house sans bags, Maxim. "This should be a fun night."

"Are you going to the wedding, too?" I ask, and I hope like hell that the answer is no. I'm sure that Justin sent the Banks an invitation. I was also surprised to find out that he invited Tess this time. Usually, he likes to serve up heaping portions of FOMO her way. The very idea of it makes my blood boil with suspicion.

"I think it's probably best if we don't." Carmen pauses and sighs, offering Maxine up a look. "Your sister's determined to go, but I'm not certain that we've fostered particularly goodwill with that man after what happened in court."

"Mm." I make a noncommittal sound. There's no cell service up here, but there is some weak, spotty Wi-Fi, and I don't know who's logged into it. Kimber was probably crying for the password halfway up the mountain. "No need. It's just a yacht party pretty much."

That's how Justin and Caroline are getting married: on a giant boat that costs more than most people's homes. Actually, on a giant boat that costs more than most rich people's mansions. It's not quite as obscene as say, a super yacht that requires dismantling a historic bridge in Rotterdam or something (gag, puke, choking on excess hubris), but it's still pretty luxe.

"*Just like Ursula's wedding to Eric at the end of* The Little Mermaid," is how Justin described it to me. Gross. Another Disney reference. I feel like he somehow missed the point of that story. As in, Ursula was defeated and Ariel ended up marrying Eric, but whatever. Let Millennials be Millennials. Will avocado toast be served at the reception is my question.

"Your grandfather committed to making chili for everyone tonight; he thought you might want to help him out in the kitchen." Carmen waltzes past, and I can't control the smile that stretches over my face.

This was how it should've been all along, right from the very start.

I never blamed Tess for wanting me back, not really. I mean, I didn't want to come here initially, but I understood her motivations. Her child was taken from her through no fault of her own, and she had a right to at least see me through my final years of high school, to build the relationship that we should've had from the very beginning.

But she shouldn't have shut the Banks out. If she'd invited us all here, wined and dined us, listened to us, let me talk to them, stopped blaming them …

"Things are finally as they should be," I say, and Maxine grins.

"God, I've missed you." She reaches out and pinches my nose, and I slap her hand away playfully. She looks over at my harem with a conspiratorial gleam in her brown eyes. "Have you guys noticed that, too? How she blurts random things out sometimes?"

"It's like her internal thoughts bleed right out of her mouth," X offers up, and then it's my turn to slap him. Only, it's like slapping marble. See? He's got granite abs, marble pecs, a face chiseled from stone by a lonely but supremely talented artist.

In that moment, it all came together.

Everything I was searching for, I found. The identity that I thought I'd lost—that is, the Dakota Banks I'd grown up with— was gone forever. But not in a bad way. In the best possible way. I'd been reborn and reforged as someone new.

Not Mia Patterson. Certainly not Mia Prior. Just ... me. It no longer mattered what name I called myself because names don't define a person. Clothes don't define a person. Houses or things or even likes or dislikes.

Heart, that's what defined me. And I had it all around me in spades. That sense of free-floating, it was gone. I felt grounded in a way I never had before. I felt—

"Excuse me." I turn and sprint into the cabin, dumping my bag out on the couch until I find the tiny glittery unicorn notebook that Maxine won for me from a claw machine at an arcade. I snatch up a pen and then I start scribbling words down because ... because, well, not because Justin wants me to.

I've just started to realize that I can communicate to the world this way, with words. Sometimes, it's hard to speak. Sometimes, I can't find the right thing to say in the right moment or sometimes I can't find anything at all. Sometimes, all I find is the wrong thing.

But with this? With words?

I start jotting the rambling, twisted ideas in my thoughts down and, as I do so, I start to feel better. *If I ever do write anything beyond these forced pages with Justin, I'll write for me. Not for anybody else. Just me. Because I'm communicating, and I'm putting my heart on the page, and I don't owe anything to anyone else.*

A smile takes over my lips yet again which surprises me.

Thursday was an awful day. Awful for me. Awful for Parrish. Awful for Maxx and Chasm. Probably pretty awful for Caroline, too, but hey, she *did* show up here in Medina looking for a dude to kill, so it's hard to be overly sympathetic.

Unfortunately for her, the black widow found herself in a very different sort of web.

"What are you doing?" Tess asks, and I feel my cheeks go beet red. I can barely convince myself to look up, knowing that my unicorn author is staring down at me. Okay, so like maybe *one* of my unicorn authors because I'd really, really like to posthumously meet Agatha Christie and maybe have lunch with Holly Black, but I digress.

"Err, writing ..." I start, and then I sit up straight and struggle to find any more words to say. Tess is just blinking down at me, and I can't believe that even after the Parrish thing and the threesome thing and the engagement and the tattoo, she's still talking to me, but ... *She knows.* The thought percolates along with another, my eyes sliding over to my grandparents as they talk in low tones in the kitchen.

Paul is sitting with Amelia and Henry at the table, playing a game of Jenga while Ben reads an *Animorphs* book by K.A. Applegate (I won't tell him that the end of that series killed me or that the letter the author wrote to her fans was poignant unless he asks). Maxine and the boys are hovering near the door as if they're not sure where to go or what to do, and Kimber is slumped in an armchair staring at me as if she has no idea who I am.

Because she doesn't.

I have no idea who she is either, to be honest. And as angry as I am at the things she did—leading me and Chas to the hedge maze and straight to Veronica's girl gang being one of them—I know that she's young (her birthday isn't until August making her one of the youngest freshmen in Whitehall history), and that we *are* strangers.

We don't have to stay that way.

I look back at Tess.

"I'm writing something down that I want to say, but that I'm not sure how to say aloud with words. At least not right now."

Tess continues to stare at me and then nods, putting her hands on her hips.

"I planned a nice hike for the morning, but we could take a

walk now. Just you and me?"

My chest tightens, and all the air escapes my lungs, but I make myself nod because I know that I need to do this. I set the notebook aside and stand up, switching out my shoes for more practical ones.

"Good luck," Parrish whispers on my way past, but I don't need it.

Luck has nothing to do with this.

Tess and I walk for a while, until we're winding down a sun dappled path beneath the trees, just as I asked for. The canopy is so thick that even though it's only five o'clock and summer is in full swing, it's a little bit dark in here.

"Do you have your phone on you?" I ask, and Tess exhales heavily before shaking her head.

"I can't keep my phone on me when I know he can listen in whenever he damn well pleases," she says, surprising the hell out of me. I actually stop walking and Tess turns to me, her face gravely serious, her expression resolute. "I know that there's something you're not telling me."

I open my mouth in automatic protest, a ready-made lie perched on my lips.

Tess doesn't even let me say it. Instead, she holds up a hand in my direction, palm out, and offers up a slight shake of her head.

"If you're not telling me, and Parrish isn't telling me, if Maxx and Chasm are going along with it, then it must be pretty bad." She refocuses her gaze on me, and I resist the urge to fidget under such an unrelenting stare. "You forget: Justin convinced me to fall in love with him." A bitter laugh escapes Tess' lips and she runs a hand down her face. "He convinced me to marry him, to have a child with him. I know how charming he can seem at first and how quickly things can go downhill once he's got you in his claws."

I say nothing. It's the best that I can do at the moment.

ENDGAME ROMANCE

"Tess …" I start and then after a brief hesitation, I say, "Mom."

That softens her a bit, but she shakes her head and continues on into the trees. I assumed she'd look at odds out here, that her oh so modern ice queen businesswoman persona wouldn't fit in with nature. That doesn't seem to be the case at all. Instead, she blends in so well that I wouldn't be surprised to find out she had survival training and could go Bear Grylls on this place.

"You don't have to call me mom if you don't want to." The words seem to pain her as they come out, but she smiles at me anyway. "If you do, I'd be thrilled, but don't force yourself."

I say nothing in response to that, pausing near a cluster of mushrooms at the base of a tree. Tess squats beside me and we examine them together. They're brown, closely clustered, and look a bit like, well, a pig's ears.

"Pig's ear mushrooms," I state, pointing at them, and Tess raises a brow at me. "I mean, I wouldn't trust my identification skills enough to eat them, but I took a class during my freshman year of high school." I rise to my feet and Tess follows along with me, studying me carefully. "My grandpa could confirm or deny my hypothesis."

"You grew up well, Dakota," she whispers, her voice edging on tears. "My only regret is that I wasn't there to see it."

I turn away from her and she reaches out to take my chin, very softly pulling my gaze back to hers. I flinch. I don't mean to, but … it happens, and her eyes widen. Then she's taking a step closer to me and staring at the edge of my mouth where Justin split my lip.

I thought I'd covered it up well enough, but …

"Did he hit you." It's not even a question. It's a statement.

"I—"

"Damn him," Tess grinds out, teeth gritted, angry tears clinging to the outside edges of her eyes. She releases my face and then takes my wrist, pushing up my sleeve. I move to jerk back, but she tightens her fingers just enough to keep me in place.

"Tess, please," I start, but she pushes the fabric up anyway, revealing several impossible to miss bruises on my upper arm. "It's not what you think."

"Dakota," she says, and it's her use of my real name that causes me to falter just enough that I know she can see the truth. There's no lie I can spout, no tale I can spin that will convince her otherwise. "How long has this been going on?"

"Please don't push him." That's what I say instead. Am I making things worse rather than better? I look up at Tess, and I hope to God that she can see how damn serious I am in my eyes. "If you push him, it'll only make things worse."

I'm breathing hard as she releases me, and I can see that she's visibly trembling with undisguised rage.

"I knew something was going on, but I …" She trails off and turns away, pushing the heels of her hands against her forehead. She closes her eyes as I move up beside her, hand hovering near her shoulder. Do I touch her? In the end, I grew up with the Banks, and we're touchy people. I lay my palm on her arm. "Can you ever forgive me, Dakota?" Tess drops her hands and looks over at me, those angry tears finding their way down her cheeks.

"Forgive you? For what?" I whisper, and she shakes her head again.

"For being selfish. If I'd left you with the Banks, if I'd never …" Tess pauses, and I can see that she really and truly blames herself for Justin's actions. Total bullshit in my opinion, but I'm not certain I'll be able to convince her otherwise. "I thought that more publicity was better, that he'd still be the wandering, penniless lunatic he was when we divorced. I didn't think he could touch me. I thought that by marrying into the Vanguards, we'd be untouchable." She bites at her thumbnail, and I almost smile.

Because Parrish does that. Because now I've started doing that a little bit, too.

Some habits are born in blood, others are learned.

It's a comforting thought.

"That's not why I married Paul, of course." She drops her hand and turns to me again, stippled shadows peppering her beautiful face. When a scarce droplet of sunlight hits her eyes, they seem to glow. It's an illusion, but it makes her look as scary, as impossible, as she was during the initial custody hearing against the Banks, when I knew I'd never be able to beat her.

It's as comforting now as it was terrifying back then.

"You love Paul?" I ask, and she forces a tight smile.

"I do. Paul is everything that Justin is not. I know he hasn't treated you as well as he should. He's a shy man, and sometimes, he can be weak." She pauses here and sighs. "Particularly when it comes to Laverne. But he's as loving and gentle as Justin is cruel."

"I don't know how you got the new custody hearing, but I don't think you can beat him, Tess." I don't mean to bring her down, but I don't know what else to do. "If your lawyer asks me about the bruises, I'll lie on the stand."

Tess just stares at me.

"It's all him, isn't it?" she asks softly. "The engagement, your behavior in court … your behavior in general." Her eyes narrow as she looks at me, and terror rips through me. "The typewriter." Tess gasps, slapping her hand over her mouth. My own eyes go wide, and I know I need to figure out a solution—and quick. This entire conversation is putting the Banks at risk. Putting the boys at risk. Tess herself at risk.

"Just wait a second," I start, forcing a laugh. "I can't deny there was a mix-up with the bruises, but you can't just start blaming everything else on Justin."

Tess turns away, paces a bit, and then spins back to stare at me.

"I may not know you as well as a mother should know her daughter, but there were so many things about that scenario that struck me as odd. You didn't know the significance of that typewriter; Justin did. How could you unknowingly recreate a scenario from the past like that?" She lifts her chin and marches up to me as I struggle to salvage the situation. She has that *look* on her face now, the one that brooks no argument. "How long has he been in contact with you? Since you came up to me and demanded to know who Justin Prior was?"

"Listen to me," I start, hyperventilating. The world is spinning around me, and it feels like everything I've done up to this point is being tossed right out the window, like all my sacrifices are being wasted. "That's not what happened!"

"You can lie to me all you want; I know he's threatening you." Her eyes fill with tears again, but her jaw is clenched, her lips pursed into a thin line. She shakes her trembling hands out, nostrils flared. "But he can't hurt you if you tell me, Dakota. There's nothing he can do when you're with me."

"That's a lie!" I scream back at her, stumbling and putting a hand out on the tree trunk beside me. "You don't know what he's really like, and if you keep pushing like this, he's going to …" I start and fail to say the words. Can I? Should I? Tess reaches out for me, but I tear away from her, and then it's me that's pacing rapidly. "No matter what you think you know, it isn't the full story. Please don't do anything with these ideas."

"Dakota, he's physically harming you," Tess says softly, taking a step closer to me. "I know you're afraid, but you have to trust me. I can't send you back to him knowing that abuse like this is going on."

"Take him to court again. However it is that you managed this new hearing, run with that. Use that against him. If you bring up any of these other accusations, I'll deny them. I'll look the judge right in the face and plead with him to send me back to Justin's."

Tess opens her mouth, closes it, opens it again. She exhales.

"Dakota, I don't understand. This is beyond childish. What can I do if you refuse to fucking speak with me?" Her voice heats up, but she quickly closes her eyes, counts to three and brings her temper under control. I realize that she's doing the best she can with a shitty situation, but I have to stay strong. I cannot give in here. If I tell her the truth now, she'll try to destroy Justin, but she won't pay enough attention to the collateral damage.

"I will—eventually. Just … give me the week." I lift my head up and meet her gaze dead-on before lifting up a single finger. "One week, Tess, and I promise that I'll tell you everything. What does it matter, right? He'll be on his honeymoon until then anyway; I'm safe for now."

"I will *never* send you back to that man's house knowing that he's throwing you around. I won't do it. There's not a thing you can say to me to change my mind about that." She turns to head back toward the cabin, but I grab onto her arm, I press my cheek into her back and close my eyes.

"Trust me, Tess. I know it's hard. I know I … I haven't given you a reason to trust anything I say. I've lied to you over and over. I slept with your son. I got engaged. I've been awful to you. But just trust me this one time, and everything will be different after."

There are several breaths between my words and her answer.

"If I give you this week, will I regret it?" she asks, and maybe she will. I tell myself this is the last lie I'm ever going to tell Tess Vanguard, and I put every ounce of conviction I have inside of myself to do it.

"Not at all. It's not as bad as you think, and in the end, Justin will get what's coming to him. Just let me have one week. Win the hearing. Do that for me, and I'll feel safe enough to talk."

She turns around slowly to look down at me, cupping my face

between her hands. Her eyes search my face, and I force a smile.

"It was just the one time anyway," I lie. "I yelled at Justin, and he lost his temper. It's the first time I've ever seen him like that, and it scared me. I won't let it happen again. If it does, I'll … I'll call you right away. I'll call the police. I'll call those FBI ladies."

Tess keeps staring at me.

"I …" she starts, and then she sighs, closing her eyes tight. "I don't like this at all. It goes against everything I believe, that I stand for. I'm fairly certain it makes me a terrible mother." She opens her eyes again, and I feel my heart seize in my chest. "Sending you back to a man who left bruises on your arms? Who split your lip like that? It's disgusting, Dakota. I'll give you the week, but only because he's out of town. That's it, the only reason."

"Th-thank you." It's all I can say. The lies are choking me, but this is an emergency.

I'm running out of time.

Rapidly.

I am rapidly running out of fucking time.

"I'm going to win that hearing, and I'm going to take you away from him forever." She lifts up a single finger. "And then I'm going to nail him to the wall by his balls and put him back behind bars where he belongs."

"Okay." There's that noncommittal word again, the most understood two syllables on the planet. I lift up a pair of fingers and make the peace symbol, flashing another pretty smile.

Tess stares at me for a second, and then she throws her arms around me.

She hugs me like she's Saffron, and I dig my fingers into her expensive (I'm sure) t-shirt, a piece of hiking gear that's clearly never been worn before. She clings to me, and I know for a fact that there's one thing Parrish was right about.

ENDGAME ROMANCE

Tess is never going to let me go.

And I'm okay with that.

When we get back to the cabin, everyone turns to look at us like a pair of blue-skinned aliens descending from the disc of some foreign star craft.

Tess clears her throat and claps her hands.

"I've heard a lot about this famous chili ..." she starts, and even if the words sound like they're scraping past a sandpaper tongue, she's trying and that's all that matters to me.

"Eww, gross, *you* are going to cook?" Kimber asks, making a gagging sound that Parrish seconds by lifting his brows. "Mom, no offense, but you're a terrible cook."

"It's pretty hard to mess up chili, young lady." Walter rummages through the cabinets until he finds a pot and then sets it on the stove. My grandmother takes a seat at the table with a glass of wine, leaning over to see what it is that Ben's reading.

"Oh, Dakota loved these books when she was your age," she says, tapping the page with a finger as I move into the kitchen and Maxine joins me. It's a little weird having Tess there, but it's a relief at the same time, the idea that we might actually be able to get along.

Please, I think, glancing over at her, *keep this promise. Even if it's the only one you ever keep for me.*

She looks back at me and smiles as Parrish sidles into the kitchen followed by Maxx and Chasm.

"I don't know about this one," I say, pointing at Parrish, "but Walter, you should see how well the other two can cook."

"I can cook better than Tess," Parrish scoffs out, lifting his chin.

"We shall see, son. We shall see." Tess grabs a series of aprons off a hook and passes them out as I glance over at the boys. They're all staring at me like they can sense something big happened in the woods.

I hope the look I give them says, *I'll tell you later* and not *we are so fucked.* But who knows? Either way, it's not time to discuss the Justin shit. It's time to cook.

"Put me wherever you need me," Chasm says, crossing his arms over his apron. "My *halmeoni* taught me well; there's nothing I can't do."

"I'm more of a line cook," X admits, reaching up to rub at the back of his head. "It's probably best if I'm not left with anything too technical."

"Boys," Maxine says, turning to stare the three of them down. "This is *chili,* like toss it in a pot chili. And corn bread. We always make homemade corn bread with this recipe."

"I've tasted it," Parrish offers up, and my mind strays back to the cornbread sitting outside my bedroom door with a slice missing. Even then, he was looking out for me.

"Too many cooks in the kitchen?" Tess asks, reaching up as if to take her apron off. I reach out and stop her before she can remove it, shaking my head.

"Food is more about family than feasting, isn't that right?" It's Paul who says that, surprising me more than just a little. That's when I notice that his gaze is on Parrish, that it's soft, that even if he's a hard man to get along with, he cares about his family.

"Paul's right. It's not about the actual food at all, now is it?" I turn back to the counter, push up my sleeves—but only to my elbows to hide the bruises—and dig in.

CHAPTER 33

Delphine and I are wearing matching off-the-shoulder cocktail dresses in a soft blush color. Paired with delicate silver heels, diamond tennis bracelets, and artful chignons, we look the part of the dutiful daughters-turned-bridesmaids.

Parrish, Chasm, and Maxx are in the audience, wearing the same suits they wore to prom. Rather, Maxx is wearing the suit he wore to the Milk Carton launch party, the white dinner jacket with the black bow tie and black slacks. *My own personal James Bond,* I think with a smile.

He's not happy, sitting there with a frown on his pretty mouth, arms crossed over his chest. His parents are in the row just in front of him, and I know he can't help but be suspicious of them.

Chasm is with Seamus, looking meek and turned-down in a way that makes me want to cry. But when he lifts his face up and swipes that lightning bolt hair from his forehead, I can see that he's far from broken. His father ignores him, staring out at the sparkling waters of Lake Washington as if he'd rather be anywhere but here.

Mount Rainier is an impossible landmark in the distance, as stoic and proud as Parrish Vanguard, seated in the front like a member of the family and not an estranged son who stabbed his birth mom in the leg with a knife.

As for Caroline herself? Well, you'd never know that Justin and his bride-to-be are more likely to kill one another than live in happily wedded bliss. They laugh along with their glittering highfalutin guests; Caroline clings to Justin's arm. And her limp? Well, you'd never know it was there if you didn't think to look for it.

"Aren't they precious together?" Delphine asks, holding a small bouquet in her hands and smiling prettily at her future stepmother. My newest bio sister looks stunning with her gold hair in a flower-studded updo, her makeup so flawless that you'd never realize she was wearing any. She's good at it. If she wanted a career as a makeup artist, I bet she could doll up the finest celebrities and Medina heirs and heiresses for big cash.

I smile back at her and nod noncommittally, but it's hard for me to want to try for anything more with Delphine after last week's incident. Either she's willfully ignorant or she's complicit. I can't seem to find any other explanation in her reaction.

"Are you nuts? He's the sweetest man in the world."

I bite my lip and taste strawberries from the gloss, wondering how long this whole affair is going to take. My eyes drift over to the Fishers, sitting in the third row on the groom's side, as if they're actually Justin's good friends instead of antagonists bent on taking him down.

This had better work, I think, turning back to see Justin watching me from the railing on the opposite side of the ship. He's surrounded by admirers, but he's only looking at me. To be quite frank, I'm afraid to be alone with him right now.

ENDGAME ROMANCE

The new hearing is next week; Justin is leaving on his honeymoon tonight.

I have until he gets back before Tess unravels—if that.

Saturday night, after she thought everyone else had gone to bed, I found her crying over a bottle of wine at the cabin's dining table. I didn't let her see me. I just stood there peering around the corner and found tears sliding down my own face until Maxx came and got me.

At least I got to sleep in the same room as the boys—albeit on a bunk bed by myself. With Maxine in the room, and the cabin bursting with parental scrutiny, there wasn't a lot of space for, um, physical exploration with the boys.

Too bad.

I adjust my sweaty grip on my own bouquet as the officiant gathers everyone together, and Delphine and I get to do what we do best: act as decorative props to Justin's theatrical performances.

Looking at him now, seeing how he behaves, the moves he makes, I feel like a moron for jumping on a livestream and asking the internet to hunt a serial killer with me. The *internet?!*

Justin Prior *is* the internet.

How funny that must've been to him.

The only way to beat a man like Justin Prior is to go in the complete opposite direction. I can never beat his tech; I can't out-hack him. What I can do is play games in the real world. I can touch some fuckin' grass.

That's how Saffron's beating him, isn't it? The old car. The lack of a phone. The snail mail. Old-school clapback.

With the sun kissing the surface of the water, Justin takes his place at the front of the yacht—whose yacht it is, I don't know, could be his in all honesty—with Caroline beside him. Bio Dad is dressed to kill in a black suit with a blue tie that matches his sapphire eyes. Meanwhile, Parrish's bio mom is decked out in the absurdly expensive white dress with the plunging neckline and the voluminous (if scandalously short) skirts that she picked out on our shopping trip.

At this point, I'm just bored of it all.

It takes considerable effort on my part not to gag my way through the vows as Justin and Caroline take one another's hands and gaze into one another's eyes. I see Raúl in the audience, Mr. Volli. He's looking a bit rough around the edges after his confrontation with Saffron, but he's still here.

He's still sending me edits via Google docs and red-penning my work.

The inner dialogue drags and drags and drags; it's repetitive at times. Do you want to bore your readers to death?

Sigh.

After the ceremony, a crowd of well-dressed employees floods the area, rearranging the chairs to make room for a dance floor. Tables are already set up, covered in fluttering white cloths, and dinner is served.

Filet mignon and butter poached lobster tails for the meat eaters; mushroom wellington and butternut squash ravioli with white wine sauce for the vegetarians. It's quite the affair. Personally, I'm having trouble choking any of it down.

"Don't stress," Maxx assures me, coming over to put his hands on the back of my chair. He leans down and puts his lips near my ear. "We've got this."

"I know we do." I turn to look at him and very nearly brush our mouths together.

Wouldn't be a good look for me, would it? Considering I'm *engaged* to Chasm. Considering Maxx brought my sister as a date. That's the part of this that freaks me out the most, her presence here. She knows we're up to something, but I don't have the heart to tell her that we're in the process of plotting the kidnapping of a seventeen-year-old girl.

Pretty gross, eh?

My stomach is queasy as I look quickly away from Maxx, and Chas reaches out to push my water glass just a bit closer to me. It's not just this whole 'lock Veronica in Laverne's vault' plot that has me on edge.

It's everything that comes after.

It's Justin.

It's taking the lesson he taught me with the cop—Heath Cousins—and amplifying it to a whole new level.

Sacrifice.

I understand, Daddy. I get it. I glance his way, handsome and charming in his suit.

"He's coming this way," Chasm mutters and Maxx very quickly moves away, retreating back to the table with his parents and Maxine.

"Care for a father-daughter dance?" Justin asks me, sweeping a bow.

I make myself smile—remember: I've been practicing these since January—and nod, offering up my hand for Justin to take. He grips my fingers just a little too hard, but I don't let on, allowing him to sweep me onto the dance floor.

On the outside, I'm as happy as can be. I'm the perfect daughter. The lost daughter. The reunited daughter.

On the inside, I'm screaming.

I don't want to do this, Justin. Please don't make me do this.

Mostly ... *I wish this were real.*

I want this to be real.

Oh how badly I want this to be real.

The sun is shining; the water is as blue as his eyes. In the distance, Seattle glimmers, a collection of silver towers with verdant green clustered at their bases. The sky is clear and open, an endless sea of possibilities.

My father is handsome and intelligent, creative and cunning. He's got a million-dollar smile, a sense of humor, a hilarious collection of charming generational stereotypes.

A penchant for blood.

I close my eyes as Justin sweeps me across the dance floor to Phil Collins' *"You'll Be in My Heart"* from the Disney movie *Tarzan*. Not my favorite movie, not my favorite song. But … it's fucking goddamn heartbreaking. It's the song that plays during a scene where Tarzan's adoptive mother is taking care of him.

Tears prick and then fall, and I can't stop them.

"What's the matter, Princess?" Justin asks, reaching up to rub one away with his thumb. "Are you that happy to see your old man married off?"

"I wish you loved me more than you loved your revenge."

He looks down at me, and he says nothing. He keeps one hand on mine, the other on my waist, and he dances with me until the song fades away and a new one starts. I don't even know what it is, but I don't care.

I take off for the stairs and head down to the secondary ballroom, the one that's lined with tables of hors d'oeuvre and full of milling Whitehall teenagers.

If you all only knew that you were on a hit list. Ticktock. Ticktock.

"Bitch," Veronica hisses as I pass, and I shove her with one hand, knocking her into one of the tables. "What the hell is wrong with you?" she screams as I shove through the crowd until I find another door and through that, the bathroom. I push my way in and flick the lock, ending up on the toilet with my head in my hands. I just sit there and pant, wondering how this can possibly end in a happily ever *anything*.

The door creaks open a moment later and there they are, my

boys.

My boys ...

They've got the bug detector in hand, too, because they're just that good. I mean, you'd think Justin wouldn't put cameras or mics in a small powder room that's basically just a toilet and a sink, but ... you never know.

"Little Sister, what are you doing?" Chas asks, coming in to squat in front of me.

"How did you get in here?" I whisper, choking on tears. Chasm reaches up to brush them away, and his touch is so reverent, so loving compared to Justin's. It just makes me cry some more.

"No locks can keep us out," X declares, sharing a look with Parrish. They squeeze into the tiny room with me and shut the door behind them.

"What if I was actually, like, peeing in here?" I sniffle, accepting the wet hand towel that Maxx passes me.

"Then I guess we'd get a lot closer a lot faster?" Parrish muses, leaning a shoulder against the wall as he studies me. "I'm not ready to see you pee yet though. Let's save that for year ten of marriage?"

"Uh, I'm the fiancé, remember?" Chasm asks, pointing at himself as Maxx scoffs.

"I'm not going anywhere unless Kota boots me to the curb. Maybe figure that into your plans, *Kwang-seon-ah*." X and Chas pretend to glare at each other, and I know they're only trying to cheer me up but ...

I burst into tears again.

"Is it the Veronica thing?" Chasm asks, trying to get me to look at him. "If it is, we can handle this without you, no problem. She gets plastered at every party; the girl might very well drink herself into a coma without the help of the sleeping pills."

"It's not the Veronica thing," I promise, dabbing at my eyes and trying not to ruin Delphine's careful makeup job.

"Tess then?" Parrish asks. "I believe she'll give you the week; she thinks she's going to crush Justin in court. Whatever it is that she's got on him, it must be big."

"No, it's not that either." I lift my hands up and shake the hand towel around for emphasis. "It's just … Justin." I look down at my lap because I can't bear to look at their faces without crying again. "It's like, I miss the father that I know he could be if he cared to try."

"I get that feeling," Chasm offers up, glancing over at Parrish. "Maybe you do, too?"

"I don't give a fuck about Caroline." Parrish huffs and then looks to Maxx. "At least you have two normal parents."

"Supposedly," Maxx hedges, and then he bites his lower lip in that way of his. "Only, you know I'm suspicious of their motives. Who knows what horse they have in this race?" X drops down to one knee beside Chasm and takes one of my hands in his. "You're not plotting anything, are you, Kota?"

Fuck.

Fuckin' Maxim freaking Wright.

"Justin is getting angrier and angrier with me. With Tess on the offensive, Saffron on the hunt, I don't have a lot of time. I have to move when his guard is down which it should be after we get Veronica."

"Meaning what?" Maxx asks in a very tight, very careful voice.

"I'm going to take matters into my own hands," I explain, and he scoffs at me.

"You're going to try to kill him? And then what? When it doesn't work, what will you do? If he has the gun he pulled on Parrish, what happens to you, Kota?" X squeezes my hand in an attempt to get me to look at him. "You cannot kill your own father."

I look him straight in his pretty green eyes.

"Only I can do it, Maxx. Only I can get close enough. He's my father; he's worked so hard to make me in his image. Well, guess what? It's working." I stop there and exhale, curling my fingers in the fabric of the feather and floral accented skirt of a dress I would never normally wear.

"Give me some time," X offers up, glancing over at the other two boys. I'm struck all over again by the insanity of this situation, by how crazy my life is and yet how solid and incredible these guys are. The three of them are stars in an ebon sky, guiding me home. "Give *us* some time."

He rises to his feet, straightening his black bow tie.

"We should probably get out of here before anyone realizes we've locked ourselves in the bathroom together." Chasm rises to his feet, rubbing his thumb across his lower lip, eyes on the door. "Don't you two have dates, after all?" He tosses this over his shoulder as he tucks his hands into the pockets of his suit jacket, kicking open the door and striding out as if it's totally normal for three teenage dudes and a teenage girl to cluster in a single-stall bathroom together.

Maxine is waiting when we come out, arms crossed over her chest. She raises her brows at the sight of us and doesn't seem particularly pleased by it. I wonder how she'd feel if she knew about the tattoo? I have yet to reveal it to either her or my grandparents. *Yet another titillating conversation to look forward to.*

"I'm not against the three of you courting my little sister, but— and pardon my French—what the fuck were you doing in there together?" She gives Maxx a look and then clucks her tongue. "I don't know the other two boys very well, but I'd expect more gentlemanly behavior out of you, XY."

He scratches at the back of his head as if he's ashamed, but

Chasm just flashes a grin.

"Gentlemanly? Ol' Maxim over here? Didn't the two of you just do it in the woods—" I clamp a hand over Chas' mouth before he can make things any worse.

Parrish sweeps right past us, yanking open the adjoining door between this room and the ballroom. On the opposite side, there's a door that leads out to the deck. From here, you can go downstairs to the bedrooms, up to the top deck, or into one of four powder rooms.

"If you're going to creep around, be a little more subtle about it." Parrish steps back and gestures Lumen and Danyella into the room.

"We didn't mean to creep," Danyella offers up, wetting her lips as Lumen looks from me to the boys and offers up the slightest shake of her head. While the former is wearing a cute little cocktail dress in a cheerful yellow, the latter has on this floor-length pink fringe crepe gown that makes her look like a princess.

I'd kill to look as elegant and mature as Lumen Hearst.

Well, okay, not a good metaphor.

You're a murderer, Kota. Don't ever forget that. No matter how this ends, your hands are stained forever. Tainted. Everyone knows it.

"Justin is looking for you," Lumen offers up, looking down at the floor instead of my face. Her golden hair is loose and waving around her face, hiding her expression for a brief moment. She sighs as she looks up again. "He said that if I were to find you, I should send you to Caroline's dressing room to help her change from her wedding dress to her reception dress."

"Sounds like a grand time," I mutter, trying to remember where exactly her dressing room is on the massive boat. "Of course she has two dresses. Anything less would be absolutely plebeian."

Maxine gives Lumen a strange look, as if she isn't sure what to make of her. After all, Maxie doesn't know that Justin is the Slayer. But Lumen? She does. We haven't discussed the incident any further for lack of opportunity, but at least she knows how to keep her mouth shut.

The door opens again and Tess appears, looking rather interested to see us clustered together the way we are. Her eyes meet mine before trailing over to Parrish, Chasm, and X. While she didn't ask how much they know, she can't possibly think they're ignorant in all of this.

"I was wondering what was taking you so long in here," she says, crossing her arms over her chest. And oh, she looks so elegant in her simple black satin gown, sharp black and red Louboutins on her feet. "I'm sure this isn't how you all wanted to spend a sunny summer day."

"I'd rather eat a wolf spider with a billion babies on its back," Parrish returns with a tight smile of his own. "But we're fine. Just gossiping. Talking crap behind the backs of Whitehall brats."

"I see." Tess looks at me for an inordinate amount of time, gaze shifting to Danyella, to Lumen, to Maxine. She probably feels better that I'm hanging out with some girls my age, but I bet she's also supremely confused as to why Maxx brought my sister as a date, why Parrish brought Lumen. "Well, I suppose there's no harm in you hiding out for the rest of the party; the boat docks in about two hours. If you want to get off then and skip the remainder of the party, I'm happy to take you … home." She lets the word drift a bit, obviously thinking about Laverne.

"That'd be nice, thank you." I smile at Tess, but she isn't buying what I'm selling. Her gaze says *one week, Dakota.* When she turns and leaves the room, I breathe a sigh of relief, putting a hand to my chest.

"That woman is intense," Maxine mumbles, watching her go. "Don't get me wrong: I'm still not a huge fan of hers, but she's not as bad as I first thought."

Parrish gives my sister one of his famous slitted stares, but then X is stepping forward and taking Maxine by the arm. She blinks in surprise at him as he lets his gaze switch over to me. *I'll take care of your sister,* he says, and even though I know I have no right to be jealous, I am. Just a little bit anyway.

"I'm sure my parents would love to see you again?" Maxx offers up, phrasing it as a question. My sister's face scrunches up slightly, and she looks to me as if for permission. I offer up an encouraging smile, and she nods.

"I'd love to see them again," she agrees, and then X is escorting her out of the room and the door is swinging shut behind them.

"I take it you all want a moment without me here?" Danyella observes, giving Lumen a very dangerous sort of look. "Don't do anything sketchy, you hear me?"

"Girl, I hear you," Lumen says breezily, waving her hand around. "Just trust us to handle this, okay? You're already way more involved than I would've liked."

Danyella adjusts her glasses and offers up an annoyed shake of her head before exiting the room.

"We can talk in here, but make it quick," Parrish informs her, lifting the bug detector up in his hand. "What do you want, Lumen?"

She narrows her eyes at him, and I see why I was so jealous of them in the first place. It might be possible to mistake their true animosity toward one another as love-hate if you didn't know them. Same deal with Chasm and Lumen.

"You basically dropped a bomb on me that night and then ghosted me after. What am I supposed to do here, Parrish Vanguard?" She huffs out a sharp breath, letting her brown eyes swing over to me. "You know why he kidnapped me from the party in the first place, right?" she asks, surprising me.

"You mean when you woke up in a field after mysteriously going missing? Yeah, not sure that I believe you for shit, Hearst." Chasm lifts his chin, hands still tucked into the pockets of his suit jacket. "My girl over here might be forgiving and sweet to a fault, but you know damn well that I'm not."

Lumen lifts her lip at him, but very quickly turns back to me.

"Did I ever tell you why Justin picked me up that first night?"

"Before you woke up with 'no memories' in a field?" Chasm scoffs, rolling his eyes and muttering in Korean. "*Gaesoli haji ma.*"

"Because you're easy to manipulate?" Parrish suggests, but Lumen ignores him, taking a step closer to me and putting her hands on my shoulders. "*Jugeullae?*"

Pretty sure Chasm said *don't bullshit me* and Parrish asked her if she wanted to die. Or something. I'm not very adept in the Korean language just yet, but I'm trying.

"Because he thought you were into me. Because he thought we were dating, Dakota." I just blink back at her in surprise. How could I have forgotten about that? *Because you've been dealing with a hundred other more important things? Give yourself a break, Kota.* "But then you and Parrish ..." She trails off and chokes on the words, shaking her head with a shudder of disgust. "So gross. I don't even know how you stomach it."

"Um." I'm not sure how to respond to that. But that is intriguing information. So Justin might've taken and tortured Lumen in place of Parrish? In addition to Parrish? Clearly, he was a target for more than just my affection; he's Tess favored son, after all. But still ...

"Just so you know," Lumen offers up, giving my shoulders a squeeze as Chasm mumbles something derogatory under his breath. She peers into my eyes. "I'm still into you, even if I don't deserve you. I might not be redeemable to you after the things I've done, but I'm not going to stop until you're free of this."

She kisses me on the cheek as Chasm curses and Parrish grabs her by the shoulder, wrenching her back a step and putting his face right up to hers.

"If you don't stop doing things like that, you'll see the full force of my wrath."

Lumen tears herself from his grip to look over at me, smoothing a hand down the pink fabric of her gown. The bottom shimmers with raffia fringe trim in a pink to red ombre; it's mesmerizing.

"I know I keep saying this, but these guys are Whitehall through and through. Just like I am. Even Maxx." She pauses there and snorts. "Especially Maxx." Lumen lifts up a single finger. "Don't let your guard down, Dakota. They might be on your side, but you might not like the things they'll do if they think it's for your benefit."

She turns and trails off for the door, offering an imperious look over her shoulder.

"Well? You're my date, aren't you, Parrish? Act like it." She turns and waits as Parrish grits his teeth, pausing to lick his thumb. I'm beyond surprised when he reaches out and scrubs my cheek with it, as if to clean off Lumen's influence.

"Next time she kisses you, I'm going to slap her." He turns away and takes off, snagging Lumen by the arm and dragging her out of the room as I sag back against the wall, eyes closed.

Chasm takes a step closer, and I can sense that he's plotting something. See, Parrish is the type to take control of a situation right then and there. X will stay calm for the most part but fly off the handle every now and again. Chasm plots behind the scenes, waits for the most opportune moment to strike.

"Please don't do anything to hurt her," I say, opening my eyes and turning to find him with his gaze on the door instead of my face. "I know you want to but save your energy. We have bigger fish to fry."

"I'm telling you, Little Sister, we can't trust her. You think Justin released her into your custody that easily? You think she *really* cares about anything but getting her family out of this mess? Think about it: if she marries you instead of Parrish, she still meets her goal of snagging a rich spouse."

"But I'm not—" I start, until it occurs to me that Tess is loaded, that she's married to Paul, and that Chasm is right.

"Uh-huh." He leans in close and then slams both palms on the wall on either side of me, getting up close and personal with my face. "*Oppa* is right, isn't he?" Chasm leans in, running his tongue along my lower lip before he draws back and offers out a hand in true dramatic fashion. "Come on. Let's go find Caroline's room."

I take his outstretched hand, heading downstairs into a well-lit hallway carpeted in champagne gold, the walls outfitted with rich dark wood molding, and dripping in chandeliers.

It doesn't take us long to find the master suite where Caroline is waiting. I knock lightly on the door and wait for her to invite me in while Chasm presses his back to the wall in the hallway.

"I'm right here if you need me, Naekkeo." He lifts his brows and I nod, slipping into the room and trying not to imagine the sound of the automatic lock clicking into place as a death sentence.

"Caroline?" I ask, looking around at the well-appointed seating area with its stark white couch, floral pillows, and porthole windows. I move into the room cautiously and then pause, a certain distinct and very sharp smell coming to me from the direction of the bedroom door.

"I'm in here."

I try very hard not to think about the box. But sometimes, it's as if the box is thinking about me, and I'm trapped inside a memory

I'd just as soon forget.

Sometimes, I think about the way Mr. Fosser's body quivered as I pulled the trigger on Mr. Volli's gun. Sometimes—far too often —I think about a serial killer turned police officer named Heath Cousins.

I hope this isn't another one of those moments.

Lifting my chin, I close my eyes and center myself before opening them again and striding forward with purpose.

I'm relieved to see my new stepmother seated at a vanity, touching up her makeup. She's wearing a crisp white robe that's slitted open to reveal the pale expanse of her thigh—and the bandage wrapped around it.

She scowls when she sees me standing there and flicks her fingers in the direction of the bathroom.

"Deal with my dress and then get the fuck out of my sight."

I just stand there blinking back at her in surprise. Thus far, she's been nothing but fake-nice to me. This is an abrupt about-face.

"Congrats again on your glorious and loving nuptials." That's what I say because apparently, I don't have many self-preservation instincts left. I move past her and then pause in the doorway to the bathroom, staring down at the spattered white gown.

My stomach flips over, and I stumble back despite myself. I know it's my reactions that Justin's always looking for—and I don't need a bug detector to tell me that he's got cameras in here— but I can't help myself. I turn away and clamp my hand over my mouth.

"Justin has high hopes for you. But in my opinion? You're as useless as Delphine." Caroline rises from her seat, pausing to sneer these words at me before she tosses her robe onto the bed and picks up her dress for the reception, this white shawl-collar minidress that gives her a much more refined look than she deserves.

It's easy to slip into, definitely not something that requires a helping hand.

But I see now that that's not why I was told to come in here.

"Deal with your dress?" I repeat. "Who the fuck did you hurt?" Caroline wheels on me, raising her hand as if to slap me. At the last minute, she draws her hand back and massages her fingers into a fist, squeezing and releasing them with considerable effort, as if she blames me for Justin's cruelty. *I* am not the one who ordered a teenager to stab her with a steak knife.

"Dispose of the dress, Mia." She grabs my chin, and I grit my teeth against the pain of her fingernails in my skin. "And don't mess this up." She shoves my face away, stepping into her heels and tossing a look over her shoulder. "But first, zip me up."

I do as she asks and then wait as she stomps out of the room before I invite Chasm in. He knows as soon as he enters that we're dealing with a situation here.

"Another maid?" he chokes out, his voice as twisted in horror as my own. I shake my head and lead him into the bathroom, gesturing at the bloodied wedding dress. We both just stand there for several minutes, likely wondering whose blood it is that's decorating the fabric.

"I just hope it's nobody we know," I whisper, moving into the room and squatting down beside the dress. It's obscene to see such a pretty white thing spattered with crimson the way it is.

I'm just happy that my grandparents didn't come to the wedding, that I just saw Tess, Maxine, and the boys, and that my little siblings are with Paul on the top deck.

"How do we get rid of this? We're on a boat," I murmur, thinking about tossing it off the side. With as many people as there are here, someone would see. I sit back on my haunches and rub at my face, trying and failing not to be annoyed right now.

It has to happen. It has to stop. I just need it to stop.

I rise up to my feet and turn toward Chasm, finding him looking at the dress in quiet contemplation.

"Easy. We burn it." He grabs my wrist and pulls me into the main living area, pointing at the fireplace that graces one wall. "This is an electric one, but there's a real firepit upstairs."

"How do we get the dress up there without being seen?" I ask, and then I answer my own question. "Cut it into strips?"

"This is an easy task," Chasm offers up, giving me a worried look. "It's not about the dress. We can get rid of it in a million different ways."

"So what is it?" I ask, and he shakes his head.

"I don't know; I imagine the answer lies with whoever's blood is on it." He moves over to a desk in one corner and starts opening drawers, finding a pair of scissors that we carry back into the bathroom, using it to shred the gorgeous gown to pieces.

We end up stuffing the pieces into a pair of stolen pillowcases.

We're going to look like total crazy people, but eh. At this point, I'm running out of fucks to give. Chasm is right though: it's not about the dress, it's about the blood.

It's Justin, making a point.

"Did you notice that he seemed to be coming unraveled?" I whisper to Chas as we walk down the hallway toward the stairs. There's an elevator, too (rich people are so fucking extra—in a really bad way), but the chance of encountering more people steers us away from that idea. "At the dinner thing with Caroline, I mean. He was pissed. It was as if he thought he was losing ground, and so he was starting to forgo the pageantry stuff. But now?"

"You think he's got something planned?" Chas whispers right back, holding his pillowcase full of bloody dress scraps like some sort of deranged Krampus creature.

"He's pulled himself back together which means he thinks he's winning again. That bothers me, *Oppa.*"

"Call me *Oppa* again, and we don't make it to the firepit. We end up in one of these guest rooms naked." Chasm grins at me, but I know he's not entirely serious. Neither of us wants to get it on with such ominous cargo on our hands.

Some of the wedding guests offer us up strange looks as we pass by with the pillowcases, but I just smile and thank them for coming. When we get to the firepit itself, Chasm sits on the edge and surreptitiously pulls out one strip after another.

With the sky darkening and booze making rounds amongst the guests, not many people seem to care that a teenager is feeding random shit into the fire. When someone does stop by to inquire, Chas lies and tells them it's a Korean wedding tradition, and they get bored very quickly. Clearly, they don't recognize the red and white strips for what they are. What rational person would?

"What if your dad hears about this? Won't he know you're full of crap?" I ask, but Chas just shrugs his shoulders.

"He's too busy licking Justin's butt to care; I'll just tell him it's all for the sake of Milk Carton." He finishes his pillowcase, tosses that into the firepit, and goes about doing the same with mine.

There's an excessive amount of ash, and the odd scent of smoldering silk, but otherwise, not much to give away our bizarre behavior but for the blood on our own hands. We retreat to the bathroom, wash up, and rejoin the crowd.

I'm a little weirded out to see Parrish dancing with Lumen while X twirls Maxine around.

"Hey." Chasm draws my attention over to him and offers up the slightest shake of his head. "Don't do that."

"Do what?" I ask, feigning total nonchalance. I mean, it's not like I'm freaking out or anything, but I'm also not super excited at what I'm seeing either.

"Believe there's anything more to this than Justin's orders." I scoff at that, but Chasm lifts a brow and pushes his razored hair off his forehead. "Seriously, Naekkeo. As much as I sorta wish they were into Lumen and Maxine respectively, it's not going to happen. You might be stuck with us until you make a choice."

I whirl on him them, the soft pink fabric of my dress rustling in the breeze.

"What if I can't, Chas?" I ask, looking down at the ring on my finger. "What if I can't choose? What if I'm never able to make a decision? What happens then?" I look back up to see him watching me, a slight half-smile on his sharp mouth that's emphasized by the black studs through his lower lip.

He reaches out and cups the side of my face in a gentle hand.

"Are you worried you're going to lose all three of us if you don't choose? Naekkeo, there's no timeline. I'll be here as long as it takes."

"You say that now, but what about in two years? Or five? What about ten?" I lift my brows and Chas opens his mouth to respond when Justin appears beside us. Even though my stomach hurts at the direction of this conversation, I let it drop, glancing over to see him smiling at us.

"A father can at least offer his daughter and her future husband champagne, can't he?" He passes over two flutes, keeping a third for himself, and forces the three of us to make a toast. "You make a handsome couple, don't you think?"

"We're a perfect couple," Chasm agrees, chugging the champagne in a single swallow. He inhales deeply, his gaze on Justin and not on me.

"Whose blood was on that dress?" I ask, because I'm done playing games. I am so sick of games that I could scream. I'm half-ready to jump off the side of this boat just so that I can have a break from it all.

But the idea of what might happen to Tess? To Saffron? To the boys? I can't do that to them. Not only would they grieve me, but I think Justin would come completely unraveled. He'd start hurting people I loved, killing them. The only reason they're all alive now is because he wants to control me, he wants to make me into a mini version of himself, and he likes to show off.

If I die, that all goes out the window.

"None of your goddamn business, that's what." Justin says that to me with a bright, exuberant smile on his face, sipping his champagne. It's quite obvious that his mood has improved substantially over the last several days.

And if it's improved? That means my situation has taken a nosedive.

I down my own champagne in much the same manner as Chasm, and Justin laughs approvingly, reaching out to give my shoulder a fatherly squeeze.

"Revealing my identity to Caroline was risky, but smart. Too bad things didn't work out quite the way you wanted them to. But ah, such is life." He takes another sip of his champagne, allowing his eyes to wander the crowd. "Look at them." He gestures with his hand in the direction of the Babylonian horde, his smile as sharp as ever. "They're finally realizing the mistake they all made, that I am and always will be their superior."

"Why not just sic your minions on them?" I ask, and I know Justin will be able to hear how tired I am in that one question alone. "Kill each and every one of them, be done with it all."

"Ah, ah, my dearest princess." He reaches out to pinch my cheek in a playful manner, and Chasm hooks a scowl his way. "What good would that do? If they're dead, they can't pay obeisance to me. If they're dead, they can't suffer. If they're dead, they're not learning the lessons they should learn. No, my way is better."

He pauses as Caroline saunters up to us, hooking her arm

around Justin's and beaming at me and Chas the way a normal person might do on the day of their wedding.

"They are clever, aren't they?" she asks, looking up at Justin with a smile. "And so obedient."

Justin nods, and offers up a very patronizing look in my direction.

"You will mind your new stepmother, won't you, princess? She's going to be a big part of both of our lives from now on." He hooks his free arm around Caroline's waist, pulling her close as if he didn't just demand for me to stab her and possibly kill her the other day.

"Caroline's nothing; she's just a user and a loser who will do anything for money, a black widow who thinks she's getting one up on me."

Justin's words, not mine.

"I'm looking forward to it." I grab Chas' hand and drag him onto the dance floor, annoyed to see that Parrish and Lumen are still at it and appear to be arguing. X and my sister, on the other hand? They're both smiling.

"Don't let him poison you against them," Chas warns me, taking me into his arms and holding me close as a slow song begins to play. We're done with Disney hits and back to classical music, as is proper Medina fashion. Just as it was at the launch party, the bubbles with the drone cameras float above us, capturing the entire scene. It'd be pretty if it weren't so goddamn creepy.

"I won't." I mean what I'm saying, even if I wish I could beg both Parrish and Maxx to stop, to come back to me, to … *How selfish am I being right now? If I'm dancing with Chasm, then they have nobody to dance with. Is that fair?*

The song finishes just at the yacht comes back into port. Most of the guests seem intent on staying, enjoying the free food, the free booze, the live music.

ENDGAME ROMANCE

Personally, I am all about taking Tess' offer to GTFO. That, and I am *beyond* thrilled to have this week to take a break from Justin's intensity.

Of course, said break includes kidnapping a classmate, but it is what it is.

Chasm and I regroup with X and Maxine and Parrish, joining Tess, Paul, and the children in the small crowd waiting for the ramp to be connected to the dock.

"Thank goodness that's over," Tess murmurs, glancing over at the three of us and sighing heavily. She looks like she's wearing an iron yoke around her neck, one that I imagine will only grow exponentially in weight when she finds out her daughter killed her own dad.

If there was any way to escape that fate, I'd take it in a heartbeat.

As we exit the boat, I notice a familiar face waiting at the edge of the marina.

It's Itsumi Takahashi and her 'bad cop' partner, Agent Murphy.

Lovely.

I expect that they're here for me which is odd seeing as I'm scheduled to meet with them yet again this week.

"Paul Vanguard," Agent Takahashi says as she steps forward. She has two uniformed police officers alongside of her, and she gestures them forward as Tess grabs Amelia and Henry by the hands, her eyes widening as a very confused Paul Vanguard is handcuffed and read his rights.

"What's going on here?" Tess demands, and my stomach drops out from under me. I'd thought that by turning myself in for the murder, I'd beaten Justin on this front.

Apparently, no such luck.

"Fuck." This from Parrish as he grits his teeth and the whole of Medina's elite—from the top deck of the super fancy mega yacht

—watch as his father, Tess' husband, and the preferred doctor of every socialite in town is whisked into the back of a cop car.

A text comes in on my phone, and even with the chaos of the situation, I know I have little recourse but to read it.

Check.

Just one word from Justin. I squeeze my fist around the phone, and I promise myself that the very next chance I get to be alone with him, I'm doing it.

It's time.

There are no more moves to make on this board.

CHAPTER 34

"This is absolutely absurd. A *Vanguard* being charged with murder? Do you hear yourselves?" Laverne is screaming into the phone which is only a change from her earlier actions in that she's not screaming in Agent Takahashi's face.

Parrish is sitting in a sea of quiet fury in the living room with me, Maxx, Chasm, and a sobbing Kimber. The younger kids are now safely tucked away upstairs, and Tess is working on legal representation for Paul.

I can only imagine the effect this is going to have on the family and on the upcoming custody battle. No matter what secrets Tess has dredged up, no matter what tricks she'd planned to use against Justin in court, what the fuck is she supposed to do with this?

Her husband is being tried for multiple murders.

"Please say something," Chasm pleads, leaning forward on the sofa and putting a hand on Parrish's knee. Parrish doesn't respond, not to pull away, not to acknowledge, nothing. He just sits there and stares at the floor as Maxx and I exchange a telling look.

I understand what Parrish is going through far better than anyone else. My father *is* the Seattle Slayer. One day, if the universe has any mercy at all, the world will know Justin for who he is, and I'll be the one with a father labelled as a killer (rightfully so, at least).

But this? This is insane. I'm not Paul's biggest fan by a long shot, but the guy is incapable of hurting a fly. Literally. He shoos them out the doors and windows with rolled-up magazines.

I don't even want to consider what my grandparents might be thinking right about now.

We had a nice time at the cabin the other night; this could undo all of that tough, emotional labor.

The front door opens and closes, and the sound of stomping heels precedes Tess into the living room.

"Oh, Kimber," is the first thing she says, coming over to sit beside her daughter on the couch and rubbing her back with a comforting her hand. Her face, on the other hand, is anything but comforting. It's resolute. Angry. Purposeful. "Please don't cry. This is all a misunderstanding. Your father will be out on bail soon enough, and we'll get this sorted."

Laverne is still shouting somewhere in the grand labyrinth of the house, but it's difficult to make out what she's saying now.

"Everyone in the world will know about this come morning." Kimber sniffles and rubs her arm across her face, shaking her head violently against the very idea of it. "I know Dad is innocent, but nobody else will believe that. We're going to have to change our names and move to another country."

"If that's what we have to do, we'll do it," Tess declares, giving Kimber's back another rub. "That's what family is all about— sometimes we have to make sacrifices for the people we love." Kimber's crying rachets up another notch, and Parrish gives his sister and mother an aghast look.

"Why would you say that to her? You're only making it worse."

"Paul is not going to jail for crimes he didn't commit; this is a reach on the FBI's part. There were too many holes in the Heath Cousins case, and they're trying to fill them in by claiming the man had an accomplice." Tess' gaze flicks to mine, and in her words, I hear that true crime writer voice of hers. She knows more about criminal law than some lawyers. Pretty sure she's like *this* close to having an actual degree in criminal justice. "Are you alright, honey?"

"I'm okay," I whisper, but I'm not really. I've put up a dam against the tidal wave of emotions that come with that night, but I don't indulge them. Later, I keep telling myself. I'll process them later. "Don't worry about me."

"I am worried about you," Tess asserts, looking over at the boys before she gently encourages Kimber to stand up from the couch. "Why don't you go upstairs and shower, change into some pj's and try to relax? Let me take care of this."

Kimber eyes her mother skeptically, but in the end, she does as she's told. Knowing Tess the way I do now, I'm starting to understand why. She might be strict as hell sometimes, but she spoils her kids and she truly does care.

Her kids.

Me being one of them.

She crosses her arms over her chest, perched on the edge of the sofa in that elegant black dress, her gaze ripping through me, Parrish, Chasm, Maxx.

"Is there anything the four of you want to tell me that might help with this?" she asks softly, and I don't know that she's quite made the connection, but she's close to it. Oh God, she is so fucking close. Maybe she suspects Justin of framing Paul, but not for actually being a serial killer. Something like that. Who knows?

"About a bunch of murdered teens?" Parrish chokes out. "Are you kidding me?"

"Don't do that to me, Parrish," Tess warns him. "Don't make me out to be the crazy one. I'm tired of it. The whole world looks at me like I'm crazy sometimes, and I'm sick of it." She stands up from the sofa and paces in front of us briefly before looking at her son again. "Is there anything more about your kidnapping that you might be able to tell the police? Something, anything that could help clear your father's name?"

Parrish looks at her for so long that I almost wonder if he isn't going to spill everything but then, with a huff of annoyance, he shoves up from the chair and takes off. It pulls at all of my heartstrings to see him like that, but I've already made up my mind that he won't be suffering for long.

I'm going to take care of this—for all of us.

"Boys?" Tess offers up, looking between the two of them. "I know there's more going on behind the scenes than you're telling me. That's just a fact at this point. But if you know anything at all that might help with Paul's case, I need you to tell me. I can protect if you let me know what's going on." When Chasm and Maxx say nothing, she looks to me next. Her brow scrunches and her lips flatten into a thin line, and I know she's thinking about the custody hearing.

Losing a second time would be devastating. It would almost assuredly mean that I'd be stuck with Justin for the next two years. That is, if I didn't plan on taking matters into my own hands.

"The Justin stuff doesn't have anything to do with Paul's case," I tell her, as if I don't understand what she's referring to. "As far as the Heath Cousins thing, I told those agents everything that happened. There's nothing else to talk about."

Tess sighs, lips pursed into a thin line, but she nods.

"I see. I suppose I'll learn more in a week then?" She cocks a brow at me and storms past as my stomach roils and I mentally kick myself for letting so much information slip. I can hear her in there making coffee, but I don't know what else to do.

I asked for a week; I imagine that's all she's going to give me.

"What do we do now?" Chasm queries, leaning back in his seat and crossing his hands together behind his head. His eyes are on the floor, but when Maxx shifts in his own seat, that amber gaze swings his way, and I recall that at one point, they both were missing from my room the other night.

It's not as if I suspect them of working with Justin. More like, Lumen was right when she said I might not like the nefarious things they'd do in order to protect me. I hate thinking that, but I can't shake the feeling that one or both of them is hiding something from me.

"You deal with Veronica." That's X, stating facts as per usual. "Although getting out of here to go to a party is going to be a tough sell on Dakota's part." He and Chasm continue to stare at one another, as if they're hatching a secret, silent plot. I suppose they must be considering that Justin warned Chasm and me from accepting outside help with this one. They can't discuss our plans aloud in here.

He's right though: how can I possibly ask to attend a high school party with this Paul thing going on? And Tess—rightfully, in this case—isn't going to allow it.

Then again, we never asked to attend Antonio's pool party way back when: we just went.

I suppose those same techniques apply here.

X turns to me, and it's as if he wants to say something but changes his mind before his mouth can fully catch up to his brain. His lips part, but then he snaps them closed and rises to his feet.

"We'd stay, if we could," is what he ends up telling me, and I nod, a lump caught in my throat that I can't seem to swallow down. Tess won't let them spend the night since, you know, she's aware they're both dating me and sort of also caught me in a threesome.

Eek. I'd almost forgotten about that.

Doesn't seem so important in light of other events, but it's certainly not been forgotten.

"It's okay." I smile and stand up, accepting an impossibly warm hug from Maxx and then another from Chasm. "We'll get through this; we're almost there."

"Just a month of summer and a handful of teenagers to torment. No biggie." Chasm shrugs his shoulders and rolls his eyes. It's not like I've forgotten Justin's itinerary either. That, or his hit list.

As in, Philippa. As in, Antonio. As in, Gavin. There are a few other names on there, too, but I'm not as familiar with the others. Am I going to have to 'kill' them all? Certainly that's Justin's ultimate goal, but we're not going to get that far.

I won't *let* it get that far.

"Get some rest and we'll talk tomorrow." I pause when I see Tess lounging in the doorway, her cup of coffee held in her hands, and her gaze impossibly locked on mine.

It's not just Justin that I'm running out of time with, it's Tess. She's made huge strides, but her grace isn't going to carry me much further than I've already pushed.

"Wake up."

It's Parrish, standing beside my bed and panting heavily. I come awake like I've been stabbed in the heart with an EpiPen, adrenaline rocketing through me as I sit up and Parrish turns away, lifting the remote to crank the volume on the massive TV that's mounted to the wall.

He takes a moment to rewind the broadcast—it's live, but like, isn't technology cool? (when people aren't using it to spy on you, I mean)—until he finds what he's looking for. Parrish presses play as I sit up and rub sleep from my eyes.

"The letter was delivered via courier late last night to the home of Jack Larae, one of the hosts of the infamous Emerald City Murder podcast. We have a copy here in our studio, but you can also download our app—" Parrish growls and fast-forwards several seconds, squeezing the remote in such a tight fist that it cracks. *"This letter—while not confirmed—is rumored to have been sent by the Seattle Slayer. It reads ..."*

And here, text pops up on the screen and begins to scroll.

"Dear Medina, you've worn a cloak of blood and diamonds for too long. You open your arms in a false embrace, but your touch is poison. Your wealth and privilege are toxins that run too deep to be purged. In the end, remember that it was a cop that brought you down. A teacher. An assistant. A maid. A postman. A butler. A DJ. A waiter. A barista. A whole host of citizens you spit on, step on, and destroy.

In the end, you made your bed and you will sleep in it. All of this, and I have but to snap my fingers. Remember that if you breathe another breath, it's only at the knife's point of my grace."

The letter stops scrolling as the blood drains from my face, and the world rocks and sways around me.

"Last night alone, there were thirteen murders in King County, each of them executed at the same time, and in a different manner. The FBI has released a statement confirming that the Seattle Slayer may be more than just one or two individuals as previously thought and instead, may be a collective of killers—"

Parrish mutes the TV and whirls around to face me, breathing so hard that he looks like he may very well pass out.

"One of those FBI agents died last night," he whispers, and that's it. I can't sit still. I throw the covers off and leap out of bed, if only because I don't know what to do with the adrenaline rush. "The redheaded one. Uh—"

"Agent Murphy." The words sound hollow and strange, as foreign as the Korean words that Chasm whispers when he holds me close, but the antitheses of their comfort.

"And Mr. Parker," Parrish continues, "the computer science teacher who gave you a B in his class."

I say nothing. What can I say? I'm … I'm in shock. Thirteen murders in one night? *And all while Justin is in the U.S. Virgin Islands on his fucking honeymoon!* But thirteen murders? I don't like that. One of them is missing. I know that because … fourteen years. Fourteen tick marks. Fourteen dead teens on the fourteenth day.

"Is everyone accounted for?" I whisper, and Parrish offers up a quick nod, cupping my face in his hands and looking me in the eyes so that I know how serious he is about this.

"Tess, the kids, my dad, Laverne. I called the Banks for you. I checked in with Lumen and Danyella." He swallows hard and closes his eyes, glancing away like he might very well be at the end of his rope. This could be positive in a way, right? Seeing as Paul was locked up during the murders … "We're meeting X, Chasm, Lumen, and Maxine in a few."

"Where's Tess?" I ask, and Parrish swallows hard.

"She left to see my dad." He releases me and runs both palms over his pretty hair, shirtless and beautiful even in the throes of emotional agony.

I snatch my phone from the nightstand and—as per usual—it's flooded with messages. I didn't even hear it ring, I was so damn tired. But there are plenty of missed calls from Maxine, my grandparents, my friend Sally from back home …

ENDGAME ROMANCE

There's a text from Justin's burner phone, too.

You see what I can do? How far I can reach? Whenever I want, however I want. Check and mate.

It takes me a second to puzzle out that message. That is, until I scroll through my texts and read what it is that Sally sent to me.

Nevaeh is dead, Dakota. She got alcohol poisoning at a party last night and passed out. She never woke up. Please call me.

Somehow, I'm sitting on the edge of the bed without realizing how I got there, and Parrish is tearing the phone from my hands to read through my messages.

"Fourteen," he murmurs, and he, too, is shaking.

Because Nevaeh was back in New York state. Because Nevaeh had nothing to do with this and didn't deserve to die. Because he killed my childhood friend for no other reason than he *could.*

I shove up to my feet and stumble into the bathroom, just barely managing to make it to the toilet before I throw up.

Justin's been playing games all this time, toying with me, with us.

I mean, I knew all of that, but I …

"Where are we meeting everyone?" I whisper, tears streaming down my face. I want to grieve my friend, but I can't. Not right now. I need to see my boys; I need all three of them; I need my sister. I want that comfort, that love, that reassurance.

"Tess isn't going to let us leave the house; they'll come here."

I nod and force myself to my feet, flushing the toilet and rinsing my mouth with water. Parrish is waiting to pull me into a tight hug, squeezing me harder than he ever has before. I can hear his heartbeat, slamming against his rib cage.

"No wonder you hated me at first sight," I whisper. "I've truly and utterly ruined your life."

"You give life meaning for me; I am *nothing* without you." He hugs me even harder, and he doesn't stop, not even when Tess comes up to find us like that, her eyes red-rimmed, but her expression strong.

This isn't hitting her like it is us because she doesn't know. She doesn't understand. She thinks Paul was framed, but she doesn't get how close we all are to the heart of the Slayer's rage.

Me and Tess.

We are his pinnacle and his epilogue.

"Are you two alright?" she asks as Parrish strokes my hair. He nods, and even though I know the sight of us embracing like this makes her uncomfortable, Tess retreats and even leaves us alone long enough to shower.

I mean, if she knew we were naked together, I doubt she'd be happy, but she's so busy talking on the phone when we come downstairs that I don't think she even notices. It's quite clear based on her conversation that she's working on Paul's case.

"Maxx and Chasm will be here in a minute," Parrish offers up, and she nods, pointing at him with the pen in her hand and tucking her phone against her shoulder.

"Do not set a *single* foot off of this property. If I find out that you have, I will send you both to separate boys' and girls' boarding schools in Europe. I swear on my *life,* Parrish Vanguard." She grits her teeth as he purses his own lips and then offers up a belated nod.

"Would she really do that though?" I whisper, and the look he gives me tells me all that I need to know.

She would.

I don't let myself think about Nevaeh. I simply force my feet to move, one after the other, until we're seated in the backyard, just out of sight of the glass doors that lead to the living room. If Tess really wanted to, she'd only have to move a few feet to spot us. This is about as far as we can go.

The sound of a car's tires on the gravel out front echoes back to where we're sitting in the sun, on this impossibly bright and cheerful day. There are flowers blooming in every garden bed, springing from baskets hung along the eaves, dripping from ornate stone pots. There's even a pond nearby with a mellifluous waterfall.

It all seems absurd, obscene really.

"I've heard you mention Nevaeh a few times. Were you close?" Parrish asks, his voice soft and low in a way I never would've expected after meeting him the way I did. Shirtless. Chugging milk. Mocking me. *Begging me not to fall in love with him.*

Only, I did. I fell in love with him, with Chasm, with Maxx, and I don't know what to do about that just now except to embrace it and enjoy it. It's keeping me afloat when all I want to do is sink.

Chasm storms out the back door, wearing a beige hoodie with an olive-green jacket over the top. He comes right over to where we're sitting and slams his palms down on the table's surface, teeth clenched, eyes glittering with rage.

"Where the fuck is he?" he snaps out, and both Parrish and I just stare at him.

"Who?" I ask, and Chasm offers up a mocking laugh, standing up straight and planting his hands on his hips.

"Maxx." Chasm looks around and then glances back at us. "We were supposed to ride together, but he took off in his goddamn Jeep before I was ready."

"So where is he?" I ask, shoving up to my feet, alarm spiking my blood. Chasm softens his expression and reaches up to brush his thumb along my lower lip, leaving a tingle in his wake.

"Don't fret, Little Sister. His car is parked on the driveway. He must be here somewhere."

I call X's phone, but I don't expect to hear it ringing from where we're at. I was just assuming he'd answer and tell us he was in the house looking for us or something. It's a large enough place that you truly could lose someone in it. For hours, probably. If circumstances were any less shit, it'd probably be a great place to play hide-and-seek.

The boys and I exchange looks and then head into the garden area, down the winding path in the direction of Maxx's ringtone. It's a song that I know well, one of my absolute favorites and oddly apropos for the situation. It's *"Good Boy Gone Bad"* by the K-pop group TOMORROW X TOGETHER.

Um.

As we move around a blind corner, Parrish and Chasm come to an abrupt halt, and I slam straight into their backs. I reach between them, shoving them apart so that I can see what they're gaping at.

That is, Maxx and Lumen.

Maxx is standing just feet from her, panting heavily as she cowers back against a decorative stone wall covered in ivy, clutching her phone and staring at him from too wide eyes.

"What the hell is going on here?" Parrish asks as X very slowly turns his gaze over to us.

In his eyes, there's an unspoken apology that I don't want to see, that I don't want to hear.

"He attacked me!" Lumen screams, pointing at him with one quivering hand as she clutches her phone to her chest with the other.

"Yeah fucking right," Chasm snaps back at her, moving forward to stand beside Maxx in solidarity. "I *knew* we shouldn't have trusted your lying ass." He sneers at her as he looks her over, glancing back at me as if to say, *I told ya so. I didn't want to be right, but I am.*

"As soon as I got out of the car, he chased me. He chased me back here and God only knows what he was planning on doing." Her voice quavers so badly that I almost believe her. Only, I would never believe Lumen Hearst over Maxim Wright.

ENDGAME ROMANCE

He stands up straight and threads his fingers in his chocolate hair, closing his eyes so tight that his skin crinkles at the edges and his brow furrows.

"What's going on?" Chas asks, looking at Lumen like he wants to spit on her.

Parrish strides forward and then pauses, cocking his head slightly to one side as he studies Lumen then Maxx. Lumen. Maxx.

"X?" Parrish queries, but he's not answering. Instead, that goddamn song keeps playing, repeating the same line over and over: *good boy gone bad.* I hang up the call just so that I can make it stop. As I do, I see a series of texts come in from Justin's burner phone, and I choke on my own heart as I notice the first message is a video.

Of Maxx.

And Lumen.

It seems to have been taken by one of the security cameras at the front of the house.

Despite my better judgment, I click it. Because surely, it'll prove that Maxx is innocent.

"The fact that you're not answering me right now is really pissing me off," Parrish breathes in his best apathetic king sloth voice. "Maxim Wright, talk to me. *Now.*"

The video starts with Maxx's orange Jeep Gladiator pulling into the driveway beside Lumen's Barbie pink car. She climbs out and then stands beside her own vehicle, as if she's waiting for Maxx to get out. As soon as he does, he approaches her and says something that I can't hear. It's video only, no sound.

Next thing I know, Lumen is backing up, and then she's running. And Maxx? He's chasing her.

I clamp a hand over my mouth, scrolling to the next video in the series. This time, it's Maxx in Justin's office. He's standing there with his hands tucked into his pockets, staring at the floor instead of at the man lounging casually against the side of his expensive executive desk.

"Well?" Justin asks, and as soon as X hears the voice coming from my phone, he opens his eyes and whirls. He starts forward as if he's going to take my phone from me, like a repeat of the incident at the coffee shop. Only this time, Parrish and Chasm step between him and me. *"Did you see her?"*

"I saw her," the Maxx on the video admits, and then he looks up, mouth in a severe frown, eyes wracked with pain. *"She was wearing a U of O t-shirt and driving a purple Chevy Camaro. It was old. Sixties or seventies I'd guess. New York license plate. I only managed to get the last few numbers."* X reaches into his hoodie pocket, withdrawing a piece of paper and tossing it onto the floor between him and Justin.

My father doesn't move to pick it up, instead waiting for Raúl to do it for him. His pet arsonist with the fancy glasses and the snappy shoes shows Justin the paper before using his lighter to set it on fire. Ashes drift to the carpet near their feet.

"Anything else you want to tell me?" Justin asks, and X looks down at the floor again, as if he's ashamed of himself.

"Dakota ... professed her love to me." The words seem to hurt as they come out, and I look up to see Maxx staring at me. That silent apology is still there, but he offers no explanation. Another text pings my phone and I glance down to read it.

As I said, choose your pawns wisely. Maybe next time, you'll listen?

I look up again, but I refuse to believe it. I flat-out refuse. Maxim Wright is too open, too transparent to be able to lie to me like that, to tell me he loves me, kiss me, fuck me ... Then I start to think about certain things that snap and gnaw at the edges of my mind.

ENDGAME ROMANCE

He knew who I was at the coffee shop and lied about it. He organized Parrish's search parties by himself. When Parrish went missing, he moved into his room on a semi-permanent basis. He took my phone from me at the coffee shop and forcibly unlocked it. He turned away Maxine at the door and brought her letter to me himself. He was willing to kill the rabbit. He trailed Delphine and found nothing amiss despite her connection to Justin. He claimed to have never kissed or fucked any other girl. He just so happened to be at the Vanguard house in time to save the family from the fire.

I feel sick. My phone drops from my hand and shatters on the cobblestone path.

"I told you, Dakota," Maxx begins, his voice harsh and pained. At the same moment, my sister comes around the corner, panting and shaking, her eyes flicking from me to Lumen, Parrish, Chasm ... X. "When I want something, I really am willing to do whatever it takes—especially for the right girl."

Whatever it takes, he'd said during sex. Whatever it takes. Whatever it takes.

"Even if that girl isn't you." He looks down at the ground as Chasm takes a step back and bumps into me, eyes wide with shock.

"You ... but ... no. I don't believe it. I don't. *Shiro.*"

"I told you," Lumen grinds out, coming over to stand beside us, pointing at X with a shaking hand. "I fucking *told* you!"

"You forget," Parrish begins, teeth gritted, hands clenched into fists. "That we know he's controlling you." It's a repeat of what he said when Justin showed him the video of me and Chasm having sex for the second time.

"You forget that I know you're controlling her."

Only ... only this time ...

Another video comes in, and I squat down to snatch my phone

631

as Maxine moves over to stand beside me. I look over and into her eyes and I see—as I always do—what I know to be true: no matter what's going on in all of this, my sister is innocent. I reach down to take her hand, and I press play one, last time.

"I won't do it." Maxx is angry in this video; he's trembling. *"Who the fuck do you think you are that you can make me do something like that?"*

"It'd be easy, right?" Justin schmoozes, walking in a circle around Maxx. They're not in his office this time, but somewhere else. I don't recognize the room, the marble floors, the soaring ceilings. Unless … is this Chasm's house? *"You want to save your girlfriend, don't you? All you have to do is convince her little sister that you're in love with her. The little sister that your best friends hate. The little sister that made your honorary mother figure, Tess Vanguard, cry. The brat. The snobby East Coast little shit. How hard would that be?"*

"Fuck you." X spits at Justin and turns to go, but my father isn't done. Oh no. Not even close. Raúl is waiting at the door, holding out a phone toward Maxx. He hesitates briefly before he takes it, and then he presses play. Whatever he sees there must change his mind because when he looks up, there's nothing but terror written into every line of his face.

"Make her fall for you. I don't care how you do it. I don't care what it takes. Just think of it as a good deed: Maxine Banks will be safe. Besides that, she'd want her little sister to be safe, too, no matter the cost, wouldn't she? She's just that sort of person."

I throw the phone as hard as I can, heaving and panting, wishing it weren't true, believing that it's not, questioning myself all over again.

"I'm sorry, Dakota," X says again, wetting his lips as Parrish stares at him like he's never seen him before. "But now, after getting to know you the way I do, I know this is what you'd want, too. Anything to keep Maxine safe. Anything."

"Keep me safe?" Maxine asks, blinking surprised eyes as she stares at me and not her ... ex-boyfriend.

"It's a complicated situation. It's not something any of us would've entered into without ... outside influence. It doesn't reflect on you at all." That's what X said to Maxine the evening of the dinner party.

"I thought I was going to break that day at the coffee shop, after you ran Maxine off and made her cry." He said that, too, didn't he?

He said all sorts of things, did all sorts of things, and I ...

"Told you that you should've dated me," Lumen mumbles, glaring at Maxx as he moves around me and over to my sister.

"What are you doing?" she chokes out as he takes her by the shoulders, leans down, and ...

I turn away. I can't look. I don't want to see.

And then I start to run, even as Parrish and Chasm call out to me, even as they chase me.

This isn't happening. I don't believe it. I refuse. I hate Justin. I hate him. I fucking hate him.

What was I thinking when I told myself it'd be hard to kill him? It won't be hard. I *want* to kill him. I want to bleed him. I want to make him hurt. I want him to suffer the way he's made me and my family and my boys and everyone else around me suffer.

So.

This is me, Dakota Banks, losing every last part of herself. Every cell. Every molecule. My very essence.

Because I've done all sorts of things I regret in the last few weeks: burned a bloody wedding dress, fell for my sister's lover, plotted to kidnap my classmate.

But this is the worst.

Truly, the worst thing that I have ever done.

Because I mean it this time: I *want* to kill my own father.

I'm going to enjoy it.

And he's never going to see it coming.

A hand reaches out from the foliage, snatches my arm, and yanks me into the cool shadows of the underbrush and into another world.

TO BE CONTINUED...

Author's Note

Originally, '*Lost Daughter of a Serial Killer*' was intended to be a trilogy. However, when the word count exceeded 400,000 words (the length of four very long books and more than double the first book, '*Stolen Crush*') I felt it could no longer be contained in one volume. Please check my website (www.cmstunich.com), social media(tiktok.com/@cmstunich or www.instagram.com/cmstunich or facebook.com/groups/thebookishbatcave), or sign-up to receive text alerts by texting BOOKS to 484848 to get news on the release.

Fun facts! Everyone knows J.R.R. Tolkien's famous series, '*The Lord of the Rings*', right? Just to put it in perspective, that **entire** series is around 576,000 words in length. The first book in this series was 180,000 words, the second was 211,000 words, and the third is 200,000 words. The fourth and final will be even longer. That means, '*Lost Daughter of a Serial Killer*' is longer than '*The Lord of the Rings*' already.

I wrote this series with the sole purpose of lingering on the characters' emotions. I was getting annoyed with movies, TV shows, and books where someone is hurt or dies or betrayed and the characters move on in a flash. I started writing this series after a personal loss, and this is the tale I needed so desperately.

It still is.

Thank you so much for reading, and Dakota and I will see you soon!

Love C. M

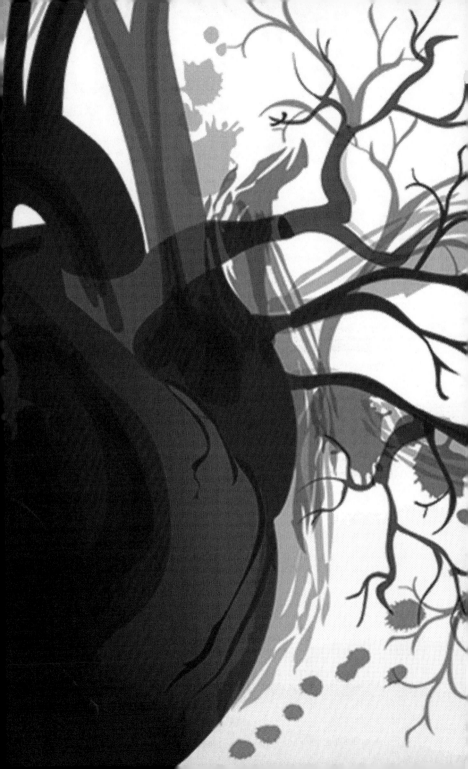

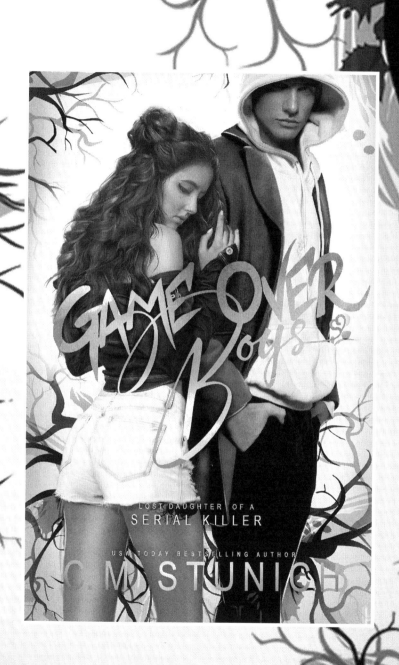

GAME OVER
Boys 2

LOST DAUGHTER OF A
SERIAL KILLER

USA TODAY BESTSELLING AUTHOR
C.M. STUNICH

A

RICH BOYS OF BURBERRY PREP × ADAMSON ALL-BOYS ACADEMY

CROSSOVER NOVEL

Orientation

USA TODAY BESTSELLING AUTHOR

C.M. STUNICH

ALLISON'S adventures in UNDERLAND

we are all mad for you here

harem of hearts series

C.M. STUNICH
international bestselling author

ORIGINALLY PUBLISHED UNDER "VIOLET BLAZE"

C.M. STUNICH

STEPBROTHER

INKED

THE SEVEN MATES OF ZARA WOLF

Pack Ebon Red

INTERNATIONAL BESTSELLING AUTHOR

C.M. STUNICH

SIGN UP FOR
THE C.M. STUNICH

Sign up for an exclusive first look at
the hottest new releases, contests,
and exclusives from the author.

@

www.cmstunich.com

JOIN THE
C.M. STUNICH

Discussion

GROUP

Want to discuss what you've just read?
Get exclusive teasers or meet special guest authors?
Join CM.'s online book clubs on Facebook!

www.facebook.com/groups/thebookishbatcave

Stalking LINKS

JOIN THE C.M. STUNICH NEWSLETTER – Get three free books just for signing up
http://eepurl.com/DEsEf

LISTEN TO MY BOOK PLAYLISTS – Share your fave music with me and I'll give you my
playlists (I'm super active on here!) https://open.spotify.com/user/12101321503

TWEET ME ON TWITTER, BABE – Recycled instagram posts but if you like to use the bird
app best then https://twitter.com/CMStunich

FRIEND ME ON FACEBOOK – Okay, I'm actually at the 5,000 friend limit, but if you click
the "follow" button on my profile page, you'll see way more of my killer posts
https://facebook.com/cmstunich

LIKE ME ON FACEBOOK – Pretty please? I'll love you forever if you do! ;)
https://facebook.com/cmstunichauthor & https://facebook.com/violetblazeauthor

CHECK OUT THE SITE – (under construction) but it looks kick-a$$ so far, right?
http://www.cmstunich.com

FOLLOW ME ON TIKTOK – There are only like three videos but ihopefully more to come
tiktok.com/cmstunich

AMAZON, BABY – If you click the follow button here, you'll get an email each time I put out
a new book. Pretty sweet, huh? http://amazon.com/author/cmstunich
http://amazon.com/author/violetblaze

PINTEREST – Lots of hot half-naked men. Oh, and half-naked men. Plus, tattooed guys
holding babies (who are half-naked) http://pinterest.com/cmstunich

INSTAGRAM – Cute cat pictures. And half-naked guys. Yep, that again.
http://instagram.com/cmstunich

ABOUT THE AUTHOR

C.M. Stunich is a self-admitted bibliophile with a love for exotic teas and a whole host of characters who live full time inside the strange, swirling vortex of her thoughts. Some folks might call this crazy, but Caitlin Morgan doesn't mind – especially considering she has to write biographies in the third person. Oh, and half the host of characters in her head are searing hot bad boys with dirty mouths and skillful hands (among other things). If being crazy means hanging out with them everyday, C.M. has decided to have herself committed.

She hates tapioca pudding, loves to binge on cheesy horror movies, and is a slave to many cats. When she's not vacuuming fur off of her couch, C.M. can be found with her nose buried in a book or her eyes glued to a computer screen. She's the author of over a hundred novels – romance, new adult, fantasy, and young adult included. Please, come and join her inside her crazy. There's a heck of a lot to do there.

Oh, and Caitlin loves to chat (incessantly), so feel free to e-mail her, send her a Facebook message, or put up smoke signals. She's already looking forward to it.